SON OF DESTRUCTION

SON OF DESTRUCTION

Kit Reed

This first world edition published 2012
in Great Britain and 2013 in the USA by
SEVERN HOUSE PUBLISHERS LTD of
19 Cedar Road, Sutton, Surrey, England, SM2 5DA.
Trade paperback edition first published
in Great Britain and the USA 2013 by
SEVERN HOUSE PUBLISHERS LTD.

British Library Cataloguing in Publication Data

Reed, Kit.
    Son of destruction.
    1. Journalists–California–Los Angeles–Fiction.
    2. Combustion, Spontaneous human–Fiction. 3. Florida–
    Fiction. 4. Suspense fiction.
    I. Title
    813.5'4–dc23

ISBN-13: 978-0-7278-8232-5 (cased)
ISBN-13: 978-1-84751-462-2 (trade paper)

All Severn House titles are printed on acid-free paper.

Severn House Publishers support The Forest Stewardship Council [FSC],
the leading international forest certification organisation. All our titles that
are printed on Greenpeace-approved FSC-certified paper carry the FSC logo.

Typeset by Palimpsest Book Production Ltd.,
Falkirk, Stirlingshire, Scotland.
Printed and bound in Great Britain by
MPG Books Ltd., Bodmin, Cornwall.

For Carl Brandt – the best of the best
with love

It won't matter how hard he runs for the car, gulping air; he will always hear her. It won't matter how fast he drives through the Florida night, how far he goes or how hard he tries, he can't outrace the horror in the house behind him, the sudden flash of orange light that stained her bedroom window.

He'll spend the rest of his life running ahead of that night: police photos of the smoking remains, coals burned to glowing cinders in her belly.

The guilt.

It's nothing I did. It's nothing I did!

Doubt overturns him.

Then what was it?

He doesn't know. Nobody does.

It's all over the news by morning. Bulletins start coming in on his car radio before he hits the Interstate. Stopping for gas at dawn in Jacksonville, he sees footage on CNN and the fiery death is bannered on newsstands by the time he reaches Savannah. In the years since, he's read magazines, books about her death and others like them – written by people compelled to explain the inexplicable because mysteries don't die until somebody comes up with the answers.

Does he only imagine that as he turned to leave, the air in the old woman's bedroom changed – or that she did?

He doesn't know. Guilt sinks its teeth into him. *Is it something I did?*

I can't be that, he thinks, without knowing what *that* is, or why it is so urgent.

I can't do that.

I won't.

He carries these things in his heart: a son that he's never seen, and a secret that he doesn't understand, but must keep at all costs. The responsibility is tremendous. Worry boils up in him. *I can't let him . . .*

Can't let him – what? He doesn't know. How do you help a son you've never met when you don't know anything but that he's yours, and you're afraid for him?

1

Dan Carteret

Burt was never his real dad. The truth is stamped in Dan's face. He was built on a different template. By the time he was tall enough to look into a mirror, he knew. He grew up knowing, but when his mother finally let go of her secret she broke it gently, like bad news.

Like, she thought he didn't know?

Even you could see it, going by at a dead run. With that bullet head and the used-car salesman's smile, Burt Mixon is nothing like him. Where Dan is tall and easy with you, Burt is mean-spirited and short. He tried to be nice to Dan, but they didn't like each other very much.

He ran that house like boot camp: spit, polish, morning runs and excruciating clap pushups, the quintessential ex-Marine. The *ex* part rankled. Something went wrong on Parris Island back in the day, but that was before he married Lucy, and she'll never tell. After he was separated from the service, Burt set himself up in New London, but he made a bad civilian. After a lifetime of pushing boots, training hick kids to shape up and snap to, he was moving used cars off the lot in a military town, and it rankled. Danny was his last recruit.

'Did you do that?' The sequence was pre-set. Burt used to stand over him, waiting for him to cry. When he was really little, it used to work. 'Well, did you?'

Whatever. That shrug. Dan is tougher now.

'Goddammit, I'm trying to make a man out of you!'

'I don't care!'

He shook off the beatings but not the guilty, conflicted look on his mother's face. She loved him, probably too much, but Burt was her only husband, and in charge. 'Don't.' He felt the edge of her hand between his shoulder blades – the gentle pressure that told him, *It's all right, love. I'm here.* 'He's your father.'

Burt was nothing to him.

His mother only ever hit him once, on a strange, sad day before he was old enough to read, and it was so awful that they both cried. He found certain things in her jewel box before she swooped down on him and snatched everything away. Underneath all her beads and bracelets, he found a snapshot of five guys in a Jeep on some beach, laughing so hard that he thought they were laughing at him, and at the very bottom there was an envelope – was that his name? There was a newspaper inside. It was awful: pictures of *somebody* or some *thing* laid out in a ruined chair like a burnt-out log in a fireplace. One bedroom slipper with a foot in it, and a naked ankle bone, like it just broke off. Lucy ripped it away from him and smacked him hard. She disappeared it but he remembers. He still can't make sense of the conflation: four laughing guys and the charred figure in the scorched chair.

Kids like Dan, even kids who grow up happy, travel on the myth: *these can't be my real parents. I'm only stuck here until they come for me.* It kept him going through the loneliness and hard times with Burt, and the snapshot fueled the myth. *Until he comes for me.*

He was fifteen before she told him the truth.

In fact, it wasn't the main business of the meeting. It came out accidentally. Even though it was late afternoon in late winter in New London, she pulled him out on the back porch and shut the door, Lucy Mixon with her sweet face tight, setting her jaw in that brave little tough-mom way. She was all hung up on it: bent on telling him, not knowing how to say it.

He wasn't about to start. They stood there shivering.

Finally she said in a tight voice, 'Honey, you know we both love you very much but I have some kind of hard news.'

He did not act surprised or upset when she explained that it wasn't going to happen right away, but she and Burt were splitting up. It was over, she had to do it. When he didn't respond she said, 'You're the only person I've told.'

He looked past her, watching it get dark.

'Danny? Dan?'

She wanted him to react, she wanted him to say, 'It's OK,' she wanted him to for God's sake *say* something but he just stood there, waiting her out.

After a long time she said, 'I'm sorry.'

An icicle dropped.

There was only the sound of her waiting.

She said what mothers do in this situation, 'Don't worry, he's not leaving you, OK? No matter what we do, he's still your father.'

It was so quiet that he could hear the ice cracking on the Thames. Lucy tried, 'You don't seem very upset.'

Like he would feel bad that this abusive, sanctimonious jarhead bastard was being kicked out of their lives. He and Burt hated each other, even though they weren't allowed to admit it.

'Danny?' Even in the dark, Lucy could see he was glad. 'Dan?'

'OK.'

The hand she put on his arm was shaking. 'I'm telling you first, so you won't feel hurt. We both still love you.'

He must have been one cold little bastard, standing there with his eyebrows clenched and his jaw carved in stone, nothing, not even an eyelid, twitching. Looking back, he feels bad about it. At the time he said, 'It's no big deal.'

'We've been a family for so long. I just.' She didn't finish. After a while she said, 'It's over and I'm sorry, OK?'

It was quiet for way too long. Oh God she was waiting for him to say something, what . . . appropriate.

All these years later he's sorry he couldn't have been nicer with her. Softer. He should have hugged her and said he loved her and let her sob into the front of his fleece. He did what he could: he shrugged, signaling *no problem*, but she was too upset to read signals. 'Dan?'

Finally he said, 'OK.'

'I just don't want you to be upset.'

Oh Mom, don't cry. 'Why would I?'

A light went on in the kitchen. Burt, looking for his dinner. For his wife, the assigned provider. 'Lucy!' He yelled loud enough for them to hear through sealed storm windows, 'Where is everybody? What's going on? Luce?'

While Danny and his mother stood out there on the back porch with icicles dropping and everything in flux.

She said, 'We've been with him since before you were born, Danny. He's just like your . . . well, he's nothing like him, but . . .'

'What?'

She covered her mouth. 'Oh honey, please don't be upset.'

He isn't? He isn't! Danny's heart did a joyful flip. *Oh God, I was right.* 'Why, Mom?'

'You mean why am I telling you or why do I think you're upset?'

Her face went to pieces. Danny's face stayed where it was.

'He tried so hard, and I know he loves me.' She was desperate to make him *like* the man she'd picked out to take care of them, she hoped for it even there, at the end of the arrangement. 'I just don't want you to miss him too much. Burt, I mean. When he goes.'

'Like I would give a . . .'

'Don't, Danny. Don't say flying fuck. Listen. I know you feel bad . . .'

'I feel fine!'

'But this might make you feel better. It. Uh. Oh Danny, I . . .'

'Dan.'

'Dan. Dan, it.'

It was cold. Spit was freezing on his teeth but they had to stay out here on the rickety back porch until she finished. 'It's OK, Mom. You don't have to tell me . . .'

'Please, I'm trying to tell you something important.'

He finished, 'You just did.'

But she didn't hear. 'I should have told you before.'

She was a mess. God he hated Burt. 'He's going. We're cool.'

'That isn't all.'

'Mom?' That little gulp of hesitation scared him. There was always the possibility that she was getting married again.

Inside, pots crashed: Burt fending for himself. Never mind what had just passed between them, or that he understood long before she tried to tell him. Lucy needed to spell it out. She took the requisite deep breath: *well*. 'About Burt.' Sigh. 'I didn't want you to go on thinking he was your father.'

An icicle dropped off the porch roof and knifed into the melting snow.

'He was just a nice guy who came along at the right time.'

Oh, is that all. Danny made her wait so she would understand what he was about to tell her. He dropped spaces between the words like bricks, to make sure she would remember. 'Like you think I didn't know?'

'How?'

Oh, Mom. Don't look so betrayed. 'How could I not?' He made a smile for her, but it was too late, or too fake. 'Mom, what's the matter?'

Water sheeted her eyes and hung, not spilling. It was a miracle of surface tension. Lucy was beaming, like, *Thank God that's over.* This is how she surprised him: 'I'm just so glad!'

'Mom!'

She rushed on. 'I'm taking my name back. It's Carteret.'

He was trying to hang tough but as soon as she said it, the surface broke. *I always knew.*

'If you want to, you can too.'

Dan Carteret.

'Yes!' He covered his face fast, so Burt wouldn't come running out to see what blazed out here in the dark just now, and shone so bright. He was that glad.

One day my real father will come for me, he told himself. Prisoner of war, he thought, superhero, Marine deserter; the myth kept him going and it crystallized that night: it had to be one of the guys in that snapshot. Why else would she keep it for so long? It didn't matter which one of the five it turned out to be, he was *Not-Burt.* Different. Unknown.

'So you're OK?'

Gulp hard, man. Breathe. Exhale carefully, so you don't spook her by shouting. 'I'm good.'

'Good,' she said. 'Now let's go back inside.'

'Not yet.' Dan put himself between Lucy and the door, trying to lead her where they had to go. 'So. Carteret. That's my father's name?'

'No. Now, move.'

He swept her hand off the knob. 'So. What's Carteret. Something you made up?'

'It's my name, Dan, that I was born with. It's who we are. Now, please. I'm getting cold.'

'I said, not yet.'

She tugged the door open in spite of him. 'We're never going to see him, you know.'

He pushed it shut. 'Why not, Mom? What is he, dead?'

'Danny, don't.'

'Married?'

'I don't know, I don't know.' She scrubbed her hands down her face. 'It doesn't matter!'

'In jail?' They were having a little battle over the door.

'No. If he was in jail we could . . . We can't.'

'Why?'

Her face went through so many changes that it scared him. 'We just can't.'

'Come on!'

Picture of Lucy, thinking. It took her a minute to come up with, 'There are people I have to protect.'

'Like who? Him?'

The look she gave him was uncompromising. Fierce. 'Starting with you.'

'Fine,' he said bitterly. 'So I don't know who I am.'

'You're my son!'

'I don't know and you won't tell me.'

'You don't have to be Dan Mixon any more, and that should be enough.' Lucy's hands were shaking. Her breath was shaking too. 'Trust me, Danny, that's all you need to know.'

'Come on, Mom!' Like a cop, he slammed the heel of his hand into his mother's shoulder; they both heard the thud. 'What's his name?'

'I can't tell you.'

'Who is he? Who is he really?'

There was a pause during which he actually believed she was going to tell him. Her head came up, but her eyes were looking past him at something else. Then her voice lifted and floated clean away. 'Just a boy I thought I loved.'

Inside, a bowl broke on the kitchen tiles and Burt squawked. 'Lucy!' Had he guessed she was dumping him? Did he hear them out here on the porch? Dan didn't think so. Burt didn't care about Lucy, he was just pissed about the no dinner. 'Lucy?'

'What happened?'

She put her fingers over Dan's mouth, shushing him. Through the back window, they saw Burt slam the oven door and stalk out into the front room. She whispered, 'Nothing. I can't tell you.'

God he was so angry. 'That's all? That's all you're going to say?'

'That's all you need to know.' She turned, as if they were done.

He pulled her back. 'No it isn't, Mom.'

'OK,' she said finally. 'It was a boy from home.'

'Where's home?'

'It doesn't matter.' Lucy sighed. It was so sad. 'He wouldn't want you to know.'

'That's a lie.' His head came up so fast that his neck snapped. 'He wrote to me.'

'Not exactly.' Her expression told him he was right.

'You tore it up.'

Stabbed in the heart. 'I'm sorry! I had to protect you.'

'What else did you tear up?' He knotted his fists to keep from shaking her. 'Marriage license?'

'There wasn't one.'

'Funeral notice? Passport?' If only he'd known what to look for that awful day when he was four, he'd know! *I know ways of hunting for things that leave no trace.* The treasures she kept hidden made no sense to him at the time: a newspaper he couldn't read with photos she would not explain, gold football, old jewelry, empty plastic shell – diaphragm case, he understood at fifteen, but not back then – night school BA from Connecticut College – he and Burt wore suits to the graduation – and, what else? 'My birth certificate?'

'I would never do that.'

'Why not,' he said bitterly. 'You trashed everything else.'

'Not that.' For a minute out there on the back porch they were like two kids squaring off. *You flinched. No,* you *flinched.* Then her face crumpled. 'Oh, honey, that would make you a stateless person. I wouldn't do that to you.'

'Prove it.'

'Of course.' She sighed. 'It's on file in Town Hall, you can get a copy any time you want. You might as well know. I had to tell them something at the hospital, so . . .' Oh, didn't she take a long breath then, and wasn't the voice she finally managed so thin when it came out that she sounded like someone else. Long breath. 'I told them it was Burt.'

'Son of a bitch!'

'I did what I had to.' Lucy had a strong, sweet face – too pale, but with those beautiful eyes. They loved each other, that was understood. She'd brought him up doing what she thought was best for him, that too was understood. She wasn't being cruel. She was doing the best she could.

'If I have a father he has a name, so, what? What's his damn name? At least you can tell me that.' When she didn't answer he took her arm. It was too thin. Even in the heavy sweater, she was rattling with the cold. Was she already sick, all those years ago? He doesn't know. That night his voice was so thin and shaky that he hated it. 'If you loved me, you'll tell me.'

'I love you, and I can't.' She looked up with tears streaming.

'Won't!'

'Won't, then.' For the second time that night, she surprised him. 'I won't tell you and you have to promise not to ask.'

Oh, Lucy. What are you afraid of? 'Mom . . .'

'I'm trying to keep you safe! Now, promise.'

'Why do I have to . . .'

This popped out in spite of her. '*Because he wouldn't want you to know!*'

'Mom!'

Then Lucy's fingers closed on his so tight that the nails dug in like little teeth. She was struggling to frame an agreement but she had run out of words. 'Please!' she cried finally, out of such grief that the implications silenced him.

For a long time they stood just there, Dan with his back stiff and chin jutting, until she jerked him into a hug. He resisted but she pulled him close. They stood, rocking. With her face buried in his chest – *When did I get this tall?* – his mother wheedled, 'And you have to promise not to look for him. OK?'

There was a technical term for the answer Dan made her then, which he didn't learn until he was in college. Let her think he was giving her what she wanted. 'As long as we both shall live.'

'Ever.'

The sound Dan came out with then, that let them end the clinch and go inside, could have meant anything. Because they had to survive the moment, she took it as a *yes*. He'd managed his first *broad mental reservation*.

He still didn't know who he was, but things were good. At least they were done with Burt.

Lucy went to court and got her old name back. Carteret. They took the birth certificate to probate court and got his name changed to match. He became Dan Carteret, and it suited him fine. He still didn't know who his father was, but he went along all right, not knowing. Lucy went back to work on the sub base; she started as clerk typist and advanced to office manager. She looked better than she had in a long time and Dan started doing better in school. They did fine together, just the two of them. The house was quieter with Burt gone, and they let things relax to the point where magazines sat on the coffee table every which-way and you could no longer bounce a quarter off beds made so tightly that it was hard to get back in at night.

There would always be the central question, but Lucy had said everything she intended to say and he loved her well enough to let it pass, at least for now. For his mother's sake Dan Carteret went along not knowing who he was. He finished high school and went to college outside Chicago not knowing; his mother loved him well enough to let him go to California to look for work. He hugged her hard, saying, 'I'll come back for Christmas.'

'Don't worry about me.' She tightened the hug and then broke it with the little push that means goodbye. 'It's your life now.'

That first year was hard: no time, never enough money. He was waiting tables, writing spec scripts because in Los Angeles, everybody hopes. He wrote for one of the free weeklies. He even sold a couple of stories to *the* L.A. *Times* magazine – a way in. Three or four Christmases went by – she was celebrating with a nice new man, his mother told him when he phoned; she said, 'Don't worry about me, I'm happy. Do you know I'm teaching myself to paint?' She said, 'Have a great life,' which he continued to do, not knowing who he was, really, or how Lucy was. By this time it was tacit that she wouldn't talk about the father, and he wouldn't ask. They loved each other that much; they understood each other that well, and he went along fine, not knowing. Dan was going along all right, not knowing whether when he went in on Monday, he'd still have his marginal job at the incredible shrinking *Los Angeles Times* because there was always something else that he could do. He was going along all right, not knowing who his father was, what he meant to her or what went wrong. For Dan Carteret in his twenties, not knowing was like the weather. A condition of life.

He went along fine, not knowing, until it became clear that not knowing was *wrong* because he didn't know Lucy was sick until they called from the hospital to tell him to come, she was sinking fast.

2

Dan

Lucy was one of those people who claimed she never got sick, which he believed, until now. She was critical – cancer, stage four and moving fast; it was time to put the central question. When they phoned, she was too far gone for him to press her on names, places, details from her past, but he didn't know that.

He flew home on the redeye, too anxious and disrupted to sleep. He and Lucy had a lifetime of unanswered questions hanging between them, but this one knifed him in the heart. *Oh, Mom. Why didn't you tell me you were sick?* She'd just say what she always said: *I wanted you to have your life.* He had to walk into that hospital and fix this. He had to badger and charm them into producing the right specialist, the right protocols, and she'd get better.

Then they could talk.

By the time he raced into her room, Lucy was beyond questions. She couldn't speak, not really. She just beamed, shaking with joy at the sight of him. Grieving, he took her hands; she was too flimsy to hug. If there really had been a new man in her life, he wasn't anywhere.

There was just Lucy, shining.

Her mouth was working and he leaned close, the way you do for a deathbed confession: *Who is he, Mom?* If she won't tell you now, she'll never tell you. Even when she knows you love her too much to ask.

She struggled to produce sound, but nothing came out. Dan bent closer, closer even, knowing it was much too late to pour out his heart; all he could do was close his hand on what was left of hers and keep murmuring – with love, 'It's OK, Mom. It's OK.'

Listening. It was too late but he listened hard. He could smell death coming out of her mouth, and there was no way to push it back; it wouldn't matter what miracle drug they fed, infused or injected, she'd never get out of that bed. She couldn't even speak, but she tried, God, she tried. He loved her, so he tried to smile and pretended that she'd spoken and he understood.

It was awful, watching her try.

He nodded as if words had come out and they made perfect sense. He said, 'Yes, Mom, uh-huh,' smiling, smiling, but he didn't fool her. She pulled him closer so he could hear what she was trying so desperately to say.

Finally he did. This is what Lucy Carteret had saved all her strength to tell her son. 'I'm so glad you're here.'

It was awful seeing her like this. 'Me too.'

They said they loved each other.

You love her and you say so, even though you can never forgive your mother for certain things. The way she put him off that night on the porch, when he asked the biggest question in his life. All she said, in a voice that floated away was, *Just a boy I thought I loved.*

All these years later, it was still a puzzle and a mystery; she was afraid to tell him. She made him promise not to ask. It was too late to ask her why.

She tried to lift her hand, but she couldn't; she was so sick, so thin, she was almost transparent. He begged her not to go.

She said what they say in the movies, 'I'm not going anywhere.' Then she died.

Like that! Part of Dan Carteret was gone. *Oh, Mom!*

And, next? Words exploded in his head – the response he'd cobbled when she made him promise never to ask about his father: *As long as we both shall live.*

She thought he'd promised, he knew he'd lied. She was gone. *OK then.*

He is free to search.

Lucy didn't leave him much to go on. The few things she'd said that night, when she first told him the truth. She loved the guy, she admitted it! Still did. Love like that doesn't vanish without a trace.

It will be in that jewel box she was so anxious to protect.

The little wooden chest surfaces when he goes through her empty apartment, padding thoughtfully through the silent, abandoned rooms. He finds it in her bedroom closet, stashed behind books on a shelf he used to be too small to reach. It's tough, going through the things she kept: bangles and mismatched earrings, his high school class ring, important papers and at the bottom items from the deep past, souvenirs of the life Lucy had before Dan was imagined and they ended up living here.

He runs his fingers over raised initials on the little gold football, a cheap high school trinket that his mother cherished or she wouldn't have kept it for so long: FJHS. OK. Tonight, he'll type FJHS into the Google search box along with her maiden name, the first step in a global search for Lucy Carteret's lost life in the years before she married Burt Mixon, who made her so anxious and sad.

Here's the picture she kept: five jocks snapped on a beach, waving and grinning like fools – a fading Polaroid that he turns over in his hands like an old friend. Wait! Here's a second one: a black-and-white of Lucy in her teens, smiling for the camera in spite of the glare. At her back, a Spanish stucco house sprawls under a row of tall Australian pines – some builder's idea of castle, with a grand stairway and two fat turrets. She's wearing a little white T-shirt that breaks his heart and – what? That corny gold football hanging between her breasts. Did his father take this? Why did she hide it for so long?

Instinct tells him this isn't all she was hiding. Troubled, he runs his fingers around the box, feeling only a little guilty because the silk lining shreds at his touch. Here. A scrap of newsprint from the paper he thought she'd destroyed before he learned to read. Well, now he can read: **Spontaneous Human Combustion.** Holy crap! He jumps, as if she'd just set her hand between his shoulders: *It's all right, love. I'm here.*

The initialed football, the snapshot. This. He feeds FJHS into the search engines, triangulates with spontaneous human combustion. Fort Jude at the top of every first page, the Florida city where – bingo: there have been three grisly, unexplained deaths by fire in the last fifty years. And, my God, the image search produces the stills that so terrified him as a kid. The crime scene photo of that bedroom slipper with a foot still in it, standing like a solitary bookend on the floor underneath the recliner where she died. He broadens the search, surfing obsessively because on the Web, everything leads to something else and in its own way, it insulates him from the ache in his belly, just below the heart.

He kept clicking; he struck gold at *howstuffworks.com*, where Stephanie Watson wrote about spontaneous human combustion at length.

> Spontaneous combustion occurs when an object – in the case of spontaneous human combustion, a person – bursts into flame from a chemical reaction within, apparently without being ignited by an external heat source. The first known account of spontaneous human combustion came from the Danish anatomist Thomas Bartholin in 1663, who described how a woman in Paris 'went up in ashes and smoke' while she was sleeping. The straw mattress on which she slept was unmarred by the fire. In 1673, a Frenchman named Jonas Dupont published a collection of spontaneous combustion cases in his work 'De Incendiis Corporis Humani Spontaneis.'

Although Lucy was sad more often than she was happy, she didn't live the kind of inner life that needs bizarre crimes and freaks of nature to explain itself. *Unless. What?* Dan is tortured by unanswered questions. *What does this have to do with us?* He browsed obsessively, lingering at this unsigned entry on *unexplainedstuff.com* and picked up later by a half-dozen other sites:

> In December 1956, Virginia Caget of Honolulu, Hawaii, walked into the room of Young Sik Kim, a 78-year-old disabled person, to find him enveloped in blue flames. By the time firemen arrived on the scene, Kim and his easy chair were ashes. Strangely

enough, nearby curtains and clothing were untouched by fire, in spite of the fierce heat that would have been necessary to consume a human being.

He should be packaging, storing, doing last things before he locks the door on his mother's life. Instead, he trolls the Internet, gleaning details. At *theness.com,* a Dr Steven Novella pushes him into murk and confusion — hey, this is an MD putting his reputation on the line — when he says:

> . . . Believers often cite as evidence the fact that a body has been completely reduced to ash, except for the ends of the arms and legs and sometimes the head. But there is a good explanation for this phenomenon. It is called the wick effect. The clothing of victims can act as a wick, while their body fat serves as a source of fuel (like an inside-out candle). The burning of the clothes is maintained by liquefied fat wicked from the body of the victim, causing a slow burn that can nearly consume the victim and resulting in the greasy brown substance often coating nearby walls.

Except for the ends of the arms and legs . . . The foot and the chair. The clipping. Another of those things she kept hidden but preserved: her secret, in code. As his mother tore the paper out of his hands that day, she smacked him hard. He reads on and on, chapter, verse, feeding on details, until he comes to himself with a shudder. *OK, lady, what does this have to do with us?*

Did she really leave Fort Jude because old women go up in flames for no known reason? He doesn't think so. Once, when she let herself talk about her life before New London, Lucy told him she'd rather die than go back there, ever.

Which she did.

Die, and she left orders. He will throw her ashes into the Atlantic thousands of miles north of her home town. What came down there, he wonders, what was so bad that she had to go? Trouble in her family, or was it something worse? He won't find the answers in his browser. He slams his laptop and turns to the pictures she kept.

If he stares at the house behind Lucy for long enough, will he see her parents grouped behind the leaded windows, snapped in black and white? Are they still in there? Would they come out and talk to him? He doesn't know. In fact, there's a lot he doesn't know. When he was a kid he wanted to go live inside that picture, hang out on the beach with those five happy guys, laughing and not giving a fuck. The problem is, they don't look carefree to him now; they look sinister and guarded.

Stupidly, he sits, half-waiting for a sign from his mother, but the dead don't leave messages, right? Reason, Carteret. Think. *One these dudes has got to be my father*, he thinks, *why else would she keep this thing?*

The hell of it is that he could stare into those faces and never know which one; he could feed the Polaroid into a scanner and enlarge it, he could analyze every facial detail down to the last pixel and still not know, but Dan does know one thing. He'll hunt down the careless, grinning bastard. He will, and when he does, he will damn well shake him until the truth falls out.

3

Lorna Archambault

Don't ask me how it happened, don't think you know what it's like. Do you know what it's like? Do you have any idea what it's like? Did you quit gossiping or leave off gawking long enough to wonder how it felt to burn alive, with your heart splitting and a furnace in your fundament?

Or were you too busy surmising? Was it all about the phenomenon, and did you give me a second thought, or were you only scared because if it could happen to me, it could happen to you? Do not send your children to visit my grave, ladies, and leave me the hell out of your little lectures on playing with matches.

I know you despised me, and you know what I thought of you.

Poor Lorna. Nobody knows what happened, but everybody knows what she looked like at the end. It was in all the papers, on TV, those pictures! How humiliating for a proud woman like her.

In this town, extraordinary things come down – Fort Jude is the lightning capitol of the world. Sinkholes yawn and eat entire cars or get big enough to devour the house, the kids' climber, the bird-bath in your front yard. People by the thousands went to light

Santeria candles outside a bank on Route 19 because they thought they saw the Virgin in the glass front. Storms blow up in seconds – hurricanes, tornados, rains that can sweep a man's car into a culvert and drown him like *that*. At sunset, sharks come in to feed in the swash. Half a boxer dog floated to the top of Circle Lake and a family in Far Acres found an escaped boa constrictor coiled under the porch, but these things happen to outsiders, not people you know, although our mayor did get struck by lighting on the eighteenth hole.

In towns like ours, where lizards come indoors and scorpions as big as lobsters can tumble off rafters in old garages, anything can happen.

Anything.

But – spontaneous human combustion?

We've had three, right here in Fort Jude!

Now, people may combust in broad daylight in London or Paris or even in downtown Dallas, but never in Fort Jude. Some poor soul may burst into flames in public where you live, but not here. The society is much too private. We will do anything to protect our own. Fort Jude's crimes and love affairs, the betrayals – our great mysteries – unfold in secret, late at night.

In Fort Jude, there are close to half a million people.

Then there are people you know.

The whole world knows about Muriel Keesler, although she wasn't from here. She's famous, because she was the first. Old Muriel combusted and burned to a cinder sitting in her chair back in the Fifties, and to this day nobody knows why. Experts still study it. People from all over the world come to Fort Jude to reconstruct the scene and come up empty. Nobody in town knew her until it happened.

Then everybody did. It's a very great mystery. No sign of arson; it wasn't suicide. Nobody broke in and set her afire. She just burned up, and nobody knows why. The only things burned were the chair she sat in and Mrs Keesler, of course. Charred bits that fell on the rug. Police and fire marshals, the coroner, scientists, nobody could explain it. Forensics experts and scientists, psychologists, journalists from all over the world came to investigate. Movie people came, even mediums came, psychic pathologists. They studied it from every angle; they wrote books about it, but it's all speculation. All that snooping, all these theories and all these years later, we still don't know how it happened, or why.

In the Sixties, a Mrs Arbruzzi flared up in her trailer and burned to a crisp, front page news in the *Star*, but she didn't gather a crowd. It was interesting, but she was a foreigner, came here from Sicily or someplace like that. Everybody ooohed and ahed, but for families that have always lived here, it was like it happened to some old lady on Mars.

Things like that don't happen to people like us.

But the third was Lorna Archambault. Lorna Archambault! Past president of the Junior League and the museum board, her father founded the Fort Jude Club, but she lit up and flamed out all the same.

As if such fires are specific to the person.

When these things happen to somebody in a society as tight as this one, the mystery lingers. Thirty years later, people still talk about it in the bar at the Fort Jude Club. What happened to Lorna Archambault, really?

How am I supposed to know?

Lorna was divorced: nobody to see, nobody to throw a blanket over her or pour water into the smoking cavity where her guts had been. Poor Lorna, how awful. And because she was prominent, it got in the papers and on TV. There were photographs of it in the *Star* – how embarrassing! Like the others, she just burned up from the inside out. As if a stealth missile homed in and exploded in her belly. Dead. The other two women had to lie in the charred ruins of their lives for hours before the landlady or some other stranger blundered in and found them dead.

When you're prominent, like Lorna Archambault, they miss you. Somebody misses you and comes looking. They find you right away.

Poor Claudia Atkinson found Lorna, they were roommates in the Pi Phi house at FSU. *We were leaving for Europe today. I brought the tour labels to stick on her bags!* Her luggage was right there by the front door, all zipped up and ready to go. Imagine. How sad.

Police came, the ambulance came, the fire truck came, although it was too late. The coroner came for Lorna, and until her son Dorian the doctor vetoed an autopsy, the cause was in dispute, but of course she ended up at DeForest, where everybody who *is* anybody goes. And oh, forensics people in flocks. Experts came. Thirty years later, they're still coming, convinced they can find the clue that everybody else overlooked. Everybody wants an explanation to things that can never be explained.

Like this one. Nobody broke into Lorna's house that night, so it wasn't robbery; her wallet and her diamonds were sitting on the dresser, in plain sight. Some of the exact same experts that came snooping around about Mrs Keesler came back to study Lorna's case, for all the good it did. She didn't use a space heater or cheap-jack kerosene stove, only poor people live like that. She used the divorce settlement to redecorate the house. Her designer had covered all the fireplaces, so it wasn't a spark popping out on the rug. She had a brand-new furnace and all the wiring was up to code. Nobody came to see her that night, at least not that they know of. There were no signs of arson, but Lorna did smoke.

One doctor said maybe her cigarette set off her own gasses. It's happened to ordinary old women in cheaper neighborhoods, but Lorna was a Southern lady. The idea! She would have died!

It could have been anything, but what? Alone in her empty house that night, snug in her nightie, Lorna Archambault kicked back in her plush recliner and mysteriously went up in flames, burning until the fire ran out of fuel. They found her lying there, split wide open like a hot dog left too long on the barbecue.

Where else but in Fort Jude? Now, the Keesler woman made history, because she was the first. Tourists still come looking for the house the way you'd visit Natural Bridge in Virginia, or in California, the Watts Towers. They keep coming even though there's nothing left where she lived but a parking lot. This Mrs Arbruzzi was just a snowbird living in a trailer park, and she was foreign. The town is filled with old people from somewhere else.

They drift in from everywhere, looking for a better life. At 4:30 every afternoon you can see them poking at ATM machines on Central Avenue and lined up for Early Bird Specials in cheap restaurants from here all the way to the beach, restless old men and sad old ladies in workout suits or spunky Florida shirts; they'd talk to you if you weren't in such a rush. They're everywhere, like the three a.m. test pattern on a TV you weren't watching.

See, Fort Jude may look like a big city to you, but to the lucky insiders who grew up on Saturday night parties and lessons in ballroom dancing and Sunday dinners at the Fort Jude Club, the ones who spend New Year's Eve in the club ballroom and children's birthdays at splash parties in the pool, it's still a small town and it belongs to the generations. For them, everybody who matters in Fort Jude knows everybody else, and everything is related. Who you are, who your people are, and in this town, the truly local families protect their own. It is a given.

At the Fort Jude Club, somebody in the family – parents or grandparents – saw Lorna in the dining room the night she died, fresh from the hairdresser and dressed to kill, sitting down for a farewell dinner with her son. Dorian didn't make his family sit down with her all that much, but it was a special occasion. Her favorite waiter brought her favorite Blanc de Noir and Dorian had a bottle sent to every table, so when he gave the toast the whole dining room stood up and drank to her. They still talk about how happy she looked.

These things don't seem important until something happens. Then the least little detail stands out. Afterward, Dorian took Lorna home. He kissed his mother good night and that's the last anybody saw of her. Except for whatever they scraped out of the chair.

What happened, really? Does a person like that feel it coming on? Maybe she mistook it for something else: *Something I ate. Pressure on the heart.* People do. For all we know, she could have been sitting in her BarcaLounger thinking, *It's just gas.*

Then she erupted.

Unless she heard something. Intruder. Raccoon in the garbage can. Maybe she looked up, startled. *Who's that?*

Or she thought horny, unfaithful Hal Archambault was coming back to her, and she lifted her head the way you do, so he wouldn't see her wrinkles sag: *You called?*

Just before she started belching fire.

The police don't really know if Lorna was awake or out cold when it started. Most people don't want to know, although everybody wondered. Did she scream for help or try to dial 911? Was she drunk or out on pills, as in, she brought it on herself? These things go down easier when survivors have somebody to blame.

What a terrible thing!

For a few seconds there, oh, lady! She must have been glorious: lit up from within, glowing like a Japanese lantern in her purple silk nightie, which is what the coroner said she was wearing when the flames consumed her. Then the fire blossomed. She split and it came gushing out. Imagine light blooming in her belly, exploding in twin gouts rushing from the holes where her eyes had been, flame shooting out of her belly and her open mouth in a celebration of light.

What was she, anyway. What did she do that brought this down on her?

Was she excited? Scared? Was she in pain?

There are no words for what I was.

4

Nenna Henderson McCall

I walked home from the office last week. It took all afternoon, minus the times I sat down to think. It's six miles from Coral Shores to our house, and I had on the wrong shoes!

I was writing speeches to Davis that I wanted to give when Davis finally came in from work. Everybody said don't marry him, you want somebody local, like Bobby, but Bobby was in love with Lucy at the time. I did want Bobby, but there was nothing I could do. They said, northerners just don't *do* like we do and that is true. Davis taught at Junior College, he had the tweed jacket with the suede elbow patches, he was cute and now I'm stuck with him – except I'm not, because it turns out Davis is a rat.

I was at the office when I found out. It was the dead, still hour after lunch. The smartass kid realtors were all kicked back, romancing would-be clients on the phone, heavy-breathing over bayfront condos, square footage and with waterfront views and I was opening my mail, everything the same.

Then it wasn't. It was the bill. The English Department secretary sends it to me because Davis is notoriously cheap. He calls long distance on the office phone. Usually I hold my nose and pay, but, *Fifty calls to Toluca Lake!* I must have yelled; when I looked up with my bare face hanging out like a wet girdle on the shower rail, seven kid realtors were texting madly, with flying thumbs and sly, snarky grins.

It's cousin Gayle. His first cousin, what kind of a failure of the imagination is that? Scrawny Gayle Carson, that Davis grew up with, it's incestuous, plus! Could he not have had the grace to call her on his cell? 'Gayle's invited us to California,' he said last Christmas, all innocence. 'Steffy's never been!' What was he thinking, using our daughter like that? 'I can't wait to see it through her eyes.' Oh, Davis. I should have known that misty smile was not for me. I didn't want to know.

I booked the trip, pretending not to know. Leaving that woman's house after the awful week we spent there, I thought, *Out of sight, out of mind.* I thought, *Got to do something about that, just not now,* when I really meant, *Not yet. Please God, just not this year.* I'd been keeping us going, things as they are, but you can't, not with everybody watching proof positive smack you in the face. All those kid realtors in their tight little outfits sitting there, just waiting for me to cry. I forgot everything and ran. By the time I realized I'd left my bag, my phone – my keys! – it was too late to go back.

Now I'm not a walker like my friends. They're mostly free to look pretty and sign up for Jazzercize and waterobics if they want to, or dress up for board meetings followed by long lunches at the club, translation: unemployed. But, frankly, we couldn't live on what Davis makes, not in this showcase at Far Acres. I wanted to live on Coral Shores with all my friends, but Davis insisted. There's a world's worth of difference between here and there; it's just too far, and last week I went the whole distance. I walked every step of the way.

It was four blocks before I felt my shoes. Mocha slides from Nine West, sand kept coming in the toes but I just went on walking, like walking was the most important thing, which in a way, it was. No. It was the only thing.

I was too upset to wait for the light, even though Harrison Rivard got hit by a truck crossing this very street last year because he was too good to wait for stoplights. He used to live in Europe and you should have seen him when he moved back, all arty and continental, although he was probably CIA, and it was a hit to make sure he didn't go spilling Company secrets in the bar at the Fort Jude Club. What a way to go, in your bloody sock feet with your groceries smeared all over the road. Poor guy, I never thought!

You don't think, not when you're sealed in your car, safe from everything, but walking, you're exposed, like poor Harrison. Walking is like opening your diary, in a way. Our whole past is out there and to get home, I had to walk through most of it. Northshore Elementary is a mini-mart now, with a parking lot where the playground was, I still have the scar where Brad Kalen jumped off the swing and it hit me in the head and I was excited and sad, remembering. We went to dances in the old box factory all through junior high, all dressed up and obsessing about sex because it was so new, thank God I know more about everything now. I walked past the lake where boys drove us to park in high school and the Dairy Queen where they took us after, and oh, oh!

It's a good thing nobody I knew saw me out in the open like that, trying not to cry. Outsiders wouldn't see me looking that much different, but all the girls from Northshore would know it in an instant. With outsiders, you can be anything you want – more interesting, younger, new – but in this town we grow up with a history. We aren't girls any more but we still know how old each other are down to the minute, we know who wet her pants in first grade and which one threw up in her desk. We've bookmarked every guy we were in love with, from third-grade crushes to the Coleman twins in eleventh grade – which twin was I in love with, really, was it Buck, or the sweet one that died? – to Bobby Chaplin in senior year . . . Oh!

Thought isn't all that good for you. You don't watch where you're going. I was walking right over my old house before I even knew it. It's buried like The Mummy's temple, down underneath that parking lot.

My whole life used to be in this block. Our parents sold out and moved into condos so the company could build the super-Publix. We were all grown and the neighborhood was going downhill anyway, but it was awful. They tore down all our houses! My whole childhood is buried underneath that parking lot, my ruby ring that I lost in Sallie's sandbox and my kitten Fuzzy, that we buried in my old back yard. I was walking over my parents' fights that always came out all right, and birthday parties and almost-sex with Bobby in the glider when we were in ninth grade. Everything I cared about is covered with tons of asphalt which is ironic, because old Lorna Archambault's house is still standing, right there on the other side of the street.

If you draw a straight line between Holt Realty and Far Acres where I was going, it would bisect the big old banyan tree in Lorna's front yard. I was like an arrow aimed at the heart of Davis McCall, I could have made it home earlier, but the snaky roots hanging off Lorna's banyan brushed my face like somebody who loved me when I was little, and it stopped me cold.

'Oh,' I said. 'Oh!'

Lorna used to chase us out of that tree, coming down off her front porch like a battleship. 'Rats,' she said, 'That tree is full of rats and scorpions.' She said, 'You girls get out of there before you get hurt, get out and go home,' but that wasn't what she meant. She meant that she didn't want her precious granddaughter playing with dirty little girls like us. She was so shaking-mad that parts of her face flapped, and I remember thinking, *You're so **old***.

'Oh,' I said to that tree even though you're supposed to be polite to old acquaintances, no matter how much they've changed, 'you're so *old!*'

And for the first time ever, I was too. My knees buckled and I slid down the big old trunk and sat there until chiggers or redbugs or something started biting, unless it was the uglies. I jumped up. By that time I was feeling so bad that I had to pat the tree goodbye, and I said, 'At least you're OK,' to make it feel better.

It was time to get home and put on makeup and pray to God that Davis got in today before high school play practice let out and Steffy came home. I wanted to face up to him and get it over with without her walking in, so I walked faster, practicing speeches, and next thing I knew, I was ranting at the stone lions at Pine Vista, two living signs of the ruination of our neighborhood.

Herman Chaplin's development scheme went bust in the Twenties land crash, before even our grandmothers were born. He had a dream, but as far as he got was the lions and stone markers at every corner and the stucco wedding cake where Bobby grew up.

The Chaplins always were a little bit too good for us, even Bobby, but in high school we never knew it, stupid me, I was in love with him. They went to college up north and settled around Boston and New York, but something happened up there and now all three of them are back, seething around in that big old house like snakes in a basket that's too small for them.

I used to dream up reasons for us to cruise Bobby Chaplin's house, back when he ruled the school, but now I drive past on my way in from Far Acres without giving Bobby a thought. Usually I'm sealed in my car with the AC on and my favorite CD, but I'd been walking for too long, and it was worse than crossing 38th Street where Harrison got hit. I ducked my head down and hurried on by, figuring out ways to get back at Davis for betraying me.

That scrawny, lascivious skank, Davis? Really? Is that the best you can do? Wrong. *Did you not think I would find out, Davis?* No. *Were you trying to torture me?* No. *What are you, retarded? Like, you thought you could get away with it?* No. *I **said**, don't ask, just get the hell out of here.* No, you need to guilt him a little bit, make him grovel before you kick him out, tell him . . .

This is embarrassing. I heard Bobby's front door open and I didn't hear it. I hoped to God it wasn't him. I kept going even after somebody called, 'Nenna?' and I went faster because I knew it was him.

I didn't stop until he caught up with me.

'Nenna Henderson!'

'Oh.' Any other day I would have hugged him: *Bobby, it's so great to see you*, even though it wasn't, but I was caught short with my messed-up life hanging out, and partly it was the shock. He'd fallen away in the shanks. In the way of redheads whose lives are over but they don't know it, his hair had faded to brown. I was too tactful to say, *What happened to you?* or ask him how he really was. I wanted to say *something*, but all I could think of was, 'Oh!'

'I saw you going by and I had to come out and say hey.'

'Hey, Bobby.' He was so friendly – did I smile? Did I look OK or did I look awful? Beyond it, I guess, because he looked all worried, and it pissed me off.

'How are you?'

'Don't ask me now.'

'I'm sorry. I . . .' Maybe he was waiting for me to spill so he could pour out his story; maybe he wanted to tell me what brought him down, and God knows we're all dying to know. I should have said, *Are you OK?* but it was getting late, I was exhausted, everybody would be home soon and I had cut him off before he had a chance to start.

'Don't be.' *Oh, Bobby, don't linger.*

He kept going along beside me. 'I thought maybe your car broke down.'

'Not really.'

'You looked like you could use some help.'

I did, but nothing I could tell him. If I'd shown him mine, he'd have shown me his. We could have hugged goodbye with, maybe, promises of more to come, but not just then. I had to keep going, so I did. 'Not really. I'm fine.'

Bobby tagged along, whether or not I wanted it. Football captain,

May King two years running and there he was following me like a dog. He'd been home in the Florida sunshine for three years but he must have spent it inside, he was that white in the face. He'd gotten skinny in there, but he was grinning and dancing along next to me as though no time had passed, 'Nenna, wait up.'

It all piled in on me and I started to run. 'Can't, Bobby. I'm late.'

'Late for what?'

It wasn't just Davis I was mad at, it was him. *When you were eighteen you wouldn't even look at me.* 'I'm in a hurry, Bobby. Why should I stop and talk to you?'

'I've missed you, Nenna. It's been forever.' He's changed but he smiled, just like in our yearbook. **Most popular**: **Bobby Chaplin and Laura DePew**. And, this is ironic. **Most Likely To Succeed: Bobby Chaplin and Lucy Carteret.** 'Nenna?'

You've been home three years. 'You could have phoned.'

'It's. I couldn't.'

'And you want me to stop and talk to you?'

'What are you doing out in this heat?'

'It's a nice day, I thought I'd walk.'

'If it's car trouble, I can call Triple A.'

'I'm almost home.' Home. Davis. Accusations and the fight.

'Let me ride you, Nenna. You look beat.'

My feet were raw but I wasn't about to stop now that I was so close. 'I *said*, I'm fine.'

At First Street, which you have to cross to get into Far Acres, Bobby did stop, exactly like your dog hitting the electronic fence. 'OK Nenna, take care.'

'I'm sorry. I have a lot to do.'

I do. In this town, there's a ritual checklist: call your lawyer, tell the kids, field a phone call from Coleman Rowell, who must have radar about these things, he's like a sex vulture waiting to pounce, the list was running through my head. OK, lady, get this over with, then tell Coleman *no*. Change your hair and dress to kill and go looking for a good man who will for God's sake do right by you. Bobby would be perfect, we could have started, but I wasn't about to stop for him. I was bent on getting home. Every nerve and muscle in me was screaming but I had to end my own business before I could think about starting anything.

5

Dan

To find out about the past, you have to go there.

Dan reduced his mother to ashes in a brass box, sealed and weighted as requested, and rented a boat so he could drop her in the Atlantic off the beach at Misquamicut, where she used to take him when he was a kid. She hadn't asked him to say a few words as the box with her in it plunged into the ocean, but he did. Never mind what he said over her. It is between them.

He did what you have to, the sad, necessary things. Filed insurance forms and settled with the funeral home. Cleaned out the apartment. Without her, the rooms were so empty that in a way it was a surgical strike. Goodwill took most of the furniture and useful small objects. He rented a storage locker for the rest. Met with her lawyer and closed up the house. His week is up, but he and his mother aren't finished.

All his life, Lucy lived as though history began when she had him. She pretended there was nothing before life in New London, and he loved her well enough to let it go, although he didn't, really.

He's been carrying it all these years, and all these years later he's found the hidden keys to Lucy's life before Burt. She kept them in her jewel box, like notes that she wrote to him, but was afraid to send. Now that she's safe from whatever she was afraid of, Dan is free to track down the answers to questions he promised not to ask. He's in Fort Jude.

It was a gut decision: no questions, no regrets. It made itself. He didn't quit his job, exactly, but he did call the office. His boss didn't say yes or no because it wasn't a question. He said, 'Remember, your mother can only die once.'

There are so many ways to parse this that he can't bear to start.

Dan Carteret doesn't want to kill his mother all over again; he just wants to put this thing to rest. He's here to strip mine her past and pull his father out.

With its flashy neon and artificial palms flanking fancy wrought iron benches, Fort Jude is nothing like New London – or Los Angeles, for that matter. It's more like downtown Oz – real palm trees and plastic flowers in cement tubs line Central Avenue, with flowers in pots hanging from the ornamental lamp-posts, and mosaic obelisks marking the major cross streets. There's so much cosmetic architecture here that it's hard to tell the difference between what is and what used to be. Brash new buildings compete with old hotels tarted up with false fronts like gaudy party masks. Dan skims the facades like a speed reader, looking for places Lucy would have gone. He wants to walk into her past and figure out what went wrong and why she tried so hard to obliterate Fort Jude.

This is not the time for a Holiday Inn, Marriott, Sheraton, any of your anonymous, clean places. It's not like he expects to run into his mother in the lobby, he just wants to stay somewhere that she might have come. He's looking for a hotel with a history, where the homefolks meet for drinks in late afternoon – people his mother might have hung out with, the ones who were born here and stayed here, so that they segued from backstory into now without feeling a thing. He'd like to slide down the bar, all, *Hi, I'm new here*. Smile and make them like him, which he's good at, even though he grew up pretty much alone. If he can make friends, maybe one of them will point him to Lucy's old neighborhood. They might even know the house. Otherwise, he'll have to go through Fort Jude street by street, block by block in his rented car, matching tree lines and front porches to the ones in his mother's snapshot until he finds the place.

It takes him two passes to find it, but the Flordana is perfect. Never mind the wrought iron fence surrounding the overgrown courtyard and the gingerbread trim bolted to the long front porch. Behind its Victorian facade, the Flordana is straight out of the 1920s, blunt and flat-footed and sweet. At odds with the false front is the Art Deco sign, blue neon winking at him from behind faded plastic ivy: FLORDANA HOTEL. Set back from the street, the hotel crouches between hulking office blocks like a nice old lady forgotten on the sofa at a high school party, wedged between two jocks too stoned to notice.

It's all cool until he parks and gets out of the car. It's hotter out here than he thought. It's . . . He doesn't know. In the courtyard he gets an attack of the dry swallows: gulp. The tiled porches are green with moss. The cement courtyard has a tired, dingy look. As if this is too little, and he got here too late. *Get over it!* he tells himself.

Don't get weird and don't pin any hopes on this. What does he think, that he can flash a snapshot of his mother and real Lucy will fall into his hands, buried secrets and all? That somebody will say, 'Why, that's Lucy Carteret, do you want to see her house?' Not really. He's a little crazy right now but he is, after all, a reporter. Was. Gulp.

Check in. Scope the place on the web before you start. This is no big deal. It's just the beginning.

But what if she and his real father actually came to the Flordana, like, after the prom? Or she stood out front waiting for her bus home from her summer job, praying he would come by in his car. Unless he parked and tugged her inside the Flordana, and she got pregnant here. *Don't, asshole.* Her lover could have been a night clerk or a waiter in the hotel coffee shop. Unless he . . .

Just don't. Hope eats him up from the inside. *He'll walk in and find me. Be here.* Would they know each other? He thinks so. It will play like a movie: *Father. Son!* Wait. The faithless shithead has a lot of explaining to do. Stupid, he knows, but losing people makes you stupid. Reporter, remember. You make your living finding out. Work this like any other story. Hit the right link and it will open up. Chapter. Verse. What happened to Lucy here. What's so terrible about it, and who his people are, really. The begats.

It lodges in his throat: the begats.

Other people take family for granted, but then other people have photos of people who look like them posted somewhere, letters, birthday cards. Family trees. A chunk of Dan Carteret is missing. It isn't just the **no father** that Lucy tried so hard to erase. It's the gap ordinary mothers fill with particulars: where she's from, who your grandparents are. What life was like before she got married and had you.

Stop that!

The woman at the desk is either a lot older or a lot younger than Lucy. She's so carefully put together and made up that it's hard to tell. Jointed silver fish dangle from her ears, very Florida. So's the aggressively blonde hair. She looks fit in her frilled tank top, although the wrinkles in the tanned cleavage give her away. Full mouth. Nice smile. 'Can I help you?'

'I need a room.'

'Lucky it's the end of the season.' She could do a commercial for those teeth whitening strips. 'Take your pick.'

Rumpled after the long flight, wrecked by the week of last things and sweating through the back of his khaki coat, Dan realizes that gross as he looks right now, she's coming on to him. 'The cheapest, I suppose.'

'Business trip?'

'Ma'am?'

'Jessie.' The grin says he must look pretty good to her, or that she thinks she's younger than she really is and he's older than he looks, unless it's just her way of adding some color to the day. 'Now, what shall I put down?'

He doesn't know.

'You don't look like a tourist.' She means, *What are you doing here?* 'If you're here on business, you get our special rate.'

Words pop out. 'I'm down here on a story.' Why does this lie make him feel so much better?

'You write books?'

'No Ma'am. For my paper.' Like a person here on real business. Smile for the lady, she believes. So can you. 'The *Los Angeles Times*? A story for the magazine.'

'Cool. What about?'

He isn't sure. 'If I tell you, I lose my job.'

'So I should put down business,' Jessie says.

Dan doesn't answer. He's thinking hard. There's some reason he burned out searching the web details on the human fires. Three old women. Here. Cool! Here's his readymade rationale; two words and he's justified. 'Research trip,' he says, grinning. 'Preliminary research.' Just saying it makes him feel better. As a matter of fact, it's a terrific story, he was just too fried to see it. Like a visa to this strange country, Lucy's fragment of newspaper justifies his presence here. 'Now if I could have my key . . .'

She isn't exactly holding him hostage, but she hasn't started checking him in. 'What are you researching?'

'Just an old story.'

'Ooooh,' she says, fishing. 'We have a lot of old stories here.'

'It's a kind of a mystery.'

'We have a lot of those. Which one?'

'I. Um. I'm not at liberty to talk about it yet.' The story shapes up in his head like one of those great unwritten novels – the kind writers only talk about in bars because by daylight, they evaporate. He frames the pitch: FORT JUDE, TOWN OF HUMAN FURNACES. His big break.

'I said, which one?'

'Ma'am?'

'Not Ma'am.' She has a very sweet grin. 'Jessie. Which mystery?'

It's been a long week. There's no logic to it but he can't be here at the desk much longer. He just can't. 'An old one,' he says, finishing with a warm smile that he hopes will be enough.

It isn't. 'Oh,' she says, all *faux naïve*, 'which one.'

'Spontaneous human combustion!' Why does that embarrass him?

'Oh, that old thing. Lorna and Mrs Keesler and that other lady.' Nice grin. 'You know, there are books.'

'I'll find a new angle.'

'Good luck with that.'

'I have to. It's my job.' He slaps his wallet on the counter: business as usual. 'Now if you'll just.'

'We'll put you down as business,' she says smoothly, scrawling in the showy red leather register planted like a stage prop on the marble counter next to the brass telephone with its standing mouthpiece and a receiver that you have to point at your ear. 'But I need to know how long you're going to be in town.'

'Good question,' he says.

'There's a rate break if you rent by the week.'

With grin that doesn't quite come off, he repeats the line written for him by the boss he probably no longer has. 'For as long as it takes.'

'OK then.' She makes a tick next to his name. 'Now, print your name in the book while I run your plastic. Folders with maps and tourist attractions over there in the rack. Nice handwriting.' She hands back his card. 'I have you on Five. Anything else I can do for you?'

'Not right now, not that I can think of. Well, one other thing.' He takes it and turns to go. Then need overwhelms reason and he pulls out his picture of Lucy, snapped in front of her house. 'So. Can you tell me where this is?'

'Sure,' she says, now that his card has cleared. Leaning over the counter, she shifts position, letting out a wave of sunscreen and perfumed deodorant compounded by body heat. 'Always happy to help.'

'I mean, this house?' She's squinting so he slides the snapshot closer adding, 'For. Uh, an architectural piece?'

That blind, vague smile tells him that she's one of those women who can't see without glasses but is too vain to put them on. Handing it back, she rests her knuckles on the counter. 'Sorry.'

He says, 'About . . . Old Florida?'

'Sorry, I can't help you.' She shrugs, rearranging her cleavage.

What is she, coming on to me? Damn, all his statements come out with question marks. Damn, he should have slept on the plane. 'So. You don't know the house?'

She isn't looking at the snapshot, she's watching him. 'Not really. Is there anything else I can do for you?'

'So,' he says, 'I have this other picture?' Knowing she'll need glasses he says tactfully, 'The faces are pretty small.' He slides it across the counter.

She may not recognize faces, but she knows shapes. Jessie slaps on her glasses and looks again. Dan is too distracted to pick up the change in her as she says, carefully, 'No, I don't know these people. From the looks of the car, that's from the dark ages. I'm a lot more recent than that.' She takes off the glasses with her foxy, jagged grin.

'OK then.' He puts it away. 'If I can just have my key?'

Odd. It's like a study in stop motion photography. Woman, arriving at a conclusion. Click. Click. Click. Let's get this done. She pulls a big brass key off the hook. 'Room 51. I'm alone at the desk today. You can find it, right?'

'Yes Ma'am.'

She does not say, *It's Jessie, please!* She dismisses him. 'OK then.'

'OK.' Dan lingers just long enough to be sure she's done with him. *What did I do wrong?* At the elevator, he turns and looks back. Jessie is doubled over the register, squinting at his entry. Then he sees her reach for the glasses again. As the elevator doors open he sees her snap open her phone. The woman who could have cared less about the snapshot stabs a number with her fingernail. She looks up with a sweet, distracted smile just as the steel doors snap shut on them.

6

Jessie

She didn't need glasses to know that was Chape Bellinger's old Jeep or name the others: Bobby Chaplin, Buck Coleman, Stitch Von Harten. Fucking Brad Kalen, God damn his eyes.

The minute the elevator doors close on the kid, Jessie hits 8 on her speed dial. She entered the number in a blinding rage when she re-entered Fort Jude. Given that she wants to smash her fist into that big, wet smacky mouth of his, she's avoided Kalen ever since. In spite of the fact that Jessie Vukovich from Pierce Point is now a member of the Fort Jude Club in good standing and last year he was the fucking Commodore, she's managed, but now . . .

She always suspected that life's a bitch. Turns out, it is.

His machine picks up, which is probably just as well. Jessie has been sitting on this for so long that acid fills her mouth. Things the bastard bastard needs to hear pile up in her head – packed in like enough nitro to blow up the world. If they spoke, it would all come out too fast, and Brad is stupid. Let the walking slime mold dangle by the short hairs for a little bit. She wants to see him hang by his guts, twisting in the wind while she takes her sweet time, laying it out for him.

As it is, the slick, radio-announcer track he laid on the machine goes on forever, smoothly supplying his cell-phone number and the number at the club. She has a full minute to compose before she spits:

'Now, don't call me back and don't ask questions. Just be aware that nothing you did is ever over. In fact, it's come to town. After what you did, it damn well serves you right.'

Shaking with fury, she ducks into the office. She has to compose herself before she can do makeup and put on her chic silk jacket and her diamond studs and high heels for lunch at the prestigious Fort Jude Club. She hates that she can't stop thinking of it as the prestigious Fort Jude Club. People who couldn't see her for dirt in high school have changed toward her since she came back to town in her Lexus and bought this hotel outright, thanks to the late Billy James, her fourth and final ex. The shittiest snots from Fort Jude High are her new best friends now, and even the boys look at her differently. Last year she sat down on the club patio with the Friday Lunch Bunch – on a trial basis, she thought, but she's been sitting down with them regular ever since.

It's silly, but given that everybody used to think of Jessie James, née Jessie Vukovich, as that cheap girl from Pierce Point, it's a very big deal. She has to get her shit together and get her smile working right so she can go down there and face them.

Even though it's the desk clerk's day off, she shuts the office. When he comes back down to the lobby, cute Dan Carteret will think she's gone for good, which is just as well. She likes the kid, but she doesn't want to talk to him, not as raw and hopeful and helpless as he is. There are things he doesn't know and things he should never have to know.

Poor kid, she thinks. Thinks he can walk in cold, ask around, and everybody will open up and tell him everything. Fat chance. There are some things only Jessie knows, and she's not about to tell anybody anything. She sighs. Poor kid, his knuckles were white when he signed the book, this is a very big deal for him.

Then she focuses on the real problem. The Lunch Bunch. What to say when they ask why she's late. They're nice enough to her now, but underneath Jessie knows who she is and they know who they are and there's still a huge difference between them. She's learned to hide it. In Fort Jude, the littlest things can give you away, so she has to be careful. Appearances are that important.

7

Bobby Chaplin

It isn't pathetic, really, it's just the kind of thing you end up doing when you're not yourself. He's been out of work for so long that he isn't sure who that person is.

For the seventh consecutive day since Nenna McCall limped by, Bobby is out in the sunshine, weeding around the cement lions on the front steps. In the dawn of his doomed real estate venture, Grandfather planted cast cement sphinxes and lions at every intersection in Pine Vista, which is what the late Herman Chaplin named his dream tract at the height of the Florida real estate boom. He poured thousands into private roads out here in the Twenties, when the sky was the limit and a thousand dollars bought something. The old man bought up every plot between here and Far Acres, in the happy expectation that the rich would come clamoring to moor their yachts on private docks behind their new houses. He envisioned a Spanish stucco wonderland out here: golf course, tennis courts, Moorish castles on the waterfront, as many as the traffic would bear. The last of his money went into building his dream house, the model home he could show buyers. One look and they'd come swarming to invest. He laid down octagonal tile sidewalks and convinced the city to pave the streets with red brick an unfortunate six weeks before the Florida real estate crash. It came a full five years before the national stock market tanked: an event that was anticlimactic down here, where land is everything.

Herman's brick streets are overgrown now, and jungle has reclaimed all his vacant lots. Most of his stony sentinels were stolen or vandalized and the ones that survive are decaying, all but the two flanking the Fourth Street approach to Pine Vista and the ones in front of his dream house. Grandfather kept them in mint condition until he died, at which point Bobby's father took over, which Bobby is expected to do. Like Bobby, the lions look tired; they've been doing what they're doing for too long.

Like Bobby, they need a change.

He isn't out here looking for Nenna, exactly, but it would be nice to talk to her. He'd like to know what brought her by here the other day, and why she was walking. The woman looked like she could use a little there-there – which he is happy to give, if she'll only tell him what's wrong. He isn't out front waiting for her, but there's always a chance that she'll come by and they can talk.

Not that there isn't plenty to do. He's yanking sandspurs out of whatever Bermuda grass remains in the doomed front lawn. Unlike his grandfather, who took to weeding the walks all the way up to Fourth Street, Bobby is not crazy, nor is he going there. He has responsibilities.

Until he lost his grip, Herman Chaplin saw to it that the pink-and-gray octagons in the front walk were lifted and leveled every year. Then Bobby's father did. His parents died gratefully, like relieved commanders turning over the helm of a doomed ship. Bobby sees to it now. As the only functional Chaplin, he sees to a lot of things. His siblings aren't fit to go out.

He wishes Nenna had let him help last week, she was so harassed. Lovely woman, looking maybe a tad old for her age – which is his age, more or less, they were in the same year all through school. Little Nenna was at the graduation house parties out at Huntington Beach, at the ruinous end of senior year at FJHS.

It was awful; he's never had more fun. Until the end.

That June he and Chape Bellinger and Brad Kalen, Stitch Von Harten and Buck Coleman stayed free in a condo Chape's aunt was stupid enough to loan. He remembers they promised to keep their feet off the furniture, which was covered in flowered chintz; there were all these little china *things* around and he remembers waking up on the pink shag rug with broken china mashed into his cheek but that's all he remembers because they were loaded for a solid calendar week.

They ran around until the sun came up and then you slept until three and got up and ran around all night, ingesting whatever until everybody was bombed into insensibility. Then they fell into Chape's Jeep and roared up and down the beach until the sun came up; at low tide the sand was packed that hard. They tore along screaming, scattering early morning walkers like gulls. Every condo and cottage on Huntington Beach was full that week; kids from five Suncoast high schools converged, so the people you fell down with just outside the circle of the bonfire weren't always people you knew.

Cathy Rhue had her folks' beach house for the week, she was famous for her body. She brought all the usual girls. Betsy Cashwell and the cheerleaders rented a cabana at the DelMar, everybody who was anybody came to Huntington Beach. Sexy Jessie Vukovich was there, but nobody knew where she was staying. Even Lucy came, but not until the last night, her grandmother was that repressive. His heart turns over whenever he thinks of Lucy, which he tries not to do. He slipped his tiny gold football into her hand after the May crowning but she never mentioned it. Everybody but Lucy was there for the week, and there were parties every night. Nenna Henderson was there, he thinks, but in the background, because she wasn't famous for anything. Not that they weren't all pretty. In high school certain elements gave you distinction and everyone else was a blur.

For instance, Jessie Vukovich was famous because she would do it with anybody, and in spite of the cold distance she kept, Lucy was famous for her looks. The cheerleaders you remembered because you all rode the bus to away games and you did what you could with them in the back. When you were team captain you had the best and the sexiest and the most famous, but that was before.

Nobody at school knew it but Bobby was also smart. He managed to hide it until he got into Harvard, the first in ten years from Fort Jude High. At the time he actually believed getting into Harvard made him better than he was, which turned their senior blast into a curious exercise in detachment.

All week, at least until that awful Saturday night, Bobby was like a passenger poised at the top of the gangplank, waving goodbye to all those little people on the dock, watching them recede as he left them behind.

Nothing turns out the way you thought. Most of us handle it, but people like Bobby are inclined to dwell. Something grave happened to Bobby Chaplin between then and now, and long before Grace left him, it broke him in two. He can't leave it alone and he can't figure it out.

People like Bobby actually believe there is a fulcrum, an exact, identifiable point when life tips and everything goes downhill. With people like Bobby, it's never who they are, or what they did. It's, *I was going along fine until X happened.* They need something to blame. The problem is, they can't put their finger on the X.

He has wasted his life on it. One of his shrinks said, *It's never what happens that makes the difference, Mr Chaplin. It's how you handle it.*

Well, he thinks, that's easy for you to say. He feels bad about what came down at senior houseparties. No. That he was involved. No. That he was out of his mind on vodka and whatever they were smoking and lying nose down in the mangroves when he should have . . . Don't go there.

Listen, he finished Harvard *magna cum* in spite of everything; he went to Harvard Law and ended up in finance, great job with a big firm so, fine.

Then, why is he here? After a year back in Fort Jude, after months of stewing over first causes, Bobby Chaplin is in no condition to analyze.

It's crazy, but there's the outside possibility that Nenna knows. He wants to ask Nenna Henderson – no, McCall – what went wrong in that wonderful, catastrophic senior week, like, what does she remember? Were there warning signs? Maybe she saw things he was too trashed to note, or deconstruct. He thinks now that the event that brought him down is located back then, but he can't be sure. Too much happened. He was drunk and lovelorn, Buck was drunk and mourning his dead twin brother, Chape was off somewhere getting it on with Cathy, Brad was drunk and vicious and Stitch was just drunk. Nothing was clear.

If Bobby had stayed sober maybe he'd remember, but you didn't. They were kids! The parties were great and you were drunk all the time, it was a given; people said things they'd never say and did things they had to be wasted to do. Worse things happened that weekend and he was too trashed to know if it's his fault.

The last thing Bobby Chaplin wants to do is stand out here on the front walk strip mining memory lane, but he doesn't want to go back inside either, not with his siblings idling in there, sour and mismatched, the moth and the toad. You can hear the TV from here. Instead he lingers, listening to the light breeze playing in his grandfather's stand of Australian pines. In the Twenties these trees were as common as pig's tracks, but the big freeze took out most of them and the ancient towering pines on the Chaplin property line are among the last. They dwarf the house. All his life Bobby has loved the dry rasp of wind in dead pine needles: the sound of something that he knows is coming, but can not yet name.

In fact what Bobby hears coming is a car, but he doesn't register until it stops and someone gets out. Startled, he whirls. 'Nenna?'

It isn't her. A young man in a new Florida shirt pulls down the brim on his airport Panama to hide whatever he may be feeling. Polite enough. Puzzled. 'Sir?'

'Are you looking for me?' He won't recognize the spike of hope in Bobby's voice.

'I'm not sure. I'm looking for . . .'

'Bob Chaplin. Goldman Sachs?' He's lost everything that he used to be, but Bobby still has that strong handshake.

'You're a broker then.'

'Was.'

The young man considers. 'Then, no.'

'Oh. You must be lost,' Bobby says, disappointed.

'Not exactly. GPS.'

Of course. Confident post-millennial dude, fully equipped. There'll be a laptop and a digicam in the backpack, enough DVDs to let him fly home without getting bored; smartphone in the pocket of the Florida shirt. It hasn't been that long since Bobby himself lived in the high end, high velocity, high tech working world – color copiers, CD and DVD burners, extra screens so you can do everything at once. Blackberry, iPhone, which is the phone of choice? He's lost track. He rocks with homesickness for all that. Whoever this kid is, he probably thinks Bobby is retired, as in, over with. Nice old fud tending his front walk. *I'm not that old!* 'iPad.' *What am I forgetting?* 'WiFi booster.' He adds, to establish his credentials, 'Next-generation everything.'

'Pretty much.' Nice grin. Nice looking kid, sandy hair, not from around here, too pale. Tourist, probably, fresh off the plane.

It's not half-bad, standing out here with him. If Nenna comes along she'll see that he is by no means Mr Lonely Guy. He has other people in his life. Nice kid, Bobby thinks. If we hit it off, ask if he'd like to meet for a drink later, down at the club. The psychic accident that brought Bobby back to Fort Jude makes him reluctant to look up old acquaintances but it would be extremely cool to walk into the Fort Jude Club with this personable young guy from up north. Don't just stand here, start the conversation. It would be rude to ask what he's doing in Pine Vista, where tourists never come.

Bobby says what you say to outsiders. 'I bet you're enjoying our sun.'

'What? Oh. Yeah, I guess.' The young man isn't attending to the conversation, not really. He's studying the house. If they were in a horror movie he'd see Maggie Chaplin's pale face bobbing at the window; she never goes out. In real life Al Junior could wander out on the porch any minute now, scratching the wedge of belly where his T-shirt has ceased to meet his jeans. To Bobby's relief the face of the house stays blank.

'Oh,' Bobby says. 'You came to see the house. It's a kind of a landmark.'

'The house.' Whoever he is, the kid jerks to attention. 'Is that your house?'

Oh God, don't ask him if he wants to look around inside. Not with things the way they are. 'If you're a contractor, we're not looking to renovate right now.'

'I'm not.'

'Who are you, anyway?'

Now the kid tilts back the hat to prove that he has nothing to hide. He has a very sweet grin. 'Nobody you'd know.'

'I guess I mean, what are you doing out here in Pine Vista?'

'Is this Pine Vista?'

Bobby says drily, 'It was supposed to be.'

'Sir?'

'Just an idea my grandfather thought he had. But you.'

'I. Um, I'm looking for . . .' Whatever he's looking for, he isn't ready to say. Instead he jerks his head at the house. 'Do you know who lives there?'

'I do. Temporarily,' Bobby adds, but not fast enough. *Who are you kidding?* 'I mean, for as long as it takes.'

The stranger looks disappointed. Bobby isn't exactly doddering but the kid says, the way you do to an old person who gets confused, 'You're sure.'

'Hell yes I'm sure.' *Oh, don't dismiss me like that!* 'What are you really here about?'

He has a hard time getting it out. 'Do you know who owned it before?'

'I told you, my father.' Bobby isn't sure why this makes him so angry. 'And his father before that. And tell whoever you're representing that we don't intend to sell.'

'I'm not here to buy anything!' Wounded, the kid thrusts a picture at him. 'Look, I just. I'm looking for this lady's house?'

Everything in Bobby stops. All he hears is the rush of his own blood. It takes him a while to drag a response out of the dead silence in his heart. 'I'm sorry.'

'Did you know her?'

Shaken, Bobby is glad that he, and not this *young guy*, is the old person here. *He is too young to know how carefully we are taught to dissemble.* 'I don't think so. No. No. It's not the only Spanish castle in Florida.'

Too much, probably, but the outsider carrying Lucy's picture is in no shape to read the fine print in Bobby's face. Every line in his body sags. He shoves the snapshot back into his pocket. 'I see.'

He looks so messed up that Bobby says kindly, 'Is there anything else I can do for you?'

The young man thinks before he answers. When he does it's nothing Bobby expects. 'Did you ever hear of a woman named Muriel Keesler, got on fire?'

'Keesler. Oh,' Bobby says, relieved. 'That. Moms used it to scare us. This is what happens when you play with matches, kids . . .'

'And two others.'

Bobby says sharply, 'What are you really here about?'

The answer is so careful that it may not be an answer. 'Going up in flames. I'm down here on a story.'

'Reporter!' This makes Bobby feel better. 'You never said your name.'

'Dan. I'm looking for the house?'

Bobby does not say, *Dan what.* They can't be out here in the road much longer. He needs to be alone so he can think. 'Where it happened? The last one standing is over on 57th.'

'You mean the one where Mrs Archambault.' Changing expressions race across his face. 'I saw the photos.'

Bobby says, 'Pretty bad. If Lorna'd seen herself like that, she would have died.'

The wind in the pines doesn't stop, but the air around the newcomer's head is still. There is an odd moment before he says, 'You mean the foot and the chair.'

'My point. In her day, she was quite the lady. If you're researching the family . . .' *Bad idea, Chaplin. Stop your mouth.*

He doesn't have to. The kid cuts him off. 'I need to see the house.'

For a frantic half-second, Bobby thinks he means this house. Maggie, doing a Mrs Rochester in the window. Al watching QVC. 'This is not the best day.'

'No. Her house.'

'Of course.' Make a smile for him, Bobby. Make it good. 'It's back that way, one block in from the corner of Fourth and 57th. Where you made the left at the Publix? If you see the water, you've gone too far. Look for the banyan, it's . . .'

'Thanks.' The kid is halfway to his car.

Bobby says anyway, 'The oldest one in town.' Then he goes inside to do what he has to do.

Maggie's fussing over her African violets. The sunlight playing on those white, white hands is just sad. After her 9/11 meltdown, it's the best she can do. Younger than he is, and she has Little Old Lady written all over her.

His big brother is kicked back in front of the Shopping Channel with a beer. If anybody asks, Al is retired, which is a good cover if you don't know. Retirement is as good a name for it as any. He's not that far north of fifty, too many idle years ahead, but is that an indictable offense? Between them, QVC and The Shopping Channel have everything Al wants and they have it in his size, second day delivery, which gives him a giddy feeling of control. Al's happy, Bobby thinks, or what passes for happy, and this is even more depressing then the set of his sister's mouth as she nips dead petals off yet another African violet.

He's going upstairs to phone when Margaret looks up from her violets. 'You had a phone call.'

'When?'

'Just now. I called you, but I guess you didn't hear.'

'I was talking to someone.'

'You.' She snaps a head off a violet. 'You're always talking to someone.'

Not really. 'Did they leave a message?'

'I am not your answering service,' Margaret says resentfully, apparently pissed off by his contact with real life.

He loves his sister, he hates seeing her like this. He says, 'Look, you can't just go into mourning and stay there.'

'OK, it was Chape Bellinger.'

'Shit.' You reach a stage in life where you can't tell whether a phone call from somebody you used to know is a good thing or a bad one. It's embarrassing, given that they were bonded in high school. They haven't spoken since Bobby got home, and that was last spring. When you get right down to it why would they, Chape is a litigator, Bobby's heard, demon in the courtroom, president of the Gryphon Club, kids' soccer coach, king of the world. Given what just happened, they have to talk anyway. Lucy's picture, in this stranger's hands. He has it planned: *Bob Chaplin, returning Chape Bellinger.* Sound official, arm's-length. Businesslike. Give him the bad news, whatever it is, and at this point he isn't sure. But the number Chape left is not the office. It's the house. They've known each other for so long that when Chape picks up, Bobby says, 'It's me.'

Big, handsome guy, big voice. 'Hey, you.'

'You called?'

'I did.' Chape's third generation Fort Jude. He never starts a meeting until he's made his manners. 'How've you been?'

'Good. You?' Bobby winces.

'I can't complain. How long have you been home?'

People gossip. It's not like Chape doesn't know. 'Too long.'

'All this time and I've been meaning to . . .'

'I know.' Chape is waiting for him to say, 'I have too,' so he does. He did mean to call Chape, really. He just hasn't, is all. Now he has to offer, 'Maybe I can give you and Sallie dinner at the club.'

'We'd love to, just as soon as . . .' Wait for it. The hesitation. The apologetic, 'You how it is when you get busy.'

'Everybody's busy.'

Like a teacher handing out the consolation prize, Chape says, 'But we'll look for you at the party tonight.'

Bobby laughs. 'I'd rather see me dead in the rain.'

'That's kind of why I called. Listen, Bob. We have a problem.'

Confused, Bobby asks, 'How did you find out?'

'Word gets around.' Chape laughs, to show Bobby he's in charge. Then he rethinks. Puzzled, he asks, 'How did you?'

'He was here.'

'Brad?'

'Brad!' Bobby's stomach sours. 'Fuck Brad. I haven't seen Brad since college. Listen Chape, we have a real problem.'

'Explain.'

'A kid was here. Could be Lucy's.'

Fucking lawyer, Chape asks in that controlled tone. 'How do you know?'

'He came looking for her house.' Bobby is deciding whether or not to tell him about the snapshot.

Chape should ask him why, but he doesn't. For a long, uncomfortable moment, he doesn't say anything. When they were kids, Bobby's pal Bellinger drove teachers nuts with his empty, innocent stare: *Who, me?* Bobby doesn't have to be there to see it – the smooth, untroubled look of a man whose mind is as empty as a pond. 'What does that have to do with me?'

'He's asking questions.' *Take that, you bland, self-important bastard. Like I'm going to spell it out.*

'I see.' Chape says smoothly, 'Let's keep it to ourselves, OK?'

Bobby groans. 'You know this town. One phone call and everybody will know.'

Bellinger uses the dramatic pause. *Take that!* Then: 'They don't have to know we're connected. Can you hold? Another call.'

Bobby holds, wondering what would be lost if he just hung up.

Before he can, Chape is back. Crisp and urgent. Agenda Man. 'Something's come up. Give me your cell number. I may need you here.'

8

Dan Carteret

Not every decision Dan makes is rational. They said, 'Your mom just died. Don't try to make big decisions or operate heavy machinery until you're over it.' Yeah, right. He dropped everything and flew to Fort Jude – on what? Two snapshots and a gold plated football.

Weird stories about human furnaces, printed out at a Kinko's in New London.

What was he thinking?

That his mother stashed her past in that box on her high dresser for him to find, but it's a long way from there to here.

His first try fell flat – ten minutes, an hour ago – how long has he been sitting here under a tree outside the Publix? Stupid, thinking he could walk up to the house in Lucy's snapshot and find Family. Grandparents. Aunts. That they'd hug him, all, *My how you've grown*, ply him with milk and cookies and tell him everything. Or that Lucy's secret lover would show up for the Greek recognition scene: *Father!* The smack of flesh on flesh colliding. *Son!*

Instead there was only Chaplin. Was the curtain moving in the Magic Kingdom turret behind him, a woman peeking out? He can't be sure. He should have stuck it to the charming bastard while he had him, flashed the Jeep snapshot, but Chaplin is too – what. Faded to be one of them. Even thinking about it makes his belly shrink. The man was laid open, standing out there in the road with his hands floating up like origami cranes.

Shit, Dan should have stuck it to him. —You knew her, you probably took this fucking picture.

The trouble is, he can't prove it. He should have homed in: — What else would she be doing out in front of your house, back when you could still afford to paint it? *Back when she was happy*.

He should have leaned on Chaplin, hard. —What changed her, or is it who? Was it you?

He was too seized up to ask, —Are you him?

He isn't ready yet. Afraid Chaplin will say yes and when Dan gets old, he'll be weak and apologetic, just like him. Coward, he took directions to the Archambault house, thanked the guy, got back his car and left. It's not like he was running away, he just couldn't be there, OK? Not that he's dodging that particular question. It's just too soon.

In fact, he is running ahead of the answer.

He used to think anything was possible; kids do. When he found his real dad everything would change. When Lucy said it wasn't Burt his heart jumped. *Now!* But she bound him with, *He wouldn't want you to know*. The rest is gnawing its way out of his belly now. What was she afraid to tell him? That his genetic package contains a wild card, he decides. That he's been holding it since birth. He knows in his gut that there's something waiting inside him that he has no name for, some buried shame or latent power or unimaginable secret, and here in the town where his mother grew up and – he thinks – met his father and fell in love, the knowledge leaves him laid wide open.

Waiting for it to show itself.

It can't be Chaplin. He has to know. He runs his fingers along his jaw, divining the bony structure. He and Lucy have the same eyes, but the shape of his skull comes from someone else, not that polished failure he left paddling in the road. He holds his hands up to the light, half-expecting to see the truth outlined in the tapering fingers or written in the network of veins on his naked arms. A man with superpowers would see everything, down to the last capillary, illuminated, but this is just Dan Carteret, hunched in the dirt under a tree in the Publix parking lot in Fort Jude Florida, wondering.

He needs to look into his father's face and see.

How he will age. Whether he can be happy.

What he will become.

Too much bad coffee, no food and no sleep breed questions. They swarm round his head like gnats. Batting them away, he lurches to his feet like Swamp Thing and goes into the Publix to refuel. He grabs potato chips, hot dog buns to sop up stomach acids – when did he eat? Nuts and Slim Jims for protein, Red Bull for that caffeine jolt and the essential sugar rush. He carts his stuff outside and sits down in the shade to eat.

He starts a list.

Scope the Archambault house, now that you're here. Take digis and make notes so you can write a feature to justify your presence here. Find neighbors who lived here back in the day, before the neighborhood went to crap. Line up interviews for tomorrow, when you're not so fried. Go back to the hotel for a WiFi connection and file a pitch. Then you can crash. Tomorrow, look for Lucy's life before him, find it in the morgue at the Fort Jude *Star*.

Good, he thinks. A sensible plan.

But Lucy's snapshots seethe in his pocket like unanswered letters or overdue bills: his smiling mother, clasping her notebook in front of Chaplin's house. She was there that day for a reason. The more he thinks about it, more he knows he isn't finished there. When the camera caught her with that lovely smile, was she coming out or going in? Chaplin damn well knows. What else does Chaplin know?

What she was really like, Dan thinks bitterly. Before.

Standing, he heads for Archambault's, but his mind is stuck somewhere between here and there.

In the lexicon of next things, there's one more thing he has to do today. If he can prove that Chaplin knows her, he'll nail the bastard to the wall. Fuck yes he knew her. In a town this small, how could he not? All he needs is a clipping, yearbook, prom photo to link the two of them, or letters . . . just something he kept.

He has to go back to Pine Vista. Tonight. When you think your source is hiding something you lean on him, hard, but Dan is too messed up to tell whether Chaplin is hiding something or just plain hiding out in that Spanish stucco heap. This time he'll go armed. *Bring takeout. This may take a while. Jumbo coffee. Maybe a six-pack. Eat while you wait. Black jeans, he decides, black T-shirt so nobody sees you out there in the night; sneakers, so they won't hear you creeping up.*

He'll hole up in the car for as long as it takes, waiting for him to go to bed. No, better. To go out.

Then he'll break in.

9

Steffy McCall

The next person to meet Dan Carteret is Steffy McCall. The last thing Steffy wants to do is meet anyone. Not today, not with her mom and dad running around crazy, all ragged and disrupted. Something happened last week, and they have gone to a place that there's no getting back from.

Steffy saw her very own mother from upstairs in this deserted house. Her mom came wandering out of the Publix lot and across the street. She was way too close to where Steffy and them hide out and smoke weed, like, right down there in the yard. She was *this close*! She plopped down under the banyan tree underneath the attic window, which scared the shit out of Steffy. Your mother, outside your private place!

Mom! She'd wreck everything if she found out.

Steffy and Carter Bellinger that she is secretly in love with, plus

Billy and lascivious Jen, have been hanging out here ever since the day Carter broke in. For the first time, Steffy had her own safe place and it was wonderful. Then, last week – last week! – her clueless, fat-assed mom wandered across the street from the Publix and sat down under the big old banyan; you could see the top of her head from here.

They were all loaded by that time, out of their heads on Jolt Cola and weed and it was killing Steffy, but she had to play mean bitch and shush them before Mom heard. 'Shut your hole,' she told Carter who she really is in love with, and she almost fucking cried. 'That's my mother, so shut your fucking hole.'

If she saw them it would be the end of parties in this house, and Mom would be up her ass with a fine-toothed comb. As it turned out Mom's mind was on something else. She just flapped like a confused penguin and went tottering off, so, whew.

It was good she was too distracted to hear them, but as it turns out, Mom was distracted by something really bad. By the time Steffy got home that day she had written a whole cover story that her folks were too upset to hear. Dad was dragging the rollaway bed to the far end of the house and everything was different.

Thank God for this place. She and Carter and them were rolling out of the Publix with the trunk full of beer and munchies that day. Instead of driving out to Pierce Point to get loaded like always, he broke into this creaky old house and they ran everywhere. In the attic, Carter said, 'This is the place.' It was like fate. *Yang.*

Steffy was all *ying,* 'And we are the ones.'

They scavenged outside the big places on Coral Shores and Carter stole some great stuff from his pool house. Jen had an air mattress and pillows and a step-on pump to keep it fat and Billy brought the beer. Their attic looks like home now – except for this ancient dressmaker's dummy, saying a snotty fuck you to their X-Box posters and Cinemart lobby cards which are kind of mocking her now that she is here alone and everybody else is on the bus.

If Carter really loved me, he'd have stayed back. But no, he was like, 'Come on, it's fun!'

Fun just doesn't seem right to her, given the way things are at home.

Nobody knows where she is.

Mom thinks she's on the class trip to Busch Gardens. Her friends think she's at the dentist. If Carter really cared, he'd have known that Steffy was too messed up to go. He'd have stayed back with her and they'd be kissing now. They might even be, oh, Steffy's too young, but she thinks about Doing It; she thinks about it all the time. Alone in the dry attic, she has to wonder: do other kids sneak in here when we're not around?

If Carter had stayed back today . . . Yeah, right. Shit. If he wants to get with Jen Cashwell in the back of the bus, OK, let him, Steffy is on to bigger things.

Like personal space. She only just found out she had one – it was in a magazine Mom had. Unless this is her own personal down time, which people need more than they need beer or weed or even Carter, that she loves so much, heavy-breathing in their ear. It's hot in here, but she's cool. Some people would say Steffy was hiding, but she's not. She just doesn't want to be around anybody right now, not even Carter Bellinger.

All Steffy wants to be in the world . . . All she wants to be is alone, which is what she is. Or she thinks she is. Even in a town as safe and sleepy as Fort Jude, you never know.

Another girl would think the attic was creepy, but Steffy and Carter and them have had so many beers and smoked so much weed and told so many secrets in this old place that it's like home.

At this point, it's better. No parents all undertones, hissing and spitting over things they don't want her to know about, and no Dad desperately pretending it's not a fight. No Mom, all smirched from crying and, like, trying to be brave.

Steffy can hardly bear the sight of her mother these days, trotting around in her perky pastel outfits and heavy makeup, with a lipstick line that she can't keep straight because her mouth won't hold still. No Mom for Steffy for a while, thank God, and please, no Dad. She doesn't know how she feels about Dad, the way he is. He is not bearing up well under the pussy whip, and, what Steffy can't stand?

All this, everything that's coming down on him? Davis brought it on himself. She found out about him and Aunt Gayle before Mom did, you know, from that time they flew out to California? Mom dyed her hair and bought outfits for the trip – gaudy colors that she hated, so she must have known something was up. You'd have to be blind, deaf and stupid not to see it. Like, from the minute they walked into the house in Toluca Lake. A blind wombat would pick up on the loaded looks, that cunty smile on Gayle, and if Steffy didn't know it for sure, by the time they got back from a day in Ventura she did. Gayle took Stef and her folks and her second husband Clueless Ed and their assorted kids for a day at the beach.

After lunch she sent Ed off for charcoal and some obscure item that she knew would take him forever to find, sunscreen SPF 2000, maybe, or eye of newt. That left Steffy and her sort-of cousins beached while Gayle took Dad body surfing and Mom sat on a rock looking confused.

That night Mom went to bed early and everybody else sat on the back deck of the house Ed built, listening to Gayle and Dad talk about the great times they had when they were kids back at the family camp in Myrtle Beach, the cousins just played and *played*. Grampa McCall was Superintendent of Schools in Columbia, South Carolina, and Dad never lets you forget it. He built the camp so the generations could gather, Dad said, and Aunt Gayle said, *We had the best time*. It was like an opera or some half-assed sentimental duet that went on and on.

Dad hardly noticed when Mom stuck her head out the upstairs window, he and Aunt Gayle laughed and talked while Clueless Ed cleaned up and toasted marshmallows for the kids, and they talked on while the kids lit sparklers and ran around screaming in the dark and they went on talking instead of putting the kids to bed, which they were supposed to do, so Steffy was up almost all night. After all, Mom said later, it's the only thing I asked you to do. This was a first in both households, surprise. The forgetting. They got laughing so hard that around midnight Mom came out in her bathrobe and rasped, 'Keep it down.'

After that trip Mom bought a whole 'nother wardrobe; she even lost a couple of pounds, but by then it was too late.

No time for that now, Abernathy, Steffy thinks, Dad's joke.

She is in a really strange mood. If she goes home any time between now and 5:30, when her folks are out the door for Patty Kalen's engagement party, they'll drag Steffy, even though the whole town knows Patty and her dad are hardly speaking because he was so drunk that he tried to pick her up outside Mook's Bar. 'You're going,' Mom said. 'Everybody who's anybody is. After all, that poor girl lost her mother. Cecilia Kalen was one of our nearest and dearest.'

Steffy couldn't say, *Mr Kalen creeps me out*, although it's true. 'Do I have to?'

'Yes. We're giving it.'

By 'we,' she does not mean her and Dad, Nenna means her and her girlfriends that she hangs out with because he and Mom live in separate worlds.

It's like Dad is here, but he isn't, and Steffy has no idea whose fault this is. If she goes home now he will be lying in wait. He doesn't pounce, it's more like lurking. Or melting into a puddle that you could fall in, which he's been doing a lot this week. Get too close and you'll sink. He schlumps around with every line in his body screaming *Hit Me*, unless it's *Forgive Me*, and Mom . . . Mom will tell her, 'Go put on something decent, you're not going out looking that.'

She's been to those parties, and those parties are crap. So are her parents, both of them. It's crap being with them right now.

She's better off here.

This is her place, if Steffy has a place, but late afternoon sun chased the last bit of shade off the roof and now it's too hot. *Hell with it. I'm not moving until the party's started and I'm sure Mom and Dad are gone.* It's harder to breathe than it was when she first lay down on the air mattress, trying to get up the strength to sob out her heart.

She'll sit out the next hour out back.

By the time Steffy hits the back porch she's gasping for air like one of those girls some creep stole and buried alive.

Oh, shit.

There's a guy on the steps. Just sitting there.

Perv alert!

Why am I not scared?

Whoever he is, he's cute. Not scared. I am sooo not scared.

Be cool. Breathe. Ask, like you belong here and he doesn't, 'Who are you?'

He looks up. Nice, like it's no big deal being a grownup, more like he's another kid. 'Oh, sorry. I didn't know there was anybody home.'

'Somebody lived here but she's dead.' Steffy ought to be on guard right now, hopping off the porch for a head start in case he lunges, but he is not that guy. 'Nobody lives here.' He is hanging in place like a sentence ready to be completed or a song waiting to be sung. She almost smiles. 'Not even me.'

His head comes up. Noted: this is not her house.

'But I sort of do,' she says, to forestall questions.

Nice guy, he doesn't ask. 'I see,' he says, waiting for whatever comes next.

God he is cute sitting there with the sunlight on his hair. God he is too old for her. Steffy should get out of this conversation and off the premises, but she won't. Not yet. 'I thought you would say, "What are you doing here?"'

'That would be a no.' He gets up. 'None of my business, right?'
He shakes one foot and then the other to see if they're still working,
like you do when you need to get the blood running so you can
move on.

'It's OK, you can stay.'

'Can't.' He grimaces. 'I've got stuff to do.'

Steffy discovers that she'll say anything to keep him. 'No problem
if you want to hang in. Really.' Question, keep him with a question.
'So. What got you here?'

'Long story.'

'Want to tell it?'

'Not really. Well, part of it.'

'Which part?'

'We'll get to that.' He has this sweet, wide open look; it's what
Steffy's guidance counselor tries and fails to hit with her because
he's a jerk. Guidance guy strikes out in spite of all the heavy eye
contact and trust exercises he makes them do in fifth period Sex
Ed, never mind that it's humiliating. But this guy . . . The smile.

Steffy is sort of smiling too.

'So. Can I see inside?'

'Not really,' Steffy says. It's not her house, but it is, and they both
know both these things.

'Look, I'm down here for a newspaper? It would be a big help
if you let me look around inside.'

'Are you writing a story or what?'

'If you're worried I can show you my press pass.'

'I believe you,' she says. 'I just can't . . .'

'Like you're not allowed to . . .'

'Talk to strangers? Not really.' She lifts her head in that proud,
cocky way her mother hates. 'I can talk to anyone I want.'

He almost-laughs. 'Because you're a big girl.' He's not being
condescending or anything, he is doing a great job of imitating Mom.

'Pretty much.' How can she not grin?

'Look, if this a bad time, no problem. I can come back.'

'That won't make it OK.' *Don't go.*

'Me talking to you?'

'Me letting you in.'

'Did you know this Mrs Archambault?'

'Not really.'

'This is her house.'

She bristles. 'Not any more.'

'I'm doing a story about some bad old stuff that happened here.'

Right, Carteret. Early American History. 'When?'

'You don't know?'

'Not really.'

Instead of hitting on her or trying one of those sinister things the TV teaches you to beware, he backs away from the house, pointing up. 'That's the room where it happened.'

Steffy moves out into the yard so she can see where he is pointing. 'Where what happened?'

'The last spontaneous human combustion.'

'Holy crap!'

'Crash, bam. Whammo, she just. Burned up.' As though he already has her cooperation, he says, 'That's why I have to get inside.'

If Carter came by right now he would be jealous, seeing the two of them standing together here. Steffy backs into the steps and sits down. He is still out there studying the second floor. 'So, what are you looking for?'

'That's the trouble. I don't know.' Unlike grownups, he doesn't sweep the step with his hand; he isn't scared of sitting on something gross. 'Why this woman burned down to grease spot, I suppose.'

'Ewww.'

'First they thought it was the husband.' He pulls a notepad out of a pocket on his thigh. Cool cargo pants. Muttering, he runs his pencil down the page. 'Harold P. Archambault.' He taps the eraser on the note.

'You have notes?'

'Big story. Research.' He looks up. 'They were divorced.'

Steffy hates that word. Divorced. 'Like, he set her on fire?'

'No. Nobody knows what did it, that's the thing.' Frustration makes him squint. 'But, you've gotta wonder. What if he was here and they had a fight?'

'People fight all the time,' Steffy says uneasily. 'It doesn't mean anything.'

'These things, it's usually the husband.'

'Just because they had a fight?' She is really uncomfortable now.

'Because usually, it is. But this guy was with his girlfriend at the Prince Edward, out at the beach, it's on the Web. They were together all night.'

Steffy gulps. *Oh God. Oh, God.* She's not afraid of this gentle guy with eyes that turn green in direct sunlight, but she is afraid. She's scared of something that she won't name and hates to think about. 'Like, he set her on fire because they had a fight?'

'No. It was spontaneous. I'm not creeping you out, am I?'

Yes. 'No.'

'Sitting there one minute,' he says thoughtfully, 'and the next minute – whoom.'

'Ewww!'

He ticks off another point. 'But the room was untouched.'

She has quit breathing. It comes out in a rush. 'Up there?'

'Yeah. And I'm here because . . .' Steffy has no way of knowing that this is not a sentence he can finish. After some thought he says, 'If I can just get into that room and mail back a couple of screen shots . . . I can buy some time.'

'Time?'

His face changes. 'It's hard to explain.' When she doesn't say anything he says helpfully, 'If you want, I really can show you my press pass.'

Steffy would like to see it; she'd like to follow up with a question but she's squirming. It's nothing he said. Something else is gnawing at her. 'So they were divorced. She burned up and it's the husband's fault.'

'The girlfriend said he was with her all night.'

Oh God. 'Girlfriend.'

'"Other woman," they called it back in the day.'

Oh, God.

'He opened a magnum and turned up the music and that was it. They didn't know until the police came.'

'So it couldn't be him.'

Bemused, he says, 'It wasn't anybody. It just happened.' He's waiting for her to follow with another question, say *something*, but Steffy is too far gone to speak. He jogs her arm. 'Are you OK?'

'Yeah.' But she is thinking, thinking, boy is she thinking. The sun burns hotter. The breeze stops. She gets up. 'So. Want to see inside?'

'I thought it was your private place.'

'Not really.' She is never coming back here. 'Not any more.'

'I did creep you out. I'm sorry.'

Still sitting, she opens the screen door. 'Really. Feel free.'

Nice, he says carefully, 'Are you sure? After all, it's, like, your house.'

She gets up. 'Come on, it's anybody's now.'

Now that she knows, the house is over with for her, but she

sort of owes it to him to show him where this lady burned up and in its own way the prurient, curious part of her has to see. In school she flunked spatial relations on the standardized tests, which means she never knows where she is in a building, which is weird. Between that and the house being all cut up after this divorced person burned up, she has a hard time leading him to the right room. Plus, she's a little scared. Like, what if the old lady is still up there, like they'll open some door and her skeleton will spring out and chase them outside and all the way down to the bay.

Upstairs, there are so many partitions that she can't tell which window he was pointing at or whether it's on this side of the dividing wall or somewhere else. Plus, she's freaking. Nothing this nice guy did, nothing he said.

The Archambaults had a fight and then the mother caught fire. After the divorce.

She says, miserably, 'I don't know which room.'

'It's that one. There.'

Everything in her sinks. 'Oh.'

He's very nice about it, really. There is nothing special or different about the right room, only that it's the right one. Yellowed window shades sag at half mast and the linoleum is pocked with dents where generations of different furniture stood after she died. The wallpaper has faded to nothing. There are no smoke marks, no charred woodwork. Just water stains and nail-holes where pictures used to be. It's as if nothing ever happened here. He studies the sketch in his notebook while Steffy fidgets. He paces, considering, until she snaps, 'Are you done?'

'What? Another minute. If you don't mind.'

Her mind roams out and when it comes back, Steffy is disrupted and writhing, so her voice comes out all freaky and weird. 'I have to go.'

'What's the matter?'

'Matter? Nothing. I'm fine. It's just. I have to go!' Gulp. Start over. 'Do you know what time it is?'

'Five.'

'Shit. I'm supposed to be home.' She isn't but she has to be; she has no idea why she's so scared.

'No prob,' he says easily. 'I'll take you.'

'No,' she says. 'No way.'

'Right. Never get into a stranger's car.'

'That isn't it. OK, I really have to go.' Steffy isn't exactly crying when she bolts, it's just sweat running down, it's . . . OK, if she starts in front of this guy she will totally lose it. What scares her second most in the world is that if she does cry, she won't be able to stop. Shit, he's following! Her voice trickles out. 'Take your time. Look around all you want.'

'You're upset.'

'I've gotta go.'

'It's too hot to walk.'

'It isn't far.'

'At least let me buy you a Coke for the road.'

'Can't,' Steffy says urgently. 'Can't!'

'What's so important that you can't wait and I can't take you?'

Grief boils up in Steffy and runs over. 'I have to get dressed for this stupid party, OK?'

She walks until she's sure he's gone back inside, where he can't see her. Then she starts to run. When she gets home nothing has happened and everybody is fine.

10

Nenna

It was weird at Lunch Bunch today, acting like everything was all right with me when everything was all wrong, what with Davis turning out to be a rat and me laying down the line and not knowing which side of it I was on. I should have stayed back, but in Fort Jude you have to go out and show yourself to the people because you don't want to hear what they say about you when you don't.

In a way it was a relief, sitting down with the girls like always, pretending nothing's changed and it's all fine. We were assigning chores for Patty Kalen's engagement party, which we're giving because her dad's a drunk and poor Cecilia died before the divorce went through. Davis or not, tonight I'm dressing, if not to kill, then at least to maim, because in this town *acte de presence* is everything, and four hundred people are coming to the club! Kara Coleman had Buck order Champagne from a Napa vineyard and the club staff is

doing the wet bar and the buffet, and if Brad bitches we'll tell him,
'Cheap at the price.' He's paying, but we're in charge. Cecilia suffered
at his hands but she loved him so we never said a word, and whatever she suffered, tonight is our big chance to make it up to her.
We're damn well helping Brad do right by their daughter, so she
can look at the pictures years later and be proud.

It was an odd day. Sallie put down her checklist. 'Wow,' she said,
and I still don't know if she was sorry. 'Lucy died. My nephew saw
it in the New London *Day*. It's not like it'll be in the Fort Jude
Star,' and then she said, because Sallie is that kind of awful, 'Turn
your back on Fort Jude and Fort Jude turns its back on you.'

We weren't close, but she was prom queen in our year! That's
too close. I saw the grave yawning and it scared me because to tell
the truth, it didn't look all that bad to me.

Sallie picked up her clipboard. 'Moving right along.'

Jessie sailed in before she could start; she looked amazing. 'Big
news.'

'You're late!' Sallie hates being interrupted and she hates women
attractive to Chape. Lucy was one, back in the day. 'We were just . . .'

'You'll never guess who just checked in at the hotel.'

I guess Jessie made two. Sallie stepped on her hard enough to
squash her flat. 'Shhh. We're mourning,' she said, although it wasn't
exactly true. 'Lucy died.'

'Oh!' Jessie said, and the ones of us that don't like Sallie all that
much listened hard. She looked shaken. 'I hadn't heard.'

'Of course not.' Sallie stuck it to her, the bitch. 'You were never
close.'

'No.' In fact, Jessie was a parade of different faces. There are things
we don't ask now that she's one of us, and with friends, you don't
really want to know about their sordid past. She got it together, but
it cost her. 'As a matter of fact, this guy . . .'

Sallie struck back. 'We were deciding on the centerpiece.'

'Shut up and listen!' Jessie pre-empted, take *that*. 'It's her son.'

Of course all Fort Jude will know by the time the party starts,
but thanks to Jessie, we were the first.

Sallie was like steel. 'What makes you so sure?'

'Name on the credit card. Dan Carteret.'

'That doesn't mean . . .'

Then Jessie shut her up for sure. 'I saw Lucy in his face.'

Now, Jessie grew up over on Pierce Point along with the Pike brothers and other people we don't know, but even then she was sharp, didn't study, never raised her hand, but you knew. What if she did leave town under a cloud? She came back a different person. The boys used to call her 'anybody's,' but Jessie Vukovich is *somebody* now. High-end car, designer clothes, bought the Flordana outright, started in with United Fund and Meals on Wheels, months and months of selfless volunteering and now she's practically one of us.

'Green eyes, I wonder where that comes from. I looked at him and I swear I saw Lucy Carteret, he must be here because she's . . .' She sort of choked. 'Now, Carteret. That's not a common name.' If there's more, Jessie wasn't saying it.

Betsy said, in that flat tone that means the opposite, 'Isn't it wonderful Lucy has a child.'

'Had.'

And one of us said what we were all thinking, 'I wonder who the father is.'

Even Sallie realized we were on Jessie's side in whatever war she thought they were having. She said, 'Poor Lucy,' and we knew we were done talking about Jessie's news. Then, *wham*! She got me in her sights. 'Nenna, what were you doing, risking death out on 38th Street last Thursday, what's going on?'

'Who, me? That wasn't me.' I thought fast. 'Listen. We should do something for poor Lucy.'

'Why? She never did anything for us.'

I saved Betsy from Sallie a dozen times back when we were little. She owes me, so she jumped in. 'Don't blame Lucy, blame her grandmother,' she said, and we were off.

Even Cathy Rhue lined up with me. 'We could have a little memorial down at Trinity, you know, since she died so far away from home.'

Sallie said, 'What for? We didn't know her all that well.'

Kara said, 'That was Lorna's fault,' so there was nobody left on Sallie's side.

'Making her ride everywhere in that big old car, like she was too good for Fort Jude.'

'It must be awful, dying up north, with nobody around to mourn.'

Jessie laid back, the way you do when you're not sure of your position, but we were all glad to have someplace new to put our miseries. I said, 'Maybe we can get the deacon at Trinity to do it here at the club.'

And everybody but Sallie said, 'Let's do!'

Things happened and we wouldn't, but planning helped. It was all the funeral we could give her, you know?

We went around the table, all, Lucy was pretty, she was nice, she was too nice for us, because you had to be a mean girl to make it through high school, you just did. So were our mothers; it's something you don't outgrow. They said Lily Archambault started Northshore Elementary with them but Lorna yanked her out, like Fort Jude was some kind of social disease that she could catch, and packed her off to Ashley Hall. She married a man in Charleston without telling her mother, things between them were that bad. Lorna brought Lily back to Fort Jude in her coffin – toxemia in the last month of pregnancy with Lucy, our mothers said, so you cut down on the salt.

She also brought home the baby like a prize.

Poor Lucy! If Hal Archambault hadn't dumped her and moved out to the beach with Eden Rowse it might have been different, but Lucy was all she had left. She was always overprotective and cranky, but it got worse after the divorce. She locked Lucy up like Rapunzel in that tower, so it's not our fault she didn't fit in.

I said what everybody else was thinking, 'I guess the old bitch got what she deserved.'

'You mean the fire.'

'Whatever it was.' My God, last week I was in her front yard!

Out of the blue, Jessie said, 'She lost her man. No wonder she was a bitch.'

I choked on my B.L.T. and ran to the john before anybody could say, 'Are you all right?'

11

Dan

Burt Mixon, that unwitting genius of negative reinforcement, taught Dan the absolute integrity of personal space when he was old enough to know he had one, but not big enough to defend it.

The gawky, anxious girl's strung so tight that the kindest thing he can do is let her go. When you get like that, you don't want people to see you. Not the way you are. Dan knows. At the corner she turns around to check. He waves and goes back into the kind of heat that stops hearts. It's exponential; even the cockroaches have died. Stalled in the sweltering shotgun hallway, Dan considers. He's looking for so many things in his life that he can't be sure what brought him here. It's those fucking news photos, he thinks. The ones Lucy tried so hard to hide. As if your mother can protect you from certain things.

The gabled frame house where the old lady died may have been nice back in the day but it morphed under the hands of multiple tenants, who made it hideous. Heading upstairs, he picks his way through a jumble of makeshift partitions, amateur wiring and crap fixtures, searching with no clear idea of what he is looking for: diaries, perhaps. Notebooks. Some trace. A hook to hang his story on. He'd settle for a note crumpled in a kitchen cabinet or a cry for help scrawled on the plaster under torn wallpaper, but all he finds are insect carcasses and desiccated mice, empty roach eggs. Dust.

'Come on,' he says to no one. 'Give me *something*.'

The attic, he thinks, even though it's clear there are no secrets there. It's hours until dark and he's running out of next things to do. The girl left her pack, he notes, disproportionately cheered. The teddy bear tag has Steffy McCall scrawled on its belly, with the address. He can always drop it off at her house. Dan shoulders the pack and with a false sense of purpose, doubles back on the room where the woman died, looking for something – emotional detritus or some forgotten object or her outline scorched in the floor – anything to mark the fact that something stupendous happened here.

He studies the splintered floor and peels away wallpaper. He peers into her empty closet, but Lorna Archambault might as well have blasted off, shooting up through the ozone layer to flame out on the surface of the moon. He needs to go, but heat drops on him like a dentist's protective lead blanket. Like a collapsing lawn chair, he folds into lotus position in the spot where her recliner stood.

Absorbing the space.

His breathing slows. His hands lie palms up on his knees, relaxed, open to whatever comes. It is the posture of meditation but there is the outside possibility that sleep throws a switch somewhere inside him; he won't know. When he next looks up, his perception has jolted into a new place. Flies drop in mid-flight in this heat; reason is stillborn. In this place, in his exaggerated state, even pragmatic reporters like Dan Carteret can inhabit the bodies of the dead.

The room is as it was in the photos, flowered wallpaper still fresh. *My mother's taste, not mine, cabbage roses and that ghastly rug*. Press photos of the death scene are black and white, the room was stripped years ago, how does he know what the colors were?

He just does.

Lavender because it's Hal's favorite . . . Lorna means the ex-husband's. This rocks him. How do I know? In that flash she is in this room with Dan, cynical realist that he is, sinking into cushions molded to her bulky form. Lodged in the spot that smoldered long after her soul fled the fire, he undergoes a profound change. *Holy fuck! . . . lavender ruffles at my throat*. Even the BarcaLounger is restored. Gold brocade, he notes, but from a recumbent position, as though this is *him* kicked back in the chair, just in from dinner with Dorian, sweet boy ('she is survived by a son, Dorian Archambault, M.D., and two grandchildren, all of Fort Jude'), a little drunk after an evening with his family, *I ate too much, but . . .* looking over the toes of her purple slippers at the TV. Studying the tiny feet on the raised footrest, *my best feature*, he notes her plush bedroom slippers, the trim, pale ankles laced with purple veins, *but for a woman my age, still sexy*.

'God, where did that come from?'

Lavender nightie, Hal's favorite color, in case he comes. If I'd worn lavender to dinner that terrible night at the Flamenco, if I'd reached under the tablecloth and touched It through his pants, would he have insisted on the divorce?

Perfume, fresh lipstick, *in case he drops in for a bon voyage*. The TV's on, but she has no interest in TV. Hoping, Hal's ex-wife waits up for him. *It is, after all, my last night at home.* She's brought a nightcap to the chair with her, a little cognac on ice because *this calls for a little celebration.* She is tired and anxious and excited, not because of the coming trip but because maybe Hal . . . *He didn't come to the club to say goodbye because he doesn't want Eden to know. I'm going around the world, of course he wants to see me alone . . . And when he comes, if I touch him the way he wants he'll forget that bitch Eden Rowse and stay.*

She waits.

Seething with anticipation, Lorna waits beyond all waiting. *If he remembers his manners, he'll come tell me goodbye.* She hopes beyond the point of hope. She is not yet angry, even though she knows the bastard is out somewhere with that woman, he took up with her before the . . . *If he loved her he'd marry her, it's just the sex.* Listening to the doleful sound of ice in her empty glass. *He's coming, he's just a little late* and then, *That selfish bitch! This is her fault.*

Sad, Dan thinks. No. Angry!

What do I care, this time next week I'll be having espresso in front of St Peter's in Rome . . . Her glossy nails knead the brocade. *Where is he, why won't he come?* She knows, but she doesn't want to know. *Dammit, Harold Archambault, come here!* Inheriting that fleshy white body, inhabiting the gold BarcaLounger, Dan Carteret moves through Lorna Archambault's hopes into grief and staggering rage because in the posture of meditation, in the hyperbaric chamber of this still, hot room, he sees. In some way he can't begin to comprehend, he and the dead woman are linked.

There are, however, things he can't possibly know.

Sweating and stultified, hallucinating or mysteriously unleashed, Dan Carteret inhabits the old lady's last night. *Damn you, Hal Archambault, I didn't have to wait up. I didn't have to sit here for so God. Damned. Long, smiling like a painted fool* . . . He plays out another scenario: *My God, Hal what are you doing, dear God, please don't light that match!*

No. The husband was nowhere near. He had witnesses, the mistress, the night clerk at the beach. The girlfriend must be pretty long in the tooth by now, did she stay in town, can I track her down for an interview?

Wait, what if Hal got fed up with her whining and actually torched the place? Why would he, he had what he wanted, boffing his girlfriend 24/7 at the beach.

Don't be disgusting.

Right. Hal doesn't care if the she lives or dies.

Stop that!

'All right,' Dan shouts at her, 'All right!'

One more sip and he'll come. She is rocking and sucking on the cognac; *if he comes in drunk all I have to do is touch that thing and he'll beg me to drop the trip and stay with him.* Even though it's too late, she plans: *I'll pull him into this chair and vulgar as it is, I'll show* **him** *around the world.*

Time dies. Resentment catches fire. *Forget me, will you, well, I'll show you.* Pills she needs in the pocket of her robe. *He'll come in and find me and then we'll see who's who and what's what.* Right, it's logical, if not inevitable. Sitting with his hands open on his knees, Dan falls into her bitterness: ***Take the pills and when he finds me with my tongue out and my eyes rolled back, it will serve him God damned right.*** Resentment twists in her belly and ignites. ***Damn you, Harold Archambault. God. Damn you.***

Something changes. She cries out in Dan's voice: 'What are you doing here?' His head comes up so fast that his neck snaps. There is somebody new in the room. Astonished, Lorna hisses, ***You.***

Dan lurches to his feet, blinking. He can't see, but he hears:

Get out.

Shuddering, he calls, 'Who! Who?'

How did you get in? She's frightened. She's furious. ***What are you doing here?*** Dan cracks his mouth wide, listening, but there is no hearing the other side of this dialog. His gut cramps as the old lady's entrails knot. ***You have no right to be here. How dare you come here, making demands?*** Disappointment boils in her belly. ***Instead of Hal.*** There is shouting: not hers – someone else.

Troubled, Dan hears only Lorna, screaming, ***Get out. Shut up and get out. What are you . . . my God!*** Livid, rocking and furious, she sees it coming.

Whatever it is.

Dan doesn't know. Then he does. *In this room,* someone else cries: 'Dear God, watch out!'

She rasps, ***I will die before I let you take . . .***

Someone who shouts, 'It's too late!'

Here in the room.

His voice. Whoever he is. 'God damn you, old woman.' The room shakes.

I'll see you dead. Words boil out of her, leaving Dan riven and shaking. ***I'll see you in hell.*** And in a plume of flames, she imagines it. She sees me writhing and howling in the heat. *But who am I. Who am I?* Rigid and furious, she envisions the murders – Hal, once she starts there will be no end to it, Eden Rowse. ***You.*** The ball of heat inside her grows; in the unlikeliest of cavities it flickers, getting brighter as she seethes in the depths of her recliner, unaware and unprotected, roaring, ***Who's sorry now?*** Furious, she is too angry to comprehend the fire inside her, any more than she will know the exact moment that her soul explodes and flies out in a shower of sparks. By the time her body splits and flames shoot up there is nothing left of Lorna Archambault but the chair she sits in and the shell of her body in its melted shreds of lavender that she put on especially for him; everything else is consumed from within, everything but the husk. For a few seconds she flames brilliantly – gorgeous, **Too bad Hal can't see**, and then collapses inward. What little is left of her curls back on itself and fuses with the melting fabric of the ruined chair. Only rage remains, a nugget of distilled evil so powerful that Dan yelps in pain.

The guilt.

Whose? 'God.' He lunges for the door.

'God!'

The guilt is terrible.

How did this door close? Did I shut myself in? Did she? Drenched and shaking, he grapples with the knob and finally breaks out. He's free, but the knowledge follows him out of the room. Changed by forces he doesn't recognize and can't name, he hurtles downstairs and out into beginning night.

12

The guys

It's a nice enough day out here on the water, but it's getting late. Not that Stitch Von Harten and Buck Coleman want their afternoon on the water to end. Every Friday they find ways to back out of the office – Stitch from Von Harten Printing, which his dad founded, and Buck from Coleman Chrysler, where he shows up only reluctantly because his father hung the business around his neck like a stone.

Every Friday they come out here with a couple of six-packs, whether the grouper are running or not. Stitch knows it sounds cheesy, but it's their special time. They're dragging their feet because of the party. They did their part – they're paying for it, stood back and admired the dresses their wives bought for the event – should be enough. The hell of it is, they're under orders to show up early, to help Cathy and Buck's pretty wife Kara cope. They're supposed to be home in time to shower and shave, break out the clippers for nose-hairs and put on the clothes the wife laid out for them and stand there until she approves.

They will do their job and walk in smiling, but, shit. All that social agro and nicey-niceness when there are egrets and blue heron in these waters, astonishing birds that take Stitch's heart with them when they take flight. If he had his druthers, he and Buck would be out in the boat watching the sun go down, but time is thumbing its nose at them and they have to go.

'Fuck,' Stitch says. 'How did we get to be so old?'

'We're not old, we're just domesticated,' Buck says. For a guy who's spent his adult life grieving, Buck is more or less content. 'We were hot shit, weren't we? Back in the day?'

Stitch laughs. 'Still are. But I see what you're saying. At reunions, they're sizing us up, looking for things to cut off.'

'Because we ruled that school.' Buck hasn't exactly pulled up the anchor. He is staring out at the bridge. 'We were good, weren't we?'

'We were.'

Moodily, Buck cracks another beer. 'We didn't know how sweet it was.'

Stitch has problems of his own, but he prefers not to dwell. He says sympathetically, 'Nut cancer. What a bitch.'

'Oh, that. That's nothing.' Buck looks up. 'We had everything, and we fucked it up.'

'Only at the end.' Stitch knows where this is going. 'Darcy. We all felt bad.'

The summer before senior year Buck's dad told the twins their future was Coleman Chrysler, no ifs, ands or buts. Darcy Coleman was drunk by noon. By four, he was crazy-ruined – they couldn't cut him off, couldn't bring him down. At midnight Buck's twin drove a demo model off the lot and crashed into the biggest tree on Beach Drive. It took hours to pry him out. Buck threw himself in on top of Darcy, like he wanted to be buried too. He's been going around like half a person ever since.

Then Buck surprises him. 'No. I mean the end of senior week. You know when.'

Stitch knows exactly when and he groans out loud. 'Right.'

'If Darcy'd been there, she'd have stayed back. No room in the Jeep.' Buck is getting weird and agonized. 'It wouldn't of come down the way it did.'

'Don't beat yourself up over things you can't help.' Stitch starts the motor so he won't have to hear what Buck says in reply. He takes off in high and doesn't slow down until they turn into the estuary off Pierce Point.

They are in low, putt-putting along the shoreline to the Marina when Buck says, 'Look!' He can't point; it's too obvious. He jerks his head at the shore. Weird business: they are being watched.

'Holy crap,' Stitch says, and he means it in a good way. 'That's Walker Pike.' Even from here, although he is half-blind without his glasses, Stitch knows. Pike is so unlike them that there's no mistaking it: that cigar-store Indian profile, the proud lift of the head. Even back in high school he was a little scary, strung tight as a string on a crossbow. Not Like Us. Stitch Von Harten personally has changed shape in the years intervening and so has Buck. It happens, but not to Walker Pike.

If anything, he stands taller, so lean and easy in his body that Buck sucks in his belly at the sight. 'Fuck, in high school he was nothing. Now look.'

'Yeah. Pierce Point trash,' Stitch says. 'What goes around comes around someplace else, I guess.' Walker Pike that they used to walk past without speaking is *somebody* now, sitting there on the deck of his neat redwood house with its glittering solar panels. 'I heard he invented Google or Ebay or some damn thing. Now he's rich as God. Look at that house!'

'Yeah. Kara says it's in *Architectural Forum*, just what you can see from here. They never got inside.'

'All that, and he wouldn't let them in?'

'He always was one weird bastard.' Stitch waves. 'Hey, Walker.'

'Look, he sees us! Walker, hey.'

'Remember us?' Not that Walker would recognize him, heavy as he is. 'It's Stitch and Buck, Buck Coleman? From Fort Jude High?'

Fluid, fearsomely easy within his body, Pike stands. Like a priest, he lifts one hand, showing them the blade but stopping short of the blessing. Then he turns and goes inside.

Stitch says, 'Well, it's nice to see you too. Son of a bitch couldn't afford a clean T-shirt when we knew him. Now look.'

Buck is slapping at his pockets. He motions to Stitch to shut the motor. 'Phone. Crap. Too late.'

'Probably the girls, getting on our case.' In Stitch's pocket, his phone is vibrating off the hook. He pulls it out and checks caller I.D. 'Wait. No. It's Chape. Buck, it's Chape. Yo, Chape!' He listens carefully. 'There's trouble with Brad. He wants us at the shack. We're on our way,' he says into the phone and slaps it shut. 'Damndest thing. He says Chaplin's coming.'

'Well, shit.' Buck looks happier than he has all day, probably because unlike them, all-American high school hero Bob Chaplin is slipping, so much for the leader of the pack. Every man needs somebody to look down on, and now it's Chaplin's turn. 'It'll be nice to see him. He's been home, how long? It's damn well time he showed himself.'

13

Walker Pike

It was funny and sad, watching the two old fuds out in their motor boat, idling a little bit too close to his house. Walker didn't mind; they looked harmless enough until they hailed him, which drove him inside. He can't be with people he knows. Walker knows them, all right, but he doesn't know them well enough to predict what they'd say or do if he let them in, or what might come down if it went wrong.

In high school he had their faces by heart, but he wouldn't have recognized either one if Stitch hadn't broadcast their names. Von Harten. Coleman. The least of the fabulous five – football captain and four rich kids from the Fort Jude Club. In high school he hated them. Face it, in high school he envied them. Well, look at them now, bobbing in that crap boat in their floppy crew hats and nose guards and zinc oxide, probably because the wives said it was that or metastatic melanoma from exposure to the sun. Poor bastards, they never had a chance.

Walker's mind usually travels on another plane but in a way it was gratifying, thinking at ground level, where he left these good old boys the night he left Fort Jude – forever, he thought. He never belonged, for which he's always been grateful. He didn't run with them in high school. He observed. An outsider then and an outsider now, Walker is a behaviorist. To him they've always been specimens from another culture because they acted so big and thought so small.

In a way, he's sorry he didn't wave back when Von Harten hailed him – they're nice enough and sad, really, with one already dead. It would be fun to see. Too bad he couldn't invite them to tie up on his dock and come up to the house for a beer.

He'd like these two old guys to see what the kid from Pierce Point made of himself with what little he was given, but it isn't safe. Now, Walker Pike is safe enough in New York or London or any of the big cities where he does business, but he can't let himself get close to anybody he knew growing up in Fort Jude. There's too much backstory between them. Interface and there's a chance that in spite of his best intentions, it will end badly.

Given the givens, Walker knows it was weird to build down here, when he fought so hard to escape. It's the terrain. He was driving along the coast outside Cape Town with the crashing surf on one side and mountains rising at his back when he was leveled by home-sickness, not for Fort Jude, for sandspurs and summertime heat mirages on blistering white sand. He came back to Florida for the sawgrass and mangroves in certain inlets and the creatures that fed among the roots, these horizons with thunderclouds at one end, and at the other, orange sunset and pink afterglow.

He's rich enough to telecommute, so he built this place. He bought the plot and surrounding property on the water not all that far from Pierce Point, where he was so miserable as a kid. It's risky, but heart-break brought him back. It's as good a place as any to be alone.

Too bad, Walker thinks, but I had to let them go. They were good old boys, Coleman and Von Harten; Chaplin was OK, although his feelings for Chaplin are ambiguous at best. The problem lies with the other two, whom he *will not name*. It's too much like summoning demons. Name them and they show up. And everything goes to hell. Trouble is, he can't say whether those two are the demon or he is, so. Sorry, Buck. Sorry, Stitch. Not today.

Even people you like may bring up things it's dangerous for you to remember. First proof of the existence of . . . No. Don't go there.

So Walker locked his door and dropped the louvered shutters, not because he's scared of those two good old boys, same as they ever were, but because he's scared of what he might do.

If.

That's the problem. It was his problem back then, it's his problem now and always will be.

The if.

14

Nenna

Crazy, but when the doorbell chimed I thought, *What if it's Bobby?* A nice man to hang out with when Davis goes. Not that I'm sure he is. Going, I mean. We haven't sat down over the details, but when I walked back from work last week, my mind ran along ahead and by the time I collapsed at home, I knew.

I can do this!

Five whole miles, and I only stopped once. I'm stronger than you think.

I know it's Bobby out front. A woman would phone ahead. It wouldn't be half bad, walking into Patty's engagement party on Bobby's arm. One look and they'd all know without me having to explain. I can ask him in and make a fuss over him, and Davis McCall, who's out in the car somewhere sulking, well, Davis can go to hell.

But my face! All dressed up, with my face all naked and smeared with grief. After days of not speaking, Davis picked today to have the fight. Frankly, life was a lot more tolerable when we weren't speaking, but these things have to be done.

I've been putting it off for months. What with parties and Steffy and my job and a hundred dozen household things, I don't have the time. I thought we might hash it out this summer when everything slows down, so I have to wonder. Did Davis plant that phone bill to smoke me out? Tomorrow, I kept telling myself, tomorrow we'll start, but we didn't. Then God cursed me with an empty afternoon – two clients canceled, no new houses to list. With Davis home early on Fridays and Steffy safely off at Busch Gardens, I walked right into it.

He let me have it before I got in the door. 'OK, Nenna. I'm done.'

All the blood rushed to my head. 'That's all you have to say?'

'I'm not spending the rest of my life on that sofa.'

Push leads to shove; I shouted, 'Then you're not spending it here!'

Crafty Davis, leading me on. 'You want me to move out?'

'I don't know what I want!'

God damn Davis, he lit up like it was Christmas morning. 'Great,

I'll need the weekend to pack. Do you want to me to pick up cartons or can I borrow the roller bags?'

I'm glad Steffy crashed into the kitchen just then, before I screamed at him. She thumped through the Florida room in a panic, calling, 'Mom?' like the world was ending. 'Dad?' She tumbled into the living room with her hair gone wild and when she saw us facing off, all hostile and stony, she stopped cold, and I can't tell if she was disappointed, or just surprised. 'Oh! You're all right.'

'Steffy!' *And we tried so hard to keep her out of this.* 'Honey, of course we are.'

'I was so scared!'

She looked so stricken that, forgive me, I yelled at her. 'Well, get a grip!'

And God damn Davis, he just blinked, sticky sweet and bland as custard pie. 'Scared, honey? Tell Daddy what you're afraid of.'

What do you think she's afraid of, you sniveling cheat. I was furious at Davis, but that's not who I hurt. 'Go upstairs and get decent. You look like shit!' She ran out sobbing even though I called after her, trying to make it right. 'I bought you a great dress. Carter's coming to the party, Sallie made him swear.'

Now she's upstairs, crying in the tub.

Davis let loose as soon as she cleared the room. At least she didn't have to hear her dad swearing and slamming as he stomped out through the Florida room and drove away. That's the beauty of central air. We're sealed up tight against heat and street noises and outside interference of any kind.

Except Bobby, waiting for somebody to answer the bell. I have to wipe my hand across my face and go to the door with a smile. Live in this town long enough and you learn how to do that in seconds, bump up the rheostat so nobody knows what just happened or how bad it was, and I will be charming. 'Bobby?'

'No Ma'am.' Who is this *lovely man*? Look at him! Good-looking in a blurred, messed-up kind of way, with such a hopeful grin that you just know he's OK. I come to the door a walking shipwreck, and here he is on my doorstep, like a gift. 'Mrs McCall?'

'Nenna. It's short for Genevieve.' As if we're already friends.

'I'm Dan. Your daughter left her backpack and I . . .' He hands it off like a calling card.

'Oh, you must be from the school.'

He takes a little bit too long to answer but that's OK, the poor thing is so rumpled and sweaty that his day was probably worse than mine. 'I'm new. She left her bag at the . . . Um.'

'Bus.'

'Anyway, here it is.' And here he is, lingering.

OK, so am I. 'Well, thanks! She'd thank you herself, but she's in the tub.'

'Tell her I said hi.' On any other day I'd close the door and that would be it, but he's the first nice thing that's happened in a week of terrible things. Besides, he's so attractive and hopeful, leaning into our lovely, cool house, *yearning* – sort of like me, looking for inspiration in decorators' model rooms.

'She'll be down in a minute. Come on in, you look dead beat.'

I park him in the Florida room with the kitchen island between us, although he's way too flustered and grateful to try anything. I duck behind the fridge door so he won't catch me smoothing my lipstick and fluffing up my hair. Then I fix two iced teas with crushed mint and sugar on the rims. He's not the only one who needs a lift. When Davis comes back and I'm sitting here sweet as Jesus, laughing and talking to a new man, he'll have to re-think the awful things he said at the end.

The trouble is, we aren't what you'd call talking. He's cradling that glass like a Magic Eight Ball, you know, if he stares long enough, the right answer will float to the top.

'How long have you been at Fort Jude High?'

'Um. I just got in today.'

'New teacher?'

'Not really.' Why does he look embarrassed? 'I'm um. I'm a reporter?'

'Oh. I thought you were from the school.'

'No Ma'am.'

'Nenna.'

'Nenna. For the *Los Angeles Times*? Here's my press pass. I'm here on a story.'

'Oh.' I can't read a damn thing without my glasses, so I pretend. 'Writing up the school trip to Busch Gardens?'

'Not really.'

'Then where did you get Steffy's . . .'

'I knew she'd want it back, and I thought maybe you'd do me a favor. There's this other thing I'm trying to . . .'

'Favor?'

'Look, Nenna. I need your help.' He pulls out a snapshot that's way too faded to read. 'I was looking for this house?'

'House.' The thing's a blur but I'd rather die than go groping for my bifocals, that's such an old lady thing, and now that he's here, I'm working my way back to being young, and if he wants to . . . Stranger things have happened. 'What are you looking to find?'

'It's hard to explain. Um. My mother was from here?' He's doing that kid thing where the voice goes up in a little hook at the end. 'Lucy. Lucy Carteret?'

God. 'She's your mother?'

'Was.'

My God. 'Oh!'

'She died.'

I know! 'I'm sorry.'

'Did you know her?'

I should be saying, *Know her, I went to school with her,* but oh, this is so stupid, pretending I couldn't be anything like that old. 'I'm sorry.'

'Yeah. Me too. Well, thanks anyway.' He has such a nice smile!

'Don't go.' I put two fingers on his wrist. *Oh, this is embarrassing. Me, flirting with Lucy's son but he's so . . . I don't want to be old!*

'Pink, much?' Before anything else can happen, Steffy blunders in, twirling her skirt. 'I look like a fucking shrimp.'

That ruffled dress looked much nicer on the dummy at Norma Jean's Boutique and I go all Mom on her, instead of whatever I thought I was when it was just us together, him and me. 'Don't use that word in this house.'

Oh, she is scornful; she hasn't seen him yet. 'Or a fucking Barbie doll.'

Sweet man, he intervenes. 'Hey Steff, I brought your backpack.'

'You!' She's embarrassed – or something. 'You told my mom?'

'I would never do that.'

'Told me what?' I'm too distracted to follow up because I hear Davis rattling around in the breezeway, just back from wherever he went to sulk, the rat. I'm hurting so bad that I want him to come in on the two of us sitting close on the sofa, me and my new man. Then he'll know who's sexy, eat your heart out, you son of a bitch.

Steffy scoops up her backpack, glaring. 'You didn't say any . . .'

Something passes between her and this Dan Carteret but there are so many particles piled up in the room by now that I can't read what he's telling her when he says, 'Nope.'

It's the proximity – his young, lean body sitting *this close* to mine, and everything – the way my body feels this minute, how hard it was with Davis and how long it's been – all piles up in me and meanwhile my girl Steffy stands there posing in the archway with her head lifted and wet lips like a model for something you want but are afraid to buy and then, damn, she gives me The Look! I saw it coming the day she was born, I just didn't know it would be so soon: *Now **I'm** the fairest in the land*, and I have to be hard as nails.

'Go upstairs and don't come back until you find the right shoes.' Meanwhile Davis slams the door and goes roaring off in that rattle-trap without saying yes, aye or no, so much for that. He hates all these parties, he always has; God knows if he'll even bother to come, and I'm damn well not going alone.

So I block what I'm thinking: *Lucy's son*, and I say, all casual, 'Want to come to this party with us?'

'I'm sorry I . . .'

'Come on, Steff and I would be thrilled.' Then, my God, I take his hands. Did Davis see us together after all, and that's why he burned rubber getting away? '*Tout* Fort Jude will be there, so no matter what you're looking for, somebody at the party's bound to know.'

'I couldn't.' He shrugs, stirring up the gators on his tacky tourist shirt. 'Not like this.'

'Oh, no problem, Davis has plenty of jackets. You'll need one from before he porked up.' I sit there, willing him. 'Hot *hors d'oeuvres* and an open bar.'

'I'm sorry, I . . .'

'And dinner.' I was thinking, *He doesn't look like Lucy at all*.

Then he got up. 'I can't. There's this thing I have to do.'

15

Bobby

Bobby didn't expect to be here, at the door to the Bellinger family fishing shack. Chape's grandfather built it in the boondocks before he or Chape were imagined, when land was cheap. It sits alone on an inlet, so far out that whatever they did there, stayed there. No outsiders saw and nobody heard. Bobby would just as soon forget some of the stuff that went down when Chape brought him and his posse out here in high school, but here he is.

As instructed, he's dressed for one more endless evening at the club. Chape phoned an hour ago. 'We have a problem.'

'Damn straight.' Lucy's son in a holding pattern, circling Fort Jude like an unanswered prayer.

'Can you come?'

'When?'

'Usual place. Six.' For a second there, Chape dropped his take-charge manner. 'I need you, dude.'

Like it or not, Bobby is walking into his past.

He's here because Chape was his best friend in high school and together they ruled. The guys he cared most about in high school will be inside. Well, all but Darcy, who wiped out at the end of junior year. Their names are carved in the unpainted door, along with the name of the one guy he ran with but never liked. If there is a call to accounting in life, this is the group he has to report to: living yardsticks, measuring him off. At another level, although he knew then that he was nothing like these men, Bobby Chaplin is thinking, *These are my people, and this is my place.*

In spite of everything, it still makes him grin.

They used to hide out in Chape's shack on the inlet; all through high school they got wasted on the Bellingers' booze. In a town where everybody knows everybody's business and your friends' parents know you well enough to call you down for bad behavior, it was the secret place in their lives. Out here where the scrub pines give way to mangroves they could do anything, and Fort Jude would never know. It was all about whiskey, weed and pipe dreams: five kids too young to drink and barely old enough to drive, kicked back around the keg mainlining Jack Daniels like good old mountain boys, the only thing missing was the coonskin caps.

Even when you look happy you aren't, really, he thinks. Even though outsiders can't see it, there's always something wrong.

They still got together here during college breaks but they were coming from different places in their heads, and that bad last night of houseparties pushed them over the edge. They landed in a new place and nobody could say which ones stood on which side of the rift, although Bobby knew that wherever he landed, he would stand alone.

The rift widened as the four of them solidified, like puppies growing into their feet. Whatever they used to be in common was no more. Chape was always going to be a lawyer like old Judge Bellinger, but until he grew into his father's face, they could pretend. Stitch Von Harten's dad set him up to take over the printing business. His family started it in Fort Jude during the Depression, so Stitch could forget the dive shop and the fishing boat, whatever he really wanted, although at that point, he still believed. By the time they were twenty his head was settling into that thickening neck; he didn't look quite like old Mr Van Harten, but it was only a matter of time, and the twins? Doomed to take over Coleman Chrysler, no wonder Darcy rammed that tree and bled his life away on Route 19. Second and third-generation businesses, Bobby thinks uneasily. That's what makes this city great. It explains a lot.

None of which explains the problem of Brad. The Kalens had him when they were too old, and spoiled the crap out of him because they didn't know what else to do. By the time he hit Northshore Elementary he was a gorilla; even teachers cringed. Old Orville Kalen used to go to the club in that white suit with a gold chain across the vest and if you ran into him it always came up in conversation that the watch fob was his Phi Beta Kappa key, he graduated *magna cum* from Yale. Brad got kept back in first grade, so he was seven when they started. They found this *big kid* slouched in his seat with his feet on the desk like a hard timer when their moms brought them in on the first day. He glared and showed his teeth, like, *watch your back,* but they did what you had to, and made friends. They used to play over at Brad's because the house was so big that nobody cared what they did and his folks were too old to do anything about it when and if they found out. Brad's mom kept cold Dr Pepper and a freezer full of Dove bars and there was an attic where she never came; 'please don't make me climb up all those stairs.' He had a toy race car you could drive around in and a Noah's Ark with thirty hand-carved animals that were supposed to be paired off on the gangplank, which they never were. Most of them were missing tails or legs and half of them were smashed because Brad used to make his animals fight and kill each other; Bobby saw it once, so he was never easy with Brad.

Kalen grew up handsome and stupid wild. He was an ugly drunk but they hung with him anyway because he was the first to turn sixteen and get his license, and until Judge Bellinger bought Chape the Jeep in their senior year, he was the only one with a car.

Six friends. Well, one's dead now and another's an alcoholic, and Bobby? He's been better. Still, he feels the same pleasure, going in. It's like slipping into a pair of hightops you've worn for so long that the canvas is like part of you, softened by wear and ripe with thirty years' accumulation of foot smell.

He opens the door, making a big smile for them.

But Chape is alone.

'Where is everybody?' He knows Chape has an agenda; he always does. Why else would he call? 'What's up?'

'Long time no see.' Of course Chape won't show his hand right away. He never does. He's set the ritual bottle of Jack Daniels out on the crate with a bowl of Cheetos and some weed, a gesture to the past. Chape is drinking Diet Dr Pepper out of the can but he greets Bobby with the usual: 'Hair of the dog?'

Bobby says the usual: 'No thanks, I'm driving.' Har har. Cheap, but it's the easy way in. They can jump cut to the present without stumbling over the years between then and now.

'Beer?'

'No thanks. You called?'

'We have a problem.'

'You said.'

'It's not what you think.'

His best friend from high school is touchy. They both are. What stands between them is the thing they never talk about. It's tacit. They never did. They've spent their lives since that night avoiding the matter even though, walking away, silent and dumbfounded, they recognized it as a central event. In a way, it would be a relief to get it out and get it over with. Chapter and verse on what happened. The guilt.

If unpacking the business of that old, bad night is on Chape's agenda, Bobby thinks, bring it on. He starts. 'About this Carteret kid.'

Chape cuts him off. 'That's not why you're here.'

'Chape, I saw him. He's got to be Lucy's . . .'

'Don't.' Chape rakes him with a look sharp enough to cut him off at the knees.

Bobby finishes anyway. '. . . son.'

'I said, don't.' There are things they never talk about. They aren't going to talk about them now.

Bobby goes cold. 'Then why am I here?'

'Yeah, well.' Amiable Chape mends it all, with that familiar, polished grin. 'I had to get you here somehow.'

Bobby shrugs. 'I'd have made it sooner or later.' They both know this is not necessarily true.

'OK. It's Brad.'

'Brad!'

'He's out there somewhere, raving, puking drunk.'

'So what else is new?'

'He's supposed to be hosting this great big fucking party at the club.'

'You got me all the way out here for this? For another stupid party at the club?'

'No. For Brad. For the Famous Five.' The tired tagline makes Bobby flinch. They are both embarrassed by what Chape says next. 'I thought maybe you could help us, you being A.A. and all.'

'How did you know?'

Chape shrugs. Everybody knows everything in this town. 'Buck is checking the bars on Baywater Drive and Stitch is covering the beach dives as we speak.' He adds, to make Bobby feel better, 'You might as well know, Buck isn't doing so good.'

'What's the problem.'

'Depression. He's scared shit he'll catch it.'

'Catch what?'

Chape gives him a you-know look. 'What Darcy had.'

'Suicide isn't catching . . .' After Darcy's funeral the Colemans took Buck away sobbing, but Bobby and Chape and the others got crazy in the parking lot, cackling with relief. Next day they brought Buck out here to the shack and they all got loaded – survivors, same as it ever was. It's funny how easy it is to get over a thing, when you have friends. He falters. '. . . I don't think.'

In that spirit Chape offers, 'Stitch has prostate cancer.'

'Men die with it, not of it. He'll be fine.'

'He hates to sit down. Says he feels all those radioactive seeds, sliding around.'

'Ow.'

Chape is studying him. 'You look good.'

Bobby approximates a smile. 'You said dress for the club.'

'With Cecilia dead, the girls are throwing the engagement party for Brad's girl. Grand ballroom, silver everything. The works.'

'Brad has a daughter?'

'Somebody has to do it,' Chape says.

'You got me here for a party?'

'I know how you feel about the club, but we're all going, for Brad.'

'You got me all the way over here for a party?'

Chape adds with a stern look, 'Even you. Re-entry.'

'I should have known.' He understands what's happening here, at least part of it. With Chape, it's never just the agenda. There's always the hidden one.

'Brad needs all the help he can get.' Chape falls into one of his rhetorical silences that he thinks of as a significant pause.

During the beat, Bobby does not say eagerly, *Whatever you say!* He narrows his eyes. *OK then. Show me your hand.*

Here it comes. When he thinks the pause has done its work Chape adds, 'If you can find him.'

'What do you mean *you*, white man?'

'Given the . . . you know.'

He sighs. 'A.A.'

'Give me a little bit of credit, Bob. It's more than that. You know that girl Brad kidnapped in college? Hauled her off the Chi Psi front porch screaming, Fourth of July in our junior year?'

'Secret marriage, Mrs Kalen's opal ring.'

'Valdosta was just a story,' Chape says. 'It cost the Kalens plenty to keep Brad out of jail.'

'I was away.' Every summer Bobby fled his parents' expectations; he can still see that sad, hopeful pair, blinking like frogs whenever he came into the room.

'But you're the only one who ever saw the woman. Remember, Labor Day?'

'Brad's Georgia girl.' Everybody has to come home sometime. He fills his cheeks with air and lets it out through tight lips. 'I did.'

'He had you out to his secret place, wherever he was keeping her,' Chape says.

'He did.'

'God only knows why you went.'

Because Chape has made clear that they aren't going there, he keeps the worst memory at bay. 'I had to see if she was OK.'

She looked OK when Bobby met her, pretty but the kind of girl who has sharp elbows, cheap clothes – not the kind whose parents call 911 when she doesn't come home; he saw Mrs Kalen's gold slave bracelet riding just above the long bruise on her skinny arm as she flashed the ring. Given Brad's history, were those K-mart rhinestones or was that a real wedding band? Kalen clamped her to his side maybe a little too tightly but he was proud and smiling, like this was the most important thing he'd ever done: 'Bobby, meet the wife.'

Even so, Bobby whispered to her while Brad poured him another of whatever they were having, *Are you all right?* She lowered those spiky eyelashes and touched Mrs Kalen's diamond lavalier with a sly smile. There were roaches running on the Formica and flies buzzing in the plastic curtains in that *awful place* but she was laughing and Brad seemed happy, maybe the only time he was allowed to be, but the Kalens put out enough money to make it all go away. Later he married Cecilia Parker. 'Her mother was an Arnault,' Bobby's mother wrote him, 'third generation in Fort Jude, charter member of the Junior League.'

Knowing how that one ended he asks uneasily, 'Did Brad ever tell you what happened to that girl?'

'There are things you don't need to know if you want to stay friends.' In a tone loaded with reproach, Chape takes Bobby where this meeting is going. 'You're the only one who knows the place.'

'It was a trailer.'

'Now you need to show me where.'

'Oh, hell,' Bobby says, and he means it on several levels. 'Don't make me go back.'

'The man is passed out in his own vomit somewhere, with that poor child waiting for him at the club. Now let's go find our friend and pick him up and scrape him off.'

'Sorry, I can't.'

'Won't, you mean. Harvard didn't do you all that much good, did it?'

Bobby shrugs.

'Look. If you won't show me where he kept her, at least tell us where to look.'

He shakes his head. 'I can't. It's all freeway now.'

It's as if Chape hasn't heard. 'OK then. One way or another, we go out there and find the bastard. We have exactly one hour to do this and get him to the club.'

16

Jessie

It's still fun thwarting Fort Jude's expectations, so for the biggest party the Lunch Bunch has mounted, *ever*, Jessie sidesteps the pudgy prospect they picked out for her and teams up with Wade Pike. She needs backup for this one.

And oh, they do turn heads, coming in. Jessie chose a simple red silk sculpted to her best self – plus diamonds, all high end and stylishly low-keyed, and bless him, Wade looks almost elegant in his bespoke linen suit. She sees people's heads snap around as they enter, and thinks, *OK. Fine.*

In a way, it's kind of funny, her new best friends' eyes glistening with envy, their tight smiles. *Look at them all, looking at us.* She elbows Wade, who hasn't noticed. 'We clean up real nice, don't we?'

For Pierce Point trash. Fort Jude society never says these things out loud, but that's what these ex-girls said behind her back, from first grade through high school graduation week and on until she left town. She came back *somebody*, and that changed. They pretend there was never any difference between them, and for complicated reasons, Jessie lets it play. She is, after all, one of them now. She almost forgives, but she never forgets. In first grade she fell down in the lunchroom and it was horrible. Girls giggled and boys and scraped their fingers at her because her mom didn't so much wash her clothes and *eewww*, she smelled. It was so bad that she got up and socked Brad Kalen. The fat little shitass started it, but Jessie's the one who got sent home for two weeks.

When you get up fighting, you get strong. From then on Jessie scrubbed out her underpants in the sink and later she shoplifted a little bit, so she'd never have to go out dirty ever again. She worked at K-Mart afternoons and the early shift at Mook's Tavern, although she was underage. She handed over grocery money, but she kept back enough for makeup and cute things. She turned heads in tank tops, hoop earrings and flippy skirts, and fuck the snots from Coral Shores, they were just girls. Jessie did what she had to, and mostly it was fun, until life boiled over and she got the hell out of Dodge.

At the time she swore she'd never come back and she didn't, not even to bury her mom. With Pierce Point behind her, she swore to God she'd make something of herself, and she has. She never intended to come here even though she could buy and sell those bitches, but Fort Jude has a way of calling you back, and here she is.

She's known the Pike brothers since forever, she and Wade used to play together in the dirt. In first grade they got bussed in to Northshore Elementary along with Walker, something about testing better than Southside Elementary kids. Walker was in second grade. He was handsome and broody and in fifth grade Jessie was sort of in love with him because he slouched around under a shadow, all, *don't bother me*. At recess he paced the playground like a captive wolf and Jessie yearned. Boy, did she yearn. If the Pike boys had a mother, she was gone. Wade never said what happened. Either he didn't know, or he didn't want to say. Wallace Pike put chicken wire over the doors to keep his babies in the house while he worked, and they crawled around filthy until Walker was big enough to take Wade outside. Mr Pike was a mechanic, running his business out of a shack, and the boys had to work in the shop. They came to school with black grease under their fingernails and raw, stained hands.

Jessie hated how the Coral Shores girls flirted with the Pike boys, smarming up against them in the halls, all excited and shivery: *Oh, you dirty boys.*

Wade's come a long, long way since their white trash days. He's not as interesting as Walker, who got a scholarship to MIT, but unlike Walker, he moves in the best circles in Fort Jude. With a shove from Coach Askew, Wade played football at F.S.U. and pledged Sigma Chi, and now he hangs with the good old boys. He started at Coleman Chrysler before Buck and he rose fast. After all, growing up in a body shop, the man knows cars. When Mr Coleman died, Wade was senior so Wade runs Coleman Chrysler now.

She's proud of him, standing here like an A-list contender in his Palm Beach suit. He looks a hell of a lot sharper than Sammy Kristofferson that the girls keep pushing at her, plus, unlike Sammy, Wade has kept his hair. The Kristoffersons may be a first family, but in the realm of survival of the fittest, Wade's the comer now. He, and not Sammy, will probably be the next Commodore of the Fort Jude Club.

Smiling her brightest smile, Jessie takes Wade's arm. Together, they'll work the room, where Fort Jude's nearest and dearest plus friends and relations from as far away as Atlanta are here in their best, making a party for little Patty Kalen.

Which is, of course, the problem, and for Jessie, it's big. Sooner or later, the creeping slime mold on the backside of the scuzziest sector of the rank, stinking universe, will have to come. The Father of the Bride.

He's also a problem for the good old girls in the Lunch Bunch, who seize on her with frantic smiles. With three bars set up and banks of white flowers and silver streamers in the ballroom, with the Tony Crimmons orchestra tuning up, the F.O.B. is nowhere around. Sallie Bellinger grips her wrist. 'Jessie, have you heard anything from Brad?'

She jerks away. 'Why would I be hearing from Brad?'

'Wade, we have to borrow Jessie for a little bit.' Betsy Cashwell separates him from Jessie with an expert sweep of the hand. 'Girls, we have to rally.'

Through locked teeth, Sallie says, 'When Brad comes in, we're reading him the riot act!'

'*If* he comes in,' Kara Coleman says. 'The boys are out looking for him.'

'He is, after all, the father of the bride.'

Jessie is a pageant of mixed emotions. 'And we're going to . . .?'

And in a frenzy of social innocence, Sallie grins, motivating like the head cheerleader. 'Why, we're going to make this the best night of Patty Kalen's life!'

17

Steffy

Steffy would rather lurk in the gold chairs babysitting Grammy Henderson than talk to her mom right now. The woman she used to think of as pretty much OK is up the wall and halfway across the ceiling tonight, and it's weirding her out. Something happened with Dad, and Mom is a different person now.

The way she dragged Steffy into this party all girly and giggly, you'd think she was back in high school and this was her fucking prom. 'Are we early? Is my hair all right,' she chattered nonstop. 'Does this dress make me look fat?' She hissed, 'Stephanie, don't slouch, I can see your boobs,' instructing through her teeth with that heinous party smile, going on as though she and Steffy are girlfriends, not mother and slave. 'Oh look, the Greenes are here but I don't see Mr Kalen, isn't everything beautiful,' she said falsely, 'I did the tables last night, don't you love all the white-and-silver, is my hair OK?' and the whole time her hand was jittering up and down Steffy's arm like a tarantula. 'Oh God, there's Kara Coleman, at least try to smile. Take care of your great-grandmother . . .'

'Mom, let go.'

'. . . and for God's sake, if your father shows up, come get me.' Then she jumped into the party like a cliff diver into a shark-infested pool.

It's a lot safer here on the shore by the bandstand, where the town's oldest old ladies are beached in gilded bamboo chairs. They sit with tilting champagne glasses stuck in rigid hands so their old, old kids and middle-aged grandkids like Steffy's mother can pretend they're enjoying the party, at least a little bit.

Thank God Grammy isn't talking tonight, she just sits like a doll on top of a cheap candy box and nods and smiles, smiles, smiles. She doesn't care how she looks or who's here and she certainly doesn't care what happens to her at this party, thank God. Furthermore Grammy always kind of likes Steffy when her brain is home, which it isn't right now. Mom's parents like to dress Grammy up and drag her out to parties even though she doesn't always know where she is. It's their way of making it up to her for sticking her in Golden Acres. Grammy's nurse put her in her best party dress and fluffed up her white hair so the scalp hardly shows. Grandpa Henderson got her a drink and plopped her down and that's fine with Grammy. She looks the same kind of happy no matter where she is.

When ladies come over to make nice, shouting to cut through the fuzz in Grammy's head, she lifts her hand like Queen Elizabeth, accepting the praise of a grateful nation with that sweet, old-lady smile. Although Grammy still has her moments, tonight she can only find one word. She says it nicely, 'My. My my my.'

The ladies all say, 'Why Grammy, how nice you look.' Then they say, 'Why Stephanie, what are you doing tending your gramma instead of dancing with cute boys?'

And with a vindictive smirk Steffy sells Nenna down the river: 'It's only until Mom . . .' so they see her Mom out there flirting. In green satin, she's hard to miss; she'd fit right in if this was the Emerald City. Ozma would have a cow.

To a woman, the ladies tsktsk. 'You ought to be the one dancing.' Like she'd dance to that crap. Plus, her friends are all at fucking Jen's party, especially Carter, so Steffy makes one of those noises where people can't tell if you're belching or answering or what.

Sweet Grammy takes up the slack. 'My,' she says, 'my my my my my.'

Then they say, 'Girls together, you and your great-grandmother,' and, the bitches, they've had enough of *old* so they run away.

Very well, Steffy thinks grandly. *Alone*. This party will never end. It's late and they still haven't had the toast so she can go. Four hundred people and not one of them Carter Bellinger, if he doesn't come she'll die stuck to this chair. Waiters know old ladies don't eat so the hors d'oeuvre trays never come here. By the time she's free, the buffet will be picked clean. Fine. They'll be sorry when they find her desiccated corpse. The band is repeating numbers, everybody's hanging in even though the party is beyond tired. Mom's getting loud; that laugh sets Steffy's teeth on edge. The grownups are drinking buckets because it's rude to leave before the father of the bride gets up on the bandstand and makes his stupid speech.

Funny. Mr Kalen isn't anywhere. Neither is Dad. Steffy would just feel better if he walked in and explained. By this time Mom's run out of people she knows. She's so lame, faking fun conversations with the bandleader and cute waiters because she can't leave until it's over, she just can't. Will Dad and Mom will dance together or fight and kill each other if he does come in? God she hates being here, listening to Grammy breathe, but it beats being out there pretending to have fun.

'Look at Nenna dancing, she's frantic!' For crap's sake, can't Mom's friends wait until they're out of fucking earshot?

'Shh, the girl! Poor thing, it's always hardest on the kids.'

That's Jen Cashwell's mother, grinning like a shark: 'It's what Nenna gets for fishing in cold water. She could have married somebody local, but no.'

And Mrs Von Harten, Mom's best friend! 'Northerners, it's anybody's ballgame. How can you tell what a man will do when you don't know who his people are?'

The worst was the Carlson sisters, after they made their manners and pushed off into the mainstream. The ugly one said to the entire room, 'Lord, Nenna's plastered to Sammy Kristofferson like a dog humping a tree.'

When Carter comes she'll get up and punch them in the face.

After a while Steffy knuckles. To survive around here you have to pretend, and she hears herself saying in her mother's fake party voice, 'Lovely party, don't you think?'

Parked next to Grammy Henderson, Carter's great-grandmother rises to the occasion. 'Yes indeed it is.'

Old Mrs Bellinger is no picnic, talks to herself, ugly things, but Carter's mom will make Carter stop by and kiss her as soon as he comes in, so Steffy sits here with the great-grandmothers on velvet seats that were new back when these old ladies were still real. He'd better not bring some skank with love bites and her boobs all smeared with whisker burn, this is one insult she is not prepared to take.

'Steffy honey, what are you doing stuck back here?' Oh shit, it's Dad, squinting like a shipwrecked sailor washed up on the beach. He looks OK, except he isn't. His outline is unstable, like a first-grader quit drawing his face before it was done.

Everything piles in on her and she cries, 'Where were you?'

He won't exactly look at her. He doesn't know where Steffy stands with the mess between him and Mom. He doesn't even know if she knows there is one, clueless Dad. He's all ulp. Blush. 'I was on the phone.'

'Where were you all this time?'

'Long distance.' There's too much to explain so he doesn't explain any of it. 'Business call.'

'Aunt Gayle.'

Does he have to yap like a dog? 'She's not your aunt!'

Crap. Steffy's just too tired to say anything back. Distressed by her silence, he adds a sweetener: 'Tell you what. I'll send Mother Henderson to rescue you, OK?'

Steffy just sits, trying to figure out how she feels about him.

'OK?' He waits a little too long for her to say it's OK, which it isn't. He gives her a miserable wink. 'Tell you what. We'll go out after, Heath Bar Mint Blizzards, my treat.'

'Whatever.'

He'll be too far away to hear her groan. Dad pushes off from the gilt chairs and he's gone for good, just like everybody else. Probably he and Mom are out on one of the long porches, having a fight.

No. Look at him, he's trying to grab Mom out in the middle of the floor. She breaks free and dances away with Mr Rivard the club tennis pro like they're in love, all sexy and *fuck you*.

Steffy hates her dad for being helpless and stupid. It's late and she's starved but the thought of chewing and swallowing in front of all these people brings up issues. Sometimes it's easier to die.

Then like a shot out of nowhere, Grammy Henderson rouses herself. It's as though all the lights in her head just went on. 'Inconsiderate, unfaithful bastard, he isn't worth it,' she says so clearly that it's scary. Then she turns to Steffy with tears in her eyes. 'Tell your mother not to be so frantic, it's mortifying. Look at her, throwing herself around like a ten-dollar whore.'

'God, Grammy.' Steffy reaches out to her oldest living relative, closing her hand on that translucent arm. 'Are you in there? Oh, Grammy. Please stay!'

But as quickly as Grammy's lucid flashes come, this one goes and the best part of Grammy is locked up inside again.

She's been stranded forever when, like one of those visions saints used to have, previews for an upcoming miracle, Carter appears. He's alone, which is good, never mind that he and not Jen Cashwell has the purple hickey on his neck. If you send your guy on an all-day field trip without you, with a long busride home in the dark, it's bound to happen. The miracle is, he's bending close, so his breath is like a kiss. 'Hey.' Like she thought he was only here for Mrs B. He's here for her! Carter doesn't even notice his great-grandmother which is OK because she doesn't much notice him, but Grammy Henderson rises to the occasion, lifting that gracious hand to Carter, saying, 'My my. My my my my my.'

'Girl,' he whispers into Steffy's hair. 'It took forever to find you in this mess.'

Over his shoulder she sees Dad approaching, all helpless and baffled, so, is Mom still with the tennis pro, or did he escape? No grandparents in sight, just Dad with his hands floating up like party balloons while Carter murmurs, 'Babe, let's go get loaded and do stuff to each other.'

Rats. Words pop into her head. *They're all rats.*

Ordinarily she'd flow upward into Carter, bod on bod; she'd grab his hand and put it *there*, but Dad is flailing in plain sight which means that her mother really is lost somewhere, glued to Mr Rivard or Mr Kristofferson, whoever she can get; Steffy caught her hitting on nice Dan Carteret in the Florida room today when it was *her* he'd come to see, she knows because of the grin he flashed when Mom started on her about the shoes.

She turns Carter slightly, scanning the surface of the party like a pirate with a spyglass until she locates Mom. Her mother and Mr Rivard are dancing close, like Steffy's awesome friend Dan means nothing to her, so that's good. Dad's crazed but hey, he brought it on himself, and meanwhile Carter's hand is winkling into her dress even though his great-grandmother is swaying and moaning and Grammy's my-my-my-my-ing because they're so tired and Steffy, well, she has fucking had enough of Carter Bellinger, she thought she loved him but he is fucking insincere.

Instead of letting him lock her in place with the other arm, she edges away. Carter doesn't get it, he leans a degree closer for every inch she slides off the gilded chair, breathing, 'Babe?'

She stands up so fast that she clips his chin with her skull. 'Go to hell, Carter. I have a new boyfriend,' she says.

The minute she says so, it's true.

18

Dan

He picks up takeout at a drive-thru and parks near the Chaplin house, munching on Slim Jims while he processes his material. He has a lot to process, starting with this compulsion to break and enter. He's fully equipped, waiting – no, praying – for Chaplin to go out so he can search the house. He has no idea what he expects to find. His mother was no stranger to this house, he's sure, but he can't start with Chaplin without proof, and this is bad.

He can't start at all unless Chaplin goes out.

It's been hours since he left the Archambault house, but weirdness filled up that stifling bedroom, weirdness drove him out of the house and followed him here, and the question is driving him nuts. What *was* that?

Where did it come from? Product of exhaustion or the heat, hallu-cination or what? Listen, it was nothing he did. All Dan was was there, laid wide open by her rage. Alone in that house, in the room where she died, he heard it! He heard her voice! My God, the woman's been dead for thirty years, but all the hatred and humiliation of the night she burst into flames exploded, boiling inside his head.

He could hear her yowling, trapped and raging inside his skull like a frustrated ghost.

Unless I am fucking nuts.

Eat. Get your shit together. Wait.

He's too jittery to eat. It's quiet in Pine Vista, nothing to see here, no signs of life in the Chaplin house, although the lights are on. The last commuters went by hours ago, heading home. He's alone on this road, as far as he can tell. If someone else is out here in the dark somewhere, if there's someone watching, Dan Carteret has no way of knowing. In fact, anybody could be parked out by the garden shed or behind the bank of oleanders that marks the property line and Dan wouldn't know because he's new to the territory. To him, Pine Vista is as bleak and strange as the face of Mars. And as still.

Waiting, he absorbs the night and silence in a neighborhood where nothing happens and nobody comes. After living on Ventura Boulevard where the traffic never sleeps, it's like a soundproof headset. The silence is profound. Then a night bird cries and he jerks to attention. *What was I thinking? Doh!*

He slithers into the garage by a window on the far side, shielding his light. It picks up a dusty SUV, and in the space next to it, a patch of oil left by a second car. Chaplin's been gone for hours. There's nothing going on inside the house that he can see, but instinct tells him to wait.

He's back in the car, gnawing his fajita wrap down to the paper when the front door opens. So he wasn't, like, fantasizing about that blur in the tower window today, the pale face that came and went faster than you can say Mrs Rochester belongs to the woman coming out. So that was her he saw, flickering like a silent movie wraith. The man is put together like Bob Chaplin, tall and loose-jointed, but he's so heavy that he shuffles. The two flick on the porch light and fuss over the keys in one of those practiced departure rituals, like pet owners patting the house and telling it be a good dog until they come back. Locking up against whatever comes.

Which will be Dan Carteret. With no evil intentions, exactly. He can't be sure what his intentions are. If he'd known there were others living here, would he have come? Belching, he slouches behind the wheel, waiting for them to roll up the garage door and get the second car started, which takes a while, and back it out into the oyster-shell driveway and go.

Then he waits a little longer, to make sure.

What else does he have to do tonight, besides go back to his room at the Flordana and brood? He's locked and loaded: flashlight and screwdriver from Ace Hardware in the messenger bag he's wearing, in case. It's big enough to conceal anything he decides to take. Another hour passes. Nothing moves. When he's satisfied that there are no signs of life anywhere, he makes a cautious circuit of the house. He doesn't know whether to be disturbed or grateful that these people are either timid or lazy. They left all the lights on.

Crunching through the bushes, he goes from window to window like a voyeur at a Times Square peep show. If he rocks forward and up on his toes, he can see in. For Dan, houses at night are like decorators' display windows, advertising better ways to live. There are complete, happy lives available inside if he can just find the right place, and come up with the cash. Walking home from school in New London, he dawdled, lingering in spite of the cold. He stood around in the snow until his toes froze, waiting until people's lights went on so he could look into those bright houses and will himself inside, happy Dan on his belly in front of their TV with brothers and sisters, snug in a tight family unit, waiting for suppertime. Night after night he prowled, stealing other people's lives.

He does not yet know what he is here to steal.

His first glimpse of the lives inside this house is depressing. Through the front window he sees Victorian side chairs and threadbare brocade sofas, nineteen twenty-something to the day. *Did Lucy sit here with Chaplin? Wait. Did they make out? More?* The idea gives him the shudders. *Next question.* The mahogany table is thick with magazines and junk mail, neatly stacked according to size and type; he sees cut glass decanters and massed house plants and art that looks like something picked out by last-century maiden aunts. Somebody has lined up a six-pack's worth of Heineken empties like soldiers on a side table by the recliner. Tropical fish hang in place in their lighted tank, fixing to float to the top, belly up. Except for the flat screen TV, the new century hasn't made its way into the living room. These are not lives he wants to walk into.

He is here to steal. Given a choice, Dan would lurk in the bushes forever, but he doesn't know how long he has. It's time.

Even though there's nobody around to see and nothing coming, Dan enters from the back. He pries the rusting screen off a back window overwhelmed by a thicket of Bougainvillea and forces it with the screwdriver. Planting his hands on the sill, he hoists himself up and inside, swift and neat as a swimmer clearing the pool.

Unlike the rest of the house, the original kitchen was redone, probably back when dinosaurs walked. Bleak under the fluorescent strip light, it's bare and stark as a biology lab. The vinyl flooring has been mopped to death; the pattern on the green Formica counters has been scrubbed white. The room is so antiseptic that it's hard to believe people eat here. It glistens like a place where food has been banned.

Sobered, Dan ducks into the shotgun hallway. In the windowless hall he can't be seen from the street, probably because the architects were under orders to keep Herman Chaplin's maids busy, but out of sight. Maids! It's a straight shot from the kitchen to the heavy front door, with hall doors opening on pantry and dining room to his right, living room to the left. Golden oak bookcases line the hall, with dusty books shelved like prisoners behind dusty glass; this house hasn't seen maids in years. The pattern in the Persian runner was worn to nothing before the present generation of Chaplins learned to walk and the place smells of mildew. Old, all these things are old.

He whirls, wondering. What is he looking for? It's not like he'll find his Lucy's initials carved into the woodwork, or a hastily lettered sign pointing the way. There must be something left of his mother in this dismal house: letters, a snapshot of the two of them together. If he has to, he'll hack into Chaplin's hard drive and find her there. Entering the dining room, he drops to a crouch so he won't be seen from the street. Not, he thinks, that there's anybody out there, but still.

It's been a long time since Chaplins sat down to family dinners here. He opens cabinets, looks in drawers, uncovering yellowed linens, mildewed table mats, tarnished silverware. The living room looks just the way he thought it would. Cluttered. Inhabited. Sad. Gnarled, hairy African violets crouch like spiders on ancient shelves in the round turret off the living room. The Naugahyde recliner dates from the Sixties, but like the art, all the other furniture looks as if it was nailed to the floor back in the day. Only the electronics are new.

Everything is in stasis.

Troubled, he stands quietly, listening. Trying to imagine his mother back when she was happy; why she was here. What she might have left behind. When you don't know what you're looking for, it takes you a while to figure out what you're looking for and even longer to find it. If you ever do.

Upstairs, he stalls outside the third bedroom door. The two others are easy to identify: the brother's is strewn with fat-guy clothes; hers is papered in violet, scented, with floral touches on everything that doesn't move. It has to be this one. Matched leather boxes on the dresser, monogrammed. Everything neat. New laptop sitting open on the table, like an invitation. He should start with Chaplin's dresser, then go in the closet and check out his jacket pockets, ransack the shelves, his desk drawers. His hard drive. Piece of cake, right?

Not so much.

Practiced reporters are trained to steal bits of people's lives when they think the conversation is about something else, but they aren't necessarily prepared to break into their subjects' empty houses and ransack their things. A normal thief would do that, no problem. To his surprise, Dan is not that guy. It takes him too long to unlock his body, joint by joint, and move on.

He has to satisfy himself with a look into the family medicine chest: Xanax, Ambien, Zantac, laxatives, estrogen, everything but Viagra; this is a family with problems. Like the kitchen, their problems just make him sad. Sighing, he goes back downstairs.

Around now, if Dan is still thinking, he should be thinking that time is running out. It's late. Chaplin has to come back sometime, and whether or not he does, the others will, probably soon. He needs to get done and get out before they walk in and find him here.

He should hurry; he can't.

Instead he is stalled in the central hallway, revolving slowly, like an extra in *Night of the Living Dead*.

Um, he is thinking, if he's thinking at all. Just, *Um*.

In fact, the only thing Lucy Carteret left in the house, the only vestige of her is here, hidden where he'll never think to look, but Dan doesn't know that. He'll have to be satisfied with the useful item he will find, assuming he gets a grip. It's in this hall.

If there's someone else in the house with him right now, and if this stranger is marking time, willing him to give up and leave, Dan is too fried to know it. Disoriented, he rubs the glass front of a bookcase out of a pressing need to see his reflected face: first proof of the existence of Dan. He's been standing between the bookcases for – how long? Stupid, but for the first time, he looks at the books behind the glass. Titles line the walls like people imprisoned here and forgotten. The history of Chaplin's world.

Browsing the titles like a speed-reader, he finds the chapter he needs.

Decades' worth of high school yearbooks fill the last bookcase, just outside the kitchen door. The logo is stamped in gold on the spine of every single fake leather binding: FJHS. *The Fort Jude High School Swordfish*, dozens of green padded covers faded in degrees, fill the golden oak shelves. The collection runs from the 1920s at the top to the late Seventies. Kneeling, Dan peers at the numerals on the books in the bottom row, chapter and verse on the last generation of Chaplins to grow up in this house.

The glass front rolls back easily. Greedily, he pulls them out, rummaging for his mother's graduation year. Finds it. Plunges in, too preoccupied to know that he isn't the only one looking for vestiges of Lucy here, or that the most important item pertaining to Lucy Carteret is not in this hall.

The object is in fact in Chaplin's dresser, in the bedroom Dan was reluctant to invade. He might feel better if he knew that there is one item in this house that says it all, but it's hidden so carefully that it's stayed hidden for thirty years. He could have torn up Chaplin's bedroom, rolled back the rug and emptied the closet and rifled his dresser, drawer by drawer without finding it, but he doesn't know.

He doesn't even know that a second intruder made his way inside while he was searching the upstairs, or that this nameless *somebody* is in the kitchen now, flat against the far side of the refrigerator, willing him to leave. Engrossed, he doesn't know anything except that his mother was so *ordinary* in her freshman year, just another clueless, pretty girl.

Squatting, he skims the class pictures, looking for Lucy among the group shots of high school sophomores and juniors, working up to the senior yearbook. He finds Lucy at her best among the senior class portraits suitable for framing that kids can also order in wallet size: white T-shirt, silver hoops in her ears, Lucy smiling brighter than he knew. And, he thinks greedily, if he keeps looking he'll identify the carousing personnel in that Jeep. All five.

Including him. Stare into their senior portraits until you know which one he is. Find your father. Then hunt him down. Shake the truth out of him.

He folds up on the floor with the yearbook open on his knees and studies it, rapt. Now, a yearbook is just a yearbook until somebody you know writes in it. Lucy has written in this one. This incriminating scrawl on the end papers: *Love ya, Bobby. And thanks for that.*

Dan is too intent on what he's doing to understand that he is being watched more closely now, or to know that the stranger who kept pace with him as he closed on the Chaplin house, greedily assessing him by what little moonlight there was, the man who has been following for longer than he knows, is very close. Absorbed, he won't be aware of exquisitely slow movement in the kitchen, as, like a sneak thief intent on stealing a closer look, his stalker fills the doorway at his back. Then the silence splits wide, torn open by a scream.

'Ou . . . hou . . .'

Thumping.

'Ouuttttt!'

The intruder is gone before Dan whips his head around.

Outside the roar amplifies, half bellow, half subverbal screech, compounded by hammering – blind Furies pounding on steel drums.

Dan leaps to his feet. He shivers at the touch of a sudden breeze blowing in from the back of the house. The muffled roar amplifies. Then something happens and the roaring stops. He grabs the last yearbook and bolts.

Escaping, he runs through the kitchen and leapfrogs the porch rail without noting that the back door is thrown wide, as is the window he thought he secured behind him when he came in. Clearing the house, Dan spins like a dime, scanning his surroundings. He expects to see trembling bushes, moving shapes, some sign that something just happened here, but he quit the house too late to see anything that will make all this make sense.

There is nothing visible, nothing to hear, just a disturbance in the air, as though something tremendous just moved out.

19

Bobby

Now that they're here, Bobby's glad Chape called them back to the cabin to regroup after the search. It's the first time he and these old friends have been together in this room since his life went south. He thought it would be hard, reading the truth about himself in their faces, but, these poor guys! Whatever life did to him, it hasn't spared them, either – except maybe Chape with his burnished, impregnable smile. This is Bobby's rehearsal for re-entry, which this party will be, unless it's death by total immersion, and so far, it's going pretty well.

Stitch and Buck were uneasy with him at first, but Bobby's always been good with people, a tremendous asset when he was in finance. A few words, a warm grin and they were his again. The unfamiliar, surprisingly old faces of his friends morphed into the kid-faces he remembers, and Brad? Passed out somewhere. Dead drunk, doubtless, he might as well be in Atlanta or on Mars.

Buck reported, 'I saw every bartender on Bay Drive. They all claimed he threw up in their toilets.'

Stitch grinned. 'He punched a guy out at Diggers.'

'There was breakage at Mook's Tavern, but I paid.' Bobby was thinking, *Schadenfreude*?

'Brad always was a schmuck.'

'Face it. Brad is one mean bastard.'

'We did what we could,' Chape said.

20

Walker Pike

'I guarded them, and none of them was lost . . .' Walker doesn't know when this verse lodged in his flank like a harpoon but day and night it goads him, trailing implications: '. . . except the son of destruction.'

Walker thinks, *He can't mean me.* The lines are, after all, two thousand years old, but he can't shake them. Truth sticks in his flank with the verse trailing behind like a whaler's line through dark waters. No matter how fast he goes or how deep he dives it follows because – whether as mandate or warning – he knows without knowing that this pertains to him.

Some translations read, 'except the son of perdition,' and boy, has he studied the translations. The one he is most comfortable with goes, 'While I was with them, I protected them in your name that you have given me. I guarded them, and not one of them was lost except the one destined to be lost, so that the scripture might be fulfilled.'

Now, that leaves room for interpretation. With the Redeemer long gone and the language diffused by centuries, who knows the exact meaning?

Hell, he doesn't even know if he's still a Christian.

He has spent his life pondering it.

He didn't live in those times; he was never that person but on bad days he has to wonder, *Did Judas ever do a hideous thing and not know it?*

Successful, a rich man or close to it, Walker Pike keeps to himself. And he has reasons. *What am I?* He paces the dock behind his house, considering. *Afraid of being destroyed? Or of being the destroyer?*

This is what circumscribes his life: the potential for destruction. He saw it once. God, it was an accident! Angry and desperate, grieving for personal reasons, he saw it unleashed and it was terrible. It happened long before Walker had any idea what it was and – God! Long before he learned to control it.

All his life since then has been circumscribed, meticulously calibrated and configured to be uneventful. His high-tech career lets him interface, but from a safe distance. He teleconferences from his tight, orderly little house in a place where no people come. In his black and stainless-steel office, he designs sophisticated applications for high level clients, and he works alone. He never sees colleagues, he won't meet clients offline, although he is famous on the Web. Only Walker knows how many patents he owns. All his conversations take place on the screen. He is comfortable at long distance, and he has options. He can always quit the application before the other party pisses him off.

Walker loves the predictability of computers. They stay where they're put and do what they're told and for every problem, there is a logical solution. All he has to do is work it out. Unlike people, computers present problems that can be solved.

He keeps the world at a distance. Walker buys most things he needs on the Web and finds the rest in all-night supermarkets that he knows will be empty at certain hours. He keeps his anger tightly controlled. And the. Ah. Incident? That was an anomaly! A freak accident that overturned him.

It scared him shit.

He doesn't know who did what to who, really. He isn't even sure what happened to her that night. Still, he lives with the risk. The weight of responsibility, which is why he avoids any circumstance that could possibly devolve into a confrontation, the unexpected friction of souls that might lead to . . .

Walker doesn't know how it would come down. The path he's set is lonely, but it's safe.

It's not his fault he fell in love with Lucy Carteret. And the rest? The rest is a source of constant pain to him.

Bad then, that Fort Jude's quintessential drunk driver plowed into the back of Walker's vintage Beemer outside the 7/11 tonight, just when he was feeling safe in life as he has defined it.

Rage kindled even before he found out who hit him.

Instead of lunging out of his car to confront the fool, Walker sat behind the wheel with his teeth locked, intent on defusing the encounter. Count down. Decompress. Get out and look at the damages. Don't say any of the things you are thinking and whatever you do, make your face do something that looks like a smile. Take this dude's license number, his insurance card and his contact numbers, and go. Stick to the particulars and if he's at all belligerent, write off the damages and split before it gets any worse. Don't argue, and whatever you do, don't . . .

Before he could get his door open a mass thudded against the car like a side of meat, followed by a greasy face that slid down to his side window, mouthing apologies.

Careful Walker, don't . . .

Don't!

A drunk, he thinks, suppressing anger. Over time, he's taught himself to keep his rage contained. It's one of the conditions of his life.

A fucking drunk. It figured. What Walker hadn't figured on was the rest. The drunk was wearing a face that he knew, even though time had morphed it into a red, bloated version of itself like a C.G. projection of the soul within: Brad Kalen. *Oh God*, he thought, even though he's not sure he believes there is God.

Oh, God.

The gross, hulking drunk he remembered as a slick, arrogant kid looked right at him – *Was he that drunk? Have I changed that much?* – and did not see. Decaying Brad Kalen blinked as though Walker was just some guy, and they had no history. Rage flared but Walker locked his teeth and held his breath for as long as it took to damp the furnace. He still could have come away clean if Brad hadn't pulled a mess of bills out of his pocket with his free hand. Grinning like a clown hired for a kids' birthday party, he mimed Walker rolling down the window so he could shove money at him and buy his way out of whatever followed.

With a grunt he smashed the door open, hitting Kalen so hard that he fell on his back, flailing. That was his first mistake, if it was a mistake. Walker still isn't sure where he is with this.

He could have cut his losses right then. He could have slammed the door on Kalen and scratched off, but he got out of the car, like, *Are you all right?* Shit, he even helped him up. The paper bag the drunk was clutching had turned into a mess of broken glass and leaking rum. Walker had to pry off his fingers, one by one. Then Kalen put his hands over his face and dragged them aside like a kid pretending to open a theater curtain, drawing little streaks of blood over his spreading grin.

'Pike,' he said, laughing as though there was nothing between them. 'Awesome!'

Never mind what the two old enemies said to each other before Brad passed out. Remember, everybody knows everything about everybody who is anybody in Fort Jude, so Walker knew that Kalen was falling-down drunk out here in the boonies on the very night that he was scheduled to go bopping down town to the local swinery. He was supposed to be toasting the bride at some big party for his daughter – things Walker knows thanks to his fool brother Wade, who chose to rise in Fort Jude society and actually feel honored to be invited.

What he doesn't know is what compelled him to lug the stupefied drunk around behind his car where they won't be seen and stuff the filthy, reeking Brad Kalen into his crumpled trunk and slam the lid on him. Or why he turned the car and headed for the Fort Jude Club, planning to roll him out of the trunk and flee before the valet parking kids came out and found him. Nor does he know what in God's name drove him to stop in Pine Vista before he made his delivery. Unless he does.

He was driving into town on Fourth Street, straight shot to the Fort Jude Club, but he failed to make the one zig-zag where Town Planning and Zoning gave Herman Chaplin his variance back in the Twenties, when he mapped out Pine Vista. Walker was driving in Fourth Street, not thinking, or trying not to think, when his body remembered what he has been working so hard to forget. He wasn't on Fourth Street any more. The road narrowed. Curbstones gave way to pulverized oyster-shell shoulders and the asphalt road turned him out on the last red brick streets that marked the entrance to Pine Vista. He was entering territory he used to know. He stopped, but it was too late to turn.

Ahead, Herman Chaplin's stone lions crouched, regarding him. Not judging, exactly. Just noting his presence. Guarding a neighborhood that never made it off the drawing board. *Like certain other things.*

Walker said goodbye to Lucy Carteret in front of those lions on that lost, terrible Thanksgiving in the year that changed his life. 'Grandmother thinks I'm out with Bobby.' She trailed her fingers across his cheek and said, 'I'm sorry it has to be this way,' and Walker groaned. In the silver twilight, the future hung between them like a veil. She walked between the cement brutes and went to Bob Chaplin's house without looking back.

He followed on foot; he had to be sure. He waited in the bushes until the big car came for her, just as she said it would. Chaplin: what the old woman wanted for her. Walker will love Lucy Carteret to the grave but nothing he said or did back then would change that old bitch or touch her heart, not given where he comes from and who his people are. He and Lucy were doomed, and that was even before he and the vindictive old bitch collided – and Walker Pike became what he is.

He thought he'd gotten past it, but here he was. Again. *Oh, shit.*

Maybe Walker zoned out; maybe he has been heading back here all his life. Never mind. A quick K turn would put him back on track to dump this drunken bastard at the club without unnecessary detours, but Walker was smoked by the past. Foolishly, he lingered. He coulda-shoulda-woulda but then in a doppelgänger moment another car – Chaplin's? – came heading out of the abandoned development.

Gulping air, Walker cut his lights and waited for it to pass.

Lucy, he thought, unless he said it aloud. *Oh, Luce.*

Like certain other things in his life, it was an accident, it just came out. He couldn't help it. With Brad Kalen in the trunk and pressing duties elsewhere, Walker found himself back in Pine Vista.

Twilights in Florida are ambiguous; there's no predicting when the day will drop off the face of the earth. The light was changing by the time he reached the Chaplin house.

A light went on upstairs. They're home, Walker thought, sagging with relief. So I can go. OK then. Time to make that K turn and get going. But he couldn't, quite. Instead he cut the motor and rolled into the long shadow of a utility shed. He had no idea what he was doing here. Maybe he just needed to think. With his captive halfway between out-cold and sleeping-it-off, he could sit here until he got strong enough to stop his inexorable slide into the past.

In fact, Walker's heart was going downhill by noon today, long before Kalen recklessly rear-ended him and came out grinning as though there was no bad history between them.

Wade called. He's sick of his brother's love affair with Fort Jude society, so he let the machine pick up. 'This just in. Jessie called, and she says . . .' Wade's voice filled the room; like everybody else in this town, he loved to beat those jungle drums. 'She says a somebody Carteret just checked in at the Flordana. Young guy, she'll tell me the rest tonight but, hey. Walker, he has Lucy's eyes.'

Walker's mouth dried out and his heart staggered. Stricken, he whirled in the beautiful space he had created, a soul circling the drain. *Fuck you, Wade. Fuck you for dropping this on me.*

Generally a strong person, Walker Pike plunged into grief for what was lost years before he even guessed what he was, or could conceive of becoming what he is. Grief drove him out of his perfect house, and although he never intended to come back to the Chaplin place, memory brought him here.

Don't, Pike. Don't be here. Get out of Pine Vista, fool.

He was fixing to scratch off when the other car approached. He tracked the headlights, troubled when the driver slowed down in front of Chaplin's house. Not Chaplin, nobody he knew, not expected here. The driver cut the motor and coasted past silently. He stopped in a sheltered spot just beyond the house, as if, like Walker, he wanted to watch without being seen.

Him, Walker thought, without knowing who he meant or why it was so disturbing. *Me.*

He should leave, he couldn't leave. OK then, wait the fucker out. A lurker had come into a place so specific to Walker that he could not bear to have him here. *When he goes, you can go*, he told himself. For years he's tried to put all this behind him. He thought he had, but here he is. Tough as he is, driven and tightly controlled, Walker

Pike understands why he's here. Part of his past is hidden somewhere inside that house, a fixed destination point in his existential GPS. When she told him goodbye, Lucy left it here, like a magnet. He still felt the pull.

He slipped out of the car and sat down on the pine needles to wait. With Kalen passed out in the trunk, he could take his time. Hey, he was doing the asshole a favor. Let him sleep it off, wake up and get his shit together before you dump him in there among his people, no hard feelings, if you can manage that.

His domesticated brother was stoked about the extravaganza at the club: 'Brad's daughter is engaged, and *I'm invited.*' In way it's pathetic, how Wade hangs on what those surface-feeders think, maybe because it's all on the surface.

And here you are, custodian of the so-called host. Wash the bastard's face even if you despise him, comb his hair and get the vomit off his shirt. It's his party, after all.

After a time, Walker saw Maggie and Al lock up the house and leave. Fine, he told himself. Now I can go.

Then the intruder's car door fell open and Walker froze. The intruder got out of his Honda and headed for the house. Quick. Anxious, judging by the angle of the shoulders. Young, judging by the lean, unfinished look. Now Walker had to wait until the stranger finished doing whatever he came to do and left.

Then he could go.

Stupid, stupid. He fell into a tracker's crouch and followed. Woulda-coulda-shoulda. The lurker snaked in through a back window and Walker groaned. *Yeah, right. And you thought you could control your life.*

He couldn't leave until the creep came out.

In the still, dense night, lost years played behind Walker's frontal bone like grainy film on a drive-in movie screen, scored by the dry needles of the Australian pines stirring in the wind: the look and feel of Lucy's body that first time, the sibilant whisper of pine branches overhead. God he loved her. God he had no choice. He gave her his mother's wedding ring, but that was much later, and in spite of forces marshaled against them. He can still see the way it looked, sliding onto her left hand.

Given what happened later he and Lucy were fated, but in his own way Walker is blind and persistent as a zombie: dead, but he won't lie down. The night he pressed the ring on Lucy they were in such distress that he was never clear where she went afterward, or where she hid the ring. He loved her so much!

The son of destruction. Walker backed out of her life to protect her, and he had to do it without telling her why; he had no choice. It destroyed him, but he would do anything to keep her safe. If only he'd been able to explain! He has spent his life since then researching the anomaly, meditating, trying to get to the truth of it. Years, with no answers. Years of grief.

Astounding need froze him where he stood, under the pines outside the Chaplin house. Whether out of need for the girl or the moment or who he used to be, Walker's heart cried to heaven, *I want it back.*

But they were gone: Lucy. The boy. Whatever they were to each other was beyond all retrieving and Walker knew it. The only thing he can hope to get back is the ring. Not that having it would make anything better; it's just an object he wants to hold. So with Brad in the trunk and certain issues pending, Walker waited for the man in the house to finish what he was doing and go.

Time wore on.

What does he think he is, Walker wondered. *Entitled? Taking his goddamn time.* It was hard at first, but he has schooled himself in patience over the years since then. The young man inside the house was nobody he knew, nobody he had any reason to hate. He had to wait. *OK then,* he told himself without affect. *For as long as it takes.*

Squatting in the pine needles, he waited beyond waiting. Shut inside the trunk of the Beemer, Brad could damn well stew in his own fumes. Eventually he'd come to. *If I'm going to do this, I have to do it soon.*

Moving so slowly that he barely disturbed the air, Walker got to his feet. He circled the old stucco, looking in. The front rooms were seedy, but so richly furnished that he was struck by the disparity. The function of money and position in this town. He entered the house through the back window. In the kitchen he paused, absorbing the space.

Where he was listening for footsteps, drawers being rifled, *something*, the sound he did hear was so subtle that at first he couldn't identify it. It was . . . Walker shrank into the shadow of the fridge while his mind scurried here, there. It was . . .

The slither of glossy pages. Slowly, he emerged, silent and insubstantial: just one more ghost of the past in this old house. Poised in the doorway, Walker studied the intruder kneeling with his back to the kitchen where he stood, absorbing the set of the kid's head, the whorl in his sandy hair, the concentration with which he studied the book on the floor in front of him. Like a high school time capsule, *The Swordfish* lay open, disgorging the past.

Him, Walker thought, riveted by an unaccountable pressure on the heart. *Me*.

He caught his breath as if to speak.

There was no time for discovery and confrontation, no time for Walker Pike and this kid to face off and say what they had to say, because out there in the damaged trunk of Walker's Beemer, Brad Kalen came awake. Walker's mouth opened; looking down at the bent head of the stupendously vulnerable new person in his life, he was on the verge when the banging and howling began, fucking Brad.

The kid's head came up.

The night cracked and Walker turned into something else. Fucking Brad. Fury boiled up. *Get out of here before . . .* He had to go! In a miracle of compression, Walker turned and left before the kid could turn and discover him.

Shit! His heart shuddered. *Shit,* he thought, without being clear exactly what he thought he was escaping. *That was close.*

21

Bobby

They rode to the party in Chape's Escalade. It made things easier for Bobby, coming in.

With Chape walking point and Stitch and Buck flanking him, it's almost like the old days. He is aroused by the stir they create even now, after so long. Women Bobby used to know turn, touching dyed hair and rearranging their faces at the sight of him. The ripple swells into the wave he and his main men made back in senior year, stalking the corridors in torn football jerseys and jeans that had gone white at the knees and over the bulge at the crotch. Kids fell away like the Red Sea, making a path for the chosen ones because he and his cadre owned the school. Now here they are again, four good buddies – too bad about Brad . . . No. He's glad he eluded them, given that Brad when he's boiled is an ugly thing. And Bobby? There are times when he trips on one of the Twelve Steps but mostly he's OK. Good, in fact.

Here in the grand ballroom of the Fort Jude Club, it's as though the bad things in his life never happened. The grappling hooks release his heart and he forgets how old he is and how long it's been. People he was afraid to see again light up. For the first time in a long time Bobby Chaplin is a kid again. He sizes up the women like an impulse shopper scanning soup can labels, thinking, *I can have any girl in this room*, the problem being that the ones he can have are no longer girls.

Oh, there are plenty of women. Dozens of foxy twenty- and thirty-somethings gift-wrapped in strappy little dresses sail past without seeing him. Like the surly teenagers with nose rings and tongue studs removed for the event and silky shifts designed to expose their precious tats, they're all depressingly young.

Well, he thinks, *fair's fair*.

Then there are the women he knows. Betsy Cashwell is as fit and cute as she ever was, but growing up in strong Florida sunlight isn't just bad for these women, it's a catastrophe. She looks like a white raisin now. Cathy Rhue's put on weight and she's not the only one. It's sad! Guys have gone bald or run to fat like Stitch and Sammy Kristofferson, who did both, and the thin ones look wasted and insecure.

You'd think an atom bomb just hit Fort Jude and when these people walked out of the ashes they were old, cardboard cutouts of people he used to know. In high school he imagined rich inner lives for them, but now he has to wonder. Then he catches them squinting at him like photographers matching negatives to prints, and thinks, *Do I look that bad?* Does he?

'Dude.' Chape snags his elbow. 'Meet the blushing bride.'

Poor kid! Patty Kalen and the fiancé stand fixed under the oleander trellis like plaster dolls waiting to be plopped on a wedding cake. Waiting for the F.O.B. Patty's smile has been set for so long that the surface is about to crack.

'Why Patty,' Bobby says, noting that her hands are slick with the sweat of too many well-wishers, 'you don't know me, but I knew your dad.'

Reloading the smile, she says miserably, 'Oh.'

'I'm sorry.' It just pops out. He covers his mouth.

Brad is famous, and not in a good way. Patty acknowledges it with a nod. 'This is Stuart, my fiancé. He's from Atlanta. And Stuart, this is . . .'

'Bob Chaplin.' His gift to the girl is not shaking her hand. 'Your mother was a wonderful person.' Young as she is, Patty is weary, weary. Her lips move in response, shaping a silent, *I know.*

'Chape Bellinger.' Chape inserts himself with that smile. The fiancé is awed by the high sheen of prosperity, but by the time he extends his hand to shake, Chape has moved on to shinier pastures. To spare him embarrassment, Bobby takes it.

'Bob,' he says, shaking firmly. 'Bob Chaplin. Goldman Sachs.'

The fiancé has one of those soft, smooth faces, like the mask of an unused baby. He says, 'Nice to meet you, Mr . . .' and hands him off as the bride's sorority sisters strike. Worn thin by waiting, Patty whirls and falls into their group hug with a grateful shriek.

Damn Brad, Bobby thinks, and not for the first time. *Damn him for everything.*

He washes up in a stagnant corner near the bar, watching bartenders pour refills. He won't deny that he's getting off on the fact that he's dry, has been for almost two years and, like Chape and Buck and everybody else here, Stitch is getting loaded.

Stitch downs his double. 'Did I tell you I lost a million bucks?'

'Shit,' Bobby says. 'At least you can cover it.'

Stitch grunts. 'Not any more. Gonna have to go Chapter Eleven soon.'

'That's terrible.'

'Don't be thinking it happened overnight.' He pats his empty pocket – he used to smoke. 'It was the alligators. Supposed to make our fucking fortune.'

'Alligators.' In high school they drove out to the reptile ranch at three a.m. Brad made them wake up Earl Havens so they could make Earl wrestle the alligator, which he did for tourists on weekends to help his dad. Earl was humiliated. He didn't want anyone at school to know. Bobby and Stitch made Brad back off before Earl lost it and broke down in front of the girls. Just remembering makes him sad.

'Alligator backpacks. Alligator boots, bags, alligator skin wallets. Do you know how much people pay for these things?'

'High-end,' Bobby offers. *Vicious bastard, Brad.*

'They're worth thousands,' Stitch says mournfully. 'You get a fortune for the hides. I went to Louisiana to see the ranch.' He lights up like an inflatable Santa. 'Bobby, I held that egg while my alligator hatched! It came to life in my hands!'

'Oh, great.' *Oh God.*

'I was in deep by the time we were done. Breeding, monthly charges, herd of vicuñas, feed 'em with the meat, sell the fleece for coats. It was a win-win, the ranch took care of everything, it would amortize when my gators grew up. We were close to the big payday when the lady called from the ranch. Thermostat busted in my sector. Do you believe my little fuckers all boiled to death?'

'That's terrible.'

Stitch brightens. 'Shit, Katrina. I would've lost 'em anyway.'

'Yeah well, we all have our losses,' Bobby says.

Then Stitch's grin splits wide open. 'Fuck, it was a scam.'

Bobby turns, distracted by laughter – clear, a little too loud. Nenna is spinning on the dance floor. Her face hasn't gone to hell and her body hasn't either – the girl he could have had in high school, he realizes, if he hadn't been wrecked in love with Lucy Carteret. Lovely Nenna, out there whirling on her own.

Buck sidles close enough to mutter in his ear. 'Trouble in the marriage.' He hocks and swallows. 'Husband's two-timing her with his sister or some damn thing.'

If there's a moment, Chaplin, this is it. The way things are for her, the way she is tonight, he could probably start the conversation and she'd be his, but miserable as she looks, abandoned on the dance floor, he can't.

Buck says, ''Nother drink?'

'Not right now.'

He just can't.

God he hates this. It will end the way these parties always do: personal disasters interwoven with thank-yous and reproaches, some-body crying in the coat room, everybody saying what a good time they had, an orgy of regret. God he wants to leave. Soon, he promises himself. When the band comes back from break I'll go out front and have Marco get me a cab.

He would have, too, but a human infernal machine slams into the bandstand before he can give it a name. The fast-moving, flailing tangle scatters chairs and music stands, toppling the microphone in a rush of static and clashing metal with one man howling like a vocalist straight from hell, and Bobby shouts in relief. 'Finally!'

It's . . . It's . . .

It looks like two bears grappling, like a baggy, snarling grizzly locked to a swift, lean black bear, the two bodies tangled and bucking so violently that the racket clears the floor. Men back away and their wives shrink behind them with little shrieks, leaving Bobby alone at the base of the bandstand as the struggle ends. The lean gladiator tries to haul the fat one to his feet and right the microphone at the same time, but it's a losing battle.

Glaring, he lets go and his burden drops, wallowing and gargling spit. As he does so, Bobby recognizes that fierce, handsome head and his heart turns over. *You look the same. After all this time.*

Blind to him, Walker Pike turns the body over with his foot and the room comes to life in a communal *Oh, no!* It's one of their own.

'The father of the bride.' Walker's rasp reaches even the clueless eddying at the fringes, laughing and talking as though nothing else is happening. 'Say hello to the people, dude.'

Brad Kalen settles into a puddle of flesh with his tongue lolling and his body bulging through gaps in his stained dress shirt like parts of a ruined, badly stuffed doll. Disgusted, Walker prods the baggy mess with his toe, but Brad is beyond speech. Did Walker bring him here to make him do right by Patty? To make a spectacle of him? He doesn't explain and Bobby doesn't know.

Looking up, Walker Pike says in a tone roughened by contempt, 'He's sorry he's late.'

Any other daughter might be in tears by now but hardship has made Patty Kalen strong. With a little nod of acknowledgement, she turns and leaves the room.

'Be careful where you leave your garbage,' he says to everyone present, and he is rigid with compressed fury. He turns and stalks out, muttering so only Bobby hears, 'It's a fire hazard.'

22

Walker Pike

So it isn't really Kalen's fault that the fat drunk imploded at the Fort Jude Club, spilling Walker out in a treacherous place – unless it is.

There was too much history in that room, repeating like something bad he ate. It cracked his protective shell, exposing the man he used to be.

What was he thinking? That he could dump Brad Kalen and get shut of him? In one of those toppling domino displays, everything Walker did that day led to something worse. The collision at the 7/11. The detour to Pine Vista. Profoundly shaken by his near-encounter with the stranger who looks like him, he teetered in Chaplin's kitchen, poised to speak. Then Kalen shattered the night, kicking and yowling, battering the interior of the Beemer's trunk until he rocked the car.

Bad things happen when Walker goes out, and he knows it.

Hurry, he told himself, fleeing the house. *Drop him at that fucking club. Vanish before you do something worse.*

He should have burned rubber and rolled Kalen out on the steps of the Fort Jude Club, but the stink creeping into his car from the trunk told Walker that he'd thrown up. He was back there rolling in it. Walker despises him, but it was so appropriate that he laughed. He stopped at an all-night car wash to hose out his trunk. To silence Kalen and clean him up. Planning, he was relieved to find that he was no longer angry, just resigned. Get him there. Dump him and go. *You have disrupted me enough.*

''Onna sue your brains out.' Brad spat on his shoes. 'Fucking Pierce Point trash.'

Walker just finished hosing him down.

'Scumbag junkyard shit.'

Pathetic.

'Your father licked assholes for a living, that fucking drunk.'

'Take this,' Walker said, throwing him the T-shirt he uses to wipe down his car after a rain. 'Yours smells like puke.'

'And your mother was a cunt.'

Walker handed him a comb. Pleased, maybe, that Kalen couldn't make him angry. 'Get the crud out of your hair.'

'I know what you are,' Brad snarled through a mouthful of spit, 'and I know what you did.'

Not likely. Nobody knows.

Walker gave him another blast with the hose. It wouldn't matter what Kalen said or did now. It took years, but Walker has gotten comfortable with, OK, he doesn't want to be pretentious, but. He's gotten comfortable with what he is. He and it have come to terms. He threw Kalen a roll of toilet paper.

'Wipe your face.'

'She'd go down on a coon dog for a nickel.'

'Get in.'

'And your father's a crap mechanic.'

'My father's dead.' Belted into the passenger seat, Brad was too drunk to continue. In spite of the hose-down, he stank; it will take more than simple detailing to get the Kalen out of this car. Leaving the Fort Jude Club, Walker rolled down all the windows but his sweet vintage Beemer still stinks. It will stink for days in spite of the towel he put down on the passenger's seat before he shoveled his captive in. Interesting, then, that he kept his cool. Intent on finishing the job.

But Brad! Brad belched insults. In the lexicon of blunt instruments, he was rummaging for the right one. As they rolled into the Fort Jude Club he came up with it, hissing wetly, 'Lucy whispers when she comes.'

I could kill him now. Walker rocked with pain. *Thank God we're here.* He reached across Kalen's baggy front, unbuckled his bulging belly and shoved him out. *Dump him and go.*

But Kalen wasn't going. As Walker leaned across the seat to close the door on him, Kalen yanked it wide. His head revolved like a cheap effect in a bad movie as he sprayed, 'You want to know what she whispers? She whispers your name.'

Whose name, Kalen? Mine? Yours?

So Walker had to jump out of the car and beat the crap out of the baboon before the thing escalated, pushing him into a dangerous place. The valet parker and the *maitre d'* guy in the uniform vaporized. *Which of us are they afraid to touch? Kalen? Me?* He doesn't know. In a way, Walker was glad nobody saw. He needed to re-organize his face before he delivered his package which, for reasons, he had to do.

Grimly, he dragged Kalen upstairs to the grand ballroom, astonished by how leaden he was. Pleased, really, that nothing worse had happened. No. Surprised and relieved. But that was last night.

Snapping awake at first light, he sits up and – God! Daylight crashes into his head, streaming into him through the crack.

Locking his arms around his knees, Walker shudders, rocked by loss.

23

Dan

This isn't where Dan expects to be, but in a strange way, he's finding it extremely pleasant.

Where he should be down at the *Star* digging up clips on the incinerations, he is in the McCalls' sunny Florida room with Mrs McCall, who for the fifth time has instructed him to call her Nenna. They're side by side on her flowered sofa, bent over Chaplin's old yearbook. Mildew has turned the faux leather to silver. Flattened insects breathed their last between these pages years ago, and a smell he doesn't recognize rises from the gutter between the glossy pages. Mrs McCall is pointing out pictures in *The FJHS Swordfish*, although for reasons that are opaque to Dan, she hasn't forgiven him for carbon-dating her.

He didn't know what he wanted when he broke in to Chaplin's house. God knows what made all that noise; he had to leave! With his search cut short, he grabbed *The Swordfish* and bolted. He got stupendously lost, escaping on back roads where everything looked like everything else. By the time he found his hotel he was too wired to sleep, but too wiped to do anything but crash. Maybe he slept, but if dreams are bookmarks, there's nothing left to prove he did. Mostly he remembers thrashing.

His eyes popped open long before it got light. **Four. Colon. Oh. Oh.**, the digital clock reported aggressively, taunting him. **Four. Colon. Oh. Eight**. Nyah, nyah. At **Five. Oh. Oh.** he declared the sun over the yardarm and opened the book. Sitting cross-legged in his briefs like a kid with a fresh porn mag, he scoured the pages, in hopes. Of what?

The answer fell into his hands like a gift. His mother's photo led the senior class portraits: pretty Lucy Carteret, silenced for once, composed for her photograph. Smiling as ordered, but with that defiant glint. Looking into her face captured more than thirty years ago, he understood that Lucy had always been the same person. At eighteen, she faced the camera with her chin lifted in the proud,

I-can-do-this way that Dan knows; seconds before the end she lifted her head and faced the future with that exact, intelligent glare.

The biography was like Lucy, short on detail. She'd listed only the necessary: May Court, 1, 2, 3, 4, May Queen, 4; *The Liveoak*, 1, 2, 3, editor, 4; president, National Honor Society, 3, 4. There was no nickname specified, even though high school kids without them usually improvised. There were no favorite sayings or flip mottoes to bring real Lucy to this page, no boyfriends named that he could interrogate and no girly lists of favorite flowers or songs to remember her by. The only thing personal about the entry was her smile. It hit him in the chest. These people, like their photos, began fading the moment the camera's iris flexed and snapped shut, fixing them in time.

Maybe cows are right, he thought. The photographer who captures your image really has stolen your soul.

He wouldn't have known the others. Chaplin's text ran for several lines, beginning with **Nickname**: 'Bobby.' The list of achievements covered every sport, plus: *FJHS Swordfish*, 1, 2, 3, editor 4. Senior musical, 1, 2, 3, 4. Fort Jude Chamber of Commerce Sun King, 4. Science Club, 1, 2, president, 3, 4. *The things they did*, Dan thought, wondering if these itemized exploits carried the same freight as objects in that Vietnam vet's story, 'The Things They Carried.'

It was hard to reconcile this jaunty, bulletproof boy and the guy with the crumbling house in Pine Vista. At eighteen, with a fresh shirt and an untarnished grin, Bobby Chaplin was a different guy, brash and freshly minted. Chaplin is not a bad-looking guy but he looks – well, defeated. Thinner, with telltale shadows in the hollows at his temples and eyes making their inevitable descent into the skull.

Where other seniors cited songs and slogans, dropping hints about epic bashes they'd survived or naming their loves, Bob Chaplin included one personal item. **Favorite saying**: 'Harvard Fair Harvard.' His staff added an editorial comment in italics: *'We always knew he was gonna be a star.'*

Yeah, right, Dan thought. Like *that* worked out. All those expectations, and now look.

He said to the photo, 'I'm sorry.'

He found Mrs McCall accidentally, because she looked exactly like Steffy on a fat day. The plump teenager's glossy hair had that freshly ironed look and her eyes gave back the bank of studio lights. She was smiling – happy and excited, open to whatever came next. Her thumbnail bio was touchingly girlish. GENEVIEVE HENDERSON, he read. *Nickname*: 'Nenna.' Pen Club, 4; Drama Club, 3, 4; FJHS Tarponettes, mascot, 4. *Slogan*: Puh-leeze. *Favorite color*: blue. *Favorite player*: Number 67, Now it Can be Told! *Favorite song:* 'The Way We Were.'

'Oh, lady,' he said to the photo, to all of them. 'What happened to you?'

Looking for his mother in endless group photos, he studied all the group shots: May Court, N.H.S., kids lined up over cutlines identifying them, left to right. Lucy wasn't among them. Pretty as she was, she didn't show up among the laughing kids caught partying or mugging for the camera in the candids either. He had to wonder, did the woman have no friends? Skimming for anything that would link her to the guys in her cherished Polaroid, he overlooked the ragged spot where somebody razored out a page. He won't find the photo of Lucy Carteret standing with Bobby Chaplin on the steps of City Hall over the cutline, *Most Likely to Succeed*.

He turned to the inscriptions in Chaplin's yearbook, loving screeds in flashy colors, but Lucy wasn't anywhere. Desperate to be different, girls wrote gushy notes with curlicues and flourishes, dotting their I's with hearts or smiley faces, scrawling cliches like, 'You're the best.' Sallie, Bethany, Betsy, Jane, began, 'Remember that time' or 'house-parties!!!' followed by paragraphs of bla, bla, bla, ending with multiple Xes and Os. He found Nenna Henderson's timid, 'Love ya Bobby,' almost by accident, she wrote so small. The guys' were briefer, scrawled in drunken haste. A gifted speed-reader, he skimmed them all.

At **Six. Oh. Oh.** he was still in lotus position, reading long after his feet had gone to sleep.

The last note he found was neatly printed. 'Thanks for that.' No explanation, no effusions in contrived script, just the signature in a spot so obscure that he had to look twice before he noticed it. 'Sincerely, Jessie Vukovich.' Flipping back, he found her photo. Less angular. Brunette back then, the woman who signed him in yesterday with the same brash smile, the same sultry toss of the hair. There it was. A plan.

He snorted orange juice and ate his way through the mini-bar before he showered and prepared for the day. Dumping the promotional bumph out of the Flordana's complimentary goody bag, he slipped *The Swordfish* inside. Flash it at the people you know. See what they do when you point to Lucy's photo. He took the stairs, peering into dim corridors as though he expected Jessie Vukovich to pop out and tell him everything.

What did she mean when she wrote, 'Thanks for that'? Do she and Chaplin have a secret history? Yesterday she handed back his snapshots with an indifferent shrug. The woman graduated the same year as his mother, could they actually not know each other in a school that small? Perched on a tapestried love seat outside the coffee shop, he mainlined swash from the coffee machine, lying in wait for her. As if he really believed that aging, overtly sexy Ms. Vukovich could solve his life.

A skinny old guy with a comb-over came out of her office at seven sharp, straightening his black string tie on his nerdy white short-sleeved shirt. Dan retreated behind the *Fort Jude Star* and settled down to wait.

At nine – late enough to make house calls, he gave up on Jessie Vukovich, FJHS grad who owed *something* to Chaplin, and what else did he have? The inscription. 'Love ya. Nenna.' He stuffed the yearbook in his Florida Trends bag and drove to her house.

Mrs McCall opened it, grinning as though something – life? – had just delivered a present, gift-wrapped, and she could hardly wait to get it inside and rip the ribbons off. She went all actress on him, trilling, 'Daniel, how nice!'

'It's Dan.'

'Come in, come in!' Was she playing to a full house or an empty one? He wasn't sure. He never saw the husband yesterday, just heard him stomping out. The lady was carefully put together for a Saturday, good hair and full makeup, yellow shoes. Was she expecting him, or did she always fix herself up like Barbie, just in case? 'Come on, you could get heat prostration out there!'

'Ma'am, if you're busy . . .'

'Who me? You've got to be kidding. Please.' She moved him along to the Florida room a little too fast. Still, it was nice to be welcome somewhere.

The Florida room was a little creepy. Where Lucy loved the light, Mrs McCall had layers of fabric covering all the glass. All Florida might be blooming outside but Nenna McCall kept this place hermetically sealed against the heat. The flowers were fake irises embellished with silk leaves so finely made that he could see the veins. Rose patterns crawled across the squashy chairs flanking the sofa and ivy crept up the legs of the wrought iron table and chairs.

Underfoot, beige roses bloomed on the Chinese rug. On the walls, he saw gaudy hibiscus prints and watercolors of the Fort Jude scenes framed in bamboo. Having shut out nature, the intelligence that chose this room had tried and failed to replicate it inside.

It made him reluctant to sit down.

She reached as if for his arm but at the last minute bent and patted the sofa. 'Sit here. I'll get us some iced tea. Unless you'd prefer lemonade,' she went on in that nervous, girlish way. 'Or coffee. Peet's, from California? It's really good.'

'Thanks, I'm pretty much caffeined out.'

'Oh,' Nenna looked at the shopping bag like a child jonesing for a present. 'Is that for me?'

'Kind of. I wanted to ask you a couple of things.'

'Sure!'

He proffered *The Swordfish*. 'You were in school with my mother?'

Guilty. She jerked away. 'When?'

'At FJHS?' He sat down so she would sit. Then he opened the book. He couldn't say what, exactly, happened to her face when he pointed out plump little GENEVIEVE HENDERSON. 'You knew my mother, right?'

She jumped up, as if to prove it wasn't true.

'So, did you?'

Her tone chilled. 'Wait here.'

What pissed her off? Waiting, he leafed through the yearbook, wondering what just went wrong. It was sweet in a way, seeing these long-ago kids' faces, because they were so *young*. Flashing on Lucy in her last hour, he saw the future; smart or stupid, pretty or not, these people were hostages to biology and destiny. Nothing that the eighteen-year-olds facing the camera with such hopes could say or do or buy or get would prepare them, or help them arm themselves against what was to come. Today Nenna wore white jeans and a tank top that exposed her tanned, buff upper arms. Her hair was almost perfect, but her face betrayed her; she worked too hard on it.

Right. Now he gets it. *She's pissed at me for knowing how old she is.*

By the time she comes back, she's forgiven him. Smiling, she puts down the tray and offers homemade cookies that he doesn't want. Offended by being nailed as a late-late Seventies person at Fort Jude High in the Middle Ages, she makes him take two before she asks, 'Who was your mother?'

He shows her the picture.

'Lucy. Carteret. You kept her name.'

'It's the only name I have.'

Her head snaps back as if everything inside it just jerked to a stop. 'I'm sorry!'

He flushes. 'It's no big.'

Recovering, Mrs McCall — sorry, Nenna — bends over the book with him, dropping details like breadcrumbs along a forest path. 'Lovely girl but she kept to herself, which is why . . . OK,' she says in that youthful tone aging women work to maintain, 'OK. We thought she was snotty.'

'She was shy.'

'It's not like we didn't like her.' Defensively, she adds, 'She didn't want to be friends. I'm sorry, we should have tried harder.'

'Don't feel bad.'

'Maybe living with your grandmother makes you weird. Her mother died having her and the old lady flew to Charleston and scooped her up.'

'Charleston?'

'Carteret's an old Charleston name. She said David wasn't fit to bring up a child, and that was that. They duked it out in court and she won.' She taps the page. 'Which is how Lucy ended up down here.'

'So you did know my mother.'

'We didn't, like, hang out with her.' She sighs. 'I'm afraid nobody did.'

Like a good student, she waits for his next question, but he is dead beat. Flat out of questions, he sinks into the down sofa cushions. The Florida room smells of cleaning products; so does nice Mrs McCall.

Finally she offers, 'She didn't hang with us. When we were little, it was the car and driver. Later she had her own car.'

'She gave my mother the car?'

'Oh, she gave her everything she wanted. Clothes. The car, when she was old enough to drive. Lucy was the only thing she had. It's sad,' Nenna adds without explanation, 'they used to be so close.'

'Lucy and her grandmother. What happened?'

'She was your great-grandmother, I suppose.' Smiling, she proffers the plate.

Deflection, so ladylike. Must be a Southern thing.

'Another cookie? I'm famous for these.'

He is both grateful and sorry that she isn't wearing perfume. For

Dan, perfume is a distinct turnoff; this lady smells of toothpaste and fresh shampoo, which makes it harder to refuse. For the first time since the hospital he is aware of his body, which is waking up after a week of grieving. *Yo, Dude!* 'Thanks, but I'd better not.'

'Do you have a girlfriend?'

He did but he doesn't. Nenna doesn't need to know. 'Did she have a boyfriend?'

'Who?'

'Lucy.'

'Oh, Lucy. Everybody was in love with her.' Nenna's face turns into a mix CD, producing music from several different albums all at once. 'We thought she and Bobby . . .' She waits a beat too long, considering, before she buys him off with a smile. 'But you never know.'

'What do you mean?'

'Hidden fires,' she says.

Reporters know silence works better than a question. 'Yes Ma'am.'

'Oh please,' she says. 'We are way past Ma'am.'

'About these hidden fires . . .'

'You never know what's going on behind people's faces, do you?'

'No.'

The pause that follows takes on a life of its own. He hears ice cubes dropping. Footsteps upstairs. The husband stomped out like Bigfoot yesterday. Must be Steffy. Wish she'd come down.

'Something happened,' Nenna says finally.

Keep your head down, Carteret. The best interviewers are invisible. 'And . . .'

'And . . .'

Repeat, so she'll have to complete the sentence. 'Something happened and . . .'

Generations of ice cubes drop before she says, 'To be honest with you, we never really knew.'

This brings his head up fast. 'Ma'am?'

'Nenna.'

'Nenna.'

She goes on, but in a new direction. 'Lucy's father went to Clemson, I think. Unless it was The Citadel. Either way . . .'

'David Carteret.' His next source. 'Still in Charleston, right?'

'We heard he died.'

Oh fuck.

'Suicide.'

Oh, fuck.

'I'm sorry.'

'I never knew him. It's OK.'

'Either way,' she finishes, as if this explains it all, 'he wasn't from around here.'

'I see.' This is a lie. He will never understand this town.

'I mean, he wasn't one of us.' Nenna pauses to regroup. When she goes on, it is about nothing he expected. 'You know, Davis and I are what Fort Jude calls *having trouble.*' She lets this float between them.

'I'm sorry.'

'You don't know what it's been like.' She reaches for his arm, rethinks and laces her hands like a child playing *this is the church and this is the steeple.* 'He fell in love with his first cousin. How obscene is that?'

Because he has noplace to go with this, he sinks the same old hook. 'Did she have a boyfriend?'

'Who, Gayle? Hell no. She's already used up one husband, and she's getting cranked up to dump number two . . .'

'I meant Lucy.'

'. . . Clueless Ed. Who knows what the law is in California. For all I know, she has Davis lined up to be number three.' Nenna raises her head, looking at him until he softens and meets her eyes. 'It's my mistake, really. Davis wasn't local either.'

The silence stretches so thin that he is obliged to ask. 'Um, about my mother . . .'

'I'm so stupid, how was I supposed to know? I mean, it's practically incest, but how could I not see the signs?' Now that she has his full attention she says, 'I may have to divorce him.'

'I see.'

Her voice lifts in a trill of discovery. 'In fact, I think I will.'

'Thanks, Mrs Um.' He's tired. They've been sitting here too long. Clumsily, he weighs exit lines. 'I've wasted enough of your time.'

'Oh, not at all.' Nenna puts her hand on his so swiftly that he jumps. 'You need more ice.'

'Not really. I should go.'

'It'll only take a minute, and I'll get more cookies too . . .'

'No thanks. Really,' he says, too late. Rounding the island that separates the territories of Florida room and kitchen area, she strikes for the interior, rattling utensils, foiling any attempt to shout goodbye and go.

Dan is alone, surprised by an unexpected message from his body. *Hi there.* Nenna's too old, but the presentation is very nicely done.

Stop that. There's only one safe way to do this. *Get the fuck out.* He can't, quite. He needs to go but now that the possibility is obvious, messages keep coming. Available. Coming on to you.

I have to get out of here.

As if she has powers and can hear him thinking, Steffy McCall slaps into the room on rubber flip-flops. Dead on target, she says, 'You don't have to stay just because Mommy says you do.'

24

Bobby

'How drunk was I?'

'You were pretty disgusting.'

'The shit I was, I don't remember that.'

'Do you remember anything?'

'Not if I can help it.' That grin.

Bobby sighs. 'Right.'

Trailing Al Chaplin's old sweats, which Bobby threw on him after the shower, Brad surges up from the sofa like Jabba the Hutt, all phlegm and bad odor. 'Where am I?'

Bobby grimaces. 'My house.'

With Brad, there is always the possibility that he will rise up and pound the shit out of you. Instead he blinks, belching, 'What am I doing at your house?'

'Beats the crap out of me.'

Some lame idea Chape had, that smug, privileged bastard, gearing up to remove his glossy nuclear family from the fiasco at the Fort Jude Club. Efficient, too. Chape couldn't herd his nuclear support group into his Escalade and return them to the safety of their showy house with its gold bathroom fixtures and terrazzo floors until he processed certain particles. Hugging busty little Sallie like a kid with his squeeze at the senior houseparties, he turned and handed Brad off to Bobby with the condescending smile of a man who was born knowing how life works.

'Best you take him. You people are supposed to be good at interventions.'

'There's a difference between intervention and garbage disposal,' Bobby said, too late.

'Carter will help you shovel him into the car,' Chape said, propping Brad up against a surly teenager who looked too much like Chape.

'But my car is . . .'

'No problem. I had Marco bring your car in from the shack.'

Astounding, the man's level of organization. He dumped Brad and that was that. Smart kid, Chape's son came armed with one of the club shower curtains, ripped off a rod in the locker room, to keep the damage contained, and there was damage. It will be days before Bobby gets the smell out of the car.

Thank God his siblings left last night to go birdwatching in Homosassa Springs. With her life in tatters, Maggie loves to study anything smaller than she is, solemnly checking off creatures sighted against her guide book. It gives her the illusion that she's getting a grip, which she isn't. And Al? Al has nothing better to do. There's a bar he likes in Homosassa, so he indulges her.

When he made it to his feet after several tries, Brad went padding out through the dining room without breaking anything, although it was close. If the gods are kind, Bobby will get shut of him and expunge all traces before they get back tonight.

The fat fuck is in the kitchen now, sticking his head under the faucet, Bobby knows the sound well enough. Then he hears the fridge door slam. He's out there drinking Bobby's seltzer straight from the bottle or orange juice out of the carton, smearing the opening with disgusting Brad-drool. Worse. Brad's always been a backwash kind of guy, you didn't want to drink after him, so he'll have to throw everything out. Bobby waits a minute because he doesn't really want to see it going down. He goes into the kitchen reluctantly. Brad doesn't see him at first.

Then he does, with a resentful, 'Oh, it's you.'

Bobby shrugs. 'My house.' He shouldn't have to explain these things.

'And I'm here . . . why?'

'Chape sent you.'

'It figures. Fucking Chape.'

'Chape is overorganized.'

'That's one way of putting it. And you brought me here after . . .'

Brad Kalen, thinking, is alarming, but Bobby isn't about to help him out.

He stands there scratching his armpits like a monkey. Oook. Oook. After a long time he asks, 'Who bailed me out?'

'You weren't in jail.'

'Where was I?'

'You don't remember?'

'Not really.' Brad's grin drips vestigial charm. 'Where was I?'

'The club. Engagement party for your daughter.'

'Oh, fuck. Patty. I forgot her fucking party.' The grin gets sweatier as he asks, 'But hey, I made it to the party anyway?'

'If you want to call it that.'

'Is she still speaking to me?'

'I wouldn't.'

'Don't look at me like that.'

Bobby says grimly, 'It's the best I can do.'

'Ug. I'm beginning to get the picture. So, the party. Um, did I do anything?'

'It was pretty bad.'

'Something I said?'

'You weren't rightly talking.'

'What did I, flash my dick? Yack in somebody's lap?'

'You were out cold. You didn't do anything.'

Brad blinks with that wide blue, innocent, *who-me?* look, he's been getting by on it ever since first grade. 'Then what was so bad?'

'If you have to ask, I can't explain it.' Bobby isn't really listening to this conversation. He's weighing his options. Chape's done with his personal *pro bono* renovation project and it's clear Brad's daughter isn't about to come and get him, she probably never wants to see him again. Is there a removal service he can call, or is he going to have to shovel rank, disgusting Brad Kalen back into the car, which already reeks of him?

'What the fuck happened?'

He says harshly, 'You landed on the bandstand like a side of beef.'

'I did?' Brad's face is working. He is casting around for ways to make the best of this, but the whole thing is too much, even for him. He tries for a smile. 'But, hey, I made my appearance.'

'If you want to call it that.'

'So Patty can stop complaining. It's not like I'm never there for her.'

'You don't want to know what Patty would say.' Bobby would do anything to scrape that pleased, smug look off Brad's fat face. 'You know who dragged you in and dumped you, right?

'Fucking Walker.'

'Right.' Funny how Brad gets this part so quickly. Is this what he does, pretend to forget things he knows, but would rather not remember?

Brad says heavily, 'Walker Pike.'

'So you did know.'

'I do now.'

'I'm surprised he didn't kill you.'

'Who, me? Why would he want to do that?'

Every muscle in Bobby's face tightens. 'After what you did.'

Brad bulks up, a monument to denial.

Stupid lout, Bobby thinks, as Brad's shoulders sag into a simian slope and his head sinks into a mess of baggy sweatshirt and rolls of flesh. Fucking Neanderthal. Standing here in my kitchen all rank and foul. Even though they aren't standing close, the hangover smell is strong enough to unpack its luggage and hang up its dirty underwear inside Bobby's head.

Eighteen months sober, Bobby hates the feeling because he knows it so well. He hates the memories filling his kitchen; they came in with fucking Brad, he's already knee-deep but they're still pouring in. Overweight, drowsy and not exactly harmless – benign for the moment at least, Kalen scratches his belly under the sweatshirt and waits for the next thing. It's like watching fruit rot. Bobby wonders how they could have been friends. If Brad's folks hadn't given him the motor bike, the car, the money, if they hadn't let him throw those big parties when they were out of town and asked no questions when they came back, would he and Chape and the others have hung out with Brad in the first place? Would they have tolerated him?

Aware that his unwanted guest hasn't responded, Bobby tilts his head and leans closer, trying to get a good look into those dull eyes. 'Are you in there?'

'Shut up.' Brad is thinking. It is excruciating to watch. Awareness comes in stages. Finally he looks up. 'Shit, he can't still be mad about that old thing.'

'He wanted to kill you after what you did.' Bobby is listening hard. He waits for Brad to fill in the blanks, which he refused to do back then. 'That night. After you guys rolled me out of the car. What happened, anyway?'

Whatever happened, Brad stonewalled Bobby then. He is stone-walling him now. 'Shit happened.' It's his way of saying: *Nothing.*

'Then why did Lucy leave town before graduation?' God he despises Brad.

'Man, that was a hundred years ago.' Looking briefly at his finger-nails, Brad lifts both hands and scratches his head: the thick gold hair has gone dark, but he still has those spoiled-rich-kid curls. 'Besides, we just got there, I barely had the girl's . . .'

'Don't say it.'

'. . . pants off. Well, I didn't.' Guilt makes him insistent. 'We didn't do shit.'

'You would have, and Walker knows it.' Bobby knows Brad is too stupid to grasp the relationship between the intention and the act: crazy night at the end of a bad week, they were all out of their mind on vodka, stoned and high on whatever else they were taking, wrecked by the pressure of last things. What would Bobby have done if he hadn't been laid out facedown in the mangroves by the time it came down? What could he have prevented, that changed certain lives? He doesn't know.

'Fuck that old shit, Chaplin, forget it. It's over.'

'That's not what Walker thinks.'

'That night is long gone.' Kalen jams his fists into his mouth, gnawing thoughtfully. Then he looks at Bobby over his knuckles and says cleverly, 'Besides. How do you know it was me?'

'Who else did you roll out of the Jeep before you got her to Lands End, Kalen? Buck and Stitch too? Chape?'

'You were too loaded to know who was there what went down, asshole. Face it, you were drunk. You're nothing but a fucking drunk.'

My name is Bob Chaplin and I am an alcoholic. If Bobby had been in his right mind he never would have let Lucy get into the Jeep that night, not after that thing with Jessie Vukovich, which was an abomination. He'd have grabbed the wheel and wrenched the Jeep off the road if he'd been in his right mind, he would have done it before they ever reached the turnoff to Lands End. Bobby groans. 'I should have stopped you.'

'Yeah, right. Like you were there at the end.'

'But Walker was.'

'Walker, Walker, what does Walker know?' There is a pause during which Brad casts around for suspects. 'It was probably Coleman, Buck always had the hots for her. Yeah, everybody knows he wanted that – what do I want to call her – that sweet little piece of . . .'

'Don't.'

'Lucy.'

So Bobby lets him have it with both barrels. 'She has a son.'

Now it is Brad's turn to shrug. 'She wasn't pregnant that summer when she left.'

'He's in town.'

'She wasn't pregnant when she came back for Thanksgiving, either.'

'That doesn't change what you did.' He means: what we did.

'Maybe not,' Brad says genially, 'but it's somebody else's problem.'

'That's what you think. He's been asking around.'

'Tell him it was Buck.'

'I don't lie.' It hurts Bobby to say, 'This isn't about just one of us, Brad, if it was, it never would have happened.' Bobby was crazy-drunk that night, yes, and psyched to be riding along in the back next to Lucy Carteret, and what would have happened if he'd had her alone, would he have gone too far because he was in love with her? His voice drops a register. 'It was all of us.' Grieving, he thinks: *It would have been different. I'm not like them.*

Brad chooses not to hear. 'Now, if you'll just get me a cab . . .'

'You can't say a thing's over just because you're done with it,' Bobby says gravely. Why is he so disturbed? OK, he loved her, he still does, and when she got into the Jeep that night he thought – he doesn't want to know what he thought; they were all crazy out of control.

'So I can get out of here and into some decent clothes. Back off.'

Bobby says, 'We're all involved.'

'You're standing too close.'

'I'm responsible . . .'

Brad pushes. 'Fuck it, Chaplin. Move.'

'. . . and you're responsible.' He pushes back.

'Shit I am. What makes you think it wasn't Walker?'

'Well now, there we have a problem,' Bobby says. In another minute he'll either have to back off or suffocate. 'You pushed her down.'

'How do you know?'

Bobby's voice is low and clear. In a kinder world, he could be heard in the back of a courtroom or in balconies far above any stage, but his life went a different way and he's just-Bobby, here with just-Brad. 'I saw you.'

Bobby is too close to the truth about himself. He did see, but he was drunk and raving, too trashed to get up off his face.

Brad's voice is a congested rattle. 'Like, you think I did all that single-handed?'

'What did you do, Brad? What happened?'

There it is: that hateful, careless shrug. 'Beats me.'

Bobby grabs those baggy shoulders and starts shaking. 'Tell the truth, you fucking asshole.'

And with a practiced, guileless, who-me grin that confirms all Bobby's suspicions, Brad glides out of his grip. 'Dude, I was too fucking drunk. How am I supposed to know what went down?'

25

Steffy

Slick as a scam artist, Steffy springs her friend Dan from Mom's lair, a.k.a. the flowered sofa, before the woman can weight him down with a ton of cookies and talk him to death. The way Nenna scowls, you'd think Steffy was running off with her new boyfriend, not saving a helpless stranger from Death by Monologue. When her mom sucks a person into those soft pillows and starts, you can practically see the cobwebs form. Usually it's one of the hags she hangs out with, but even though the big party was last night, not one of her Lunch Bunch phoned and nobody came by. It's weird. Unless it's sad.

Steffy might stop to feel sorry, if she wasn't in such a rush. Poor Mom was spilling her troubles to a stranger because her friends don't call and she's had a shitty week. God, how embarrassing! She probably went off on Dad in gross detail, up to and including the humiliating fact that he has to drag his pillow downstairs after Steffy goes to bed, like they don't think she knows that he's slept on the rollaway ever since the fight.

Please God, don't let her complain about the sex. Mom is so pissed off right now that she doesn't care what comes out of her mouth. Right now it looks like she's quit caring what she does. The woman is flat-out flirting, when she needs to get her ass to a marriage counselor and buy lessons in putting everything back where it belongs. She can vent for $150 an hour *and* do something useful at the same time and, boy, does her mother love to vent. Steffy read a book once that had a whole chapter called 'The Human Swamp.' Well, that's Mom.

'Hey, Dude!' She storms the room and Dan lights up.

'Steffy. Hey!'

'So, Mom,' Steffy calls, releasing him from the sofa. 'Dan and I have a Thing we have to do.'

'Wait! Oatmeal cookies!'

Steffy nudges Dan through the door with a bright, 'He's going, Mom.'

Behind them, Mom bulks up like Swamp Thing, all waving tendrils and mournful eyes. 'Where?'

'Emergency,' he chokes, clicking his cellphone open and shut to prove it. 'I'm sorry, and thanks.'

Bingo, zot, it's like magic. They're out the door.

26

Jessie

Out of nowhere, Sallie Bellinger says, 'If you want to know the truth, I always thought it was a gang bang.'

Oh shit, Jessie thinks. Just when she was getting comfortable, chattering over coffee with the Lunch Bunch. *Let's don't go there.* 'I thought we were talking about . . .'

Sallie's voice drops. 'Shhh! Here she comes.'

Rounding up the usual suspects at the club's beachfront annex, they'd agreed to skip Nenna this time because she, and not Brad Kalen, was topic A. That dress! The way she ricocheted from man to man, making all those desperate ex-wife moves, they should warn her, but her best friends can't say anything or ask her about

it because she hasn't told them. And here she is, coming in all
la-la-la, like Davis isn't a philanderer and everything's just fine. Like
every woman at this table but Jessie, she's practiced at glossing over
life's dirty parts.

Entitled insider that she is, Nenna nudges Kara aside and slides
into the banquette. Jessie's pleased to be included, but, wow. Last
night's party lies like a patient etherized upon a table, but this patient
is kicking and screaming because the anesthetist didn't show up and
the dissection is well under way. The sunlight is dazzling even through
layers of tinted glass. The water glistens and from here swimmers bob
like lazy ants in the gentle swells. Dolphins and egrets and gulls wheel
against the cloudless backdrop, but given all they have to talk about,
nobody but Jessie sees.

'Jessie?' Sallie Bellinger elbows her. *You're on.* 'You were saying
what he's like.'

'Who?'

Betsy does that thing with her eyebrows. 'You know. Lucy's son.'

Sallie serves a hard ball. 'If he really is her son.'

Cathy Rhue enters the game. 'Is Carteret really his name, or is
it some kind of scam?'

'It was on his credit card, Cathy.'

'Not to put too fine a point on it, but. Does he look like her?'

'Yes.' Jessie's uncomfortable with this, but if she wants to stay, she
has to play. 'Same hair, just a little darker. Green eyes.'

Sallie serves. 'Wonder who that comes from.'

'Oh, the father, I suppose.'

Betsy hits it over the net. 'Whoever *that* is.'

'As a matter of fact, he looks a lot like Lucy. I should know.'
Heads whip around. Nenna! Jessie has to admire the woman; she
knows she was topic A. before she walked in, but she volleys like a
pro. 'He was at my house!'

Score! New to the game, Jessie slips. 'No shit!'

Nenna grins. 'We were having iced tea.'

'Get out!'

'And my oatmeal cookies. That's why I'm late.'

'You're not late, you're . . .'

Cathy says kindly, 'Just in time. We were just starting.' Never mind
the empty coffee cups and pastry crumbs and ruined paper napkins;
they've been at it since ten.

'Good thing I baked last week.' Nenna glows – not like she's lost her man, more like she just scored a shiny new one. 'He ate about a dozen.'

'What's he doing in Fort Jude?'

'He's here on some big story.' In training since nursery school, Nenna waits a beat before she adds, 'For the *Los Angeles Times*.'

'Is he really Lucy's son?'

'He says he is.'

'I could say I'm the queen of France, but would you believe it?'

'Where else would he get *The Swordfish* from our year?'

'He had *The Swordfish*?'

Topic A. when she came in. Now look at her, with yellow feathers in her teeth. 'Bobby's, actually,' she tells Betsy and Jessie relaxes, but only a little bit.

'He knows *Bobby*?'

'I saw what you wrote to him in *The Swordfish*, Betsy. And I thought you were my friend.'

'Houseparties. It was a crazy time,' Betsy says, propelling Jessie into a bad place.

Kara's from Chicago, but that doesn't stop her. 'I hear they were pretty wild.'

Sallie says, too fast, 'Don't believe everything you hear.'

'You're the ones who laid it all on me, how crazy it got, especially the last night when your friend Lucy showed up . . .'

'We were never really friends.

'Lucy kept to herself until that night.'

'White bikini, see-through shirt, you might call it her coming out party.'

Resentment crackles in the room. 'Like she was asking for it.'

And Jessie's automatic censor breaks down. 'Nobody asks for a rape.'

'A *rape*! At *houseparties*? Don't even *think* it.'

'Puh-*leeze*.' Sallie's smile scrapes Jessie raw. 'People like us don't do things like that.'

Don't, Jessie thinks. *Just don't*, but she's sliding into the zone. Everybody who was anybody was at the beach the week before graduation, running around crazy, like it was the night before the Battle of Waterloo, and this was the Last Good Time. She hadn't exactly been invited to camp out in one of the beach houses because she had, OK, she had a reputation, so she crashed at home and slipped into the parties in all those houses after it got dark, stayed up all night when the parties spilled out on the beach and never left until the last dog was hung and the last of them staggered off to bed and, man! It was almost like she belonged.

So she was at the bonfire on the famous last night when Lucy showed up for the first time ever, all gorgeous and sexy and brash. She sneaked out. That grandmother kept her on a short leash.

Jessie knows how her own night ended – *Don't go there* – but Lucy? The girl was everywhere, she danced with everybody, all these aging girls' boyfriends, captains of this and that and a bunch of guys that nobody knew. They rolled in from Broward and Sarasota and as far away as Tarpon Springs. Fort Jude houseparties were that famous. By the time the night ended Jessie knew why Sallie and Betsy and all were so pissed off at her, she just didn't know who Lucy left with or what happened after that, and the rest? She jerks herself back into the present, where it's safe.

Fucking Sallie is going, 'These things do happen. Just not to people you know.'

'Don't be so sure.'

And as if she knows what Jessie's thinking, Betsy scowls. 'Probably one of the Pierce Point boys, you know, like the Horshams or the Ackleys, Lanny Rucker or the Pikes.' Take *that*.

And Sallie drives in the stake. 'People like that don't get invited to our things, they just don't.' She covers her mouth like a priest crossing himself after the stake goes in. 'Oh! Sorry, Jessie. Wade is soooo *not* the same person now. He was much, much different back then.'

'So was I.'

'No offense!'

Jessie does not back off with the traditional, 'None taken.' She won't. But leaving is out of the question. All she can do is sit, waiting for this to end.

As if to make up for what she just did, Sallie Bellinger diverts the pack. 'I wonder if Brad's OK. Brought down in front of all of us, and by . . .' It's a close thing. She almost says, 'Pierce Point trash,' but substitutes, 'Walker Pike.'

'Poor Brad!'

'We ought to go check on him. He could be a danger to himself.'

'Brad hates these things, now tell me he didn't get belching, puking drunk so he wouldn't have to come.'

'And he wouldn't, if Walker hadn't dragged him kicking and screaming. We should be over at Patsy's, apologizing.'

'Frankly, I don't think she wants to hear from us. We talked her into that humongous party, and now look.'

'Cecilia would have died.'

'I bet Brad's ashamed.'

'Humiliated, I hope.'

'He ought to check himself into rehab.'

'Or do us all a favor and hang himself.'

'Oh, he's much too self-centered to do that. Like, what would Fort Jude do without studly, stupid old Brad?'

'Who would we have to talk about?'

It's interesting, watching Nenna writhe, Jessie thinks, but after a lifetime with these women, she's expert at the quick save. 'But if he *did* do anything drastic . . .'

Sallie twists her beads in a show of remorse. 'It would be on our heads. We made him give that party, after all.'

'For Cecilia. She'd want us to make sure he's OK.'

'After the way he did her?'

'Because he did.' Nenna is all wronged wife today, rehearsing for the divorce.

'Did you *see* how he threw himself on her coffin down at St Timothy's? He loved that girl in spite of everything.'

'If Brad wants to kill himself, let him! It's not our fault.'

Betsy sighs. 'Unless it is.'

'It isn't safe. You know what he's like when he gets mad. Let one of the guys check on him. Buck, maybe, or Stitch. They're still friends.'

Kara says, 'Not after last night. They're over him.'

Betsy turns to Sallie. 'Chape can do it. After all, they're best friends.'

'They weren't *that* close,' Sallie says. 'Besides, Chape's at the Florida Bar Association in Deland, and he won't be back until tonight.'

'By then it might be too late.'

Oh, Betsy, head cheerleader. 'OK, then. It's up to us.'

'We can't all go.'

'You brought it up, Nenna. Maybe you should . . .'

'Can't.' Their old friend's mouth narrows. Her eyes are gun slits with a massed army behind them, glaring out. 'I have a lot on my plate right now.'

'It's our duty.'

'I would, but this is my acupuncture day.'

'I promised to take Gramma Bellinger shopping after lunch.'

Betsy sets her cup down hard, like a gavel. 'After all, we started it.'

Somebody ought to do it but nobody really wants to do it. Nobody present really likes Brad. Jessie gets up, broadcasting contempt. 'When the check comes, my number is V48. Since you're all too chicken, I'll go.'

27

Steffy

And how she brought it off? Timing. When Mom went into the kitchen, she hissed, 'Don't tell Mom. I found something scary at the house.'

She didn't have to say which house. He dropped that ancient yearbook he came with. Now all she has to do is make up some story, right?

But Dan's all over it, like white on rice. 'OK. What did you find in the house?'

'Yeah, well. Whatever. It's hard to explain. You kind of have to see it.'

'Letters? Papers? Skeleton? Disembodied corpse?'

It's just something she made up to spring him. 'You mean, like, ghost? Not really.' She fishes, but comes up empty. 'It's a lot and a lot stranger.'

'Explain strange.'

Come up with something, quick. All she hears in her head is, duh. Duh. Duh. Only three more blocks. Duh! 'So, where did you get that old *Swordfish*?'

'Yard sale!'

Did he just turn red? Her tone says, *Gotcha.* 'Yeah, right.'

Dan counters with, 'So, what's this, like, *scary thing* you found at the Archambault house.'

And Steffy knuckles. 'Oh, that. That was just a story to get you out of Mom's clutches. Like, you were desperate. Look, we're here.' Carter is here too. Her heart leaps up at the sight of his car. She jumps out.

He says, 'OK then.'

'Are you coming or what?'

'Can't. Researching down at the *Star*.'

'OK. The something strange was just a story, but it wasn't,' she says heavily. 'There's. Um. Something in the attic that you have to see.' That, at least, is the truth. She needs to get him in there long enough to mess Carter up a little bit, you know, to get him back for the hickey Jen plastered on him like a fruit label, then he can go. She leans into the car, wheedling. 'Really.'

'Look, you got your ride. If you'll just close the door?'

'Come on, it won't take long.' When he greets this with an apologetic shrug, she comes clean. 'OK, I need a favor. It's my boyfriend? It'll only take a minute, just enough to make him jealous, please?'

'You're kidding.'

'It's important. You don't even have to talk to him.'

He cuts the motor. 'OK.'

It's kind of trippy, going into *their place* with a gorgeous man, knowing that Carter, who might actually be watching from the attic window, will hear them talking on the stairs. But of course they aren't talking. Dan just follows politely so she is rummaging again, weighing setup lines. Think of something to say that will make him answer, Stef, think fast. She blurts, 'I told him you were my boyfriend!'

'What?'

'Carter. Carter Bellinger. It's a long story,' she says, thinking: *Take that, perfidious Jen.*

'I bet.' He isn't listening, he's inspecting the scarred wallpaper as they climb the stairs, as though what he needs is written there.

'So if you wouldn't mind . . .'

'What, holding your hand?'

'Playing like you care.'

But he is running his fingers over initials carved in the old newel post with a weird, visionary squint.

'Come *on!*'

Opening the attic door Steffy says, to keep the conversation going, 'Mom told me you have, um, family down here?'

'Sort of. Maybe. I don't know.'

'Where else would you get a copy of the world's oldest *Swordfish*? I mean, fuck, it's from my mother's year.'

And for the first time since they left her house, her new guy smiles. 'It was my mother's year too. Her name was Lucy,' he adds, as though she'll recognize it and start to talk. 'Lucy Carteret?'

'Awesome!' she says as her head clears the top of the attic stairs. *We're practically the same age.* This makes her so happy that she laughs. She's trying hard to make this sound like a party. 'That is sooo cool!'

What follows is everything Steffy hoped and more. 'Babe!' Carter is energized by the unfamiliar voice. He greets her with a studly hug. At the same time he is craning over her shoulder to see who . . .

'This is my friend Danny,' she says carelessly, as Dan Carteret emerges from the stairwell. 'Danny, Carter. Carter, Dan.'

Nicely — he really is a good guy! — her friend slips a possessive arm around her. 'Any friend of Steffy's . . .'

Carter gives him a diffident, 'Hey.'

'He's a reporter. How cool is that?'

'Really.' Not a question. Period. Carter is trying way too hard to sound unimpressed. 'And you brought him up here because . . .'

Steffy says, all, everybody-knows-this, 'You mean you don't know what happened here? When you get home, Google Lorna Archambault. She burned up right here in this house.'

'No shit.'

'Yeah, shit. Dan's doing a story about it, for his paper? It's . . .'

But her trophy is too absorbed to pick up on his cue. Instead he spooks around the attic, peering into gables, turning over trash with his toe, running a hand over the dressmaker's shape which might in fact be dead old Lorna's shape, poking at defunct Venetian blinds. When he does speak, he says nothing that Steffy expects. Instead he pulls out a tired old picture, which he hands to Steffy first. 'I can't stay, but, hey. Do you know these guys?'

More than anything, Steffy wants to help him, but she doesn't know these guys. She hands off the snapshot to Carter, who's so close that her flank twitches, from her armpit all the way down. His warm breath swirls around in her ear; she wants to finish this fast so Dan will leave. Then she'll do whatever she has to with Carter, to get him back from Jen.

But the least likely person to recognize somebody in Dan's crap snapshot turns out to know. Carter yips like a pirate with a treasure map. 'Well, yeah!'

'No shit!'

'Yeah, shit. There's one a lot like it tacked up at my dad's fishing shack? Except my dad isn't driving in that one, go figure. I mean, it's his Jeep. That's Millicent Von Harten's father in the back with Mr Coleman and his twin brother, the one that died in the wreck?

And the guys hanging off the sides? Oh hell, I don't know who this one is, that has all the red hair? But the one on the driver's side is definitely Mr Kalen, you can tell by the unibrow.'

28

Dan

A quick study, Dan leaves the attic before the kids can distract him, rehearsing their names. Coleman. Von Harten. Kalen. Bellinger. Four names, sixteen steps. It won't take long. Chaplin's off the list – those watery blue eyes. With four locals to research, it won't be hard. Then he can hunt down and slay, or . . . He doesn't know. It's like that old movie: *I know who you are and I know what you did.* Except he doesn't.

He aches all over, as if they just told him that his father died. How do you grieve for somebody you never knew? It's odd. He does. He always has.

Get down on your knees and thank your God.

What? He trips, nicking his hand on a latch. 'What!' *Oh, crap, this house is not good for me.* Why is he still on the second floor?

It's in the blood.

'Get the fuck out of my head!'

Not him. Never. Do you hear?

The hell of it is, he does. Where he should be downstairs and out of here at a dead run, Dan's like a car with a dead battery, stalled in front of her bedroom door. Either he's batshit crazy or the old bitch really is yelling, **It's in the blood.**

Out, he thinks, *got to get out,* but he lingers, boiling with questions. Then, my God! At his back, there's a disturbance in the air. Before he can swivel to see, there's a thump between his shoulder blades. *Mom!*

Air knifes into his chest.

Liberated, he runs for the exit, wondering how the fuck his mother got into this house.

29

Jessie

Jessie has been in worse places. The cavernous front room of the Sixties Modern shrine to Orville and Mildred Kalen is littered with the expected: crumpled beer cans, miniature airline empties and ranks of full-sized dead soldiers; clothes strewn every whichway; unopened bills and second notices, sleazy skin mags and months' worth of old newspapers, some still in their plastic wrappers like snakes that died before they could slough their skin.

The architect's vision went to hell the day Brad Kalen shipped his ancient parents off to Golden Acres, that'll teach you to have a baby way too late in life, that'll teach you to spoil him rotten. Mold overtook the white stucco walls the day they left; their pictures faded. It's been a long time since anybody opened the dusty fiberglass curtains on their panoramic view of the inlet, or opened the sliding doors. Dead dieffenbachia droop in porcelain urns on the filthy terrazzo and the whole place smells of sour laundry.

He's here, she thinks, sailing into the kitchen as though she'd swept down the curved staircase all dressed up for the next party every night of her life here, the privileged child of the house.

Yes she has been here before. No she doesn't want to talk about it. Junk from Brad's tux pockets litters the kitchen counter: wallet, keys, dented silver flask. Somebody jammed last night's dress clothes into the washer, tuxedo and all, and started it; through the glass she sees the stuff revolving, a study in black and white. A stinking load Brad washed but left to mildew in the machine is heaped on top; it was too vile to put into the drier. Brad's black patent leather dress shoes sit in a bucket of suds, he'd probably puked on them. Somebody – not Brad – somebody's fastidious.

Bobby, she thinks. He lugged Brad out of the club last night, an unlikely pairing. Sure, they hung out back in the day, but they were never friends: the gorilla and the thinking stork. That load is sloshing into the rinse cycle; he must have just left. *Good old Bobby.* She nukes water in one of the few clean mugs she can find and with a grimace, takes the only thing available – instant – and makes coffee. *Get the bastard up. Then we can start.*

She goes up the pink granite stairs, wondering whether she'd rather find him awake or stupefied. All she has to do is see whether or not he's dead, but Lucy Carteret's son is in town, and Jessie has questions. Snores rip through the upstairs hall: asleep, not dead. Too bad. It would have settled a lot of things.

Fuck. He'll be hard to wake up.

Brad is on the rumpled platform bed in the ruined master bedroom, drooling on his black satin sheets. Round bed, mirrored ceiling. Looks like a set for a porn shoot, but not anything you'd want to watch. Bobby maxed out on Brad around the time he should have been shoveling him into the shower. The room stinks of puke and hangover.

There are things it's OK to do in high school. Kids don't cut as fine a line when it comes to niceties, but adults discriminate. People who used to hang out together stop being friends or realize they never were friends, really. Age makes men cautious. Judgmental, and once they judge, it's final. Yeah, Bobby dumped Brad on the bed naked and filthy, and walked away. He was that anxious to get shut of him.

A rank pile of grey sweats by the bed tells her Bobby did finish the job and left before Brad yacked again and crawled away from the stink. She has no problem seeing him like this. Because she was a Pierce Point girl, not one of the cool kids, it's the only way she's ever seen him. Not naked, necessarily, but real Brad, neither charming nor social in the Fort Jude way. Underneath, he's always been willful, brutish and blunt.

Now it shows, and if it hadn't been for Walker taking control last night . . .

Fucking Brad will strut right back into that circle like the gypsy's daughter, miraculously turned back into a virgin again. It's the Fort Jude way. The Fort Jude way is a little miracle of denial. Jessie should know. There's a thin line between organized society and raw nature. She knows how the town's anointed nice boys looked at her back then; she heard the girls' savage whispers snaking down the halls, but now everything is pretty, pretty, now everybody's nice. *Nice* is the product of a powerful group effort. Societies like this one survive on the strength of a pact created by the group and mutually agreed upon. **Nobody needs to know the truth if we act the part.**

In this town the chosen are born smoothing over rough spots and ignoring the boggy ones – even Brad, at least they do in public, where people can see. Jessie shudders. As a kid, she envied that entitled, happy little circle. Now she's in it – more or less. The kid who used to be nobody is *somebody* in this town. It's comfortable. Fort Jude's chosen do what they have to, to keep their pretty creation intact.

She's been studying it ever since first grade. In a way, she's like the anthropologist who moves into a jungle village, alien at first, fitting in so she can crack the place open for examination even as she's welcomed into the tribe.

She knows now. Boy, does she know.

Before they bussed her across town to Northshore Elementary she was happy. She played in the dirt with kids who could care less who had what or who got invited or who your folks were, and if somebody pushed you down, you got up and started over. At Northshore, she spent solitary lunch hours and moody afternoons on the school bus, scheming all the way across town. Sure she could talk the talk and walk the walk if she had to, but she despised the superior little snots with their cotillions and sailing lessons at the Fort Jude Club. She loved to push their buttons. Never mind the cute outfits. She could turn heads, just boogieing down the hall in her trashy clothes.

Back in the day, there were still things nice girls just didn't do, whereas Jessie didn't give a crap. At Fort Jude High she sent those girls – the very friends she sits down with now – a different message: *I can take your boy away from you, no matter who you think you are. I can have any guy you have and every one you want.* Those girls used to look right through her, like, *slut.*

Well, she has their number now. But Jessie has mellowed.

Defiance sat better on Jessie back then. Odd how in the end you always come home to the town you stepped out of like dirty underwear and kicked away. Back in Fort Jude thirty-some years after the fact, she chose to assume protective coloration because for Jessie Vukovich these days it's restful, fitting in.

Like a declared state of peace.

She has money; she still has her looks and she doesn't want to spend the rest of her life alone, rising on company ladders in strange cities. She's proved herself. She doesn't need to prove anything to these candy-faced, aging girls and she certainly doesn't need to fight them. In fact, they've grown into nice, likable women that it's fun to sit down with. Every one of them has been seasoned by troubles they don't talk about: fucked-up kids, unfaithful or insufficient mates, some illness. They've all suffered losses and every one of them has chosen to smile in spite of it and keep going. These people have welcomed her, and at her age, Jessie is grateful. She needs a context, so she can rest.

There isn't much else she needs, except a new man that she can go to all their parties with; she wants this one to be a keeper, so that when push comes to shove, they'll both be around to help each other die. Odd what passes for happiness. Jessie's led several lives outside Fort Jude so far, starting as a Blackjack dealer in Vegas at nineteen – high-end table at La Mirage, she might still be there if she hadn't started marrying up. Her men were all good in their own ways, just not good at love.

It's time to decide which of the good old local boys will wear well, and settle down.

First, Brad. Wake him up. Ask.

Even though the smell is disgusting, she puts coffee on the bedside table and jiggers the alarm clock to go off in five. She opens the heavy, lined curtains so the room is bright and pushes aside the sliding door. Then she sits down to wait.

In a way, it's kind of wonderful. Pavlovian. He slams the clock off at the first beep, stumbles down the carpeted steps from the bed and lumbers into the shower. He comes out toweling his head with that useless dick flapping under his slack belly.

God she despises him.

'What are you doing here?'

'I'm supposed to see if you'd offed yourself.'

'Why would I do that?' He does not move to cover himself.

'Call it wishful thinking.' She tosses him a throw from Mildred Kalen's brocaded *chaise longue*. 'Give me a break. Put this on.'

Only a fool with no sense of how he is perceived by others would crack that lewd grin, like, *woo hoo*. 'I thought I was giving you a break.'

'While you're at it, cover that smirk.'

He drapes the Afghan over one shoulder and lets it drop as he heads into the walk-in closet, finishing his turn with a stripper's bump of that hairy butt. She hears hangers sliding on the rack, drawers opening, Brad farting. When he comes out, the shorts and polo shirt hide the worst of the damages. Matchy green, one of those golf outfits Orville left behind when Brad shipped him off to Golden Acres. He faces her in an old man's coordinated colors. 'What are you really doing here?'

'Lucy Carteret.'

Offhand: 'I heard she died.'

Jessie's head snaps back. 'Who told you?'

Lucy? Dead? How does word get around anyway, zeitgeist? Jungle drums? Or do these people communicate like certain kinds of trees – bamboo, she thinks – with a common root system deep underground, woody tentacles interlocking?

He doesn't answer. Instead he burps a question like that old TV comic who played the belching drunk, 'What about her?'

Fuck if she'll tell him that Lucy's kid is down here from the north, Brad may not know he exists. Let him sop up that information like some fucking tree draining its secret life from the sandy Florida dirt. Better yet, let the kid smack him in the face with it. Let this Dan Carteret track him down and put the fucking question, and when Brad answers, she hopes the kid beats the crap out of him.

She hates this but she has to stay until she gives him the last, hard shove down the road to hell. The question she came to ask, and, as it turns out, can't leave until she asks. 'So. That time. Did you rape her?'

He picks up the mug like a defensive weapon. 'When?'

'Don't insult me. Did you?'

'Did I rape you?'

Vile, she thinks. Filthy, she thinks. Bitter. Bitter. 'You know fucking well what you did.'

Instead of answering, Brad says, 'Shitty coffee.'

'So did you? Rape her?'

Brad raises the mug to mask whatever is going on with his face, which is not necessarily completely under control. He looks at her over the rim, snarling, 'Why would I do that?'

She does not have to say, 'You have a history.'

Brad does not have to say, 'I suppose you want to know if she enjoyed it.'

They have no need to dig up old shit. He does not have to respond with another insulting question, or force her to deconstruct the only possible response she can make to it. Instead she fixes him with a look that makes even Brad crumble. He seems to be melting all at once, a decomposing lump of flesh like Jabba the Hutt, or a monster from a kids' picture book.

Jessie watches.

Then Brad says through a spurt of bile, 'You might wanna split before it hits the fan here. I'm gonna puke.'

30

Bobby

Al and depressed Margaret just came in from Homosassa Springs with a pelican mounted on driftwood, a souvenir for him. Al is busy putting his arrangement of newspapers and empties back exactly how he had them, although Brad didn't disturb much that Bobby can see. Margaret is tending her African violets with that apologetic air, as though she's lamenting something so intense that she's sorry Bobby's not in on it. She bobs in the turret like a faded paper doll, picking off dead blossoms with a half-smile because death, at least, is something she can count on.

Ever since 9/11, Margaret's had trouble going out. Bobby only lured her into the yard last month and Al got her into the car so she's improving, but it's slow. She claims it's chronic fatigue syndrome, but Bobby is secretly convinced that after she lost the baby and her husband bailed, she just quit. She hasn't exactly turned her face to the wall, but it's close.

He's grateful and singularly touched when he makes her smile.

Al is the most nearly content of the three. He never aimed all that high, which means he's always been pretty well satisfied with whatever mark he happens to hit. Golden parachute, few demands, why not? He has something going with a waitress out at the Lighthouse; that's all he seems to need, but Bobby. He had dreams.

He walks through these rooms grieving, but the other two will never guess. He's that good at dissembling. It isn't exactly the Fall of the House of Usher, but it's close. *How did we get this way*, Bobby wonders. *How did we go from being what we were to this?*

Margaret floats by. 'Have you eaten?'

'Not really.'

'You look awful.'

'Late night.' Before they can ask questions he adds, 'No big.'

Al says, 'I've got Domino's on speed dial.'

Margaret shudders. 'All that grease! I'll thaw my turkey soup.'

She'll cry if Bobby doesn't say, 'Sounds good.'

'And hot croissants,' she adds. 'Poppin' Fresh.'

In New York, Bobby ate business lunches in the Oak Room and dinners at Lutèce and the old Le Cirque – all places, he realizes, that have ceased to exist, at least as he knew them. 'That would be lovely,' he says, just to see her smile.

'I'm at the Lighthouse,' Al says. 'If anything comes up, you've got my cell.'

'You don't mind canned peaches, I hope.' Margaret drifts into the kitchen. It's a foregone conclusion that he'll sit down and pretend to enjoy her idea of food.

How did it get to be twilight? Hard night, he supposes. Long day. It was nearly noon by the time he offloaded Brad and hosed down the Kalen laundry room, and the afternoon? He doesn't know. He spent a certain amount of time roaming the house because he thinks somebody broke in last night, but he can't prove it.

In the uncomfortable fug of Brad's incursion he didn't pick up on it, but when he walked into the house after delivering him, he got the idea that the air in here had changed. First he checked the obvious: strongbox. Yes. Family silver. Untouched. Then in a panic he upended the right-hand top drawer to the dresser he had as a kid.

The ring was still taped to the underside where he put it for safekeeping. He closed the drawer with an almost-sob, unless it was a groan.

Alarmed, he scoured his hard drive, but he found no tracks. Every file is timestamped: last accessed 6 a.m. yesterday, when he gave up on his piece about Fort Jude in the late 1800s and shut down. He headed downstairs, relieved.

There had, however, been a breach in security. He just didn't pick up on it. Now, lingering in the shotgun hallway because he can't bear to watch Margaret stirring her gummy turkey soup, he jerks to attention. The shelf with all their copies of *The Swordfish* is missing a tooth. He drops to his knees, disturbed.

His yearbook, the one with so much of his past in it, is gone.

Like the maid in that Ionesco play Bobby liked in college, he thinks, *My name is Sherlock Holmes.* He is sitting on the hall floor, double-checking, when Margaret sticks her head in. 'What's the matter with you?'

'I was just. Ah. Getting a rock out of my shoe.'

'Don't give me that. You were looking at Lucy's picture.'

She doesn't need to know that he razored it out. It's in the back of his closet in a morocco frame. She doesn't need to know that his yearbook is gone. He cares even though Lucy is long gone, so even though his sister is all too prone to psychic disruption he has to say, 'No. Something's missing.'

Her eyebrows shoot up but she decides to forget it, for now. 'Dinner.'

At the kitchen table he sits with his head bent as though they are Pilgrims waiting for somebody to say grace. He is looking into a bowl of Margaret's turkey soup, the last cube of a batch she froze in a post-Christmas fit. Glutinous rice, cubed celery and overcooked carrots float among shreds of white meat in gray broth. She's waiting for him to say, 'It looks great.'

'It's my specialty.'

Oh, God he is tired of sitting down to awful dinners under fluorescent light.

They're going along safely enough, hiding behind his dutiful Q. and A. about Homosassa, when Margaret pounces. 'So, what are you going to do about it?'

'About what?'

'Lucy had a baby, and he's here!'

Even she knows. Like the soup, it is depressing. 'What do you mean, what am I going to do?'

'Is it yours?'

'What?'

'You heard me. I saw you and him out there yesterday, talking. What's he like?'

A direct answer would give her too much pleasure. He parries. 'Like, you think he'd drop by? Just another stupid tourist, lost in Pine Vista.'

'Did she have your baby, Bobby.' It's supposed to be a question but Margaret lets her voice drop at the end, like a person setting down a rock.

She doesn't know. A part of him unclenches. 'Where's this coming from, Mag?'

'Who else would come looking for you, Bobby? Who else could it be? Tourists don't come here. Turns out Nenna invited him to the Kalen party so you saw him, what's he like?'

This town, he thinks. *This town*. 'I wouldn't know.'

She removes his half-full soup bowl as if to punish him, and dumps it in the sink. Because her parts are not all that carefully strung together, he has to be careful not to let her see that this is a relief. She squints. 'Were you finished?'

'It's wonderful, but I had a huge lunch.'

'At the Flordana.'

'No.'

'That's where he's staying, I just thought . . .'

'Who?'

He has to be grateful that she does not say 'your,' or 'Lucy's.' Just, 'The son. It's time you and he connected.'

'Margaret, I don't know what you've heard or who you've been talking to, but they're full of shit.'

She sets down bowls of canned peaches with blobs of Cool Whip. Margaret isn't speaking to him, but he's too preoccupied to notice. The missing yearbook, the Kalen disaster at the club, the last thing Brad said to him, run on a loop inside his head. He can't stop cross-hatching the territory, chasing a question he can't quite frame. OK, maybe he's been silent for too long, but he's closing on it.

Then his sister, *who he thought he was being strong for*, astounds him. Reaching across the table, she grips his arm in a spasm of sympathy, crying, 'Oh, Bobby. How can you stand your life?'

I'm fine, eighteen months sober and still counting. Consolidating. Trimming the portfolio and fixing up the house for sale. Walking into that party was a piece of cake, so it won't be hard to re-connect. 'You know what, Mags? It's probably time we got you to a better shrink.'

'Oh, Bobby.' When she raises her hand like that he thinks he can see light through it. 'Don't do me like that.'

'No no, I mean, you're doing so well. Al says you were great in Homosassa,' he says, and the whole time his mind is racing after its quarry. 'You're getting strong.'

Her face clouds over. 'You didn't hear about the trouble. At the Dairy Queen.'

'Even the best people have setbacks, Mag.' Last night's train wreck had common ingredients: Kalen. The kid. Pike. And . . .

'What makes you so sure?'

'Eighteen months sober, remember?' And the last element – Ionesco's maid would be proud. The final ingredient is . . . 'If somebody as lame as me can get my shit together, so can you!'

Margaret's big problem is that in every respect, she's too easy. Her eyes are brimming. 'I'm so glad.'

The final ingredient is. Finally. Bobby knows. 'I have to go out for a while, OK Mag? You'll be fine.'

Performative utterance or self-fulfilling prophecy, she buys it. She says firmly, 'I'll be fine.'

'Hang in and tomorrow we'll go out to lunch.' Her face does that jerky, frightened thing. 'Nowhere scary. Just the Pelican.'

'Where are you going?'

'Pierce Point,' he says. 'It's hard to explain.'

It's either hard to explain or hard to orchestrate, because Bobby is gearing up for a confrontation. He takes the long way because he and Pike haven't spoken since that night Walker came to the house, OK, thirty years ago. They were never friends, although he suspects they're a lot alike. Oh, God this is hard. He takes the oyster shell road that hugs the shore, making time to write the necessary speeches. For all the good that does. When he arrives at Walker Pike's neat redwood house on the far side of Pierce Point, the only opening line he's managed to come up with is, 'You have something of mine.'

Like Florida beach houses in the 1920s, Walker's place is built with a tin roof and wooden shutters that drop to protect the glass from storms. Even though it's late spring, he has the shutters down. Except for running lights on the deck and the yellow bulb in the lantern above the door, no light shows. For all he knows, Walker is gone. He goes up on the deck and knocks, rehearsing his opening line.

OK then. Knock again. Again. If nothing happens, walk away. Go on, admit it, it would be easier. Unless you think you can break in.

The door opens.

Everything Bobby lined up to say evaporates. 'Hi.' *Weak, Chaplin. Fucking lame.*

Standing on bleached teakwood planks worn smooth as the deck of a square-rigger, Walker Pike regards him. Like silvered teak, he's weathered well.

'It's me.' Bobby adds foolishly, 'Bob Chaplin, from school?'

'What are you doing here?'

'I had to see you.'

The face Walker has prepared for him is carefully assembled. Neutral. Handsome. He's lost the hungry, vulpine look he had as a kid. 'I don't *do* drop-ins,' he says in a level tone but he adds, to make clear that he is by no means hostile, 'If you want to know the truth, I don't do people.'

Write too many undelivered speeches and you write yourself backward, into cliché. Bobby blurts, 'We need to talk.'

'No we don't.'

'You have something of mine.'

'No.' Then Walker astounds him. 'You have something of mine.'

Troublesome facts drop into place like tumblers, with an audible *snick.* Suppressing a groan, Bobby dips his head in acknowledgement. 'I do.'

Walker snaps to attention. 'I *thought* she'd sent it to you.'

'Let me in?'

'I'd rather not.'

'If I go home and get it, then will you let me in?'

'No,' Walker says, and that's the last thing they'll say about Lucy's wedding ring.

Desperate, he tries, 'Lorna.' Walker's face clangs shut, which makes Bobby babble on about her snobbery, that big old car, her outfits with matching gloves and shoes until he hits, 'All she cared about was Precious. Fat as a toad. And *mean.*'

'She loved that dog.'

Bobby does not have to add, *Probably the only thing she loved.* 'Some expert came all the way from Tampa to do its hair.' *Walker speaks. I'm almost there!*

But Walker ends it. 'Precious was mostly bald.'

It's weird. Bobby's articulate by nature and by no means a stupid person but thirty years of pain and confusion, the bulk and weight of raw experience compressed, boil up and present as a single word. 'Please!'

Walker stops Bobby with the flat of his hand and holds him in place. 'Wait.'

'It's urgent.'

'Not yet.' The green eyes move faster than any scanner, assessing. His fingers tighten on Bobby's arm as if he's testing for vibrations. Fiber. Intent. Something inside Walker goes: Click. He says, 'OK. You're safe.'

Relief makes Bobby too bluff, too hearty, just one of the guys.

'Shit yes I'm safe.' What is the man, a walking metal detector? 'I'm not here to rip you off.'

Walker says coldly, 'Safe, as in, I can't hurt you.'

'I think you ripped me off,' Bobby blurts. '*The Swordfish.*' Oh shit. *Oh, shit!*

Walker's face changes, perhaps too fast. 'That wasn't me.' He stands aside, revealing polished floors, teak furniture with clean lines, shelves filled with books by the thousands. 'Come in.'

31

Dan

Exploding into the *Fort Jude Star* parking lot, Dan finds a note on his windshield. The oversized sheet of rag paper is neatly folded and tucked under the wiper blade. Whoever left it has an enviable printer; the heavy stock unfolds to poster size. The writer chose quality paper, 72 point type, to deliver a message that there is no mistaking:

DON'T BE HERE
DON'T DO THIS
IT ISN'T SAFE

Dan grunts. It's like taking a blow to the heart – not fatal, but he feels it. The puzzle is not that somebody has been watching, or why the note. This is the mystery: the design, the quality of the stock. The message is the medium. He knows without being told that this is not a threat. Carefully matching the original fold lines, he zips the paper into his messenger bag. He locks it in the car and walks away, pacing the streets with no certain destination.

He has to think.

When he left Archambault's this morning he came directly to the *Star* building, jittering and loaded for bear. His thinking has done a 360 since then, and it's getting dark.

He went in to research the story he devised to justify his presence here. His projected in-depth story about Fort Jude's spontaneous human combustions got him into the morgue, a.k.a. library. Three unexplained deaths by fire in the same city within thirty years – what a story! If he could find something new on them and get it right and sell it, Fort Jude's incendiary women would jump-start his career. If he could force himself to go back into that terrible house.

It's in the blood.

The librarian brought him everything he needed: photocopies of front pages and folders of individual stories, folders of cracked photos, city directory, tax records on the one burn site still standing police reports, personal data on the victims – everything he needed – but he could not bring himself to look at them.

In a miracle of avoidance, he cut to the chase.

He called for everything they had on Chaplin and the four names supplied by this guy Bellinger's kid. The boys snapped in that Jeep on a prehistoric beach before he was imagined are middle-aged men now, but if his mother kept that snapshot she kept it for a reason, maybe as a message to him.

Maybe Lucy, who told him nothing, saved the big stuff for last so she wouldn't have to sit through a painful Q. and A. Searches always begin in crazy hope and end in the usual way, but, hey. Maybe he can find and confront the guy.

Maybe she knew he'd use the photo to track the suspects to their lairs. She never said much but she loved him, she'd want him to get what he wants. What he wants? He wants to bag his biodad like a deer and take him home tied to his roof rack, antlers and all. Then the fight, the joyful reunion, whatever Dan Carteret really needs – an *explanation* – will follow. To hell with the story. He can get out of this town without going back to the Archambault house.

Meeting Bob Chaplin yesterday, Dan never would have guessed that the miserable, defeated guy he found weeding his sidewalk in Pine Vista used to be a big deal. Amazing, he's front and center in a full-page spread in the Sports section, flanked by his main men Bellinger, Von Harten, Coleman, Kalen, holding their helmets like trophies – five guys with Seventies sideboards and toothpaste grins.

All but Chaplin stayed local. He moved north and rose fast in the food chain, up to a point. Eagle Scout, Harvard graduate, summa cum; Harvard combined law degree and M.B.A., Goldman Sachs; New York wedding, reception at the Metropolitan Club but no photo, wonder what happened with the wife; regular promotions. Then the stories stopped.

Scowling, Dan studied young Chaplin the way he used to study

Burt Mixon's blunt, mean face, convincing himself all over again: *It isn't him.*

He thinks.

The others? Their lives continued, boring or not. The Bellinger kid's father did well over the years, still is: high school fullback, University of Florida all the way, marriage to a local girl, partner in a leading law firm, officer in the Florida Bar Association, ecology activist, local tennis star, all good. There wasn't much on Von Harten or Coleman; Jaycees, pillars of the community, printing company, car dealership, prizes for whatever they're still doing, no big, but at least they're still doing it. Possible. They're all possible.

The thick Kalen file started with a sixth birthday party – carousel and pony rides, family must have a lot of jack; at six the kid had the same bulldog scowl as Chaplin's beefy tackle. Dan scowled reflexively. Kalen smiled for his photo in suit and tie graduating from some jerkwater college, *couldn't get in anywhere decent,* Dan thought; *could he be that stupid and be my dad?* Wedding photo: Kalen in a tux, strong-arming his cute, tiny bride with big boobs out of the Episcopal cathedral in a shower of rice, reception at the Fort Jude Club. There were mug shots with announcements of each new job – **Bradley J. Kalen, second V.P., Bradley J. Kalen, publicist, Bradley J. Kalen, representative** – about two a year until they stopped. *Bradley J. Kalen, unemployed?* Divorce notice buried in City Briefs: irreconcilable differences, one of those legal niceties constructed to protect the perp. Drunk driving arrests starting in high school, ongoing. Assault, probably bar fights, ongoing. Charges filed, charges dropped. *Oh, fuck. It better not be him.*

Sitting there in the library, a.k.a. morgue of the *Star,* he could not have told you whether he came in to research the whole human torch thing because it was a good story or because of the newspaper photo that Lucy ripped out of his hands when he was five years old. It may be a message too.

Dan still doesn't know why she kept it, but that's not the worst thing he doesn't know. What is it with that house? Yesterday something happened to him in the old woman's stifling bedroom and for longer than he can say, life as he knows it stopped dead. Hallucination or fever dream? He doesn't know. She came boiling into his head, ugly and raw and raging over something that he sure as hell didn't do. Wherever she is in time, she smacked into him again today. While he was in the attic with Steffy, he was OK. He was OK talking to her boyfriend Carter. He was OK starting downstairs. Then outside her bedroom, she crashed into his head again roaring, **Not him. Never. Do you hear?** The words scorched, driving him out of the house a fraction of a second too late. There in the hallway, hot as a branding iron he can still feel, she marked him:

It's in the blood.

Things we think of to say after the moment for that pissed-off, snappy comeback evaporates: *Chill, lady. You're just a story. If that's the way you feel about it, then fuck you.*

In a day centered on searching, why did he save his mother for last? Achievement, achievement, achievement, high school P.R. boilerplate with a head shot of Lucy Carteret smiling like any pretty girl. Then, three grafs under a mug shot. **Local Girl Wins Radcliffe Scholarship**. Radcliffe?

One of those things about his mother that she never told. Lucy loved talking to him, she'd say anything, but when he asked her about her life before him, when he asked her about anything in it, she shut down. He always thought she was smarter than he was; he knew she'd dropped out of college. He never knew which one, or why she quit. A *Star* staffer wrote the scholarship story. It ended:

'Daughter of the late Lorna Carteret of this city and the late William Carteret of Charleston, S.C., the FJHS senior lives with her grandmother, Mrs Lorna Archambault at 4343 Azalea Street.'

This is how Dan Carteret, a good reporter in normal times, ran head-on into the detail he did not know he was avoiding. Like a crash test dummy in a high-speed experiment, he hit the wall. Something inside him went *splat!*

No wonder he couldn't get out of that house fast enough. No wonder Lucy kept the tearsheet from the *Star*. No wonder he didn't know – and after he knew, which he freely admits, now that he is up against it, he didn't want to know. The ruined foot. The chair. Images long burned into his brain expanded and magnified until they filled the world. Directly related to him.

Fuck, she was his great-grandmother. **It's in the blood.**

All this unexplained fire and probable damnation is specific to him.

The discovery drove him boiling out into the twilight, to the rented Honda and the note on the windshield. A demon in his head is busy writing background music for what lies ahead: possible scoring for the Greek Recognition Scene.

DON'T BE HERE
DON'T DO THIS
IT ISN'T SAFE.

Fuck. He has to source the note.

32

The Lunch Bunch

There's nothing like a good fire to bring out all your best friends.
It's ghoulish but true, it's a fantastic bonding time. Thank God
nobody was hurt.

Most of us went to bed early – imagine, on a Saturday night, but
it was the day after the biggest bash of the year and the Kalen party
wiped us out! We went to the Colemans' for cocktails about Kara's
brother from Detroit but it was a done deal; since we were getting
over Friday night, we'd be at Kara's all dressed up and smiling at
five sharp and out by eight. No stylishly late arrivals for us and no
kicking back with the Colemans after, dishing the other guests and
finishing off the wine. When everybody's seen everybody for two
nights running, you just get tired.

Some people went out for fried shrimp and slaw at the Shrimp
Tank afterward, but most of us were so worn out by all the work
we did on that party and drained by the disaster that we ate all
Kara's hot *hors d'oeuvres* and went straight home to crackers and
cheese, TV in our jammies, early to bed.

Our kids might be out helling around but nobody begrudges
them; our good old boys were thinking, shit, it's their turn. Then
they thought, but it's still my turn! We felt it in the way they shifted
in the bed, twitchy as horny high school boys, and we knew what
was up front and center in their heads. Then we rolled them over
and they forgot.

The sirens woke us up.

We went running out, and everybody that wasn't within earshot,
Cathy or Betsy Cashwell phoned. We have everybody that matters
on speed dial. Even Nenna snapped to, although of course by the

time she got here there wouldn't be much left to see – her fault, really, for letting Davis stick her in that corny Venetian knockoff over in Far Acres, where only rich outsiders live.

We ran out in our sweats, shortie gowns, raincoats, kaftans, the first thing we grabbed; lipstick, of course, but no makeup, we barely had time to comb our hair. Half of us look OK when we're *au* pretty much *naturel*, but the other half are a fright – no names, please! Face it, some women should never be seen without a bra, insulting the public with native-lady boobs and bellies rolling out of control, and, you want to know what's unfair? This is unfair. Except for the stubble and their hair being mussed up, our men looked pretty much the same as they do in the day.

Outside the sky was all the wrong color, talk about your unearthly glow.

Every piece of rolling stock in the city came pouring in to Coral Shores; they rushed down Coral Boulevard like the spray out of a fire hose, cop cars and fire trucks, city cars with giant speakers and ambulances toting machines to restore breathing, or jump-start your heart. Our street looked like a laser tag park, what with all the revolving strobes and all those sirens! Cop cars, yowling like cats in heat. The Bellingers came boiling out of Sallie's Lexus; naturally they were the first people Betsy phoned. They were first over the bridge after the rescue units passed, too bad they have to live in town, but Grammy Bellinger's Victorian on Bay Drive is too nice to leave. Poor Chape looked distracted and crazy with worry, and Sallie, my God! She almost got hit by TV Nine. We lit out after the news van, crazy to see what burned. Sallie got up and dove into the mainstream along with us, running down the road to Coral Circle. The night turned orange, what a sight!

God-almighty, the Tills' house was on fire.

Now, Boyd and Carole Till fly to Paris every spring even though it's still beautiful down here, and they jet to Maine as soon as they get back from France. With Boyd's money, everybody could. Easter Monday rain or shine they pull down their teakwood Rolos and arm the alarms and walk away without a care. You can do that in Coral Shores; we are protected. Shoresafe Security is that good.

Besides, we watch out for each other here.

Why, in Coral Shores you can throw a stone in any direction and hit a friend. We all grew up together, like one big family! We learned manners and flirting at the cotillions in junior high; never mind that we smoked grass outside the Malobar at intermission or that in eighth grade, sex disrupted the flirting and we cried all the way home in the car. We've been through so much together that whatever happens to you, there isn't a one of us who can't sign her sympathy note: Been There.

We live so close that we can walk to our friends' parties in our Manolos, all silky in the night. At Christmas if it's cool enough, we throw on our furs that we bought for New York and go house to house. Last year the Tills had a living crèche outside, with people in robes and shepherd outfits in a life-sized manger; we thought Boyd hired them but Betsy says they were volunteers from Carole's church.

The Tills can take off whenever they want because they have more than Shoresafe Security. They have friends! We watch out for their house, and for more reasons than Carole thinks. Sad to say, Boyd has some pretty weird friends dropping by when his wife goes away. Stitch picked up on it when he was out speed-walking last year, bikers and worse people spilling out at dawn.

Richer than God, and Boyd has a personality disorder. You wouldn't know it to look at him and we've never seen it in Fort Jude but, poor Carole, Boyd is a cross-dresser, which is probably why they travel so much. Maybe that kind of thing goes over better in Paris than here. If he'd let Carole have that baby she wanted so bad, maybe he wouldn't be flouncing around in Carole's pretty things. Once she came back from her Godchild's christening in Atlanta and found grease spots all down the front of her black velvet, and he ruined her Fortuny pleated dress! Carole started FJHS after we left for college and Boyd is way older, which probably explains a lot.

But why did Boyd's house get on fire?

Fortunately, it stands all by itself the far side of the circle, so nothing else caught. With the circle jammed with city trucks, we ended up in Lillian Lipton's front yard. Buck and Stitch had to bang on her door because Miss Lillian isn't deaf exactly, but age has made her just a little dumb, and they didn't want her to see the fire and get confused. She came out blinking, but she has the *sweetest* smile, and she was thrilled to see them. Of course they promised to keep the flames off her roof. She thanked them and invited us up on the porch, so we'd get a better view. Then she went in the kitchen to make coffee, which is what you do.

It was interesting, being together with nothing but our nightclothes between us and all the others' bodies; it made us softer, unguarded and rumpled from our beds. Man, woman. Woman, man, with only the smoke and the products we put on to keep us sweet to mask our body smells. Here in the night we had a choice between flirting and the usual sibling etiquette, which protects us all.

Generally we treat each other's men like sandbox friends – big smile, no agenda, it's for the best, but seeing Buck in briefs and a dress shirt and baggy old Stitch in his striped pajamas and Chape with those ripped-looking abs and thighs, with nothing between us but the underwear he slept in, brought it home:

How many things polite society protects and defends, in and of itself.

Watching Chape, we had to wonder whether Sallie has a harder row to hoe than she lets on, as in, whether Chape is gone for a reason all those times he says it's work. Then there was Al Watson, twenty years younger than Bette so we only see them at big parties, but who could keep from looking at Al?

Miss Lillian came out with a nice coffee tray and she put on the porch light so she could see to pour; the Nabisco wafers were a nice distraction, which was just as well. Then the light went off and we focused on the fire.

Tills' kitchen wing roof caved in and flames shot up. You wouldn't expect a tile-roofed stucco to burn so bright, but the parquet floors and poor Carole's antiques and draperies fed it for quite a while. When the firemen bashed out the Rolos we half-expected to see kids in drag screeching and flailing inside, you know, Boyd's special friends, or Boyd himself in one of Carole's shifts or at the very least some vagrant running out with his hair on fire, but whoever broke in was either dead already, or long gone.

Thank God our kids are OK. As soon as we heard the sirens, we phoned.

At first there was so much racket that we couldn't hear ourselves think but finally even the TV people and the ambulances left. The fire had died and officials were going into the wreckage to inspect. Sane people would have gone home, but we weren't finished here.

We had to talk. Not that we hadn't already begun to speculate.

Somebody said, 'Good thing they weren't home.'

'Just so you know, the paramedics took Cal Simmons away on a stretcher. Heart failure.'

'Good thing they found him in time.'

'Good thing,' everybody said. Good thing this. Good thing that.
'Thank God nobody was hurt.' Good thing.

'That we know of. Boyd was into people we don't know about.'

'What do you mean?

'What if one of Boyd's scuzzy bikers . . .'

'You don't know that they're bikers.'

'They sure as hell aren't regulars at the Fort Jude Club.'

'Whatever they are. Shit, so, what, he gave one a key to the house?'

'Like, it was a grudge fire? Like, because Boyd pissed off someone?'

'What makes you think it was arson?'

'It had to be arson. Look how fast it went up.' Buck is on the City Council, so he's in tight with the police and fire chiefs, who were buzzing around in yellow-taped slickers like hornets looking for somebody to sting. 'I'll find out.' he said, and trotted across the street to ask.

'These things don't just happen.'

Sallie was maybe too quick to reassure us. 'Sometimes they do. Could have been the furnace.'

'In April?'

'Or their wiring!'

Somebody snapped, 'Or their grandmother blew up,' and everybody laughed.

Old stories never lose their power. Tribute to maturity: only one of us brought it up. Testimony that even accidental fires make us nervous? We had to turn it into a joke, although it was nervous laughter.

Mariel said, 'Well, it's not like there haven't been a lot of little fires.'

'You mean the Warrens' trellis.'

'And the Boyles' garage.'

'Plus, our cabana at the beach!'

'That was nothing like this. Those were all nuisance fires.'

'Little things. Things kids do. Hell, we set a few in our time.'

'This is different.'

'Kids,' Chape said stiffly, and God only knows why he scowled the way he did. 'What makes you think it was kids?'

At that very moment Sallie clapped her hands to her face. 'Oh my God,' she said, loud enough to distract us. 'Poor Carole! What'll she do when she hears?'

Naturally Betsy already knew. 'It's insured. The adjuster's on his way.'
'Who says?'

'Carole, of course.' We had to forgive Betsy for being just a little
smug. She's the only one of us with Carole's Paris hotel on speed
dial. 'After all, somebody had to break the news.'

'How did she take it? Did she scream when you told her? Did
she cry?'

'It's morning in Paris. She was very calm.'

'Poor Carole! Is she OK?'

'I'm worried about her, if you want to know the truth. She was
too calm. Everything burned to a cinder and all she said was, "You
know, Betsy, it might be just as well."'

'What might be just as well?'

If it had been one of us asking we would have ragged on her,
what are you, clueless? But it wasn't any of us, standing here in our
jammies, it was Nenna, showing up late in high heels and full makeup,
a living reproach.

'I came as soon as I heard.'

After an hour in front of the mirror. We could tell.

'Too late, you missed it. It's nothing but cinders now.'

We love Sallie, she's so forgiving. 'Come on up here, girl.'

'Miss Lillian made coffee.'

We gathered around, hot to fill her in. Kara said, 'Look! I've got
pictures on my phone.'

Then our voices went from warm to cold. 'Oh, Davis.'

'Hello, Davis.'

We all said hello although we aren't speaking to him after what
he did to her.

Ironic, in a way, that the group's known philanderer was the only
man out here fully dressed. He and Nenna didn't look too happy,
really. They looked like they were fighting when the phone rang
and on the long car ride over they fixed their faces so we wouldn't
know.

It's interesting. We were all furious at Davis for how he did Nenna,
but even though we'd always thought he was not nearly good enough
for her, now that we knew about his secret lover, he almost looked
good to us.

Where our men were running around looking like they'd been
slept in, Davis looked cool in an oxford cloth shirt and ironed jeans,
new topsiders, no socks. He had his collar open and the cuffs rolled

back, and something about standing out here in our night-things talking to Nenna's soon-to-be-ex husband made us over-conscious of bodies: his, ours.

Davis did a pretend salute with the smile he'd probably been using on girls behind Nenna's back for years. 'Ladies . . .'

Then something better came along and we forgot.

Whoever he was, this new man looked good, exciting, and only partly because he was new. Young. Very much himself out here in the dark with us. Tall, with a forelock that kept falling in his face.

Then somebody whispered, 'It's him!'

It was. Dan Carteret, that we'd heard so much about. He was the spitting image of Lucy, and now that he was here, we wondered why Jessie didn't say he was gorgeous, like, was she was trying to keep him for herself? What was she, sitting down there at the Flordana thinking up ways to lure him into her suite, like, *Me first*? Well, tough. Instead of falling down with Jessie Vukovich who, sweet as she is, would do it with anybody, he was here among us, and back-lit by the cops' headlights and the smoking afterglow of the Tills' ruined house, like maybe he'd come to tell us who did what to his mother that we still talk about, but never actually knew.

Somebody turned on Miss Lillian's burglar light so we could all take a better look. He stood down there on the walk, knuckling his head until Nenna – no, *our friend Nenna* – turned to see what we were staring at, and didn't she light up.

And didn't she trill, all surprised and charmed, 'Why, Dan!'

We thought he'd bound up the steps so she'd be forced to introduce him but he hung back, swiveling from us to the smoldering remains and back with a baffled squint. Then he said, 'You called?'

Oh, you clever bitch.

Well, didn't Nenna rush down the steps like a girl on prom night – and who could blame her, with Davis the rat standing *right there*, picture of a man asking for it?

For a woman who's been flattened and tromped on by a slick liar like Davis McCall, it was like landing a karate kick in his whitened teeth: take *that*. No, better. And why shouldn't she leave with him, she's practically single now . . . but, Lucy's son! We'd give anything to know what Nenna told this lovely man to get him here, and more to know what happened after they got in his car and rolled out of Coral Shores.

Things finally died down but we were all too disrupted to go

straight home, so Betsy had us over for toast and coffee in the glossy
new kitchen she built with the settlement from Clive. Kara ran home
for her banana bread and Cathy went next door for butter and that
calamondin marmalade she loves to make. Somebody thought to
bring Miss Lillian and she sat among us in her chenille bathrobe,
looking thrilled. Nobody saw where Davis went. He knew we didn't
want him here.

We looked at our men, who were sweet and rumpled and ordinary
now that we had all come in out of the dark, and we thanked
whatever gods take care of us that we were here with them, not
Davis. We took turns talking to poor Carole in Paris while our men
pestered Buck for details he'd picked up from the fire marshal.
Somebody turned on the TV and we waited for video of the fire
to show up on the news.

Of course we were upset!

If a thing like that could happen to Carole, what could happen
to us?

Being together like this, homefolks getting down in Betsy's kitchen,
made us feel better. It always does. The coffee was good, and worn
and frazzled as we were, we felt more or less restored. While we
were still debriefing, rehashing everything we knew and guessing at
the rest, the sun came up and there wasn't a one of us who wasn't
thinking: *Too bad it has to end*. It took us a long time to say good
night because we were tired as hell but we didn't want to let it go.
We and our men started home, walking through the early morning
two by two, and that weird, weird night ended up in a normal
morning way.

33

Walker Pike

Every time a siren sounds the vibration starts, deep in Walker's belly.
It turns him into a tuning fork, but you wouldn't know it to look
at him. It's been this way for longer than he cares to remember.
Going in to confront Lorna Archambault at twenty-one, he had no
idea what he was, or that it would end in fire. He was young and

so in love that he'd do anything. He met the perfumed monster smiling, even though she despised him.

How could he guess that he was the monster?

He didn't know. He didn't know!

Tonight he hears the sirens long before Nenna wakes Dan Carteret out of a sound sleep to stage her rescue from the scene on Coral Shores. Walker shudders as engines from North and Southside stations roar past the Flordana, screaming down Central Avenue toward Bayfront Drive and over the bridge to the island. Something's ablaze out there. The sirens tell him it's big. Good thing he's parked here in front of the Flordana, praying – insofar as Walker prays – that the kid will sleep through the racket and stay inside. He does not want to go out to Coral Shores where the commotion is and he certainly doesn't want the kid to go. Walker hates to see anything burn, won't let Dan see. Or put either of them out there, where they can be blamed.

The trucks recede and Walker shakes himself, trying to unclench. Nothing to see now, Pike. Nothing to do here but sit behind the wheel, waiting. Stay until morning, just to be sure this new person in his life is safely stashed. Now that his son is here, it's his duty to – he supposes it's: *protect*, and if Dan wakes up and races out to chase fires, he'll follow, and . . .

He doesn't know what comes next, only that it's important.

Yes, Walker's been tailing him. When he left the warning on Carteret's windshield today he thought his job was done, but it isn't. He went home thinking, *He'll be fine*, but that was a lifetime ago. Chaplin showed up at his house tonight. He looked like a carcass washed up on the beach, standing under the porch light leached of substance. 'We have to talk.'

Walker didn't want to. They did.

When it was done, Walker did what he had to. He came here. He's been standing vigil ever since. Responsible.

Sad, square old Bob Chaplin came inside all shaky and diminished. God, that was weird. He begged Walker to hear him out, all, *I alone am left, I alone am left to tell*. It was hard for him, just being there. It was hard for Walker too, but he let Chaplin talk, and Chaplin brought it back. All of it.

Walker gritted his teeth and held back, even during the hardest part, because he must never even *think* what he's thinking. He can't go there. Correction: must not go there. Ever.

At the end, Chaplin choked out an apology for everything he'd ever done and the one grave thing that he had failed to do. *Protect her.* In a way, it released both of them.

It was the first time they'd ever sat down together, and in another life, in a different society, Walker thinks, he would have liked the guy.

As it was, they were alike, with Fort Jude society like a ditch between them. The grimy kid whose dad ran a failed body shop out on Pierce Point came into Northshore Elementary under deep cover. The Coral Shores kids thought he didn't belong. When he shambled off the bus at Northshore Elementary in Pop's flapping shoes and torn castoffs they laughed at him. They pointed, they mocked his walk. Hurt, he turned his back on them, even on Chaplin, who tried to make nice when they landed in the same advanced math class. Nobody gets to see the cluttered, filthy rooms where Pop raised him and his little brother. He'd die. The grilled windows. The chicken wire that kept them inside before Walker got big enough to look after Wade and strong enough to work in the body shop. Nobody. He turned away in a protective slouch, put on a scowl that hid whatever he was thinking.

To his surprise, compared to most of those kids he was pretty smart, but you hide smart because you know it will make them hate you. In classrooms he grabbed the last seat in the back, kept his head down, never raised his hand, solved math problems no problem, but he did it on paper only. Teachers knew he knew, but he wouldn't go to the blackboard, so they stopped asking. They got along with Walker after they stopped trying to praise him. They never pressed because even adults were a little scared of him; by then he'd perfected the glare, growing up under deep cover. He graduated a year ahead of his class; nobody noticed, nobody cared.

Chaplin was just as smart, but he was better at dissembling. He knew how to please the people. In high school he was way too smart to show how smart he was, although Walker knew.

Once, they bumped into each other in Cambridge – the high school hero was at Harvard and Walker was on scholarship at MIT. Surprise. Tight smiles. *Oh, it's you.* He could see Chaplin reassessing him. Grinning, he asked Walker to come back to Eliot House for a drink, but he refused.

In Cambridge, he was a new person. It made him wary of people who knew where he came from. More important: by then he had more important secrets to keep. In Cambridge he and Chaplin never mixed – they never would, but tonight they sat down as equals, although in real life Walker has the edge and Chaplin said as much, coming in. *Failure humbled him*, Walker thinks over coffee. *He has nothing left to lose*. When they got down tonight, talking in Walker's beautifully spare, well-ordered living room, he and Bob Chaplin turned out to have more in common than he knew, because for all those years when Chaplin was being noble, he was in love with Lucy. They have plenty to talk about, but he let Chaplin do the talking.

Skirting certain matters. *The ring. What did she do with the ring?* The guilt. Where, exactly, that guilt should lie.

The ex-Harvard, ex-golden boy cradled his coffee, careful not to mar the polished teak table Walker designed and had made especially for this house. Grimacing, Chaplin talked about his failure – and not in a twelve-step way, although Walker noted the watery eyes and unsteady smile, the classic recovered-alcoholic's way of putting things. He laid it to one spectacular mistake at Goldman Sachs, although they both knew his grief was lodged farther back and somewhere much deeper. Fort Jude's golden boy was in mid-divorce when he messed up at the brokerage, he was fighting tooth-and-claw with Bethany and her lawyers, which skewed his judgment, and that was just before the crash. He jumped too fast on a major I.P.O., it tanked and he cost the firm their biggest client.

'It's like falling off a horse,' Chaplin told him. 'It shakes your confidence and day after day you have to get up and go out riding, but you're scared. You seize up and everything you do from then on goes wrong.'

It was only the first in a string of wrong calls that unspooled and ruined him, and that was the end of Bob Chaplin, Goldman Sachs. Now, Walker could have warned the man off that particular transaction. When he isn't working with the A.I. boys in public and private sectors, Walker Pike codes models of everything from stock market futures to burgeoning world wars. An intuitive coder, he's a genius at projection.

As he is living his life alone in every sense, it's what he does for fun. He could have warned Chaplin off that first I.P.O., and that just on the basis of what he has stored on his hard drive, which is only the beginning of what Walker knows. He could have warned Chaplin off a lot of things. He's never been much of a drinker but Pop was, so he could have warned him never to take a drink just because he felt bad, which is what tipped Chaplin down the chute into blackouts, rehab and the remaining eight yards into A.A.

If life is a race and he used to think of Chaplin as running way ahead, Walker passed him a long, long time ago.

Funny, the fourteen-karat kid from the right side of town told Walker Pike more than he needed to know about his own life and about what went wrong with his marriage, and Chaplin did all that on the way to talking about the last night of houseparties in his drunken last year at Fort Jude High.

Because the mangrove patch at Land's End was where their separate lives and this conversation had been heading from the beginning, Chaplin doubled back on the matter of that chaotic night at Huntington Beach. It hurts to know that polished failure that he is, Chaplin can tell Walker things he'd never have found out alone, because he shut himself up inside his head and locked all the exits a long, long time ago.

No matter how many models he runs on his powerful machine, Walker Pike was and always will be a terminal outsider.

'That last night of houseparties,' Chaplin said, underscoring the difference between them with a rueful, insider's grin. 'Oooh, man! You know what that's like.'

'No. I don't.'

'But you understand. Dude, you've gotta remember those parties.'

'Not so much. Not invited.

'Shit, everybody's invited.'

Walker's voice flattened. 'Not everybody.'

'Oh, shit.' Like Walker, Chaplin has been brooding over the matter of that night. He was brooding long after the particles settled because unlike Walker he felt responsible for what happened. Walker wouldn't know until Chaplin confessed to him, but the football hero blamed himself then and on and on, to this very moment.

'You might as well know, I was in love with her. I thought I could tell her and she'd love me back, if I could only get her to come! Last party of the year, my last chance. Please try to understand.'

'I'm trying.'

'So it's my fault she came out to the beach to spite that bitch grandmother. I begged. She had her own money by then, from her dad's family. She had a new car so she could come and go when she wanted, and the hell with the queen of the Fort Jude Club. Did you know our moms were scared of her?' Walker keeps his face so tightly closed that Bobby added, 'You know, big old Lorna. Lorna Archambault?'

Tightening every thread in his body in a miracle of compression, Walker kept it all in. Regret. Rage. Everything that could send this encounter to the old, bad place. 'Yeah.'

'I begged Lucy to sneak out and come with me.' Chaplin sighed. 'I waited for hours before I gave up and the hell of it is, by the time she walked down on that sand in *that silky white thing* I was too drunk to take care of her!'

'Not the first time,' Walker said, too low for Chaplin to hear. He would get through this without hurting anybody; he had to. He gripped the arms of his chair and filled his head with white sound, through which Chaplin's voice still came, but buffered. Remote.

'I was so fucking drunk!' Chaplin was the dog, begging to be whipped.

'I saw.'

'I loved her so much! It was my last chance to tell her, so I pulled her into that Jeep.'

Everyone has to sob out their story, Walker thought. Letting Chaplin talk was an act of mercy.

'Beautiful girl, us guys puking drunk. What was I thinking?' Chaplin wanted Walker to cry with him.

'In hell,' Walker said without explaining. He was at the beach that night, but for a different reason. Too late to protect her.

Then Chaplin told him a lot of other things: what happened before Walker caught up with them, what was said, and who . . . Walker would never show it, but it left him sick with anger. Clamped shut. It was unfair, really, letting the poor guy strip naked without giving anything back, but before everything, he had to keep control. There are things Bob Chaplin doesn't know that Walker will never tell him.

There are things about Walker that nobody needs to know. That he struggles to keep hidden.

'It's OK,' Walker said. 'You can stop now.' *Please.*

'I was so wasted.' Chaplin was bent on laying down his burden. At the end he looked relieved, like a Catholic coming out of Confession. As if he'd finally shaken off whatever sat on his head – monstrous, leaden. 'Please try to understand.'

Grieved as he was, shaken and suffering, Walker overrode it. He stood, and Chaplin stood. Surprised, Walker found himself raising the blade of his right hand – not as weapon and not in warning, but as though to bless the man before he released him.

'OK then.' Then he let him go.

'Oh, thank you.' On the porch, Chaplain cried, '*I'm so sorry.*'

'Don't.'

It saddens him to think that men like Chaplin actually believe that there are things you can get off your back by confessing them, as though destiny is fair and open-handed. That he can get past what he did by giving it a name.

The poor sod believes there is in life an identifiable moment at which, when *for good reason*, everything goes bad.

Well, Walker is here to tell you that's a crock of shit. Whatever is wrong within Walker Pike has been burning in there since the day he tumbled into the world, hopeful and unaware.

What happened with the old lady was inevitable.

He knows what he is and he fears it. The potential staggers him. *I've always been this way.*

Knowing circumscribes his life in ways he freely acknowledges and does not resent. Walker is a solitary. He lives alone and walks shy of others' lives. He stays out of their houses because it is important – not to keep his secret, but to keep them safe.

Please God, the kid will stay safe in his bed inside the Flordana tonight.

But when the last sirens die, just as the first EMS van comes back up on Central Avenue, he sees young Carteret come barreling out of the Flordana. Some kind of reporter, Bob Chaplin told him. Of course he chases fires, but the damn thing must be out by now. With a groan, Walker kicks his car into gear and coasts downhill as Carteret runs for the garage. He keeps the motor running while the kid goes inside. When the grate comes up and the rented car rolls out Walker falls in behind, gliding along behind.

He is here to follow, not stalk, Dan Carteret. He keeps pace, thinking as long as he stays in the shadows and keeps his distance, they'll both be safe.

There is this with the kid, but there's more.

If they see him, he may be blamed.

He goes over the bridge and along Coral Boulevard with his lights off, turning into a side street when the kid turns, parking at the corner so he won't know. Out in the circle, people he knows by sight are kicking at the embers of Boyd Till's pretentious, ruined house. He can smell the size and scope of the fire. Walker wants to see, he isn't here to see, he is here to protect Dan Carteret, although he does not know why and could not say from what, exactly.

Much as he'd like to walk up to this decent, attractive kid who looks like him, much as he wants to clamp Carteret's skull in his hands and pull him close, look in the eyes and see into his soul so he can confirm the likeness; much as Walker wants to grip the kid's hands and sense the truth of him, he'll keep a safe distance, and he must never, ever identify himself or tell Dan that he loves him, and he does. He may want to let his son know him and know everything about him, but the burden of knowledge that Walker Pike carries and has carried all these years must, at all costs, be contained.

It's for Dan's protection.

This is why he stays put when the kid finally comes back to his car – and not alone, which is a surprise. Dan comes back to the car with a woman Walker recognizes. That he knew, but not really, no big thing.

Keeping his charge's tail-lights in sight, Walker follows the rented Honda to the house where Nenna Henderson – no, McCall – seems to live; he pulls past the Honda and stops in the shadow of the jacarandas two doors beyond Nenna's house. He tilts his mirror, watching as Dan follows her inside.

When his son leaves here, Walker needs to see that he makes it safely to the next place. For reasons not altogether clear, he'll wait here for as long as it takes, wondering what's going on behind the Florentine façade and whether the sun will come up on the new day before he gets through doing whatever he's doing in there, and comes back to his car.

Dan, he thinks. He lets the word out. 'Dan.'

34

Dan

'Why am I here?'

Poor lady, she looks tired now that they are in the light, uncertain and wounded by Dan's tone, does she have any idea how late it is?

Did she expect him to thank her for yanking him out of a stone sleep to chase a dead fire? After which she scammed him into this ride home, getting into his car on the strength of information that she shows no sign of delivering; you bet he's pissed.

She says lamely, 'I thought you were into fires.'

'Who told you that?'

'Everybody knows.'

His eyebrows shoot up.

'After all, you told Jessie. You're not in Los Angeles with a billion strangers, this is Fort Jude.' She's maneuvered him into a chair in the French Provincial living room – one of those orderly, hushed places where no people come. Cold, like a decorator's model room. 'Davis won't be back tonight.'

'Ma'am . . .'

'Don't.'

'I have stuff to do.'

'We won't bother Steffy, she's over at Jen Pritchard's.'

Oh, lady. Don't smile at me like that. 'It's late.'

'It isn't late, it's early.' Mrs Um, Nenna will say anything to keep him, lilting, 'So. Talk about your suspicious fires. Want to hear what they're saying about Boyd Till?'

'I'd rather hear about my mother – whatever you know.'

'They're saying some bike buddy of Boyd's set it, you know Boyd goes around in Carole's evening dresses when she isn't . . . Oh, please don't look at me like that!'

'Look, you said . . .'

'I know what I said. I had to tell you something.'

And don't scrunch up your face like bubble wrap, it's disfiguring. And would you stop sighing? 'If you don't have anything . . .'

She blurts, 'I was afraid you wouldn't come!' Everything is sliding around now. Her face, her stated reason for this encounter.

'. . . I'll just go.'

'I couldn't bear to get back in that car with Davis. Not with everybody knowing. Not after I kicked him out for good.'

'Right.'

He can leave, but he can't stop her from following him to the door with that sweet, frenzied smile. 'This is a really hard time for me.'

'I'm sorry.'

'So am I. If you want the whole truth, I just wanted to show Davis.'

'Show him what?'

'That I have friends!' She grabs his arm. 'Was that so terrible of me?'

Pressed, Dan bares his teeth. As a smile, it sucks, but at five a.m. it's the best he can do – a rictus to get out the door on.

But she goes all life-or-death on him. 'Wait! Ugh.' Nenna groans. Something inside her is struggling to the surface. 'Agh. This is hard. I . . .'

Shit. He has to stay until she coughs it up.

Finally she blurts, 'I had to show them all I'm still attractive. Is that so terrible?'

'You don't have anything on Lucy, do you.' *Say no, so this night can end.*

'No.'

'OK then.'

'I mean. No, I do!'

Now it's his turn to groan. There is no way of seeing into urgent, worn-out Nenna, no telling what she has stored up for him. To find out, Dan has to follow her back into that Louis-Whatever parlor, sit down and wait.

'Coffee?'

'No.' He sits, but does not speak: an interviewing tactic he learned on the job. Let silence do its work.

'I should have told you yesterday,' she says, 'but it's hard. We never talked about it at the time and we didn't talk about it afterward and we don't talk about it now because you don't in Fort Jude, especially since nobody's sure what went down and it would ruin one of us. Am I making any sense?'

Looking into his hands, he waits.

'See, certain things are best forgotten. Everybody has something to live down and we respect that, aren't we all here to help each other through?'

They sit until the period clock on the marble mantel strikes again.

'When you get mixed up in something shameful in Fort Jude you'll shoot yourself dead before you let on, because your nearest and dearest will badger you until the story comes out – and when it does, you are implicated. Tarred with the same brush, you just are. We think your mother was . . .' She blushes. 'Well . . . A thing like that can toxify your life. You don't talk about it with your best friend, you don't even whisper it to your lover, you wouldn't dare because we are all connected. Tell *one single human being* and they all know. You have to protect yourself!'

Oh fuck, he thinks. *Talking in circles.*

'What if people found out that was you, laid out drooling by the bonfire when it happened, squealing drunk with a bunch of boys so out of control that there was no telling what they'd do? What if people knew you were so loaded that you don't even remember what you stooped to or with who, what would everybody think of you then?'

'Ma'am?'

'What if they started asking why didn't you stop them?' All her breath comes out in a sob. 'Understand, when these things happen, they always blame the girl.'

'What things?'

'Like it's all your fault,' she says bitterly, 'for being jealous of her and so wasted that you didn't lift a hand. You didn't *make* it happen but you let it happen. Do you know what that's like?'

He needs his digital recorder. The tangle of words is unraveling too fast, with loose ends everywhere.

'I mean, look at poor Jessie. It took her years to live down all the things she did with all those boys, because everybody knew. She had to make all those donations, drive all those miles for Meals on Wheels to . . . What do I want to say here? Atone for whatever she did with those boys. And she enjoyed it!' Frowning, she corrects. 'Or what we think she did.'

A bad wind blows in out of nowhere. 'At least I'm not the only one.'

'The only one what?' *Shut up, Carteret. Just let her do this.*

'The only one they blame for letting Lucy go off with them,' she says impatiently.

'Off with who?'

'If our folks knew their girls were laid out on the sand with their knees up just like Jessie Vukovich . . . Oh, that sounds terrible, but this is Fort Jude.' Another long, time-sucking sigh. 'Around here we drag our pasts around like Marley's ghost, because whatever you do, if even one person finds out, everybody knows it. You'd have to move to Alaska to escape it! In Fort Jude people forgive, God knows we all do it every single day, but nobody ever, ever forgets,' she says.

She says, 'And if you're a slut, that's what everybody thinks of you.'

'You're saying my mother was a slut?'

'Hardly.' Something ugly breaks the surface. 'She thought she was too good for us!'

The thing about period clocks is the pendulum. Every fucking tick.

Nervously, she zips and unzips the hoodie she threw on to go out tonight. Color keyed to the silk tank top, what was she thinking? Was she dressing for him? 'Oh this is embarrassing. Girls like us, no matter what we did back then or where we did it or who we did it with, the day we get married we're all virgins again.' She rocks with anger. 'Because it's expected! If nobody finds out, it just — un-happens. It has to. Am I making any sense?'

'Not really.'

'It doesn't matter. I'm sure up north things are a lot freer, but this is a small town locked up inside a big city and down here everybody minds everybody else's business — that is, everybody that matters.' She fixes him with her eyes. 'It's how we keep each other safe.'

He lies politely; anything to keep her going. 'I see.'

'We keep quiet.' She spreads her fingers in apology. 'It's what we do, and I'm sorry. If the truth came out, it would ruin more lives than just Lucy Carteret's. So I hope you understand, and I'm sorry.'

He doesn't. He wants to pick this woman up by her hoodie and batter her with questions but he has to wait until her head comes back from wherever it's wandered off to. It takes longer than it should.

'OK,' she says finally. 'So what I wanted to tell you was, it got way too late that night; there were at hundreds of us there, everybody that mattered and all their friends, all the team captains, cheerleaders, prom queens and the whole May Court except, of course, for Lucy because she was beautiful but she was never one of us, which is why . . .'

He leans forward to catch what comes next.

Instead she takes him on a detour. 'It's like Lucy was above us all even in first grade, birthday parties in the club ballroom and we had to dress up for old Lorna's little princess, unless . . .'

'Unless?'

'Unless she was her prisoner! Then Lucy's dad died up in Charleston and she came into some money. All those years trapped in the tower. She bought a convertible! Came down on the beach at the tag end of houseparties, amazing body and her hair was perfect.

It just was too much. We hated her. I'm sorry, that's the way it was, like, if it had happened to another girl, we might have—'

'What?'

'Warned her off!' Is she drunk or just used up? The girlish way Nenna rearranges her breasts inside the tight tank top makes clear that she'd have sex with him to keep from having to explain. 'I must look awful.'

'You look fine.'

'I don't, but thanks.' *Oh, lady, don't sigh!* 'Sometimes I wonder how it would have come down if we'd been friends. But she was not like us!'

'You said that.'

'God knows what her problem was.'

Carefully, he leads her back into the interview, asking little, giving nothing – no hint of an agenda, framing a question from what he knows. 'Shy?'

'Like, we were never close. I don't know if she was shy or just too good for us. She just didn't *do* like we do. She lived in her own little world, and maybe if she'd stayed there, she wouldn't have . . . And the saddest thing?' Her face is all messed up.

'Ma'am?'

She wails, 'Not Ma'am!'

In the silence, he counts heartbeats.

'Bobby Chaplin was in love with her. He begged her to come out in his car so maybe it was his fault, what happened. She came sailing down at the tail end of a long week fresh and shiny as the sun goddess, when the rest of us were wrecked. Did you know that when you're sleep-deprived, it's like being drunk?'

Just when he thinks she's getting to the point, Nenna lapses. He nudges. 'You were saying . . .'

'I was saying Lucy came down on the beach because Bobby begged, but she didn't come with him. Maybe she was a little bit in love with Bobby too, but I doubt it or she wouldn't have come so late. He gave up on her and got blind drunk plus whatever else Chape and them were taking. Listen, there's something you should know.' It takes her some time to formulate what she has to tell him and when she does, it's nothing he expected.

'You know, when you hang out with people all your life, you learn some necessary things. What to look out for. How to handle yourself. But Lucy was like Edie Sedgewick at her first party.'

'Who?'

'Crazy-wild. Too wild.' She leans in, desperate to explain. 'We sure as hell never would have . . . She shouldn't have . . . Well, she just shouldn't!'

This is harder than he thought. He's tried all his life to get inside that head but when he thinks of Lucy, even at eighteen, it's as going along with that brave chin up and her elbows clamped to her sides, resolutely on her own. In all the time he knew her, the only stupid thing she ever did was marrying Burt. 'Shouldn't what?'

'Oh.' She hesitates. 'A lot of things.'

'Like . . .'

'White bikini bottom and nothing under the white gauze shirt, no matter how gorgeous, that's one. Two, the way she drank and what she was smoking, and three, going off with those boys. You don't do that, not the way they were.'

'Which boys?'

'I guess you had to be there. It was the last night of life as we knew it — you know, dance, drink and get loaded, for tomorrow you die. Well, not really, but Sunday was graduation and the end of everything that mattered. We had a humongous bonfire, with a ton of hot dogs and hamburgers from Sharp's Market — our graduation present from Stan Sharp's dad, even though they lived on the south side. Nobody ate, but we were drinking, people brought six-packs and pints, airport minis and whatever pills our mothers were taking, stole pills, uppers, downers, believe me, we had everything out there, along with everybody you could hope for, even sluts and skanky glue sniffers from junior high that we never saw any more. The sand was hard enough to dance on, and the music, oh my God, the music.' She names a bunch of bands from the dark ages. 'Can you see what it was like?'

'Who did she go off with?'

'Crazy. It was that amazing, wonderful kind of crazy. Lucy Carteret waltzes into the mist of it, for the very first time. It's a wonder we even noticed, we were so blasted, I mean, what's one kid more or less in that mob? Except, she looked so hot! If you want to know the truth, it pissed us off. Boys forgot who we were and went lusting. It's not fair!'

'Ma'am?'

She doesn't bother to correct him. 'She was a perfect size four, except on top, where she was bigger.'

In spite of himself, Dan blushes.

'Now that I think about it, she probably stayed over at the Carleton Inn and left after her grandfather went to bed. He and Eden Rowse were shacked up in there, had been for years before the divorce. Probably that's why old Lorna was so mean. She hated Lucy. She hated everyone. She hated us.

Oh, Lucy. Oh, Mom. A good reporter, he prompts: 'Why?'

'She hated us for, I don't know, corrupting Lucy. I'm surprised she didn't show up with the cops and wreck the party. God knows what-all she had bottled up inside. No wonder she burned to death.'

'So.' Shaken, Dan sets his jaw. *Do this like a professional. Just do it.* 'You were at the beach.'

'I was? I was. We all were.'

'That night.'

Mrs McCall's eyes are shifting here, there. 'Oh, God. I'm thirsty, are you thirsty? A little brandy? Coffee? It's hard to know what to offer at this ungodly hour.'

'No thank you.'

'I need some water. Be right back.'

It takes forever. She returns like a car just out of a cheap body shop, with all the dings and scratches retouched, but not repaired. 'There.'

'The beach. You were telling me about the . . .'

She says apologetically, 'There isn't that much more to tell.'

He is careful to control his tone. 'What do you mean, there isn't that much more to tell?'

'Understand, by the time Lucy got there we were all pretty far gone. Then at the ass end of that night Lucy went off in the Jeep. We saw her go.'

Her voice drops. 'God help us, we were thinking, *Serves her right.*'

'Ma'am!'

She sighs. 'That's pretty much it.'

'Wait!'

'Remember, we were eighteen. So Lucy went off with them and that's the last we saw of her, she was valedictorian, but she didn't show up for the speech. Something went down, nobody will talk about it and we try not to ask. The School Board never did get names so everybody's safe – Sallie's dad let that cat out of the bag and he never guessed what a big relief it was for all of us. See, those were not boys from South Side High that Lucy went off with and it wasn't that gang from Bradenton, they were our boys that we wanted to grow up and marry, and some of us have.

'By the time the School Board met on it we were all off in college in Gainesville or Tallahassee or Atlanta so we couldn't forget it, but we didn't have to testify.'

'And?'

'That's it.' She spreads her hands, and they are empty.

'That's all you have to tell me? That's your big secret?'

'Yes. Lucy went off with them and we let her go!' She's trying hard to come up with something more for him, but this is all she can manage. 'We weren't there and God knows the boys won't tell.' She takes his hands. She is desperate to explain. 'We protect each other, OK?'

'No.' He finds it necessary to drive it in. 'You wouldn't even tell me who was in the Jeep,' he adds, although he already knows.

A bad sound comes out of her. It is the sound of a woman losing it, so when Nenna answers it's a partial answer. 'Brad was driving.' Tears are coming down her face, so swift and dense that they roll into her mouth and a bubble seals it as her mouth stretches wide in soundless grief. It shimmers until finally it pops. Words come out, but nothing he can use. 'We saw what was happening and we let her go!'

35

Steffy

They've been riding around in Mr Bellinger's ragtop Buick, like, forever. Wild, being out with Carter at this strange, still hour when real people are locked inside their houses, but while they were running free at the tippy end of Pierce Point the dark bled out of the night; too late turned into too early and Steffy is fucking exhausted.

Carter looks tired too, hunched over the wheel with his cheeks caved in, but Steffy isn't about to end this, even though she's beyond ready to go home.

She can't.

She loves him so much!

Plus, she can't go back to her house just yet. It's way too early to get caught sneaking in, and her mom hasn't been sleeping much since the big fight. Cough in the night and the woman comes in to check on you; get up to pee and she springs out. Steffy doesn't dare show until it's time for breakfast somewhere, or her mom will find out that instead of staying over at Jen's house as advertised, she's been out all night, running around with Carter Bellinger.

When he yanked her aside after the Saturday night movie she thought, *OK then. This is it.* He grabbed her elbow in the parking lot, clamped her hand under his arm and growled into her hair, 'Want to do something really trippy?'

Steffy's heart jumped. In a shitty week, maybe things weren't so shitty after all. She had to act like she could care less – because this was Carter, that she was in love with, asking her, and it was so very, very important to her, so she shrugged him off and mumbled, 'Sure.'

Perfidious Jen smiled that smile and pretend-zipped her mouth as though she and Carter never did Whatever: *Nobody will ever know.*

Pathetic, her being this excited. God only knows what she was expecting when they headed for Bayfront Drive. It's been this and that with Carter for so long that Steffy needs it to get serious, even though she's scared. It's way past time.

When was that, around midnight? Forever ago. She was excited to be in the convertible, which Carter's dad loans him even though his license got suspended last month. She wished he'd put the top down so all Central Avenue could see the two of them going along together in that cool car: her and Carter Bellinger, Carter and her. Probably he wanted privacy, given what they were just about to do.

When they left the Cineplex she thought tonight was the night, they were finally going to do the scary, private thing that would bond them forever, body and body, heart and heart. Naturally Carter would want to keep the top up, so nothing could interrupt and no fool cruising on Bayfront Drive that late would accidentally see in. When they finally Did It, she thought, it would be a relief. Then Carter would be hers and Jen and every Tiffany and Britney in Fort Jude could go the fuck to hell.

Now she's not so sure.

They didn't park on the bay they just drove on, past the usual place where she and Carter almost got started once. He kept going even though the makeout spot was deserted and the moon was making one of those paths of light on the water that your heart follows to the stars. They didn't park, at least not then. Carter just kept going along the waterfront to the two big old cement sphinxes guarding the bridge to Coral Shores. It was so late that all the houses on Coral Boulevard were dark; they were all safe in bed while she and Carter . . . She doesn't know.

They sneaked into the Tills' house on Coral Circle, they were there for hours and she still doesn't know!

Carter had her breaking into somebody's house in the dead of night and messing with their belongings, and the weird thing? She never gave it a thought.

She would have followed him anywhere.

Never mind that everyone knew the Tills were in Europe and the house was alarmed, never mind that or that Shoresafe Security could put them in jail. Carter walked her up to the side door just like they'd been invited. He found the key under the cement hoptoad and let her in! How did he know what numbers to tap into the alarm? The Tills have a deal where when you walk into a room the whole ceiling lights up – awesome, right? It was like walking into a private club with the floors waxed and everything set up and waiting, just for them.

'This is the place.'

'What about the Tills?'

'Fuck 'em.'

The minute the lights went up on the humongous playroom, Steffy freaked. 'They'll see us!'

Laughing, Carter pointed. 'No they won't.'

She saw stainless steel Rolos locked over the windows like armor on a tank. If the Tills ever had kids it was a long, long time ago, but somebody spent a lot of money on this paneled rec room with fake stuffed grouper and swordfish on plaques, a pool table and a pinball machine complete with flashing lights and a bucket full of quarters so anybody could play. They had an old-timey soda fountain left over from Early America – Mr Till's bar. Champagne glasses and Gators mugs stood on glass shelves under a barroom mirror with an alligator at the top in frosted glass.

'There's beer in the fridge.'

'How do you know?'

His voice got raw. 'He has parties here.'

'What . . .'

'You don't want to know.'

There were squashy sofas and fat chairs at the far end of the room so Steffy thought probably this was the place where she and Carter were finally going to get down to it; he'd picked here because it was private, she just hoped to God they didn't get caught. It was exciting and scary and weird.

Instead they played pool for, like, a hundred hours. She didn't think it was because she kept winning, but the longer they played the madder Carter got and the more she won, the more he wouldn't let her quit.

Her boy was pissed at something; he started out pissed tonight. He was pissed before they broke into the house. Then he was pissed because all he found in the minibar was Diet Coke, like Mr Till hid all the liquor because Carter was coming, or Mrs Till had put Mr Till into rehab and poured his booze down the sink. In fact, Carter was pissed about a lot of things, which was odd since Mr Till nicely left the key for him, and Carter tapped in the alarm code like it wasn't the first time.

Maybe if she'd let him win the trouble wouldn't have started, but Steffy wouldn't lose. The more games she won, the madder Carter got. What was his problem? Losing at something as stupid as pool wasn't that big of a deal but he got a little crazy, like he'd dropped something nasty into his Diet Coke. Then it got worse. When Steffy broke down and pretend-lost so they could get the hell out of there, he jerked her around so sharply that he hurt her arm.

'Don't pull that shit on me,' he yelled. 'Do this fair and square and I promise, we're done in one game.' Of course they weren't. The more they played, the more bent Carter became, turning the game into pool hell. He made them play until Steffy felt tears running, and Carter was furious and out of control. Thank God the fury ended it, but not like you'd think. Steffy was winning for, like, the hundredth time and Carter freaked. He ripped the crap out of the pink felt top of Mr Till's pool table trying to kill her last ball.

'Oh, shit,' Steffy said. 'Let's go!'

'We can't have *that*!' Carter shouted, loud enough to wake up the neighbors even though the Rolos were down. He kept stabbing the felt with his pool cue as if he hadn't already done enough, gouging like he could make the table bleed, yowling, 'We can't have that!'

It was awful. He was out of control and nothing Steffy said or did could move him away from the table or get him outside, where it was safe.

By the end she was praying to him, 'Please. We have to go!'

He showed big square robot teeth in a yellow robot grin. 'Not yet.'

With security off, Carter got into the Tills' storage no problem by punching a panel to open a secret door. He dragged in a pile of old newspapers and crumpled them on the pool table, grinning. 'Smart, right?'

He was trying to make it look like it was *not* a kid with a pool cue who wrecked Mr Till's special watermelon felt, it was death by accidental fire. Steffy was not about to help him. She stood back while he kicked the slats out of a chair; there was no stopping Carter now. She couldn't stop him from sticking them underneath the newspaper either, when any asshole knew you piled the kindling on top. At the end she ran outside because she couldn't bear to see him light the match.

It's OK, she told herself, shivering in the dark, and on quiet Coral Shores she could almost believe it. She had to! *It's only a **little** fire.*

By the time Carter came back to the car, she was telling herself that he hadn't just done that. This was her boyfriend, after all. He might get mad and do stupid things but nobody starts a fire in an empty house. In fact she was sure of it, because he got in the car grinning like nothing had happened, and they both started to laugh. A song they liked came on the radio and Carter was singing which made Steffy feel better, so she sang too.

They ended up on Bayfront Drive after all. He put the top down so if kids saw them together, they'd be impressed. At the curve nearest the bridge, they parked. It was sweet, very sweet, sitting under the palm trees with Carter's lips going all those nice places. It was sweet and sexy and sad, clinging in the dark. Steffy thought they were just making out, but she knows now that while Carter was doing all those nice things to her, his mind was not on it. It was somewhere else.

God she was scared when the sirens started to howl.

Carter quit doing what he was doing and faced forward.

They watched the sky light up over Coral Shores.

They quit talking, too. It was too weird out; Steffy was too scared. Even Carter was scared; she felt him jittering, pressed close with one leg over the stick shift and Steffy pulled so tight that the ridge on the bucket seat hurt her ass.

Heavy trucks rumbled past. There were so many that the street shook.

When it was all done they just sat. Finally when the glow died and the sky was empty over Palm Shores, a long time after the last city truck rolled past on its way back to town, he grunted and started the car.

Then he said, 'You know I love you.'

'I'm so glad.'

The next thing Steffy knew the two of them were way the hell out here on Pierce Point, walking around on crushed shells and dead mangrove leaves in the sand spit at the end, picking up driftwood and bits of shell that might turn out to be pretty or useful which was hard to tell, because it was too dark. Sheltered by the mangroves they wandered, talking only about stuff they found in the sand, hanging out in that nice, nowhere place as if nothing strange had come down, wandering until it got light. When the first trawler rounded the point on its way to the Gulf, Carter bundled her back into the car.

They've been riding around ever since.

This is sad, Steffy thinks, looking at the boy she's loved for so long. Now she's not so sure. Wait. Didn't she just get everything she ever wanted? Carter Bellinger all to herself, and for a whole, entire night? Here they were in his car. With the top pulled up over them like covers, they could be lying close in bed, and didn't he just tell her again that he's in love with her, which she's been waiting to hear since fifth grade?

She and Carter are close now, closer than she's ever been to anyone. They just went through *so much*. She ought to feel happy, but she doesn't. She wants to feel excited and loving and totally bonded, like they are the same person under the skin, but she can't.

She just feels bad. An entire night together and she doesn't have enough from him, or he doesn't have enough from her.

Steffy's not sure what this means, only that where she ought to be feeling all the right things, all she has is a terrible, terrible sense of loss.

'Oh,' she murmurs accidentally. *This is just so sad.*

God forgive her, Carter takes it wrong.

'Oh Steffy,' he barks, so abruptly that it startles her. 'Let's drive to Valdosta and get married!'

This makes her feel so guilty that she can't stand to look at him.

She does not say the obvious. She doesn't even say, why should we, we haven't even had sex? What she does say, and it takes her a while to think of it, is, 'I can't, Carter. I'm babysitting Grammy Henderson today. I have to go home.'

36

Nenna

I woke up feeling awful. If I slept at all. I mean, by the time I fell down on the bed it was light outside.

How can you grow up along with all your friends, smart women who talk about everything all the time and still end up knowing the tune, but not all the words to your life? I tried to tell Dan how it happened, I mean, I opened up my *soul* but my nice new friend ran out of the house at dawn like his hair was on fire and it breaks my heart.

On top of Davis, it was just too much. At least that's done. Kicking him out was like lopping off a foot to stop necrotizing fasciitis or gangrene; you have to amputate to save your life. You're not dead but you *hurt* so much that you roll around on the bed, too messed up to sleep.

Oh, I know where he is. Davis, I mean. He's out at the Pierce Point Marriott where every other man in God's creation is having more sex than Davis ever had with Gale. Instead of screwing, he's on the phone with that quasi-intellectual skank, do you know what he said to me? He said, 'She may not have her doctorate but she's the most intelligent woman I know,' but he means she will go down on him in a broom closet if she has to, anything to get what she wants and what she wants is my husband.

Well she can have him, credit card debt and all, thank God Chape Bellinger's office made me separate our finances before this thing blew up in my face. God, I'm depressed. It's lonely in here without Davis, the rat, and Steffy's off at my friend Cathy's house for a sleepover with Jen, I'm one woman alone in here with no one to talk to, but at least Steffy has a best friend.

No Davis coughing or thumping around downstairs; it's so quiet that I can't sleep, I'm too tired to do anything, but it was almost time to start getting ready for church, so I shuffled downstairs and made coffee – instant, since it's just me. I was half minded to call Cathy and ask her to wake my daughter, say I need her to . . . *something*. Too early. Instant coffee and.

And nothing.

Morning paper, for all the good that does me, nothing I really need to know, like what in God's name made Davis bump fronts with his own first cousin. It's practically incest. Or what's going to happen to me.

'Mom. Mom?'

'Steffy!' *Rescue! Thank heaven you've come.*

But she was running in like I just saved her from sudden death and before I could say, 'Why are you home so early,' or, 'Did Cathy drive you,' or, 'Where's your stuff,' she ran smack into me with this ginormous hug. 'I'm home!'

'Sweetie, you're early!'

Her smile was so wide that I should have started with the questions, but she headed me off with such a nice surprise. 'It's Sunday, right?'

'I guess so.'

'Duh, Mom. Church.'

'Church!'

'No way are you going to church alone.'

And my heart went out to her; there are things about your nearest and dearest that you know, and things you don't want to know, and what's important to me right now is making it through. That's the only thing any of us really needs – somebody to help us make it through; I was so excited! 'Aren't you sweet! I'll make blueberry muffins.'

'If you want, I'll wear the pink dress.'

'You hate that dress.'

She looked at me, all, *Oh, Mom.* 'It's church.'

'I thought you hated church!'

'You're not going in there all alone.' She gave me the sweetest smile. 'Since Dad . . .'

'Say no more.' *You understand!* And didn't I hug her then, and didn't I think we might make it without him after all. 'Don't you worry about Dad. And don't you worry about me. We'll both be fine.'

Now Steffy's sitting at the kitchen table with her head bent in the morning sunshine, as if we're already in church. She has the funnies open in front of her but she isn't reading, she's just sitting like a little sponge, soaking up the room, and me? The kitchen smells so good with my muffins baking, the sunlight looks so pretty on my daughter's hair that I don't feel half as bad as I thought. It'll be nice living here, just the two of us. We can be ourselves. Now that I know prickly, resentful Steffy's on my side, I can handle this. I can do anything, now that I know.

I turn the oven up a notch so the muffins will be ready sooner and I can slather them with butter and honey and serve them to my wonderful, loyal only daughter and best girlfriend before the mood evaporates and we have to go out and face the rest of my life.

37

Walker Pike

'What are you doing here?'

Blinking, Walker jerks to attention so smartly that his head bumps the glass. Is he drooling? God. A minute ago it was dark and he was asleep, and now he's in his Beemer on the main drag of Fort Jude in broad daylight, across from the Flordana Hotel. Even though he's parked in the shade, the heat's piling up in the vintage car. Downtown Fort Jude on a Sunday is deader than a beached manatee, but his brother Wade is at the window on the passenger's side, making a comic fish-in-a-fish-tank mouth on the glass. Walker rolls it down so they can talk. 'What do you want?'

'I said, what are you doing here?'

'Oh. This.' Walker comes back to himself in stages. 'Waiting for a guy.'

'On Central Avenue?' This gives Wade such comprehension problems that he is blinking too.

'Pretty much.'

'On Sunday morning?'

'Is that a problem for you?'

'Dude, look at you!' Wade is all dressed up today: white shirt with white-on-white striped tie, white handkerchief tucked into the breast pocket of his light-weight French blue suit. 'Are you sleeping in your car?'

'No.' Countering his kid brother's suspicion with suspicion, Walker squints. 'What are you? Going to a funeral?'

'It's Sunday,' Wade tells him. 'I'm taking Jessie to church.'

'Jessie.' In high school Walker and Jessie had a history, but he's not the only one of her men, and that's not all he was to her. There's something bigger between them. He trusts her. She trusts him. They'll always be friends. Nice woman. He's glad she's happy now. 'Nice.'

'In case you haven't noticed, I think we're an item.'

'So, cool!'

'And in case you haven't noticed, you're parked in front of her hotel.'

'I am?' Walker hesitates just long enough to make it look as though this is a surprise. 'I am.' Then, 'Church,' he says thoughtfully.

Grinning, Wade touches the silver cross locked to the buttonhole in his lapel. 'I'm getting elected head of the vestry today.'

He doesn't envy Wade, but in a way he envies Wade. 'Pop would be proud.'

For a second there, his staid younger brother shows a gleam of the old Wade sparkle. 'Pop would be astounded.'

Where he hasn't smiled in days, Walker breaks wide open in a grin. Put it to the lazy morning, the sunshine, the fact that soft as he is, tubby and out of shape, his baby brother cleans up real nice. And unlike his older brother, Wade Pike is happy now. 'OK then, enjoy.' Walker starts the motor.

'I thought you were waiting for a guy.'

'I am. But he said if he didn't show up by ten, I should look for him in front of the Fort Jude Club.'

Wade says, 'We don't open until noon.'

'We?'

His brother grins that insider's grin. 'I'm the next Commodore.'

'Well, look at you.' Walker takes off the hand brake and lets the car roll an inch or two, to let Wade know that talking or not, he has to go. 'Better step back, you don't want to crud up your suit.'

'Noon sharp. For the champagne brunch.' Even though the car's moving, Wade sticks his head in the window to add, 'When we all get out of church.'

'Bye, Wade.' Walker pulls away gradually, so his brother has time to jump aside. When he comes around the block again he sees Wade handing Jessie into that shiny Explorer he likes so much, *What is it with these people and big cars.* Jessie has the pocketbook with matching shoes today, Manolos, he thinks, take *that*, motherfuckers. He sees that for Morning Prayer at the Fort Jude Episcopal Cathedral, his childhood friend from Pierce Point is elegant and subdued in silk. He also sees that Jessie's body is sexy as ever and every man in that church will know it, no matter how carefully she pins up the front of her staid little dove grey wraparound dress, but nothing will come of it. They are, after all, in church.

He is struck by the way ritual keeps these people in place. Dates marked on every monthly calendar. Everything by the book.

Watching the Explorer go, Walker marvels at how sweet this is.

He loves this town in spite of itself because in Fort Jude at least, for some people, Sunday mornings are boring and predictable because the core society works hard to keep everything in place. They set store by ritual. The inevitability of certain things. People here rely on the power of shared history, ceremony and the continuity of the seasons to reinforce and support them, beginning with Buccaneers and Gators games in the fall and the Chamber of Commerce Harvest Festival on through the Christmas debutante ball and January Superbowl parties, relying on the predictability of meetings and fundraisers, cocktail parties and dances to keep them in place until baseball season starts for the Devil Rays and members gather for the big Easter egg roll at the Fort Jude Club, the first big event of the spring. In a subtropical city with no autumn, no dreary winters to mark the seasons, Wade's friends use these events to signify the time of year as surely as church bells remind them that it's Sunday again.

The Pikes' position in this tight society was always marginal, predetermined by birth and signified by their location, clinging like sandspurs to the sandy tip of Pierce Point. His parents were peripheral personnel that the inner circle of Fort Jude might recognize on sight, but wouldn't know, because in this town there are people you know, and people you don't need to know. Walker saw it in the way they looked at him when he got off that school bus at Northshore, and if Wade wants to change that? Fine.

When Wade Pike goes out now, they all know him. He's one of the invited. The society tells him who he is, even as each occasion tells him what to do. The Fort Jude his brother fits into so smoothly is a complex living organism, a self-contained, self-sufficient unit, but it's nothing Walker wanted, then or now.

It took Wade years to slip into the stream where he flows along with the others, serene and comfortable, perfectly safe. No matter what hopes or doubts or what burden of dread or private grief keeps pace with them, on Sunday mornings these people get up and dress nicely and go to church, where they can sit or kneel under colored light filtering in through stained glass windows, thinking whatever they're usually too busy to think.

It makes life so simple, Walker reflects – lovely, in fact. *Too bad I'm not that person.*

He knows what he is.

Sometimes Walker wonders if the dead stay around, watching even though you don't know it. He used to wake up screaming, with the old woman roaring around inside his head. *Nightmare*, he told himself. *Vicious, revolting. Done*, but now that Lucy's dead, he has to wonder if these things are ever really done.

He wonders if Lucy's spirit is out there, if it ever comes near enough to know how he feels, whether she knows all the things he wishes he'd said when he left her run on a loop, filling his head. Whether she understands now why he had to keep his secret, or how hard it was to keep from running back to hug her, so she'd know.

How do you explain to the woman you love that fate or physics or bad chemistry or a great psychic accident transformed you into a toxic avenger, a ticking bomb?

When he fell in love with Lucy Carteret it was forever, but look at the sorrow that brought down. When he left this town he thought it was forever, but even when you are unarmed but dangerous, you never know which things are forever or how much you can lose in a flash. Far as it was from Florida, Cambridge wasn't far enough; he ran into Chaplin in Harvard Square in his troubled third year at MIT.

By then Walker was living two lives, ambitious and conflicted and in love.

—Bob Chaplin, imagine. Small world.

—Why, Walker, what are you doing in Harvard Square?

Chaplin was friendly; Chaplin had no idea what Walker Pike was hiding, his sweet life with Lucy in that wonderful, tiny room. Swift and intuitive – *interested*, Chaplin never guessed. They should have talked but Walker was with Lucy, which was intensely private, and they were pledged to keep it that way. He was busy reinventing himself, bent on protecting her, so he muttered politely and backed away from Chaplin and his old life in Fort Jude as if from the far side of a chasm he'd crossed safely.

Protective and cautious Walker, months before it all blew up.

He had no idea what was coming; who would? Nobody in his right mind could divine or even imagine such a thing. Then his life went up in flames and, sobbing, he left Lucy behind – no farewell, no warning, no explanation. A thing like that. How could he explain? He loved her so he left her in the middle of the night.

Love, he thinks, or prays, now that there's a chance that Lucy's spirit can hear him, *I hope you can forgive me now that you know,* but nothing happens, really, except raindrops on his windshield when the hotel sprinkler starts up.

A man like Walker has resources. A man like Walker knows how to disappear in the same big city without running away. The year he got his doctorate in computer science from UMass, Boston, not even Wade came to see them put on the hood and shake his hand. Wade didn't know. With his life with Lucy destroyed, Walker did what he had to, losing himself in the stream of thousands driving to high tech jobs in the ring of glossy megaliths lining Route 128. Blending in. He reinvented himself as safe, boring, reliable, and up to a point, it worked.

Too bad things went wrong whenever he tried to start over with someone new.

Which he did once too often, because he was alone and grieving and afraid. He left Lucy to save her but he could not stop looking for her in other women's beds. When they disappointed him: not-Lucy, the anger grew. The last thing he can allow back into his life is anger, so that ended that.

Picture Walker Pike: backing out of life.

He can't get close to anyone. Not the way he is. For Walker, human contact beyond the simplest transaction is dangerous.

What he does for a living he can do anywhere, so at forty he doubled back on Pierce Point. Kicking off his shoes to walk in the sand where he dug as a kid, Walker considered. It was home. Lucy would never go back to Fort Jude; at the time it felt right. The sand here is, after all, what he came out of. He fit. Using profits from one of his software patents, he bought Pop's garage back from the bank. He tore down the building and commanded a house where he might not be happy, but he could be content. Contractors built to his design. Brass fittings. Teak floors, everything perfect.

When things are good in his heart, which they aren't right now, he can sit on his deck and watch sailboats and trawlers and fishermen go past on their way out into the Gulf. He loves the light on the water and the restless, panoramic skies; he loves feeling the people he grew up with living with their children in the growing city at his back, souls joined and familiar as the ganglia in his right hand.

Walker loves this place. He loves it even though unlike Wade he hates the society. They've always been different people. Wade's a sweet, ordinary, even-tempered guy, while he . . .

Oh God, Walker thinks because at bottom what he is, is so terribly wrong. *This is so awful.* He never should have come home to this town!

Just then a shadow moves in the hotel courtyard. He snaps to attention. It's the kid.

38

Bobby

Over at the Chaplin house in Pine Vista, Bobby's on the phone with Nenna McCall, a fact that both delights and frightens him, the latter because of what prompted this call. Talking in the shotgun hallway, he can hear his sister rushing around overhead. Al is off somewhere. It doesn't matter that they never know where.

Instead of getting to the point Nenna says, 'I can't talk long, just while Steffy's in the shower.'

'You called to tell me.' He waits for her to fill in the blank.

'I did. Maybe I should stop by after church.' Her voice lifts in surprise. 'Do you believe we're going to church?'

'In this town most people do,' Bobby says sadly. He used to have a place in this tight little community of the like-minded, good people all. He left for Harvard belonging, but in the years since then he's gone too far in this life of false steps and unexpected complications to be comfortable with them.

'They're inducting the new canon today with coffee and mimosas afterward,' Nenna says. She called with an agenda, but she's eminently distractable. 'And sticky buns in honor of Wade. If you happen to drop by.'

Hope surfaces. He doesn't always have to be this way. 'I'll try.'

'Buffet at the club afterward?'

Then reason kicks in. 'I wish. I promised to take Margaret to Shell Art for supplies.' He also promised his sister brunch at the Pelican afterward, although since the misery and confusion of that stupid, botched high school party, he's never been comfortable at the beach. The memory, he can handle. It took him years to process, but he can. It's the flashbacks that bother him. He never knows when they will hit. 'So probably you should tell me now.'

She can't seem to begin. 'Just so you know.'

'Please. I have to go.' Margaret will be coming downstairs dressed for the Pelican in another minute, nervously gnawing the edge of her purse. His sister feels safe there because the family went on special occasions when they were small. As Margaret clatters out of the upstairs bathroom he hurries Nenna along. 'About the Carteret kid . . .'

'Believe me, he's not a kid.'

'Neither are we,' he says mildly when he wants to bark at her.

Nenna sighs. 'Not any more.'

'Could you just say what you called to say?'

'OK. Here's the thing. I . . .' Another false start.

'What!'

'Look,' she says finally, 'it was an accident. I had him here for no reason, and I couldn't just send him home, so I . . .'

From upstairs comes the sound of Margaret psyching herself up for the excursion, nervously trotting back and forth from mirror to mirror while his anxieties keep pace with her. He snaps, 'You what?'

'I didn't mean to, but I told him what happened that night.' Nenna sighs.

'That night!'

'You know, when Lucy was . . .' She breaks off. 'Was whatever she was that night.'

The sound Bobby makes comes from somewhere deeper than a groan. 'I didn't know you knew.'

'When whatever happened – happened.' Waiting for him to supply the details, she lets it hang. 'I tried to tell him but I don't really know.'

Then, frustrated by the long silence, Nenna cries, 'I don't know anything! I'm sorry, Bobby, but she was his mother. I'm just so sorry she's dead, and besides, I got him all the way out to my house last night for no real reason, poor guy, I felt so *guilty*. I couldn't send him off empty-handed. I . . . I had to give him *something*.'

'I see.'

'Maybe I was just tired.'

During the pause that follows, he hears Margaret circling like a 747 in a holding pattern. 'Nenna . . .'

'Look, I know it was a mistake but I ended up saying a lot of things that we don't talk about to somebody who doesn't know us, and that's really bad. About that Saturday night, and Lucy coming down on the beach so late, after you'd given up on her and gotten . . .'

'Don't.'

'. . . so drunk. I just thought you should know. In case he comes your way? To ask? The thing is, he . . .' In a heartbeat, her tone veers from dark to festive. 'Oh, Steffy, look at you! Bobby, Steffy's here, I have to go.'

'Thanks for the heads up.'

'Just so you know.'

'Just so I know.'

Nenna covers the mouthpiece while she and the girl confer. Then she says in that bright, artificial, Fort Jude way, 'Right then. Take care, Bobby. Lovely to talk.'

'Wait. I need to know what you told him.' What he really needs to know is how much Nenna knows.

But his friend is caught up in her daughter's rhythms now. Like a girl she says, 'Later, OK?' Giggling, she delivers a punchline dug up from the deep past when they were so young that it was still funny, 'See you in church.'

39

Dan

Confused by the scene he played with Mrs McCall after the fire, too wired to sleep, Dan lurched into the lobby of the Flordana. He ran his credit card in the crap business center and starred their houses on the grainy printout of the Internet map.

Done. Sleep.

When he emerges, the town is preternaturally quiet. Jazzed on caffeine and carbs from the machines, with no Fort Judeans around badgering him with guilty secrets, he comes out into the sunlight feeling, well, what passes for happy in this weird time.

He has a plan. This one looks rock-solid: grill the peripheral witnesses, one, two, three, building questions on answers, fact-checking as he goes. Nail them at home before he grills the prime suspect, who, although the northerner hunting his father can't know it, is still snoring on stinking satin sheets in a house suffering a steep descent from shiny high tech into deep slobbery.

It's a curse, having an orderly mind, but how is he supposed to know? OK, he'll start with Carter Bellinger's dad, in hopes. It was, after all, his Jeep. But there's more. There is always more. He knows from what the McCall woman said that his mother suffered. He still doesn't know exactly how, or why. First he will identify the bastard and confront him. Then he will . . . OK. This is the thing. Does he not look more like Bellinger in that Polaroid than Kalen, with his leering, gorilla grin? Squint and he can almost see himself in Bellinger's face. Nose to nose with George Chapin Bellinger, LLD, he'll can him: face, body mass, stance. Soul, which is what rules Chaplin out. If there's anything in the configuration; if, counter to expectations, Bellinger's the guy, he can forget the other two – forget Kalen! – and put his heart to rest.

Otherwise, it's on to Coleman and Von Harten, solid Fort Jude business types with houses on the same block in Coral Shores, because he needs to triangulate. If it really is Kalen, then he'll damn well go in there armed with facts. Sick of hints, slippery truths and polite evasions and sick to death of Fort Jude, Florida, Dan's given up on that heartwarming 'Father!' 'Son!' moment. He won't even hit the guy. He just needs to know, so he can walk away. He thinks: *Closure.* Damn that orderly mind.

Leaving the Flordana, he's too preoccupied to notice the car keeping pace as he heads down Central Avenue and around the corner to the hotel garage. He's trying out lines.

'You don't know me, but . . .'

'I think we have something in common.'

'You remember Lucy, right? Lucy Carteret?'

'Um. Hello.'

Lame, but better than, 'Are you him?'

Fuck, Bellinger's house is sealed up tighter than an entomologist's catching jar. It's a vintage Spanish stucco with a contemporary add-on doubling its size. They keep the king-sized yard beautifully groomed, like women of a certain age. The ancient Royal palms in front look like fat cigars with Sideshow Bob fright wigs bobbing at the tops. The long porch overlooks the water between here and Coral Shores.

Trying on speeches, Dan rings. *Well, hi.* Nobody comes. He bangs with his fists. He shouts. Nothing.

He circles the house on thick, springy Bermuda grass, dodging hibiscus and gardenias and crunching through Mrs Bellinger's bougainvillea hedge to get a closer look. Boat trailer's here, convertible with FSU decal and wife's coupe gleam in the driveway, no Escalade. The Bellingers are gone.

All right then. Coleman's. Nobody answers at Coleman's house, even when he quits knocking and yells. They were just here, he can smell coffee. Now they're not. The windows stand open behind their ironwork grills. The Von Harten house around the corner is deserted too. His orderly plan disassembles, with parts rolling away in all directions.

Dan tries a dozen other houses, thinking the neighbors will know when his marks will be back, but the Sunday morning streets in Coral Shores are like the decks of a ghost ship. Where is everybody? Why aren't they firing up the BBQ or sitting over late morning coffee with the Sunday *Star*? Only the sound of a baby crying tells him that he's not in some crap movie where the hero wakes up to discover that everybody else on the planet has been wiped out by a neutron bomb.

He calls, 'Anybody home?'

He gets back the sound of nothing.

'Where is everybody?' Dazzled by sunlight bouncing off the white sand that borders the road, the white cement underfoot and bleached pastel houses with flat, white roofs, he whirls under a bleached sky. All his opening lines evaporate, replaced by a crap line from the end-of-the-world movie playing inside his head. 'Where is everybody anyway?'

Frustration drives him back to his car and on, cross-hatching the deserted city. In the absence of a plan, he circles new and old neighborhoods, searching because for once contingencies elude him, thinking, thinking, until this rises up in front of him like Munch's screamer and stops him dead:

It's in the blood.

He is at the Archambault house.

Why here? Dan wonders. *Why today?* He is also thinking, *Why me?* but he knows. Shivering, he enters the hundred-degree temperature and makes his way up the stairs and into her bedroom, thinking, *What does she want from me, human sacrifice?*

He shouts, 'What do you want from me!'

Dan Carteret, apparently related by blood to the woman who died in this room, folds up on the floor like a contemplative, waiting for the bitch to answer.

It's time to come to terms with who he is.

Or what he is.

Whether it's really in the blood. The foot, the chair. Twenty-some years later, and at the visual memory of that newspaper, he still shudders. Everything changed the day he opened Lucy's jewel box. In a flash she snatched it away: that's *that*. As though she could throw away the past and protect him. As if he could forget what he saw. The photo burned into the soft tissue behind his eyes. It brought him here.

Scorched, he gasps.

Behind the curtain of the known, something stirs, signaling the presence of the unknown fury, unless it's a terrible power.

Which? This is the mystery that keeps Dan Carteret fixed in lotus position in the house he vowed never to come back to. Sitting in Mrs Archambault's abandoned bedroom that first day in Fort Jude, he comprehended her. Old Lorna occupied him in a way he can't specify. Rage flickered in his belly and he cried out, unless she did.

Who's there?

Was the old woman really inhabiting him, squalling and raging inside his head? Did she really scream at him yesterday, when he fled the house? God knows he felt the heat – whether fever dream or hallucination, he can't say. He's been running ahead of it ever since. He and the fury that flamed out in this room hang from the same tree. Like armed thugs in a home invasion, Lorna broke into his head and he thinks, asks, wants to know and is afraid to know: *Is it something I did?*

Fixed in lotus position in the spot where the Barcalounger stood, Dan closes his eyes and summons her. He expects some intimation – insight, shared memory, altered consciousness, *something* – but nothing happens and nothing comes. Flies buzz. Sweat runs down. Whatever vibe he got in this overheated room is gone. Instead his mind scrambles like a cockroach circling the drain in a summer flood. What did he think: she would come down on a fluffy cloud and explain everything? Resolutely, he occupies the splintered floor like a player in Sartre's *No Exit*, unless it's the schlub in that movie *Groundhog Day*. Shit, he thinks because he could sit here forever and still not know. Just, shit. *What do you mean, it's in the blood?*

In the end he begs, but he is nothing more than Dan Carteret, alone in an empty room. Extreme, sitting on the splintered floor in the heat, but he has been driven to extremes. *One thing. Just tell me one thing. Did someone strike a match or is it in the blood.* Stretched to the limit by waiting, he explodes.

'Damn you, answer me!'

Outside a car door slams and whatever he thought was coming . . . evaporates. A girl shouts, 'I *said*, I'll *get* a ride home from *here*.'

He hears the tiresome, reasonable sound of a mother intent on making her point, '. . . budda-budda-mumble, you . . .'

'I *told* you, Carter's driving me!'

The woman goes on with her 'but, but, budda-budda' in that sweet, sweet voice. It's distracting, but at this point Dan could use a little distraction. He came into this house alone. He got down in all humility and he laid himself wide open but nothing came in. Face it. Nothing will.

'Three on the dot, I promise. If I have to, I'll call a cab!'

The girl's voice rises in a stagy sing-song. 'Bye-eeee . . .'

Pathetically grateful, he unlocks his joints and scrambles to his feet.

Steffy McCall to the rescue. She comes in the back, calling, 'Carter? Carter honey. Dude!'

Shit, is that kid Carter in the house? Did he hear me screaming like a psycho? Dan goes into the hall, half expecting Carter to come thudding down the attic stairs all onka-bonka, but there's nothing moving overhead and nobody around but the girl calling from the front hall, 'Carter, is that you?'

Dan hangs over the banister. 'It's only me.'

Sighing, she starts upstairs. Her hair is combed out today; she's wearing pink lip gloss and a pink headband that matches her dress. She doesn't exactly hide her disappointment. 'Oh, OK.'

'You're all dressed up.'

'Church. Then the club, like every other stupid Sunday. Is Carter here?'

'I told you, no.' She looks like a doll set up in real Steffy's place. He eyes the matching bag and shoes. 'Patent leather.'

She scowls. 'Is that a problem for you?'

'Looks nice.'

'You're sure you haven't seen him.'

'No, and I've been here since . . .' He looks at his watch. 'Wow. Since one.'

'He would of bombed in here straight from church, he felt so awful. Like, because of the fight? So you didn't see him? Carter? Carterrrr!'

'I told you, nobody's here but me. What fight?'

'Are you sure you didn't see him?' Dan shakes his head but she goes on calling. She cranes, trying to see past him. 'Carter? Carter, it's me. He could be hiding. Maybe he sneaked in.'

'Nobody gets past me.'

She tilts her head, studying Dan like an entomologist coming to conclusions about a bug. 'I don't know, you look kind of . . . Are you sure?'

Dan knows he lost time sitting there in the ruined bedroom, but he would never lose control. 'No,' he says firmly. 'No way.'

'He could be hiding.'

Now he's getting pissed. He says meanly, 'Because he set that fire last night.'

Astonished, she swivels: *Is it that obvious?*

Dan shrugs: *It is.*

And they're friends again. 'OK,' she says. 'His dad found out it was Carter and he went ballistic at church. He went off on Carter just as Mom and me were coming out, like, right in front of everybody who's anybody in Fort Jude? He said a whole bunch of shitty, shitty things to Carter and Carter punched him in the chest. Mr Bellinger went ooof and slugged Carter in the belly, like, wham. Shit! They couldn't stop.' She isn't exactly crying, but she's close. 'Mr Pike had to help Mrs Bellinger pull them apart, and they aren't even friends!'

'Church,' he says thoughtfully.

'Everybody saw. Now they're all down at the club, talking about it over sticky buns, you should hear it, you wouldn't believe what they're like. I hate them all. I hate this town!'

Musing, he shakes his head. 'They were all in church.'

'Where else? They always are, and then they come out and say the shittiest things! It was awful, like, right up there the main archway? It was like he was reviling him in the middle of Sunshine Stadium and you could watch Carter crying on the giant screens. Everybody in Fort Jude saw Mr Bellinger beat the crap out of Carter and they heard what he called him. No wonder Carter bailed. Shit,' she says, listening at the bottom of the attic stairs, 'he's not up there either.'

'I told you . . .'

'Right.' Her face fragments like a bad transmission and snaps back into focus: resilient kid. Big, getting-down-to-business sigh. 'Guess I'll go get Grammy over with.'

'Do what?'

'At the old folks' hatch. It's my Sunday, we take turns.' She is busy brushing schmutz off her pink dress. 'It's not so bad, except for the smell. Lysol or some shit, like, they even disinfect the food. So. Was my mother hitting on you?'

Now it is his turn to be surprised. He gets to the answer in stages. 'Not really. I'm sorry. Yeah, pretty much. What are you doing?'

'Calling a cab.'

'Don't bother. I'll take you.'

'It's out in west hell.'

Church, he thinks. Then the club. They won't be home for hours. 'Come on,' he says. Whatever he thought he was doing here is over now. 'I've got nothing but time.'

'Awesome!' The crafty look she gives him is a masterpiece. 'Would you mind coming in with me? Grammy doesn't talk much, and it's a lot and a lot easier with two.'

40

Walker

It's not unpleasant, sitting here in the car outside Golden Acres, although after a day spent stalking, he's sick of being in the car. Grief has taught him patience; he'll live. He always does.

Meanwhile, it's pretty out here on the bay, at a point that's a little too close to the end of the world, given the function of this place. Low-lying Spanish stucco apartments and a handful of cottages sit in the landscape like Herman Chaplin's dream community compressed by the exigencies. Some people say he started this miniature village as a demo model, some say the grand old entrepreneur was planning an amusement park, but the compound went up so long ago that nobody is sure. When the Methodists bought the property from Herman's estate, several problems were solved. Fort Jude society had a place to stash its frail and unpredictable parents when they got too old or too crazy to take care of themselves. They were installed at Golden Acres well before the likes of Wallace Pike came to town with his pregnant wife and first-born son – not crazy yet, but there were intimations. Generations of oldsters had passed through by the time Anna Pike ran away from her husband and, with Pop the way he was, six-year-old Walker understood he was in charge of every-thing, including Wade.

Pop was good enough at what he did, running the garage and taking care of the bills, but daily life dumbfounded him. By the time Walker was old enough to worry, he thought that sooner or later, he'd have to make the money so Golden Acres could deal with Pop. When the old man set the shop on fire in Walker's first year at MIT, he and Wade checked into it, even though old Wallace swore it was an accident. He was erratic, forgetful. You never knew.

Walker came down from Cambridge during term to scope the place, and this was after he'd vowed never to come back to Fort Jude. He and Wade went around with the girl from the front office; she was new. Golden Acres looked pleasant enough, with an activi-ties director and a pianist in the dining room every Sunday. They even had a little pool. There were parties in the Health Center for every hundredth birthday, of which there seemed to be a lot. You could see they took good care of people, photos of hundredth birthday parties lined the halls. Fragile guests posed for the photog-rapher in wheelchairs and on walkers, all dressed up and smiling bravely in their party hats. The aides and social workers Walker met were all nice enough, but when they met the director, everything changed. Odd that in an establishment depopulated by death on a regular basis, there were no vacancies. Walker was still in college but he was already earning, and Pop was slipping fast. Together he and Wade could cover it somehow, but the woman in charge took one look at them and said with the nicest smile, 'Your father wouldn't be comfortable here.'

It's a cool afternoon for April and Walker has the windows down. He is parked in a spot the shade will protect until late afternoon. As Sunday is the world's official visiting day no matter what the institution, he won't be noticed in this crowd. Everybody in town seems to be out here, visiting somebody from the generations that went before – and there are several degrees of age from the look of it, from hale but vacant-looking grands who got struck sick or stupid too early in life on up to the wispy great-greats, skeletal old people with only a few white hairs left standing on their pink heads. Considering where he is right now and where he's followed Dan Carteret so far today, and considering how close he's come to being seen at every stop the kid has made, Walker finds this parade of residents extremely peaceful. Nice old couples just about his age come past, pushing old parties in wheelchairs or supporting elbows so their shaky friends and relations can totter along the walks with blissed-out smiles. The visitors all come out of the building headed for the choice benches overlooking the water, but nobody seems to mind when their charges cut out, homing in on the first available place to sit down.

Some visitors from the outside world have brought gift baskets and some go by carrying flowers. As the afternoon flows past, Walker watches as the young and healthy run out of conversation and begin picking at the contents of the baskets, proffering food they'll end up eating themselves, nibbling out of sheer nervousness. Nobody wants to admit that fruit and candy are nothing to passengers on the long slide to the exit interview. They are beyond being interested in food. They're beyond being interested in much of anything, and it is this that Walker finds so restful – the absence of striving. Ambition went to sleep in these old people before they lost it, or consciously relinquished control, turning over the pressure of responsibility to whoever checked them into this place.

Driven as he is, ambitious and highly competitive, Walker is happy to be surrounded by people who have just . . . let go. In a lot of ways, it's a relief.

His . . . No. This Dan Carteret and that girl, Nenna Henderson's daughter, have been inside the main building for a long, long time. Ten more minutes and he'll be gnawing his wrists to keep from lapsing into a doze. Walker loves sleep, thinks about it, misses it and invites it, but he works so hard that he never has much time for it. Sleep is the one place in his life where it's more or less safe.

Sleeping, he can let down his guard because whatever it is that drives him is quiescent, enclosed. Locked inside his skull. Then he can rest. Only then. The power or potential for destruction, whatever

Walker Pike chooses to call the force that changed him forever, will lie dormant until he awakes. He can't hurt anybody.

He's in the zone when a tap on his windshield rouses him. It's Jessie, still in that slinky dove gray silk she had on when he saw her going into church with Wade but the neckline's looser, she undid a pin or took off a belt – something – he doesn't know.

She comes around to the open window. 'What are you doing here?'

'Visiting an old party.'

'Who?'

'Nobody you know.'

'Then why are you alone?'

'He can't come out until they change his bag.'

But they've known each other for much too long. 'I don't think so,' Jessie snaps, 'it's not like your dad's in there.'

Your father wouldn't be comfortable here. His teeth clamp. 'You remember! Yeah, I wanted to firebomb this place.'

'But you didn't. You hired Florence Rivers to take care of him.'

'Damn near broke us. There was a lot of stuff missing after he died.'

'Cheap at the price.'

'She cleaned us out.' Walker says thoughtfully, 'We were so broke we had to plant him out in the boonies. Or let the city plant him.'

'The boneyard.'

'Public, the city calls it. It was sad. We did what we could afford. He went into Poinsettia Gardens, out by the Interstate. Probably right next to yours.'

'You'd be right on that,' she says, grinning, 'if I'd ever had a dad.'

'You told everybody he died in Vietnam.'

'Unless I told them he was lost at sea.' They fall into the rhythm like the old, good friends that they are. 'You have to tell people something, you know?'

Walker grins. It's been a long time since he's been this easy with anyone. 'Unless you don't.'

'Like you, Mr tight-mouth. Wade says you're making a bundle in stuff so techy that he can't get a grip on it.'

God, did she really make him laugh? 'It's just computers. That's giant electronic brains to you.'

'Why aren't you off floating around on a yacht?'

'Can't swim.'

'Son of a bitch, I miss you!'

'Me too.' *Don't explain it. Never explain.*

'Why don't you ever come around?'

'I can't,' he says, and that's that.

Her voice drops into a new place. 'I wish you had.'

Walker sees his whole life passing before his eyes, and it is over. 'Oh, Jessie,' he says with real regret, 'Wade says you guys are getting close.'

'He's a good man.' She can't hide the sigh. 'Yeah, we are.'

He does not say what he is thinking. *I wish it could be me.* With Jessie, he is never angry. They go back so far that he knows what she will and won't do, and there's so much between them that the main ingredient is trust. Right now she is listening. She's listening hard, but Walker is too much what he is to risk it.

He will *not* mess up another life. He loves her, just not the way he loved Lucy, and it makes him generous. 'Go for it, Jess. Enjoy your life.'

She says for both of them, 'I am.'

'You've been through a lot.'

'So have you.'

'Wade will take good care of you.'

Walker tried to relinquish the possibility; she's trying too, but she's still out there, waiting for something he can't give. It's hard, watching her face come to terms with the future she's trying to project. 'After a while you just want somebody to be there when you get old.'

'You deserve the good stuff.'

'We all do.' Her tone lifts. 'Wade and I are looking at a wonderful house in Coral Shores.'

'Coral Shores. Where everybody who is anybody . . .'

'They're nice people, Walk.'

'I'm sure.'

'And you won't be a stranger, will you.' Statement, done deal, as far as Jessie's concerned. 'Sunday dinners, after we move in?'

'I don't know.' Walker wants to tell her he'd love that – he would, but he's much too conflicted to guarantee anything. His temper is such that he can't be sure what will come down in any given situation. At bottom, he's always aware of the potential and it makes him afraid, not for his own safety but theirs. Because of what could happen to people he loves if something comes down and they are standing too close. 'I don't think so.' But this is Jessie. Like a dedicated artisan, he makes a smile for her. 'But I'll try.'

Then her voice changes. 'I don't know if I ever thanked you for what you did.'

'Please don't.' Brad Kalen. Fucking Brad fucking Kalen, with Jessie flattened in wet sand under the mangroves where the rich bastard dragged her one drunken night, bent on battery and humiliation. After the rape. Heedless and stripped right down to his hairy, brute arrogance, convinced they were alone. After he beat the crap out of Kalen, he should have turned him in. For all the good that would do. Old Orville's money will get him out of anything – it always did. Then the part of Walker that he can not suppress pre-empts with: *If I'd had the power then . . .*

But Jessie's saying, 'It changed a lot of things for me.' She adds sweetly, 'How I valued myself.'

'You don't need to thank me, it was a given.' He pulled Jessie out of the sand and took her home crying; at the front door she hugged him and they never spoke of it again. Fucking Brad Kalen. Walker's belly tightens and his fists clench. Yeah, he had to lay waste and pillage on the way to Jessie's rescue. Years before he knew what he was. Is.

'That's not what Brad thought,' Jessie says without inflection. 'He said since I was everybody's, he should get the biggest piece.'

'I should have killed him.' It would have prevented a lot of things. Walker is too distressed to number them, but the worst one ended in the release of the terrible power that changed his life. He grips the steering wheel, anchoring himself. It takes him a moment to realize that Jessie is still talking.

'It made a tremendous difference to me.' Framed in the car window, she bends down to make clear how important this is. 'Like, all the difference in the world, and I never really thanked you.'

But Walker can't keep on talking about it this way; the **ugly** inside him is simmering. *Shit,* he thinks. *And I hoped I was done with that.* Reaching up, he touches her face to get her attention. 'I knew,' he tells her. 'I love you Jessie, but you'd better go.'

'It's OK.' They know each other so well that he doesn't have to explain. She knows he's upset. 'Wade and I came out here to see our old kindergarten teacher, remember old Mrs Earlham from Pierce Point?'

He doesn't, but he needs to release her while he can still contain himself. If he doesn't he'll start ranting, and that is the best-case scenario. 'OK then,' he says nicely, 'I'll let you go. Tell her I said hey.'

'You aren't here to visit an old party, are you?'

He shakes his head.

'I know you're following the kid.'

'You what?'

'Dan Carteret, Lucy's son.'

'Who says?'

'Somebody on Coral Shores saw you. Everybody knows. What do you want with him?'

'I'm just following, it's no big deal.'

'He's a nice kid,' she says. 'Just, whatever you do, don't hurt him.'

Walker cries, 'I'm here to protect him!'

'Dear one, here's Wade. I have to go. Oh, Walker, take care!'

41

Dan

'You never know what you're gonna get. Sometimes she's all talka-talka, and the rest, she just stares. *You're not leaving now.*' Steffy pushes Dan into the room and closes the door as far as the institutional doorstop permits, giving it a kick to make her point. She peers into the Geri-chair where her great-grandmother is tipped back, apparently to help blood make it all the way up there to her brain. In spite of the touch of lipstick put on by an aide, she looks transparent, like what's left after an insect sheds its carapace.

'Oh.' Dan has never seen anybody this old. 'Oh!'

'GRAMMY, ARE YOU IN THERE?'

Where she had been staring at the TV in its ceiling mount, old Mrs Henderson turns to see who yelled. She lights up like a paper lantern.

Triumphant, Steffy hisses, 'See? She knows me. That's why somebody has to come.'

'Can she hear us?'

'Sort of.'

'Hello, Mrs Henderson.'

Just as suddenly, she lapses. All the lights go off inside.

Sighing, Steffy studies the lunch tray with its plastic dishes and plastic-looking food. 'GRAMMY, YOU HAVEN'T TOUCHED YOUR CUPCAKE. HAVE A BITE.'

Dan turns to go.

'LOOK, GRAMMY, IT'S CHOCOLATE. Sugar usually perks her right up.' Steffy will say anything to keep him here. 'When she gets going it's a riot. Plus, you're looking for something or somebody, right? Give her a minute to perk up, OK? She knows some amazing shit.'

'She doesn't look very perky to me.'

Everything is in stasis here. Dan delivered Steffy as promised, and when she asked him to come up to the room it was clear that she needed it so he walked point, seeing her up the stairs and down terrible pastel halls lined with saccharine repros chosen to help people forget that they came here to die. He kept Steffy talking to cover the babble in the health care wing, which is where they are. They talked about her boyfriend Carter, but not really; they talked about why stain-proof flooring, why the wide bedroom doors; they talked about Nenna not at all. They jabbered, trying to blur the occasional outraged cry coming from rooms they passed, the spontaneous groan, but old voices knife into a sensitive nerve. Dan came inside Golden Acres because the girl needed it, but he can't stay. He doesn't have the time.

'If she comes to, tell her I said hi.'

'Give me a minute!' Steffy's fingers lock on his arm like teeth. She yanks him into the space between Mrs Henderson and the TV. She mutes the set. 'That's better, isn't it, Gram? Dan,' she says in her mother's exact ceremonial voice, 'this is Grammy Henderson.'

'I don't think she's in there any more.'

'Fuck she isn't. Grammy!' She ratchets up the volume. 'Grammy, this is my friend Dan.'

'Look, I really can't . . .'

'You have to! GRAMMY, THIS IS DAN.'

'Hello, Grammy.'

'Her name is Blanche.'

'Hello, Blanche.'

Waiting, Dan is aware of life going on elsewhere – conversations hitting the same dead end in rooms all along the hall. Sudden, inadvertent cries. Half Fort Jude's history is deposited here, stored inside of old people a lot like this one, who remember, but can't explain. Did Steffy's great-grandmother know the incendiary Lorna Archambault? God knows she's old enough, but at the moment she is beyond speech. He can wait forever and never find out. He imagines every room in Golden Acres is like this one, dense with history, but history under lock and key.

In a city where everyone seems to know everything that goes on, these old parties have probably processed and stored all the information he needs. If age didn't kill, they could tell him everything. Solve his life. Decades worth of answers are layered inside these old patients' heads. Soon they will all be gone. Their random access memories are shot. Death will erase their hard drives and local funeral directors will deal with what's left. He's running out of time! *Talk to me.* What would he uncover if he could go from room to room, cracking secrets out of their shrinking heads?

Shit, Dan thinks. It's just as well I didn't come here for answers. Look at her!

Dressed in pink seersucker today, with knotted bones that used to be feet tucked into sheepskin booties that have never walked a step, Blanche Henderson stirs. There's a button missing on the dress and someone has closed the neck with an oval brooch which, he notes uneasily, seems to contain human hair. Other people have the good grace to die off before they reach this age, but Grammy is still among them. Studying the husk of a woman who's been around too long, Dan marvels. *How did you get to be so old?*

Sensing his impatience, Steffy says, 'Grammy?'

The old woman's body has given up on her but the spark won't let go, no matter how much she wants it to fly up.

Grammy's in there somewhere, fixed on something only she can see. Great age has one compensation. Time and space are nothing to her. Dan has no idea how long it will take Grammy to get back from wherever she is roaming; she could be anywhere, wandering around in search of the white light or spinning her wheels on memory lane or excavating truths that at the time she didn't recognize as such.

Is Blanche aware that Steffy has brought an outsider into the close, obscenely intimate space where – soon, if she's lucky – she will die? Does she have any idea that Dan is willing her to speak so he can escape? He gnaws his lip until blood comes.

'Hang on and I'll get some cupcake into her.' Patiently, the girl holds a sticky cube to her great-grandmother's lips. Steffy tickles Grammy's cheek until the mouth pops open. She slips in the cake like mail into a letter slot. 'There.'

Like a vet giving a dog a pill, she strokes Grammy's throat. It takes a long time for her mouth to move. They wait a long time for her to swallow. Watching for signs of life, Dan thinks: *Steffy's right about the smell.* Then he thinks: *There isn't enough Lysol in the world.* Everything is desperately pretty in Grammy's room. Pink eyelet curtains, matching dust ruffle, pink comforter and ruffled eyelet pillow shams that in no way obfuscate the fact that this is a hospital bed. Aqua walls. Above the bed hangs a framed repro of that pretty-pretty painting of a Southern belle at a piano; Dan thinks the dress comes in different colors according to which company supplies the repro, but he isn't sure. Then the chair clanks into upright position and he jumps out of his seat.

'Hello,' the old lady says, blinking. 'Hello?'

'It's me, Grammy. Stephanie. Nenna's girl?' She shoves him closer. 'And this is Dan.'

'How do you do,' Dan says, looking into opaque eyes. The disturbing thing about Grammy Henderson is that she is pretty much bald. What little hair she has stands up bravely, a handful of white threads that one of the attendants has brushed to a shine and fluffed so it will look like more. She doesn't exactly look at him. She just holds up the knot of bones that passes for a hand as though she's used to having it kissed. Instead, he bends down and carefully – every segment of this lady ought to be stamped FRAGILE – he takes it. It's like shaking a bunch of dried flowers.

Startled, she looks up, shouting, 'Company! Stephanie, get my wig!'

Steffy whispers, 'It's been years since she wore the wig. This is a very big deal.'

'What did you say your name was?'

'Dan. Dan Carteret.'

'Little Lucy's boy!' That flash. As suddenly, Blanche goes back inside.

How does she know? Did Nenna come running with the news? He snaps forward, hanging on the next word, but Grammy's gone. Amazing how still a person can be, for so long.

Long becomes too long and Dan gives up on her. It's late. He turns to Steffy, assuming they are done. 'OK then. Where do you want me to drop you?'

'Oh, I have to stay. Staff's night off, I have to feed Grammy when her dinner comes.' She turns with a steely glare, all teeth. 'You're hanging in with me, right?'

This is a moral dilemma that Dan will not have to face.

Grammy has fought her way to the surface. 'Those poor babies!' she pre-empts, rolling down a track that was laid more than thirty years ago. 'I warned Lorna not to steal Sam Carteret's baby away after Lily died, but she didn't care. She went up to Charleston with lawyers and took Lucy away from him. I said, "Lorna, that baby is all he has left!" I said, "You'll be sorry," and she was. I said, "That girl will never forgive you," and she never did.'

The next thing Blanche says is so bitter that it astounds him. 'No wonder Hal Archambault divorced her. She was a mean, willful . . .' Her mouth is working, but lady that she is, she can't use that word. Instead she spits. 'We used to be friends!'

Steffy dabs at the glob with a tissue and Grammy goes on. 'The Carteret boy was sick with grief, but she was bent on it. I said, "Lorna, if you do this you will live to see history repeating," but I swear, that woman marched on Charleston like Hitler, she hated all men. That's why Lily sneaked off to Valdosta to marry Will, and Lucy . . .'

'Lucy.'

Thoughts rush across the space behind Grammy's eyes like cloud formations; she reaches out and snatches one. 'Sam sent Lorna a post card. **Your new granddaughter is named Lucy. P.S., it killed Lily. In case you cared.'**

Lily was Lucy's mother. Chapter. Verse. Verified. Thud. *My great-grandmother. It's* . . . Blinking, he tries to shake it off. *In the blood?*

'Lorna had a hard heart before Hal Archambault left her for that tramp, so no wonder, but the divorce turned it to stone. Poor Lucy! She was Lorna's perfect dollbaby, all dressed up with nowhere to go. No boys allowed in that house, and as for men, men! She looked at men and she saw . . .'

'Wait.'

'Liars, fornicators and cheats. Lucy couldn't go with any boy her grandmother didn't approve, and nobody was good enough for Lorna Archambault. She had to sneak away from parties at the Fort Jude Club to see poor Hal! I said, "Give that girl little freedom or you'll lose her," but she was like the Gorgon, beating Lucy to death with snakes. No wonder it ended the way it did.'

His mouth forms: *How?*

With a tremendous effort, Grammy spits, 'Her girls fell in love and she couldn't keep them. We all know how that ended, with Lily dead and Lucy dead to her.'

Dan is aware that he is holding his breath.

'She was awful to those boys,' she says without naming them because at Grammy's age people become interchangeable and time is all the same. 'Both times.'

This rolls in like news in a foreign language. Beggared, he murmurs, 'Ma'am?'

'Lily eloped – so sad – and then she died and Lorna swooped down like the wolf upon the fold and took Lucy away from poor Sam, she was a spiteful, controlling old . . .' Grammy's mouth knots, twitching while she searches for the euphemism. Finally it pops out like a cherry pit. 'Witch!'

Steffy murmurs, 'Wuow, that's the most I've heard out of her in weeks! Here, sweetie, just a little more cupcake, OK?'

But Grammy is rolling now, heading for the exit ramp. 'It was spite, pure and simple,' she says, just before she runs down. 'Spite!'

Dan gives her a gentle push to keep the recital rolling, 'You said, both times.'

'She didn't care how much in love they were. She saw Hal in every man. At least Lucy was forewarned.' Grammy's eyes crackle. 'Thanks to me.'

'You knew my mother?'

'Lucy was too smart for her. Sweet girl!' Abruptly, she seizes Dan's hand and pulls him close. He can smell death coming out of her mouth. 'You look like her.'

It hits like a mallet and his breath catches. 'Yes Ma'am.'

'Your mother fell in love but she kept it a secret. She had been warned.'

Everything in him rushes forward. 'You warned her?'

'God help me, I tried to warn them both!' Grammy is tiring. She drops his hand.

'I tried to tell them history repeats itself. It always does.' She sighs. 'When she got pregnant, she went where Lorna couldn't hurt her.'

More, Grammy. More. 'Who did?'

'Oh, those poor boys!'

'Boys? Which boys, Ma'am? Ma'am!'

Lapsing, she comes back with, 'He was devastated.'

'Who?'

Used up, Grammy Henderson waves her hand, fighting off invisible flies, but she's still in there, and at some level she knows that Dan is waiting with teeth clenched so tight that the enamel cracks. She says with finality, 'Terrible, what got old Lorna, but she brought it on herself.'

Oh, lady, don't stop now. 'How? Oh, please, Mrs Henderson, just one more answer. What set her on fire?'

But Blanche has talked a lot for a woman her age – what is her age? Half past ninety and hurtling to the finish line – and she's spent. She says crossly, 'That's enough.'

'What did it?' *Oh, please.* 'What?'

With the wave of a southern lady banishing anything unpleasant, she changes the subject. 'Nenna, has my dinner come?'

'Not yet, Grammy,' Steffy says.

'You were telling us about Lucy.'

Blinking, she asks politely, 'Who?'

'Lucy Carteret, remember?' Dan presses even though he knows Grammy is shutting down. He gives her everything he has. 'I'm her son.'

'Don't.' Feebly, she swats him away.

'Please!'

'Oh, don't!' Exhausted, the old woman cries, 'I want my dinner now!'

Silence overtakes them.

'I have to go,' Dan says when it's clear that this time, Grammy won't be back.

'Dude . . .'

He turns. 'And I'm not kidding.'

'Dude!' Then Steffy sees his face, and lets him go.

42

Jessie

Alone in her office, Jessie is both glad and sorry she ran into Walker out there at Golden Acres. She loved talking to him after all this time. He's so dark and remote that these old girls – her friends – are scared of him, but she and Walker go way back. With her, he is so easy! They'll always pick up where they left off even if it's another hundred years. It was the best thing about a routine, perfectly pleasant

Sunday in Fort Jude. Then on the way out of Mrs Earlham's room she got in a fight with Wade, but that isn't the downside.

It wasn't really a fight, just one of those emergency exits women build out of words when they're feeling crowded by a lover who is not quite enough and expects too much. Everybody needs a little down time, but Wade got pissed – hurt feelings, she supposes. 'All right then!' he said, and dropped her here. After a long day with big old Wade, who wouldn't know a boundary if he fell over it, she's relieved to be by herself again, in a place where she won't be distracted by the pressure of his expectations or weighed down by that sweetly persistent, clueless will.

Jessie did not flee Golden Acres because she was freaking – unlike Dan Carteret, who will admit as much when he comes back to the Flordana at dusk. Old people are ancient history to her. She'll be living among them when her time comes and she knows it. She just hopes that if he survives her, Wade sees to it that she gets a single room. Hell, even if they check in together she needs a single room.

Yep, she tells herself, and this is not such a bad thing. It's gonna be Wade.

Seeing Walker today disrupted her; there is shared history. The crackle of what might have been. As long as she was inside Mrs Earlham's sunny corner room in the assisted living wing, she could put it aside. Their spunky old kindergarten teacher is still bright, and she laughs a lot. She gets around her quarters better than can be expected; she knows more gossip than Jessie. She's cool; they let her keep her dog. She asked after Walker who, she would not stop reminding Wade, was handsome as Lucifer and smarter than a bundle of whips. 'I always knew that boy would go on to do great things,' she said, and when Wade didn't respond she said, 'what's he up to, honey? How is he, anyway?'

'Oh,' Wade said carelessly, and Jessie cracked her mouth open wide as a baby bird, hoping to be fed. 'He's fine,' Wade said, and that's all he said.

When they came outside Jessie couldn't help checking – was the car still there? – and she can't help what her heart did when she spotted Walker slouched behind the wheel, but that isn't it, not really. That isn't the downside.

Everything came back in on her. Everything.

Hurting, she started in on Wade, but she shut down the fight before it could get too bad. She said what with the party and the fire, the pile on her desk back at the Flordana was so high that scorpions were nesting in it.

Wade came back with: no problem, he'd come in and smash the little suckers flat, so she had to tell him she was really, really tired – which she is, but not in a way Wade Pike would understand. When she flared up at him he got over-solicitous, which he always does. He still thinks that Jessie, who had it all scooped out at nineteen – thank God she would never be pregnant – isn't really upset when she gets mad at him, it's only P.M.S. which, OK, it's a little late for that. She was out of the car and halfway across the courtyard before he could open the door for her.

She needs time and space to sort out the *sorry* about running into Walker, which at the moment is overriding the glad. She sent the desk clerk home and slipped into the office, where she can keep an eye on the front desk and the entrance, in case.

It doesn't take long to figure out what the matter is. Memory has been rolling in from so far off that for a long time she didn't hear it coming. Now it hits with all its terrible freight, and mashes her flat.

The tastes, the sounds, the crap they were all drinking that lost, bad night come back in on her, everything rank and sour and so sudden that she shudders. The pain is old but still fresh. Her mouth fills with the taste of mingled snot and blood the way it did when it happened; she feels the cold, hard sand behind her head and under her bare back and she can feel wet sand creeping into her crotch as she gasps under the weight of the sleek, arrogant, angry bastard grinding the sand deeper into her most private part, and before anything she feels the humiliation.

She was never sure which ones ran off and which ones stayed to watch.

A high school sophomore. Stupid kid, what was she thinking, crashing the seniors' houseparty when it wasn't even her year, and they couldn't see her for dirt? Lord knows she was pretty enough, stacked and sexier than those fucking Barbie cheerleaders, and with people who didn't know, she could easily pass for older which is how she got in the door in the first place, but she was too young! The trouble was, Mollie Regan knew her from church and she never liked her – jealous, Jessie supposes, that woman was still stuffing her bra when she was old enough to afford implants. Jessie blended in fine, she was dancing with Billy Pouncey when Mollie spotted her. Ms. Head Cheerleader dug those purple fingernails into her arm, hissing, 'You don't belong here,' and yanked her off the floor, which is how she ended up out on the curb in the middle of the night.

Her own damn fault for crashing, everybody knew houseparties were for seniors only and it didn't matter how cute or sexy you were. She was sitting on a cement sea turtle out there on Coquina Alley waiting for Billy or some other boy to come out that she would consent to ride home with in exchange for a little of the one thing Jessie did best. But then Chape's brand new Jeep came along, filled with sophomore boys scoping the scene like it was their senior year and they were the killer dudes laying waste and pillaging the maidens, come what may. Six first-string players from the FJHS Tarpons riding around drunk as bastards, acting like they ruled the world which they did, in a way, rolling to a stop at the sight of her.

'Girl, you want a ride?'

Stupid, she thinks now. Stupid, heedless little bitch.

Stupid ever to get in any car with Brad Kalen, never mind who else was along. The boys were all loaded but so was Jessie, so what else is new? Besides, she recognized the car which was Chape Bellinger's sweet sixteen present before she saw Brad was behind the wheel. She thought it was Chape stopping for her which, given who he was and given where Jessie came from, was an honor. Plus, given how late it was, she could use the ride. But Brad was driving, with Chape out cold and insensible, wedged in the back behind the bench seat, which was full of guys. Brad gunned the motor, laughing. 'Are you getting in or what?'

He was a little heavier set than most even back then, but he was also a year older than them. Back then he worked out and Jessie is here to tell you that he oiled the biceps and the pecs. With tight gold curls and that big, heavy head Brad Kalen looked like fucking Tiberius, riding in to take the throne. She was a little scared of him so she said, 'There isn't room,' but the guys in the back all said like one person, 'You can sit on my lap.'

Cute Bobby Chaplin was riding shotgun, smart and safe as houses, so why not? If the look Bobby shot her should have told her that he had misgivings, she wasn't about to pass up a ride. Who wouldn't want to be seen out riding around these cool guys? She tossed her hair like a cheerleader and jumped into the back.

Stitch Von Harten and the Coleman twins skooched over so she could slip in between Buck and Darcy instead of jouncing along on their knobby knees – too bad about Darcy but who knew he was already doomed? Brad passed the bottle – God only knows what they were drinking – and Jessie knocked one back. Stupid, stupid, stupid, she thinks now, but in the beginning, so crazy and so very much fun, being with these guys – top of the line, leaders of the pack. They were singing, and she remembers riding along thinking, *Now I'm in with them, these are my main men.*

When you grow up on the outside and something like this happens, you think, *Now everything is going to be different.* They'll want you at all the parties now, and not just because you have big knockers. Yeah, right. Brad took a turn nobody expected and her neck snapped. They were at the head of a coral road going nowhere. 'Shit,' Bobby said, and Brad said, 'No shit.' Then Bobby, who Jessie was so psyched to be hanging out with, said, 'This is where I get off.' She remembers just exactly how it sounded. 'This is where I get off.' He reached over the seat and grabbed her hand. 'And you should come too.' He was asking her to jump down and come along but she was out with the boys and they liked her and by that time frankly, she was too fried to think about that big of a decision.

Oh shit, Jessie thinks, jumping up so fast that she upsets her chair. *Done is done.* She can't go back and she can't make it change. The trouble is, she can't get rid of it, either, and seeing Walker again today the way she did on a bright Sunday afternoon after so long and just when she thought she was on top of things – she can't handle it. She just can't.

It isn't the pain or humiliation, it's the knowledge that Walker Pike saw her like that, tattered and bawling in the sand, which he did because it was Walker who ended it. Just when she thought she was going to die – and by God she wanted to die that night and at certain times every night for years afterward – Walker came. Alone by that time, and she can't know when the others fled – alone, and brutish, vengeful Brad Kalen was rolling her over to try something new when headlights exploded the night and everything changed. A car door slammed and Walker Pike came down on them like the Trojan army and ended it.

Everything stopped in a shower of sand and flying spit and her attacker's bloody teeth and the hell of it is that every time she sees Walker now, and she does love Walker, Jessie knows he is remembering.

No matter how old they get or how pretty she makes herself, Walker is seeing her like that. *Like that.*

It isn't fair, she thinks bitterly, he never looked that way at Lucy. In spite of all that.

Distracted and miserable, she finds herself running around the lobby of her hotel thumping tapestry pillows and misting her bromeliads – anything to escape the sense memory, which is overwhelming. She is straightening lampshades when the kid from up north comes out of the elevator with a Jiffy bag under his arm – when did he come in? Was she so wrecked that he went past the desk without her noticing?

Lucy's boy.

It breaks her heart to see him. Then she looks at his face and her heart goes out, and for more than one reason.

She chooses the easy one. 'You look like you've been hit by a truck.'

He grins, probably because Jessie is smiling. 'Long day.'

'Bar's closed, but I can buy you a cup of coffee.'

'I just came to pick up something. Gotta be somewhere.'

'Have you eaten?'

'Not so's you'd notice.' Now, why does this embarrass him?

She says kindly, 'You need a Flordana burger so you don't die on your way to wherever you're going. Chips on the side, and guaco. Come on, come and sit five minutes while Sibby fixes it, it looks like you could use the mercy.'

'Mercy?' He stands there, juggling the Jiffy bag while he thinks it over. Should he stay or should he go? His lips aren't moving but they might as well be. It's not clear what he is considering, but she can see that he's sifting through significant material.

'I can get it to go, if you're in that much of a rush.'

'OK.' It's a good smile. Honestly pleased. 'Thanks.'

This is nice, Jessie thinks, studying the kid while he stirs too much sugar into the iced tea she ordered for him because, she said laughing, he needs a caffeine jolt to keep him going while Sibby gets his hotel Happy Meal into the clamshell. All these years childless and she's sitting here with a great-looking man, and instead of flirting she's coming on like Mrs Mom. It's kind of restful. Besides, it's taking her out of herself. *Sweet, sitting here with a sweet guy who doesn't know how they did me, talking about nothing.* 'So,' she says, 'Fort Jude. Scary, right?'

Then he puts the snapshot on the table. Yes, she saw it the first day. Yes, she knows what he wants. No. She knows what she wants. It's time.

'Do you know these guys?'

Him. She puts her finger on the snapshot so she won't have to see that face again. 'Oh,' she murmurs, 'Oh, shit.'

'So you do know them.'

She grimaces to mask what she is thinking. 'Always did.'

'I'm looking for my father?' Not a statement, a question.

Jessie says gently, 'We don't always know what we're looking for.'

'You're going to help me, aren't you.' Not a question.

'If I can.'

'These guys.'

She takes a long breath. OK, as the guy who led her business seminar in Vegas said, *Let us begin.*

'Lucy should have known better than to get in a car with those guys, no matter how many there are. There is no safety in numbers in this town.' Like it or not, she is back there. 'You don't do that when you see him, not even when it's full of boys which is why you get into the car in the first place. Son of a bitch loses the others along the way, he just throws them out the back or they get fed up and jump out because they can't stop him and they know where this is going, and where you thought you were safe . . .' She breaks off, hoping she can jump from here to the business about Lucy without telling him too much about herself, but it's too late.

'When you get to be my age, you get used to a lot of things and you learn how to handle it, but I was only fifteen!'

'You.' Daniel is too quick for her. 'You?'

So she has to tell him. 'Yeah. Me.'

'Same guy?' He grimaces. 'Same guy.'

'After he did it he beat the crap out of me.' This pops out even though she is trying hard not to talk about herself. She pulls her voice back together and starts over. 'Your mother should have known better, she was eighteen.'

Sad, what his face does then.

'It's OK, it ended differently.' Then without explaining because she can't bear to tell another living human what happened to her when she was young and stupid, Jessie makes the jump cut to Lucy's story, that is, as much of it as she knows.

'Nobody in her right mind gets in a car full of drunks, but look.

She was sheltered, it was her first beach party, how was she supposed to know? Oh shit, I should have warned her but we didn't talk – not that she was snotty, just standoffish, and besides, I was distracted. I was with Clete Rucker that night and hey, I was *invited*, getting down with all the kids out there just like I belonged, down with the bonfire and great music and moonlight on black water, God only knows what we were drinking; we were all crazy and by the time I looked up, she was getting into that Jeep and it was too late to warn her.

'When I saw what was happening I screamed and ran after them but by that time they were bombing down the beach and I knew. I ran along after them it seemed like all night, crying and screaming to stupefy the dead. I yelled, "Lucy, watch out," but the wind took it. Forgive me I ran screaming and forgive her she didn't hear and then I lost sight of them.' She is swallowing tears. 'There was sand in my eyes and in my mouth and in my hair and my God, I cried and cried.'

Ashamed, she meets his eyes; it's what honest people do. 'I should have called the beach police, I should have brought the Air Force down on them, I should have taken their guns and shot him dead or howled to break glass and kept on howling until she heard me and took warning, *Watch out for Brad . . .*'

'Brad. Kalen, you mean.' **Click.**

'. . . but I was so drunk I was puking sand, and . . .' She breaks off. The kid is sitting across from her with his mouth cracked open, not drop-jawed, just trying to hear more than she is willing to say.

'And what?' He drops a warm hand on her wrist, squeezing until she flinches and pulls away. 'And what?'

Now they arrive at the heart of her pain and, OK, Jessie thinks, it's time to admit it, her bitter, bitter jealousy. She tells him, 'Thank God Walker saw them go.'

'Who?'

Jessie Vukovich loves Walker Pike, she always will and they both know it but that's as far as it goes; Walker is a very private person. Never mind that she knows without having to look that he's parked out front on Central Avenue right now, that he's sitting out there in the dusk waiting for the kid to come out so he can follow him, and never mind that Jessie isn't sure why Walker is tailing him, but she has her suspicions.

She says lightly, 'Just a boy I used to know,' and the kid's irises explode. Then because she can't just drop it and leave it lying there she says, 'But he got there in time. Walker caught up with the son of a bitch, which is why the ugly fucker graduated missing three teeth. I guess he beat her pretty bad. Walker had to clean her up before he took her home, and Walker . . .' She is rolling into a little threnody when Dan Carteret lunges up like a shark, all teeth. 'Wait! Your food!'

'I can't.' Choked with anger, he wheels. 'I have to go.'

'Not yet. This is important. You might as well know . . .' The details pile in on Jessie and she is surprised that even though she will never outlive her own misery and humiliation, what became of perfect Lucy after Walker saved her from Brad Kalen is a source of greater pain than anything Brad did to her. 'Wait,' she cries. 'Wait for the rest!'

Too late. He's out the door. Running for his car so hard and fast that he won't see Walker parked there.

She says anyway, 'If you're looking for your father, Kalen's the wrong guy. You got born a lot later. A whole year later, at the very least.'

43

Bobby

The sun is over the yardarm, always a bad time for Bob Chaplin, Goldman Sachs. There will be no drinking, but his hands shake and his mouth waters every evening just about this time. His brother and sister are no help. Margaret's trotting around upstairs, pray God she isn't planning another of her Sunday night suppers, and Al is off at his favorite bar, leaving Bobby alone to replay tapes in his head – all those lost conversations, old and recent – with no way to rewrite them and nothing to take his mind off it. He won't call friends. He found out last night that it really has been too long. He loves Von Harten and Coleman but they have their own problems, and after seeing his designated best friend up close last night he remembers what he always knew. Bellinger was never his friend, not really.

No problem. He's used to being alone. He'll be fine.

He is surprised and grateful when the doorbell rings. 'Nenna! This is nice.'

'Are you busy?' She's holding a basket covered by a checkered dishtowel with that freshly washed look, as if it just came out of the drier. She looks pretty in the creeping dusk, maybe a little shaky but hopeful. 'I made too many corn muffins this morning, I hope you like . . .'

'I just started a pot of coffee.' Bobby is hopeful too.

'I hope you don't think it's too late for . . .'

He lifts a corner of the cloth and peeks in, quick to reassure her. 'They look great. Hey, Margaret brought orange blossom honey back from Homosassa Springs. Would you like . . .'

'I'd love to.' She smiles. 'Can I come in?'

Her smile makes him smile. But, this house! He covers quickly. 'It's too pretty out to be stuck inside.'

'The light really is beautiful at this time of day.'

He walks her around to the picnic table. 'Let's sit out here.'

'Let's do.'

'Wait here, I'll bring a tray.'

He likes the way she scoots her legs over the bench and sits. Bobby notes that unlike the girls when he knew them back in high school, Nenna does not jump up and offer to help, which is the Fort Jude way. She seems to know that he'd find it intrusive. When she had him at the front door she didn't try to push her way inside. Maybe she knows he'd rather not have her nosing around in there feeling sorry for him, he thinks, going into Margaret's dim kitchen.

She doesn't need to see how he lives, which . . . yes!

Which he is going to change. Apartment down town, he'll gentrify a neighborhood. Fresh resume; he'll add a line that says **consultant** to explain the gap. With his credentials, he can get a new job.

Bobby collects coffee cups and the full pot, sugar bowl and two spoons, butter and two butter knives, honey with its wooden dipstick, proof against drips. Two of his mother's Minton dessert plates. He works quietly because he doesn't want to bring Margaret downstairs. He's rather not hurt her feelings – which he would, if she found the tray and asked him to explain. When he comes back outside Nenna is waiting nicely in the twilight, sitting there with her head bent, like a child. He sets down the tray. 'I'm sorry it took so long.'

'This is so nice!' She smiles.

'I'm glad.'

She breaks one of the muffins and puts it on a plate. She butters the halves, drizzling them with honey and pushing the plate across the table. 'Here, this one's for you.'

'Wonderful.' Soberly, he pours the coffee, setting the first cup down in front of her. 'Sugar?'

'No thanks, Bobby, I'm fine. Nice to see you.'

'You too.'

She is sitting there fishing for thoughts. Surprised by what surfaces, she laughs. 'And let's don't talk about our problems!'

Bobby grins. 'Let's don't.'

'It's just so nice to *see* you.'

He jumps up. 'I forgot napkins!'

'Don't worry, we're fine.'

'I guess we are.'

She says, 'We have a lot to talk about.'

They are both smiling now. Bobby says, 'We do.'

44

Dan

Rushing out of the Flordana, overcharged and crackling with frustration, Dan feels like a fugitive from the static Fort Jude Sunday afternoon. In Grammy's room, in the Flordana coffee shop, he turned into a convict in a holding pen, waiting for – helicopter rescue? Darkness, so he could swarm over the wall and escape?

The key, he realizes. Jessie Vukovich told her story, liberating him. He drives through the soft Florida night like a death-row murderer with a last minute reprieve. He is going to confront the man Lucy sent him all this way to meet. He knows she did: the whole jewel box thing, the contents she left behind like a message to him. The thump between his shoulder blades. He finds certain details encoded. How could she not want this?

He isn't sure how the encounter with the father will end, but tonight by God he will end it.

Darkness changes everything. By day Coral Shores looks orderly and civilized, bisected by the boulevard, with neat cross streets intersecting. It looks like a grid, but only to outsiders. At night it turns into a warren. Coordinates keep sliding around, defying his GPS. In a better world it would be a straight shot to the peninsula, but in a community committed to privacy no road is straight and nothing is clear-cut. The route Dan mapped so carefully sends him down identical side streets that turn suddenly, looping back to Coral Boulevard, unless they dead-end at a stand of trees or dump him at the edges, stymied by yet another private driveway to a protected house with its private waterfront. At night all these houses look alike; every tree on Coral Shores looks like every other tree and landmarks repeat themselves so he can never be sure whether he has been this way before.

In the dark on Coral Shores nothing is as advertised, and to make things worse he almost sideswiped a stranger's heavy car the last time he went around that circle and discovered it was the same old circle all over again.

He's pissed off at himself for being careless and for getting lost, and he is even more pissed because angry as he is, Dan is torn. Where he grew up hoping for better – forget Jor-El, he thinks bitterly. Werewolf is more like it, if werewolves have were-children, which would explain a few things.

This is the hell of it, then. All his life Dan has traveled on the knowledge that the man he looks like – who looks like him! – is out there, a loving stranger built from the same genetic material as him, blood and bone, fiber and mysterious power, but now . . . He's not searching for his father the defrocked superhero, he is tracking a monster.

In a way, he's grieving for the myth. Dan's last remaining suspect was never a brave prisoner of war, government witness, valiant secret agent under deep cover. It's hard, letting go of the idea of his father as a silent hero walking out of his only son's life for good and compelling reasons. Heroic elements like honor, valor, duty did not call his real dad to serve just when he most needed him. Those are stories unhappy kids tell themselves so they can keep on going just like all the other kids.

Now, in the realm of suspects Kalen looks like the biodad. The father Dan is tracking tonight turns out to be a drunken ape who beats the women he forces into sex. Or, and this is what troubles him. Destroys them. The template he appears to be modeled on is all that and, worse: he doesn't even know what the fucker looks like.

Like me? He says through locked teeth, 'I don't think so.'

When he finds Kalen, he'll drag the designated father-to-be outside and beat him with a tire iron, one lick for every soul he's ruined or betrayed, including Lucy's, *One lick for every year he stole from my life*. Unless all he wants is to get him down and beat the truth out of him – whatever it is. Fuck knows there are questions. Fuck knows the bastard deserves it. But even though he's rigid with anger, a vulnerable part of Dan is in stasis, poised for the exculpating 'Father!' 'Son!' moment in which things are made right and everything is explained.

A crazy thing to expect. Kalen, *in extremis*, yacking up truth?

Fuck! Wrong turn.

Question. Is Kalen also a murderer? The thought darts across his mind like a spray of sparks running along a fuse. What if he torched old lady Archambault?

Fuck! Another wrong turn. Fuck! Another question.

Did he?

Wrong turn . . .

He has to wonder: wrong question?

A voice he barely recognizes fills the car. 'Asshole, what do you want here?' Yes he is shouting.

Not knowing makes him even angrier.

When he gets to the house he'll break in and pounce, drag Kalen out into the street and then he will . . . Imagination betrays him. *Father! Son!* What would that be like? It makes him shudder.

Whatever Bradley J. Kalen is to him, whatever the gross, rotting brute of a rapist says or does or denies doing when he confronts him, *He is no father to me*. **I will not have it**. OK then, he thinks, smoking with fury. When you get to the house, smash the lock and yank him out the door no questions, no explanations, and when you drag your quarry into the light, take your long look into its face, God knows you've been waiting long enough. Then beat the crap out of him.

Roaring with frustration, he shouts, 'If I can find the fucking place!'

45

Walker

Maybe some deep, unsuspecting part of Walker wants to get caught but it's unlikely, given the care with which he circumscribes his life. More likely he's played out his string, trailing young Dan Carteret night and day without stopping for more than the rudimentaries, running hard last night and all day and into tonight, blindly rushing along on no sleep, on exhaustion compounded by intolerable tension and aching grief. Although he refuses to acknowledge it, Walker Pike is strung out on hours of following without being seen, taut and driven because he does not know how to do what he has to without hurting anyone.

In fact he isn't sure what he has to do, but that's not the hardest thing. The hardest thing is being *this close* to his son without showing himself, even when he most wants to speak to him. With no idea what he would say if they did talk, because they are strangers and he's afraid to find out what said son, the baby he, OK, the child he walked out on, would have to say to him.

Or maybe he's sitting out here in plain sight because he is flat-out exhausted.

Unless it's the function of geography.

At night on Coral Shores it's harder to follow a man without his picking up on it. Bright moonlight defies him. This is, furthermore, a tight community where solid citizens hunker down at home after dark, particularly on Sunday nights when the nesting instinct strikes. All partied out after the weekend, they hole up in front of the electronic fire, snug and sanctimoniously self-satisfied.

There's nobody on the streets but Walker Pike and the man he is following.

Inevitably, the kid will pick up Walker's headlights in his rear view mirror; he'll notice that when he turns, Walker turns. They've already come close; that rented tin can almost nicked him back there on the circle. He had to lay back and run with his lights off for several blocks, until the driver was done stopping to see if Walker would pass him, and fed up with screeching around corners to trick the driver keeping pace with him. Out on the barren peninsula road even a blind monkey would know that he was being followed.

Better get there first, Pike, if you hope to control what goes down out there when the kid comes charging in to storm Kalen's house.

Walker will wait for him outside Orville Kalen's dream house. It's easy enough for Walker to find – not because he's local, but because this is not the first time he's been here, parked outside. Never mind when that was, or what Walker Pike considered when he stopped in front of the gleaming modern house one night not that long ago, riveted and trembling with suppressed rage. Shattered, he hit the gas and scratched off while the enemy he most wanted dead was still alive. Correction. Still safe.

Unlike the northerner from the real world, who will keep cross-hatching Coral Shores until he hits the right road, Walker goes like an arrow to the end of the peninsula. Out here, planting is sparse. Scrub pines and travelers' palms cling to sandy dirt that blows across the city's poshest piece of real estate same as it did in the white trash neighborhood on Pierce Point back in the day, when Walker and Wade lived with Pop in four rooms above the garage.

In denser neighborhoods on Coral Shores where Walker Pike never comes and certainly would never be invited, homeowners have trees and topsoil, tons of sphagnum moss and fertilizer delivered by the truckload. Gardeners roll out sod richer than Persian carpeting and set down plants like bric-a-brac, whereas Pierce Point families cemented over front yards to get rid of sandspurs, or battled nature with rye grass and supermarket shrubs doomed by the sandy soil before they patted dirt over the roots. Like the others in his part of town, Orville Kalen had all the right things trucked out to garnish his expansive Sixties modern house at the nether end of Coral Shores, but without constant attention nothing lives long, not even a man with all the money in the world.

When you die, they die.

There are days when Walker wishes that he could.

Kalen is home, right where Chaplin dumped him yesterday – yes, Walker knows. Over the years, he kept track. All that money made Kalen lazy and self-indulgent. Careless about how he got what he wanted. At this hour he'll be staggering from bed to the fridge and back to bed with an overloaded plate, unless he's sprawled on those greasy sheets with a freshly opened fifth, stupefied. First prize, he has choked to death on his own vomit, but that kind never dies. The rangy kid from New London will find the place; it is inevitable. He'll bang on the door and something terrible will come down.

What Walker is most afraid of: fire.

He has to stop the kid before he gets close enough to knock. Until then, he waits. He cuts the motor and glides in next to the house. Yes he's exposed, but his son won't see Walker parked in the shadows with his lights off, at least not right away. Walker needs to be where he can see him coming. *My boy.*

Given who he is and the line he has walked with such vigilance, Walker Pike is far from careless, but sometimes you just. Get. Tired.

He closes his eyes but does not sleep. Exhaustion greases the ways and instead Walker recedes into reverie, slipping away from solid ground as smoothly as a newly launched ship; he is adrift now although he doesn't know it, that's how bad it is.

Put it to too many hours behind the wheel. He is stretched to the limit by proximity and the need to keep his distance. All those years keeping them safe. Lucy. The boy. He loves them so much!

'Don't give your heart to anyone,' Pop said to his sons after their mother ran away, 'look what it made of me,' and Walker took it to heart.

He took it to heart and didn't let go until he followed Lucy Carteret to Huntington beach that night for no known reason except that she was lovely and she didn't know he was alive. As far as she knew, he was just the guy who fixed her grandmother's car, a necessary piece of the infrastructure, but he was his own person by that time, with a real life three thousand miles away from Pop's garage and the judgmental society of Fort Jude. She didn't need to know.

She smiled at Walker without seeing beyond the smudge on his face or the grease on the coverall. He wouldn't tell her that he'd been called home from Cambridge during exams because Pop was in the hospital. Wade phoned him, sobbing; he had to come. Nor did she have to know what the old man said to him that same night, tossing in the bed with his belly swollen and the toxic whites of his eyes the color of Betadine from the years of drinking that did in his liver and brought Walker home from MIT.

Pop was drunker than shit when he said it, Walker told himself, then and now. That damn fool pint of Jack Daniels on top of what the hospital was giving him; didn't they frisk his friends before they let anybody in to visit him?

Pop was dead drunk when he said that terrible thing to me, Walker told himself resolutely; Pop didn't know what he was saying; Pop was disconnected and raving. He was out of his mind with pain and alcohol and heavy duty meds compounded by whatever was in the IV flowing into him.

That night Pop raged for hours and Walker discounted it. Overturned, he took it for what he thought it was, but truth will always find you. The words followed him out of the room like a plague of hornets. Then the old lady died and for all these years he has wondered.

Were you trying to warn me, old man?

'Walker, watch out! I see it!' Wallace Pike rose up out of the bed in a surge of blankets like a shark attacking. Words came out of his face in a spray of spit and alcohol fumes. 'It's in you too.'

'What is, Pop? What is?'

'It's in you, I can see it.'

'Pop?' He shuddered: bad memories. Certain fires. 'Pop?'

The old man gargled words but couldn't spit them out. *What were you trying to tell me?*

At the time Walker thought it was sheer agony that unhinged Pop and set him to screaming; he asked, 'Are you in pain?'

'Hellfire,' Pop howled like a man running ahead of a pack of demons and it came out like vomit, 'the flame!' He thrashed and bellowed until the nurses came and shot him full of downers; his flame died and the next day he forgot.

By the next day, Walker was in love with Lucy Carteret.

It still mystifies him because the fact of it is so profound: that a man can fall in love in a single night. That it can happen in a flash. They went to the same school but Walker didn't know her. He finished Fort Jude High a year ahead of his class; there was no reason for her to know him. If you didn't play sports or do any of the stupid things that kept all those fresh-faced, privileged Fort Jude insiders at school for hours after the last bell rang, you could spend three years there without knowing anyone. Walker went home after school to work for Pop. He didn't mix with people outside the classroom. He didn't much want to. Even before the trouble, Walker kept to himself.

At MIT he was a new person. Dean's list, all that. Easy among people as smart as he was, and there were many. Then Wade phoned. His baby brother took on like Pop was on his deathbed, which wasn't exactly true. Wade's 'emergency' put Walker right back where he started, in the Pierce Point Garage, finishing the job Pop was doing the day he went belly up in the grease pit.

Lucy came in on his first morning. 'How soon can you have it back?' Shredded jeans on her, tie-dyed T-shirt, which was big that year, she was dressed just like everybody else but not. Diamond studs in her ears – her dead mother's, he learned later; that nice-girl hair held back by prescription sun glasses – how does Walker know? There's not much Walker doesn't know. She apologized, the way you would to any man who was doing a job for you, 'It's my grand-mother's. She always expects things back yesterday.'

It was graduation week. Turned out this was Wade's big emer-gency. He couldn't deal with Pop because it was Senior Week; he was too busy out at the beach, carousing. Walker said, 'When do you need it?'

She gave him a nice, indifferent smile. 'Um, tonight? I'm going to the beach and she won't let me out of the house until she gets her car back.'

'Right,' he said. He did not say: senior houseparties – not Walker in his old man's coverall, with his hands filthy and his face thick with sludge. Not Walker, who knew as well as anyone what house-parties were, but had never been to one. Not Walker, looking the way he did. Pop was replacing a cracked block when he took queer and Wade rushed him to the E.R.; he had to finish the job.

There was no way she could know who Walker Pike really was. Not that day. 'If you could do it by six . . .'

Why was she so anxious? You'd think it was her first beach party. He pretended to mull the estimate. In fact, he was taking her in – not the face, not even the body. He was absorbing the truth of her: the intelligence. The touching vulnerability. 'Six o'clock, no problem. Ride you home?'

'No thanks.' She gestured to the road outside. Walker saw that redheaded Chaplin kid out front, idling in his father's car: brainy Bob Chaplin, he noted. Safe as houses. Apologetic smile. 'I have a ride.'

Walker drove to the beach that night anyway. In case.

Houseparties, what was he expecting? He wasn't sure, but he knew what happened to Jessie after one of those things; it ate at him. He pulled her out, but too late. His heart told him to watch out for this one. No. He had to see her. He had to let her see him when he looked like himself, not like a greasy swamp bunny in Pop's big old coverall. He would never walk into a private party even with an invitation, but everything opened up on the last night of Senior Week. The parties merged for the big bonfire on the beach. All creation would be down there on the sand, partying. Walker hated himself for knowing those things about matters he had moved beyond and could care less about, but he had to go.

On Huntington beach in a crowd that size Walker could lurk without having to explain himself; he could take all the time he needed to scope out Lucy Carteret and watch her from a distance; he would lay back until it seemed like the time was right. Then he'd invent a reason to speak to her. She probably wouldn't recognize him right away, all cleaned up and looking fine. When he reminded her who he was she'd be surprised. She'd thank him for getting that grandmother's car fixed in time. Then he could ask where she was going to college in September and the conversation would start. She'd have to ask him where he went. Then he could tell her he went to MIT, which even people down here admitted might be as good as Duke.

Driving out to Huntington beach that night Walker wrote dialog in his head. It's where all his best conversations take place.

The party wasn't hard to locate. From the causeway he could see the bonfire staining the night sky. He turned off on beach road and left his car on a side street. He walked the half-block to the path over the dunes where high school seniors and hangers-on chattered like monkeys, going back and forth from the beach. There were too many; they might ask who he was, or what he was doing here if he ran into them, so he stopped short of the path and started up through sawgrass and sandspurs, climbing the steepest part of the dune. When he reached the top, the spectacle stopped him cold.

The party sprawled on the beach below.

He couldn't make himself go down. There was Walker Pike, all cleaned up tonight and looking pretty good in his white linen shirt and faded cutoffs, with his sandy hair washed until it shone, combed wet and pulled into a pony tail, in preparation. Why could he not go down there on the sand like a normal person, walk into that crowd and find the girl?

In Cambridge, Walker had no problem going out and showing himself to the people. In Massachusetts, it was easy. He was lean and handsome and good at what he did. Reclusive as he was in

high school, he had changed. MIT turned him into a good talker
– better company, he supposes. They got what he was saying. All
those smart people with no crippling preconceptions. In that world,
Fort Jude dichotomies did not pertain.

Now he was back home, poised at the crest where he could study
the people on the sand. He stood there for a long time, scanning the
crowd, looking for Lucy Carteret until his feet went to sleep and his
muscles twitched as the sand shifted under him. A term on the Dean's
List, headed there again this spring, work-study job in Computer
Science, the chairman wanted him to go on for an advanced degree,
and he was still reluctant to go down there on the beach. The hard-
packed sand was swarming with the cream of Fort Jude society, a
distinction he hated as much as he hated this town. He couldn't bring
himself to penetrate that mob of heedless drunks and acid heads who
knew Walker Pike as Pierce Point trash, if they knew him at all.

Bad idea, Pike. This was a bad idea. He turned to go.

He would have, too, but the angry snarl of a motor filled the
street below. Walker wheeled to see what it was. Then he jumped
aside as a Jeep rolled over the curb, aimed up the path through the
dunes. Howling, the driver came on, and to hell with anybody who
happened to be coming up from the beach. To hell with everybody,
they could get the fuck out of his way. Near the top the Jeep
foundered, wheels spinning. When he recognized Bellinger's
Wrangler, Walker's heart seized up, and that was before he saw who
was at the wheel. The car wasn't the only thing he recognized.
Memory told him where this would end. Rehearsing the future in
a spasm of nausea, he saw it all. Hulking Brad Kalen was behind
the wheel, filthy-drunk and fueled by rage, hollering at the others
to get out and push the fucker, get moving you sniveling assholes,
I smell pussy down there.

If Walker thought Lucy would be safe tonight, he was a fool.
Like an obedient footman, Bob Chaplin – the kid he thought was
Lucy's protector tonight – jumped out of the Jeep like an obedient
lackey and put his shoulder to the car, along with the others. Walker
should have acted then; he should have yanked Kalen out of the
Jeep and throttled him on the spot. He should have shaken him
until his ears bled but before he could shout, the Wrangler belched
and started moving. Chaplin jumped in with the others as it pitched
over the crest and headed downhill, hurtling out of Walker's reach.

The despicable bastard Walker had to pry off of Jessie Vukovich that time went roaring down on the crowd with sand flying and music blaring out of the speakers and his main men screaming as he aimed for the heart of the party.

The Jeep breached the crowd and everybody scattered. Walker started to run. As he did, he spotted the girl he knew he was in love with dancing with her lacy shirttail flying out from her long body, white lace skimming the white bikini. Lucy let go of some boy's hand and spun out, laughing. Oblivious. She was oblivious. Walker saw that his beautiful, stupid girl was stoned out of her mind, loose-limbed and weaving in front of the fire with her arms flying and her mouth open to the skies. Then he saw her whirl at the sound of her name and he saw her wave, laughing. Like a fool she trotted over to the Jeep, flattered and ignorant. He saw Kalen laughing and waving.

He shouted, but he was too far away. He ran, but it was too late.

Walker died. He saw the future, and it was vile. The night he pulled Kalen off Jessie Vukovich, Jessie sobbed all the way home. Dripping bloody snot, she explained, 'You only get in because there are others in the car. You think you're safe.'

Crafty in the way of stupid people who know how to get what they want, Brad Kalen used his buddies like inflatable state troopers when he went stalking, propping them in place before he made his move to signify that this would be a safe ride. Then – how many times has this happened? He knew how to lose his buddies along the way; either he was too selfish for a gang rape or they weren't the type; Walker didn't know, any more than he knows what binds them to him. He did know where the bastard would take her to do it because they had both been there before. Walker was pounding back over the dune, running for his truck before Kalen and his cohort left off grinning for Bethy Bellinger's camera like rock stars and helped Lucy into the Jeep. Walker knew, if not to the minute, how long all this would take and he would damn well get to Land's End before Kalen did.

This time, he wouldn't fuck up. He would be there in time to stop it.

Which Walker did, springing on Kalen before he could get that flimsy shirt off Lucy although, God, he had already hauled off and split her lip with his fist. Even tonight, Walker doesn't know why he didn't shout or throw something or figure out how to warn the girl before it came down. He should have plowed into Kalen the minute he nosed that Jeep into Lands End Road and stopped. Maybe it was Pierce Point wariness – cops would assume he was the offender – or maybe he was waiting for the son of a bitch to convict himself. *You fool.* Either way he still grieves over the pain his waiting caused her. Whatever ate Walker up evaporated when Kalen pushed her down and started pounding; Walker was on top of him, snarling and dragging him off before Lucy understood what was happening to her.

'What are you doing,' she cried, and Walker didn't know whether she was talking to him or her assailant. 'What are you *doing!*'

He dragged Kalen's bloody hand out of her tiny white bikini pants and beat the living shit out of him, noting with satisfaction that there was no way they could get false teeth into that blunt, brute face of his in time for him to make that big smile for the graduation-day group photograph. He kicked Kalen over onto his face and left him in the sand. *Too rough, Walker,* he realized when he saw how the girl looked at him, shrinking, terrified and sobbing.

'Oh, please,' he cried, holding his hands out to her like a plaster St Francis.

'Oh,' Lucy sobbed, covering her mouth.

'I had to.'

She looked into her hands and saw blood. 'Oh, oh!'

'I had to stop him.'

Her wild face was just now coming back together and she did not back away. Lucy came back into herself in stages – aware and thinking. When she could speak she acknowledged this in a voice so low that he had to guess at the tone, 'You had to stop him.' Then everything lifted. 'You did!'

Then, with Kalen laid out in the mangroves like an eviscerated shark, Walker hugged her close, crying, 'I'm sorry, I am so goddamn sorry,' because he was afraid that he had in fact fucked up, just not in the same way as with Jessie Vukovich. Then Lucy bowed her head and leaned into him, so he could feel her lips moving on his chest and he felt the warmth of her mingled blood and wet breath through his shirt as she said loud enough so that there would be no question, 'I'm sorry too.' He wouldn't kiss her – that torn lip – but he wrapped her in his shirt and took her home, riding along with the extraordinary sense that his life was about to change. It was, just not the way either of them in their wildest feat of clairvoyance or naked intelligence could possibly imagine.

Yes he was in love with her. He knows she was in love with him too, which is why he tried so hard with the old lady and how his heart broke afterward.

The next day she was gone. 'Up north,' he was told by the smug old woman when he went to ask for Lucy at her house. Mrs Archambault filled the doorway with her tidy permanent wave and perfect choker pearls and fixed glare. *Why are you here?*

'She's on a trip,' she told him in that cold, flat tone she kept for people who came to cut her grass or repair broken windows. That sneer: *Yard men.*

'I need to see her.' He meant, *I need her.*

Then she looked at him and said, in a voice that tore him in half and made tears choke Walker Pike, who never cries, 'Did you do that to her? Did you?'

'No,' he shouted. He was still shouting when she slammed the door on him. 'Dear God, no!'

Like she would believe anything he said.

Well, fuck her. They were both home over Labor Day Weekend, Lucy with all her bruises healed and only a small white scar on the lip because while Walker struggled with Kalen, the bulky drunk struck out and clipped his captive again with the back of his hand, tearing it with his ring. Now she was home.

His brother Wade was the social one so he knew who was in town, and when. Walker phoned the house. She muttered, afraid of being overheard. Colluding. His heart sank. The grandmother would never approve of him. That night Lucy came out to meet him on the waterfront across the street from the Fort Jude Club. The old woman thought she was inside, at the big party. They rode out to Land's End; it was something they had to do.

They parked near the spot. They got out. They had to, given her pain and his determination to save her again and again. Without discussing it, they walked out on the strand where the mangroves were thick, studying the sand until they found the place. They didn't do anything; they just stood, looking. For a long time they were silent. Then she turned and started back to the car.

He touched her cheek. It was one of those things.

Immediate and sure. No transaction needed. It fell into his hands like a gift.

They loved each other: she loved him. She was starting Radcliffe. Perfect.

In Cambridge they were equals, close and getting closer in love. They saw each other some nights and every weekend; they saw each other whenever they could. Walker thought they could be together on Thanksgiving weekend in Fort Jude, but Lucy went back to her grandmother's and he went home to Pierce Point.

'I'm so sorry. Grandmother.' Her face told him the rest.

He cried, 'If I could only talk to her!'

'Not yet,' Lucy warned and she was begging. 'Just not yet.' It was Wednesday of the long weekend. She touched his cheek. 'Pick me up at the club. She's running the Thanksgiving dance – Friday night? She'll be too busy to notice.' She saw his face. 'Please, hiding is only for a little while. She just doesn't need to know.'

His heart staggered. 'So nothing has changed.'

'Not yet.' She touched his lips, sealing them. 'Not yet.'

He picked her up outside the club just the way he had on Labor Day weekend. The ballroom windows were ablaze. Another big party that she could leave without being noticed. They drove to the beach; it was what they did. She'd booked a room. They made love for the first time.

Walker thought: *Now. Everything will be different.*

Coming in on the causeway, she had him take the Fourth Street exit. Walker said, 'Why?'

'Please, just drop me in Pine Vista?'

'Why, Lucy? Why should I do that?'

Her face went eight ways to Sunday. Her voice was so low that he could barely hear. 'I told her to pick me up at Bobby Chaplin's house. She thinks he's OK because his great-grandfather started the Fort Jude Club. It's crazy, but I had to tell her something.'

Like a fool, he pressed for reasons. The more she tried to explain, the worse he felt and the more he pressed.

Finally Lucy pushed him away with both hands, crying, 'I can't let her find out about you and me!'

The bitch found out anyway. Somebody saw them coming out of the Laughing Gull Motel and phoned the house. Lucy never told Walker what went on between her and the old woman at the end of that long weekend. She came to his room in Cambridge, ashen. 'I love you. She and I are done.'

It wasn't only the old woman. The society stood between them. Walker said, 'And Fort Jude?'

'Hush. I'm never going back.'

Didn't he take her into his arms and hold her tighter than ever then, and didn't he love her even more?

He and Lucy were together in Cambridge all that spring. They made love in Walker's cubicle in the cold cement block dorm at MIT and because he loved her so much they were careful, so very careful. Just not careful enough. In May, he gave her his mother's ring.

When he slipped it onto her hand, she flinched. 'What's this?'

'I love you. It's time.'

'I can't,' she said, but she didn't take it off.

'Please!'

'I can't,' she said, and his world crumbled. 'I just can't.'

'Why?'

Emotion reamed Lucy out and left her transparent. Everything showed in her face. Her choice and the consequences, what he was and who she was. Her voice was low; he could barely make out what she was saying but he could not deny that she'd said it. 'I won't let her hurt you!' The next words came from some dark place that Lucy had never let him see. 'You have no idea what she can do.'

'She won't hurt me.' Walker was desperate. Angry. 'And she won't hurt you.'

God help them both, she was crying. 'Don't worry, I won't let her. I'm out of there, I'm done with all that.'

Why did it kill him, knowing how much this cost her?

In Cambridge he and Lucy could be anybody they wanted, but Fort Jude was another story. He hated that she cared what the city thought; it ran in her blood. Without telling her, he drove to Florida to confront the old lady. Lucy was pregnant. They would be married. She would have his baby and Mrs Lorna Archambault, pillar of Fort Jude society, would damn well acknowledge it.

What Walker will never know is why old Lorna left her front door unlocked and ajar that night, or what she was waiting for.

He let himself in and went upstairs to the room where she sat with the television blaring. The door was closed. He could have left; the TV was so loud that she'd never know. Instead he knocked. Like a prom queen the woman inside lilted, 'Harold, is that you?'

'No Ma'am,' he offered in the cultivated tone that pleased people in Cambridge. 'I'm sorry to disturb you, but.'

'Hal?'

'It's Walker Pike, Mrs Archambault. It's about your granddaughter.'

'At this hour?'

'I'm sorry. I came about Lucy.'

The voice went cold. 'Lucy is dead to me.'

You bitch! 'It's urgent.' He opened the door.

The old woman was sitting right where he thought she'd be, commanding that recliner like the evil queen on her brocade throne. Regal bathrobe. Monograms on the purple slippers. Lipstick. Salon blue curls and massed diamonds on her knobby hands. That look. Everything about her telegraphed contempt. *Oh, it's you.* 'What are you doing here?'

'Lucy and I are getting married.'

'Oh. No. You're not.' She spat questions like poison darts. Walker did his best. Everything he offered made her angrier. Never mind what she said that set him off. It was vile. Never mind what Walker spat back. She used every word she had to revile him, pushing, pushing, 'She's an Archambault.'

'Fuck that,' he said finally, 'she's having my baby.' It was all he had.

'In hell.' She coughed it up like blobs of phlegm. 'I'll get it reamed out of her.'

'No.' He was controlled. Drawn tight and vibrating with rage. 'You'll never see her again.'

Fuming, she rapped the wooden claws of her brocade chair with such force that her diamonds left scars. 'I'll file charges. I'll see you in jail.'

The sound that came out of Walker then left him white and shaken. The terrifying words. 'I'll see you in hell.'

He said it more out of grief than anger although inside he was blazing with it. Rocking with hatred, murderous and stricken, Walker fled the place before he lost control and hurt her.

So in fact Walker may have done it; decades spent pondering and he still doesn't know.

How could an unwitting kid like him suddenly set a woman on fire? With no matches, no flaming torch, only his consuming rage in the room between them, with nothing to strike sparks on but the hatred that consumed her, had he actually done this? She was smoldering before he cleared the city limits, although it would be hours before Walker knew it.

Nobody saw him come or go.

There was nothing going on in the darkened house behind him that Walker could see in his rear-view mirror. Still he left Fort Jude pursued by a sick, bad feeling. The encounter left him feeling soiled, corrupted by emotions like sparks that ignited somehow, filling the room behind him. Furious, he tried to outrun his rage. Anger kept pace, but whether it was his or hers, he is still not certain. He hit the accelerator hard, hurtling away from the house, but the anger followed, with guilt sniffing at its heels. In the dark street behind Walker Pike, something happened. He didn't see it, but at the exact moment his gut twisted.

Knowledge went through him like a tremor along a fault line.

He drove straight through to Boston.

By the time he got there it was all over the news.

The *Globe* carried photos courtesy of the *Fort Jude Star*.

Walker locked himself in his room at MIT, reflecting. *So that's what I am.*

Lucy telephoned; she called and called but he was too deep in self-disgust to pick up the phone. Recognition came in stages. It marked him to the bone. Lucy knocked on his door, crying out, but he sat there like a figure cast in bronze, the image of what he had become. *The son of destruction.* She went away. For a long time he kept to his room, riven and terrified.

Before that night Walker Pike lived safely on the fringes but he was in it now, body and soul; he had no name for the power that rocked him.

He couldn't begin to know what it meant, he only knew that he was dangerous. What he was, or what he was becoming put him outside society. He loved her so much! He couldn't see her again. Not if he loved her and wanted to keep her safe. It moved and terrified him to care so much about a woman, and to be afraid to be around her for fear it would happen again. *Whatever I did.* His body shook to the foundations as certainty took hold. He was afraid for Lucy's safety and the safety of the child he knew he would never see, and that was the end of them as a couple. Walker. Lucy Carteret.

He had to let her go.

Walker let her go because he saw what he was, and it was terrible. The knowledge and the potential. *That kind of thing doesn't happen just once.* What kind of monster sets an old woman on fire without touching a match to her? What awful power does he have, that made him destroy another human being without getting close enough to light a fire?

He had too much to tell Lucy, too much he couldn't tell her. To keep her safe, he telephoned. It almost killed them both. 'I just want you to know, I love you.'

'Did you do it?' Her voice shook.

I love you and I always will. 'I don't know.'

'Did you murder her?'

'I love you, and I have to go away.'

'Did you?'

He wanted to say he loved her at least once more; he knew it would be the last time, but the words seized up in his throat and he choked, 'Forgive me, I have to go!'

He left for a year to take the job his department chair had lined up for him with Sony in Tokyo. He sent money to her at Radcliffe. It was the only address he had. Somebody rubber-stamped the envelope: NO FORWARDING ADDRESS and sent it back. Back in Cambridge, he went to see the Radcliffe registrar. With Walker sitting across from her, visibly distressed, she broke precedent and told him Lucy dropped out of college. Nobody knew where she went, the dean told him with a judgmental scowl. She was having a baby. He left Lucy to save her life. Its life.

That should have been the end of loving her, but it wasn't. Some things don't end.

He loved their baby too. He loved them both but given what he was, he walked away from them. He had to. For years Walker slouched along alone, miserable and shaggy. He went inside his work to hide.

On bad days he thinks of himself as the sea captain in the story Pop loved to tell back when he and Wade were small. The captain's wife promised to keep a candle in the window until his whaler came back into port. Instead his ship went down with all hands on board, and he was reported lost at sea. The widow mourned, but finally she gave up hope and remarried. Pirates plucked the captain off a desert island – not dead! Joyful, he headed home, looking for the candle in the window. The house was bright but his candle was gone. When the long-lost husband looked inside he saw his wife, his children at the hearth with another man sitting in his chair, a nice, happy family gathered around the fire with their heads bent in the golden light. His heart blazed and then died.

For her sake, he turned and walked away.

For her sake he lived on other people's happiness, glimpsed through lighted windows at night.

Walker became that person. He never went where Lucy was, but he kept track. He located her in New London; he knew their baby was a boy; he knew when she married Mixon; he's never followed because he can't let her be with him or come anywhere near, but he kept track. Dear God, has he kept track.

It was hard. He loved her. He missed them to extinction, but he managed. He managed until that freakish night when the kid turned five and he weakened and sent the clipping, as though one day he would find it and know. Walker left Lucy Carteret to keep her safe – to keep *them* safe – but he sent the clippings, trying to explain. He sent them because from the brain he was given to the whorls in his fingertips, this boy was his, and he should know.

But, God. What is he? What kind of monster abandons his only son?

46

Both

Wham!

Walker jumps. This is what you get for drifting.

Someone's banging on the roof of his car.

'What,' Walker shouts. 'What?'

It's the kid.

It's Dan Carteret, with his angry mouth squared like the door to an open furnace and his eyes peeled stone naked, wider than Pop's, glaring in at him. He rocks the car, shouting at Walker through the glass: 'WHY ARE YOU FOLLOWING ME?'

Shit, Walker thinks, I guess this is what I saw coming. Sighing, he rolls down the window. 'No real reason, son,' he says evenly, although he has damn good reasons.

'Don't call me son!'

'I'm sorry.' Anything to talk him down. 'Quiet. He's sleeping in there.'

'I know. I know!'

'You don't want to wake him up.'

'The fuck I don't!'

'Shut up, will you? Shut up!'

Dan grabs the door handle, shaking it violently. 'Get out of the fucking car!' He kicks the door with each word.

With Walker unshelled, his son starts pounding on him instead of the car, livid, and yelling so loud that the commotion sets off Kalen's automatic burglar lights. Suddenly the driveway is brighter than day. 'What the fuck,' he shouts, blinded by the glare. 'What the fucking fuck?'

Walker takes advantage of the distraction and grabs the kid, holding him at arm's length to make him stop hurting himself. Not only are his eyes peeled wider than Pop's, they are the exact same cobalt as Pop's eyes and Walker's eyes, and the set of the brows, the whorl of hair at the top of his head, everything – even the line of that jaw – signifies that this crazed, out-there guy directly related to Walker can do more damage than he knows.

Straight-armed by Walker Pike, he digs his fingers into Walker's forearm. 'Let go.' Wild, he is shouting loud enough to wake the dead-drunk.

'Shhh, honey.'

'I said, let go!'

'Shut up,' Walker says in a level tone, 'shut up, if you don't want the cops.' He has been following this boy it seems like forever, frightened and proud and dubious and hungering for a glimpse, a moment in which he knows and the kid knows. For the first time since this thing started they are close enough for Walker to see him plain. Certain now, stricken and joyful, Walker lets go. *He looks like me.*

The kid's eyes fly even wider.

Walker is used to dissembling. He covers quickly. 'Keep it down or Brad will . . .'

'You mean Kalen.' Astounded, Dan softens. *He looks like me.* All those years looking for the truth in a mirror and here is the man he was looking for, blood and bone, spit and image. Right now, it's too stupendous to process. Like Walker, he has grown up vigilant. Schooled in protecting himself. 'Yeah. That's who I'm looking for.'

'He's usually passed out stone drunk at this hour.'

Walker should know. He drove back to Fort Jude years after the fact, grieving for his life and bent on satisfaction. He sat in front of the Kalen house, considering. What he is: *the son of destruction.* What happened to the old lady was a mystery. If he caused the fire, it was accidental. Unless. He hated her, but he walked away. He walked away and she caught fire anyway. What would he become if he knowingly torched the slouching monster he's hated ever since that night? He tries too hard to sound easy, adding, 'Dead drunk and senseless.'

'I heard.'

'He usually is,' Walker says easily, trying to discourage this kid who is by no means a kid. He must be thirty now. Lucy's baby is a grown man, older than Walker was when he lost them both. No. Loved, wanted to keep, but for their own peace and safety, let them go. *Don't. You're too strong to go there now.* 'You better be glad he's put himself away, so he's no threat to the population. He'd be out here charging us with his SUV.'

Not Walker's fault the kid is struggling with this. All of it. Frustrated and raging. 'Fuck that shit!' Pulling free of Walker he wheels, shouting loud enough to wake the dead but not the dead drunk. 'Come on out here, asshole. I know what you did to my mother.'

'He's beyond hearing you now.'

The next thing Dan says overturns him. He turns back to Walker so fast that pain smears his face. 'Well, so is she!'

Walker staggers.

Reflexively, Dan reaches out to steady him. 'You didn't know?'

'I didn't know.'

'I'm sorry.'

Tears start in the stranger's eyes, but the desperate man Dan found here in the dark is no stranger. Where he had been struggling, Daniel Ames Carteret comes to a full stop.

My God, he really does look like me.

There is so much to say, so much to tell and so much to ask boiling up in him that he can't breathe. For the first time in his life, he's flat out of words. All he can come back with is that name. It comes out like a sob. 'Lorna Archambault.' What is he trying to do, repel all boarders with his lame cover story? Get this man *who looks like me* to reassure him, tell him the old woman is no kin? 'Fucking Lorna Archambault.'

Walker doesn't want the kid to know who he is or what he is — what his son may, under pressure, become. He shouldn't, he can't, but at bottom he does want the kid to know and it's killing him.

He doesn't know whether to unburden himself or deny everything, but he will not let Dan Carteret see him crying. 'Yes. Lucy's grandmother.'

The next thing comes out of his son in a great rush of air – is it a sigh of relief or an agonized groan? Walker can't tell. 'She got on fire.'

'You're Dan Carteret,' Walker says. 'Lucy's son.'

Dan dips his head in acknowledgement. 'Lucy's son.'

'I'm Walker Pike.' It's as close as they will get to the *Father! Son!* moment.

Words boil out of his son. 'He has to pay for what he did to her.'

Walker says, 'I know.'

'I'll make him pay. He has to pay.'

'No!' It's all coming in on Walker, whole and fully realized: what happened back then and why he thinks it happened, the scream of rage that overflowed the old woman's bedroom; it could have been hers; the anger flickering between them, what his anger did to her . . .

Or what he thought it did to her.

He will not pass this burden on! Walker is frightened not for himself or for Brad Kalen but for Dan Carteret, *the son of destruction.* He will not have it! He grips his son's arm, profoundly moved by the contact after all these years. Walker wants to keep him here, he wants to sit with him, talk and keep talking until certain things are understood between them but all he can do now is what he has to do. He starts moving Lucy's son – their son – back to his car and he keeps pushing in spite of the fact that Dan digs in his heels, resisting every step of the way. Walker says through tightly locked teeth, 'Now, leave.'

'No!'

'I mean it. You can't be here.'

Naturally he's struggling. This is Walker's flesh and blood! 'Not until I . . .'

Swift and urgent, Walker backs him up against the rental car. 'You have to go.'

'But this dirty, fucking . . .'

'Go,' Walker says firmly, forcing his will on his son without being able to explain why this is essential. Central to both of them. 'Leave it to me.'

'No way.' Anger makes Dan incoherent. 'That fucking bastard

fucking hurt her and I'll make him pay. He wrecked her life! I have
to . . .'

He shoves Dan backward, into the car. 'No, I do.'

'But the bastard, bastard . . .'

'I'll take care of it.' Here is Walker Pike, the most father he will
ever be, speaking to the only living person he loves, and he does
love Dan Carteret in ways he will reflect on from now until his
death: Walker Pike, sending his only son away. A light goes on inside
the house. Walker closes the car door on him. 'Now, go.'

Sure and gentle as Lucy, his father thumps him between the shoulder
blades. Dan backs sags, but he can't give up. Quite. 'Wait.' Torn, he
cries from the gut, 'Wait!'

Everything Walker is thinking and everything he is afraid of rushes
into his face. Words pile up, but they stay locked inside. Then Kalen's
front door opens and Walker slaps the car door like a NASCAR
starter, dispatching everything in the world that he cares about,
sending it away with an order that will not be defied because Walker
Pike is taut with urgency, his mouth an open grate, the air bright
with his soul blazing. 'Just go.'

Dan dips his head in acknowledgement. That's all.

Later that night Kalen's bedroom window will bloom for no known
reason, and not for long enough to cast any light on the deserted
street.

Presented to

by

_____

_____

on the occasion of

_____

_____

_____

D A T E

Like I always say,

"There's nothing like a great book." *And God's Word is the greatest!*
        Happy reading!

Hi, McGee
here

I'm sure you
will enjoy these Bible
stories as much as I do. They're filled with action,
adventure, romance, heroics, mystery, and bravery.
You will read about great escapes, battles, visions,
and miracles. You will meet kings, queens,
prophets, warriors, giants, angels, priests, disciples,
missionaries, and ordinary people who do amazing
things. And you will learn about God.

McGee's
FAVORITE
Bible
Stories

KENNETH N. TAYLOR

Illustrated by Richard and Frances Hook

TYNDALE HOUSE PUBLISHERS
WHEATON, ILLINOIS

God's Word Is True

What makes these stories so special is that they are all from the Bible. That means they are true—the events that you will read about actually happened many years ago. What's even more important is that these stories are given to us by God—the Bible is *God's Word*.

Here's what God tells us about his Word: "The whole Bible was given to us by inspiration from God and is useful to teach us what is true" (2 Timothy 3:16).

WOW! That's pretty amazing isn't it! God inspired human beings to write his message to us in the pages of a book, the Bible.

God's Word Is a Light

Psalm 119:105 says, "Your words are a flashlight to light the path ahead of me and keep me from stumbling."

Isn't that great! The Bible shows us the way to go in life. Like a flashlight shining on the path through the woods on a dark night, God's Word helps us see the right way and helps guide us home.

The Bible sheds light on how we should act . . . everywhere.

Library of Congress Cataloging-in-Publication Data

Taylor, Kenneth Nathaniel.
    McGee's favorite Bible stories / Kenneth N. Taylor; illustrated
  by Richard & Frances Hook.
        p.   cm.
    Rev. ed. of: The book for children. c 1985.
    Summary: Introduces over 300 illustrated Bible stories, ranging
  from Genesis to Revelation.
    ISBN 0-8423-4142-0
    1. Bible stories, English.   [1. Bible stories.]   I. Hook,
  Richard, ill.   II. Hook, Frances, ill.   III. Taylor, Kenneth
  Nathaniel. Book for children.   IV. Title.
  BS551.2.T3757   1992
  220.9′505—dc20   92-20265

Printed in the United States of America

98 97 96 95 94 93 92
 8   7   6   5   4   3   2   1

God's Word Is for You

Some kids think the Bible is just for adults or for people who have been trained in how to read it. That's silly. God's Word is for all people, of all ages—and that means you!

When you read these stories and other passages in the Bible, often you will think that God is speaking right to you (and he is!). And you will never outgrow the Bible. As you get older, you will continue to discover new and exciting lessons from God.

Well what are you waiting for? Look up the story you want to read and get to it! If you have any questions, ask a parent or your minister.

READ

God made you and knows you completely. He also made the world and knows what it takes to make everything work well. And he knows how to solve all your problems and answer all your questions. So wouldn't it make sense to see what God has to say? You bet it would! That means reading the Bible.

I love reading these stories because they're fun, exciting, and interesting. But even better than that, they answer my questions and teach me great lessons about life.

THINK

After you read a Bible story, take time to think about what God is telling you. I find it hard to read a whole book straight through. So I read one story and then think about it. Later, or the next day, I'll read another story. That way I get to imagine myself in the story, the book lasts longer, and I learn more.

Whatever your reading style, here's a tip: look deeper than the story—look for the lesson. In other words, think about what God could be telling you through what you just read.

DO

The next step is to obey God. This means doing what he wants you to do; it means putting into practice the lesson you learned from the Bible story. When you read, ask, What does God want me to do? How does he want me to act? God's lesson for you may involve relationships, habits, attitudes, words—he's interested in every area of your life.

Don't just read the Bible stories, do something about what you learn in them.

Here's how to find your favorite Bible stories

• You will find the number of each story on the left, followed by a title that tells you what the story is about.

    9 God Keeps His Promise

• Just to the right of the title is another number. That number tells you the page where the story begins.

15 A Stairway That Reached to Heaven 57

If you turn to page 57, you will find story number 15 that tells about Jacob's amazing dream of a stairway from earth to heaven.

• To help you find these stories in your own Bible, the Scripture passage is in parentheses just under the title.

133 The King Who Ate Grass 384
(DANIEL 4)

This tells you that the story about the king eating grass can be found in the Bible in the book of Daniel, chapter 4.

• At the beginning of every story, there is a splash of color, like this:

The blocks of color are there to help you find where the stories begin.

• As you turn the pages, you will discover a lot of great drawings. Those illustrations will help you see the story better in your mind.

• Then, at the back of the book, you will find an index of important people and where you can read about them. For example, if you wanted to learn about AARON, the brother of Moses, you can turn to story 29.

I've listed the stories and where they can be found. But now I've gotta go help Nick out of another sticky situation. I don't know what he'd do without me.

Happy reading!

Check out our ancient ancestors!

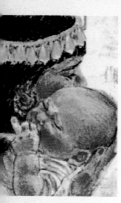

And you think you have problems!

What would you do if your pet talked back?

This guy had muscles in places that most people don't have places!

I get tired just thinking about all the running David had to do!

A boy king—now that's what I call cool!

I love a party!

Here's a fast-food feast!

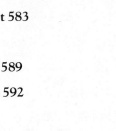

Talk about a great escape!

Oooh—this message hits home!

GOD MAKES A BEAUTIFUL WORLD

GENESIS 1, 2

LONG, LONG AGO, long before anyone can remember, God made the world. But it didn't look the way it does now, for there were no people, animals, birds, trees, bushes, or flowers; everything was lonely and dark.

Then God made the light. He said, "Let there be light," and light came. God was pleased with it. He gave the light a name, calling it Day. And when the day was gone and the darkness came again, he called that darkness Night. God did these things on the first day of creation.

Then God made the sky above the earth; and he gave the sky a name, too, calling it Heaven. God did this on the second day of creation.

Now God said that the waters covering the earth should become oceans and lakes, and the dry land should appear. Then he made the grass grow, and the bushes and trees. All this was on the third day of creation.

On the fourth day God let the sun shine in the daytime, and the moon and stars at night.

On the fifth day he made great sea monsters and all the fish. And he made the birds—some, like the ducks and geese, to fly over the water and swim on it and live near it; and others, like eagles, robins, pigeons, and wrens, to live in the woods and fields.

On the sixth day of creation God made the animals, those that are wild and live out in the forests, such as

15

elephants, lions, tigers, and bears; and those that are tame and useful, such as rabbits, horses, cows, and sheep. And he made the little insects, such as the ants that crawl around on the ground and the little bees.

Then God made a man and named him Adam.

This is how God made him. He took some dust from the ground and formed it into a man's body, and breathed into it, and the man began to breathe and became alive and walked around. And the Lord God planted a beautiful garden as a home for the man he had made, calling it the Garden of Eden; in it God planted lovely trees full of delicious fruit for the man to eat.

God told Adam he could eat any fruit in the garden except the fruit from one tree called the Tree of the Knowledge of Good and Evil. If he took even one bite from that tree's fruit, God said, Adam would begin to die.

Adam was the only person in all the world and he was lonely. God decided it wasn't good for him to be alone, so he made another person to be with Adam and to help him. This is how he did it: he put Adam to sleep; and while he was sleeping, God took one of Adam's ribs and made a woman from it. Then God brought the woman to Adam, and she became his wife. Her name was Eve.

Then God looked at all he had made in those six days, and he was very pleased. So the earth and skies and all the plants and animals were finished in six days of creation.

On the seventh day, God rested; so it was a quiet and different day from all the others, a holy day of rest.

The first man and woman, Adam and Eve,
lived in the Garden of Eden.

17

THE WORLD'S SADDEST DAY

GENESIS 3

THERE WAS someone else in the Garden of Eden besides Adam and Eve and God. Satan was there, in the shape of a serpent. Satan is the wicked spirit who tempts us to sin. So now the serpent came to Eve and told her to do something that was wrong. He asked her, "Did God tell you not to eat the fruit of any of the trees in the garden?"

"We can eat any of it except from one tree," she replied. "We can't eat the fruit of the Tree of the Knowledge of Good and Evil, for if we eat it, we will begin to die."

"That's not true!" Satan told her. "It won't hurt you at all! God is just being mean to tell you that! Really it's good and will make you wise!"

Eve should have gone away and not listened to Satan, but she didn't. Instead, she went over and looked at the tree. It was beautiful! And the fruit looked so good! When she remembered that Satan had said it would make her wise, she took some of the fruit and ate it and gave some to her husband, Adam; and he ate it too.

After they had eaten it they heard a voice calling to them. It was God's voice. But they didn't come; instead, they hid among the trees, for now they were afraid of God. God called to them again.

"Where are you, Adam? Where are you?"

"I'm hiding," Adam finally replied, "for I'm afraid of you."

"Have you eaten the fruit I told you not to?" God asked.

Then Adam began to make excuses and blamed Eve. He said, "The woman you gave me, she gave me some of the fruit and I ate it."

God asked Eve, "What is this you have done?"

"Satan fooled me," she said, "and so I ate some of it."

God was very angry with Adam and Eve and with the serpent. He said that the serpent would be punished by having to crawl on the ground in the dust all its life. He told the woman that when her children were being born she would have sickness and pain. And God sent Adam and Eve out of the beautiful garden and wouldn't let them live there any longer; for if they stayed they might eat fruit from the Tree of Life and live forever. So he sent an angel with a sword made of fire to stop them from ever going back into the garden again.

God told Adam that because he had listened to his wife and eaten the fruit, when the Lord had told him not to, the ground would no longer grow lush crops for him as it had in the Garden of Eden; instead, it would grow thorns and thistles. As long as Adam lived, he would have to work hard to get enough food to eat; and when he died, his body would become dust again, like the dust he was made from.

But even though they had sinned, God made a way for Adam and Eve to be saved from punishment after they died. He promised to send a Savior who would be punished for their sins so that they wouldn't have to be punished. God said that if people would ask God to forgive them and would trust the Savior to save them, and would try to obey God and be good, God would take them to heaven when they died.

When the Savior came, he died for Adam and Eve's sins, and for their children's sins too, and also for ours. We are all sinners. But God forgives us if we ask him to, because Jesus died to take away our sins.

THE FIRST FAMILY FIGHT
GENESIS 4, 5

AFTER ADAM AND EVE were sent out of the Garden of Eden, God gave them two sons. The older one was named Cain; the younger one, Abel. When they grew to be young men, Cain became a farmer while Abel was a shepherd with a flock of sheep. They both had wicked hearts like their parents, and they often sinned. But Abel was sorry about his sins and believed the promise God had made to send a Savior.

One day Abel brought a lamb from his flock and offered it as a gift to God by killing it and burning it on the altar. The altar was a pile of stones which was flat on top. He built a fire on the altar and put the dead lamb in the fire to burn up until only ashes and bones were left. This was called a sacrifice. By giving God his lamb, Abel showed God that he loved him.

God was pleased that Abel worshiped him in this way, for the lamb was in many ways like the Savior God would one day send to die for people's sins. The Savior would be gentle and patient and innocent like the lamb, and would be killed as a sacrifice just as the lamb was.

But Abel's brother Cain did not turn from his sins or believe God's promise to send a Savior; and when he brought his offering it was not a lamb, which was what God wanted, but some things from his garden. So God was not pleased with Cain or his offering.

Adam's first two sons
were Cain and Abel.
Cain was angry
because Abel obeyed God
and he did not.
Cain killed Abel.
God severely punished
him for doing this.

*Here is a picture
of the oldest man
who ever lived.
His name is Methuselah.
He was 969 years old
when he died.*

When Cain realized that God wanted a lamb as a sacrifice, and had accepted Abel's sacrifice but not his, he was angry with God. Yet God spoke kindly to him and asked why he was angry. If Cain would bring a lamb, God told him, then God would accept his gift and be pleased with him.

Cain was angry with God but took his anger out on Abel. One day when they were in the field together, Cain killed Abel, and the ground was wet with his blood.

Then God called to Cain, "Where is your brother Abel?"

"How should I know?" Cain answered. "Am I supposed to look after my brother?"

But God had seen what Cain did, and now declared that all the rest of his life Cain must wander from place to place as his punishment for killing Abel—always afraid, and with no home to stay in. And when Cain planted a garden, it wouldn't grow well, so Cain would hardly have enough to eat.

Adam lived for many years after this. Finally, when he was 930 years old, he died, and his body became dust again as God had said it would, because he ate the forbidden fruit in the Garden of Eden. Nine hundred and thirty years is a very long time for a man to live, but in those days God allowed people to live much longer than now.

During those years Adam and Eve had many children, and the children grew up and had children, and then those children grew up and had children, until there were many, many people in the world. One of them was Enoch. The Bible tells us that Enoch walked with God. This means that he loved God and thought about God all the time. It was as though he and God were walking along like friends, with Enoch listening to what God was saying and trying to please him and obey everything he said.

When Enoch was 365 years old, God did a wonderful

thing for him: he took him up to heaven while he was still alive! So Enoch didn't die like other men; God just took him away to live with him.

Enoch had a son named Methuselah who lived to be 969 years old. The Bible doesn't mention anyone else who lived to be older than that, so Methuselah is called the oldest man who ever lived.

STORY 4

NOAH AND THE GREAT FLOOD
GENESIS 6, 7, 8

AS THE YEARS went by, the world became more and more wicked. People did all kinds of bad things. They didn't want to please God and didn't even try to obey him. So God was angry with them and said he would punish them by sending a flood to cover the earth with deep water, drowning them all.

But there was one good man whose name was Noah. God loved Noah and told him about the flood he was going to send, so that Noah could get ready for it.

God told Noah to build a huge boat as high as a three-story house, filled with many large rooms, and having a long window and a big door in the side. He said that when the boat was finished, Noah and his sons and their wives would live in it and float away safely when the flood came.

God also told him to bring into the boat a father and mother animal of every kind there was, and birds and even insects, so that when the flood came, some of each kind would still be alive; for everything outside the boat would be drowned.

So Noah began to build the boat. It took him a long, long time, more than a hundred years; but as you know, at that time men lived much longer than they do now.

Noah did something else, too, besides building the boat—he was a preacher, so he talked to the people about God and warned them about the flood that was going to come because of their sins. But the people didn't believe him and they weren't sorry for their sins.

When the boat was finished, God told Noah to bring all his family and the birds and animals into the boat, for in seven days the rain would begin and the flood would come, and everyone outside the boat would be drowned.

So Noah brought his wife and his three sons and their wives into the boat. And he brought in at least two of each kind of animal and bird. These were in pairs, a father and a mother of each kind. Two of some kinds came and seven of other kinds.

When all were safely inside, God closed the door and locked it.

Seven days later it began to rain; in fact, it poured. It rained without stopping for forty days and forty nights. The rain came down as if it was being poured from great windows in the sky. The creeks, the rivers, and the great oceans all began to rise, and water covered the land. After a while there was so much water all around the boat that it was lifted off the ground. Higher and higher the water rose, with the boat floating on it.

But what about those people who had refused to obey God and wouldn't listen to Noah's warning? They had

25

laughed at Noah for saying there would be a flood; they said Noah was only trying to scare them. But now, too late, they saw that all he had told them was true. Oh, if they could only get into the boat! But now it was too late.

So all the people in the world were drowned except those in the boat. And every animal and bird and insect, except those in the boat, died in the flood, for all the earth was covered with the water. There was no land to be seen anywhere; only the boat could be seen, floating alone upon the water.

God did not forget Noah. All through that dreadful storm he took care of him and of all those who were with him. God kept the boat safe. Finally the rain stopped and the water began to go down again.

After Noah had been in the boat for 150 days, almost half a year, the water had gone down so much that the boat rested on the top of a mountain called Ararat, but Noah and his family stayed inside, for God wasn't ready to let them out yet. Two months later the flood had gone down even more, so that the tops of other mountains could be seen peeping above the water.

When the ground finally dried enough, God told Noah and his wife and his sons and their wives to come out of the boat and to let out all the animals and birds. At last they could walk around outside.

Then Noah built an altar, as Abel had done, and sacrificed animals and birds upon it to the Lord. This was his way of thanking God for saving him and his family from

At God's command, Noah brought animals of every kind to live in the huge boat he built. Noah, his family, and the animals were saved from the flood.

26

the flood, though all the other people in the world had drowned.

God promised that he would never send another flood to drown all the people. As proof, he gave Noah a sign—a beautiful rainbow in the sky where Noah could often see it when it rained; and whenever he saw it, he would remember God's promise not to send a flood like that again.

STORY 5

A HUGE TOWER
GENESIS 11

SOON AFTER the flood ended, Noah became a grandfather, for God gave children to Noah's sons and their wives. These grandchildren grew up and had children too, until after a while the world was full of people again.

Don't you suppose these people would be very careful not to make God angry? They knew about the terrible flood and what had happened to all the people before. But no, they didn't care, and kept on doing all sorts of bad things. Perhaps they weren't afraid of God, because of the rainbow and God's promise not to send another flood. But there were many other ways for God to punish them. He could send sickness or war or not enough food, or he might send down fire from heaven to burn them up. But they seemed to forget this; their hearts were bad so they acted just like the people before the flood, and constantly sinned against God.

God wasn't happy about this tower because the people building it were trying to prove that they could get along without God.

There was only one language in the world at that time. Today there are hundreds of languages, like English, Spanish, French, and German. But in those days the people all talked alike, so everyone in all the world could understand everyone else!

One day the people said to each other, "Let's build a high tower, as high as heaven!"

So they began to build it. We are not told why they wanted this tower, but probably it was because they were proud and wanted everyone to see how great they were to build such a high tower. But it is sinful to be proud, and God knew what they were thinking.

One day the Lord came down from heaven to see the tower, and he was not happy about it. He decided to stop the people from building it. So he made them begin to speak in different languages! Now they couldn't understand each other. One man would ask another for a hammer, but the other man couldn't understand him! This made them angry with each other, and soon they stopped working and went home.

They didn't even want to live near each other any more, so all those speaking the same language lived together, and moved away from those who didn't speak their language. That is why different languages are spoken in different parts of the world today.

So the tower, which was called the Tower of Babel, was never finished. The word "Babel" means "mixed up." When people began to talk in different languages and couldn't understand each other any more, they got all mixed up. That is why the tower was called the Tower of Babel.

GOD'S FRIEND ABRAM

GENESIS 11, 12, 13

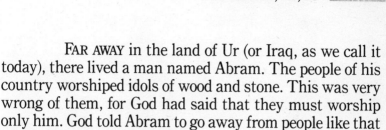

FAR AWAY in the land of Ur (or Iraq, as we call it today), there lived a man named Abram. The people of his country worshiped idols of wood and stone. This was very wrong of them, for God had said that they must worship only him. God told Abram to go away from people like that and to move to another country.

So Abram left his home and relatives and friends and traveled far away to a distant land with his wife Sarai, his nephew Lot, and his servants. He had never been in that land before, but he believed God would take care of him. Abram was seventy-five years old at that time.

It was a long, hard journey. They had to cross wide rivers and a desert where the country was lonely and wild. Yet God took care of them and brought them safely to the promised land. It was called the land of Canaan. Today we call it Israel.

"I will give all this land to you—this whole country," God told him. "It will belong to you and to your children forever."

Then Abram built an altar and worshiped God by killing an animal and burning it on the altar.

Other people were living there in the land who might have harmed him, but God made sure that they didn't. It was a time of famine when Abram arrived. Famine means that the grass and the grain didn't grow well, so the people had little to eat.

One day God told Abram
to move far away to another country.
He took his family, his servants,
his sheep, and his goats
and started out.

Now Abram went away for a while to still another country called Egypt, and waited until there was more food for them in Israel. Then he and Lot and their families returned to Israel again, and Abram sacrificed to the Lord again by killing a lamb and burning it on the altar.

Soon Abram became very rich and owned many, many cows, goats, and sheep. Lot had many of them too.

But the men who took care of Lot's animals quarrelled with the men who took care of Abram's animals. When Abram heard about this, he talked to Lot about it. Do you think Abram said, "This is my land, Lot, and you get out—God has given it to me, and you must move away somewhere else"? No, Abram was very nice to Lot and said, "Let's not have any fighting and quarrelling between us."

Then Abram and Lot divided the land. Abram gave Lot first choice, even though he didn't need to—it was his land, for God had given it to him.

Lot chose the very best part of the country, the valley of the river Jordan. One of the cities there was named Sodom. The men of Sodom were very bad, but Lot went to live among them anyway. He was not a bad man himself, for he worshiped God, but he went to live among these wicked men because he thought he would have better pasture for his cattle in their country and that he soon would become rich. He shouldn't have done this, and we will soon see how much trouble it caused.

After Lot had moved away to his new home, the Lord said to Abram, "I will give you all of the good land Lot chose. Lot is living there now, but some day it will all be yours!"

God also said he would give Abram so many children and grandchildren and great-grandchildren that they would become a great nation. That promise has come true and today we call Abram's people the Israelis, or Jews.

Abram could have kept all the land for himself,
but he offered to divide it with his nephew, Lot.
And he let Lot take
first choice.

ABRAM GETS A NEW NAME
GENESIS 13–17

ONE DAY GOD told Abram, "I am your friend." So Abram reminded his great friend that he wanted a son, for he had no children. God promised to give him one.

Then he took Abram out under the night skies. He told him to look up at the stars and asked him whether he could count them. Abram couldn't do it because there were so many. Then God told him, "You will not only have a son, but many, many grandchildren and great-grandchildren. Their families will be like those stars up there—too many to count!"

But God also told Abram that these people of his would be taken away to another country as slaves and be treated cruelly for many years. "But afterwards," God said, "I will punish those who hurt them, and I will bring them back to the land of Israel, and they will be very rich."

God also said that Abram would live to be an old, old man, and would die happy.

Abram's wife, Sarai, owned a slave girl named Hagar. She was Abram's other wife. But Sarai was angry with her and punished her. Then Hagar ran away into the lonely wilderness where no one lived.

The angel of the Lord found her beside a spring and asked her where she had come from and where she was going. She answered that she had run away from Sarai. Then the angel told her to go back to Sarai again and to obey her.

The angel also said that Hagar would have a son whose name would be Ishmael and that he would be a fighter—he wouldn't like other people, and they wouldn't like him! So Hagar went back to Sarai, and afterwards God gave her the son he had promised, and she named him Ishmael.

When Abram was ninety-nine years old, God talked with him again. (Abram lay face downward on the ground while God talked to him.)

God said again that he would give Abram many, many grandchildren and great-grandchildren—a whole country full of them—and some of them would be kings. God now made a promise to Abram and his children: "I will be your God," he said, "and you will be my people."

Then God promised again to give the land of Israel to the Jews.

Now God gave Abram a new name! "Your name isn't Abram any more!" God said. "From now on it is Abraham!" (Abraham means "the father of a whole country.")

And he gave Sarai a new name too. Her name became Sarah (which means "princess"). So the Lord changed both their names, and promised again to give him a son, whose name would be Isaac.

GOD'S VISIT TO ABRAHAM
GENESIS 18, 19

ONE HOT DAY as Abraham was sitting at the entrance of his tent, he looked up to see three men coming towards him.

He ran to meet them and threw himself down in front of them with his face to the ground, for that is the way strangers were welcomed in that land. Abraham invited the men to rest in the shade of a tree while he brought some water to soothe their tired feet. In those days people either went barefoot or wore sandals, so their feet became very dusty. One of the things a friendly man did for his guests was to give them water to wash their feet after a long, hot walk.

Abraham ran to the tent and told Sarah, "Quick, bake some bread." Next he ran out to where the cows were and selected a fat calf to be killed and cooked.

When the meat was ready he set it before the men, with some butter and bread and milk, and they had a picnic beneath the tree while Abraham stood nearby to serve them.

After they had finished eating they started off towards the city of Sodom, and Abraham walked along beside them.

Now I must tell you that these three men were really not men at all. Two of them were angels, we believe, and the other one was God.

Could God look and talk like a man? Yes, several times

in the Bible he appeared in the form of a man and talked with someone.

God told Abraham that he had decided to burn up the cities of Sodom and Gomorrah. Why was he going to do this? It was because the people who lived there were so bad. Abraham was very sad when he heard about this, for Sodom was the city where his nephew Lot lived.

That evening Lot was out by the city gate; for in that country the cities had walls around them to keep out enemies, and there were gates in the walls to go in and out.

As Lot was sitting there, suddenly the two angels stood before him. But Lot didn't know they were angels because they looked just like men. They were the same angels who had come with God to Abraham's tent. Lot stood up to meet them and invited them to come to his house to spend the night.

"No," they replied, "we'll just camp out here."

But Lot was afraid of what the bad people of the city might do to them, so he begged them to go home with him. Finally they agreed.

After supper the angels asked him whether he had any other sons or daughters in the city besides those who were with him at home.

"Go and warn them to leave Sodom at once," they told him, "for the Lord is going to destroy this city."

Lot ran quickly to the homes of his married daughters and said to his sons-in-law, "Quick, get your families out of the city, for the Lord is going to destroy it."

But they didn't believe him, and Lot had to come back home without them.

Lot's family was escaping the destruction of Sodom and Gomorrah. The angel told them not to look back, but Lot's wife disobeyed. She became a statue of salt.

Early the next morning, while it was still dark, the angels said to him, "Leave the city at once, or you will be burned up along with all the other people living here. Take your wife and your two girls and get out right now. *Hurry!*

"Don't look behind you," they said. "Hurry to the mountains where the fire won't kill you."

But as they were going, Lot's wife looked back toward Sodom, even though the angels had told her not to. She died right there and became a statue of salt.

Then the Lord rained down fire from heaven on Sodom and Gomorrah, completely destroying both cities. All the people in them died, and all the grass and plants and trees were destroyed.

God saved Lot and his two daughters, but Lot lost everything, including all the nice things he took to Sodom when he and Abraham left each other.

STORY 9

GOD KEEPS HIS PROMISE
GENESIS 20, 21

ABRAHAM MOVED AGAIN, this time to a place named Gerar, in what is now the land of Israel. The king of Gerar gave Abraham a present of sheep, oxen, and slaves, and told him he could live anywhere he wanted to in ·his country.

Abraham was the very first Jew.
He loved God very much. In the
picture you can see him with
his wife Sarah and his
son Isaac.

Hagar and her son Ishmael
were sent away from home
into the desert.
Ishmael was dying from thirst.
But God provided water for him
and he got well again.

At this time God gave Abraham and Sarah a little baby son, just as he had promised them. Abraham named him Isaac, for that is the name God had told him to give him.

Abraham was 100 years old when Isaac was born. What a happy day it was!

The baby grew and was soon old enough to play with other children. So his father gave him a nice party. But during the party another boy, whose name was Ishmael, made fun of Isaac. Ishmael was the son of Abraham's other wife, Hagar, who was a slave girl. When Isaac's mother saw the slave girl's son mocking her son, she was very angry.

Sarah told Abraham to get rid of Ishmael and his mother, because she couldn't stand the sight of them. Abraham didn't want to send them away, but God told him to do as Sarah demanded. So Abraham got up early in the morning, gave some bread and a bottle of water to Ishmael and his mother, and sent them away.

They walked a long way into the wild country. Soon all the water in the bottle was gone. Ishmael became so weak with thirst that his mother thought he was going to die. She laid him under a bush in the shade and went a little farther on and sat down and cried, for she didn't want to see him die.

But God heard her, and the angel of God called to her out of heaven, "What's the trouble, Hagar?"

The angel told her not to be afraid and showed her where there was a well! So Ishmael had a drink and felt all right again.

God was kind to Ishmael and took care of him. Growing up in the country, far away from any city or town, he learned to shoot birds and animals with a bow and arrow.

Meanwhile Abraham was still living at Gerar. When the

king of Gerar realized that God was Abraham's friend, he asked Abraham to be his friend too.

Abraham promised to be friends, but he told the king about a problem. Abraham's servants had dug a well. But then some of the king's servants said it was theirs, and they wouldn't let Abraham use it! It was hard work to dig a well in the rocky ground of that country, so Abraham didn't want to have to dig another one.

The king said he didn't know his servants had done this and he was sorry about it. Then Abraham took seven lambs from his flock and gave them to the king. The king asked him why he was giving these lambs to him. Abraham replied that they were a present to remind the king that Abraham had dug that well and that it belonged to Abraham.

So the king and Abraham made an agreement always to be friends. Abraham called the name of the place Beersheba, which means "the well of promise," because it was there that he and the king promised to be friends.

STORY 10

GOD GIVES ABRAHAM A TEST

GENESIS 22, 23, 24

DO YOU REMEMBER that Abel sacrificed a lamb to God? Do you remember how pleased God was with him for doing this?

Well, one day God said to Abraham, "Abraham, take

your son Isaac whom you love so much, and go to the land of Moriah and burn him as a sacrifice upon one of the mountains I will point out to you!"

How could Abraham ever do this? How could he kill his own dear son? But God told him to do it; Abraham heard him speak. He knew that he must do whatever God said.

So Abraham got up early in the morning and saddled his donkey. He took two young men with him, some wood to lay on the altar, and Isaac, his son.

They started towards the mountain God had told him about. They traveled all that day and the next day and the next, before Abraham finally saw the mountain far ahead of them. Then he told the young men to stop and wait. He and Isaac would go to the mountain and worship, he told them, and then would come back to them.

Why do you think Abraham said that both of them would come back? I think it was because Abraham believed God would bring Isaac back to life.

Isaac carried the wood, and Abraham took some fire to light the wood (since they had no matches in those days). The two went on together.

Isaac did not know what God had told his father to do, nor why his father was taking him to the mountain. He knew they were going to offer a burnt offering, but he didn't know he was going to be burned up on the altar as a sacrifice. So, as they walked along together, he said to his father, "Father, we have the fire and the wood, but where is the lamb for a burnt offering?"

Abraham answered, "My son, God will find himself a lamb for the burnt offering."

When they came to the place God had sent them to, Abraham built an altar and laid wood on it. Then he tied Isaac and laid him on the wood, and Abraham lifted the knife to kill his son.

But at that instant the angel of God shouted to him from heaven. "Abraham! Abraham! Stop!"

Then the angel told him not to hurt Isaac. Abraham had proved that he feared God. He had been willing to obey God's command even if he had to sacrifice his and Sarah's only son.

Then Abraham noticed a ram caught in the bushes by its horns. God had sent it there to be used as a burnt offering instead of Isaac. Abraham killed it and burned it on the altar.

God was greatly pleased with Abraham for being willing to obey. Then the angel of God spoke to him from heaven again and told him that God would bless him by giving him many, many grandchildren and great-grandchildren. His family would some day be so large, the angel said, that no one could even count them! And they would help all the other people in the world.

(The angel said this about helping other people everywhere, because the Savior of the world was going to be born into Abraham's family.)

Then Abraham and Isaac came back to the young men who were waiting for them, and they all returned home.

Sarah, Isaac's mother, died when she was 127 years old. Abraham and Isaac cried a lot because she was dead.

Isaac became a full-grown man and wanted to get married. But his father Abraham didn't want him to marry any of the girls in that country, because they all worshiped idols instead of worshiping God. He wanted Isaac to marry a girl from the country where his relatives lived, where the people obeyed God and didn't worship idols.

But that country was far away. So Abraham called his oldest servant, the one who was in charge of all his business, and asked him to go to that distant land where his relatives lived and to bring back a girl for Isaac to marry.

So the servant loaded ten of Abraham's camels with beautiful presents and started off. After many, many days of hard travel he finally arrived at the town where Abraham's relatives lived. He made the camels kneel down by a well that was just outside the city.

A WIFE FOR ISAAC
GENESIS 24

IT WAS EVENING when Abraham's servant arrived at the town, and the girls were all coming out to draw water from the well. As the servant watched them coming, he asked God to help him to find the right one to be Isaac's wife.

How could he ever know? This is what he decided to do. He would ask one of the girls to give him some water from her pitcher. If she answered him with a smile and said, "Yes, and I will water your camels too," then she would be the one God had chosen to be Isaac's wife. But if she grumbled and wouldn't give him the water, then she wouldn't be the right one.

While he was still praying, a beautiful girl named Rebekah came, carrying her pitcher on her shoulder; she went down to the well and filled it with water.

The servant ran over to her and said, "Please give me a drink from your pitcher."

"Certainly, sir," she replied, "and I'll water your camels too!"

She set down her pitcher from her shoulder and gave the servant a drink, then ran back to the well and began drawing water for his camels!

After the camels had finished drinking, the man gave Rebekah a gold earring and two gold bracelets. He asked her whose daughter she was and whether there was room at her father's house for him and his men to spend the night. Rebekah told him she was the daughter of Bethuel and that there was plenty of room.

When the servant heard her say she was Bethuel's daughter, he realized that she was a cousin of Isaac's, for Abraham was Bethuel's uncle. He was glad, so he bowed his head and worshiped the Lord, thanking God for helping him to find the right girl so quickly.

Rebekah ran home to tell her mother that the men were coming. When her brother Laban heard about it and saw the earring and the bracelets, he ran to the well to find the man and to bring him home. After Laban had helped him unload the camels and feed them, it was time for supper, so Laban took Abraham's servant in to meet the family.

But the servant said he couldn't eat until he had told them why he had come to their country. He said that he was Abraham's servant and that the Lord had blessed Abraham and made him very rich. He had silver and gold, flocks and herds, camels and donkeys; God had also given him a son, Isaac, who needed a wife.

He told how he had come to the well that day and had prayed that God would help him to find the right girl to be Isaac's wife. He had prayed that if she was the right one she would answer pleasantly when he asked for water. He

Abraham sent his servant to find a wife for Isaac. God helped him find the right one. Her name was Rebekah.

told them that while he was still praying, Rebekah had arrived. When he had asked her for a drink, she had said, "Of course, and I'll water your camels too!"

Then the servant asked them whether or not they would let Rebekah go with him to marry Isaac. They said yes; since it was the Lord who had brought him to them, Rebekah could go.

When the servant heard this he was very happy and worshiped the Lord. He brought out other beautiful presents—jewels of silver and gold, and beautiful clothing—and gave them to Rebekah. And he gave her mother and her brother presents too.

At last he and his men were ready to eat, and afterwards they stayed at Laban's house all night.

STORY 12

REBEKAH SAYS YES
GENESIS 24

IN THE MORNING, Abraham's servant wanted to take Rebekah and leave at once to return to Abraham.

But her mother and brother said, "Let her stay with us a few days at least, and then she may go."

The man begged them not to delay him, for he felt that he should hurry back to his master again.

They said, "We'll call Rebekah and ask her if she is willing to go so soon."

She replied, "Yes, I'll go now."

So they sent her to Isaac and never saw her again, for Isaac's home was hundreds of miles away.

After many long, hot, weary days of camel travel, they came at last to Canaan just as the sun was going down. Isaac had gone out into the field for a walk, to be alone with his thoughts. Perhaps he wondered whether the servant would soon be back and whether God had helped him to find a girl to be his wife. What would she be like?

Just then he looked up, and the camels were coming!

When Rebekah saw Isaac walking in the field, she asked the servant who it was, coming to meet them. The servant told her it was Isaac. Then she took a veil and covered her face with it. Isaac brought her into the tent that had been his mother's before she died. And Rebekah became his wife, and he loved her.

Abraham gave all that he had to Isaac and died at the age of 175. He was buried in the cave he had bought from Ephron, where he had buried Sarah.

STORY 13

ESAU'S TERRIBLE MISTAKE
GENESIS 25

AFTER ISAAC AND REBEKAH were married, God gave them twin sons! The babies' names were Esau and Jacob. Esau was born first, and Jacob was born a few minutes later. So Esau was the older.

In those days the oldest son in every family had what was called the birthright. This meant he got more of the money and property when his father died. In fact, he got twice as much as the other children.

In Isaac's family, Esau was born first and had the birthright.

When Esau and Jacob grew up to be men, Esau was a hunter; he went out into the fields and woods and killed deer and brought the meat home to his father, Isaac. How his father loved that meat!

Jacob stayed at home and helped to care for his father's flocks and goats.

One day Jacob was at home cooking some especially good food when Esau came in from his hunting. Esau was very tired and hungry and asked Jacob to give him the food. Jacob said he would if Esau would give him his birthright! Esau didn't care about it, so he told Jacob he could have it; then Jacob gave him some food.

It was wrong for Esau to sell his birthright. God had given it to him, and he should not have sold it. It was wrong, too, for Jacob to take it.

STORY 14

JACOB LIES TO HIS FATHER
GENESIS 27, 28

ISAAC WAS getting very old and couldn't see; he called his oldest son, Esau, and told him to take his bow and go out into the field and get a deer. "Cook the meat just the way I like it best; then I will bless you."

Esau made a terrible mistake.
He sold his birthright to Jacob
for a bowl of food.

He meant that he would ask God to be kind to Esau and give him many good things. So Esau went out into the field to hunt the deer for his father.

Rebekah heard what Isaac said, and she wasn't happy about it. She didn't want Esau to get the special blessing from Isaac, even though he was her oldest son; she wanted the best for Jacob.

When Esau had gone to hunt for deer, Rebekah told Jacob to kill two lambs from their flock of sheep and bring them to her. She cooked them so the meat tasted just like the deer meat Jacob's father loved so much. Then she got some of Esau's clothes for Jacob to put on and she put goat skins on the back of his hands and neck. She told him to take the food to his blind father and to say that he was Esau.

So Jacob took the food to his father. His father was surprised that Esau was back so soon. Because he was blind, he asked if it really was Esau. Jacob said yes, and that he had brought the deer meat his father had asked for.

His father put his hands on Jacob's hairy neck—remember, Jacob's mother had put a goat skin around his neck!—and smelled his clothes and was convinced that it was really Esau, even though his voice sounded more like Jacob's. And of course, it was Jacob, and not Esau at all. Jacob had fooled his father. So his father ate the food and blessed Jacob.

As soon as Isaac had finished blessing Jacob, and Jacob had left the room, Esau came in from his hunting, with the deer meat he had cooked.

Isaac asked him, "Who are you?"

Esau answered, "I am Esau, and I have the meat you told me to get for you."

Isaac began to tremble, "Who was it, then," he asked, "who was just here? I gave him your blessing!"

Isaac knew now that it was Jacob who had come in first,

*Jacob worked for Laban
for many years
so that he could marry
Laban's beautiful daughter
Rachel.*

and he told Esau that his brother had been there before him and had stolen his blessing.

Esau cried and begged his father to bless him too. So Isaac did, but he had already promised the best things to Jacob, and now he couldn't take them away from him.

Esau hated Jacob for what he had done, and said to himself, "My father will soon die and then I will kill Jacob."

Esau was not a good man; he did not love God. When a good man has done something wrong, he is sorry afterwards and asks God to forgive him and tries not to do it again. But when a bad man has been wicked, he does not repent and ask to be forgiven; he goes on and does the same thing again. Jacob did a wicked thing in lying to his father, but afterwards he became a good man who loved and served God as long as he lived, and God forgave him for his sin. But Esau was not willing to forgive Jacob; instead, he said he would kill him after his father died.

When Rebekah heard what Esau was saying, she sent for Jacob and told him to leave home and to go away to the country where she used to live, to the home of her brother Laban, so that Esau could not hurt him. But how could she get Isaac to agree? This is the way she did it.

She reminded Isaac that the girls of Canaan didn't love God, but prayed to idols. She reminded him that Esau had married two of these girls; she said she would rather die than see Jacob marry a girl who didn't love God.

Isaac agreed that Jacob must not marry a Canaanite girl. He called Jacob to him, blessed him again, and told him not to marry a girl of Canaan, but to marry one of his mother's relatives who lived far away in another country.

Then Isaac sent Jacob away to that far-off land where his Uncle Laban lived, to see if he could find a girl there who would marry him. It was the same land from which Isaac's mother had come with Abraham's servant.

A STAIRWAY THAT REACHED TO HEAVEN

GENESIS 28–31

AS JACOB TRAVELED, he had a dream one night. He thought he saw some stairs in front of him reaching to heaven, and angels were going up and down them. God stood at the top of the stairs and told Jacob about the country he was going to give him and his children. And God said he would be with Jacob and take care of him wherever he went and would bring him safely home again.

Jacob woke up, and was afraid because God had been there and had spoken to him. So, very early the next morning, he got up and worshiped the Lord. He called the place Bethel, which means "the house of God."

Jacob kept traveling a long, long time until he came to Haran, where Laban lived. He saw a well there in the field, three flocks of sheep lying around it, and the shepherds with their flocks. A large rock was rolled over the mouth of the well to cover it; when all the flocks arrived each evening, the shepherds would roll away the stone and get water for the sheep. Afterwards the stone would be rolled back over the mouth of the well again.

Jacob asked the shepherds where they lived, and they told him at Haran.

"Do you know Laban?" he asked them.

"Yes," they said, "we surely do."

Jacob asked if he was well.

"Yes, he is," they replied, "and look, here comes his daughter Rachel with his sheep."

Jacob went over to the well and kissed Rachel, then rolled away the stone and watered her sheep for her. He explained to her that he was her cousin, her Aunt Rebekah's son, and she ran and told her father.

When Laban heard that his nephew had arrived, he ran out to meet him. He gave him a warm welcome and brought him home. After Jacob had been there about a month, Laban asked him to stay and work for him.

By this time Jacob was very much in love with Rachel, and he told Laban he would work for him for seven years if he could marry Rachel afterwards.

Laban was delighted. So Jacob worked for him for the next seven years. Even though it was a long time, the years went by so fast they seemed like only a few days to Jacob because he loved Rachel so much.

But when the time was up, Laban would not let him marry Rachel. He said her older sister Leah should be married first, so Jacob had to marry her in order to marry Rachel afterwards. He had to work seven more years for Rachel. This was very unfair of Jacob's uncle, but Jacob agreed to it because of his love for Rachel. So he stayed and worked seven years more, and both Leah and Rachel were his wives. Afterwards, he married two more girls, so he had four wives in all.

Jacob wanted to take his wives and children back home to the land of Canaan to see if his father and mother were still alive. But Laban wouldn't let Jacob go. Laban said he realized that the Lord was blessing him because Jacob was there, and he asked what wages Jacob wanted in order to stay longer.

Jacob said that if Laban would give him some of his sheep and goats he would stay. So Laban did. Jacob's flock soon grew very large. After a while he was rich and had many slaves and camels and donkeys, as well as large flocks of sheep.

One day Jacob heard Laban's sons talking angrily about him. They said he had stolen their father's sheep and that was why he was so rich. Jacob noticed that Laban was not as friendly to him as he used to be.

Then God told Jacob to return home to his father in the land of Canaan. God said he would be with Jacob and take care of him and keep him from harm.

Jacob sent word for Rachel and Leah to meet him out in the field where he was caring for his flock. He wanted to talk with them where Laban couldn't hear what he said. He told them that their father wasn't friendly to him any more and that the Lord had told him to go back to Canaan.

Rachel and Leah both agreed he must do whatever the Lord wanted him to.

STORY 16

JACOB'S SECRET ESCAPE
GENESIS 31, 32

JACOB GOT READY to return home to Canaan, to see his father and mother again after being away for so many years. He put his wives and children on camels, took everything that belonged to him, and started back towards the land of Canaan, driving his sheep and goats ahead of him.

Laban was away when Jacob left, for Jacob had kept it all a secret. But three days after Jacob was gone, someone told Laban about it. Laban quickly set out after him. He was angry, for he didn't want Jacob to go. But that night, in a dream, God spoke to Laban and told him not to harm Jacob or even speak roughly to him.

It took seven days for Laban to catch up with Jacob, for Jacob had gone a long way—across a river and through a wide, lonely country—to a mountain called Gilead. There Laban finally found him.

He asked Jacob why he had gone away secretly, taking his daughters Rachel and Leah and their children, without letting him know; he wanted to kiss them all good-bye before they left.

Jacob said he kept it a secret because he was afraid Laban wouldn't let Rachel and Leah go. Then Jacob got angry. He reminded Laban of the twenty years he had worked for him taking care of his sheep and goats, day and night, winter and summer, in the heat and the cold. And now, he said, Laban would have sent him away without paying him a penny for all the work he had done.

Laban replied. "Your wives are my daughters, and your children are my grandchildren. I would never harm them. Let's be friends and promise that we will never hurt each other."

Jacob agreed, and they made a huge pile of stones as a monument to remind them of their promise. If they were ever angry and came to harm each other, they would see that heap of stones and, remembering their promise, would go back home again.

Jacob then built an altar and offered up a sacrifice. Afterwards he and Laban and the men who were with him ate together and camped together that night.

Early the next morning Laban kissed Rachel and Leah and their children good-bye and blessed them. He went back home and never saw them again.

As Jacob and his family traveled on towards Canaan, some angels met them. Perhaps God sent them to help Jacob, for soon he would be coming to where his brother

These two brothers haven't seen each other for many, many years!
   The one with the bow and arrows is Esau, and the other one is Jacob.

Esau lived. Esau might try to kill Jacob for stealing his birthright so long before.

Jacob sent messengers to tell Esau about all that had happened during the twenty years he had been away. He was afraid. Though it had been twenty years since he had lied to his father and stolen Esau's blessing, Jacob still remembered his sin and was afraid of what Esau might do to him in revenge.

Jacob's messengers returned with the fearful news that Esau was coming to meet him with four hundred men. Jacob's heart sank. He divided all his flocks, herds, camels and men into two groups. If Esau attacked one group, the other group might be able to escape.

Jacob prayed and asked God to save him from Esau, for he was afraid Esau would kill him and his wives and his children. He thanked the Lord for being so very kind to him before. He admitted he did not deserve the good things God had given him. When he had left Canaan twenty years before, he had owned only the staff he carried in his hand. But now, coming back, he had all these men with him, plus flocks and herds and camels. He had been very poor before, but God had made him very rich. He thanked God for this.

The next morning he sent some of his cattle as a present to Esau—220 goats, 220 sheep, 30 camels with their colts, 40 cows, 10 bulls, 20 donkeys, and 10 donkey colts. Jacob hoped these gifts would make Esau so happy that he wouldn't hurt Jacob or his family or steal his flocks and herds.

IS ESAU STILL ANGRY?

GENESIS 32, 33

THAT NIGHT JACOB got up, awakened his family, and sent them across the river while he stayed behind alone.

Then a Man came and wrestled with him until dawn. Jacob was strong and kept on wrestling until the Man touched Jacob's thigh. Just by that touch, Jacob's thigh was put out of joint, and he became lame.

The Man said, "Let me go, for dawn has come."

But Jacob replied, "I won't let you go until you bless me."

"What is your name?" the Man asked.

So Jacob told him. (In their language Jacob's name means "tricky" or "unfair.")

The Man said, "I am giving you another name. You are no longer Jacob, but Israel." (Israel means "a prince of God.")

Who was this Man? He was the same person who had talked with Abraham about destroying Sodom and Gomorrah: this Man was the Lord. The Lord was glad that Jacob wanted God's blessing so much that he kept on asking for it all night; for Jacob refused to stop wrestling with God until God had given him a blessing.

Then Jacob said to the Man, "Now tell me *your* name."

But the Lord answered, "Do not ask!" And the Lord blessed Jacob there.

Jacob was afraid something dreadful would happen to

him because he had seen God and talked to him. But God blessed him instead. Then Jacob (or Israel, as we can call him now) named that place Peniel, which means "the face of God." For he said, "I have seen God face to face."

The sun was rising as he limped back across the stream. He limped for the rest of his life because the Lord had touched him. Probably the Lord did this to make him always remember that God had blessed him.

When Jacob saw his brother Esau coming with four hundred men, he divided his wives and their children into groups. If Esau attacked, perhaps some of them could run away and escape, and not all be killed. Then Jacob went on ahead by himself to meet his brother.

He bowed low before him seven times. Esau was pleased by Jacob's humility and ran to meet him. He put his arms around him and kissed him on the cheek, as men still do in that country when they meet friends. Then they both started crying.

God had promised Jacob that he would be with him and keep him from harm, and now we have seen how God kept his promise. First, he hadn't let Laban hurt Jacob or even speak roughly to him; then, he made that angry brother Esau, who had wanted to kill him, feel so good towards him that he cried!

Then Esau asked, "Who are these women and children?"

"They are all mine," Jacob replied. Then the slavewives and Leah and Rachel came with their children, and the children met their Uncle Esau for the first time.

Esau asked Jacob, "Why did you give me all of these sheep and goats?"

"They are a present for you," Jacob replied.

"No, you shouldn't do that," Esau said, "I have enough, my brother; keep them." For Esau had plenty of flocks and herds of his own.

But Jacob said, "Please accept my present," and he begged him until Esau finally did.

Esau suggested to Jacob that they travel together as they returned home, but Jacob was afraid to. He told Esau to go on ahead while he followed more slowly.

"Some of the children are too little to go very far at a time," he explained, "and the flocks and herds cannot be driven too fast or they will get sick and die."

Esau agreed and offered to leave some of his men with Jacob to help him and to protect him from robbers, but Jacob said he didn't need them. Finally Esau went back home.

A GREAT PILE OF STONES
GENESIS 35, 36

AFTER ESAU had gone, Jacob traveled to a place called Succoth. Here he stopped and rested his cattle before he went on to the land of Canaan.

Now God spoke to Jacob again. He told him to go to the city of Bethel and to build an altar there. Bethel was the place where Jacob had dreamed many years before about the stairs reaching to heaven with angels going up and down on it. In that dream God had promised to be with him wherever he went and to bring him back safely, and now God had done this.

Although it was more than twenty years since he had gone away, the Lord had taken care of him all that time, and at last he was safely home in his own country again. That is why God told him to go back now to Bethel where the promise had been given to him and to build an altar there and worship the Lord.

So Jacob said to Rachel and Leah and to his sons, "Let's go to Bethel and build an altar there to God."

He told them how kind the Lord had been to him many years before when he was in trouble, when he was running away from his brother Esau, and how the Lord had been with him ever since and had taken care of him.

On the way to Bethel they passed through cities where the people might have robbed or killed them. But God made the people afraid, and they didn't try to harm Jacob and his family in any way.

They arrived safely at Bethel and built an altar there and sacrificed to God to show him how thankful they were.

Then God spoke to Jacob, blessed him, and told him again, "Your name isn't Jacob any more, but Israel." (Remember, Israel means "a prince of God"; this new name showed how much God loved him.)

God told him again that he would give all the land of Canaan to him and his children and his children's children, that they would become a great nation, and that some of them would be kings.

Then Jacob set up a great pile of stones at Bethel, so that everyone would always remember that this was the place where God had spoken to him.

Afterwards Jacob and those with him started off to Bethlehem. Before they arrived, Rachel had another baby, and they named him Benjamin. But Rachel died soon afterwards, and they buried her beside the road. Jacob was extremely sad, for he loved Rachel very much. He piled stones over her grave to show where she was buried, and the stones stayed there for hundreds of years.

Finally Jacob came to Hebron, where his father lived. Yes, Isaac, his father, was still alive. Though it had been so long since he had become old and blind, God had kept him alive until Jacob came home again.

But Isaac died soon afterwards and his sons, Jacob and Esau, buried him in a cave where Abraham and Sarah were buried. He was 180 years old at the time of his death.

Then Esau took his wives, his sons, his daughters, his cattle, and moved everything he owned to the land of Edom. For he and Jacob had so many cattle that there was not enough food for all of them to live together in the same part of the country.

STORY 19

JOSEPH'S DREAMS
GENESIS 37

ONE OF JACOB'S twelve sons was named Joseph. He was the youngest in the family, except for Benjamin.

When Joseph was seventeen years old, he went out into the fields one day to help his ten older brothers, who were taking care of the sheep and the goats. But while he was there he saw his brothers do something they should not have done. That night when he got home, he told his father. This was a good thing to do, for then his father could talk to his brothers about it, so that they would not do it again. But of course his brothers were angry with him for telling on them.

Joseph was his father's favorite son, so his father gave

him a present of a beautiful coat. But this made his brothers jealous.

One night Joseph had a strange dream, and the next morning he told his family about it.

"In my dream," he said, "all of us were out in the field tying bundles of grain stalks. Then your bundles stood around mine and bowed to it!"

This dream made his brothers even angrier. They thought Joseph was saying that they should bow to him as though he were their king.

Then Joseph had another dream. This time he dreamed that the sun, the moon, and eleven stars all bowed to him. His eleven brothers knew he was talking about them when he talked about the eleven stars bowing to him, and the sun and moon must mean their father and mother. This made them angrier than ever.

When he told his father about the dream, his father scolded him.

"Do you think your mother and brothers and I are going to bow to you?" he asked. "Don't be foolish!"

Soon after this his brothers took their father's flocks to Shechem to find pastures for them there. Shechem was a long way off. It took several days to walk there with the sheep.

Not long afterwards Jacob said to Joseph, "Go and find your brothers and see how they are getting along and how the sheep are." So Joseph went to find them.

But his brothers weren't at Shechem. He was wandering around in the fields looking for them when he met a man who told him, "Your brothers are at Dothan. I heard them

Joseph was his father's favorite child. He gave Joseph a very pretty coat, but this made his brothers jealous and angry.

say that they were going there." So Joseph went on to Dothan.

When his brothers saw him coming, they began talking to each other about killing him.

"Here comes that dreamer," they said. "Come on, let's kill him and throw him into a well, and we'll say some wild animal has eaten him. Then we'll see what happens to his dreams!"

When Joseph's brother Reuben heard them talking like that, he didn't like it at all. He wanted to save Joseph, so he persuaded his brothers to put Joseph into the well without hurting him. Reuben planned to come back after the others were gone and take Joseph out and get him home to his father again.

Joseph came, and they grabbed him and took away his beautiful coat and put him into a well that did not have any water in it.

Then they sat down to eat their lunches. Just then they saw some men coming along on camels. These men were taking things to the country of Egypt to sell. When Joseph's brother Judah saw them, he said, "Let's sell Joseph to them! We'll get rid of him and get some money, too."

The other brothers thought this was a good idea, so they pulled Joseph out of the well and sold him for twenty pieces of silver. The merchants put him on a camel and took him far away to the land of Egypt.

Reuben had not been there when Joseph was sold. When he came back to the well to get Joseph out and send him home, he was very sad.

"Joseph is gone," he exclaimed. "Oh, what shall I do?"

Joseph dreamed one night that all of his brothers would bow down to him as if he were their king. This dream eventually came true.

70

The brothers killed a young goat and dipped Joseph's coat in the blood. They brought the coat to their father and told him they had found it on the ground.

"Is it Joseph's coat?" they asked.

Jacob knew it was and began to cry. "Yes," he said, "it is Joseph's coat; a wild animal must have eaten him. Joseph is dead." Jacob said that he would mourn for his boy all the rest of his life.

STORY 20

STRANGE DREAMS IN A JAIL
GENESIS 39, 40, 41

THE MEN who had bought Joseph took him to Egypt and sold him to a man named Potiphar, who was an Egyptian army officer. Joseph became his slave and lived in his house.

The Lord helped Joseph to work hard. His master was pleased with him and put him in charge of all his other servants. God blessed Potiphar because Joseph was in his home.

But after a while Potiphar's wife wanted Joseph to do something very wrong. Joseph said no, and that made her angry. She decided to get even with him, so she told her husband a lie. She said that Joseph had tried to hurt her. Her husband believed her and put Joseph in jail.

One day Pharaoh, the king of Egypt, became angry with two of his officers; one of them was his baker, and the other was the man who brought him wine whenever he wanted a drink. Pharaoh put them both in the jail where Joseph was.

One night both of these men had dreams. When Joseph saw them the next morning, they looked very sad.

"What's the matter?" he asked. "Why so sad this morning?"

"We had strange dreams last night," they told him, "and there is no one to tell us what they mean."

"Tell me your dreams," Joseph said, "and I'll ask God what they mean."

So they did, and Joseph was able to tell them what their dreams meant. He said to the wine officer, "When you get out of jail, ask the king to let me out too."

Both dreams came true just as Joseph said. The king sent a messenger to the jail to bring back to the palace the man who was in charge of his wine, to work as he had before. I'm sorry to say that the man promptly forgot all about Joseph and didn't bother to tell Pharaoh about him or try to get him out of jail.

Two years later King Pharaoh had a dream. He was standing beside the Nile River in Egypt and saw seven cows coming up out of the water. They were fat and healthy, and they went into a meadow to eat grass. Then seven more cows came up out of the river. These cows were thin and scrawny, and they ate the fat and healthy cows! Just then King Pharaoh woke up.

Soon he went back to sleep and had another dream. This time he thought he saw seven ears of corn growing on one stalk. They were plump ears, well filled with grain. But afterwards seven other ears of corn grew on the stalk. These were thin and withered, and they ate up the seven good ears! Then Pharaoh woke and realized it was a dream.

The dreams bothered him so much that he sent for all

the wise men of Egypt and told them his dreams, but they couldn't tell the king what his dreams meant.

Then the man in charge of the king's wine remembered the young man in jail who had told him and the chief baker what their dreams meant. He remembered that the dreams came true just as Joseph had said.

So the king sent for Joseph. He quickly shaved and put on other clothes and was brought to Pharaoh.

Pharaoh said to Joseph, "I had a dream last night, and no one can tell me what it means; but I'm told that you can."

Joseph said he could not do it, but that God would. Then Pharaoh told Joseph his dreams: the one about the cows and the dream about the corn.

Joseph told him that both dreams meant the same thing: God was telling Pharaoh what was going to happen in the future. The seven fat cows and the seven good ears of corn meant seven years of wonderful crops, when everyone's gardens would grow. The seven thin cows and the seven withered ears of corn meant seven years when nothing would grow. First there would be seven good years in Egypt. The corn would grow tall, and there would be plenty to eat. But afterwards there would be seven years of poor crops when people would be hungry, for nothing would grow in their gardens.

Joseph told Pharaoh to put someone in charge of making the people of Egypt save up corn during the seven good years. Then during the hungry years, the people would have enough food. The king thought this was a good idea and he put Joseph in charge!

JOSEPH'S DREAMS COME TRUE
GENESIS 42

So PHARAOH didn't send Joseph back to jail any more, but made a great man of him instead. The king took off his own ring and put it on Joseph's finger and dressed him in beautiful clothing and put a gold chain around his neck. He was in charge of all the land of Egypt and was almost as great as the king.

During the first seven years, when all the farms had such good crops, he went to all the farmers and made them give some of their corn to Pharaoh. Joseph took this grain and stored it in the nearby cities, keeping it safe until the seven years of famine came.

Then the seven years of good crops ended, and the seven years of poor crops began. Soon everyone began to be hungry because there was so little to eat. When all their food was gone, the people came to Pharaoh to ask for something to eat.

"Joseph is in charge," Pharaoh said. "Go to him and he will tell you what to do."

Then Joseph opened up the buildings where the grain was kept and sold it to the people.

Joseph's brothers were still living in the land of Canaan when the famine came. Soon their grain was gone, and they needed food for their father and for their families.

Then their father said to them, "I hear there is grain in Egypt; go and buy some for us, so we won't starve to death."

Joseph predicted
that there would be
seven years
of good crops
and seven years
of famine.
The Egyptians
saved their corn
during the
seven good years.

So Joseph's ten brothers got on their donkeys and rode for many days until they came to Egypt.

Since Joseph was the governor of Egypt, he was in charge of selling the grain to the people. His brothers didn't recognize him in his Egyptian robes, but Joseph knew them right away.

Imagine Joseph's surprise and joy to see his brothers again, even though they had been so cruel to him. But he pretended he didn't know them at all. He spoke roughly to them and asked them, "Where are you from?"

"From the land of Canaan," they said. "We have come to buy food."

Then Joseph said, "No, you are spies and have come here to see what trouble we are in, so that you can bring an army and attack us."

"Oh, no, sir," his brothers answered, "we have come to buy food. We are all one man's sons. We are men who speak the truth. We are not spies." They said one of their brothers was with their father in the land of Canaan far away, and one was dead.

Joseph still pretended not to believe them and said he would find out whether they were telling the truth or not. This was what he would do. He would send one of them back to Canaan to get their youngest brother they had told him about and bring him to Egypt. All the others must stay until he returned.

Then he put them in jail for three days.

On the third day he talked with them again. This time he said that only one of them must stay, and all the others could go home to take food to their families. One must stay so that Joseph would be sure the others would come back again and bring their youngest brother with them.

When his brothers heard this, they were very sad. They said God was punishing them for their sin of selling their brother as a slave along ago. Reuben (the one who had intended to take Joseph out of the well and bring him back to his father) said to his brothers, "Didn't I tell you not to sin against the child? But you wouldn't listen to me."

Joseph listened to them talking to each other. They didn't know he could speak their language and understand them, but of course Joseph understood every word they said.

He took Simeon and tied him up while all the others watched, for Simeon was the one he chose to stay in Egypt while the others went home for Benjamin.

Then Joseph told his servants to fill his brothers' sacks with grain and to put into the tops of their sacks the money they had paid for the grain; but he didn't tell his brothers that the money was there.

Finally their donkeys were loaded, and all except Simeon started back home to Canaan. That night when they stopped to eat, they opened a sack to get some food. There was the money right at the top of the sack! They were frightened, for they didn't know how it got there.

STORY 22

JACOB SENDS GIFTS TO JOSEPH
GENESIS 43

AFTER MANY HARD DAYS of travel Joseph's brothers finally returned home and told their father what had happened.

When they went out to unload their donkeys and empty the grain out of their sacks, can you imagine their surprise when each of them found his money at the top of his sack? There it was, lying right on top of the grain! When Jacob saw the money, he was afraid.

"You have already robbed me of two children," he said, "for Joseph is gone and Simeon is gone. And now you want Benjamin, too."

Then Reuben said to his father, "Kill my two sons if I don't bring Benjamin safely back to you! I will take care of him."

But Jacob said Benjamin couldn't go. Joseph was already dead; if anything happened to Benjamin, it would be too much to bear.

The famine became worse and worse. Soon the grain brought from Egypt was almost gone and Jacob said to his sons, "Go back to Egypt again, and buy us a little more food."

But Judah told his father they couldn't go unless Benjamin was with them; for the governor had told them, "You must not return without your brother."

"I'll see that nothing happens to him," Judah said, "and if I don't bring him safely back again, then I will bear the blame forever. If we had not stayed at home so long, we could have gone to Egypt and been back by now."

Finally their father agreed. He told his sons to take presents to the governor. Then Jacob prayed for his sons and begged God to make the governor kind to them, for if his children were taken away from him, he would die with sorrow.

The brothers took the presents, the money, and their brother Benjamin and went back to Egypt.

JOSEPH'S FAVORITE BROTHER

GENESIS 43

SOON JOSEPH SAW them standing before him again. When Joseph saw Benjamin with them, he said to his servants. "Take these men home to my house and get dinner ready for them, for they are going to eat with me."

Joseph's brothers were frightened when they saw where the servant was taking them. They thought Joseph was going to keep them as his slaves and never let them go home again. They thought it was because of the money they found in their sacks.

Joseph's servant told them not to worry, there was nothing to fear. He brought their brother Simeon to them, the one who had been left as a prisoner while they went home for Benjamin.

When Joseph arrived, they brought his present to him and bowed low before him.

He spoke kindly to them and said, "Is your father well, the old man you told me about? Is he still living?"

They answered, "Yes, he is in good health, he is still alive." And they bowed to him again.

Then Joseph saw his brother Benjamin and said, "Is this your youngest brother you told me about? May God be good to you, my son."

Then Joseph hurried away to find a place where he could be alone. He went into his bedroom and started crying because he was so happy at seeing his little brother again.

But then he washed his face, and when he came out again he kept back the tears so that his brothers didn't know what he had been doing!

Then they all sat down to eat. Joseph ate by himself at one table, and his brothers were at another table, for Egyptians never ate with Hebrews, and everyone thought Joseph was an Egyptian!

Joseph seated the oldest brother at the head of the table, with the next oldest next to him, and so on down the line according to their ages. Who could have told him their ages, they wondered! But you and I know that no one had to tell him, for he knew it all the time!

Joseph served all the food from his table, and waiters took it over to the table where the brothers were. He gave Benjamin five times as much as any of the others! You see, he loved Benjamin more than the others because he and Benjamin had the same mother, Rachel, who died when Benjamin was born. (All the brothers had the same father, Jacob, but there were four different mothers.)

STORY 24

A BIG SURPRISE
GENESIS 44, 45

JOSEPH TOLD one of his servants to fill the men's sacks with grain and to put back their money in the top of the sacks, just as he had before.

"And," Joseph said, "put my silver cup in the sack of the youngest boy, Benjamin." So that is what the servant did.

In the morning, as soon as it was light, the men got on

their donkeys and started back to Canaan.

But they were hardly out of the city when Joseph told his servant to chase after them and stop them and ask them why they had stolen his silver cup. So the servant hurried and caught up with them.

They were very much surprised and wondered what the servant was talking about when he asked them about the cup.

"God forbid that we should do such a thing as to steal the governor's cup," they said.

"If any of us stole it, we ourselves will kill him," they said, "and all the rest of us will go back and be slaves."

The servant said that only the one who had stolen the cup would be a slave; the rest of them could go home.

Then they all took down their sacks from the backs of their donkeys and opened them so the servant could look. He began with the sack of the oldest, but the cup wasn't there. He went on down the line, but none of them had the cup. Then he came to Benjamin. And there was the cup, right at the top of Benjamin's sack.

Now the poor brothers didn't know what to do. They tore their clothes in sorrow and finally loaded up their donkeys and went back to the city with Benjamin and the servant.

Joseph's brothers were surprised that the stolen cup was in Benjamin's sack.

When they saw Joseph they all fell to the ground before him. Joseph pretended that he thought Benjamin had really stolen his cup and said they should have known that he would find out about it. Judah stood up and spoke to Joseph for all of them.

"Oh, what shall we say to my lord?" he asked. "God has found out our wickedness; we are all your slaves."

But Joseph said that only the one who had stolen the cup would be his slave; the rest of them could go on home to their father.

Judah pleaded with Joseph. He explained that when they went home, they had told their father what he had said. Their father had told them that if they took Benjamin, and anything happened to him, he would die of sorrow. So now, Judah said, if they went home without Benjamin, their father would die of shock and sorrow. Then Judah begged Joseph to let him stay and be a slave instead of Benjamin, and to let Benjamin go home to his father.

Joseph couldn't stand it any longer. He ordered all of his servants to leave the room, and Joseph was left alone with his brothers. Then he began to cry. His brothers watched in surprise.

Finally, when he could speak, he told them, "I am Joseph! Oh, tell me more about my father!"

His brothers were too surprised and frightened to say anything. Then Joseph called them over to him.

"I am your brother Joseph!" he said again.

Then at last they realized what he was saying—and what excitement there was as they all hugged and kissed each other!

Joseph told them to stop being sad for what they had done to him, because God had turned it all into good. Joseph loved his brothers and didn't want them to be unhappy and afraid, and that is why he told them this.

He explained to them that the famine would last another five years, for God had said that there would be no crops for all that time.

"Hurry back to my father," he told them, "and tell him that his son Joseph says, 'God has made me ruler over all of Egypt. Come down to me, and you will live in the best part of the land. Bring your children, your flocks and your herds, and all that you have, and I will take care of you.' Tell my father how great I am in Egypt, and describe all you have seen. Hurry home and bring my father here."

Then Joseph hugged his brother Benjamin and cried again, for he was so glad to see him. And Benjamin cried too, and so did all the brothers.

STORY 25

A FAMILY REUNION
GENESIS 46, 47

WHEN PHARAOH HEARD that Joseph's brothers had come, he was very glad.

He told Joseph to tell them to return for their father and their wives and children and bring them all to Egypt where there was plenty to eat.

"Take some of my wagons for your wives and little ones to ride in," he said. "Don't bother to bring any of your furniture and other things, for I will give you everything you need."

Then Joseph gave new clothes to each of them—giving Benjamin more than any of the others! And he sent his father twenty donkey-loads of food and other good things.

Then at last he let his brothers start for home again to get his father and their families.

When they finally arrived home, what joy there was!

"Joseph is alive," they shouted. "He is governor over all the land of Egypt!"

It seemed too wonderful to be true, and Jacob did not believe them at first; but when he saw Pharaoh's wagons that he had sent, he finally realized that his sons were telling the truth.

"It is proof enough," he said at last. "Joseph is alive! I will go and see him now before I die."

So Jacob and his children and their families all left their homes in Canaan and started off for the land of Egypt. They stopped briefly at Beer-sheba, where Grandfather Isaac had built an altar many years before and had sacrificed to God.

That night God spoke to Jacob and said, "Don't be afraid to go down to Egypt, for while you are there I will make your family grow into millions of people."

God told Jacob that he would take care of him in Egypt, and that when the time came for him to die, Joseph would be by his side.

So Jacob and his sons and their families left Beer-sheba and went on to Egypt. They took their cattle with them and all of their belongings.

Jacob sent Judah ahead to tell Joseph that his father was on the way. When Joseph heard this, he jumped into his chariot and raced out to meet him. He and his father wept for joy when they finally saw each other again after all those long years apart.

Israel—that was Jacob's other name, remember?—said to Joseph, "Now I can die in peace, for I have seen you again. To think that you are still alive!" He could scarcely believe it.

Then Joseph invited some of his brothers to come with him to meet Pharaoh and to tell him that they had arrived with their flocks and herds. When Pharaoh asked them what kind of work they did, they told him they were cattlemen just as their grandfathers had been. Joseph told them to say this because it was the truth, and also because Joseph wanted Pharaoh to send them to live in Goshen, which was the best part of the land of Egypt for raising cattle. So Pharaoh gave them permission to go there.

Then Joseph took his father to meet Pharaoh and to bless him.

STORY 26

Jacob Blesses His Children

GENESIS 48, 49, 50

JACOB LIVED in the land of Goshen with his children and their families for seventeen years, but at last the time came for him to die. He became very sick, and a messenger came to tell Joseph that his father was getting worse and wouldn't live very much longer.

So Joseph took his two sons, Manasseh and Ephraim, and went to visit his father. Jacob sat up in bed and talked with him, and told him how kind God had been to him during his long life. He told Joseph about the time in his youth when God had spoken to him in a dream—the dream about a stairway going up to heaven, with angels walking up and down on it.

Joseph told his father that he had brought his two sons with him so that Jacob could bless them. Jacob told him to bring them close to him. Then he put his arms around them and kissed them and asked God to help them. What a happy day that was for Jacob and Joseph and the two boys!

Then Israel called in all his other sons and blessed each one of them. He told them he was going to die, but that God would be with them and bring them back to the land of Canaan. He commanded his sons to take his body back and bury it in the same cave where his grandfather Abraham was buried, and his grandmother Sarah, his father and mother—Isaac and Rebekah—and his wife Leah.

When Jacob had finished all he had to say to his sons, he lay back on the bed and died. Joseph put his face down to his father's face and wept over him and kissed him. Then he commanded his servants to embalm his father. This meant to put spices and other things into his body to prepare it for burial. All the Egyptians mourned for him for seventy days.

Joseph told Pharaoh that his father had made him promise not to bury him in Egypt, but to bury him back in Canaan. So Pharaoh granted him permission to leave the country for a while.

After the funeral, Joseph's brothers were afraid. They thought that now, with their father dead and unable to defend them, Joseph would surely punish them for all the bad things they had done to him. But he told them not to be afraid, for though they had wanted to hurt him by selling him as a slave, yet God had turned the harm into good by putting him in Egypt where he could save many people from starving to death from the famine. And he spoke kindly to them and comforted them.

Joseph was in Egypt all the rest of his life, and lived to see the birth of his great-grandchildren. But after many years he sent for his brothers and told them that the time had come for him to die.

He asked that his bones be taken back to Canaan when God took the nation of Israel back there again. This didn't happen for four hundred years, but when Moses led the people of Israel back into the Promised Land of Canaan, he took along Joseph's bones just as Joseph had requested.

So Joseph died when he was 110 years old. His body was embalmed and put into a coffin in Egypt.

THE PRINCESS FINDS A BABY

EXODUS 1, 2

AFTER HUNDREDS OF YEARS Jacob's children and grandchildren and their children became a great nation in Egypt. There were so many of them that it took many days to count them all.

Then a new king began to rule over Egypt who didn't care at all about Joseph and all he had done to save Egypt. When the new king saw how many of Jacob's descendants there were, he was afraid of them. He thought that some day when his enemies came to fight against him, Jacob's huge family would turn against him and help his enemies, then run away and go back to their own country. He didn't want that to happen; he wanted them always to stay in Egypt as slaves to do his work.

So this wicked king persuaded the Egyptians to treat Jacob's family (now known as the Israelis, or people of Israel) very cruelly. They made slaves of them, making

A princess found baby Moses
in the little boat
his mother made for him.
She adopted him
and he became her son—
a grandson of
Egypt's king!

them build houses for the Egyptians and work in their fields. But the more cruelly the Israelis were treated, the more of them there were. God had promised Abraham and Isaac and Jacob that their children would become a great nation, and now God was doing as he had promised.

Pharaoh told his people that whenever they saw a baby boy among the Israelis, they must throw him into the river so he would drown or be eaten by the crocodiles. What a cruel king he was! But God protected his people from this evil king.

Now I'm going to tell you about what happened to one of the little Israeli babies, whose name was Moses. Moses became one of the greatest men in all the world when he grew up.

His mother and father loved him very much, and they were afraid that the Egyptian king's men would come and take their baby away and kill him. So the baby's mother hid him at home for three months after he was born. Then she made a little basket from the stems of long weeds that grew by the river and smeared the outside of it with tar to keep the water out. It was a little boat that would float safely on the water.

She put her baby in the little boat and floated it out among the bushes at the edge of the river. She told her daughter, whose name was Miriam, to hide there and watch to see what would happen to the baby and to try to help him in any way she could.

Soon a princess came along. She was one of the daughters of Pharaoh and had come to bathe in the river. She and her maids were walking along the river's edge when she saw the little boat in the bushes. She sent one of her maids to get it and bring it to her so that she could open it and see what was inside. And when she opened it, there was a little baby! She felt sorry for him and decided to adopt him as her own son.

"This must be one of the Hebrew children," she exclaimed. Miriam, the baby's sister, had been watching, and now she went over to the king's daughter and asked, "May I go and get one of the Hebrew women to take care of the baby for you?" The princess said yes, so Miriam ran home to get her mother! When her mother came, the princess said to her, "Take care of this baby for me, and I will pay you well!"

So the baby's mother took him home again!

STORY 28

MOSES RUNS AWAY
EXODUS 2

WHEN THE LITTLE BABY was older, the princess sent for him to come and live in her palace and be her son. She called him Moses, an Egyptian word that means "taken out," because she had taken him out of the water. He lived with her for many years and was a prince.

One day when Moses was grown up, he went home to visit his birth father and mother and the other people of Israel to see how they were getting along. While he was with them, he saw an Egyptian hitting an Israeli. Of course this made Moses very angry, for the Israeli was one of his relatives. Moses looked to see if anyone was watching, then killed the Egyptian and hid his body in the sand.

The next day as he was walking around he saw two Israelis quarrelling. He scolded the man who was in the wrong and asked him why he had hit the other man. This made the man who had done wrong very angry.

"You can't tell *me* what to do," he shouted. "Are you going to kill me as you killed that Egyptian yesterday?" Then Moses realized that someone had seen him kill the Egyptian and that everyone knew about it.

When Pharaoh heard what Moses had done, he wanted to arrest Moses and have him executed for murder, but Moses ran far away to the land of Midian, where Pharaoh couldn't find him. He sat down beside a well trying to think what to do next. Soon some girls came to get water. There were seven of them, all sisters. They wanted to water their father's flock, but some shepherds who were standing beside the well told them to go away.

Moses told the shepherds to be quiet, and he helped the girls water their flocks. When the girls got home, their father asked why they had come back so quickly. They told him that an Egyptian had saved them from the shepherds and helped them get the water.

"Where is the man?" their father asked. "Why didn't you bring him home with you?" He told them to go back and find him and invite him home for dinner. So Moses went home with them. They all wanted him to stay and help them. He liked it so much that he married one of the girls and lived there for many years, caring for their father's sheep.

THE VOICE IN THE BURNING BUSH

EXODUS 2, 3, 4

ALL THE TIME MOSES was living in the land of Midian, the Egyptians were being very cruel to the people of Israel. Finally the people of Israel cried to the Lord because of their sufferings, and the Lord heard them and looked down from heaven and pitied them. He decided to send Moses to help them.

One day while Moses was taking care of his sheep out in the country near Mount Horeb, suddenly he saw fire flaming up out of a bush. Moses ran over to see what was happening and saw a strange thing: the bush was on fire but didn't burn up! Just then God called to him from the bush, "Moses! Moses!"

We can hardly imagine how surprised and frightened Moses was, but he said, "Yes, Lord, I am listening." God told him not to come any closer and to take off his sandals because the place where he stood was holy ground, for God was there.

God said, "I am the God of your fathers—the God of Abraham, Isaac, and Jacob." Moses hid his face, for he was afraid to look upon God.

Then God told him that he had seen the sorrows of the people of Israel, and had heard their cries, and had come down from heaven to set them free from the Egyptians.

There was a new king in Egypt by this time, not the one

Moses was surprised to see a bush on fire that kept burning and burning without burning up! It was because God was there.

who had chased Moses out of the country. This new king was called Pharaoh just like all the other kings of Egypt. The Lord told Moses to go to Pharaoh and to tell him to stop hurting the people of Israel and to let them leave Egypt and go back to Canaan. The Lord told Moses he was to lead them out of Egypt and to bring them to that very mountain where he was talking with Moses.

Moses said he was sure that no one would listen to him or believe that the Lord had really sent him. He had a shepherd's rod in his hand, which the Lord told him to throw on the ground. Moses did, and God made it change into a snake! Moses was afraid of it and ran away.

Then the Lord said, "Grab it by the tail." Moses did, and it was changed back into a shepherd's rod again!

Then the Lord said to Moses, "Put your hand into your coat." When he took it out, his hand had turned white! It was covered with a dreadful disease called leprosy that made it white.

"Put your hand back into your coat again," God said. When Moses took it out this time, it was well again!

God gave Moses power to do these two wonderful miracles so that when the people of Israel saw him do them, they would believe that God had sent him. But if they still would not believe him, even after he had done these two miracles, then Moses must take some water out of the river Nile and pour it on the ground, and the water would change to blood!

Moses had a brother whose name was Aaron. God said that Aaron could go with Moses and make the speeches to Pharaoh and the people of Israel. God would tell Moses what to say, Moses would tell Aaron what to say, and Aaron would tell the people and the king what God wanted them to know.

When the Lord had finished talking with him from the

burning bush, Moses went back home and received permission from his father-in-law, whose name was Jethro, to return to Egypt to visit his people.

BRICKS WITHOUT STRAW

EXODUS 4, 5

THE LORD told Moses' brother, Aaron, to go and meet Moses at Mount Horeb. When he got there, Moses told him all about everything that had happened and what God had told him to do.

Moses and Aaron went together to Egypt and talked with the Israeli leaders. They showed them the two miracles. Moses threw down his shepherd's rod and it became a snake; then he put his hand into his coat, and it became white with leprosy. When the leaders saw these two miracles, they believed that God had sent Moses and Aaron, and that Moses was to lead them out of Egypt.

Then Moses and Aaron went to Pharaoh and told him, "The Lord God of Israel says, 'Let my people leave Egypt and worship me in the desert.'"

"Huh!" Pharaoh scoffed. "Who is the Lord, and why should I obey him? I've never heard of that god, and I certainly won't let these Israeli people out of my sight."

One of the jobs of the Israeli slaves was to dig clay and make bricks by drying the clay in the sun. The clay was

97

mixed with pieces of straw to make the bricks tougher and stronger. This straw was given to them by Pharaoh.

But now Pharaoh was so angry that he said from now on they must get their own straw, but still make just as many bricks as before. Pharaoh said they were lazy, and that was why they wanted time to go and worship their God.

So the people of Israel went out into the fields and gathered straw. But though they worked very hard, they could not make as many bricks as when the straw was brought to them. Some of the people were brutally beaten because of this.

The leaders of the people of Israel told Pharaoh that he wasn't being fair. How could he expect them to make as many bricks, now that he was not giving them the straw?

He replied, "You're lazy! You're lazy! That's why you say, 'Let us go and sacrifice to the Lord.'" And he told them to get to work, for no straw would be given to them any more.

Then the Israelis saw that they were in real trouble, and some of them went to Moses and Aaron and accused them of making things worse for them instead of better.

Moses complained to the Lord about it and asked why he had sent him. He had only made things worse for the people, and now the Egyptians were more cruel than before.

"Just wait," the Lord told Moses, "and you'll see what I am going to do. Tell my people that I will rescue them from their slavery, and they will be my special people. I will lead them into the land I promised long ago to Abraham, Isaac, and Jacob."

Moses told the Israelis what God said, but they wouldn't listen to him any more.

Then the Lord sent Moses and Aaron to talk to Pharaoh

again. "When Pharaoh tells you to do a miracle, throw your shepherd's rod on the ground," the Lord said, "and it will change into a snake, just as it did before."

So Moses and Aaron went to Pharaoh. Aaron threw down his rod, and sure enough, it changed into a snake. Then Pharaoh called for his magicians. They brought some shepherds' rods and threw them down, and their rods changed into snakes too. The Lord let the magicians do just as Aaron had done!

But Aaron's snake swallowed up all the other snakes! Even so, Pharaoh wouldn't let the people go.

STORY 31

THE TERRIBLE TROUBLES BEGIN
EXODUS 7, 8

THE LORD told Moses to go to Pharaoh the next morning when he would be taking a walk beside the river. When Pharaoh came along, Moses must go up to him and say, "The God of the Hebrews has sent me to tell you, 'Let my people go. They must sacrifice to me in the desert.'"

So the next morning Moses went to the river. Sure enough, Pharaoh was out for a walk, and Moses told Pharaoh what the Lord had said. But Pharaoh refused to let the people go.

The Lord told Aaron to strike the river with his shepherd's staff, while Pharaoh and his men were watching. When Aaron did this, the water in the river changed to blood! Suddenly all the water in Egypt, in all the streams

99

and ponds, changed to blood too! So the fish died, and the Egyptians had no water to drink.

The Egyptians dug holes in the ground near the river to get water fit to drink, for the blood stayed in the river seven days.

The Lord now told Moses to announce to Pharaoh that unless he let the people go, God would send millions of frogs that would cover the entire nation and be in the Egyptians' houses and even jump into their beds.

But Pharaoh said he didn't care, he wouldn't let the people go.

So God told Aaron to point his shepherd's staff over the rivers of Egypt. Suddenly, millions of frogs came up out of the water.

Now Pharaoh and the people of Egypt were in real trouble. Frogs were everywhere. He called for Moses and Aaron and asked them to pray to God to take the frogs away. "If you do," Pharaoh said, "I'll let the people go to sacrifice in the desert."

"When do you want the frogs to die?" Moses asked.

Pharaoh replied, "Tomorrow."

So the next day Moses prayed to the Lord, and the Lord did as Moses asked. The frogs in the houses and villages and fields all died, and the people gathered them in great heaps. The smell of dead frogs was all over the land. It was terrible!

But when Pharaoh saw that the frogs were dead, he wouldn't let the people go.

Then the Lord commanded Aaron to strike the dust on the ground with his shepherd's staff, and the dust changed into very small insects called lice that covered the people and the cattle.

But Pharaoh's heart was wicked. He wouldn't let the people go.

FLIES, BOILS, AND HAIL

EXODUS 8, 9

THE LORD again told Moses to get up early the next morning to meet Pharaoh as he went to bathe in the river. Moses must tell him again to let the people go. If he still refused to let them go, the Lord would send swarms of flies all over Egypt.

Moses did as the Lord commanded, but again Pharaoh said no, he wouldn't let the people go. So the Lord sent the flies and they covered the whole country.

But in the land of Goshen, where the Israelis lived, there were no flies at all, because the Lord did not send them there.

Pharaoh was very much upset about the flies, as he had been about the frogs. He called Moses and Aaron and told them, "All right, the people of Israel can sacrifice to their God, but they must stay in Egypt to do it. They mustn't go out into the desert."

Moses told Pharaoh they must leave Egypt and go three days' journey into the desert to sacrifice to the Lord, for that is what God had told them to do. Then Pharaoh said all right, they could go, but not that far.

"Please," he begged Moses, "pray to your God to get rid of the flies." Moses said he would, but he warned Pharaoh not to lie to him again by not letting the people go. When

Pharaoh saw that the flies were gone, he changed his mind again and wouldn't let the people go!

Next the Lord commanded Moses to tell Pharaoh that a great sickness would destroy the cows and sheep of Egypt, but the cows and sheep of the Israelis would not be hurt at all.

But Pharaoh still said no, the people could not go.

So the Lord sent the sickness. The Egyptian cows and horses and donkeys and camels and sheep began to die. Pharaoh sent to see if any of the Israelis' cattle were dead, but not one of them was even sick! When Pharaoh found that the animals belonging to the people of Israel were all right, his heart grew even harder and more wicked than before, and he would not let the people go!

Then the Lord told Moses and Aaron to stand where Pharaoh could see them and to toss handfuls of ashes into the air. So Moses stood before Pharaoh and tossed the ashes into the air; and sores broke out on the Egyptians and on their animals throughout all Egypt, except where the Israelis lived.

But Pharaoh's heart was still wicked, and he wouldn't let the people go!

Then the Lord told Moses to get up early the next morning and tell Pharaoh that God would send a great hailstorm—a storm such as there had never been before. Moses told Pharaoh to get all his cattle in from the fields quickly, for everything out in the storm would die.

Then the Lord told Moses to point his hand towards heaven, and suddenly a terrible hailstorm began, and lightning ran along the ground. Never before had there been

Flies, flies everywhere. They filled the houses and swarmed outside. No one could escape them.

such a storm in Egypt. The hail crashed down onto the fields, killing men and animals alike.

But in the land of Goshen, where the people of Israel lived, no hail fell at all!

Then Pharaoh sent for Moses and Aaron and said, "I have sinned; the Lord is good, and I and my people are wicked. Beg the Lord to stop the terrible thunder and hail, and I will let you go right away."

Moses said that as soon as he was out of the city he would ask the Lord to stop the thunder and hail. When he prayed, the thunder and hail stopped.

And when Pharaoh saw that it had stopped, he changed his mind and wouldn't let the people go!

STORY 33

LOCUSTS AND DARKNESS
EXODUS 10

MOSES AND AARON went to Pharaoh again to tell him that if he wouldn't obey the Lord, tomorrow the Lord would send locusts to destroy everything that was left. Locusts are like grasshoppers, but they eat gardens and crops.

Pharaoh said to them, "All right, go and sacrifice to the Lord your God, but which of the people do you want to go?" Moses answered that all of the people of Israel must go—young and old, sons and daughters, flocks and herds—for they must have a religious holiday.

Pharaoh said that only the men could go—the women and children must stay in Egypt. Moses and Aaron were then dragged away by Pharaoh's guards and told to get out and stay out.

Then the Lord told Moses to lift his hand towards heaven, and the locusts would come. Then the Lord caused the east wind to begin blowing, and it continued blowing all that day and all night too. In the morning the wind brought great clouds of locusts that filled the sky and covered the ground! They were all over Pharaoh's palace and in all the houses of the Egyptians. The locusts ate everything that the hail had left.

Pharaoh hurriedly called for Moses and Aaron and said, "I have sinned." He asked Moses to forgive him only this one more time and to pray that God would take the locusts away.

So Moses went out and prayed. The Lord sent a very strong west wind that blew the locusts into the Red Sea, where they drowned.

But when Pharaoh saw that the locusts were gone, he wouldn't let the people go!

Then the Lord commanded Moses to hold up his hand towards heaven, and it became dark all over the land. The Egyptians couldn't see one another for three days, and couldn't leave their homes.

But in the houses of the Israelis it was as light as usual.

Then Pharaoh called for Moses, and said, "All right, go and worship the Lord! Take your children with you, but not your flocks and herds." But Moses told him no, they wouldn't go without their animals. That made Pharaoh angry. He told Moses again to get out of his sight and never come back again. If he did, Pharaoh said, he would kill him.

THE WORST PUNISHMENT OF ALL

EXODUS 11, 12

MOSES BECAME ANGRY and told Pharaoh that God was going to send one last terrible punishment. The Lord himself was coming to Egypt and in the middle of one night soon, he would cause the oldest son in every Egyptian home to die. Even Pharaoh's oldest son would die. There would be a great cry of grief all through the land, such crying as there had never been before and would never be again. But not one of the Israeli children would be hurt in any way; then Pharaoh would know that he and his people were the ones the Lord was punishing, and not the Israelis. Moses told Pharaoh that after this punishment the Egyptians would come and beg Moses to take his people and leave the country.

Moses stalked out in great anger, leaving Pharaoh sitting there.

Then the Lord instructed the Israelis to be ready to leave Egypt in four days. He told them to ask the Egyptians for jewels and silver earrings and gold necklaces to take with them. And the Lord caused the Egyptians to want to give their jewels to the people of Israel.

The Lord said that each family in Israel should get a lamb and kill it on the fourth evening. Then they must take the blood of the lamb outside and sprinkle it on each side of the door and up above the door, making three marks of blood on the outside of every Israeli home. They must stay in their houses and not come out again until morning, for that night the angel of the Lord would come and kill the oldest child in every home where the blood was not on the door.

On that fourth evening they must roast the lamb, God said, and everyone in the house must eat some of it. They must be dressed to travel as they ate it, all ready to go, with their shoes on and their walking sticks in their hands. And they were to hurry as they ate, for when the Lord went through the land on that night and caused the oldest sons to die, at last Pharaoh would really let them go.

God promised that he would pass over the houses where the blood was on the door and not harm anyone inside. The supper of lamb they ate that night was called the Lord's "Passover," because the Lord passed over the houses where he saw the blood on the door.

At last the terrible night came. In the middle of the night the Lord passed through the land. Wherever he saw the marks of blood, he passed over that house and no one there was harmed. But there were no marks of blood on the houses of the Egyptians, and the Lord sent his destroying angel into every one of those homes and caused the oldest son to die. Even Pharaoh's oldest son died that night.

The king got up in the night with all his people, and there was a great cry of sorrow and despair through all the land, for in every home the oldest son was dead.

Pharaoh called for Moses and Aaron and told them to leave Egypt at once and to take all the people of Israel with them. "Take all your flocks and herds," he begged, "and leave tonight." All the Egyptians begged them to go quickly, for they were afraid the Lord would kill them all, not just their oldest sons.

So the people of Israel left Egypt that night, carrying

their clothes on their shoulders. And the Egyptians gave them jewels of silver and gold, and clothes too; so they went away with great riches. And many of the Egyptians went with them. The lamb that was killed in every Israeli home that night was in some ways like our Savior. The lamb died for the people, and its blood saved them. That is what happened again many years later, when Christ the Savior came as the Lamb of God to die for each of us.

And just as God passed over those who had the marks of the lamb's blood on their houses, and did not punish them, so it will be when Christ comes back again. He will not punish those who have the marks of the Savior's blood in their hearts—those whose hearts have been cleansed from sin by his blood.

That night as they left Egypt, the Israelis took the body of Joseph with them, for Joseph had made his brothers promise four hundred years before that they would take his body home again to Canaan! At last his dying wish was being fulfilled.

STORY 35

A PATH THROUGH THE SEA
EXODUS 13, 14

FINALLY THE PEOPLE of Israel had escaped from Egypt. At last they were free. What a wonderful feeling it must have been—they were no longer Pharaoh's slaves.

The Lord led them toward the Red Sea to a place called

Etham, on the edge of the desert. There they set up their tents and made camp.

As they traveled along, the Lord was very kind to them; he went before them in a cloud to show them the way. The cloud was shaped like a pillar reaching up towards heaven. They could see it all the time. As they walked along, it moved on ahead of them so that they could follow it and know where God wanted them to go. In the daylight it looked like a cloud, but at night it became a pillar of fire. It gave them light at night, so they could travel whenever the Lord wanted them to, day or night.

Almost as soon as the Israelis left Egypt, Pharaoh and his officers were sorry they had let them go. "Why did we ever let them get away from us?" they asked.

Then Pharaoh and his soldiers got into their chariots and chased after the people of Israel. They caught up with them as they were camping by the Red Sea. The Israelis saw the Egyptians coming and were frightened and cried out to God. Then they turned against Moses and blamed him for getting them into this trouble. It would have been better to stay and be slaves to the Egyptians, they said, than to be killed in the desert. But Moses told them not to be afraid. "Wait and see what the Lord will do for you," he said. "For the Egyptians you have seen today will never be seen again. The Lord will fight for you, and you won't need to do a thing."

When Pharaoh and his army had almost caught up with them, the cloud in front of them moved behind them, and came between them and Pharaoh's army. The cloud was dark on the side where Pharaoh was, and his soldiers couldn't see. But the side of the cloud that was turned towards Israel was as bright as fire and gave the people light in their camp!

The Lord said to Moses, "Tell the people of Israel to start

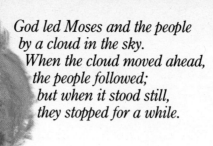

*God led Moses and the people
by a cloud in the sky.
When the cloud moved ahead,
the people followed;
but when it stood still,
they stopped for a while.*

marching to the sea. When they get there, point your shepherd's staff toward the sea, and a path will open up in front of you through the water, and my people will go across on dry ground!"

So Moses pointed his staff towards the sea, as the Lord had told him to, and the water opened up ahead of them, making a path across the bottom of the sea. The water was piled high on each side of them like walls, but they walked across on dry ground and were soon safe on the other side!

The path through the water was still there the next morning, so when Pharaoh saw what had happened, he and his chariots started across between the walls of water. But the Lord made the wheels come off the Egyptian chariots, so they ground to a stop.

Then the Egyptian soldiers panicked. "Turn around! Let's get out of here!" they shouted. "The Lord is fighting against us; he is for the Israelis."

But before they could get out, the Lord told Moses to point his staff towards the sea again. When he did, the water came together and covered the Egyptians, drowning the entire army. Not one soldier was left alive. The Israelis saw them lying dead upon the seashore where the waters washed them up.

But Moses and the Israelis were safe on the other side of the Red Sea. There they sang a song of praise to the Lord for saving them from Pharaoh.

FOOD FROM HEAVEN AND WATER FROM A ROCK

EXODUS 15, 16, 17

THE ISRAELIS now found themselves in a great desert between Egypt and the Promised Land, Canaan, where God was leading them. Soon their water was gone and they were thirsty. They finally arrived at a place called Marah and found water there, but it was too bitter to drink. But instead of asking the Lord to help them, they blamed Moses.

Moses prayed to the Lord about it, and the Lord showed him a certain tree and told him to throw it into the water. He did, and suddenly the water was no longer bitter, and the people could drink it!

They traveled on and came to Elim; there were twelve wells there and seventy palm trees. Going on farther they came to the desert of Sihn. But now a rebellion broke out; the people began to riot against Moses and Aaron because they were hungry. They said they had had plenty of food in Egypt and they wished God had killed them there instead of bringing them out into the desert to die of starvation.

The Lord heard their complaints and told Moses he would send meat for them that evening, and as much bread as they wanted in the morning. Then they would know that the Lord was taking care of them.

The Lord did as he promised, for that evening about the

time the sun was going down, huge flocks of birds called quail came flying just above the ground. The people killed them with clubs and ate them for supper.

The next morning after the dew was gone, small white round things were all over the ground. No one knew what it was, so they called it "manna," which in their language means, "What is it?"

"This is the bread the Lord promised you," Moses told them.

The Lord told the people to go out each day except Saturday and gather as much as they wanted. He told them not to take more than they needed for one day, since there would be a fresh supply each morning. The Lord wanted them to trust him one day at a time for their daily bread. Some of the people didn't obey, and gathered enough for two days instead of one. The next morning the extra manna was spoiled, with worms crawling around in it. They had to throw it away and get fresh manna off the ground.

Each morning when the sun warmed the ground the manna melted away and disappeared. But early the next morning there was always more waiting for them.

The only exception was on the seventh day of each week. That was the Sabbath day when God told them not to work. On that day there was no manna on the ground. The day before the Sabbath they gathered twice as much as other days, and what they saved to eat the next day didn't spoil. Some of the people went out on the Sabbath anyway to try to get some, but there wasn't any. And the Lord was angry, so they didn't do it any more. After that they rested on the Sabbath day as the Lord had told them to.

The manna was small and round, and white like coriander seed. It tasted like bread made with honey. Moses told Aaron to get a bottle and fill it with manna. He wanted to

God
rained
down food
from heaven!
This food was
called "manna."

keep it forever, so that the children who weren't even born yet would be able to see a sample of the food the Lord fed his people with in the desert. Moses did this, and God kept the manna from spoiling for hundreds of years until they finally lost it.

The Israelis ate manna every day for forty years until they finally came to the land of Canaan.

As they traveled they came to a place called Rephidim, but found no water there. So they complained again. "Get us water," they demanded of Moses.

"Why blame me?" Moses asked.

"Because you brought us here," they retorted.

Then Moses cried out to the Lord and said, "What shall I do? For they are almost ready to stone me."

By this time they were close to Mount Horeb where Moses had seen the fire burning in the bush. The Lord told him to lead the people to a certain rock on Mount Horeb and to strike the rock with his walking stick. Moses did as the Lord said, and water poured out, giving everyone enough to drink!

STORY 37

A MEETING ON THE MOUNTAIN
EXODUS 17, 19

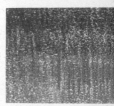

THEN SOME SOLDIERS from the country of Amalek attacked them. There was a brave man among the people of Israel whose name was Joshua. Moses said to him, "Choose the men you want, and go out tomorrow to fight with the army of Amalek. I will stand on top of the hill with the rod of God in my hand."

Joshua did as Moses told him to. As Joshua's men fought with the Amalekites, Moses, Aaron, and a man named Hur went up to the top of a hill where they could watch. Moses pointed his staff towards the men fighting in the valley below. As long as he held it up, the people of Israel were winning; but whenever he let it down, the enemy began to win. Soon Moses' arm became very tired, so Aaron and Hur rolled a rock over to where he was standing, and he sat on it. They stood on each side of him and held up his hands all day until the battle finally ended at sunset. So God gave the victory to the Israelis.

God was angry with the Amalekites for fighting against his people and said the time would come when all the Amalekites would be destroyed.

The Israelis arrived at Mount Sinai three months after leaving Egypt. They camped at the bottom of the mountain while Moses went up and talked with God. God told Moses to remind the people how he had helped them by protecting them from the Egyptians, and he said that he would love them more than any other people if they would obey his commandments.

God told Moses to go down and call the people together. In three days God would return to the top of the mountain to talk with Moses there, and all the people would hear him. He told Moses to tell the people to wash their clothes and to be very careful not to sin, in order to get ready for God's visit. None of them was allowed to go up onto the mountain, for anyone who did must die. A loud trumpet blast far up on the mountain would be the signal for everyone to gather quickly at its foot and wait there for God to speak.

Moses went down and told the people, and they put on

fresh, clean clothing for the awesome occasion. On the morning of the third day there was a terrible thundering and lightning, and the Lord came to the top of the mountain in a thick cloud. And there was a trumpet blast so long and loud that the people trembled with fear.

Then Moses led them out of the camp to the foot of the mountain. The whole mountain was covered with smoke because the Lord was there. The smoke climbed skyward as from a furnace, and the mountain shook. The trumpet blast grew louder and louder. Moses called, and God answered him, summoning him to the top of the mountain.

STORY 38

THE TEN COMMANDMENTS
EXODUS 20-24

THEN GOD GAVE the people of Israel these Ten Commandments:

1. YOU MUST NOT HAVE ANY OTHER GOD BUT ME

This means that we must love God more than anyone or anything else, for anything we love more than God becomes our god instead of him.

2. YOU MUST NOT MAKE ANY IDOL,
   NOR BOW DOWN TO ONE, NOR WORSHIP IT

Many people in the world make statues, or idols, and believe that they are gods which can help them. But in this commandment God forbids making such statues or bowing

117

God called Moses
to the top of Mount Sinai,
where he gave him
the Ten Commandments,
written on two tablets
of stone.

down to them or worshiping them. God is the only one who can save men, and we are to worship him alone. This commandment also means that we are not to worship money or clothes or anything else but God.

3. YOU MUST NOT TAKE THE NAME
   OF THE LORD YOUR GOD IN VAIN

This means that whenever we speak God's name, we must do it reverently, remembering how great and holy a name it is. If we speak it carelessly or thoughtlessly, we offend him. This commandment teaches us not to swear.

4. REMEMBER THE SABBATH DAY, TO KEEP IT HOLY

In this commandment God instructed his people not to work on the Sabbath. This was because God rested on the seventh day after his six days of work when he created the heavens and the earth.

5. HONOR YOUR FATHER AND YOUR MOTHER

Next to obeying God, we should obey our parents. We must not delay doing what they tell us to, and shouldn't even wait to be told. This is God's commandment.

6. YOU MUST NOT KILL

We break this commandment by murdering, but we also break it when we are angry with someone and wish he were dead. For then we have the wish for his death in our hearts, and God sees murder in our hearts.

7. YOU MUST NOT COMMIT ADULTERY

When a man lives with a woman as his wife when he is already married to somebody else, it is adultery. God says we must never do this, and it is a sin when a man and a woman sleep together when they are not married. He commands us to be pure in all our thoughts, words, and actions.

8. YOU MUST NOT STEAL

You must not take anything for your own that belongs to someone else. If you have ever done this, whether by mistake or on purpose, God commands you to give it back or pay for it.

9. YOU MUST NOT TELL LIES

This means that you must never say anything about another person that isn't true. And when you are saying what is true, you must be very careful how you say it. Don't leave out a little or add a little to make it different from the real truth.

10. YOU MUST NOT COVET ANYTHING THAT IS YOUR NEIGHBOR'S

To covet a thing is to wish it were yours. We must not do this. God, who knows best, gives to each of us just what he wants us to have.

When all the people heard the terrible thunder and the blast of the trumpet and saw the lightning and the smoke and heard God's voice, they were terrified. They said to Moses, "You tell us what God wants, and we will do it, but don't let God speak with us, or we will die." Moses told them God hadn't come down to kill them, but to make them afraid to sin against him.

The people stood a long way off from the mountain while Moses climbed up to the dark cloud where God was. There God talked with him and gave him many more laws for the Israelis to obey.

When the people heard these laws, they promised to obey all of them.

A SPECIAL HOUSE FOR GOD

EXODUS 25-28

THE LORD told Moses to come up to the top of Mount Sinai again, so that he could give him two tablets of stone with the Ten Commandments written on them. So Moses went up, along with Joshua, his assistant.

Then a cloud came down and covered the mountain for six days. On the seventh day the Lord called to Moses from the cloud. Moses stayed there on the mountain for forty days and forty nights. The people at the bottom of the mountain saw the glory of the Lord like a bright, burning fire at the top.

The Lord told Moses that the people should build a Tabernacle, or church, where they could worship him. He showed Moses just how to do it; he even gave Moses a pattern of the building, so he would know just what it should look like.

God also commanded Moses to make an Ark to be placed inside the Tabernacle. This Ark was a beautiful gold box— it was made of wood and then covered inside and outside with pure gold.

God said that when the Ark was finished, Moses was to put into it the two stone tablets God would give him—the tablets with the Ten Commandments written on them.

The Ark was to have a cover of solid gold, with two gold angels standing on it, one at each end, facing each other with their wings spread out. This cover with the angels on it would be called the mercy seat.

There was to be a gold table, too—made of wood and covered with gold—to stand in the Tabernacle, and a gold lampstand to give the Tabernacle light.

God told Moses just how to construct the Tabernacle. It would be portable, easy to take apart and put together again, for the people were to carry it with them on their journey to the land of Canaan.

The sides of the Tabernacle were to be made of boards covered with gold. The door of the Tabernacle would be a curtain; and another beautiful curtain, called the veil, would hang across the inside of the Tabernacle, dividing it into rooms. In the inner room Moses was to place the Ark with the mercy seat. The gold table and the gold lampstand would go in the outer room.

There was to be a little yard all around the Tabernacle and a wall to protect the yard. An altar would stand in the yard in front of the door of the Tabernacle. It would be made of wood covered with bronze, large enough to sacrifice oxen, sheep, and goats on it.

The Lord said that Aaron and his sons would be God's priests. They would sacrifice to God the animals brought to the Tabernacle by the people of Israel. Aaron would be the High Priest; he would be in charge, and his four sons would be his assistants.

Beautiful clothes were made for Aaron. There was a linen turban for his head, with a plate of gold fastened to the front of it, and these words written on it: "Holiness to the Lord." This reminded Aaron that God commanded him to be holy, and it reminded the people to honor Aaron as God's High Priest.

Next to his skin Aaron wore a robe made of embroidered linen. Over the linen robe he wore a long, sleeveless blue coat. Hanging from the lower edge of this outer robe were

*The Ark
was the most
important part
of the Tabernacle.
Its cover, with the cherubs
on it, was called the mercy seat.*

decorations made to look like pomegranates—blue, and purple, and scarlet.

Over the blue robe, Aaron wore a many-colored vest, called the ephod.

Over the front of this vest was a square piece of richly embroidered cloth with twelve different kinds of jewels on it, called the breastplate. These jewels were of the most beautiful kinds, including a ruby, a sapphire, and a diamond, each in a beautiful gold setting.

STORY 40

AARON MAKES A GOLD CALF

EXODUS 29–32

THE LORD told Moses to bring Aaron and his sons to the door of the Tabernacle and bathe them there. Then he put on them the special robes made for them and poured olive oil on Aaron's head, anointing him as God's High Priest. Afterwards Moses gave sacrifices to God on their behalf. That is the way Aaron and his sons became priests.

They sacrificed two lambs every day for the sins of the people. These lambs were killed and then burned before God on the great bronze altar, one in the morning and the other in the evening.

God told Moses to make another altar, too, of wood covered with gold. This altar was not to sacrifice animals on, but for burning incense. When incense burns, it sends up a smoke that is sweet to smell.

The animals sacrificed on the bronze altar represented the Savior being offered up for our sins. The incense sending up its sweet smoke from the gold altar represented the prayers of God's people.

When the Lord had finished talking with Moses, he gave him the two tablets of stone on which he had written the Ten Commandments. Moses had been with God on Mount Sinai for forty days and forty nights learning about all the things God wanted made.

124

★ THE TEN COMMANDMENTS
EXODUS 20:3-17

1. You may worship no other god
   than me.

2. You shall not make yourselves
   any idols;
   you must never bow to an image
   or worship it in any way.

3. You shall not use
   the name of Jehovah your God
   irreverently,
   nor use it to swear
   to a falsehood.

4. Remember to observe
   the Sabbath as a holy day.

5. Honor your father and mother.

6. You must not murder.

7. You must not commit adultery.

8. You must not steal.

9. You must not lie.

10. You must not be envious
    of anything your neighbor has.

Meanwhile the people of Israel were in their camp at the foot of the mountain. They became impatient when Moses stayed so long. They went to Aaron and said, "We don't know what has become of Moses. We want to worship idols, like all the other nations do."

"All right," Aaron said, "bring me your wives' and children's gold earrings." Aaron melted the earrings in a fire and poured out the gold into a big lump, which he then made into the shape of a beautiful gold calf.

The people bowed to the calf and said it was their god who had brought them out of the land of Egypt. Aaron built an altar in front of it and told the people to come back the next day for a big celebration. Early the next morning, they sacrificed burnt offerings to the calf instead of to the Lord. They had a great party, feasting and getting drunk and dancing around the calf.

All this time Moses was still on the mountain. He couldn't see what the people were doing, but God could. "Quick! Go on down," God told him, "for the people have done a very wicked thing. They have made a calf and worshiped it and sacrificed to it and called it their god."

Moses hurried down the mountain with the two tablets of stone in his hand. Joshua, his helper, was with him, and as they came near the camp, they heard the noise of the people shouting.

Joshua said to Moses, "It sounds as if they are getting ready for war."

"No," Moses said, "it isn't the noise of war; they are singing."

When they came nearer Moses looked down and saw the gold calf and the people dancing before it. He could hardly believe it. In great anger he hurled the two tablets of stone down the mountain and they broke in pieces as they smashed against the ground.

THE IDOL IS SMASHED

EXODUS 32, 33, 34

WHEN MOSES SAW the people worshiping the gold calf, he ran all the rest of the way down the mountain and smashed the calf and ground it into powder. Then he threw the powder into the water and made the people drink it.

Moses turned to Aaron and demanded, "Why have you helped the people do this great sin?" Aaron tried to excuse himself. He said the people told him to make the calf or they would hurt him. They brought him their gold, he said, and when he put it into the fire, it just happened to come out in the shape of a calf. What a wicked thing for Aaron to say!

A terrible punishment from the Lord came upon his people because of their sin. Moses stood at the gate of the camp and told everyone who was on the Lord's side to come and stand there with him. All the men of the tribe of Levi came. He told them to take their swords and to go from one end of the camp to the other, killing every man they met. In this way God punished the people for their wickedness. That day the Levites killed about three thousand men.

The next day Moses told the people that although they had sinned so greatly he would pray for them, and perhaps their sin would be forgiven. So he talked with the Lord about it. He confessed that the people had sinned terribly because they had made the idol and worshiped it, but he begged God to forgive them. But God said no, he would punish those who had sinned. He would not go with them

127

to the Promised Land and he would not give them the cloud to lead them any more.

Moses begged God to stay with them, and the Lord finally listened to his prayer and promised that he would.

Then God told Moses to make two stone tablets like the ones he had broken, and he would write the Ten Commandments on them again.

He told Moses to come up alone to the top of the mountain in the morning. No one could be anywhere near the mountain, and no flocks or herds were to graze there.

So Moses chipped out two tablets of rock, just like those he had broken, and went up to the top of Mount Sinai early in the morning, carrying the tablets. And the Lord came down in the cloud and passed before him. When Moses heard his voice, he bowed quickly to the earth and worshiped. He prayed again that the Lord would forgive the people of Israel and would let them be his people again.

The Lord accepted Moses' prayer and took the people back again as his own. He promised that he would do wonderful things for them and drive out the wicked nations of Canaan to make room for his people to live there instead.

STORY 42

THE WORKMEN FINISH GOD'S HOUSE
EXODUS 35–40

NOW MOSES INVITED the people to bring their gifts of gold, silver, bronze, wood, and whatever else was needed, to begin building the Tabernacle. The people gladly brought their gold and silver bracelets and earrings and other ornaments. Some brought jewels for the breastplate for the High Priest, and olive oil for the lamp. They kept on bringing more and more. Finally there was enough, but still they kept on bringing things. Moses had to tell them to stop! He handed their gifts to Bezaleel and Aholiab and the other men chosen and trained by the Lord to do the work.

These men made curtains to spread over the top of the Tabernacle as its roof. They also made a beautiful curtain to hang inside the Tabernacle, to divide it into two rooms, and a curtain for the front door. The sides of the Tabernacle were made of boards covered with gold.

It was at this time that Bezaleel and Aholiab made Aaron's beautiful clothes—his linen coat, and the blue, purple, and scarlet vest.

Then they made the breastplate with twelve jewels attached to it. Each jewel was set in gold. Aaron wore this breastplate over his chest, suspended by two gold chains coming down from his shoulders.

The robe beneath the vest was all blue, and around its lower edge hung what looked like blue, purple, and scarlet pomegranates. Between the pomegranates were gold bells that tinkled as Aaron went in and out of the Tabernacle.

Then Bezaleel made the Ark. It was a wooden box covered inside and outside with solid gold. The cover of the Ark, called the mercy seat, was pure gold without any wood. The Ark was the most important part of the Tabernacle because God was there.

Then Bezaleel made two gold angels to stand, one on each end of the cover. Their faces were turned towards each other, with outspread wings.

Coats and trousers of soft linen were made for Aaron's sons, too, and a turban for Aaron's head, with a gold plate on it that read: "Holiness to the Lord."

At last the different parts of the Tabernacle were finished and ready to be put together. The workmen brought them to Moses, and he inspected them to be sure everything was just as God had said.

God told Moses to go ahead now and put the parts together to make the Tabernacle. So the Tabernacle was finished, with the yard around it, and everything in place inside. Then the pillar of cloud that went ahead of the people of Israel as they traveled, came and stood over the Tabernacle and covered it.

And the glory of the Lord filled the inside of the Tabernacle so that Moses couldn't go in.

These children are bringing their gifts to the Tabernacle. God is pleased because they want to help.

TWO SONS OF AARON DIE
LEVITICUS 10-14

AARON'S FOUR SONS were in charge of worshiping God at the Tabernacle; they saw to it that everything was done properly, in just the way God wanted it done.

God commanded incense to be burned on the gold altar. This incense was placed in a kind of cup, called a censer, probably made of bronze. The priest carried coals of fire in the cup into the Tabernacle and set it on the gold altar. He sprinkled the incense on the coals so that it would burn and send up its sweet smoke. The fire in the censer was taken from the burnt offering altar, from the fire God had sent down from heaven.

But two of Aaron's sons, Nadab and Abihu, put other fire in their incense cups because they didn't want to obey God. God was angry at their sin and sent down fire from heaven that burned them to death. Their dead bodies were carried away from the Tabernacle, out of the camp. God told Aaron and his other two sons not to show any sign of grief for them, for they had been put to death because of their sin against God.

The Lord told Moses what animals and birds and fish the Israelis could eat, for they were not to eat every kind. They could eat oxen, deer, sheep, and goats, but not camels, rabbits, or pigs. They could eat fish that had fins and scales, but not those with smooth skins. They could eat doves and pigeons and quail, but they were forbidden to eat eagles, ravens, owls, and swans.

Do you remember about the leprosy that came suddenly upon Moses' hand, making it white as snow until he put it back into his coat again? God sent it upon Moses so that he could show this miracle to the people of Israel in Egypt. Leprosy was a very dreadful disease that sometimes spread over people's entire bodies, for no one knew how to cure it. After a while the leprosy would eat away the person's fingers and toes.

God told Moses and Aaron that when a man had a spot or sore on his skin that seemed like the beginning of leprosy, he must go to the priest. The priest could look at it and say whether or not it really was leprosy. If it was, the man had to go away from his family and from all the rest of the people and live alone.

If it seemed that God had made him well, the priest would look at him again and decide whether he was well. If he was, he could come back again and live in the camp.

But he must bring three lambs, or, if he was poor and could not bring so many, he could bring one lamb and two doves or young pigeons to the Tabernacle as offerings to the Lord who had healed him.

STORY 44

THE HIGH PRIEST'S SPECIAL JOB
LEVITICUS 16–22

DO YOU REMEMBER that there was an inner room in the Tabernacle where Moses put the Ark and where God came in a cloud above the mercy seat? That room was the most holy part of the Tabernacle; it was called the Holy of Holies. The Lord told Moses that no one but Aaron, the High Priest, could ever go in there. Even Aaron could go there only once every year, very carefully.

Before going he bathed thoroughly. He took off his splendid High Priest's robe and put on plainer clothing of pure white linen, for he must go in humbly before the Lord. Before going in, he offered up sacrifices for his own sins and for the sins of all the people. He took the blood of those sacrifices with him into this most holy place and sprinkled it with his finger on the mercy seat and in front of it; there Aaron prayed that the Lord would forgive him and all the people.

What did it mean when the High Priest did these things? He was showing what the Savior would do for all who trust in him. For the High Priest went into the most holy place on earth to pray for the people; the Savior, after he was crucified, went up to heaven to pray for us. The High Priest asked God to forgive the people because animals had been sacrificed for them. The Savior asks God to forgive us because he died for us. Aaron is dead and cannot ask God to forgive us, but the Savior is alive in heaven and is there every day asking God to forgive us.

On the day when Aaron went into the most holy place, the people were not allowed to work, but spent the time thinking about their sins and being very, very sorry for them. Anyone who did not do this was punished, for that day was the most solemn day of all the year. It was called the Day of Atonement.

God said that when the people of Israel arrived in the Promised Land and went out into their fields to cut their grain and bring it into their barns, they must never bring in quite all of it, but must leave a little. And when the grapes became ripe, they must not pick every grape, but must leave some for the poor who had no fields or vineyards of their own. The poor could come and gather what was left.

And the Israelis were not to hate each other, but to love each other. If one of them saw another doing wrong, he must tell them kindly not to do it any more. Then he might repent of his sin.

When people from other countries came to live among them, the Israelis were not to treat them unjustly nor steal their things. They must be as kind to them and love them as much as though they had always lived with them and were their own people.

The nations living in the Promised Land of Canaan, where the Israelis were going, worshiped a huge idol named Molech.

This idol, with the face of a calf, was made of bronze and was hollow, so that a fire could be lighted inside it like a furnace. After it had become very hot, those wicked people would put their little children into the idol's arms, and there the babies burned to death. The people beat drums while the babies were burning, to keep from hearing their screams. They burned their children in this way because they thought it pleased the idol; they called it giving their children to Molech.

God told Moses to kill any of the Israelis who gave their children to Molech. If the people refused to kill a man who did that, pretending not to know what he had done, God said that he himself would punish the people for not punishing that man.

These children and their parents are celebrating one of the three great national holidays. Each holiday was a time of joy and thanksgiving.

THREE HOLIDAYS
LEVITICUS 23, 24

THE LORD commanded the people of Israel to have three religious holidays each year.

The first was called the Passover. This celebration was to remind everyone about the night they came out of Egypt, for it was a great victory over the Egyptians. Each year when this event was celebrated, the people ate a lamb during the night, just as they had done that first time. Then for seven days afterwards they ate bread made without yeast. God wanted the people to have this celebration each year so that they would always remember how God had punished Pharaoh until he finally set the people of Israel free, even though he was determined not to let them go.

Seven weeks after the Passover, there was the Harvest Festival. This lasted only one day and came after the grain had been gathered into the barns. The people thanked God for sending the rain and the sunshine that made their crops grow out in the fields and for giving them food enough for another year.

At the end of the year, there was the Tabernacle Festival. This celebration lasted seven days. During those seven days all the people of Israel moved out of their homes and lived in huts made from branches of trees because the Israelis lived like that for forty years while they were traveling through the deserts. The Lord wanted them to remember this when they arrived in Canaan and were living in houses again.

At each of these three celebrations every man of Israel was to come to the Tabernacle and bring an offering to the Lord.

One kind of gift God told Moses to tell the people to bring was olive oil for the lamps in the Tabernacle. Olives are a fruit that grow in Canaan. When the olives are pressed, a very pure vegetable oil runs out of them. It was this oil that the people were to bring to burn in the seven lamps that were in the gold lampstand.

God told Moses to take finely ground flour and to bake twelve loaves of bread with it. These were to be placed on the gold table which stood in the Tabernacle near the gold candlestick. He was to put them there on the Sabbath day and leave them a whole week until the next Sabbath. Then a priest took them away and put fresh loaves in their place. Aaron and his sons could eat the bread after it was taken away, but they must eat it at the Tabernacle because it was holy bread; they could not take it home, for it had been set on the gold table before the Lord.

STORY 46

THE YEAR OF JUBILEE
LEVITICUS 25

GOD SAID that when the Israelis came into the land of Canaan, they could plant their crops for six years, but every seventh year they must not plant any seed at all, but just let the land alone. If any grain grew without being planted, they must not cut it, and the grapes on the vines must not be picked; this seventh year was to be a Sabbath year, a year of rest for the land! Yet there would be enough to eat that seventh year because the Lord would give them enough extra crops the previous year to last for two years.

Every fifty years was the year of Jubilee. This was a glad and happy year. The day it began, trumpets were blown all through the land. No one planted crops or harvested them that year, for God promised to give large crops the year before, enough to last through the entire year of Jubilee. If anyone had been so poor that he had had to sell the field his father had given him, he got it back free when the year of Jubilee came! For the Lord said that the person who bought it had to give it back at that time.

Or if anyone had sold himself as a slave, he became free when the year of Jubilee began. What a wonderful year!

God told the people that if they would obey his commandments, he would send them rain so that all their crops would grow well, there would be luscious fruit on their trees, they would have plenty of bread to eat, and no one would hurt them. The Lord would destroy or drive away the dangerous wild animals. He himself would take care of his people and make all their enemies afraid of them.

But if they didn't obey his commandments, God said they would have sickness and trouble. When they sowed their grain, it wouldn't come up, or if it did, their enemies would come at harvest time and steal it from them. Wild animals would carry off their children and kill their cattle. Only a few people would be left in all the land. The Lord would send disease and famine upon them. Their enemies would make war on them, and the people of Israel would be taken away to other countries where the people would hate them, and many of them would die there.

But if those who were left would confess that they had been wicked and that it was God who had punished them, then he wouldn't punish them any more. He would be kind to them and bring them back again to the land he had promised to give to the children of Abraham, Isaac, and Jacob.

THE PEOPLE OF ISRAEL FOLLOW A CLOUD

STORY 47

NUMBERS 1–4

MORE THAN A YEAR had passed since the people of Israel left Egypt, but they had gone no farther than Mount Sinai.

They had stayed there for forty days and forty nights while Moses was on the mountain getting the two tablets of stone from God, with the Ten Commandments written on them. But Moses had angrily thrown down the two tablets and broken them because the people were worshiping the gold calf.

Then they waited for forty more days and nights while Moses went back up the mountain with two new tablets and the Lord again wrote his Ten Commandments on them.

Afterwards they waited while the Tabernacle was built and while God spoke to Moses inside the Tabernacle, giving him many new laws for the people of Israel to obey.

But at last the time had come to leave Mount Sinai and

to continue the journey to the Promised Land of Canaan.

The Israelis were divided into twelve large groups, called tribes. Each group was descended from one of the sons of Jacob.

The Lord told Moses and Aaron to count all the men of Israel who were able to be soldiers. There were 603,550 of them.

The men of the tribe of Levi were not counted with the others, because the Lord didn't want them to go to war. He chose them to stay near the Tabernacle to take care of it. Whenever God told the Israelis to move to a new location, the men of this tribe took down the Tabernacle and carried the different parts, and whenever the people of Israel stopped and made camp, these men set the Tabernacle up again.

There was much work for these men of the tribe of Levi to do. Besides sacrificing the two lambs every day, the people brought many other offerings. Wood was cut to burn these. Water was brought for washing. The ashes were taken away from the altar, and the yard where the offerings were killed was cleaned.

Aaron and his sons could not do all these things by themselves, so God chose the Levite tribe to help them. Moses and Aaron counted 8,580 men of the Levite tribe.

The twelve leaders of the tribes now brought presents for the Tabernacle in six wagons pulled by twelve oxen. Moses gave the wagons and the oxen to the Levites to carry the different parts of the Tabernacle when the people of Israel were traveling. Two wagons were used to carry the heavy curtains; four other wagons carried the boards covered with gold for the sides of the Tabernacle, and the brass pillars that stood around the court. But there was no wagon to carry the Ark, the gold lampstand, the gold altar, or the bronze altar, for God said that these should never be

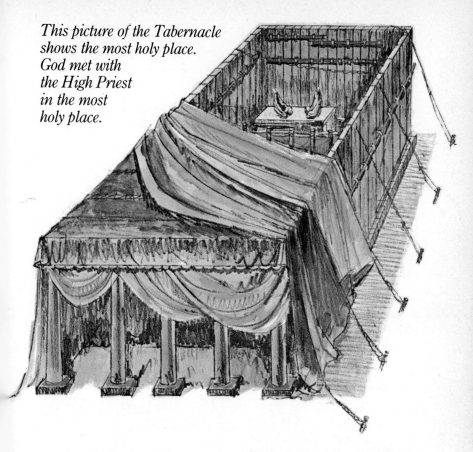

This picture of the Tabernacle shows the most holy place. God met with the High Priest in the most holy place.

carried in wagons. They had to be carried on the shoulders of the men of the tribe of Levi.

All this time the pillar of cloud stood over the Tabernacle. During the day it was the color of a cloud, but every night it became a pillar of fire. It came there on the very first day when Moses put up the Tabernacle, and there it remained above the roof of the inner room, called the most holy place. It stayed there except when the Lord wanted the people to move. Then it lifted and waited for the people to get ready to follow, and as the cloud moved forward, the people walked behind it.

As long as it was moving, everyone followed, but whenever it stopped, everyone stopped and set up the camp. If the cloud stayed over the Tabernacle only one day, they stayed only one day. If it stayed two days, they stayed two days; or if it stayed a whole year, they stayed a year. But whenever the cloud lifted, whether by day or by night, they traveled. It was the Lord who made it stay or go, and he was guiding the people through the wilderness.

The Lord commanded Moses to make two silver trumpets for the priests to blow when Moses wanted to call the people together, or when they were about to start traveling.

While traveling, the people of Israel carried banners and flags and marched like an army. Each tribe kept in its own place, and each one had a captain in charge of it.

The Levites carrying the different parts of the Tabernacle were surrounded by the other tribes. Wherever the cloud stopped, the people stopped, and the Levites set up the Tabernacle again.

The Levites put up their family tents next to the Tabernacle, and the other tribes put their tents all around them, farther away from the Tabernacle than the Levites.

STORY 48

ALWAYS COMPLAINING

NUMBERS 10, 11, 12

NOW IT WAS time for the Israelis to leave Mount Sinai, for the Lord told them they had been there long enough. They should move on towards Canaan, he said.

So the cloud rose from the Tabernacle and moved on before them, and they followed it for three days until they came to the wilderness of Paran. There it stopped and there they camped.

We would suppose that when the people saw the cloud going along in front of them they would be very thankful to God. We would expect them to be satisfied with whatever he chose to give them until they reached that good land to which he was leading them. But no, they complained that there was no meat for them to eat. "We remember the fish we had in Egypt," they said, "and the cucumbers, the melons, and the onions, but now we have nothing at all beside this manna."

The Lord was very angry with them, and Moses was discouraged. Then he complained to the Lord, too. He asked the Lord why had he been given the care of all these wicked people. It was too much for him, he said, and if the Lord was going to send him such a burden as this to carry, he wanted to die and end it all.

Moses sinned when he talked to God like that, for God had always helped him when he was in trouble, and he was willing to help him again now. Moses should not have complained—he should have trusted God.

God told Moses to tell the people that he would give them meat, for he had heard their complaining. They would have meat not only for one day or five days, but for a whole month until they couldn't stand the taste or sight of it.

Moses could hardly believe it. He said, "Here are 600,000 families, and yet you say you will give them meat to eat for a whole month? Must we kill all the flocks and herds that we brought out of Egypt? Or shall all the fish of the sea be caught to give them enough?"

The Lord answered, "Have I grown weak? Is that why

you think I can't do it? Wait, and you will see whether my words will come true or not."

So Moses told the people what the Lord had said.

Then the Lord sent a wind that brought quail from the sea, and they flew down all around the camp. There were so many that the ground was covered with them. The people went out and gathered them all that day, all that night, and all the next day. But as soon as they put the meat in their mouths to eat it, the Lord sent a great plague among them, and many of them died for their sin and were buried there in the wilderness.

Then the cloud lifted again, and the people followed it until it stopped at a place called Hazeroth; there they stopped and made their camp.

Moses was their leader because the Lord had chosen him. Yet the Bible tells us he was more meek and humble than any man alive. But Miriam, his sister, and Aaron, his brother, found fault with him for marrying a woman who was not an Israeli. They said God had chosen them also, and that they, too, should be rulers over the people.

The Lord heard what Aaron and Miriam said, and he was angry. He told them to go with Moses to the Tabernacle. While they were there, the pillar of cloud came down and stood by the door. Then the Lord called to Aaron and Miriam from the cloud and they came and stood before him. The Lord told them he had chosen Moses, and he asked them why they were not afraid to speak against Moses as they had been doing. When the pillar of cloud rose again, Miriam was covered with leprosy; her skin was as white as snow. God had sent the disease upon her as punishment for their wickedness.

When Aaron saw it, he was terribly frightened and said to Moses, "We have sinned." He begged that Miriam might be healed.

Then Moses prayed earnestly to the Lord for her, saying, "Heal her now, O God, I ask." And the Lord listened to his prayer and healed her from her leprosy.

Then the people traveled from Hazeroth back again to the wilderness of Paran.

THE TWELVE SPIES
NUMBERS 13, 14

THE PEOPLE OF ISRAEL had almost reached the Promised Land of Canaan now. Moses told them to go in and conquer it, for the Lord had told them to. But the people begged Moses to send spies first, to go through the land and come back and tell them what it was like.

So Moses sent twelve men, one from each tribe. He told them to look at the land to see whether it was good or bad, what sort of people lived there, how many there were, and whether they lived in tents or in cities with walls around them.

Moses told the spies not to be afraid, and to bring back samples of the fruit that grew in the Promised Land. So the spies walked through the land from one end to the other, and the Lord kept the people who lived there from hurting them. At a place called Eschol, they cut a branch of grapes with a single cluster so large that it took two men to carry it! They hung the cluster on a pole with a man at each end, carrying it between them! They also brought back to Moses some samples of the wonderful pomegranates and figs that grew in the Promised Land.

They were away for forty days before returning with their report and with the samples of fruit they had found. They said the grain and grapevines grew tall and strong and that there was plenty to eat and drink. But there was one problem: there were walls around the cities, and the people were fierce and strong. The spies were afraid and didn't think the Israelis would be able to conquer people like that.

But two of the spies, Caleb and Joshua, remembered God's promise that he would give the land to the Israelis. They knew he would keep his promise, for they had faith in him. Caleb begged the people to enter the land at once; they were well able to capture it, he told them.

But the other spies persuaded the people not to go. There were giants there, the spies said, so large that ordinary people seemed about the size of grasshoppers in comparison!

So the Israelis refused to enter the Promised Land.

Moses and Aaron felt terrible about this; so did Joshua and Caleb, the two good spies. Once more they told the people what a wonderful country the Promised Land was. They begged the Israelis not to be afraid of the people living there, for the Lord would help his people. But the people were angry at Caleb and Joshua for saying this, and wanted to kill them.

Then God was very angry with the people of Israel. He told Moses that he would send a terrible plague to destroy them; they could no longer be his people, he said. Instead he would give many children to Moses, and they would become a greater nation than the people of Israel were.

But Moses begged the Lord not to kill them. Moses said that if God destroyed his people and didn't bring them safely into the Promised Land, all the heathen nations would say it was because God wasn't able to do it!

The Lord listened to Moses' prayer and promised not to kill the people after all. But because the people had disobeyed God so often and wouldn't believe his promises even though they had seen him do such wonderful things for them, God said they couldn't enter the Promised Land for forty years. They must wander around in the wilderness all that time until all of them were dead. At the end of the forty years, God said, he would bring their children into the land. And he promised that the two good spies, Caleb and Joshua, would live and enter Canaan with them.

The Israelis returned to their camp and stayed there several days. Then the Lord led them back into the wilderness.

STORY 50

AARON'S AMAZING STICK
NUMBERS 15–18

THE SABBATH was the seventh day of each week; the Israelites were commanded not to work on Sabbaths.

One Sabbath day a man was noticed at work gathering sticks. Since this was against God's law, he was put in jail until the people could find out how God wanted them to punish him for his sin.

The Lord told Moses to sentence the man to death. "Tell the people to take him out of the camp and throw heavy stones upon him until he is dead," the Lord said. So they did.

After this, three men named Korah, Dathan, and Abiram, and 250 other Israelis, started a protest movement against Moses and Aaron. They said Aaron had no right to be the High Priest and that they didn't want Moses as their leader.

Korah was one of the Levites. He helped the priests at the Tabernacle, but he was not satisfied with doing this. He wanted to be a priest. That was why he had urged these 250 men to come with him to speak against Aaron.

Moses heard what they had to say and told them to return the next day, each with an incense cup and some incense. Then the Lord would show them whether or not he had chosen Aaron alone as his High Priest.

So they all returned the next day with their incense cups, put a fire in them, and sprinkled incense on the fire just as the priests did at the Tabernacle. All the rest of the people of Israel came out to watch and to encourage and support the rebels against Moses and Aaron. But the Lord was very displeased with them for coming. He commanded them to get back away from Korah, Dathan, and Abiram. So the people drew back.

Then Moses announced what God's proof would be that he had chosen Moses and Aaron: the ground would open up under Korah, Dathan, and Abiram and swallow them alive.

Moses had hardly finished speaking before the ground opened up and swallowed them—Korah, Dathan and Abiram, with their tents and families—screaming as they went down alive into the ground, and the earth closed over them again.

All the people standing near them ran for their lives, fearing that the earth would swallow them too. And the

Lord sent fire from the sky that killed the 250 other rebels.

But the next day all the people murmured against Moses and Aaron again. "You murdered Korah, Dathan, and Abiram and those 250 other good men," they said.

Then the Lord was very angry. He said to Moses and Aaron, "Get away from these people, for I am going to destroy them." But Moses and Aaron lay flat on their faces before the Lord and prayed for all the Israelis. The Lord refused to listen, for even while they were praying he sent a terrible plague among the people and many of them died.

When Moses realized what was happening, he said to Aaron, "Quick! Take an incense cup and put fire on it from the altar of burnt offering. Sprinkle incense on the fire, and run out among the people and offer up the incense to the Lord."

Aaron did as Moses said. He ran out among the people and stood with the burning incense between those who had died and those still living, and the Lord stopped the plague. But 14,700 people had already died.

Then God reminded the people again that the men of the tribe of Levi would be helpers to Aaron and his sons and would do the work at the Tabernacle.

STORY 51

MOSES' DISOBEDIENCE
NUMBERS 20, 21

NOW ALL THE ISRAELIS moved their camp again, this time to the Zin Desert. Moses' sister Miriam died and was buried there.

Once again they ran out of water, and the people rebelled

against Moses. "Why didn't you murder us along with Korah and the others?" they shouted insolently. "You might as well have done that as to kill us now with thirst."

Then Moses and Aaron went to the Tabernacle and threw themselves flat on the ground before the Lord, and the glory of the Lord appeared to them.

Then the Lord told them to take Aaron's stick from the Tabernacle and as all the people watched, to stand before a certain rock God pointed out to them. "Speak to the rock," God told Moses, "and water will gush out before their eyes."

So Moses took the stick from its place in the Tabernacle and summoned the people. But instead of just speaking to the rock as the Lord had told him to, he yelled angrily at the people. "Listen, you rebels, must we get water for you from the rock?" Then he struck the rock twice, though God had not even mentioned striking it. He had only told Moses to speak to it.

Suddenly water began flowing from the rock and all the people and their cattle drank and drank until they had enough.

But God said to Moses, "You didn't believe me, did you? You didn't think it was enough just to speak to the rock as I told you to. So you struck it twice. The people would have respected me more if the water had started flowing from the rock when you only spoke a word. Your punishment is that you may not lead my people into the Promised Land."

How sad that Moses did wrong and had to be punished! How he had looked forward to going into the Promised Land! But now he would never get there.

When the people arrived at Mount Hor, almost forty years had gone by since they left Egypt. At Mount Hor the Lord spoke to Moses and Aaron and told them that the time had come for Aaron to die. "You and Aaron and Aar-

The Israelis complained;
they wanted water.
Moses struck the rock
and water came out.
But God had told
Moses to speak to
the rock. He was
disobedient.

on's son Eleazar are to go up to the top of Mount Hor," the Lord told them. "When you arrive, take the High Priest's garments off Aaron and put them on his son Eleazar. Aaron will die while you are up there, and Eleazar will be the new High Priest."

Moses did as the Lord commanded. While all the people watched, he and Aaron and Eleazar went up the mountain. When they got to the top, Moses took the High Priest's clothes from Aaron and put them on Aaron's son Eleazar. Then Aaron died on the top of the mountain. So Eleazar became the High Priest in the place of his father.

When Moses and Eleazar came down from the mountain and told the people that Aaron was dead, they had a time of mourning for him that lasted thirty days.

The Israelis were very tired of traveling, and again they sinned by rebelling against God and against Moses. "We have no bread and no water, and how we hate this manna," they complained.

The Lord was angry and sent serpents into the camp to bite the people, causing many of them to die.

They ran to Moses, screaming, "We have sinned, for we have complained against the Lord and against you; please pray that the serpents will go away."

So Moses prayed for them. The Lord told Moses to make a bronze snake that would look like the poisonous snakes that were biting the people.

"Put the bronze snake on a pole," God said. "Whenever anyone is bitten, if he just looks at the snake on the pole, he will get well again."

So Moses made the bronze snake and put it on the top of a pole. Many people looked at it and lived instead of dying from their snake bites.

But it wasn't the bronze snake that made them well. It was the Lord who did it. The bronze snake on the pole reminds us of the Savior. He was lifted up on a wooden cross to die for our sins. If we look up to the Savior on the cross, and realize that he died to take away our sins, God will give us eternal life just as he gave life to the people in Moses' time who did as God said, and looked up at the bronze snake.

STORY 52

BALAAM'S DONKEY SPEAKS!

NUMBERS 22, 23, 24

AS THE ISRAELIS went on, they came to the plains of Moab, where Balak was the king.

When Balak saw them coming, he was frightened. He thought they wanted to fight with him, and he knew there were too many of them for his soldiers to win. So he sent for a man named Balaam to curse the people of Israel. To curse someone means to ask God to send some great evil upon him.

The king told Balaam he would make him rich and great if he would curse the people of Israel.

Balaam loved money, so although the people of Israel had done him no harm, he was willing to curse them to get the money the king promised to give him. He got up early in the morning, saddled his donkey, and started off with the men whom the king had sent.

But God was angry with Balaam for agreeing to curse his people. So God sent an angel with a sword to stand in front of Balaam in the road. Balaam couldn't see the angel, but his donkey did and ran into the field by the side of the road to get away. Balaam beat the donkey and told her to behave!

The angel went on farther and stood in the road at a place where there was a wall on each side. When the donkey came to the place, she pressed up very close to the wall to get by the angel. In doing this she crushed Balaam's foot against the wall, and he hit her again.

Then the angel went on still farther and stood in a narrow place where there was no room at all to get by. The donkey saw the angel standing there with the sword and was so afraid that she fell down under Balaam. This made Balaam very angry, and he beat her as hard as he could.

Then the Lord made the donkey speak like a person! She said, "What have I done to deserve your hitting me these three times?"

Balaam said it was because she had disobeyed him and had turned off the road when he wanted her to go straight ahead. "If I had a sword with me, I'd kill you," Balaam said.

Then the donkey spoke to him again and said, "Haven't you ridden on me ever since I was yours until today? And have I ever done anything like this before?"

"No," Balaam said, "you haven't."

Then the Lord opened Balaam's eyes, and he saw the angel standing there in front of him with a sword, ready to kill him. Balaam was very frightened and threw himself flat on the ground before the angel. Then the angel said to him, "Why have you struck your donkey these three times? I came here to stop you from doing wrong. The donkey saw me and got out of the way. If she hadn't, I would have killed you and saved her alive." Then the angel commanded Balaam to go on to the king, but to say to King Balak only what God would tell him to say.

So Balaam went with the king's men, and the king came out to meet him and welcome him.

God gave this donkey a special message for Balaam because Balaam did not see the angel in the road. Balaam paid attention when he heard the donkey speak.

CURSES TURN TO BLESSINGS

NUMBERS 23, 24

THE NEXT DAY the king took Balaam up on a hill where he could look down and see the entire camp of Israel. Balaam told the king to build seven altars and to prepare seven young bulls and seven rams to sacrifice as burnt offerings to God. Balaam went off by himself, and the Lord met him. Balaam told the Lord about the altars he had built and the animals he had sacrificed. But the Lord wouldn't let him curse the Israelis; he sent him back instead! He said only good things about them and promised that God would care for them and help them.

King Balak was very disappointed and angry when Balaam blessed the Israelis instead of cursing them. He decided to try again. The king took him to a different place from which he could look down upon the people of Israel. He built seven more altars there, and again they sacrificed a young bull and a ram on each altar. Balaam thought that by building so many altars and offering so many sacrifices, he could persuade the Lord to let him curse the people. But he should have known that the Lord wouldn't let anyone harm his people no matter how often he was asked, and no matter how many sacrifices or gifts were given to him.

Balaam told the king to stay there while he went again to ask the Lord for permission to curse the people. The Lord met Balaam but, of course, wouldn't let him curse them. He made him bless them instead!

156

By now King Balak was very angry with Balaam. "I sent for you to curse my enemies, and instead you have blessed them three times," he growled. Then he told Balaam to go home. So Balaam didn't get any of the silver and gold he wanted so much.

When King Balak realized that he couldn't bring evil on the people of Israel by getting Balaam to curse them, he tried another way. He knew he could get the people of Israel to make God angry by sinning against him. For Balaam had told King Balak to invite the Israeli young people to parties honoring idols.

The Lord was very angry with the people of Israel for doing this and sent a disease which killed them by the thousands.

STORY 54

ALMOST THERE
NUMBERS 25–36

THE PEOPLE OF ISRAEL wandered around in the wilderness for forty long years. God wouldn't let them go into the Promised Land of Canaan during all that time. Do you remember why? It was because they had refused to go in when God had told them to; they had listened to the ten spies who were afraid. So God said they must all die in the wilderness, and only their children could enter Canaan, the land God had promised them.

Those forty years finally ended, and God brought them back again to the edge of the Promised Land. He told Moses and Eleazar to count the men old enough to be soldiers.

They discovered that every one of the men who had refused to enter Canaan the first time had died in the wilderness, as the Lord had said they would. Only Caleb and Joshua, the good spies, were still alive, for God had promised that they could go into the Promised Land. Everyone else who had been twenty years old or older at that time had died during those forty years.

Now the Lord led the Israelis to the river Jordan where they waited for him to tell them when to cross. On the other side was the Promised Land of Canaan. But two of the tribes of Israel came to Moses and requested permission to live on this side where they were, instead of on the other side. They asked this because there was good pastureland for their cattle on this side.

At first Moses was angry with them; he thought they wanted to stay behind because they were afraid of the wicked nations in Canaan on the other side of the river.

"You want to stay here while your brothers go over to fight?" he demanded.

"No, no," they replied, "we don't mean that. We'll cross over with the others to fight, but we want to leave our families and cattle here. Then afterwards, when the war is over, we will come back here and live on this side of the river."

So Moses agreed. He spoke to the rest of the people and told them to let the two tribes have the land they asked for. So it was agreed that they should do this.

These two tribes were the tribes of Reuben and Gad. The tribe of Manasseh also asked and received the same permission.

The Lord told Moses that the Israelis must drive out all the heathen nations living across the river. They must destroy all their idols and break down all the heathen altars they would find there.

Every Israeli family was to be given enough land for a home and farm.

The reason why the Israelis must drive out and destroy the heathen nations was so that the Israelis wouldn't be tempted to worship their idols. For if they worshiped them, the Lord would need to destroy his people because of this sin.

MOSES' LAST WORDS
DEUTERONOMY

WHILE THE PEOPLE of Israel were camped beside the river Jordan, waiting to go across, Moses spoke to them for the last time. He knew he couldn't go into Canaan with them because he had angrily struck the rock with his rod instead of just speaking to it as God had told him to.

He was afraid the people would forget God's laws when he was gone. In this last talk to them, Moses told them again how kind the Lord had been. He reminded them of the time forty years before when they were so close to Canaan, but they had refused to go in because the spies told them the people in Canaan were too strong to fight against. He reminded them how angry the Lord had been with them and how God had sent them back into the wilderness for forty years.

Moses told the people that he had begged the Lord to let him cross the river with them, to enter the good land there in Canaan. But the Lord had said no, he must speak of it no more.

But the Lord told him he could see the Promised Land even though he couldn't go into it. So he climbed a high mountain and saw it far away in the distance.

Moses asked the Lord to give the people of Israel another leader to take his place. Otherwise, he said, the people would have no one to guide them and care for them. They would be scattered and lost, like sheep without a shepherd. The Lord announced that he had chosen Joshua as the new leader, so all the people must obey him just as they had obeyed Moses.

Moses told the people to teach God's commandments to their children. They must talk about these laws in their homes, and when they were out for walks, and before going to sleep at night, and when waking again in the morning. Everyone must talk about God's laws many times each day and remind each other about how great and good God is.

They must never forget how God had led them through the wilderness for forty years and fed them with manna. In all that time their clothes had not worn out, and their feet had never become sore from traveling. God had led them through that lonely wilderness to a better land where streams ran through the fields and where springs of water poured down from the hills. In that good land across the river the grain grew plentifully and there were huge crops of juicy grapes; there were fig trees and pomegranates and olive trees—food enough and to spare. And there was iron and copper in the hills, which they could dig out and use to make many wonderful things. They must never become proud and say that they had got these things by themselves, for it was the Lord alone who gave everything to them. The Lord said that if they forgot about him and worshiped other gods, they would be killed.

When the Lord gave them victory over the people living in Canaan, the people of Israel must never say God had done this for them because they were so good! No, they weren't good at all. Rather it was because the people living in Canaan were so wicked. And it was because God had promised Abraham, Isaac, and Jacob that he would give the land of Canaan to the Israelis.

STORY 56

THE CITIES OF SAFETY
DEUTERONOMY

GOD ALSO TOLD his people that some of their cities must be set aside as safety zones, where a man could run and be safe from punishment if he had accidentally killed someone. For instance, if he was cutting down a tree and the head of the axe flew off the handle, killing someone standing there, the man with the axe must run to a city of safety. Otherwise the dead man's brother or son or some other relative might try to kill him in revenge. But if he escaped and ran to the city of safety, no one could hurt him there. If anyone did, that person would himself be killed.

When a person who had accidentally killed someone arrived at the city of safety, he would tell the judges what he had done. They would take him into the city and give him a place to live. Then if the brother or the son of the man he had killed came and asked for him, they would protect him because he hadn't meant to hurt or kill anyone.

But if some wicked murderer came to the city and asked

for safety, the judges wouldn't let him in, and he would be put to death for his sin.

Moses told the people that on the very day they crossed the river and entered the Promised Land, they should build a monument of stones with the laws of God written on them for everyone to read.

Moses said that if the people of Israel obeyed the Lord, the Lord would make them the greatest nation on earth. He would bless them and their children, their land, and their cattle. Their enemies would be afraid of them and would stay far away.

But if the people of Israel didn't obey God, then they would have constant trouble. The seed they planted in their fields wouldn't grow, locusts would come and destroy their growing grain, and worms would eat their grapevines. The people would be weak and sickly, and the Lord would send fierce warriors against them who would not pity the old or the young, but would take them all away as slaves to other countries.

Moses told the people that they must choose between the good and evil ways. He begged them to choose the good way so that they and their children would live long and well.

Then he presented Joshua to them as their new leader.

The Lord now summoned Moses and Joshua to the Tabernacle. He appeared to them there in the pillar of cloud, and consecrated Joshua as the new leader of Israel.

Moses wrote down God's laws and ordered that every seven years the priests, elders, and all the people, including the children, must be called together to listen as these laws were read aloud to them. For they needed to hear them again and again and to remember to obey them. Moses gave the book of laws to the Levites, and told them to keep it inside the Ark.

After this the Lord told Moses to climb to the top of Mount Nebo to look across the river Jordan into the Promised Land. Then he would die on the mountain, just as Aaron had died on Mount Hor.

Moses was an old man now, but still as strong as many young men. He said a last good-bye to his people and climbed to the top of the mountain. There he looked across the Jordan at the Promised Land of Canaan—the land God had promised long before to Abraham, Isaac, Jacob, and to their descendants.

Then Moses died there on the top of the mountain, and the Lord buried him in a valley in the land of Moab, but no one knows where. He was 120 years old when he died, but he was well and strong until the day of his death.

After that, Joshua ruled the Israelis and they obeyed him as they had obeyed Moses. The Lord gave Joshua wisdom and made him able to teach and guide them.

STORY 57

A NEW LEADER
JOSHUA 1, 2, 3

THEN THE LORD said to Joshua, "Moses my assistant is dead, and you must lead the Israelis across the river Jordan into the land I promised them. Be strong and brave, and be careful to obey all of my laws. Then everything you do will be successful. Don't be afraid, for I will be with you and help you wherever you go."

Then Joshua spoke to the Israeli officers. "Go through the camp," he said, "and announce to all the people that three days from now we will cross the river Jordan into Canaan, the Promised Land!"

Meanwhile, Joshua had already sent two spies across. They came to the city of Jericho and went into the house of a woman named Rahab. Someone told the king of Jericho that two spies had come to the city and were at Rahab's house, so the king sent police officers to Rahab's home and told her to bring out the men who were hiding there.

Instead, Rahab took the two men up to the flat roof of her house and hid them under some stalks of flax spread there to dry. The king's messengers looked everywhere, but since they couldn't find them, they finally went away.

After they had gone, Rahab talked with the men and said she knew that the Lord had given her country to the Israelis. The people of Canaan had already heard how the God of Israel had dried up a path for them through the Red Sea and how he had helped them in fighting against their enemies. Rahab said that when her people heard these things they were very much afraid of the people of Israel. Then she asked the two men to promise that they would remember her kindness in protecting them, and not let any of her family be killed when Israel captured the city of Jericho.

The men said that if she would keep it a secret about their being there, they would protect her. They told her to hang a red rope from the window of her house to help them recognize it again. When the Israeli army came to destroy the city, no one inside her house would be harmed.

The city of Jericho had a high wall around it, and Rahab's house was built on the wall. The king had ordered the

Joshua led the Israelis around Jericho for six days.
On the seventh day they marched around it seven times.
Then they all blew their trumpets and shouted.
The walls crumbled!

gates of the city to be closed to keep the two spies from getting away, so Rahab let the two men down by a rope on the outside of the wall. She warned them to hide in a nearby mountain for three days until the soldiers stopped looking for them.

They did this, then crossed the river to tell Joshua all that had happened.

Joshua and all the people got up early the next morning and traveled to the banks of the river Jordan, where they stayed for three days. Then Joshua told them, "Get ready! Tomorrow we will cross the river, and the Lord will do wonders among you. The priests will go first, carrying the Ark. As soon as their feet touch the water, the river will stop flowing, and the priests will walk through on dry ground!"

Everything happened just as Joshua had said. The next morning the priests carried the Ark towards the river, and all the people followed them. When the priests stepped into the water at the river's edge, the water opened up in front of them, and they walked on dry ground into the middle of the river! The priests waited there with the Ark while all the people walked past them to the other side, into the Promised Land of Canaan.

After all the people had crossed, the priests carrying the Ark followed. As soon as they stepped out of the river onto the shore, the river began flowing again!

The Israelis made their camp at a place called Gilgal. There they found some corn in the fields, which they roasted and ate. It was the first time they had eaten anything but manna for forty years! The next day, the manna stopped coming. For the forty years while they were in the wilderness where no grain grew, the Lord had sent manna to them every morning without fail. But in Canaan there was plenty of food, so the Lord stopped sending the manna.

166

JERICHO'S WALLS FALL DOWN

JOSHUA 5, 6

JOSHUA LEFT THE CAMP and went on foot to inspect the city of Jericho with its high walls. Glancing up, he saw a man with a sword in his hand. Joshua strode up to him. "Are you friend or foe?" he demanded.

"I am the general-in-chief of the Lord's army," the man replied. He was telling Joshua that he had come to be their leader and to show them how to win the battles against their enemies. Joshua realized that this man was the Lord, so he fell to the ground and worshiped him. It was the same Man who had come to Abraham's tent long before to say that God was going to destroy Sodom. And he was the Man who had wrestled with Jacob when he was returning to Canaan from Laban's house.

The people of Jericho had shut the city gates to stop the Israelis from coming in. But the Lord said he would give Joshua the victory anyway. He even told him how to plan his attack.

All the Israeli soldiers, he said, must march around the city once every day for six days, and the priests must go with them carrying the Ark. Seven priests were to walk ahead of the Ark, blowing trumpets made of ram's horns.

On the seventh day the Israelis were to march around Jericho, not once, but seven times while the priests blew the trumpets. As they finished the seventh time around, the priests must blow a loud, long blast, and all the army must give a mighty shout. Then the walls of the city would fall down flat, and the Israelis could walk right in!

Joshua told his army that only Rahab and those with her in her house would be saved alive. The Lord had commanded that all the rest of the people of Jericho must die for their sins. All the silver, gold, brass, and iron in the city belonged to the Lord and must be put into the treasury where gifts to the Lord were kept. Joshua told the people not to take any of it for themselves, for the Lord would send a great punishment upon them if they did.

The people did as the Lord commanded. The first day they all marched around the city once, the priests following behind blowing the trumpets. Then came the priests who carried the Ark.

On the second day they marched around the city again, and so on for six days.

But on the seventh day they got up early, before it was light, and marched around the city seven times. The last time around, the priests blew a great blast on the trumpets, and Joshua called out to his army, "Shout, for the Lord has given you the city!"

They gave a mighty shout, and at that moment the walls of the city tumbled down before them, and they rushed into Jericho and captured it. Joshua told the spies who had been at Rahab's house to protect Rahab and everyone with her, just as they had promised her. So they saved Rahab, her father and mother, her brothers, and all who were with her in the house. Afterwards the army of Israel burned the city; but the silver, gold, iron, and bronze were put into the treasury of the Lord.

A Thief
Is Punished

JOSHUA 7, 8

THEN JOSHUA SENT scouts to Ai, another city of Canaan. When they came back they told him that it was a small city and not many people lived there, so only a part of the Israeli army was needed to capture it. Two or three thousand men would be enough, they said.

So Joshua sent about three thousand men. But when the men of Ai came out against them, the Israelis suddenly became afraid and ran, and the men of Ai killed about thirty-six of them.

Joshua didn't know what to do. Israel had been defeated! He tore his clothes, and he and the elders of Israel lay on the ground praying until the evening. Joshua cried out to the Lord, saying, "All the people of Canaan will hear how the Israeli army has run away from its enemies; and they will gather around us on every side and kill us, until not one of us is left."

But the Lord said, "Get up! Why are you lying there? There is sin among the people of Israel; that is why your enemies have defeated you."

Then the Lord told Joshua that one of the men of Israel had kept some silver and gold taken from the city of Jericho. He had taken it for himself instead of putting it into the treasury of the Lord. The Lord said he would not help the people of Israel any more unless they punished the man who had done this.

God told Joshua to bring all the people before him, and he would tell Joshua who the thief was. The man who had done this thing must be burned alive in punishment for stealing from the Lord and for not obeying him. So Joshua got up early in the morning and brought all the people before the Lord, and the Lord showed him the man who was guilty. His name was Achan.

"Tell me what you have done," Joshua demanded.

Achan then admitted that he had seen a beautiful garment and some silver and a piece of gold, and that he had taken them and hidden them in the ground beneath his tent.

Joshua sent messengers who ran to Achan's tent and found the things buried there. They brought them to Joshua and to all the people of Israel and laid them out before the Lord.

Then Joshua and all the people took Achan and the beautiful garment, and the silver and gold, and his sons and daughters, his tent, his cattle, and everything he owned, to a nearby valley. There they were stoned to death and burned. A great heap of stones was piled over Achan's dead body to show where it lay. After that the valley was called the Valley of Achor, which means "The Valley of Trouble."

Then the Lord said to Joshua, "Now you can conquer the city of Ai." And the Lord commanded Joshua to put all the people of Ai to death for their sins. This time, he said, the Israelis could keep the gold and silver they found, instead of putting it into the treasury of the Lord.

So Joshua and all his army attacked Ai. He sent thirty thousand men around behind the city during the night to hide where the people of Ai couldn't see them. The rest of the army attacked from the front.

170

Joshua killed all the people of Ai, as the Lord had commanded. But the Israelis kept the gold, silver, and cattle for themselves, for God had said that this time it was all right for them to do this.

Joshua then built an altar of great stones on Mount Ebal and wrote God's law on it, just as Moses had told him to.

JOSHUA GETS FOOLED

JOSHUA 9, 10

WHEN THE OTHER KINGS in Canaan heard how Israel had destroyed Ai, they brought all their armies together to fight against Joshua and his people.

But one of the cities, named Gibeon, refused to join the others. The people of Gibeon didn't want to fight, for they knew that the Lord was helping the Israelis and would destroy anyone fighting them. Instead, they sent men to Joshua wearing very old clothes and worn-out shoes and carrying dry and moldy bread, pretending that they had come from another country far away.

They came to Joshua and told him, "We have come from a distant land, for we have heard of your God and of all the great things he has done for you. Our people have sent us to ask you to make a treaty with us and be our friends."

Joshua and the men of Israel didn't ask the Lord what to do, as they should have done; they agreed at once to be friends with the people of Gibeon.

Three days later they learned the truth. These men had not come from a distant country at all, but lived close by, in Canaan, and were among the wicked nations the armies of Israel had been told to destroy.

Then Joshua called for the men of Gibeon and demanded to know why they had lied to him. They said it was because they feared for their lives, for they had heard that God was going to destroy the people living in Canaan and was going to give their land to the Israelis. Joshua couldn't kill them because only three days before he had promised not to. But he said they must be slaves, and work for the priests and the Levites, cutting wood and carrying the water needed at the Tabernacle.

When the king of Jerusalem heard that the people of Gibeon had surrendered to the Israelis, he was very angry. He and four other kings put their armies together and went to Gibeon to fight against it in revenge.

Then the men of Gibeon sent a messenger to Joshua. "Quick! Come and help us," they said, "for the kings of the mountains have come to punish us."

Joshua and his army fought against the five kings attacking Gibeon, and the Lord made them become afraid of the Israelis and run away. But as they ran, the Lord caused great hailstones to fall upon them out of heaven, so that more of them were killed by hailstones than by the Israelis.

As the Israeli army was chasing them, the sun began to set, for it was evening. Joshua was afraid that God's enemies would escape in the darkness, so he commanded the sun not to go down, and he told the moon to stay where it was and not to move farther across the sky.

There was no day like it either before or afterwards, for the Lord, at Joshua's request, made the sun and moon stand still in the sky so that the Israelis could keep on chasing and destroying their enemies.

THE LONG
JOURNEY ENDS
JOSHUA 18-21

JOSHUA AND HIS TROOPS won many, many more battles against many kings, but there was still much land remaining to be conquered.

All the people of Israel went to the city of Shiloh to set up the Tabernacle there. They had carried the Tabernacle all the way from Mount Sinai, taking it down when they traveled and setting it up again when they stopped. But they had come to Canaan to stay—their long journey was ended. The Tabernacle wouldn't have to be moved again.

The priests and Levites brought the Tabernacle to Shiloh, a city near the center of their new country, and set it up permanently as the Lord had told them to.

But although Israel had conquered only part of Canaan, they had grown tired of war and wanted rest and quiet. It seemed as though they did not want all the good land God was willing to give them.

The Lord spoke to Joshua and reminded him that a large part of the land had not yet been taken away from the Canaanites. So Joshua asked all the people how long it would be before they would be ready to continue the war against the heathen nations still living in Canaan. He asked them to choose twenty-one scouts, and Joshua sent them out to inspect the land that was still unconquered. He told them to give him a written report.

The chosen men walked through the land, made maps

of it, and brought their report to Joshua in Shiloh. Then Joshua drew straws for the different tribes of Israel so that the Lord could tell them which part of the land each tribe should have. God told them to finish driving out the heathen nations so that they could have the land for their own use. Joshua promised that the Lord would help his people do this.

God said that the priests and Levites were not to own farms like the men of the other tribes, because he wanted them to stay at the Tabernacle and work for God there. But God said they could have cities of their own to live in. The priests and Levites came to Joshua and the leaders of Israel to find out what cities they could have, and they were given forty-eight cities where they could bring their wives and children and have their homes.

STORY 62

THE PEOPLE CHOOSE GOD
JOSHUA 22, 23, 24

THE MEN OF THE TRIBES living across the river Jordan had stayed with the Israeli army ever since crossing the river and had fought against the heathen nations in Canaan. They received a full share of the cattle, gold, silver, and anything else taken from the enemy.

Joshua called these men to him and thanked them for their help. "You have obeyed me, whatever I told you to do," he said. "You have not let your brothers fight alone,

Joshua drew straws
for the different tribes of Israel
so that the Lord could tell them
which part of the land
each tribe should have.

but have stayed with them and helped them. Now go back to your homes on the other side of the Jordan. But be very careful, after you get there, to obey all the commandments Moses gave us, and to love and to serve the Lord your God with all your hearts."

So they started back home. When they came to the river Jordan, they stopped and built a great altar, shaped like God's altar at Shiloh, where the Tabernacle was. But God had told the Israelis not to sacrifice on any other altar but the one at the Tabernacle. When the men of the other tribes heard that they had built another altar, they were angry, and sent their armies to fight them.

Phinehas, the High Priest, and ten Israeli leaders arrived ahead of the army to ask why they had built this altar.

"We want to know," they said, "why you have built another altar to offer sacrifices on, when the Lord said we should have only one altar—the one at Shiloh. Don't you remember how God sent a great plague on us for worshiping the idols of the Midianites and the Moabites?"

The tribes from across the river were very surprised. They said they had never dreamed of using the altar for sacrifices. It was just a monument, in the form of the altar at Shiloh. In years to come, they said, the people on Joshua's side of the Jordan might say that the tribes on their side of the river Jordan weren't really Israelis, because they didn't live in the Promised Land of Canaan. They could then point to the monument as proof that they were truly people of Israel, just like the others. They fully understood, they said, that there must be no sacrificing except at Shiloh.

So then everyone was happy again.

Joshua had become an old man. One day he summoned the leaders of Israel and reminded them of all the Lord had done for them and urged them always to honor God in everything they did. Then the Lord would greatly bless and prosper them, he said.

"The Lord has driven out your enemies and given you cities, fields, vineyards, and a land of your own to live in," Joshua reminded them. "Fear the Lord and worship him. If you don't want to worship him, then choose the idols you would rather worship. But as for me and my family, we will worship the Lord."

The people answered, "God forbid that we should leave the Lord to worship idols. For it was he who brought us out of Egypt and gave us this land. We will worship the Lord, for he is our God."

Then Joshua took a great stone and set it up beneath an oak beside the Tabernacle in Shiloh. That stone, he said, would be a witness to remind them of the promises they had made to worship only the Lord.

So Joshua died. This godly man had lived for 110 years.

GOD KEEPS ON HELPING HIS PEOPLE

JUDGES 3

AFTER JOSHUA'S DEATH, the Israeli army continued to fight the heathen nations as the Lord had told them to; and God helped them and made them victorious. But they stopped fighting before they had driven out all the nations of Canaan. They allowed some of the heathen nations to stay.

Then the Lord said to the people of Israel, "I brought you out of Egypt into this land I promised you. I commanded you to destroy the idols of the nations living here, and I told you never to make peace with them. But you have not obeyed me. Now I will not help you any more. The rest of the nations shall stay, and they will tempt you to sin and cause you great trouble."

Then the people of Israel began worshiping idols named Baal and Ashtaroth, who were the gods of the people of Canaan. The Lord was very angry about this and sent enemies to fight against his people and to make them their slaves.

But when they turned away from the idols and turned again to the Lord and asked for his help, he helped them by raising up leaders, called judges. These men helped them fight against their masters and win. Yet, as soon as the Lord set the people free, they would forget him and sin again by worshiping idols and ignoring the Lord. This sinning and repenting continued for more than three hundred years! During that time fifteen judges were their leaders.

The first judge was Othniel; he was the younger brother of Caleb, one of the good spies. Othniel fought against the king of Mesopotamia, who had kept the Israelis as slaves for eight years. And God helped Othniel and the men of Israel conquer their master's army, so they were free again for the next forty years.

But after Othniel was dead the people of Israel began to worship idols again. Then the king of Moab led his army against Israel and enslaved them for eighteen years. But when the people of Israel cried to the Lord for help, the Lord appointed Ehud as their leader.

Ehud made a dagger, hid it under his coat, and came to the king of Moab's palace while the king was sitting in his summer parlor. "I have a secret message from God for you, O king," Ehud said to him. The king sent everybody out of the room so he could hear the secret. Then Ehud pulled out the dagger and killed the king.

Ehud ran out of the house, and shut and locked the doors behind him. When the king's assistants returned, they saw that the doors of his room were locked and said to themselves, "The king must want to be alone; we'd better not go in." But after they had waited a very long time, they took a key and opened the doors and found the king lying dead on the floor.

By this time Ehud was far away, and they couldn't find him. Ehud went to Mount Ephraim, in the land of Canaan, and blew a trumpet to call the men of Israel to him.

"Follow me," he told them. "The king is dead, and the Lord will help you conquer the army of Moab."

The men of Israel fought and killed ten thousand brave soldiers of Moab; not one escaped. So the Israelis were again free from the Moabites. This freedom continued for the next eighty years.

STORY 64

TWO BRAVE WOMEN
JUDGES 4, 5, 6

SHAMGAR WAS the next judge of Israel. He led his people against the Philistines; and all by himself, with nothing but a sharp stick and the Lord's help, he killed six hundred of the enemy.

But when the people of Israel began to worship idols again, God let them be conquered again. This time they were slaves for twenty long years. Then the Lord gave them another judge to help them in their troubles. This judge was a woman named Deborah. She lived near Bethel in a house beneath a palm tree.

Deborah sent for a man named Barak and told him that the Lord wanted him to lead ten thousand Israeli soldiers against Sisera, the captain of the enemy army. But Barak was afraid and wouldn't go unless Deborah went with him. Deborah said she would, but the honor of the victory would go to a woman!

So Barak and Deborah led the ten thousand men of Israel against Sisera. Sisera called up all his reserves, including nine hundred iron chariots, and came out to fight. But the Lord gave Israel the victory.

Sisera jumped from his chariot and ran away to the tent of a woman named Jael. He didn't know she was a friend of the people of Israel.

"Give me a little water," he begged her, "for I am very thirsty." So she gave him some milk to drink.

"Stand in the door of your tent," he told her, "and if anyone comes by and asks if you have seen me, tell him no."

He was so tired that he lay down and slept. Jael took a sharp tent peg that was used to fasten the tent to the ground, went quietly over to him, and drove it into his head with a hammer, killing him.

Soon afterwards Barak came by looking for Sisera. Jael went out to meet him and said, "Come here, and I will show you the man you are looking for." Then she took him into the tent, and there lay Sisera, dead.

So the Israelis were freed from the king of Canaan that day.

But after forty years of freedom, the people of Israel began worshiping idols again. Then the Midianites came and fought them, and made slaves of them and treated them very cruelly.

Then, as they had before, the Israelis cried to the Lord to help them. The judge the Lord sent this time was Gideon.

Gideon was threshing wheat one day and trying to hide it from the Midianites, when the Lord came to him in the form of an angel and spoke kindly to him. Then Gideon told the Lord about the troubles the people of Israel were having because of the Midianites.

"You will free the people of Israel from the Midianites!" the Lord told him.

"But, Lord, how can I do that?" Gideon asked.

"That's easy!" the Lord replied, "I will be with you, and you will destroy their whole army as if it were only one man!"

STORY 65

GIDEON AND HIS WOOL
JUDGES 6, 7, 8

SOON A GREAT ARMY of Midianites arrived and camped in the valley of Jezreel. Gideon blew a trumpet and called the men of Israel to go with him and fight them.

Gideon asked God to do a miracle to prove to him that it was really God who had promised to help him when he went to fight against the Midianites. This is the miracle Gideon asked God to do. Gideon said he would leave some wool out on the ground all night. In the morning, if the wool was wet with dew and the ground all around it was dry, this would be a miracle and he would know that the Lord was going to help him in his fight to free the people of Israel.

So Gideon left the wool on the ground all night. Early the next morning he went out and found it full of water. He wrung the dew out of it with his hands and filled a bowl with the water, but the ground all around was dry! Why wasn't the ground wet too? You see, it was a miracle.

Then Gideon asked the Lord for permission to try it again; but this time he asked God to make the ground wet with dew and to let the wool stay dry! God agreed, so Gideon left the wool out another night, and in the morning the wool was perfectly dry, but the ground all around was wet!

Gideon knew by these miracles that the Lord would certainly help him when he went out to fight against the Midianites. Gideon's little army got up early in the morning and started towards the vast army of Midian. But the Lord told Gideon that his little army was too big!

"Send some of your men home," God said. "Tell anyone who is afraid, to leave."

When Gideon told his men this, twenty-two thousand of them went home, while ten thousand stayed.

"There are still too many!" the Lord said. "Bring them

God told Gideon to send his soldiers home except for three hundred of them who drank from their hands. God would use these to defeat an army.

182

down to the river, and I will choose the ones I want in the battle."

So Gideon brought them to the river. All the men were thirsty and began to drink. Some lifted the water to their mouths in their hands, and some stooped down and put their mouths into the water. The Lord said that only the ones who drank from their hands (there were three hundred of them) could go with him to the battle!

Gideon told the three hundred men to get up and come with him, for the Lord would give them the victory. He put them in three different groups and gave each man a trumpet and a pitcher with a lighted lamp inside. He told them that when they came to the camp of the Midianites, they must do exactly as he did. When he blew his trumpet, they must all blow theirs and shout, "The sword of the Lord and of Gideon!"

In the middle of the night he and his three hundred men arrived in the camp of the Midianites. Suddenly he and all of his men blew their trumpets and broke the pitchers and shouted, "The sword of the Lord and of Gideon!"

When the Midianites heard the noise and saw the burning lamps that had been hidden in the pitchers, they yelled in fear and ran for their lives. The Lord made them afraid both of the men of Israel and of each other, too, so that they were killing and fighting one another all over the valley.

Gideon and his men chased them as they fled across the river Jordan. The two kings of the Midianites raced ahead of him with fifteen thousand soldiers. But he caught up with them and overcame them and took the two kings captive.

So the Midianites were driven out of Canaan, and the people of Israel were no longer their slaves.

Gideon was the judge of Israel for forty years. God gave him many sons, and he lived to be an old man.

ABIMELECH KILLS HIS BROTHERS

JUDGES 9, 10

AS SOON AS GIDEON was dead, the Israelis promptly forgot about the Lord. They turned away from God again, and worshiped the idol Baal.

Gideon's son Abimelech was king of the city of Shechem, but his friends wanted him to be king over all of Israel instead of just one city. They gave him seventy pieces of silver taken from the temple of Baal, and he used the money to hire men to go with him and help him.

First he killed all his brothers except the youngest, who ran away. Abimelech did this because he was afraid the people might become tired of him and ask one of his brothers to be king instead. So he became the king of all the land of Israel.

After Abimelech had been king for three years, God sent him trouble. Instead of being his friends, the people of Shechem became his enemies. While he was away on a trip, they decided to kill him.

The governor of the city, who was still Abimelech's friend, sent him this secret message: "Be careful. The people of Shechem have rebelled against you. Come in the night with your men, and hide out in the field until morning. As soon as the sun is up, march towards the city, and when the people come out to fight you, you can defeat them."

So Abimelech did this. He brought his men to the city

185

during the night and hid them in the fields near the city. In the morning the people saw him and came out to fight, but he chased them back into the city and killed many of them.

Later, some of the men of Shechem escaped to the temple of their idol Baal and barred the heavy gates so that Abimelech couldn't get to them. He led his troops up a mountain and cut off large branches from the trees, then returned to the temple. They piled the branches against the door and set them on fire, burning up the temple and all the people inside.

Then Abimelech went to the city of Thebez, fought against it, and captured it. The people who lived there fled into a strong tower, locked the door, and climbed to its top. Abimelech tried to burn the tower as he had the idol temple in Shechem, but a woman threw down a huge rock from the top of the tower. It hit him on the head, crushing his skull.

When he knew he was dying, he called one of his young men and said to him, "Draw your sword and kill me so it won't be said I was killed by a woman."

The youth thrust his sword through Abimelech, and he died. In this way God punished Abimelech for killing his brothers and also punished the people of Shechem for helping him do it.

After Abimelech was dead, Tola was the judge of Israel for twenty-three years.

After him, Jair, who lived across the river Jordan in the land of Gilead, was judge for twenty-two years. He had thirty sons, and each of them was the governor of a city in Gilead.

Then the people of Israel turned away from the Lord again and worshiped Baal and Ashtaroth, the same idols their fathers had worshiped. So this time when the Philistines attacked Israel, the Lord didn't help his people. They became slaves again for eighteen years.

In their trouble they cried out to the Lord for help; but he reminded them of how often he had set them free from their enemies, only to see them turn their backs on him again and worship heathen idols. Let them go to the idols they had chosen, he said, and ask them for help. But the people of Israel confessed their sins and asked God to punish them, but please to set them free from their enemies. They destroyed the idols they had worshiped, and worshiped the Lord again, and he pitied them in their sufferings.

JEPHTHAH'S FOOLISH PROMISE
JUDGES 11

THE AMMONITES CAME to attack Israel again and were camped in the land of Gilead, on the other side of the river Jordan. The Israeli men organized an army, too, but they had no leader; they needed a general to tell them what to do.

One of the Israelis, named Jephthah, was a great and brave soldier, but the men of Israel had been unkind to him, so he moved away to another country. But when the people wanted a man to lead them against their enemies, they remembered Jephthah. The elders of Israel went to him in the land of Tob, and said, "Come and be the general of our army."

Jephthah answered, "You hated me and sent me away. Why come to me now when you are in trouble?" But the elders promised before the Lord that they would make him their king if he won the war for them. So Jephthah went with them.

He sent messengers to the king of the Ammonites, asking him why he had come to fight. The king answered that hundreds of years before, the Israelis had taken away his land when they came up out of Egypt. "Give me back my land," he said.

But Jephthah sent messengers to say that the land they had taken was given to them by the Lord, and they were going to keep it. Then Jephthah and the men of Israel went out to fight the Ammonite army.

Before the battle, Jephthah made a promise that if the Lord would give him the victory, he would offer up as a burnt offering whatever came out of his door to meet him when he returned home from the battle. Jephthah did wrong in making such a promise, for he had no idea who or what might come to meet him.

When he led his troops against the Ammonites, the Lord

Jephthah made a foolish promise.
The one who first met him
was his only daughter.
Can you imagine how he felt?
He should not have
kept his promise.

gave him the victory, so the Israelis were free from their slavery again. When the battle was over, Jephthah returned to his home. His daughter, his only child, came running out to meet him, full of joy at seeing her father again.

Can you imagine how Jephthah felt? He tore his clothes in his sorrow and finally told her of his promise.

She said, "Father, if you have made a vow to the Lord, do to me as you have said."

Jephthah should not have kept his wicked promise. God had commanded the Israelis to sacrifice oxen, goats, and lambs as burnt offerings. God had told them never to sacrifice their children; this was what heathen nations did and were punished for doing. Jephthah should have repented of his promise and asked God's forgiveness; but instead, he kept his evil promise.

STORY 68

A VISIT FROM AN ANGEL
JUDGES 13

AFTER THIS the people of Israel sinned again and displeased the Lord by worshiping idols. Again they became slaves, this time to the Philistines for forty years.

A man named Manoah and his wife were among those who still worshiped the Lord, but they were sad because they had no children. One day the angel of the Lord came and told Manoah's wife that she and Manoah would have a son. The angel said their son was set apart for God and must never drink wine or whiskey and must never have his hair cut. The angel also told them that when their son was grown, he would free Israel from the Philistines.

The woman ran and told her husband that a prophet had spoken to her, for she did not realize he was an angel. Then Manoah prayed, "Lord, let the prophet come again and teach us how to raise the child you are going to give us."

The Lord heard Manoah's prayer, and the angel came again to the woman as she was out in the field. She ran to her husband and told him the man had come again. Manoah went with his wife and said to him, "Are you the man of God who was talking to my wife?"

"I am," he said.

Then Manoah asked him, "How shall we raise the child you have promised us?"

The angel answered, "Be sure to do everything I told your wife before."

Manoah begged the angel to stay and eat with them, for they still didn't know it was an angel. But the angel said, "Even if I stay I will not eat your food."

Then Manoah said, "Tell us your name so that we can honor you when the child is born as you have promised us."

The angel answered, "Why do you ask my name? It is a secret."

Then Manoah took a young goat as a burnt offering and sacrificed it upon a rock. The angel did a wonderful thing as the fire was burning on the rock, its flame going up towards heaven. The angel of the Lord went up in the flame and disappeared! When Manoah and his wife saw this, they fell flat upon the ground in worship.

Manoah was frightened. "We have seen God," he said, for he believed the angel was the Lord. "We shall surely die because we have seen him."

But his wife said to him, "If the Lord had intended to kill us, he wouldn't have accepted our burnt offering nor promised us a son."

A few months later, God gave Manoah and his wife the son he had promised them, and they named him Samson. As the child grew, the Lord was kind to him and blessed him.

SAMSON'S RIDDLE
JUDGES 14

WHEN SAMSON WAS GROWN, he went to a city called Timnath, where he fell in love with a Philistine girl. She was not a Jewess, but when he returned home he told his father and mother about her and asked them to get her as his wife. His father and mother told him he should marry an Israeli girl, not a Philistine girl, for the Philistines were enemies of the Israelites. Besides, God had told his people not to marry non-Jews.

But Samson was not willing to give her up. He said to his father, "I want her, so get her for me."

His father and mother went back with him to Timnath. On the way there, a young lion came roaring out at Sam-

Samson was so strong that he could break
the strongest ropes his enemies tied him with.
They had not yet discovered
the secret of his strength.

son, and the Lord gave him strength to kill the lion with his hands as easily as if it had been a young goat.

When Samson finally met the girl and talked with her, he wanted all the more to marry her. A wedding date was set, and he and his parents went back home. When he returned to marry her, he came to the place where he had killed the lion and went over to look at it. Its body was all dried up, and a swarm of bees was living in it, storing honey there. He took some of the honey in his hands and ate it as he walked. Afterwards he gave some to his father and mother, but he didn't tell them he had taken it out of the dead body of the lion.

Samson gave a big party for the young men of the town, for that was one of the marriage customs of those days. Thirty Philistine youths came, and the party lasted seven days. During the party Samson decided to tell them a riddle. He promised to give each of the young men a suit if they found out what his riddle meant before the seven days of the party ended. But if they couldn't find the answer to his riddle, then each of them must give *him* a suit! The Philistine boys agreed to his bet.

"Go ahead," they said, "tell us the riddle."

"All right," Samson replied, "Here it is: 'Food came out of the eater, and sweetness came out of the strong!'" (He meant that he had taken honey from a lion, and eaten it. But of course he didn't tell the Philistines the answer because then he would lose the bet!)

For three days they tried to find the answer, but couldn't. Finally the young men went to his bride and told her they would kill her and her whole family unless she found out from Samson the answer to the riddle.

She knew they would kill her, so she asked Samson to tell her, but he wouldn't. Then she started crying and saying he didn't love her or he would tell her.

"I haven't even told my father or my mother," Samson answered; "why should I tell you?"

But she kept on begging and crying, and he finally told her just to keep her quiet. Then of course she went and told the Philistine boys.

They came to Samson on the seventh day, just before the end of the feast, and pretended they had thought up the answer by themselves. "What is sweeter than honey?" they asked. "And what is stronger than a lion?" But Samson knew his wife had told them.

SAMSON THE STRONG MAN
JUDGES 16

ONE DAY SAMSON decided to visit a Philistine girl friend of his named Delilah. When the kings of the Philistine cities knew he was there, they promised to give Delilah eleven hundred pieces of silver if she would help them capture him. So Delilah begged Samson to tell her the secret of his great strength and how he could be made as weak as other men.

Samson told her a lie. He said that if he were tied with seven ropes made from green flax, then he would be as helpless as any other man.

Delilah told this to the kings of the Philistines, and she tied him with the ropes while he was asleep. He didn't know there were men hiding in the room to grab him.

When she had tied him up she cried out, "The Philistines are here to get you, Samson!" Instantly, Samson woke up and broke the ropes as easily as if they were threads.

Delilah said he had mocked her and told her a lie and begged him to tell her the truth. How could he be tied up so that he couldn't get away? This time Samson said that if he were tied with two new ropes that had never been used before, he would not be able to break them. So she took two new ropes and tied him, while men hid in the room, then called out to him as before that the Philistines were coming to get him. But he broke the new ropes as easily as before.

Delilah scolded him for lying to her again, and again she begged him to tell her how to tie him so he couldn't get away. Samson said that if she would weave his long hair into a loom, his strength would leave him and he would be helpless. So she did this. But when she told him the Philistines were coming, he was as strong as ever.

"How can you say, 'I love you' when all you do is make fun of me and lie to me?" she asked. Day after day she begged him to tell her and would give him no rest. At last he told her the truth. He said that he had been a Nazarite since he was born. His hair had never been cut, and if it were, he would no longer be strong, but as weak as other men.

Delilah realized that this time Samson was finally telling her the truth. She sent this message to the kings of the Philistines: " Come once more; this time he has told me the truth!" So they came again and brought her the money they had promised.

Samson is standing against two pillars and pushing against them with all his might. He has pushed them apart and the building is falling down.

196

Then, while Samson was asleep, a barber came and cut his hair.

Delilah woke Samson up and told him that the Philistines were coming to get him. He thought he could easily get away as he always had before, for he didn't realize that the Lord had let his strength go away. But this time the Philistines caught him, for he could no longer fight against them, and they bound him with bronze chains. They poked out his eyes, making him blind, and shut him up in prison where they made him work very hard turning a millstone to grind their corn.

But while he was in prison, his hair began to grow longer again, and the Lord gave him back his strength.

One day the kings of the Philistines called the people together in their idol's temple to offer a sacrifice to their god Dagon and to rejoice because Samson had been caught. Everyone present praised Dagon (he was an idol), because they thought he had helped them catch Samson! They were all very happy.

"Send for Samson so we can tease him," someone suggested. So they brought blind Samson out of the prison and set him between the two pillars that held up the roof of the temple and made fun of him there.

The temple was packed with people, including all the kings of the Philistines. Many of the people were having a party on the roof, while those inside the temple were laughing at Samson. A boy held him by the hand to lead him because he couldn't see. Samson asked the boy to place his hands on the pillars that held up the temple roof, so he could lean against them. The boy did.

Then Samson prayed, "O Lord, help me, and give me strength only this once." He gave a mighty push against the two pillars as he stood there between them, and said, "Let me die with the Philistines." As he pushed, the pillars

moved apart, and the roof fell on the kings of the Philistines
and on all the people inside, killing great numbers of them.

Samson died with them, but in his death he killed more
of the enemies of Israel than he had while he was alive.
Then his brothers came and took his dead body and buried
it.

A BEAUTIFUL LOVE STORY

RUTH

DURING THE TIME judges ruled Israel, a man
named Elimelech and his wife, Naomi, moved from Israel
to the land of Moab.

His sons married Moabite girls, and they all lived together for about ten years. Then Elimelech and his two
sons all died, leaving Naomi alone with her two daughters-
in-law.

Naomi decided to go back to her home in the city of
Bethlehem in Israel. She asked her daughters-in-law if they
would rather stay in Moab, the land where they were born
and where all their friends and relatives lived, or whether
they wanted to move to Israel with her.

When her daughters-in-law learned of her decision to
return to Israel, they cried. One of them, Orpah, decided to
stay in Moab; but the other, Ruth, didn't want to leave
Naomi.

"I'll go with you," she said, "and live wherever you live.

Your friends will be my friends, and your God will be my God."

When Naomi saw how much her daughter-in-law Ruth loved her, she didn't urge her to stay in the land of Moab, but agreed to let her come with her to the land of Israel.

So they came to the city of Bethlehem where Naomi had lived before moving to Moab.

One day during harvest time, Ruth said to Naomi, "Let me go out to the harvest fields and pick up grain dropped by the harvesters." She said this because one of God's laws for his people was that poor people must always be allowed to pick up any bits of grain that dropped to the ground at harvest time. Ruth wanted to get some of this grain for them to eat.

Naomi agreed to this. Ruth went to a field belonging to a man named Boaz and began picking up the grains behind his workers.

When Boaz came out to the field later that morning, he asked the foreman in charge of the reapers, "Who is that girl over there?"

"She is the one who came with Naomi from the land of Moab," the foreman replied.

Boaz went over and talked to Ruth. He was very pleasant to her and told her to stay with his reapers and not to go to some other field, for he had warned his young men not to bother her. When she was thirsty, he said she should get water from the pitcher placed there for his workers and drink as much and as often as she wished. And he told her to eat lunch with his workers from the food he provided for them.

Ruth thanked him very much and asked him why he was so kind to her since she was only a stranger. Boaz said it was because he knew about her kindness to her mother-in-law: how she had left her father and mother and the

Ruth was a young widow who
came to Israel from another land.
She came with Naomi, her
mother-in-law. Ruth
worked hard and God
helped her. Her great-
grandson was
King David.

land where she was born, and had come to live among the people of Israel. He said he hoped God would bless her because she had done these things. He was glad, he said, that she had left the land of Moab where the people worshiped idols and had come to Canaan to worship the Lord.

Ruth stayed in his field until evening, then beat out the barley grain she had gathered, and took it to her mother-in-law. When Naomi saw how much Ruth brought, she was glad, and asked the Lord to bless the man who had been so kind to her. She asked who it was, and Ruth said, "The man's name is Boaz." Naomi was surprised and told her he was a close relative of theirs! He was a very rich man, Naomi said.

Ruth said he had asked her to keep coming back to his field until the harvest ended. Naomi, too, told her to do this; so Ruth went back day after day until the end of the harvest.

One day Naomi said to Ruth, "Boaz is threshing barley tonight at the threshing floor." She told Ruth to go to the threshing floor and find Boaz. Then she told her what to say to him.

Ruth did as her mother-in-law said. Boaz and his workers winnowed his barley that night, and after a hearty supper he lay down for the night beside a stack of sheaves. When it was dark, Ruth went over and lay at his feet! Around midnight he woke up, startled and afraid. "Who's there?" he demanded.

"It's only me, sir," Ruth replied. Then she said what Naomi had told her to say. Because he was a close relative, she wanted him to take care of her and marry her.

The idea pleased him very much. "May the Lord bless you, my child," he replied. He said he would gladly marry her if he could, because all the people of Bethlehem knew what a fine person she was.

That day Boaz called together ten of the city officials and told them that he wanted to marry Ruth. All the city officials prayed that the Lord would bless Ruth and make Boaz still richer and greater than he was already.

So Boaz married Ruth, and Naomi was very happy. The Lord gave Boaz and Ruth a son, and grandmother Naomi loved the baby very much. They named the little boy Obed.

JOB'S TERRIBLE TROUBLES

JOB

THERE WAS A MAN in the land of Uz named Job, who worshiped God and was careful to do good at all times. God gave him seven sons and three daughters, as well as a lot of money. He had three thousand camels, seven thousand sheep, one thousand oxen, five hundred donkeys, and many servants; in fact, he was the richest man in that part of the world.

After Job had enjoyed this good life for many years, God sent trouble upon him to see whether he would bear it patiently and be willing for his heavenly Father to do what he thought best. God allowed Job's money and children to be taken from him.

Job tore his clothes and bowed down to the earth and worshiped, saying, "I had nothing of my own when I was born and I will have nothing when I die. It was God who gave me my children and my riches, and it is God who has

203

taken them all away again. He knows what is best for me, and I thank him for all he has done."

After this, to test Job even more, God sent him sickness and pain. He was covered with boils from head to foot, and he sat on the ground beside the city gate in great distress. His wife was angry because God had sent him so much suffering. She came to Job and said, "Why do you still trust God? Speak against him for treating you like this, even though he kills you for saying it."

Job answered her, "You are talking like a foolish woman. After we have had so many good things from God, shall we not be willing to have evil things too?"

So Job still said nothing that was wrong.

He had three friends who came to talk with him and comfort him. When they saw him, he was so changed that at first they didn't recognize him. Then they tore their clothes and cried and sat beside him on the ground in silence for many days because they could see his grief was very great.

These friends thought his troubles had been sent upon him because he had done something bad. After a while they spoke to him and said, "You must have sinned. But if you will be sorry for your sins, God will forgive you and make you get well again."

But Job knew he had not done those bad things. He said

*Job was a servant
of God. God blessed him
with seven sons, three
daughters, and great wealth.
He owned many servants,
sheep, camels, donkeys,
and oxen.*

to them, "You came to comfort me, but what you say doesn't help me at all. I would rather you hadn't come."

Then Job talked about his troubles. "The Lord has sent great troubles upon me," he cried out. "Oh, that he would put me to death so that I wouldn't need to suffer any more! Oh, that I had someone to speak to God for me, for he doesn't listen to my prayers any more. Yet I know that my Savior is alive, and that after many years he will come to earth, and I shall rise from the grave and see God for myself."

But when Job saw that he could neither die nor get well, but must bear his pain, he grew impatient. He was willing to have these troubles for a little while, but not until God saw best to take them away.

Then he began to find fault and to say that his troubles were too great and that God was being cruel and unfair to him. And his three friends, instead of trying to encourage him, still told him he was bad and had made God angry. They said God didn't punish good people, but only bad people, so Job must have been very, very bad to have so much pain.

This made Job angry at them, and that made them angry with him. They kept on talking back and forth for a long while, and each of them said many things he shouldn't have.

Then they heard the voice of God speaking to them out of a whirlwind. God reminded Job that he had made the earth, the sea, and the sky. It is God who gives the wild animals their food and feeds the young birds when they are hungry. It is God who gives the beautiful tail to the peacock and the feathers to the ostrich. He makes the horse swift and strong and unafraid. He teaches the eagle to build her nest on the high rocks and to fly away to hunt for food for her young ones.

Then Job saw that he had sinned in finding fault with

God. "I am bad," he said, "and have spoken of things that I don't understand; I am sorry for my sin and bow down in the dust before you."

After this, the Lord made Job well again. God blessed Job twice as much as before and made him twice as rich. Now Job had fourteen thousand sheep, six thousand camels, two thousand oxen, and one thousand donkeys. He also had seven more sons and three more daughters; so now, including those in heaven, he had twice as many children as before.

Job lived 140 years more after all these things had happened to him, and he died when he was a very old man.

STORY 73

JONAH AND THE GIANT FISH

JONAH

LONG AGO NINEVEH was one of the greatest cities in the world, but it was also a very wicked city.

One day God spoke to the prophet Jonah and said, "Jonah, go to Nineveh, and tell the people about the punishment I am going to send them because of their sins."

But Jonah didn't want to go, so he ran away to Joppa, a city by the sea. There he found a ship headed in the opposite direction from Nineveh, so Jonah bought a ticket and got on board to try to get away from God.

When the ship had sailed out to sea, the Lord sent a strong wind and a great storm. The ship was in danger of sinking. But Jonah didn't know the danger they were in, for he had gone down to the bottom of the ship and lay there fast asleep. The captain found him and woke him up.

"How can you sleep like this?" the captain shouted at him. "Get up and pray to your god; perhaps he may pity us and save us from dying."

Then the sailors talked together and said, "This storm has been sent because someone in the ship has been bad. Let's draw straws to find out whose fault it is."

They did, and Jonah drew the short one. They said to him, "Tell us, what wicked thing have you done? What country do you come from?"

Jonah replied, "I am a Hebrew, and I am running away from the God who made the sea and the dry land, because I don't want to obey him."

Then the men were very much afraid and said, "Why have you done this? What should we do to you so that the storm will stop?"

Jonah told them, "Throw me into the ocean; then it will become calm again. I know it is my fault that this danger has come upon you."

As soon as they had thrown Jonah in, immediately the sea grew still and calm. The men were amazed and offered a sacrifice to the Lord and promised to serve him.

The Lord had sent a huge fish to the side of the ship to swallow Jonah as soon as he fell in! Jonah stayed alive in the fish three days and three nights. He prayed to the Lord while he was in the fish and confessed his sin. God heard him and commanded the fish to swim to the shore and vomit him out.

Then the Lord spoke to Jonah a second time. "Go to Nineveh," he said, "and give the people there my message."

So Jonah went to Nineveh. He walked through the city for many hours and finally came to the center and he

After he was swallowed
   by a giant fish,
Jonah was sorry.
So God told the fish
   to vomit him out
onto the shore.

shouted out God's message: "Forty days from now Nineveh will be destroyed because of the sins of its people."

When the king of Nineveh and the people heard this, they believed God had sent Jonah and they knew what he said would come true.

God saw that they were sorry and that they had stopped being bad, so he took away his punishment and didn't destroy the city after all.

Jonah was very angry about this. He wanted Nineveh to be destroyed because the people who lived there were enemies of Israel. Also Jonah was afraid that now the people would laugh at him and say he didn't know what he was talking about.

He spoke angrily to the Lord and said, "I knew you wouldn't destroy the city, and that is why I ran away. Now please kill me; I would rather die than live." But the Lord spoke pleasantly to Jonah and didn't punish him for talking like that.

Jonah went to a place outside the city and waited to see whether the city would be destroyed or not. That night the Lord caused a vine to grow, and the next day its thick leaves shaded Jonah's head from the hot sun. He was very glad it was there. But soon God sent a worm that gnawed through the stem of the vine, and the vine died. Then God sent a hot wind on Jonah, and the sun beat down on his head. Since the vine was no longer there to shade him, he grew sick and faint from the heat. Again he became angry.

Then God said, "You are angry because I have destroyed the vine that protected you, and yet you want me to destroy Nineveh, that great city where there are more than 120,000 little children so young that they cannot tell their right hands from their left!"

So God taught Jonah how selfish and wicked he was to wish that Nineveh would be destroyed.

SAMUEL HEARS GOD'S VOICE
1 SAMUEL 1, 2, 3

THERE WAS A MAN of Israel named Elkanah who lived in the city of Ramah. Every year he took a trip to the Tabernacle in Shiloh to sacrifice to God. His two wives, Hannah and Peninnah, always went with him. Elkanah loved Hannah more than Peninnah and gave her many presents. But Hannah was unhappy because Peninnah had children and she didn't, for the Lord hadn't given her any.

One day Hannah came to the Tabernacle and prayed. She promised the Lord that if he would give her a son, she would give him back to the Lord again, and he would be set apart to serve the Lord all his life at the Tabernacle.

Eli was the High Priest at the time. Hannah was crying as she prayed. Eli was sitting there and saw her lips moving but couldn't hear her speaking. For some reason he decided that she was drunk, and scolded her for it.

But Hannah told him, "Oh, no, sir, I am not drunk. I am praying in my heart to the Lord."

Then Eli told her he hoped God would give her what she prayed for. Then Hannah was glad.

The Lord answered Hannah's prayer and gave her a son. She named him Samuel, which means "Asked of God."

Soon after Samuel was born, the time came for his father to go to Shiloh again to sacrifice as he did each year. But Hannah didn't go this time; she wanted to wait until her little boy was older. Then she would take him with her and leave him at the Tabernacle to help God and his priests

211

with their work, for this is what she had promised the Lord.

Finally the time came when he was old enough, and she took him to the Tabernacle.

"Do you remember me?" she asked Eli. "I am the woman who stood here praying to the Lord that time, and you thought I was drunk. I was praying for this child, and the Lord has given me what I asked for. Now I am giving him back to the Lord again; as long as he lives he shall be the Lord's." And so she left little Samuel at the Tabernacle to stay and help Eli.

Eli had two sons whose names were Hophni and Phinehas; they were priests at the Tabernacle. The Lord had said that all his priests must be holy and good because they were God's ministers. But Hophni and Phinehas were not good men. They were very bad.

Eli was very old. He heard about all the bad things his sons were doing and he scolded them, but he didn't punish them or make them stop being priests as he should have done.

Samuel, although he was only a child, did what was right and pleasing to the Lord. His mother made him a coat each year and brought it to him when she came with her husband to offer their sacrifice. Eli was, of course, very friendly to them and asked the Lord to bless them because they had given Samuel to the Lord.

Samuel helped Eli in any way he could. One night when Samuel had gone to bed, he heard a voice calling him.

"I'm here," he answered and jumped up and ran to Eli. "What do you want?" he asked him.

But Eli said, "No, I didn't call you; go back to bed."

But then Samuel heard the voice again, so again he ran to Eli and asked him, "Why are you calling me, Eli? What do you want?"

It was nighttime, and Samuel was awakened by God speaking to him. "Samuel, Samuel," God called. Then God told him what was going to happen to Eli and his sons.

"I didn't call you, my son," Eli said. "Go and lie down again."

But Samuel heard the voice a third time and went to Eli and said, "I'm sure I heard you calling me. What do you want me to do?"

Then Eli knew it was the Lord who had called the child. He said to him, "Go, lie down; and if he calls you again say, 'Speak Lord, I am listening.'"

So Samuel went back to bed. And the Lord came and called as before, "Samuel, Samuel."

Samuel answered, "Yes, Lord, speak, for I am listening." Then the Lord told him he was going to punish Eli and his sons because his sons were so wicked and Eli hadn't punished them.

STORY 75

ENEMIES CAPTURE THE ARK
1 SAMUEL 4–7

EVERYTHING GOD SAID to Samuel came true. One day the men of Israel went out to fight against the Philistines, and four thousand Israeli soldiers died in the battle. The leaders of Israel wondered why the Lord had allowed so many to be killed. They decided to get the Ark from the Tabernacle and take it with them into the next day's battle to see if that would help them.

So they sent messengers to the Tabernacle at Shiloh to ask for the Ark to be brought to them. The two sons of Eli, Hophni and Phinehas, took it out to the army. When the

Israeli soldiers saw it, they shouted for joy, and the noise was heard far away on every side.

The Philistines heard the shouting and said, "Why all the noise in the camp of the Hebrews?" When they were told that the Ark had arrived, they were very frightened. "Who can save us now?" they asked. "Let us be strong and fight like men, or we will become slaves of the Hebrews."

That day the Philistines killed thirty thousand Israelis and captured the Ark! And the two sons of Eli, Hophni and Phinehas, were killed. A messenger ran to Shiloh to tell Eli. He sat waiting on a bench by the road, for he was afraid of what might happen to the Ark. The messenger ran to him and said, "The men of Israel have run from the Philistines, and a great many of them have been killed. Your two sons Hophni and Phinehas are dead, and the Ark of God has been captured."

When the messenger told him about the Ark, Eli fainted and fell backwards to the ground, breaking his neck; and so he died.

The Philistines carried the Ark to Ashdod, one of their cities, and put it in the temple of Dagon, their idol. They set it down by the idol and left it there all night.

When they got up in the morning and came to Dagon's temple, they found that their idol had fallen on its face on the floor in front of the Ark. They set it up again, but the next night the idol fell down again in front of the Ark, and this time its head and hands were cut off!

Soon afterwards a terrible sickness came upon the people of Ashdod, and many of them died. Then those who were left said to each other. "The Ark of the God of Israel must not stay here." So they called together all of the rulers of the Philistines and asked, "What shall we do with the Ark?"

"Let's send it to Gath," they replied. Gath was another city of the Philistines. So they carried it to Gath, but as soon as the Ark arrived there, the people living there began to die. The Philistines kept the Ark for seven months, but all that time the Lord sent great trouble upon them. Then they asked their wise men how to send it back to the land of Israel, for they were afraid to keep it any longer.

The wise men told the Philistines to make a new wagon and hitch two cows to pull it, but to take their calves away from them and tie them up at home. Usually cows wouldn't leave their calves unless led away by hand.

"Now put the Ark on the cart," the wise men said, "and let the cows pull it wherever they want to without anyone leading them. If the cows leave their calves behind and take the Ark to the land of Israel, it will show that the Lord is making them go there and that he is angry with us for keeping the Ark, and has sent all these troubles as a punishment. But if the cows turn around and go back to their calves, we will know it was not the Lord who punished us, but our troubles have come upon us just by chance."

The Philistines followed the directions of their wise men. As soon as the cows were let loose, they started off straight into the land of Israel, leaving their calves behind.

The Israelis who lived near the border of the country were reaping their wheat harvest in a valley near the city where the cows were going. When these men looked up and saw the Ark coming, they shouted with joy.

The cows brought it into the field of a man named Joshua and stood still beside a great stone that was there. Then some men of the tribe of Levi carefully took the Ark down from the cart and laid it on the stone. They broke up the wagon for wood, killed the cows for a burnt offering, and sacrificed them to the Lord.

Then the Ark was taken to the city of Kiriath-jearim, into the house of a man named Abinadab. It stayed there for twenty years, and God blessed him.

216

THE PEOPLE DEMAND A KING
1 SAMUEL 8, 9

AFTER ELI WAS DEAD, the Lord chose Samuel to be the new judge of Israel. Samuel lived in the city of Ramah where his father Elkanah and his mother Hannah lived.

Then the people of Israel began to sin again, for they worshiped the idols Baal and Ashtaroth. So the Lord sent the Philistines to fight them.

Samuel said to his people, "If you will destroy your idols and obey the Lord, he will save you from the Philistines." So the people knocked down their idols, and then Samuel told them, "Come, all of you, to the city of Mizpeh, and I will pray for you there."

So they came to Mizpeh to confess their wickedness and said, "We have sinned against the Lord."

But when the Philistines heard that the people were at Mizpeh, they went to fight them there. The Israelis were frightened and said to Samuel, "Pray hard that God will save us." Samuel took a young lamb and sacrificed it as a burnt offering, and then prayed to the Lord for the people. And the Lord listened to him. As Samuel was sacrificing the lamb, the Philistine army was coming closer and closer. But God sent a great storm of thunder and lightning upon them, and they ran away in fear. So the Lord gave the men of Israel the victory.

When he was old, Samuel let his two sons help him rule.

But they weren't fair like their father. If two people had an argument and came to his sons to decide which was right, his sons would ask for money and would say that whoever would pay them the most was right. This is taking a bribe and is a very wrong thing to do.

Then all the leaders of Israel came to Samuel at Ramah to tell him he was too old to keep on being their judge and that his sons were bad. They asked him to choose a king for them so that they would be like the other nations around them. Samuel was displeased when they asked him to choose a king and asked the Lord what he should do.

The Lord said it was not Samuel the Israelis wanted to get rid of, but the Lord himself. The Lord told Samuel to warn the people what it would be like to have a king, and how cruelly he would treat them. So Samuel told them the king would make their sons work in the fields and make their daughters be cooks and bakers in his kitchen. He would steal the best of their lands and vineyards, their cattle and sheep. They would cry out because of the trouble their king would bring upon them, but the Lord wouldn't listen to them.

But the people insisted. "We must have a king just like the other nations," they said. "We need him to help us fight our battles." Then the Lord told Samuel to do as they asked and choose a king for them.

There was a young man named Saul, who was good-looking and taller than anyone else in Israel. One day some donkeys that belonged to Saul's father ran away and got lost. Saul's father said to him, "Take one of the servants with you, and go look for the donkeys."

Saul started out, but after he had gone a long way and couldn't find them, he said to the servant, "Let's go back; probably by now my father has stopped worrying about the donkeys and is worrying about us!"

218

God wanted to lead
his people personally,
but they insisted on having
a king like the ungodly
nations around them.
So God let them have
their own way.

By this time they were near the city where Samuel lived. The servant told Saul that a prophet lived there whose words always came true. "Let's go and ask him where to find the donkeys," he suggested.

"That's a good idea," Saul replied. "Come on, let's try it."

The Lord had already told Samuel, "Today I will send you the man who will be the king of Israel." When Samuel saw Saul, the Lord said to him, "This is the man I told you about."

Saul didn't know Samuel, and he went up to him and asked, "Can you tell us where the prophet's house is?"

"I am the prophet," Samuel answered. Then he told Saul to bring his servant and come to a celebration. As for the donkeys, Samuel told him to stop worrying about them—Saul's father had already found them!

Samuel brought Saul and his servant to the celebration and gave them the best places to sit among the guests. Samuel told the cook to bring in the food he had told him to save for an important guest, and the cook brought it and set it before Saul. Samuel told Saul to enjoy it because it had been chosen especially for him. So Saul stayed with Samuel all that day. How surprised he was to receive all this special attention!

SAMUEL'S WARNINGS

1 SAMUEL 10, 11, 12

EARLY THE NEXT MORNING as soon as they got up, Samuel had a long talk with Saul. Afterwards he went with him to the gate of the city. As they were walking together, he said to Saul, "Tell your servant to go on ahead, but you stay here so I can show you what the Lord has commanded me to do."

When the servant was gone, Samuel took a bottle of olive oil and poured it on Saul's head. We have read about Moses doing this to Aaron to make him the High Priest. Kings were anointed in the same way. When Samuel poured the oil on Saul's head it meant that God had chosen Saul to be the king of Israel. But no one except Saul and Samuel knew that God had chosen him, for the Lord was not yet ready to announce it to the people.

One day not long afterwards Samuel made a speech to the people and reminded them of the way God had brought them out of Egypt and set them free from their enemies. But they were not satisfied with God's care for them, and now they were asking for a king to rule them instead. Samuel told them to come to the city of Mizpeh to see their new king. When they came, Samuel announced that Saul was the one. Everyone wanted to see him, but they couldn't find him anywhere. So they asked the Lord where he was, and the Lord answered, "He is hiding," and told them where to look for him!

221

Then the people ran and brought him out of his hiding place. He was a big, handsome fellow, taller than any of the rest of them. Samuel said, "See, here is the man the Lord has chosen for you; there is no one like him among all the people of Israel." And they all shouted, "God save the king!" Then Samuel told them again how much trouble they would have. He said that Saul would be a very bad king, and Samuel wrote it all down in a book.

After this the Ammonites came up to fight against the Israeli city of Jabesh-gilead. The men of Israel who lived there were afraid and said that if the Ammonites would be kind to them, they would surrender without a fight. But the Ammonites wouldn't promise. Instead, they said they would punch out the right eye of each of them. When the men of Jabesh-Gilead heard this, they asked the Ammonites to give them seven days to send messengers to the Israelis in other parts of the land. If by that time no one would come to help them, they promised to surrender and let the Ammonites do as they pleased!

Then the leaders of the city sent messengers to Gibeah, where Saul lived, and told the people what the Ammonites had said. The people cried out in fear. Just then Saul came in from the field with a herd of cattle, and asked what the trouble was.

When he found out, he took two oxen, cut them in pieces, and sent a piece to each part of the land of Israel with this message: "I will do this to the oxen of anyone who doesn't come at once to fight against the Ammonites."

Three hundred thousand came to Saul immediately when they heard this threat. Early one morning he led them out against the Ammonites, and Saul and his army won the battle. The Ammonites who weren't killed in the battle ran away, so the Israelis won a great victory.

After this triumph Samuel made another speech to Israel. He told them again that they had done wrong to ask for a king. The Lord was their king, and they shouldn't want another. "Now see what the Lord is going to do," he said. "This is the time of harvest, when we don't have rain, but I will ask the Lord to send a great storm of thunder and rain to make you realize how much you have offended him."

So the Lord sent a terrible storm of thunder and rain until all the people finally honored the Lord and respected Samuel. And they begged him to pray for them, for they were afraid that they would all be killed by the storm.

Samuel said, "I will never stop praying for you. Only worship the Lord and obey him with all your hearts, and always remember the great things he has done for you." They had sinned, he said, but now if they would obey the Lord, the Lord would forgive them and take care of them because he had chosen them to be his people. But if instead of obeying him they kept on being bad, they and their king would be destroyed.

STORY 78

TWO MEN AGAINST AN ARMY

1 SAMUEL 14

TWO YEARS after Saul became king, he formed an army of three thousand soldiers. Two thousand of them were under his personal command, and the other thousand were commanded by Saul's son Jonathan.

One day Jonathan went to fight some Philistines who

had invaded the land of Israel. The Philistines gathered together a great army and came with thousands of chariots and horses and so many soldiers that they couldn't be counted. When Saul's little army saw the tremendous forces coming to attack them, they were terrified, and hid in caves and bushes and among the rocks on the mountains, and in holes in the ground. Some of them fled across the river Jordan into the land of Gilead, where the other tribes of Israel lived. Only a few soldiers stayed with Saul, their king, and they were trembling with fear.

Saul came to Gilgal, for Samuel had promised to meet him there to sacrifice burnt offerings and peace offerings and to get God's directions for Israel's battle plans. Saul waited seven days for Samuel, but when he still didn't come, Saul became frantic. "Bring an offering," he commanded—and he himself sacrificed the burnt offering. This was a terrible thing for him to do, for God permitted only the priests to sacrifice offerings.

Just then Samuel arrived in town, and Saul went to meet him. Samuel said at once, "You have done a terrible thing." Saul began to make excuses and said he had been afraid to wait any longer for fear the Philistines would come. But Samuel said it was wrong to disobey the Lord no matter what happened, and the Lord would not let him be king any more, but would choose someone else in his place. Samuel didn't mean that Saul would stop being king right away, but that the Lord would choose a new king soon.

The Philistine army was camped nearby and Jonathan, Saul's son, asked his armor-bearer to go with him to the camp of the Philistines. Jonathan thought the Lord might allow the two of them to defeat all that great army of Philistines! And, of course, it is true that the Lord can give victory to anyone, whether they are many or few. The armor-bearer agreed to go with him.

David was a shepherd before he became the king of Israel. One time he killed a lion in order to protect his sheep from harm.

Jonathan told him how they could find out whether the Lord intended to help them or not. They would go and stand where the Philistines could see them. If the Philistines called out to them and told them to wait, they would go no further, for it would mean the Lord was not going to help them. But if the Philistines said, "Come on up and fight!" they would know that the Lord would give them the victory.

So Jonathan and his armor-bearer climbed up to where the Philistines were and stood where they could be seen. The Philistines made fun of them and said, "Look, the Hebrews are coming up out of the holes where they were hiding!" and they called out, "Come on up, and we will show you how to fight!"

When Jonathan heard them say this, he told his armor-bearer, "The Lord has given us the victory!" Then Jonathan climbed up the rocks to the Philistines' camp, using his hands as well as his feet to climb the steep hill, and his armor-bearer climbed after him. When they got to the top, they fought and killed about twenty men.

Then the Lord sent an earthquake. The ground shook, and all the Philistine army trembled with fear and ran away!

When the Philistines started running away, Saul and his men went up to join the battle. Many of Saul's soldiers who had been afraid and had hidden in the mountains came out now and joined him again. The Lord helped the Israelis so that the whole huge Philistine army ran away from them.

The Israeli soldiers were very hungry that night, for Saul had ordered them to eat nothing until evening because he wanted them to go on chasing their enemies. So none of them had tasted any food all day.

They came to a wood where honey was dripping on the

ground from a beehive in the trees. But though the men were so hungry, they were afraid to eat the honey for fear King Saul would kill them for disobeying him. But Jonathan didn't know what his father had said, so he reached out the end of a stick he was carrying, dipped it into the honey, and ate it. When Saul heard about this, he was furious at Jonathan for disobeying him. "You must die, Jonathan," he said.

But the people said, "Jonathan must die? He is the one who has given us this great victory!" So they saved Jonathan from being put to death.

STORY 79

KING SAUL
DISOBEYS GOD
1 SAMUEL 15, 16

AFTER THIS, Samuel told King Saul that the Lord wanted him to destroy the entire Amalekite nation because the Amalekites had fought the people of Israel when they came out of Egypt hundreds of years before, though the Israelis had done them no harm.

So Saul got together a great army of more than two hundred thousand men and fought with the Amalekites and defeated them. He killed the people, but he kept their king alive, along with their sheep, oxen, and lambs.

The Lord was angry with Saul for not destroying everything as God had told him to. "I am sorry that I made Saul king," God told Samuel, "for he has not obeyed my command."

When Samuel heard the bleating of the sheep and the lowing of the oxen Saul had taken from the Amalekites, he said to Saul, "What does this mean—the bleating of the sheep and the mooing of the cows?"

Then Saul began to make excuses. He said that the people had insisted on saving them alive to sacrifice to the Lord. But Samuel asked Saul whether he thought the Lord was better pleased to have sacrifices offered to him or to have his commands obeyed. Then Samuel told Saul again that because he had disobeyed the Lord, the Lord would not let him continue as king.

God told Samuel to go to Bethlehem, find a man there named Jesse, and anoint one of Jesse's sons as the new king.

But Samuel answered, "How can I? If Saul hears about it he will kill me."

The Lord told Samuel to take a sacrifice with him and to ask Jesse to come to the sacrifice. Then the Lord would show him what to do next.

Samuel did as God commanded. He came to Bethlehem, prepared his sacrifice, and invited Jesse and his sons to come and watch. When they came, Samuel thought that Jesse's oldest son was the one the Lord would choose because he was such a fine-looking young man. But the Lord told him no, he was not the one. Then Jesse called his second son, but the Lord said no. Then he presented in turn his third, fourth, fifth, sixth, and seventh sons. But Samuel said, "The Lord has not chosen any of these. Are these all the sons you have?"

"No," Jesse answered, "there is one other, the youngest, but he is out taking care of the sheep."

"Send for him," Samuel said. So they brought in David.

Then the Lord said to Samuel, "Anoint him, for this is the one."

After David was anointed, the Lord sent his Holy Spirit into David's heart to make him wise and good, but he took his Spirit away from Saul.

We have already read about the angels—those good spirits who serve God. The Bible tells us there are evil spirits, too, who serve Satan. One of these evil spirits went into Saul and troubled him by making him discouraged and angry. Saul's assistants suggested that harp music would chase out the evil spirit whenever it troubled him.

One of Saul's men knew David, and knew that he could play the harp well. So Saul sent messengers to Jesse and told him to send him his son David. Jesse loaded a donkey with bread and wine and a young goat, and he sent them with David as a present to King Saul. But he didn't tell Saul that Samuel had anointed David to be the new king! So David came to Saul and stayed with him and helped him. Whenever the evil spirit troubled Saul, David played sweet music on a harp to quiet him, and the evil spirit would go away. When David was no longer needed, he returned home; and Saul soon forgot about him.

STORY 80

DAVID KILLS A GIANT
1 SAMUEL 17, 18

ONCE AGAIN the Philistine army decided to fight Israel, and Saul and the men of Israel got ready for the battle. One of the Philistine soldiers was a giant named Goliath. He wore a lot of armor—a bronze helmet to protect his head, an armored coat, and sheets of bronze to cover his legs so that no sword or spear could wound him.

He strutted into the valley between the two armies and yelled to the army of Israel, "I'll fight the best man in your army. If he can kill me, we Philistines will be your slaves; but if I kill him, then you must be our slaves!"

Saul and the men of Israel were frightened; no one in Saul's army was willing to go out and fight with the giant. For forty days he came out every morning and evening to defy the men of Israel.

Meanwhile, David was feeding his father's sheep at Bethlehem, but his three oldest brothers were in Saul's army. One day David's father said to him, "Take this food to your brothers, and take this present of a cheese for their captain, and see how they are getting along."

David managed to find his brothers, and as he was talking to them, the giant, Goliath, strutted out and gave his usual taunt.

"How dare this giant defy the armies of the living God?" David demanded. When the men standing near him heard David say this, they realized that David wanted to fight Goliath. They told Saul, and Saul sent for him.

"You can't possibly do it," Saul said. "Why, you're only a youngster, while Goliath has been a tough soldier for many years."

"But I can!" David answered. "One day while I was watching my father's sheep, a lion grabbed a lamb and I went after it and struck the lion and he dropped the lamb. Then he came after me, but I caught him by his beard and killed him. Another time I killed a bear with my hands. And I'll do the same to this wicked giant, for he has defied the armies of the living God. The Lord who saved me from the jaws of the lion and the bear will save me from the sword of the giant."

230

Goliath laughed
at David's sling.
But David used it
to shoot a stone
that hit Goliath
in the forehead.
And Goliath
fell down dead.

"All right," Saul said, "go and fight him, and the Lord be with you."

Then Saul gave David his own armor—his bronze helmet, his armored coat, and his sword. But David said, "I'm not used to these," and took them off again.

He took his stick with him that he used to protect the sheep, and his slingshot. Choosing five smooth stones from the brook, he put them into his shepherd's bag, and started towards Goliath. The giant saw him coming and rushed out to fight him. But when he saw David he didn't think he was worth fighting. David didn't look like a strong, brave soldier, but like a shepherd boy who had never fought before.

"Am I a dog, that you come at me with a stick?" the giant asked angrily. And he called on the idols he worshiped to curse David. "Come over here so I can kill you," he yelled.

But David answered, "You come to me trusting in your sword, your shield, and your spear; but I come to you trusting in the God of Israel. Today he will give you to me, and I will kill you and cut off your head. The army of the Philistines will be killed, and the birds and wild animals will eat them!"

As Goliath came closer, David ran towards him. Putting his hand into his shepherd's bag, he took out a stone, put it into his sling, and sent it sailing towards Goliath. It struck him square in the forehead, broke his skull, and he fell down dead. So David defeated the giant with a sling and a stone. David ran over to him and used Goliath's own sword to cut off his head.

When the Philistines saw that Goliath was dead they started to run. The army of Israel gave a great shout and started after them, killing many of them. Afterwards the men of Israel came back and went into the Philistines' camp and took all the gold, silver, and clothing from their tents.

David came from the battle with the head of Goliath in his hand. Then Abner, the captain of the army of Israel, took him to Saul.

"Who are you, young man?" Saul asked.

David answered, "I am the son of Jesse of Bethlehem." For some reason Saul didn't realize that this was the same boy who used to play the harp for him. He made David a captain in his army.

STORY 81

SAUL IS JEALOUS OF DAVID
1 SAMUEL 18

AFTER THE BATTLE with the Philistines, King Saul and David were traveling together through some of the cities of the land. The women came out with songs and dances to praise them for their victory, but they praised David more than they did Saul! They said that Saul had slain thousands of the Philistines, but David had slain tens of thousands! Saul was very angry about this, and from then on he was jealous of David.

The next day an evil spirit came into Saul's heart and troubled him while David was playing before him on the harp. Saul had a spear in his hand and he threw it at David, intending to pin him to the wall, for he wanted to kill him. But David saw it coming and jumped out of the way just in time.

Saul was afraid of David because he saw that the Lord was with him. The Lord helped David do everything well, and all the people loved him.

One day Saul said to him, "I will let you marry my daughter Merab if you will go out and fight against the Philistines." Saul said this because he hoped the Philistines would kill David.

So David went out and fought with the Philistines. He won the battle, but Saul didn't keep his promise, for he made Merab marry someone else instead.

One day Saul heard that his younger daughter Michal loved David. He said David could marry her if he would go and kill one hundred Philistines. Saul hoped that this time David would surely be killed.

So David went with his soldiers and fought the Philistines. This time King Saul was true to his word and let Michal marry him.

When Saul realized how much the Lord was helping David, he became more and more jealous and afraid of him. He became his enemy and hated him. He told his son Jonathan and all his friends that they ought to kill David.

But Jonathan loved David and told him what his father had said. "Go and hide for a while until I talk with my father," Jonathan said, "and I will tell you what he says." So David went away for a few days.

Jonathan begged his father not to harm David, for David had done nothing to hurt him but had only helped him. He had risked his life to kill Goliath the giant, and afterwards the men of Israel had won a great victory. Saul had been happy when these things happened, so why, Jonathan asked, should Saul now be trying to kill David? For David was a good man and had done nothing which deserved death.

Saul listened to Jonathan and promised before the Lord

that David would not be killed. Then Jonathan called David from his hiding place and told him what his father had said. He brought David to Saul, and David stayed at Saul's house as before.

DAVID'S BEST FRIEND

1 SAMUEL 19, 20

AGAIN THERE WAS war in the land, and again David led the army of Israel in its fight against the Philistines, and again he won. But Saul was not pleased, because now the people loved David even more than before.

Once again the evil spirit came into Saul's heart. He sat holding his spear in his hand while David was playing the harp. Again Saul threw the spear at David, and again David jumped away just in time, and the spear went into the wall. Then David ran for his life.

He fled to Ramah, where Samuel lived, and told him all that Saul had done. Afterwards he went to the town of Naioth. But someone told Saul that David was there, so he sent men to capture him, but the Lord saved him from them. Then he fled from Naioth to the place where Jonathan was and asked him, "What have I done? Why is your father trying to kill me?"

Jonathan hadn't heard that his father was after David again. He promised to do everything he could to help.

The next day was a special religious holiday, and Saul would expect David to eat at his table. But David was

David and Jonathan
were good friends.
They helped each other,
and enjoyed
being with
each other.

afraid to go and begged Jonathan to let him stay away for three days. If Saul asked why he was not at the feast, Jonathan would answer that he had given David permission to go to Bethlehem, where his father lived, to be with his family when they offered their yearly sacrifice. David said that if Saul was angry when he heard this, it would show that King Saul was determined to kill him. But if he wasn't angry, then everything was all right. Jonathan agreed to this plan.

"But how will I find out what your father says when he hears that I have gone?" David asked Jonathan.

"Come out into the field with me and I'll show you what to do," Jonathan replied.

Jonathan showed David a large rock and told David to hide behind it the next day. Then Jonathan would come out into the field and shoot three arrows and send a boy after them to pick them up. If Jonathan called out to the boy, "The arrows are on this side of you," David would know that Saul was not angry with him, and he should return. But if Jonathan called, "The arrows are beyond you," David would know that he must stay away because Saul meant to kill him.

Jonathan suggested this plan because he thought Saul's spies would be watching him, and it would not be safe to go and talk with David.

The next day was the holiday, but David's seat at the table was empty. Saul didn't ask about him, for he thought something had happened to keep him away. But the next day, when David still wasn't there, Saul asked Jonathan, "Where is David? He hasn't been here either yesterday or today."

Jonathan replied, "David asked if he could go to Bethlehem, for his family is having a sacrifice, and his brother commanded him to be there."

Then Saul was very angry with Jonathan for allowing David to go. He said Jonathan would never be king as long as David lived. "Bring David to me," he said, "I'm going to kill him."

The next day was the day when David was to hide in the field behind the rock Jonathan had pointed out to him. Jonathan went there with a boy to chase his arrows. Then he shot an arrow over the boy's head.

"The arrow is beyond you. Hurry, hurry," Jonathan shouted to him. David heard him and knew he must go away, because Saul was planning to kill him.

The boy found the arrows and brought them to Jonathan. Then Jonathan gave his bow and arrows to the boy and told him to take them back to the city.

As soon as he was gone, David came out from his hiding place, and he and Jonathan cried together over what was happening. Jonathan said David must go away and hide from his father. So David became a fugitive, like a person who has done something wrong and has to hide.

STORY 83

DAVID'S LIE BRINGS TROUBLE

1 SAMUEL 21, 22

DAVID WENT FIRST to the city of Nob where the Tabernacle was, for it had been moved from Shiloh after the Ark was captured by the Philistines. Ahimelech, the High Priest, was surprised to see David and asked him why he had come. David was afraid to say he was running away, because somebody might send word for Saul to come and capture him.

So he told a lie.

He said Saul had sent him on a secret errand, but he couldn't tell anyone what it was. This was very wrong of David. The Lord who had saved him from the lion and the bear and from Goliath the giant was able to save him from Saul. He should have spoken the truth and trusted in God. Because he didn't, he got his friends into terrible trouble.

There was a man there at the Tabernacle named Doeg, who was in charge of King Saul's cattle. Doeg told Saul that he had seen David talking with Ahimelech, the High Priest. Then King Saul blamed Ahimelech, and said that he was a traitor for helping David, and Ahimelech must die. But, of course, Ahimelech didn't even know that David was running away. This was very unfair of King Saul.

Meanwhile, David was at the Tabernacle. "Is there a spear or sword here that I can have?" David asked. "I didn't bring my sword with me."

"The sword of Goliath is here, wrapped in a cloth," the High Priest replied. "If you want it, take it, for it is the only one here."

So David took it. "It's the best!" he said.

Then David went to Gath, a city of the Philistines. The leaders of the city brought David to their king and told him, "This is the man the women of Israel sing about, saying he has killed ten thousand of us Philistines."

Then David was afraid and pretended he had lost his senses: he scratched on the doors and acted like an insane person. King Achish said to his men, "Anyone can see the man is out of his mind! Why have you brought him to me? Do I need a madman? Shall such a fellow as this come into my house?" So they chased him away.

He fled from Gath and went into a great cave, called the cave of Adullam, and lived there. When his brothers and his parents heard about it, they came to be with him; and others came too, until there were four hundred people living with him.

One day David was thinking about the good times he used to have when he lived at Bethlehem, tending his father's sheep. He thought of the well by the gate that he used to drink from as a boy. "How I wish I could have a drink from that well!" he said. Three of his men heard him say it and wanted to please him. They went to Bethlehem and broke through the Philistine guards and got some water from the well and brought it to David. But then David wouldn't drink it! When he realized that his friends had risked their lives to get the water for him, he poured it out on the ground as an offering to the Lord instead.

Meanwhile, Saul and his soldiers had gone to Gibeah to search for David there. One day as Saul was resting beneath a tree, with his spear in his hand and his generals standing around him, he began complaining to them that they were not his friends. "If you are my friends, tell me where David is," he begged.

It was then that Doeg the Edomite told Saul he had seen David at the Tabernacle, and that Ahimelech the High Priest had given food to David and had given him the sword of Goliath, the Philistine giant.

The king angrily sent for Ahimelech to come to him with all the other priests who worked at the Tabernacle. Saul asked him why he had helped David. Ahimelech replied that he didn't know David was running away from Saul. Shouldn't he help the king's own son-in-law in any way he could? he asked.

But Saul was very angry. "You must die, Ahimelech," he shouted, "you and all your relatives too." He turned to

THE SHEPHERD PSALM
PSALM 23

Because the Lord is my Shepherd,
I have everything I need!

He lets me rest
in the meadow grass
and leads me beside
the quiet streams.
He restores
my failing health.
He helps me do
what honors him the most.

Even when walking through
the dark valley of death
I will not be afraid,
for you are close beside me,
guarding, guiding all the way.

You provide delicious food for me
in the presence of my enemies.
You have welcomed me
as your guest;
blessings overflow!

Your goodness
and unfailing kindness
shall be with me all of my life,
and afterwards
I will live with you
forever in your home.

the soldiers standing there and said, "Kill these priests, because they are on David's side." But the soldiers refused.

Then he said to Doeg, the Edomite, "You do it." And that wicked man killed all eighty-five of them. Then Doeg went to the Tabernacle at the city of Nob, where the priests lived, and killed all their wives and children. But Abiathar, one of Ahimelech's sons, escaped and fled to David to tell him what Saul had done.

David said, "I knew when Doeg saw me at the Tabernacle that he would surely tell Saul. It is my fault that your father and all your relatives have been killed." Then he asked Abiathar to stay with him and promised that no one would ever harm him.

STORY 84

A PIECE OF SAUL'S ROBE
1 SAMUEL 23, 24, 25

AFTER THIS, someone told David that the Philistines had come into the land of Judah again. They were fighting against the city of Keilah and robbing the people of their grain. David asked the Lord whether he should go and fight against them.

"Yes," the Lord answered, "go and destroy them, and save the city of Keilah."

But the men who were with David were afraid to go. David asked the Lord again, and the Lord told him to go, for he would give him the victory. So David and his men went and fought with the Philistines. They won the battle and saved the people of Keilah.

When King Saul learned that David was at Keilah, he said, "Now I will catch him; I'll surround the city with my soldiers, and he won't be able to escape."

Saul called together his entire army to go down and get David. David asked the Lord whether the people of Keilah, whom he had just saved from the Philistines, would fight against Saul or whether they would let Saul capture him.

The Lord answered, "They will let Saul capture you!"

So David and his men (there were, by this time, about six hundred of them) left Keilah and hid in the wood. Saul searched for him everywhere, but God kept him safe.

One day Prince Jonathan, King Saul's son, came to see David to renew their friendship. "Don't worry," Jonathan said, "for my father will never find you. You are going to be the next king of Israel." And again they promised always to be friends. Then Jonathan went back home, but David stayed in the woods.

Some people called Ziphites came to King Saul now and said, "We will show you where David is hiding." So Saul and his men went with them. But just as they were closing in on David, a messenger came to Saul, saying, "Hurry back, for the Philistines have invaded your land." So Saul had to return, and the Lord saved David again. Now he went to a new place in the wilderness to hide.

Saul went back to Keilah after fighting the Philistines, but David had escaped. So Saul chose three thousand of his soldiers and took them out into the wilderness to hunt for David among the rocks where the wild goats lived.

Saul went into the same cave where David and his men were hiding! They were lying along the sides of the cave where Saul couldn't see them! Saul didn't know they were there, of course, so he walked into the cave alone. David's men wanted to kill Saul, but David wouldn't let them. But David sneaked up behind Saul and cut off a piece of Saul's robe, then hid again.

When Saul had left the cave, David shouted to him, and Saul looked around to see who was calling him. Then David asked Saul why he listened to the wicked men who said that David wanted to harm him. He could easily have killed Saul, he said, and some of his men wanted him to do it, but he had told them he would never kill the man whom the Lord had anointed to be king.

Then David held up the piece of robe he had cut off. "See this piece of your robe!" he exclaimed. "I cut it off but I didn't kill you; now you know that I'm not trying to hurt you. So why are you trying to kill me? Let the Lord judge between us and see which one of us is doing wrong. Let him punish you for your cruelty to me, but I will never harm you in any way."

When Saul heard David speaking like this, the feeling of hatred went out of his heart, and he started crying. Then he said to David, "You are a better man than I am, for you have done good to me, while I have done wrong to you; even today you have shown me your great kindness, for when I was in your power you didn't kill me. May the Lord reward you for the good you have done. I know very well that some day you will be the king of Israel. Promise me that when you become the new king, you won't kill my children." And David gladly promised.

Then Saul went away to his own home, but David and his men stayed out in the wilderness.

Soon afterwards Samuel died, and all the people of Israel came for his funeral and buried him at Ramah, the city where he had lived.

A CRUEL MAN WITH A KIND WIFE

1 SAMUEL 25

DAVID WENT DOWN to the wilderness of Paran where a very rich farmer lived, who owned three thousand sheep and one thousand goats. His name was Nabal, and his wife's name was Abigail. She was a kind and beautiful woman, but he was a bad, quarrelsome man.

David and his men had their camp near where Nabal kept his flocks. David needed a lot of food for his men, but he never stole a single sheep or goat from Nabal and didn't let anyone else steal them.

When the time came for Nabal to shear his sheep, David told ten of his young men to go and talk with Nabal and ask if he would give David and his men some food in exchange for all their help.

But when they talked to Nabal about it, he laughed at them. "Who is David?" he asked. "There are plenty of men like him nowadays who run away from their masters!"

So David's young men came back and told him what Nabal had said. Then David said to his men, "Get your swords." They would go to Carmel, David said, and punish Nabal. David meant that they would kill Nabal.

So they started out. But before they got there, one of Nabal's young men went to Abigail, Nabal's wife, and told her that David had sent messengers to Nabal, and how unkindly Nabal had treated them. "Yet David's men were very good to us when we were out in the wilderness," the young men said. "They kept us safe night and day, all the time we were there."

Abigail hurriedly took two hundred loaves of bread, two casks of wine, five sheep, five sacks of parched corn, one hundred clusters of raisins, and two hundred cakes of figs. She loaded them on donkeys, and went out to find David. But she didn't tell her husband.

She met David and his men coming towards her house, ready to fight. She got down from her donkey and bowed low before David and told him, "Here is a little present I have brought for your young men." She told David that the Lord would surely bless him and save him from King Saul, and that he would be the new king of Israel. Then she pleaded, "Don't do something you'll be sorry about later on."

David listened to her and thanked the Lord for sending her and for the good advice she had given him, because it had kept him from going on in his anger to kill Nabal. He took the food Abigail brought, spoke to her in a friendly way, and sent her safely away. Then he and his men went back to their camp.

When Abigail came home, Nabal was having a big party and was drunk. So she said nothing to him about David until the next morning. Then, when she told him of the danger he had been in, all his strength left him. He lay paralyzed, motionless as a stone for about ten days, and then died.

When David heard that Nabal was dead, he sent messengers to Abigail to ask her to come and be his wife.

DAVID STEALS THE KING'S SPEAR

1 SAMUEL 26, 27

SOME ENEMIES OF DAVID came to King Saul and told him where David was hiding in the wilderness. Saul's bad heart hadn't really changed. Although the hatred had gone for a little while when David spared his life, it soon came back again. Now Saul was as eager as ever to kill David. So when he was told where David was hiding, he took three thousand men to look for him.

David heard about it and sent spies to watch; they soon brought back word that Saul had arrived. Then David and his nephew Abishai went secretly to Saul's camp at night. Saul lay sleeping with his spear in the ground by his pillow. Abner, the general of Saul's army, and the rest of his soldiers, were sleeping around the king. Abishai begged David to let him go and kill Saul. He would strike the sharp spear through Saul's body into the ground, he said, and Saul would die at once.

But David said no. "Don't do it," he said, "for it is a great sin to kill the king whom God has given us. Perhaps the Lord will kill him, or he will die in battle, but I won't kill him."

Then David had an idea.

"Let's steal his spear and the bottle of water there beside his pillow!" David said. So they crept close and took them, but no one woke up, because the Lord had sent a deep sleep upon Saul and his men.

Then David stood up on the top of a hill, a safe distance away, and shouted to Saul's men and to Abner. Abner woke up suddenly and jumped to his feet.

"Who is it?" he called.

David shouted back, "Why haven't you kept better watch over the king, so that no one could come and kill him? Where is the king's spear and the bottle of water that was beside his pillow?"

Saul recognized David's voice, and asked, "Is that you, David?"

Then David asked Saul why he was still chasing him and trying to kill him.

Saul said, "I have sinned; I have been wrong. Come back, my son David, for I won't harm you."

David replied, "Here is your spear; let one of the young men come over and get it."

Then David went away into the wilderness again, and Saul went back home.

David didn't believe that Saul would stop trying to kill him, for he had talked that way before and had cried and called him his son, but afterwards he had come out with three thousand men to get him.

"Someday he will finally find me and kill me," David said to himself. "I must go and live in the land of the Philistines. Then Saul will give up looking for me."

So David took his six hundred men to the Philistine city of Gath. Achish, the king of Gath, welcomed David and let them stay in his land and gave them the city of Ziklag to live in. For he hoped to have the help of David and his men in times of war.

When Saul heard that David had fled to the Philistines, he stopped searching for him.

King Saul has been trying to catch and kill David. Now David is taking the king's spear, but doesn't try to hurt him.

KING SAUL GETS INTO TROUBLE

1 SAMUEL 28

DAVID STAYED in the land of the Philistines a year and four months. While he was there, the Philistines declared war on King Saul.

When Saul saw how many Philistines had come to attack him, he trembled with fear. He asked the Lord what to do, but the Lord didn't answer him.

At that time there were people in the land of Israel who could talk with the spirits, and the spirits would tell them what was going to happen in the future. It was a great sin to do this. The Lord had commanded that anyone who did this must be killed, and Saul had chased many of these people out of his land.

But Saul was in great trouble. He had asked the Lord what to do, but the Lord wouldn't answer him. So he said to his men, "Try to find a woman who can talk with the spirits of dead people, so that I can ask Samuel what to do."

"There is a woman at Endor who can do this," his men told him.

Then Saul put on other clothes instead of his royal robes, so that the woman he was going to see wouldn't know who he was. He took two men with him and came to the woman at night. He told her he wanted to talk to a certain man who was dead and asked her to have this dead man's spirit come and talk to him. "Bring me Samuel," he said.

Then Samuel stood before them. Saul fell to the ground before him.

"Why have you disturbed me by bringing me here?" Samuel asked him.

"Because I am in terrible trouble," Saul replied; "for the Philistines are making war against me, and God has gone away from me and won't talk to me. I have called for you so that you can tell me what to do."

"Why ask me, if the Lord has left you and become your enemy?" Samuel asked. "The Lord has done what I told you he would do: he has put you down from being king and has made David king, because you didn't obey God. And he will give the Philistines the victory over Israel tomorrow, and you and your sons will be here with me among the dead."

STORY 88

KING SAUL DIES IN BATTLE

1 SAMUEL 29, 30, 31

THE PHILISTINE KING brought along David and his six hundred men to help him fight against King Saul. But the Philistine army officers didn't want David. They were angry at their king for bringing him. "Make this fellow go back," they said, "for if he comes with us he might turn and fight against us to win the good will of his master Saul."

Then King Achish called for David and told him, "You'd

better go back. I can't fight my generals." So David and his men got up early in the morning and left.

When they got home three days later, they found their houses burned down, for the Amalekites had been there and destroyed the city, and carried off their wives and children. David's men wept until they could weep no more.

David called Abiathar, the High Priest, and told him to ask the Lord whether he should go after the Amalekites.

The Lord answered, "Yes, go after them, and you will get back all they have taken." David took his six hundred men with him, but by the time they reached Besor Brook, two hundred of them had to stop and rest because they were so weary and faint that they couldn't keep going. But David went on with the other four hundred.

David and his men found the Amalekites having a big celebration—feasting, drinking, and dancing because of all the booty they had taken from David's city and from the other places they had robbed.

Then David and his men rushed upon them and killed them. Only four hundred escaped on camels.

David's men got back their wives and children and everything the Amalekites had taken, as the Lord had said they would. And they also took the flocks and herds of the Amalekites.

David and his men now returned to Besor Brook. The two hundred men they had left behind came out to meet them.

Then some of David's men who were selfish and wicked said, "These two hundred weren't with us, so we won't give them any of the booty we captured from the Amalekites, but they can have their wives and children back."

But David said no. He told them they must share and share alike—those who were left behind and those who were in the battle should all get the same rewards.

Meanwhile, the battle between King Saul's army and the Philistines had begun. The army of Israel was defeated and many were killed. Then the Philistines began moving in on Saul, and killed Jonathan and two of Saul's other sons. The archers shot at Saul with their arrows, and hit him and he was badly wounded. Then he said to his armor-bearer, "Kill me with your sword, because I fear the Philistines will get me and torture me." But his armor-bearer was afraid to, and wouldn't do it.

Then Saul took his own sword and stood it on the ground with its point upward, and he purposely fell on it so that it ran into his body and killed him.

When his armor-bearer saw that Saul was dead, he also fell on his sword and died. So Saul died, and his three sons and his armor-bearer, and great numbers of his men. The Philistines won, as Samuel had told Saul they would.

The next day, when the Philistines returned to the battlefield to get the clothes of the men they had killed, they found Saul and his three sons lying dead on Mount Gilboa. They cut off Saul's head and took his armor, and sent word to all the Philistines that Saul was dead, and that the Israelis had been driven out of their country. They put Saul's armor in the house of their idol, Ashtaroth, and fastened Saul's body to a wall, along with the bodies of his three sons.

But when the Israelis who lived in Jabesh-gilead heard what the Philistines had done to Saul, the brave men of that city traveled all night and took down the bodies of Saul and his sons from the wall, and brought them to Jabesh-gilead; there they burned them, and then took their bones and buried them under a tree.

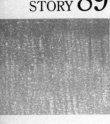

DAVID BECOMES THE KING

2 SAMUEL 1–5

MEANWHILE, DAVID was still at his home in Ziklag, and didn't know that the Philistines had beaten the Israelis in the battle. But soon a messenger arrived from the battlefield to tell David, "The Israelis have lost the battle and many are dead, and Saul and Jonathan are dead too."

"How do you know Saul and Jonathan are dead?" David demanded.

The young man replied, "I was with Saul when the Philistines surrounded him with their chariots and were ready to kill him. When he saw me he shouted, 'Quick! Come and kill me before they capture and torture me.' So I did, for I was sure he was doomed. And I took the crown from his head, and the bracelet from his arm; here they are, for I have brought them to you."

But the young man was lying to David; for as you know, Saul had killed himself. The young man said this because he thought Saul's death would please David, and David would give him a reward. But David wasn't pleased at all. He tore his clothes in sorrow, and all the men who were with him tore theirs too. And they mourned and wept for Saul, and for his son Jonathan, and for the men of Israel who had died.

David asked the young man why he wasn't afraid to kill the king God had chosen. "You must die for this," David told him. And so he was killed instead of getting a reward.

Years before David came to the throne, God had told Samuel to anoint the shepherd boy as the future king of Israel.

Afterwards, David asked the Lord whether he should go to the land of Israel. And the Lord said yes. Then David asked him what part of the land of Israel he should go to. And the Lord told him, "To the city of Hebron." Hebron was one of the cities of the tribe of Judah, to which David belonged.

David was now thirty years old. Upon his arrival at Hebron, the leaders of the tribe of Judah asked him to be their king, and he agreed.

But the other tribes of Israel didn't come to him, for they already had a king. His name was Ish-bosheth, a son of Saul. But one day about noon when Ish-bosheth was taking a nap, two of his army captains came into his house pretending they wanted to bring him a gift. But when they came into his room, they killed him.

They cut off his head and brought it to David at Hebron. "Look," they said, "we have brought you the head of Ish-bosheth, the son of Saul your enemy, who wanted to kill you."

But David was very angry. He reminded them that when he was living at Ziklag he had killed a man for killing Saul, and now these two army captains must die, too, for killing Ish-bosheth.

When the other tribes saw that Ish-bosheth their king was dead, they asked David to be their new king. So at last David was king over all twelve of the tribes of Israel.

David now captured the city of Jerusalem and lived there in a strong fort. He became a very great man, for the Lord helped him in everything he did.

King Hiram of Tyre was a good friend of King David's. King Hiram's people were expert construction workers. So Hiram sent builders and carpenters to build David a palace in Jerusalem.

THE ARK COMES BACK HOME
2 SAMUEL 6, 7

DO YOU REMEMBER that after the Philistines sent back the Ark to the land of Israel, it was carried to the city of Kiriath-jearim, and left there in the house of a man named Abinadab? It had been in Abinadab's house ever since—for more than seventy years—because the people of Israel didn't care any more and had forgotten all about it. But now King David asked his people to come with him and bring the Ark to Jerusalem. So they set the Ark on a new cart and started off to Jerusalem with it.

Now remember, the Ark was very holy. When it was first brought inside the Tabernacle, God came in a cloud that stood above the Ark, showing his deep interest in it. And when the people of Israel went through the wilderness and took the Ark with them, they were not allowed to put it on a cart, for it had to be lifted up on poles and carried on the shoulders of men called Levites, whom God had chosen for this work. And the Levites were not allowed even to come near it until the priests had covered it with the curtains of the Tabernacle. That is how holy the Ark was.

So when David wanted to bring the Ark to Jerusalem, he should not have put it on a cart. It should have been carried by poles on the Levites' shoulders. But instead he put it on a cart driven by two men whose names were Uzzah and Ahio.

257

When they came to the threshing floor of Nacon, the oxen pulling the Ark stumbled, and Uzzah, forgetting what the Lord had said about not touching the Ark, put out his hand to steady it. And the Lord killed him instantly for doing this.

David was displeased with the Lord for killing Uzzah. And David was afraid that he, too, would be punished. So he took the Ark no farther, but left it in the house of Obed-edom, a Levite.

It stayed there in Obed-edom's house for three months, and the Lord blessed Obed-edom and all his family because of its being there. When David heard how the Lord was blessing Obed-edom, he called the priests and Levites and told them to get ready to bring the Ark to the new Tabernacle he had made for it in Jerusalem.

When the priests and Levites went to get the Ark, David and the leaders of Israel went too, to show their joy and respect. This time David commanded the Levites to carry the Ark on poles across their shoulders. Do you remember why? It was because God had commanded that it be carried in that way only. David didn't want anything to happen again like what had happened to Uzzah.

So they brought the Ark to Jerusalem with joyful shouts and the music of trumpets, cymbals, and harps. Every time the Levites who carried it went a few steps, David offered

up sacrifices to the Lord. He was so glad to be allowed to bring the Ark that he couldn't just walk quietly along, but had to leap and dance for joy. But when Michal, his wife, looked out of a window as he passed his house, and saw him leaping and dancing, she was disgusted. She told him afterwards that he looked silly. But David told her he had done it to please the Lord, and he was willing to look even more foolish than that if it would please the Lord.

So they brought the Ark to Jerusalem and put it into the Tabernacle David had made for it.

One day as David was sitting in the beautiful palace he had built for himself at Jerusalem, he started thinking

David was so glad to bring the Ark to Jerusalem that he couldn't just walk quietly along, but had to leap and dance for joy.

about the Ark's being out in the Tabernacle, which was really only a great big tent. He felt in his heart that he should build a temple for it more beautiful than his palace. At that time there was a prophet named Nathan, and David told Nathan what he wanted to do. Nathan said, "Go and do it, for the Lord is with you and will help you."

But that night the Lord spoke to Nathan, and said, "Tell David not to build the temple." The Lord was glad David wanted to build it, but he said David's son was the one God had chosen for this job. So David stopped his building plans and left it for his son to do, as the Lord had told him to.

David conquered many heathen kings in the countries near Israel, and took away their horses, chariots, gold, and silver. He gave part of the gold and silver to the treasury of the Lord. And the Lord was with him and helped him in all he did; he was a good ruler over his people.

STORY 91

ONE SIN LEADS TO ANOTHER
2 SAMUEL 11, 12

JOAB WAS THE OFFICER in command of David's army. Once when Joab and his soldiers went to fight against the Ammonites, David stayed in his palace in Jerusalem instead of going with them. It was a warm summer evening, so he went up on the flat roof to walk around and cool off. While he was standing looking out over the city, he could see a beautiful woman taking a bath. Instead of looking the other way, he sent a messenger to find out who she was. The messenger reported that she was Bathsheba, the wife of Uriah the Hittite, who had gone with Joab to fight against the Ammonites.

David sent for her and made her come and sleep with him, even though she was already married to Uriah. This was, of course, a very great sin. Soon afterwards she sent word to David that they were going to have a baby. David sent immediately for her husband Uriah to come back from the army. David wanted everyone to think, when the baby was born, that its father was Uriah instead of David. So David told Uriah to go home to spend the night with his wife. But Uriah didn't do it.

Then David sent Uriah back to the army with a letter to Joab. In the letter David told Joab to put Uriah in the most dangerous spot in the battle, and then for all the other soldiers to run away and leave Uriah by himself against the enemy, so he would be killed. David wanted Uriah dead so that he could marry Bathsheba.

Uriah gave Joab the letter, but didn't know what it said. Joab did what David told him to: he sent Uriah out into the front line of the battle, and he died there. Then David married Bathsheba as soon as Joab notified him that Uriah was dead.

But the Lord was very angry at what David had done. He sent Nathan the prophet to tell David, "A terrible thing has happened. A rich man who has great flocks of sheep has stolen a lamb from a poor man. It was the only lamb the poor man had. It was his children's pet and he himself loved it very much. But a friend came to visit the rich man and he wouldn't use one of his own sheep as meat for dinner, but stole the poor man's lamb and killed and ate it."

When David heard about this he was furious. "The man who has done this thing deserves to die," he shouted.

Then Nathan said to David, "You are the rich man I am talking about! For the Lord chose you to be king, and gave you many wives and children, and made you rich and great. Yet you murdered Uriah to get his wife." Nathan said the Lord would send a dreadful punishment upon David for doing this.

Suddenly David seemed to realize how wicked he was. "I have sinned against the Lord," he admitted.

When David and Bathsheba's baby was born, David loved him very much. But the Lord sent a sickness upon the little boy. David prayed that the baby wouldn't die, and lay all night on the ground, crying to the Lord. The chief men of the city came and talked to him and tried to get him to eat, but he wouldn't.

Finally, seven days later, the baby died. David's servants were afraid to tell him, for they said, "While the baby was alive, King David was so sad—what will he do now that the child is dead?"

But when David saw them whispering together, he knew what had happened. "Is the child dead?" he asked.

"Yes," they said, "he is."

Then David got up and washed and dressed himself, and went out to the Tabernacle where the Ark was kept, and worshiped the Lord. Afterwards he came back and asked for his dinner. His servants were very surprised, and asked him why he had refused to eat while the child was alive, but now that it was dead, he was willing to eat again.

David answered, "While the baby was alive I fasted and wept because God might be kind to me and let the child live. But now that he is dead, what good does it do to refuse to eat? Can I bring him back again? I will go to him when I die, but he will never return to me."

DAVID'S REBELLIOUS SON

2 SAMUEL 14, 15

DAVID HAD OTHER WIVES besides Bathsheba, and they gave him children too. One of these sons was named Absalom. When he grew up, he was the best looking man in all Israel, and was the best athlete in the entire country. His hair was so thick and long that when he cut it at the end of each year, there were three and a half pounds of it!

Absalom bought some chariots and horses, and had fifty men running ahead of him wherever he went, so that all the people would notice him and think he was very great. Early each morning he went out to the gate of the city, and when he saw anyone coming to speak with the king, to ask for help, Absalom called to the man and talked with him and said that if only he were king he would give the man everything he wanted. And whenever anyone bowed to him because he was the king's son, Absalom was very friendly and told him not to do it. So everyone liked him because he fooled them into thinking he cared about them when he really didn't care at all.

One day he asked his father for permission to go to Hebron to offer a sacrifice. The king said go ahead. But the real reason Absalom wanted to go was to start a rebellion and try to get himself made king instead of his father. He sent spies all through the land to persuade the people to come to Hebron and make him their king. The spies told the people that on a certain day when Absalom's friends blew their trumpets long and loud, they should all shout, "Absalom is king in Hebron." Two hundred men from Jerusalem went along to help him.

David finally heard about what was happening and when he realized how many of his people wanted Absalom to be their king, he said to his officials, "Hurry! We must run away before Absalom comes and kills us." So the king and many of his loyal friends fled from Jerusalem, crossed the brook Kidron, and headed towards the wilderness.

When David had gone a little way out of the city, Hushai, one of his friends, came to be with him, for he loved David and didn't want to stay behind. But David told him to go back to Jerusalem and stay there until Absalom came, and to watch and see what he did, and then secretly send messages to David telling him what was happening. So Hushai went back to Jerusalem.

STORY 93

ABSALOM FIGHTS WITH DAVID
2 SAMUEL 16, 17

WHILE DAVID was hurrying out of Jerusalem, a man named Shime-i, one of King Saul's relatives, came and cursed David and threw stones at him. Shime-i hated David just because his relative, Saul, had hated David. Abishai, David's nephew, asked, "Why should this dog be allowed to curse my lord the king? Let me go over and cut off his head."

But David said no, probably the Lord had sent Shime-i, and it was all part of the punishment the Lord was sending him. "My own son Absalom is trying to kill me," he said, "so is it any wonder that this man, who is my enemy, would like to do the same?"

Absalom arrived in Jerusalem just after King David left. Absalom asked his friends what to do next. His friend Ahithophel said, "Let me take twelve thousand men with me and start after David tonight. We will catch up with him while he is tired, and all his men will run away, and I will kill him. And when the people see that he is dead, they will come and want you to be their king."

This advice sounded good to Absalom, but first he asked David's friend Hushai what he thought was best. Hushai told him not to go with only twelve thousand men, but to wait until he could get up a great army. Hushai said this because he wanted to give David more time to get away.

As soon as Hushai knew that Absalom had decided to wait, he went to the priests in Jerusalem, who were David's friends, and told them to send a messenger quickly to David and tell him to hurry across the river Jordan before Absalom's army could get there.

There were two young men, sons of the priests, who were hiding from Absalom outside the city, and a woman gave them Hushai's message. They started off to find David, but a boy saw them and told Absalom, and he sent some men chasing after them. The priests' sons ran to a house by the road, with a well in the yard. They climbed down inside and hid there and a woman spread a covering over the top of the well, and sprinkled corn on the covering so that no one would think of looking inside.

Absalom's men came to the house to look for them, but couldn't find them, so they went back to the city again.

Then the young men came up out of the well, and carried

Hushai's message to David. So David and all who were with him crossed the river that night.

After David had crossed Jordan, an old man named Barzillai, who lived there, and some other people too, brought all kinds of food for David and his men to eat.

As soon as Absalom had gathered his army together, he chased after his father.

Meanwhile, David's men went out to fight. David stood by the gate of the city while his men were going out, and as they passed him, he spoke to all the captains, saying, "For my sake deal gently with Absalom."

The battle was in a wood, and God gave David's army the victory.

STORY 94

ABSALOM HANGS BY HIS HAIR
2 SAMUEL 18, 19

AFTER THE FIGHTING, Absalom was riding on a mule, and the mule galloped under the branches of a great oak tree. Absalom's thick hair caught among the branches. The mule galloped away and left him dangling there.

One of David's soldiers ran to Joab and told him, "I saw Absalom hanging in an oak tree!"

Two young men, sons of the priest, were going to David to give him a message from Hushai. Absalom's men pursued them, so they hid in a well.

"Why didn't you kill him?" Joab asked. "I would have given you a big reward."

"I wouldn't kill the king's son no matter what you gave me," the man replied. "The king commanded us not to harm him."

"I can't stand here and argue about it," Joab said. Then he took three darts and thrust them into Absalom's body while he was still alive, hanging in the branches of the oak. So Absalom died.

Then Joab blew a trumpet as a signal for his army to come back, for now that Absalom was dead, there was no need for any more fighting. Joab's men threw Absalom's dead body into a pit in the woods and piled a great heap of stones over him.

After the battle was over, one of the priest's sons, whose name was Ahima-az, said to Joab, "Let me run and tell King David how the Lord has punished his enemies."

But Joab said no, and told another man, named Cushi, to go and tell the king.

"Please let me go too," Ahima-az pleaded.

"What for?" Joab asked him.

But he said again, "Please let me."

So finally Joab let him.

David sat at the gate of the city, waiting to hear news from the battle. His watchman on the top of the wall saw a man running towards the city, and shouted this news down to the king. Then the watchman saw another man running too, and he told the king that now two men were coming.

Ahima-az arrived first. He came panting to the king,

Absalom's thick hair got caught in the tree branches. As he hung there helpless, his enemy Joab came and killed him.

shouting, "All is well!" Then he threw himself down before the king and exclaimed, "Praise God! He has given us the victory!"

The king asked him, "Is Absalom safe?"

Ahima-az answered, "When Joab sent me, I saw a great commotion, as if something had happened, but I don't know what it was."

Then Cushi, the other messenger, arrived. He said, "I have news, my lord king: the Lord has punished all those who rebelled against you."

The king asked, "Is Absalom safe?"

Cushi answered, "May all the king's enemies be as that young man is."

Then David knew that Absalom was dead. He went up into the room above the gate, crying, "O my son Absalom! My son, my son, Absalom! Would that God had let me die instead of you, O Absalom, my son, my son!"

When David's army learned how deeply the king was mourning for Absalom, they were afraid to return to the city. They stole in quietly by another gate, and were like people ashamed of fleeing from a battle, instead of like those who had just won a great victory. But the king kept on mourning. He covered his face, and wept aloud. "O my son Absalom! O Absalom, my son, my son!"

Joab was angry. He came to the king and said, "You have made us all ashamed. We have fought for you and saved your life and the lives of your wives and your children. You seem to love your enemies more than us. I can plainly see that if Absalom had been saved alive and all the rest of us had been killed in the battle, you would have been very happy! If you don't go out and say 'Thank you' to your troops, I am warning you—they will all desert you and you will be worse off than you've ever been from your youth until now."

Then the king went out and talked with his soldiers and thanked them for saving him.

When the people in Jerusalem learned that Absalom was dead, they invited David to return and be their king again. So David started back to Jerusalem.

KING DAVID GETS OLD
1 KINGS 1, 2

THE YEARS WENT BY and King David was getting old now, and knew he soon would die. He remembered what God had said, that David was not the one to build a beautiful temple for the Ark, but that his son would do it. So David collected stones and timber and iron—everything his son would need to build the temple when he became the new king.

David decided the temple should be built on the top of the hill where Araunah's threshing-floor had been. He put masons to work shaping the foundation stones, and carpenters cut great beams from cedar trees. Other men made iron nails. David bought huge piles of gold and silver and bronze, for large quantities of these would be needed. "My son Solomon is inexperienced," he said, "and isn't able to decide about these things yet, and the temple must be very, very beautiful, and admired among all nations."

271

Then David explained to Solomon that many years before, he himself had wanted to build God's temple, but God had told him not to, because David was a soldier and had killed many people. God had helped him win great victories over the enemies of Israel, but God wanted a man of peace to build his temple. God had promised that Solomon's reign would be peaceful, and so Solomon could build God's temple.

But David had another son, Adonijah, who wanted to be king instead of his brother Solomon. And now that his father was old and weak, he thought this would be the best time to try to become the king. So he had a great party for his friends, and persuaded them to let him be their king. When David heard about it, he commanded his government officials to take his own mule and let Solomon ride on it to a fountain just outside Jerusalem, and to anoint him as king over all the land. "Blow the trumpet," he said, "and shout, 'Solomon is the new king!' Then bring him back here to the palace and let him sit on my throne, and he will be the new king of Israel."

So that is what they did, and that is how Solomon became the new king. Solomon's brother Adonijah and the men who were with him heard all the shouting and asked, "What is all that noise?" Just then someone came and told them that David had said that Solomon was the new king, and all the people were shouting for joy. Then Adonijah was afraid that Solomon would kill him because he had tried to be the new king. But Solomon said that if he would behave himself from then on, no harm would be done to him.

Before King David died, he called together all the leaders of his kingdom and told them that the Lord had chosen Solomon to build the temple. Then David said to these princes and great men, "You must be very careful to do whatever the Lord tells you to, for then you will always have this good land which God has given us, and you can leave it to your children when you die."

Then David said to Solomon, as all the others listened, "Solomon, my son, obey God and worship him with all your heart. If you do, he will be your friend, but if you turn away from him he will destroy you."

Then David gave Solomon the plans and drawings of the temple and of all the furniture inside. The Lord had given David these plans, and now he was passing them on to Solomon. And David gave Solomon all the gold and silver he had collected. "It is a big job," David said to his son, "but don't be afraid to begin building, for the Lord God will help you all the way until the temple is finally built."

David prayed very earnestly for the people, and for Solomon his son. He asked the Lord to help them keep on loving the Lord and keep on obeying his laws.

David finally died after being king for forty years. All the people loved him and they buried him in the city of Jerusalem.

GOD'S BEAUTIFUL TEMPLE
1 KINGS 3–7

SOLOMON FEARED GOD, and was careful to do what was right. One night God spoke to him in a dream, and told him he could have anything he wanted! What would you have asked for? Solomon finally decided to ask for wisdom! He wanted always to know what was best to do to help his people the most.

God was pleased with Solomon for asking for wisdom, and told him that because he had not asked for money or for a long life or for victory over his enemies, God would give him the wisdom he asked for and all these other things besides! So God made Solomon very rich as well as very wise.

Solomon now got ready to build the temple. He asked David's friend, King Hiram of Tyre, to send lumbermen into the forests to cut down trees for him to use in the building, because Hiram's men were experts at cutting down trees. Hiram agreed, and sent his men into the forests of Mount Lebanon, where cedar trees grew. Solomon sent many thousands of his own people, too, and they worked together with Hiram's men in cutting down the trees and afterwards bringing them to the sea, which was not far away. There they made them into rafts, and floated them along the shore towards Jerusalem.

Hiram also sent one of his best workmen to Solomon to help make the temple as beautiful and perfect as possible. This man would make beautiful things from gold, silver, bronze, iron, wood, and from expensive linen cloth.

Now Solomon began to build, carefully following the pattern his father David had given him. The temple was to be about 100 feet long, 33 feet wide, and 50 feet high. In front of it there was a 200-foot tower, soaring far above the rest of the temple.

No noise was heard all the time the temple was being built. Can you guess why?

It was because the foundations of the temple were built of stone, and each stone was cut into its proper shape before it was brought to the temple site.

When the walls were up, Solomon covered them on the

These two women are fighting about which one can have the baby. Each one claims to be the mother. King Solomon, the wisest king who ever lived, found out which one was telling the truth.

inside with cedar boards carved with the shapes of flowers, then covered with gold. Even the floor of the temple was covered with pure gold.

Across the middle of the temple he hung a curtain colored blue, purple, and crimson, called the veil, to make two rooms just as there were in the Tabernacle. The innermost of these rooms was for the Ark, and was called the most holy place. The inside walls of the most holy place were covered with wood carved into shapes of angels, palm trees, and flowers. These walls and the floor were then covered with gold. In this inner room he made two statues of angels with their wings spread out. The statues were fifteen feet high. They were carved out of the wood of olive trees, then covered with gold. They stood with their faces turned to the wall, and their wings reached from one side of the room to the other.

Solomon made two great bronze pillars to stand in front of the temple, one on the right side and the other on the left. And he made a bronze altar, which was four times as large as the one Moses had made for the Tabernacle. There was also a great tank of water that rested on the backs of twelve bronze oxen.

He also made ten huge brass tubs set on wheels, so they could be moved from one place to another. These were to hold water for washing the sacrifices.

Next he made ten gold lampstands to give light inside the temple.

It took seven years to finish all this work.

It took Solomon and all Israel seven years to build this beautiful temple for the Lord. The people brought lambs, goats, and cattle to be sacrificed.

K. Hook

SOLOMON FORGETS GOD

1 KINGS 8–11

Now SOLOMON summoned all the leaders of the nation to Jerusalem, to be there when the Ark was taken from the Tabernacle to the temple.

The priests carried the Ark into the most holy place, and set it under the statues of the angels. And when the priests came out again, leaving the Ark behind, a bright cloud of God's glory filled the temple.

The king stood before the people and publicly thanked God for helping him build the temple. Then as all the people watched, he knelt down, spreading out his hands towards heaven, and asked the Lord to hear and answer all the prayers the people of Israel would ever pray there. And if their enemies ever conquered them because of their sins, Solomon asked that the Lord would help his people when they came to the temple and prayed. Or if the Lord had to punish them by not sending rain on their fields, so that their crops wouldn't grow; or if sickness came into the land; or if swarms of locusts and caterpillars came and ate their grain—whatever trouble might come, he asked that the Lord would always help them when they came to the temple and prayed.

Then the king gave many animals to the people to sacrifice—22,500 oxen and more than 100,000 sheep! So the king and all the people dedicated the temple to the Lord as a place for his Ark, and as a place where sacrifices would always be offered to him.

One night soon afterwards the Lord appeared to Solomon and said that he had heard his prayer, and would accept the temple as his home. He promised that when the Israelis sinned against him, and he punished them for their sins, he would forgive them and take their punishment away if they would be sorry and would come to the temple and pray to him there. And he promised again that if Solomon would obey him, Solomon could be the king as long as he lived, and his children and children's children would be kings after him.

But if Solomon and his people turned away from God and worshiped other gods, God would no longer bless them but would drive them out of the good land he had given them. And he would no longer stay in the temple—so glorious and beautiful now—but would destroy it so that all who passed by would be astonished and ask, "Why has the Lord done such terrible things to this land and to his temple?" And the answer would be, "Because the people disobeyed the Lord God of their fathers who brought them out of Egypt. They chose other gods and worshiped and served them!"

The queen of the far-away country of Sheba heard of Solomon's wisdom and his knowledge of the true God, so she came to visit him. She brought many servants with her, with camels carrying rare and expensive spices, and gold and precious stones. She talked with Solomon and asked him hard questions about many things she wanted to know. Solomon answered them all and explained about everything she asked. When she saw his beautiful palace and the expensive foods on his table, and the number of servants he had, and the temple, she could hardly believe it. "I heard of your riches when I was in my own land," she exclaimed, "but you are far richer and wiser than I was told!"

Solomon was wiser than all the other kings of the earth, and they came to learn from him.

But Solomon had many wives; he married many beautiful heathen girls, even though the Lord had told him never to do this because they didn't know or love the Lord. And sure enough, when he grew old his wives persuaded him to worship their idols, so he didn't keep on obeying God as his father, David, had done. He even built beautiful temples for these idols.

The Lord was very angry with him and said that because he had done these things his son could not be king of all the land. Yet for David's sake the Lord didn't take away all the kingdom from Solomon's son; he let him be the king of two of the twelve tribes of Israel, but gave the other ten to someone else. And the Lord raised up enemies to trouble Solomon because of this great sin.

STORY 98

TWO KINGS AND TWO KINGDOMS
1 KINGS 12

ONE DAY a youth named Jeroboam was leaving Jerusalem, and a prophet came up to him and grabbed hold of the new coat he was wearing and tore it into twelve pieces! Then the prophet gave Jeroboam ten of the pieces. The prophet exlained to Jeroboam why he had done this. It

280

was because the Lord was going to let him be king over ten of the tribes of Israel!

When King Solomon heard about this, he tried to kill Jeroboam, but Jeroboam ran away into the land of Egypt where Solomon couldn't hurt him.

Solomon was the king of Israel for forty years, and he died and was buried in Jerusalem. Then Jeroboam's friends sent a message to him in Egypt, telling him to come back home again, and he did. Then he and all the people went to Solomon's son, whose name was Rehoboam, to make him their king.

First, however, they talked with him about the harsh, cruel way his father had ruled them. They wanted to know if Rehoboam planned to treat them better than his father had. If he would promise, then they would let him be their king.

Rehoboam told them to come back in three days, and he would give them his answer.

After they had gone, Rehoboam went to the old men who had been friends of his father, and asked their advice. They told him to speak gently to the people and to promise to rule them with kindness and love. They said that if he did this, the people would gladly choose him as their king for as long as he lived.

But Rehoboam was not satisfied with this good advice from the old men. So he asked the young men who had grown up with him what they thought. The young men told him to speak roughly to the people and to tell them that if they thought his father had been cruel to them, they hadn't seen anything yet! For he would be even more cruel. His father had been a little harsh, but he would be *very* harsh.

When the people came back for his answer three days later, Rehoboam spoke roughly to them, as the young men had advised him to. He shouted, "If you think my father was cruel to you, well, I'll be much more cruel; and if you think he was harsh, you'll think it was nothing by the time I've finished with you."

Most of the people went away in great anger and said that he couldn't be their king; they wanted Jeroboam instead.

But the tribes of Judah and Benjamin stayed and made Rehoboam their king. The other tribes chose Jeroboam. So Jeroboam was king over ten tribes, as the prophet had said, and Rehoboam was king over only two.

When Rehoboam saw that the ten tribes had left him, he sent a messenger to them, asking them to come back, but they threw stones at the messenger and killed him. Then Rehoboam hastily called together all the soldiers of Judah and Benjamin, 180,000 of them, and formed them into an army to go out and fight against the ten tribes. But God sent a prophet to tell them that his people must not fight against their brothers in the other ten tribes, but to go on back home.

So now there were two kings ruling over the people of Israel. Until this time, one king had ruled over all of them—first Saul, then David, and then Solomon. But now Solomon's son Rehoboam was king over the tribes of Judah and Benjamin, and Jeroboam was king over the other ten tribes.

Rehoboam's kingdom was called the kingdom of Judah; and Jeroboam's, the kingdom of Israel.

King Jeroboam not only disobeyed God himself, but he led the people of Israel to break God's Law by worshiping these gold idols.

R. Hook

A PROPHET IS KILLED BY A LION

1 KINGS 13

WE HAVE READ about the way the ten tribes chose King Jeroboam and deserted King Rehoboam.

One day King Jeroboam said to himself, "If my people go to Jerusalem to offer sacrifices and to worship at the temple, they will see King Rehoboam, the son of the great King Solomon, and they will want him to be their king instead of me."

So King Jeroboam made two gold statues of calves and placed them in two temples, one at Bethel and the other at Dan, in different parts of his land; and the people went there to worship them. For he said to the people, "It is too far for you to go to Jerusalem to worship God. These gold idols are your gods; worship them, for they brought your fathers out of Egypt." What a wicked thing for Jeroboam to say!

Jeroboam chose wicked men as priests to sacrifice to his calf idols. But he wouldn't allow the priests of the Lord to offer sacrifices to the true God. Because of this, all the good priests and Levites who lived in his land moved to Jerusalem to live; and many other good people who would not worship his calves went with them and chose Rehoboam as their king.

One day Jeroboam was standing in his idol's temple beside the incense altar, preparing to burn incense to the gold calf, when a prophet came to him from the land of Judah. This prophet said that a king named Josiah would be born in Judah, and this king would come and wreck Jeroboam's idol! The prophet said this was not going to happen for many years, but to prove that it would surely happen some day, God would now break Jeroboam's altar, and its ashes would spill to the ground.

Jeroboam was very angry with the prophet for saying such a thing, and tried to grab him, but as he reached for him, the Lord instantly made Jeroboam's arm grow stiff, so that he couldn't draw it back again! And at that moment the altar cracked in two, just as the prophet had said it would, and its ashes were scattered on the ground.

Then Jeroboam begged the prophet to pray that his arm would be all right again. So the prophet prayed for him, and his arm was made well.

Then King Jeroboam said to the prophet, "Come home with me and rest yourself, and I will give you a reward."

But the prophet answered, "If you gave me half the riches in your palace, I wouldn't go with you, nor eat in this place. For the Lord told me not to." Then the prophet started back to the land of Judah.

Now there was another prophet, an old man, living there at Bethel. His sons came and told him about the prophet from Judah, and all he had done to Jeroboam and his altar. The old prophet asked his boys which way the prophet from Judah had gone, for they had seen the road he had taken; and the old man followed after him.

He caught up to him, and found him resting under an oak tree, and said to him, "Are you the prophet from Judah?"

"I am," he replied.

Then the old man said, "Come home with me and eat."

But the prophet from Judah said, "I can't go with you,

nor eat or drink in this place, for the Lord has commanded me not to."

Then the old man said to him, "But I too am a prophet, and an angel spoke to me, saying, 'Bring him back with you to your house, to eat with you.'" But the old prophet was lying, and made up the story about the angel.

It was wrong for the prophet from Judah to listen to the old man, for the Lord himself had already told him what to do. But he went home with him and ate with him. The Lord was angry because of this, and while the two men were sitting at the table the Lord made the old man speak to the prophet and tell him that because he had disobeyed the Lord and come back to Bethel and eaten there, he must die.

And sure enough, as he started back to the land of Judah, a lion met him and killed him, and his dead body lay on the road.

When the old man heard about it, he said, "It must be the prophet from Judah who disobeyed the command of the Lord.

"Saddle my donkey," he said to his sons. Then he rode until he found the body of the prophet and saw the donkey and the lion standing there. The lion had not eaten the body nor killed the donkey.

The old man lifted the prophet's body onto the donkey and took it to Bethel, where he buried it in his own grave. Then he said to his sons, "When I am dead, bury me here in this same place; lay my bones beside his bones, for the words that he spoke against the altar in Bethel shall surely come true."

Instead of doing exactly what God had told him to do, this old prophet listened to some bad advice. God punished his disobedience by letting a lion kill him.

A LITTLE PRINCE DIES

1 KINGS 14, 15, 16

AT THAT TIME the son of King Jeroboam was sick, and Jeroboam said to his wife, "Take off your fine clothes and put on something so old that no one will recognize you, and go to Shiloh, and visit the prophet who told me I would be king. Take him a present of ten loaves of bread and a bottle of honey, and he will tell you whether the child will get well."

Jeroboam's wife did as he had told her to. She put on a cheap dress instead of her queen's gown, and went to Shiloh, and came to the prophet's house. The prophet was old now, and couldn't see very well, but the Lord had told him that the wife of Jeroboam was coming to ask about her son.

So when he heard the sound of her feet as she came in at the door, he said, "Come in, wife of Jeroboam; why are you pretending to be someone else? I have a sad message to give you. Go and tell Jeroboam, 'The Lord says, I raised you up from among the people, and made you king over ten of the tribes of Israel. I took those ten tribes away from Solomon's son and gave them to you. Yet you have not obeyed my commandments, but have turned away from worshiping me and have worshiped idols instead. Therefore I will destroy you and your family. Not one will be left alive. Dogs will eat those who die in the city, and the birds will eat those who die in the field; for the Lord has told me so.'"

Then he said to Jeroboam's wife, "As you enter the door of your house, your child will die. And all the people shall mourn for him and bury him. He is the only one of Jeroboam's family who will be buried in a grave."

So Jeroboam's wife went home, and as she came in at the door, the child died. And they buried him, and all Israel mourned for him as the prophet had said.

Jeroboam was king for twenty-two years; then he died, and his son Nadab became the new king.

Nadab didn't obey God either, but worshiped the golden calves his father had made. But after two years a man named Baasha rebelled against him and killed him; then Baasha became the king.

The first thing King Baasha did was to kill every one of King Jeroboam's family. So the words of the prophet came true, for he had told Jeroboam's wife that the Lord would bring evil on Jeroboam and his family, until not one of them was left alive.

King Baasha was as wicked as King Jeroboam, and he too worshiped the gold calves. He was king for twenty-four years; then he died and his son Elah became the new king.

Elah was king for only two years. One day he was drinking in the house of one of his friends when Zimri, the captain of half of his chariots, came into the house and killed him. Then Zimri said that he was the new king.

The men of Israel were away at the time, fighting against the Philistines, but as soon as they heard what Zimri had done, they said they didn't want him to be their king, so they chose their army general, Omri, to be their new king instead.

Then King Omri and the men of Israel came to the city of Tirzah, where Zimri was, and surrounded it. When

Zimri saw that he couldn't prevent them from capturing the city, he committed suicide by going into his palace and setting it on fire, and he died in the flames. So Zimri was king for only seven days.

After Omri became king he bought the hill of Samaria and built a city on it and called it the city of Samaria. King Omri lived in this city, and for nearly two hundred years afterwards the other kings of Israel lived there too.

King Omri sinned as Jeroboam did, for he worshiped the gold calves and encouraged his people to worship them. He was king for twelve years, and died and was buried in Samaria, the city he had built; then his son Ahab became the new king.

STORY 101

A DEAD BOY LIVES AGAIN!

1 KINGS 16, 17

UP TO THIS TIME, six kings had ruled over the ten tribes of Israel, and every one of them had been bad. But the Bible tells us that King Ahab, Omri's son, was worse than any of the others.

He married the daughter of a heathen king. This girl's name was Jezebel, and she worshiped the idol Baal. King Ahab built a temple for this idol in the city of Samaria and chose bad men as priests to offer sacrifices to the idol. So King Ahab caused the people of Israel to worship Baal just as the heathen nations did.

290

The Lord was angry with King Ahab and sent the prophet Elijah to tell him that as punishment there would not be any more rain in the land of Israel for many years, until Elijah asked God to send it. Ahab was very angry with Elijah because his God had stopped the rain, and he wanted to kill Elijah, so the Lord told Elijah to go and hide.

"Go and hide beside a brook in the wilderness," the Lord said. "You can get drinking water from the brook, and I have commanded the ravens to feed you there!" So Elijah hid by the brook, and the ravens brought him food every morning and evening. But after a while the brook dried up because there had been no rain, and a great famine came over the land.

Then the Lord said to Elijah, "Go to the city of Zarephath, for I have commanded a widow to feed you there."

When Elijah came to the gate of the city he saw a woman gathering sticks, and he called to her and said, "Please bring me a cup of water to drink." As she was going to get it he called to her again, and said, "And a piece of bread, too!"

But she answered, "As surely as God lives, I have no bread. I have only a handful of meal in a barrel, and a little olive oil in a bottle; and now I am gathering sticks to bake a little loaf of bread for me and my son to eat, and then we must die of starvation."

But Elijah told her, "No, you won't! Go and bake the bread, but make a little loaf for me first, and bring it here, and there will be plenty left for you and your son! For the Lord says that although you have only a little flour and olive oil, it will last until the famine ends!"

She did as Elijah said, and sure enough, there was always olive oil left in the bottle and flour in the barrel, no matter how much she used! It was a wonderful miracle! This went on for a whole year until the famine ended.

One day the woman's son became sick and died. Elijah took him out of her arms and carried him up to his own room and laid him on his bed. Elijah pleaded with the Lord and said, "O Lord, why have you brought evil upon this woman in whose house I stay, by slaying her son? Please, O Lord, let the child live again!"

And the Lord heard Elijah's prayer, and the boy came back to life, and Elijah took him down to his mother. What a wonderful miracle!

STORY 102

ELIJAH FACES BAAL'S PROPHETS
1 KINGS 18

THERE WERE many other prophets of the Lord besides Elijah in the land of Israel. But Queen Jezebel, the wicked wife of King Ahab, hated them all and tried to kill them.

Obadiah, the manager of Ahab's palace, was a good man who feared the Lord, so he hid a hundred of the Lord's prophets in caves where Jezebel couldn't find them, and sent them supplies of food and water.

After the famine had lasted for more than three years the Lord said to Elijah, "Go to King Ahab, and I will send rain."

King Ahab didn't know Elijah was coming, or that the Lord had promised rain, so King Ahab and Obadiah were out looking everywhere to find grass to save the horses and mules from dying of starvation. They went in different directions so they could finish their work faster.

As Obadiah was walking along, Elijah met him. Obadiah recognized him and said, "Are you Elijah, sir?"

"I am," Elijah replied. "Now go and tell King Ahab that I am here."

So Obadiah found the king and told him, and he came to meet Elijah. When King Ahab saw Elijah he exclaimed, "There you are, you traitor." He said this because he blamed Elijah for the famine.

But Elijah answered, "I am not a traitor, but you and your family are, because you have forsaken the Lord and are worshiping Baal."

Then Elijah told King Ahab to send for all the people to come to Mount Carmel, and to bring with them all 450 of the priests of Ahab's idol, whose name was Baal. So all the people came with the priests.

Elijah asked the people, "How long will it be before you decide whether you will serve God or Baal? If the Lord is God, obey him; but if Baal is God, then obey him.

"Now bring two young bulls," Elijah said, "and let Baal's prophets kill one of them and lay it on Baal's altar, without any fire under it. And I will take the other young bull and kill it and lay it on the Lord's altar, without any fire under it. Then let them pray to Baal to send down fire from heaven to burn up their young bull. And I will pray to the Lord for fire to come from heaven to burn up the young bull on the altar of the Lord. Whichever god sends fire from heaven to burn up his offering, he is the real God." And all the people agreed.

Baal's prophets chose a young bull and killed it, and laid

it on the wood on the altar, but put no fire under it. Then they cried out to their idol, Baal, from morning till noon.

"O Baal, hear us!" they shouted, and leaped up and down on their altar. But no voice answered them, and no fire came down from heaven to burn up their offering.

About noon, Elijah mocked them and said, "Call louder, for perhaps your god is talking to someone and isn't listening, or maybe he is away, or is asleep and must be awakened!"

So they yelled and shouted to Baal until evening, and cut themselves with knives until the blood gushed out, hoping it would attract Baal's attention and make him answer them. But no fire came.

Then Elijah gathered all the people around him and used twelve stones to rebuild the altar of the Lord that had long lain in ruins, and dug a trench around it. He put wood on the altar and cut the young bull apart and laid the pieces on the wood.

Then he said to the people, "Fill four barrels with water, and pour it over the sacrifice and over the wood." When they had done this, he said, "Do it a second time." And they did it a second time. "Now do it a third time," he said. And they did. So the water ran down over the sacrifice and over the wood, and filled the trench around the altar.

That evening, at the time when the priests at the temple used to offer a lamb for a burnt offering, Elijah came near the altar and prayed to the Lord, saying, "Hear me, O Lord, hear me, so that these people will realize that you are the true God."

Then the fire of the Lord fell from heaven upon the altar and burned up the offering and the wood, and even the stones of the altar, and licked up the water in the trench.

When the people saw it, they all fell face downward on the ground, shouting, "The Lord, he is God! The Lord, he is God!"

And Elijah said to them, "Grab the prophets of Baal! Don't let a single one escape!" So the people arrested them and Elijah took them down to Kishon Brook and killed them there; for the Lord had commanded that anyone who told people to forsake God and to worship idols must be executed.

STORY 103

ELIJAH'S STRANGE PICNIC
1 KINGS 18, 19

ELIJAH TOLD KING AHAB that now he could celebrate, for the rain was coming and the famine would soon be ended. Then Elijah went up to the top of Mount Carmel and kneeled down with his face to the ground, and prayed that God would send the rain. After he had prayed he said to his servant, "Go and look out towards the sea. Are there any clouds yet?"

The servant went and looked, but came back and said, "I couldn't see any."

"Go again seven times," Elijah ordered him.

So the servant went six more times and finally the seventh time he said, "There is one tiny cloud."

Then Elijah knew the Lord was going to send the rain, so he said to his servant, "Go and tell Ahab, 'Quick! Get your chariot ready and get down off the mountain, before the rain stops you!'"

295

While his servant was going to tell Ahab, the little cloud grew larger and larger until the entire sky was black with clouds, and the wind began to blow, and there was a very heavy rain. Then Ahab rode in his chariot to the city of Jezreel. And the Lord gave Elijah strength to run before the chariot until he came to the gate of the city.

When he got home, King Ahab told his wife, Queen Jezebel, all that had happened, and how Elijah had killed the prophets of Baal. Jezebel was very angry and sent this message to Elijah: "By tomorrow at this time you will be dead, for I will kill you." When Elijah heard this he was badly frightened and ran for his life, and came to the city of Beer-sheba in the land of Judah. There he left his servant, while he himself traveled on for another day and hid in the wilderness.

He sat down under a juniper tree and asked the Lord to let him die. "Now, O Lord, take away my life," he said, for he was very tired of running away from his enemies. But he did wrong in asking to die. God had sent the ravens to feed him, and had saved him from Ahab and from the wicked prophets of Baal.

Finally he fell asleep, and as he lay there under the juniper tree, an angel came and touched him and woke him up. "Get up and eat," the angel said. Elijah looked, and there was a loaf of bread baked on some coals near him, and a bottle of water by his head. So he ate and drank, and lay down and slept again.

Then the angel of the Lord came a second time and touched him and told him to eat, so that he would have strength enough for the journey that lay ahead of him. So he got up and ate again, and the Lord gave him strength from that food to live for forty days and forty nights without eating again, until he came to Mount Horeb, and he lived in a cave on the mountain.

God sent Elijah
away to hide.
He camped
beside a brook
and ate the food
the ravens
brought him
in their beaks.

Then the Lord's voice came to him and said, "What are you doing here, Elijah?"

"The people of Israel have broken their promise to obey your laws," Elijah replied, "and have torn down your altars, and killed your prophets, and now I am the only one left, and they are trying to kill me too."

"Come out and stand at the entrance of the cave," the Lord told him. Then the Lord passed by. A terrible wind tore up the earth on the mountain, and even moved the rocks, but the Lord was not in the wind. And after the wind came an earthquake, but the Lord was not in the earthquake. And after the earthquake a fire, but the Lord was not in the fire. After the fire there came a still, small voice. When Elijah heard the voice, he knew that God was there. He wrapped his face in his cloak, for he was afraid to look upon God.

Then the Lord told Elijah to leave the cave and return to the land of Israel. When he got there he must anoint a man named Elisha to be the Lord's prophet instead of himself, for the time was coming soon when Elijah must leave the world behind and go to heaven.

So Elijah returned to Israel as the Lord had told him to. As he was walking along, he saw Elisha plowing a field. Elijah went over to him and threw his coat over Elisha's shoulders. Elisha knew that when a prophet did this to someone, it meant that that person should leave his home and become a prophet. So he left the plowing and ran after Elijah.

AHAB STEALS A VINEYARD

1 KINGS 20, 21

KING BEN-HADAD of Syria now summoned his army and went to fight against the city of Samaria, where King Ahab of Israel lived. He sent messengers to Ahab to tell him, "Your silver and gold, your wives and children, all are mine."

But the Lord sent a prophet to Ahab who told him not to be afraid, but to go out and fight the army of Ben-hadad.

Ben-hadad and his captains were having a drinking party in their tents when Ahab and his little army arrived. The huge Syrian army was taken by surprise and ran for their lives in great panic. When Ben-hadad saw what was happening, he jumped on a horse and got away.

The next year Ben-hadad's advisors persuaded him to gather together another army as great as the first, and they came up and spread over the whole country.

After seven days the battle began, and the Lord gave Israel another mighty victory, for they destroyed 100,000 of the Syrians. The rest escaped to the city of Aphek, and there a great wall fell down and killed many more. But Ben-hadad fled into the city and hid.

Ben-hadad's men came to him with the suggestion that he throw himself upon the mercy of King Ahab. "We have heard," they said, "that the kings of Israel are merciful; we will dress in sackcloth to show that we are sorry, and go to the king of Israel and ask him to save your life. Perhaps he will let you live." So they put on clothes made from old sacks, to show their humility, and came to Ahab, and said, "Your servant Ben-hadad begs, 'Please let me live.'"

"Wasn't he killed in the battle?" Ahab asked. When he heard he was still alive, he told them to go and bring him. When Ben-hadad arrived, Ahab let him ride with him in his chariot as though they were friends. Then Ben-hadad promised to give Ahab some of his cities, so Ahab allowed him to return again to his own land.

But God was angry with Ahab for doing this. He had given Ahab the victory over Ben-hadad so that Ahab could put him to death. Now God sent a prophet to Ahab who said, "Because you have let this man go, you must die instead of him."

Soon afterwards Ahab wanted to buy the vineyard of a man named Naboth because it was near his palace. "I'll give you a better vineyard for it," he said, "or else I'll pay you whatever it's worth."

But Naboth didn't want to sell his vineyard. It had belonged to his father and he wanted to keep it. So he refused to sell it.

Ahab returned home angry and unhappy, and lay down and sulked and refused to eat! When Queen Jezebel came home she asked, "What's the trouble? Why are you so sad?"

"Because Naboth won't sell me his farm," Ahab replied.

"Are you the king of Israel or not?" Jezebel demanded. "Get up and be happy—I will give you the farm!"

Then she wrote letters, and signed them with Ahab's name, and sealed them with his seal, and sent them to the elders of the city of Jezreel where Naboth lived. In the letters she told them to find some bad men who would tell lies about Naboth, and say that they had heard him speak evil of God and the king.

The elders did as Queen Jezebel commanded. They found two men who lied about him. Now the Lord had commanded that anyone who spoke against God should be stoned. Naboth had not done that terrible deed, but the bad men lied and said that he had. So the people took Naboth out of the city and threw stones at him until he died, and the dogs came and licked up his blood. Then they sent a message to Jezebel: "Naboth is dead."

When Jezebel heard it she said to Ahab, "Go and take Naboth's vineyard, for he is dead." So Ahab went down to the vineyard to claim it.

But the Lord told Elijah to go out and meet him at the vineyard and say to him, "So you have murdered Naboth and taken his vineyard, have you? Well, where the dogs licked up the blood of Naboth, dogs will lick up your blood too."

STORY 105

FIRE FROM HEAVEN
1 KINGS 22; 2 KINGS 1

ONE DAY King Jehoshaphat of Judah went to visit King Ahab of Israel. King Ahab asked him to help him fight against King Ben-hadad again. King Jehoshaphat told Ahab to ask God first, and find out whether God wanted them to do this or not.

So King Ahab summoned his 400 false prophets and asked them, "Shall I go to battle or not?"

"Yes," they answered, "for the Lord will be with you." But King Jehoshaphat didn't believe these men, for he knew that they were not real prophets at all, but only said whatever they thought would please King Ahab.

301

"Isn't there a prophet of the Lord around here somewhere?" King Jehoshaphat asked. "Let's ask him, too."

"There is one," Ahab answered, "a man named Micaiah; but I hate him because he doesn't prophesy good things about me, but always something bad."

"Let's ask him anyway," King Jehoshaphat said.

So Ahab sent a messenger to bring Micaiah. The messenger came back, bringing Micaiah. King Ahab asked him, "Shall we go out to battle, or not?"

"Certainly," Micaiah said, "go right ahead!"

But the king saw that Micaiah didn't really mean this. "How many times must I tell you not to lie to me?" he demanded.

Then Micaiah answered, "I saw Israel scattered upon the hills like a flock of sheep that is lost and has no shepherd."

But despite Micaiah's warning, the king of Israel and the king of Judah went out to the battle. Ahab said to Jehoshaphat, "I'll not wear my royal robes; then no one will know me. But you wear yours and let them see you are a king!"

But an arrow hit Ahab between the pieces of armor that covered his chest. No one was aiming at him, for no one knew he was Ahab; the arrow just happened to hit him there.

"Turn around and get me out of here, for I am badly wounded," Ahab said to the soldier driving his chariot. Ahab sat in his chariot all day watching the battle, but that evening he died.

Ahab's body was taken to Samaria and buried there. And as his chariot was being washed beside a pool of water near the city, the dogs came and licked up his blood, just as Elijah had said they would.

Ahab's son Ahaziah now became king. But he was as

bad as his father. One day he fell from an upstairs room in his palace and was seriously hurt. He sent messengers to Baal-zebub, the idol of the Philistines, to ask whether he would get well again. Then the angel of the Lord said to Elijah, "Go to meet King Ahaziah's messengers and ask them, 'Is it because there is no God in Israel that you have to go and ask Baal-zebub, the idol of the Philistines? For doing this, the Lord says that King Ahaziah shall not get well again; he will surely die.'"

Elijah told the messengers what the Lord had said, so they returned to Ahaziah.

"Why have you come back so soon?" he asked.

"A man came to meet us," they told him, "and told us to return to you and say, 'Is it because there is no God in Israel that you have come to inquire of Baal-zebub, the idol of the Philistines? Therefore you will not get well but will surely die.'"

"What did he look like?" the king asked the messengers.

"He was a hairy man," they said, "with a leather belt."

"It was Elijah!" Ahaziah exclaimed.

The king was angry and sent a captain of his army with fifty soldiers to capture Elijah, and to bring him to the king. They found him sitting on the top of a hill. The captain yelled at him. "Hey, you prophet, the king commands you to come on down."

"If I am a prophet," Elijah answered, "let fire come down from heaven and burn you and your fifty men." And fire came down from heaven, and burned them up.

Then Ahaziah sent another captain with fifty men, and he came to Elijah and called to him, "Prophet, the king says come right away."

Elijah answered, "If I am a prophet, let fire come down from heaven and burn you and your fifty men." Then fire came down again from heaven, and burned them up.

Then Ahaziah sent another captain with fifty men, and he came to Elijah and called to him, "Prophet, the king says come right away."

Elijah answered, "If I am a prophet, let fire come down from heaven and burn you and your fifty men." Then fire came down again from heaven, and burned them up.

Ahaziah sent a third captain with fifty men. But when he came to Elijah, he fell on his knees before him, and said, "O prophet, please save my life and the lives of these fifty men, your servants. Don't let the fire come down from heaven and burn us, as it burned the two captains with their men who were here before."

Then the angel of the Lord said to Elijah, "Go with him, don't be afraid." So Elijah went with him to the king.

Elijah told the king, "The Lord says that because you sent messengers to your god Baal-zebub, the idol of the Philistines, instead of sending them to me, the God of Israel, therefore you shall not get up from this bed, but shall surely die."

So Ahaziah died as Elijah said, and Jehoram his brother became king instead.

STORY 106

A CHARIOT RIDE TO HEAVEN
2 KINGS 2

THE DAY soon arrived when the Lord was ready to take Elijah up to heaven. Elijah wanted to be alone when the Lord took him, so he said to Elisha, "Stay here, please, for the Lord has sent me on to Bethel."

God took Elijah
to heaven
in a fiery chariot.
As he left,
he gave his coat to Elisha.
This showed that
Elisha was to be
the new prophet.

But Elisha said, "I'll not leave you." So they went to Bethel together.

The young men from the school for prophets there came over to Elisha and asked him, "Do you know that the Lord will take away your master from you today?"

"Yes," he said, "I know."

Then Elijah said to Elisha, "Stay here at Bethel, please, for the Lord has sent me to Jericho."

But Elisha said, "I'll not leave you." So they came to Jericho.

The young men who were in the school for prophets there at Jericho came to Elisha and asked him, "Do you know that the Lord will take away your master from you today?"

"Yes, I know," he replied.

Then Elijah said to Elisha, "Stay here, please, at Jericho, for the Lord has sent me to the river Jordan."

But Elisha answered, "I'll not leave you." So they went on together. Fifty young men from the school of the prophets followed them, to watch and see what would happen.

Elijah and Elisha stood at the edge of the river, and Elijah struck the water with his coat, and the river divided before them so that they went over on dry ground!

When they were on the other side, Elijah said to Elisha, "Tell me what you want me to do for you before I am taken away."

Elisha asked to have even more of God's Spirit upon him than Elijah had.

"You have asked a hard thing," Elijah answered, "but if you see me when I am taken from you, you shall have what you are asking for; but if not, you will not get it."

As they walked along and talked together, suddenly a chariot of fire, with horses of fire, swept between them and snatched Elijah away from Elisha, and took him up to heaven in the chariot. Elisha saw it, and cried out, "My father, my father, the chariot and horsemen of Israel!"

Elisha never saw Elijah again on earth. He picked up Elijah's coat that had fallen on the ground, and with it he struck the river, and the water divided before him as it had for Elijah, and Elisha went over on dry ground!

Then the men of Jericho came to Elisha and told him, "Our city is pleasant to live in except that the water is no good. It ruins the ground so that nothing will grow here."

"Bring me a water jar and put some salt in it," Elisha told them. So they brought it to him. He went to the spring where the city got its water and threw the salt in and said, "The Lord says, 'I have made these waters pure; they shall never again cause the people to be sick, or ruin the ground.'" So the water was pure from that day on.

THE OIL THAT KEPT COMING

2 KINGS 3, 4

AFTER THIS, King Jehoram of Israel gathered his army together to fight against the Moabites. He asked King Jehoshaphat of Judah to help him.

"All right," Jehoshaphat said, "I'll go with you."

The king of Edom went with them too. So these three kings took their armies with them and marched for seven days, and in all that time they found no water to drink. Then the king of Israel was frightened, for he knew that his soldiers were so thirsty they couldn't fight.

King Jehoram of Israel worshiped idols, but King Jehoshaphat worshiped the Lord. So Jehoshaphat asked, "Isn't there a prophet here who can find out from the Lord what we should do?"

One of the king of Israel's officers said, "Elisha is here; he was Elijah's assistant."

"Let's ask him," Jehoshaphat said. So the three kings went to visit Elisha.

Elisha was angry and disgusted when he saw the king of Israel. "Why have you come to me?" he asked. "Go to the false prophets of your father Ahab, and of your mother Jezebel; let them help you!"

Elisha said this to him because the king didn't ever obey God except when he was in trouble. Then Elisha said to him, "If King Jehoshaphat of Judah were not with you, I wouldn't even listen to you."

The Lord told Elisha to tell the kings to command their soldiers to dig many ditches in the valley where their camp was. The Lord said there would be no wind or rain, but the ditches would be filled with water! Then all the soldiers could drink as much as they wished.

"You will destroy the cities of the Moabites," Elisha said, "and will cut down their trees, and fill up their wells, and spoil the best of their land."

Elisha's words all came true the next morning, for the Lord caused water to flow along the ground and fill the ditches, and so everyone had plenty of water to drink. And when the enemy soldiers from Moab looked across the valley to the camp of Israel, the sun shone on the water in the ditches and made it look red. When the Moabites saw the redness, they thought the armies from Israel had been fighting and killing each other, and that the red water was blood!

This mother had waited many years to have a little boy. When he suddenly died, she was very sad. But the prophet Elisha brought him back to life.

"We've defeated them," they shouted. "Let's go and see what we can loot from their tents."

So they ran to the Israeli camp. But suddenly they realized that their enemy was still there! Now they fled back in disorder.

The men of Israel ran after them and chased them all the way back to their own country. Then the Israelis cut down their trees and destroyed their cities, filled up the wells, and scattered stones and boulders on every piece of ground, just as Elisha had said they would. Afterwards the men of Israel returned to their own land.

One day the wife of one of the college students came to Elisha with a serious problem: "My husband is dead," she said, "and you know that he loved the Lord. But he owed some money and I can't pay it back, and now the man I owe it to has come to take away my two sons and make them his slaves."

Elisha asked her, "What do you have that you can sell?"

"Nothing," she answered, "except one jar of olive oil!"

"Well," he said, "I'll tell you what to do. Go and borrow empty jars from all your neighbors, and take them into your house and shut the door. Then take your jar of olive oil and begin pouring it into the jars you borrow."

So she borrowed empty jars and pots, and took them into her house and shut the door. Then as her sons brought the empty jars to her, she poured olive oil into them from her one little jar, and the oil kept coming until all the jars were full! Finally, when she said to her son, "Bring me another jar!" he answered, "There is not another empty one left!"

She came and told Elisha, and he said, "Go and sell the olive oil and pay the man what your husband owed him, and take the money that is left to buy food for yourself and the children."

ELISHA DOES GREAT MIRACLES

2 KINGS 4

AFTER THESE THINGS, as Elisha was traveling around through the land, he came to the city of Shunem, where a rich woman lived, and she invited him to stop at her house for dinner. And always after that, whenever he passed that way, he stopped for a meal.

One day she said to her husband, "I'm sure this man is a prophet of the Lord. Let's give him a little guest room and whenever he comes to visit us, it will be ready for him." So that is what they did.

Once when Elisha was there with his servant, whose name was Gehazi, he said to him, "Call this woman."

When she came, Elisha told Gehazi to say to her, "You have been very kind to us; what shall we do for you in return? Is there anything you want me to ask the king to give you?" But she replied that she needed nothing.

After she was gone Elisha said to Gehazi, "Can you think of anything we can do for her?"

"Yes," Gehazi said, "she has no child."

"Call her again," Elisha said. So Gehazi called her and she came again and stood at the door. Then Elisha told her that the Lord would give her a son. And Elisha's words came true the following year.

When the child was old enough, he went out one day to the field with his father, to watch the reapers. While he

311

was there he became sick, and cried out to his father, "My head! Oh, my head!"

His father said to one of the young men, "Carry him to his mother." So the child sat in her lap until noon, and then died.

She took him up to Elisha's room and laid him on the bed, and shut the door and left him there. Then she sent a message out to the field to her husband asking him to send one of the young men and one of the donkeys so she could hurry to the prophet and come right back again. She didn't tell him that their boy was dead, and so he said to her, "Why today? There isn't any special meeting today!"

"I need to go today," was all she would say.

So he told her to go ahead. "Drive hard," she said to the servant. "Hurry, don't stop for anything." So she came to Elisha at Mount Carmel.

Elisha saw her in the distance and said to Gehazi, "Look, here comes that Shunammite woman. Run to meet her and ask, 'Is everything all right? Is your husband well? How is your child?'"

Gehazi ran and asked her and she replied, "Everything is fine." When she came to Elisha, she knelt down and caught him by the feet, and Gehazi came to push her away.

But Elisha said, "Let her alone, for she is in some sort of trouble, and the Lord hasn't told me what it is."

Then the woman said to Elisha, "Why have you told God to give me a son, and then take him away?" So then he knew that her boy was dead.

When Elisha came into the house the dead boy was lying there upon the bed. So Elisha went in and shut the door and prayed. Then he lay upon the child, and put his mouth upon the child's mouth, and his eyes upon the child's eyes, and his hands upon the child's hands; and the child's flesh grew warm!

Elisha came out of the room and walked back and forth for a while in the house. Then he went up and stretched himself upon the child again; and the child sneezed seven times, and opened his eyes and came to life again!

Then Elisha said to Gehazi, "Call her!" So Gehazi did.

"Take your son!" Elisha said to her as she came into the room.

Oh, how thankful that mother was!

STORY 109

A LITTLE GIRL HELPS NAAMAN
2 Kings 5, 6

THE KING OF SYRIA liked Naaman, the general of his army, because he had won so many battles against his enemies. But Naaman was a leper. A leper is a person with a sickness which affects the skin and finally makes the nose and fingers and toes rot away.

Now it so happened that when the Syrians conquered the land of Israel, they brought back with them a little Israeli girl who became the slave of Naaman's wife.

One day she said to her mistress, "I wish my master could go and see God's prophet in Samaria, for he would cure him of his leprosy."

Someone told the king what the little girl had said, so he told Naaman to go to Samaria and be healed.

Naaman took a fortune in silver and gold with him, and

ten sets of new clothing. All this was a present for the prophet if he would heal him. Naaman came in his chariot and stood at the door of Elisha's house. Elisha didn't go out to meet him but just sent this message to him: "Go and wash yourself seven times in the river Jordan and you will be healed of your leprosy."

But Naaman was angry. "Do you mean to tell me the prophet isn't even going to come out here and pray to the Lord his God for me, and put his hand on me and make me well?" he demanded. "Aren't the rivers in my own country better than all the rivers in the land of Israel?" So he turned around and went away in a rage.

But then some of his men came to him and said, "Sir, if the prophet had told you to do some hard thing to make you well, wouldn't you have done it? So when he tells you just to go and wash, and you will be healed—why don't you at least try it and see?"

So Naaman went down to the river Jordan and dipped seven times, and suddenly his skin became as new and fresh as a little child's, and he was healed of his leprosy. He went back to the house of Elisha and said, "Now I know that there is no other God in all the earth except the God of Israel."

He wanted to give Elisha a present, but Elisha said, "No, I won't accept it." Naaman begged him, but Elisha wouldn't take it.

Then Naaman asked for two mule-loads of earth from the land of Israel to take home with him, and he would make an altar from it, for he never again would offer a burnt offering to any other god but the Lord.

General Naaman had leprosy. His servant girl, a captive from Israel, told Naaman that the prophet Elisha could cure him by God's power.

Naaman started home to his own country, but when he had gone just a little way, Elisha's servant Gehazi said to himself, "It's a shame my master wouldn't accept the present Naaman wanted to give him. I'll run after him and ask for something for myself."

When Naaman saw Gehazi running after him, he stopped his chariot and stepped down to meet him, and said, "Is everything all right?"

"Yes," Gehazi answered, "but my master has changed his mind. He sent me to tell you that after you left, two young men, prophets' sons, came to visit him. He asks you to give them a wedge of silver and two sets of clothing."

"I'll give *two* wedges of silver!" Naaman replied.

So Naaman gave Gehazi two wedges of silver and two sets of clothing, and sent two servants to help Gehazi carry them, for the silver was very heavy. But when they were near Elisha's house, Gehazi took the silver from the servants and sent them back to Naaman again. Then Gehazi hid the silver and clothing for he didn't want Elisha to know about it. But the Lord had already told Elisha. So when Gehazi came and stood before him, Elisha asked him, "Where have you been, Gehazi?"

"Nowhere," Gehazi said.

Elisha replied, "Didn't I know it when Naaman stepped down from his chariot to meet you? Is this a time for us to take money and clothes? And now, because you have done this, Naaman's leprosy shall be on you and on your children forever." And as Elisha spoke, the leprosy covered Gehazi, and he went out with white splotches of leprosy all over his body.

FOUR LEPERS FIND FOOD FOR A CITY

2 KINGS 7

NOT LONG AFTER THIS, King Ben-hadad of Syria mobilized his army again and returned to Samaria to attack it. His soldiers surrounded the city to keep anyone from getting in or out. No one could take any food to the people inside, so there was a great famine. As the king of Israel walked among his soldiers on the top of the city wall, a woman called to him for help.

"What's the matter?" he asked.

She answered, "Another woman here suggested to me that we should eat my little son one day and her son the next day. So we killed my son and ate him, but the next day when it was time to kill her son, she hid him."

When King Jehoram heard this, he tore his clothes in anguish over the dreadful famine raging over the city, and that such a thing had been done among his people. But Jehoram was as wicked a man as his father Ahab, and that is why God sent these terrible troubles upon them. Jehoram should have repented and asked God to help him. Instead, he blamed the troubles on Elisha and said the prophet would be put to death that very day.

Elisha knew the king was planning to kill him, so when the executioner arrived at his house, Elisha told those with him to lock the door and keep the man out.

Afterwards the king himself came to Elisha's house with one of his assistants. Elisha told them that the famine would end the next day, and there would be plenty of food, for the Lord had told him this. But the king's assistant wouldn't believe it. Elisha told him that because he didn't believe the words of the Lord, he would see the food, but wouldn't taste one bite of it. Soon we shall see how Elisha's words came true.

That night four lepers were sitting outside the city walls. They said to each other, "Why sit here until we starve? If we go into the city we'll die from the famine. If we sit here, we have nothing to eat, and will die. Come on, let's go out to the army of the Syrians. If they don't kill us, we will live; if they kill us, we will only die like we're going to anyway."

So they went across the field to where the Syrian army was camped—but no one was there! For the Lord had made the Syrians hear the noise of a great army coming out against them. They fled in the night, leaving their tents and horses and everything else. But really there was no one attacking them at all!

When the lepers had walked through the entire camp and found no one, they went into one of the tents and ate the food they found there, and took money and clothing, and hid them. Then they went into another tent, and carried away more silver and gold, and hid it too. But then they stopped and looked at each other. "This isn't right," they said. "We have good news for our people, and yet we aren't telling them."

So they returned to the city that night and shouted to the guards on the wall, "We have been to the camp of the Syrians and no one is there! The horses are tied, and the tents are standing there, but no one is around!"

God frightened the Syrian army away. Four lepers found food in the deserted Syrian camp. They shared it with all the other starving Israelis.

318

The guards rushed over and told the king. "It's a trick," he said. "The Syrians know we are starving and so they are hiding outside the camp. When we go over, they will rush back and capture us."

One of the king's assistants said, "We still have a few horses. Let's ride over and see."

So the king sent a few of his men over to the Syrian camp and sure enough, no one was there. They searched as far as the river Jordan, and all along the road there were clothes and equipment thrown away by the Syrians as they ran. Then the men returned to Samaria and reported to the king.

When the news reached the people, everyone rushed out to the camp of the Syrians and brought back huge supplies of flour and grain left by the Syrians when they fled. So the famine was suddenly ended, and now there was plenty of food. The king sent his assistant—the one who wouldn't believe Elisha—to stand at the gate and keep the people in order. But he fell beneath the surging crowd and was trampled and killed. So it happened to him as Elisha had said: he saw the food but never tasted it.

STORY 111

GOD TELLS ELISHA THE FUTURE

2 KINGS 8

ONE DAY ELISHA said to the woman whose son he had brought to life again, "Move to some other country for a while, for the Lord is going to send another seven years of famine to the land of Israel."

So she took her family to the land of the Philistines, and lived there for seven years. Then she returned to Israel, but found that while she was gone, someone had moved into her house and claimed her fields.

Taking her son with her she went to see King Jehoram, to plead for her right to her farm again. When she arrived at the palace, Gehazi, the servant of Elisha, was there and the king was talking with him.

"Tell me about some of the wonderful things Elisha has done," the king said. Gehazi was just telling him how Elisha had brought a boy back to life, when that boy and his mother came in to speak with the king!

Gehazi said, "My Lord, O king, this is the woman I was talking about, and this is her son who came to life again!" When the king asked her whether it was true, she told him it was. Then the king told one of his assistants to see to it that she got back her house and land, and to pay her for any fruit and grain that her fields had produced while she was in the land of the Philistines.

Elisha now went to Damascus, where King Ben-hadad of Syria lived. Ben-hadad was sick at the time, so he said to Hazael, one of his assistants, "Take a present to Elisha the prophet, and tell him to ask God whether I will get well again." So Hazael went to visit Elisha, and took a present to him—forty camel loads of the good things of Damascus.

He said to Elisha, "The king of Syria has sent me to ask you whether or not he will get well again."

Elisha answered, "Go and tell him he can get well. But the Lord has shown me he will die."

Elisha stared silently at Hazael, as though reading his thoughts, until Hazael was embarrassed; then Elisha started crying.

"Sir, why are you weeping?" Hazael asked.

Elisha answered, "Because I know the horrible things

you will do to the people over in Israel; you will set their cities on fire, and kill their young men, their women, and their little children."

Hazael was astonished. "Am I such a dog as that?" he asked.

And Elisha replied, "The Lord has shown me that you will be the king of Syria."

So Hazael went back to King Ben-hadad.

"What did Elisha say?" the king asked.

"He told me you'll get well," Hazael lied.

But the next day Hazael took a thick, wet cloth and spread it over the king's face as he lay sick and helpless, so that he couldn't breathe. Thus King Ben-hadad was murdered and Hazael declared himself king.

STORY 112

JEZEBEL'S TERRIBLE DEATH
2 KINGS 9–13

AT THIS TIME ELISHA summoned one of the students at the college and said to him, "Get some anointing oil and go to the city of Ramoth-gilead and look for Jehu, who is a captain in the king of Israel's army. When you have found him, take him into a room alone, and pour the oil on his head, and say, 'The Lord has anointed you to be the king of Israel.' Then open the door and run."

So the young man went to Ramoth-gilead and found the captains of the army sitting around, with Jehu among them. The young man went up to him and said, "I have a message for you, sir."

"For which one of us?" Jehu asked him.

"For you," the young man replied.

Jehu took him into a room in the barracks and the young man poured the olive oil on his head, and said to him, "The Lord says, 'I have anointed you to be the king of Israel! And after you become king, you must punish Ahab for killing my prophets by putting to death all who are left of his family. Dogs shall eat Queen Jezebel in the city of Jezreel, and no one will bury her because of all the people she has murdered.'"

Then the young man opened the door and ran.

When Jehu rejoined the other captains, one of them asked him, "What did that crazy fellow want?"

"Well," Jehu told them, "he said the Lord has appointed me as the king of Israel."

Then the captains blew a trumpet and shouted, "Jehu is king!" So, backed by the army, Jehu became king instead of Jehoram.

Jehu rode to Jezreel in his chariot. As he came near the city, the watchman who stood in the tower over the gate saw him coming and told King Jehoram. Jehoram jumped into his chariot and rode out to meet Jehu. "Is it peace, Jehu?" he demanded.

Jehu answered, "How can there be peace with your sinful mother, Jezebel, still around?" When Jehoram heard this, he tried to get away, for he saw that Jehu had come to fight. But Jehu drew a bow with all his might, and shot an arrow at Jehoram. It went into his heart, and he fell down dead in his chariot. Then Jehu commanded his captain to throw Jehoram's dead body out onto the ground. And the place where he threw it was in the vineyard his father Ahab had stolen from Naboth.

As Jehu arrived in the city, Queen Jezebel, Jehoram's mother, heard the commotion and put on her ornaments and makeup, and looked out from a window. As Jehu came in at the gate she called down to him.

He looked up at the window and shouted to the men in the house with her, "Who is on my side?" Two or three people stuck their heads out and said they were.

"Then throw her down," Jehu instructed them. So they threw her out of the window, and her blood was sprinkled on the wall, and the horses of Jehu's chariot trampled her. Then Jehu went into the palace and had a celebration feast. Afterwards he said to his assistants, "Go out and get the body of that wicked woman and bury it, for she was a king's daughter." But they could only find her skull, feet, and the palms of her hands, for the dogs had eaten her.

Jehu reigned for twenty-eight years in all, and was a very bad king. Then his son Jehoahaz became the new king. After seventeen years, King Jehoahaz died, and his son Jehoash followed him upon the throne.

One day Elisha became sick and realized he would soon die. King Jehoash of Israel came to see him and stood beside his bed with tears running down his cheeks. Elisha said to him, "Get a bow and some arrows. Now put an arrow in the bow and aim it through the open window." As the king did this, Elisha placed his hands over the king's hands. "Now shoot!" Elisha said, and the king did. Then Elisha told him what the arrow meant; it meant that the people of Israel would defeat the Syrians, and be free.

Next Elisha told the king to take some arrows and strike them against the ground. The king struck the ground three times and stopped. Elisha was angry, and said, "You should have struck five or six times, for then you would have

Jezebel looks out her window.
Soon she would be thrown
out the window to her death.
God used Jehu to get rid of
this wicked woman.

struck the Syrians until they were all destroyed; but now you will win against them only three times."

So Elisha died, but even after he was dead he caused another miracle! For as some people were carrying out a dead man to bury him, they saw some bandits coming towards them. In their haste and fright they quickly placed the dead man in Elisha's tomb, and when the dead body touched the bones of Elisha, the man came back to life again!

THE END OF THE KINGDOM OF ISRAEL
2 KINGS 14, 15; AMOS; HOSEA

AFTER THE DEATH of Elisha, King Jehoash of Israel mobilized his army against the Syrians and defeated them three times, just as Elisha had said he would. Jehoash was king for sixteen years, then died and was buried in the city of Samaria; and his son Jeroboam II became king instead.

The Lord was kind to Jeroboam and the people of Israel, for he pitied them for all they had suffered from their enemies. So he helped Jeroboam defeat the Syrians and conquer two of their cities, Damascus and Hamath. But the people of Israel didn't thank God for his kindness. Although he helped them in their trouble, and saved them from their enemies, they still worshiped the statues of the gold calves instead of worshiping God.

The Lord sent Amos the prophet to talk to them about this. The Lord had seen all of their sins, Amos told them, and so he had kept back the rain from their fields, and had sent famine and disease and hunger to show them he was angry. But still they hadn't turned from their evil ways, so an even greater punishment would now be sent upon them. There would be crying in their streets and on their farms; for an enemy would come and defeat them and treat them cruelly, and they would be carried away as slaves to other lands, and their king would be killed. But Amos told them that if they would only repent and obey the Lord, the Lord would even now forgive them, and these terrible things wouldn't happen to them.

Amaziah, who was the head priest at the idol temple at Bethel, was furious when he heard Amos tell the people these things. He reported to King Jeroboam that Amos was talking against the king, and saying that the king would be killed and the people taken away as slaves. Amaziah told Amos to run for his life and get out of the country.

The prophet Hosea, too, came and warned the people, telling them about the great punishment the Lord would send upon them. He too begged them to repent so that the Lord could forgive them. But they wouldn't listen. Finally, after being king of Israel forty-one years, Jeroboam died, and his son Zachariah became the new king.

But Zachariah was the king for only six months. Then a man named Shallum rebelled against him and killed him, and became king. But Shallum reigned only one month! For a man named Menahem killed him and became the king!

Menahem ruled for ten long and evil years, then his son Pekahiah became the new king.

But Pekahiah was as great a sinner as King Jeroboam was. Jeroboam, you remember, was the king who first set up the images of gold calves and told the people to worship them. And now King Pekahiah didn't destroy these idols as he should have, but worshiped them himself and taught the people to do this too, instead of worshiping God. He had been king for two years when one day a man named Pekah, the son of one of his army officers, came into the palace and killed him. Then Pekah became the new king.

From these true stories about the evil kings of Israel you can see how very wicked the people of Israel were. Instead of doing as God had taught them, they chose to worship idols, just as the heathen nations living around them did. They even burned alive their little sons and daughters as sacrifices to the idols.

God was very angry with the people of Israel for doing such things. Yet he waited patiently for them to stop doing wrong. He sent famine and disease and war into their land to show them he was angry. And when they continued to disobey him, then he sent his prophets to warn them again and again. These prophets preached to the people, telling them of the terrible punishment ahead, and begging them to stop doing wrong so that God could forgive them and keep them as his children. But they wouldn't listen. So at last God did as the prophets had warned and sent an enemy to conquer them and take them far away to another country to live as slaves, and they never saw their own country again.

So the kingdom of Israel was finished. It had lasted 254 years, ever since the ten tribes chose Jeroboam as their king. Nineteen wicked kings had ruled over them during that time. Now the king of Assyria sent people from his land to live in the cities of Israel. We do not know what happened to the ten tribes. They never returned to their own country again, and nothing more is said about them in the Bible or in any other history book.

That is the end of the story of the kingdom of Israel, so now we will go back 254 years and begin the story of the kingdom of Judah.

THE LITTLE KINGDOM OF JUDAH GROWS

STORY 114

1 KINGS 14, 15

WE HAVE already read about what happened after King Solomon died. His son Rehoboam became the king of the two tribes of Judah and Benjamin, but the other ten tribes didn't want him as their king and got someone else instead. Rehoboam lived at Jerusalem near the temple built by his father, King Solomon.

Rehoboam was forty-one years old when he became king of Judah, and he reigned seventeen years. Then he died and was buried in Jerusalem, and his son Abijah became king instead.

Soon there was war again between the armies of Judah and Israel. The army of Judah had 400,000 men in it, but the army of Israel had 800,000. Before the battle began, King Abijah of Judah stood on a mountain and shouted down to King Jeroboam and the men of Israel, "Don't you know that God has said that only the sons of King David should be your kings? Your king Jeroboam isn't a son of David. Yet he has declared himself to be Israel's king. This is wrong. And you have twice as large an army as we do, but you worship the gold calves made for you by Jeroboam; he says they are your gods. We worship only the Lord, and he is with us, and is our captain. O men of Israel, do not fight against the Lord, for you can never win against him."

But while Abijah was speaking, Jeroboam led the army of Israel into action against him and the battle began. Then the men of Judah cried out to the Lord for help, and the priests who were with them blew on their trumpets. Then the men of Judah gave a great shout, and as they did, God helped them, and Jeroboam and his army ran away. So the men of Judah won the victory because they trusted in God.

King Abijah reigned for three years, then died, and his son Asa became the new king of Judah.

Asa was a good king who tried to please the Lord, so the Lord gave his people rest from war. Then King Asa said to them, "Let us build more cities in our land, with walls, towers, and gates, so that our enemies can't conquer us." So the kingdom of Judah grew strong and prosperous.

Thirty-five years after Asa became the king of Judah, King Baasha of Israel declared war against him. But instead of praying to the Lord for help, King Asa took the silver and gold from the temple and from his palace and sent it to the king of Syria, to hire him to come and help him fight the king of Israel. The king of Syria did as Asa asked and sent his army to attack some of the cities of Israel. So King Baasha returned to defend his country, ending the war against Asa.

But the Lord sent a prophet to rebuke Asa for asking help from the king of Syria instead of from God. "The eyes of the Lord are looking everywhere around the world to find those who love him, so that he can help them. You have done foolishly because you trusted the king of Syria instead of trusting God. From now on your enemies shall conquer you."

Asa was angry with the prophet for saying this and put him in jail.

Three years later Asa became ill with a disease of the feet. His trouble grew worse and worse, yet in his sickness he didn't ask the Lord to heal him, but trusted only in his doctors. After three years of illness he finally died. The government officials of Judah laid him in a bed perfumed with sweet-smelling spices, and then buried him in a grave he had made for himself in Jerusalem. And his son Jehoshaphat became the new king.

GOD HELPS A GOOD KING
1 KINGS 22; 2 CHRONICLES 18, 19, 20

THE LORD was with Jehoshaphat because from the time he was made king he did what was right. All his people brought him gifts, and he had riches and honor. In the third year of his reign he sent teachers all through the cities of Judah, with the book of God's laws as their textbook, to teach God's will to the people.

One day he went down to the city of Samaria to visit King Ahab of Israel. King Ahab prepared a great party for him, and then persuaded him to go with him to fight against the king of Syria. One of the stories in this book has already told us how Jehoshaphat put on his royal robes and went into the battle, and how the Syrians thought he was Ahab, and tried to kill him. But when he cried out, then they saw their mistake and stopped following him, because God would not let them kill him. When the battle was over, Jehoshaphat came back to Jerusalem.

The Lord sent a prophet to ask him, "Was it right for you to help a wicked man like Ahab, and to be a partner with a man who hates the Lord? The Lord is angry with you. But you have done well in other things: you have taken away the altars where the people worshiped idols, and you have been anxious to serve God." So Jehoshaphat stayed at home in Jerusalem after that.

Once the Moabites, the Ammonites, and the Edomites came up to fight against King Jehoshaphat. When he heard that they were coming, he sent word to all his people, asking them not to eat for a few days but to pray hard asking for God's help. People came from all over Judah to the temple at Jerusalem to pray.

Then King Jehoshaphat stood up before them and prayed, "O Lord, are you not our God who drove out the heathen from this land, and gave it to your people? But now the Ammonites, the Moabites, and the Edomites are coming to drive us from the land you have given us. Will you let them do this? For we are not able to fight against this great army they are bringing. We don't know what to do. But we are looking up to you for help."

Then the Lord sent a prophet to tell King Jehoshaphat and the people, "Don't be afraid of this vast army. Tomorrow go out and face them. Just stand still when you get there, and you shall see how the Lord will save you. O men of Judah and Jerusalem, don't be afraid, for the Lord will help you."

Then King Jehoshaphat fell flat on the ground with his face in the dust, worshiping God. And all the people of Judah and Jerusalem did the same.

Early the next morning they went out to meet their enemies. As they were going, King Jehoshaphat said to his soldiers, "Trust in the Lord and believe what his prophet has said; then you will be victorious." And Jehoshaphat placed a choir at the head of the army to sing praises to God!

As the choir began to sing, God helped the men of Judah: for the Moabites, the Ammonites, and the Edomites began fighting and killing each other! When the men of Judah arrived, they saw their enemies lying dead on the ground. The people blessed and thanked the Lord for giving them the victory. And always after that the valley was called Berachah Valley, which means, "The Valley of Blessing." Then King Jehoshaphat and the Judean army returned to Jerusalem, led by a band and orchestra of harpists and trumpeters, and went to the temple to express their thanks to God.

The heathen nations feared to fight him after that, and God gave him and his people rest from war.

But afterwards King Jehoshaphat did wrong again, for he joined with the wicked king of Israel to send ships to a land called Ophir, to bring back gold. A prophet came and told him that because he had done this, his ships would be wrecked. And what the prophet said came true.

King Jehoshaphat was king for twenty-five years, and for the most part he did what was right and was pleasing to the Lord. Then he died and was buried in Jerusalem.

GOD MAKES A BAD KING SICK

2 CHRONICLES 21, 22

JEHOSHAPHAT HAD seven sons. At his death he left part of his treasures to each of them, and put them in charge of some of the cities of Judah; but he appointed his oldest son Jehoram to be the next king.

Jehoram wasn't like his father, though, for he didn't worship God. And he was afraid his brothers might lead a revolt and take the kingdom away from him, so he had them murdered.

King Jehoram also sinned by building altars in the mountains where the people went to worship idols.

King Jehoram's reason for doing all these wrong things was that he had married the daughter of Ahab, the wicked king of Israel, and she encouraged him to worship idols instead of worshiping God.

One day a letter came to King Jehoram from the prophet Elijah, and this is what it said: "The Lord says, 'Because you have not obeyed me as your father Jehoshaphat did, but have been wicked and have made the people wicked, and have killed your brothers who were better than you are, I will send many troubles upon you. You will become sick with a terrible sickness.'"

Then the Lord sent the Philistine and Arab armies to attack King Jehoram and his people. They came to Jerusalem and plundered his palace of its riches and took away his wives and his sons as captives, so that not one of his sons was left except Ahaziah, the youngest. After all this, the Lord sent a dreadful disease upon him, just as Elijah had said. He was sick for two years and grew worse and worse, for he couldn't be cured. Finally he died in the eighth year of his reign. But the people didn't mourn for him. He was buried in Jerusalem, but not where the other kings of Judah were buried. Then his son Ahaziah became king instead.

Ahaziah reigned only one year. Like his father, he was a very bad man, for his mother, who was the daughter of wicked King Ahab, taught him to sin.

One day King Ahaziah went to visit King Jehoram of Israel, at Jezreel. While he was there, Jehu attacked King Jehoram and killed him. We have already read about this, how Jehu drew a bow with all his might and shot an arrow at King Jehoram that went into his heart and the king fell down dead. King Ahaziah tried to help King Jehoram, and so Jehu told his men to kill him, too, and they did. Afterwards, the servants of King Ahaziah brought his body in a chariot to Jerusalem and buried him there, in the graves of the kings.

STORY 117

A LITTLE BOY BECOMES A KING

2 CHRONICLES 23, 24

WHEN AHAZIAH'S evil mother, Athaliah, heard that her son was dead, she killed his sons (who were her own grandchildren), so that she could be the queen. But

one of his sons, a little boy named Joash, was hidden from her in the temple, along with his nurse, for six years. Jehoiada the High Priest, and his wife, who was the little boy's aunt, took care of him, and in all that time Queen Athaliah never found out that he was still alive. But after six years Jehoiada showed the little prince to the Levites, and said that it was time to crown him king of Judah.

Then they brought out little Joash, who was now seven years old, from the room where he had been kept hidden, and they anointed him as king of Judah by pouring olive oil upon his head, and then crowning him. Then they all clapped and shouted, "God save the king!"

When the queen heard all the noise and shouting, she ran to the temple to see what was happening, and saw the little king standing there by a pillar with the crown on his head. The leaders of the nation stood beside him and all the people rejoiced and blew trumpets, and the singers in the temple sang, accompanied by the royal band and orchestra. The queen ran in shrieking, "Treason! treason!" The High Priest told the Levites to take her outside, for she must not be killed in the Lord's house. So they dragged and pushed her over to the stable of the king's palace and killed her there.

Afterwards, the High Priest made an agreement with King Joash and all the people that they would obey the Lord. Then Jehoiada directed the priests of the Lord and the Levites to go to the temple of God and to begin worshiping God again. He put guards at the gates so that no one could go in to rob or wreck it.

When Joash grew older he decided to repair the temple of the Lord, for it was in very poor condition. He called the

Queen Athaliah murdered her own grandchildren so she could rule Judah. Only little Joash escaped. He was hidden until he was old enough to be king. Then Athaliah was executed.

priests and Levites and said, "Go into all the cities of Judah and collect money from the people to repair the temple of the Lord. And see that you hurry." But the Levites didn't get started on this project for a long time. Finally the king sent for Jehoiada the High Priest and asked him, "Why don't the Levites collect the money and repair the house of the Lord?"

Then Jehoiada took a chest and bored a hole in its lid and set it at the door of the temple. Word was sent throughout the nation that everyone coming to the temple should bring some money as an offering to the Lord. Everyone was happy to do this and brought the money willingly and dropped it into the chest. Whenever the chest was full, the High Priest and the king's treasurer came and emptied it out and counted it, and put it in bags, and gave it to the men who were in charge of the carpenters, masons, and builders.

Jehoiada arranged for sacrifices to be offered at the temple every day, and persuaded the king to obey the Lord. For although Joash had wanted to repair the temple, he didn't really love God in his heart. Yet as long as Jehoiada lived to advise him, he did what was right. But Jehoiada finally died at the age of 130 and was buried in Jerusalem in the graves of the kings, because he had done so much good for the nation. He had not only obeyed the Lord himself, but had taught the people to obey him, too.

But the nation's leaders were wicked men; for although they had worshiped at the temple while Jehoiada was alive, it was only because Jehoiada had persuaded the king to worship there, and they had to go to the temple with him. But as soon as Jehoiada was dead they told the king they didn't want to worship God any more, and the king, whose own heart was wicked, gave them permission to stay away from the temple. They went and worshiped idols instead.

GOD'S TEMPLE IS ROBBED

2 CHRONICLES 24, 25

WHEN ZECHARIAH the priest, Jehoiada's son, saw the wickedness of the people and their leaders, he spoke up. "Why do you disobey the commandments of the Lord?" he demanded. "You will bring great trouble upon the land. For you cannot prosper when you disobey God."

King Joash was angry with Zechariah for saying this, and issued orders to kill him. So he was killed with large stones in the court of the temple. Joash forgot about the kindness of Zechariah's father, who had protected him as a child and made him the king.

As Zechariah was dying, he said to the people, "The Lord will see what you have done, and will punish you for it."

What Zechariah said came true; for at the end of the year the Syrians attacked Judah. A terrible sickness now came upon King Joash, and after the Syrians were gone, his own people rebelled against him and killed him as he lay in his bed. He was buried in Jerusalem, but not in the graves of the kings. He had reigned forty years at the time of his death. Then his son Amaziah became the new king.

Amaziah led his army against the Edomites, and the Lord gave him the victory. But when he came back from the battle he brought with him the idols of the men of Edom, and set them up to be his gods! The Lord sent a prophet to him. "Did those idols help the Edomites when you fought against them?" the prophet demanded.

But Amaziah was angry with the prophet, and said to him, "Who are you to interfere and tell me what to do? Be quiet or you'll be sorry."

Then the prophet said, "I know that God has determined to destroy you because you have done this wicked thing, and because you will not stop despite his warning."

King Amaziah of Judah now sent this message to the king of Israel: "Come with your army and let us fight each other."

But the king of Israel said, "Just because you have beaten the Edomites, don't be so proud and ready to boast. Stay at home. Why should you meddle with me, and bring trouble on yourself and all the people of Judah?"

But Amaziah wouldn't listen, because the Lord meant to punish him and the people of Judah for worshiping the idols of Edom.

So King Amaziah went with his army to attack Israel, and the king of Israel came out to stop him. But then King Amaziah's army panicked and ran away! The king of Israel captured King Amaziah and took him back to Jerusalem where he broke down the walls of the city. Then he went into the temple and took the gold and silver bowls that were there, and the treasures from the king's palace, and carried away some of the people as captives to his own city of Samaria. Later the people of Jerusalem rebelled against King Amaziah and killed him as he tried to escape from them. They brought his body to Jerusalem and buried him there. He had been the king of Judah for twenty-nine years.

ISAIAH TELLS THE FUTURE

2 CHRONICLES 26; ISAIAH

AFTER KING AMAZIAH's death his 16-year-old-son, Uzziah, became the new king. At first he did what was right, for he had a good and wise counselor named Zechariah whose advice he followed; as long as he did right, the Lord caused him to prosper. He owned a great many cattle and many wells. He loved to sow grain and plant vineyards, and he had many farmers working his fields for him.

There were 370,000 men in his army, all armed with shields, spears, helmets, bows, and slings. He built war machines to shoot arrows and stones from the walls against his enemies. These "cannons" were mounted on the walls of the city of Jerusalem. And God helped him in fighting against the Philistines so that he conquered many of their cities.

But that made him proud, and he began to disobey the Lord. He went into the temple where only the priests were allowed to go, and took a censer in his hand to burn incense on the golden altar. Then Azariah the High Priest and eighty other priests went in after him, and told him, "Get out! You have no right to burn incense to the Lord; only the priests, the descendants of Aaron, may do that. Leave at once, for you have sinned! The Lord may punish you for doing this."

But instead of being afraid and hurrying outside, Uzziah

was angry with the priests for talking to him like that. Then suddenly the dread disease of leprosy appeared upon his forehead; and the priests saw it there as he stood beside the gold altar. Then they took hold of him and pushed him out of the temple. Now he himself hurried to get away because the Lord had sent this punishment upon him.

The king never got well, but was a leper until his death. He had to live in a house by himself because God had said that no leper should live with the rest of the people. His son Jotham ruled the land in his place. King Uzziah died at the age of fifty-two and was buried in Jerusalem. Then Jotham became the king.

Jotham was twenty-five years old when he began to reign, and he reigned sixteen years, in Jerusalem. He built cities in the mountains of Judah, and built castles and towers in the forests. He fought the Ammonites and made them his servants. Each year they paid him thousands of pounds in money, wheat, and barley. And he became very great because he always tried to please the Lord.

But though he himself worshiped the Lord, his people were wicked; so God sent Isaiah the prophet to warn them. But the people didn't pay any attention, for their religious and political leaders were mostly wicked men. The Lord was very angry with them because of their sins, Isaiah said, so he would call their enemies from far-off countries to come and conquer them. These enemies would be as fierce as lions, and no one could stop them. The people of Judah would be taken away to distant lands as captives. Their land would be left lonely and desolate, covered with briars and thorns, their cities empty and deserted, with Jerusalem and the temple destroyed. But after many years, Isaiah said, the cities would be rebuilt, for the Lord would raise up a great king, named Cyrus, who would command that the city and the temple should be built again.

Isaiah told the people many other things about the future. He said that Jesus would be born in the family line of King David, and that he would grow up to have sorrow and suffering and afterwards be put to death for the people's sins. Isaiah told about these things 700 years before they happened, for he was a prophet and God told him about future events. He told them about John the Baptist, too, saying that someone else would come before the Savior did, to preach out in the wilderness, telling everyone to get ready to receive the Savior by turning from sin.

But the people of Judah wouldn't listen to the preaching of Isaiah, so God took away their good king from them when Jotham died. Then his son Ahaz became their king instead.

STORY 120

KING AHAZ CLOSES THE TEMPLE
2 CHRONICLES 28, 29

AHAZ WAS twenty years old when he began to reign. But he didn't obey God as his father had done, but worshiped idols instead. He even sacrificed his little sons as burnt offerings to the idols, just as the heathen did. So the Lord sent the kings of Syria and Israel against him.

They came and attacked Jerusalem and took away many of the people as captives to the city of Damascus.

The king of Israel now fought against Judah, too, and killed 120,000 of the army of Judah in one day. He sent

great numbers of women and children far away to another land.

But it was not only the kings of Syria and Israel who declared war against Judah, but the Edomites and Philistines too. Then the king of Judah took some of the silver and gold from the temple and some of the treasures from his own palace, and sent them to Tiglath, king of Assyria, to hire his army to fight against the enemies of Judah. King Tiglath accepted the present and did as King Ahaz asked him to: he fought against the Syrians, and took the city of Damascus from them. But it did Ahaz little good, for the Lord was against him because he had sacrificed his sons to idols.

After this Ahaz became even more wicked. For he broke up and destroyed the temple wash tanks, placed there by King Solomon hundreds of years before, and took down the great brass basin resting on the backs of the twelve oxen, and set it on the pavement of the court instead. He also cut apart the sacred bowls of gold and silver, and boarded up the temple so that no one could go there to worship. But he placed idols all over Jerusalem, and not only in Jerusalem but in every city throughout the land. So the Lord was very angry with Ahaz and the people of Judah because of all their wickedness.

Ahaz was king for sixteen years, then he died and was buried in Jerusalem, but not in the graves of the kings. Then his son Hezekiah became king instead.

Hezekiah did what was right and followed the Lord. As soon as he became king he reopened the temple, which his father Ahaz had closed, and called back the priests and

King Ahaz led the people of Judah away from God. He even closed up the temple so that the worship of God would stop.

345

Levites, who had been sent away from the temple by his father. He ordered them to put everything back in order so that the people could come and worship God again.

Then the priests went to work and after fifteen days of hard labor they came back and reported to the king, "It's all finished! All the cleaning has been done, the altar is ready for use, and we have brought back the gold and silver bowls taken away by Ahaz. Everything is ready."

Then King Hezekiah got up early the next morning and went up to the temple with the leaders of Jerusalem. They took with them seven young bulls, seven rams, seven lambs and seven goats. Hezekiah commanded the priests to kill and burn them on the altar as a sacrifice to God for all their sins. He also organized a great choir and orchestra from among the priests and Levites to sing praises to the Lord. As the offering began to burn on the altar, the people began to sing praise to God, accompanied by music from the cymbals, harps, and trumpets. So all the people worshiped, and the singers sang, and the trumpets sounded, until the burnt offering was finished.

After the king and the leaders had sacrificed, King Hezekiah invited the people to bring their offerings. They brought 70 young bulls, 100 rams, and 200 lambs, and the priests offered these for the people's sins. The king was glad, and so were all the people, because the Lord had caused everyone to want to bring offerings to God, and because the temple was open again and the Lord was being worshiped.

A HOLIDAY IN JUDAH

2 CHRONICLES 30, 31

KING HEZEKIAH now wrote a letter to all of his people in Judah, and also to the people of the land of Israel, asking them to come to Jerusalem and to celebrate the feast of the Passover. For it had been many years since the people had celebrated it as the Lord wanted them to.

Messengers carried the king's letters throughout the whole country of Judah and Benjamin, but when they came to the land of Israel, the men of the ten tribes wouldn't listen to them, but mocked and laughed at them. However, a few confessed their sins and were sorry for them, and came to Jerusalem.

But in the land of Judah, the Lord made all the people want to come. So there was a great crowd in Jerusalem to celebrate the feast. Before beginning it, they fanned out through the city and knocked down all the idol altars and threw them into Kidron Brook.

Then the Passover festival began. Each father brought a lamb to the temple, where it was killed before the altar. Afterwards, he took it home to roast it, and he and his family ate it that night as the people of Israel did on the night they came out of Egypt. The Lord wanted the people to remember that night in Egypt, and how he had saved them from Pharaoh and the cruel Egyptians. That is why he had commanded them to celebrate this Passover festival each year. But they had stopped doing this long before. That is why Hezekiah called them to come to Jerusalem to begin to obey the Lord again, so that he would be pleased with them and bless them.

They celebrated happily for seven days. The priests and Levites sang praises to God every day, playing on harps and trumpets. And the Levites went out among the people and taught them the law of the Lord so that they would know what he wanted them to do.

At the end of those seven days of celebrating, they all agreed on seven more days of praising God. King Hezekiah and the leaders gave them a vast number of cattle for sacrifices—3,000 young bulls and 17,000 sheep. So all the people of Judah, with the priests and Levites and the men who had come from Israel, were filled with joy. Since the times of Solomon there had never been such a wonderful time in Jerusalem.

When the celebration finally ended, the people went out to the cities of Israel and Judah and broke up all the idols, and destroyed the altars where the idols were worshiped.

Afterwards, King Hezekiah set up a schedule for the different groups of priests and Levites to take turns in assisting the people to worship the Lord at the temple. He organized morning and evening sacrifices, and special sacrifices on the Sabbath and on feast days. The king told the people to bring to the temple a tenth of all their crops so that the priests and Levites would have enough to eat, just as Moses had commanded; for the people had not done this for a long time. Now they obeyed the king, and so did many who lived in the land of Israel, bringing their gifts to the priests.

When the king and the leaders came to the temple and saw the great heaps of food brought in by the people, they thanked the Lord for making them want to bring so much.

GOD'S ANGEL DESTROYS THE ENEMY

STORY 122

2 CHRONICLES 32

THE KING OF ASSYRIA and his army now invaded the land of Judah again, and conquered some of its cities. When King Hezekiah of Judah learned that the invading army was on its way to Jerusalem, he quickly repaired the walls of the city and set the people to work making huge quantities of shields and darts. He told his army, "Be strong and brave. Don't be afraid of the king of Assyria or his mighty army, for there are more on our side than on his! For we have God fighting for us!"

But for all his brave words, King Hezekiah was badly frightened, and he sent great quantities of gold and silver to the invading Assyrian king, hoping he would accept these gifts and go away.

And that is just what happened. The king of Assyria took the gold and silver and returned to his own land. But afterwards, he came back!

On the way back he stopped at a city called Lachish to attack it, but sent some of his officers to Jerusalem to tell the people he was coming to destroy it. His messengers shouted up to the people watching from the top of the Jerusalem wall, "The king of Assyria says, 'Don't listen to King Hezekiah when he tells you he is able to fight against me, and that the Lord will save you from my power. Pay me more money and come and be my slaves. If you do, then I won't hurt you, but if you don't . . . .'"

349

When Hezekiah heard what the messengers were saying, he tore his clothes and put on sackcloth, and went up to the temple to pray to the Lord. And he sent messengers to Isaiah the prophet telling him what the king of Assyria had said, and asking him to pray for the people.

Then the prophet Isaiah sent back this message to King Hezekiah: "The Lord says, 'Don't be afraid of the words spoken against me by the king of Assyria. For I will send a great punishment upon him, and he shall turn and go back to his own land, and there I will cause him to die.'"

So King Hezekiah refused to give up the city to the king of Assyria. But the king of Assyria sent his officers back again, this time with a letter to Hezekiah that said, "Don't let your god fool you into believing that I can't conquer Jerusalem. You know how the kings of Assyria have destroyed other nations. Their gods were not able to save them. Why do you think your god can do any better?"

When Hezekiah read the letter he was very much afraid. He took the letter to the temple and spread it open there before the Lord. Then Hezekiah prayed and said, "O Lord, you are the only God. You made the heaven and the earth. Lord, look and see and hear the words spoken against you by the king of Assyria. What he says is true, that he has destroyed many another nation and tossed their gods into the fire. Those gods were only lifeless idols made of wood and stone; so of course he was able to destroy them. But now, O Lord, he is planning to destroy Jerusalem. Please save us from him, so that all the kingdoms of the world will know that you are not like the idols of the heathen nations, but that you are the Lord, and that there is no other God besides you."

The Lord listened to this prayer of Hezekiah, and then told Isaiah the prophet to take this message to him: "The Lord says, 'I have heard your prayer and I will do as you

King Hezekiah foolishly showed off his treasures to visitors from Babylon. Years later these treasures were stolen and carried away to Babylon.

asked. The king of Assyria shall not come here or build forts around this city, or shoot an arrow into it! He will go home! For I will save Jerusalem!'"

And what Isaiah said came true. That night the Lord sent his destroying angel into the camp of the Assyrians and killed 185,000 of them.

So the king of Assyria went back in shame to his own land. And while he was worshiping there in the house of his idol, two of his sons killed him. That is how the Lord saved Hezekiah and the people of Judah from the king of Assyria, and from all their enemies.

STORY 123

THE SAVIOR WILL COME!
2 KINGS 20; 2 CHRONICLES 32

IN THOSE DAYS King Hezekiah became very sick from an infected boil, and the prophet Isaiah said to him, "The Lord says to get ready to die."

Then Hezekiah turned his face sadly to the wall and prayed, "O Lord, remember how I have tried to please you in all I do." Then he broke down and cried.

So the Lord told Isaiah to return to Hezekiah, and to tell him, "The Lord says, 'I have heard your prayer, and seen your tears, and I will make you well again. Three days from now you will be well enough to go to the temple, and I will add fifteen years to your life!'" So Isaiah told this to the king. And he said to the king's assistants, "Take a lump of figs and lay it on the boil." And they did, and he was soon well again!

King Hezekiah became very rich and famous. He had great flocks and herds of cattle, horses, and sheep. For the Lord helped him so that he prospered in everything he did.

But strange as it seems, Hezekiah did not stay humble and thankful to God for his blessings. He grew proud of his riches and power as though he had got these things by himself. Then the king of Babylon heard of his greatness, and sent messengers with letters and a present for him. When the messengers came to Jerusalem, Hezekiah was proud to have them visit him because they represented a great king, and he boasted to them about his great wealth and showed them his silver and gold, and his horses and armor, and all the wealth of his kingdom.

Then Isaiah the prophet came to Hezekiah and said, "What did these men say? And where did they come from?"

"They came from Babylon," Hezekiah replied.

"What have they seen in your palace?" Isaiah asked.

And Hezekiah answered, "Everything! There is nothing among my treasures that I haven't shown them."

Then Isaiah said, "Hear what the Lord says to you. 'After you die, all your wealth shall be carried to Babylon; nothing shall be left.'"

Hezekiah answered, "Whatever God does is right. At least there will be peace while I'm alive."

King Hezekiah had persuaded the people to put away their idols and to worship the Lord, but soon they began praying to idols again. God sent the prophet Micah to speak to them about this.

"All God requires," Micah said, "is for the people of Israel to be just and kind and merciful to each other, and to be humble and obedient to the Lord!" Micah, like Isaiah, prophesied of the Savior, telling where he would be born—it would be in the city of Bethlehem. (Not only Micah and Isaiah, but almost all the prophets told about him hundreds of years before he was born. Because they predicted this, we who are living today can know the Savior is the Son of God, just as the prophets said, and that God sent him.)

Hezekiah was the king of Judah for twenty-nine years, then he died and was buried in Jerusalem in the best of the graves of the kings. His son Manasseh became the new king.

Manasseh was twelve years old when he became king. But he was a bad king and did many wicked things. For instance, he worshiped the sun, the moon, and the stars. And he built the idol altars again which his father Hezekiah had destroyed, and even set up an idol in the temple of the Lord.

The Lord sent prophets to warn Manasseh and his people to stop sinning, but they wouldn't listen. So the Lord sent the Assyrian army to capture King Manasseh, and they caught him as he was trying to hide from them in some bushes. They bound him with chains and took him to Babylon. When he was there far from home and in great sorrow, then he thought about his sins and finally was sorry for them. He prayed with all his heart to the Lord, and the Lord heard him and was kind to him and brought him back to Jerusalem.

Then Manasseh knew that the Lord was the only true God, and he took away the idol he had set up in the temple, and tore down all the altars he had built in the courts around the temple and threw them out of the city. He also repaired the altar of the Lord and presented sacrifices to God upon it.

Manasseh was king over Judah for fifty-three years, then died, and was buried in the garden of his palace in Jerusalem; and his son Ammon became king instead.

*The Law
of Moses
had been lost
and then
discovered
in the temple.
It was read
to Josiah,
who had
never before
heard
the words
of God's
Law.*

Ammon was twenty-two years old when he began to reign. But he was a bad king, for he offered sacrifices to all the gods his father Manasseh had worshiped. And he wasn't sorry afterwards and didn't destroy them as his father had, but went on sinning more and more. After he had been king for two years his people rebelled against him and killed him, and chose his son Josiah as their new king.

STORY 124

KING JOSIAH AND THE LOST BOOK

2 KINGS 22, 23; 2 CHRONICLES 34, 35

JOSIAH WAS eight years old when he became king. He reigned thirty-one years and did what was right; for while he was still a boy he began to serve the Lord. He went all through the land of Judah and destroyed the altars of Baal wherever he found them, and tore down the idols. He also traveled out among his people who were living in the land of Israel (for the ten tribes who had been living there were gone, having been captured and driven away), and did the same thing there. Then he returned to Jerusalem and set his men to work repairing the temple, for it had fallen into disrepair. The people brought gifts of money to pay the workmen.

One day Josiah sent one of his officers to the High Priest to tell him to count the money the people brought, and then to give it to the carpenters, builders, and masons for repairing the temple. As the officer was talking with the High Priest about these matters, the High Priest happened to remark to him, "I've found the book of Moses' laws! It was here in the temple!"

Hundreds of years before this, Moses had written down the laws God had given him. He commanded that these laws must be read out loud to all the people every seven years. But the wicked kings and people of Judah hadn't cared to hear God's laws, and had let the book be lost and forgotten, so Josiah had never seen it before. But now while the temple was being repaired the High Priest had found it again. He gave it to the king's officer, who took it to Josiah and read it to the king.

When King Josiah heard the words of God's laws, and learned about the punishments God said he would send on the people for not obeying, he tore his clothes and wept.

Josiah immediately summoned to the temple all the priests, the Levites, and the people, and read the book to them. Then the king made a covenant with the Lord and promised to obey his commandments with all his heart and soul. The people promised, too, that they would obey God's laws.

We have already read about King Hezekiah's great celebration of the Passover after many, many years of neglect. But after he died, the Passover was again forgotten for a long, long time. But now Josiah called everyone to Jerusalem to celebrate it again. He gave the people 30,000 lambs and young goats, and 30,000 young bulls, so that everyone would have a sacrifice to offer. But although the people obeyed the command of the king and came to celebrate the feast, they didn't truly love God or sincerely worship him, for in their hearts they still trusted in their idols.

The prophet Jeremiah reminded them of how God had brought them from slavery in Egypt and had given them this good land he had promised their fathers; but they hadn't thanked God nor obeyed his commandments. God had seen their wickedness and was angry with them, Jeremiah said. Yet if they would turn from their evil ways he would forgive them and not punish them. But the people wouldn't listen to Jeremiah. They weren't at all sorry for their wickedness, but sinned more and more. Even while Jeremiah was speaking to them they said, "Let's kill him." But God saved him from them.

Then the king of Egypt came with his army, and Josiah went to fight him. But the Egyptian king sent a message that he was merely passing through on his way to make war against the king of Assyria, and he told Josiah to let him alone. But Josiah wouldn't turn back. He took off his royal robes and put on others so that no one would recognize him and went into the battle. There an arrow struck him.

"Get me out of here, for I am badly wounded," he said to his servant, and then he died.

They brought him in a chariot to Jerusalem and buried him in the graves of the kings, and everyone was sad. His son Jehoahaz now became the king of Judah.

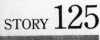

STORY 125

JEREMIAH WRITES A SAD LETTER
2 KINGS 24; 2 CHRONICLES 36

JEHOAHAZ WAS twenty-two years old when he became the king, but he reigned only three months. He didn't do right as his father had, and the people disobeyed

God. So Pharaoh, king of Egypt, came and attacked him and took him in chains to Egypt. There he remained until his death.

Pharaoh appointed Jehoiakim, the brother of Jehoahaz, to be the new king. Then he forced Jehoiakim and the people of Judah to pay him thousands of dollars in silver and gold. Afterwards, when Pharaoh had gone away with all the money, the people of Judah faced a new danger. For now King Nebuchadnezzar of Babylon arrived to attack them. Nebuchadnezzar took some of the sacred vessels from the temple and carried them to Babylon, and put them in the temple of his idol there.

In the fourth year of Jehoiakim's reign, the Lord told the prophet Jeremiah to write down all the punishments that were still going to come upon the people of Israel. The Lord said that when the people heard about those punishments, perhaps they would turn to God so he could forgive them. Jeremiah dictated God's message to a good man named Baruch, and Baruch read it to the people at the temple, and to the king and his officers. The king was sitting beside the fireplace, for it was winter. As soon as his officers read to him three or four pages of God's message, the king would use his penknife to slash the pages and throw them into the fire. Some of his men begged him not to do this, but he wouldn't listen; he wasn't afraid of God's punishments, he said. He was very angry with Jeremiah and Baruch for writing these messages, so he sent his guards to arrest them, but the Lord hid them.

Then the Lord said that because the king had burned up God's messages, Jeremiah must dictate it all again. So Baruch wrote it all down once more, and a lot more besides.

The people hated Jeremiah for telling them about their sins, and he complained to the Lord about it. "I have done them no harm," he said, "yet they all curse me."

Then the Lord promised that when the enemies of Jerusalem arrived to capture the city, they would not harm Jeremiah. "I will make them treat you well," the Lord said.

Jehoiakim reigned eleven years, then died, and Jehoiachin his son became king instead.

Jehoiachin was eighteen years old at the time, but he reigned only three months, for King Nebuchadnezzar of Babylon came and defeated him. Nebuchadnezzar took away more of the golden bowls made by Solomon, and took away the treasures from the king's palace, and captured the king, his mother, his wives, the leaders of Judah, the builders, smiths, carpenters, and all the soldiers. He drove them all before him to far-off Babylon.

After they had gone, the prophet Jeremiah wrote a letter to them, telling them to build houses and plant gardens and be content in that distant land of Babylon, because the Lord said they must stay there seventy years and serve the king of Babylon. But when the seventy years ended, and they had repented of their sins and prayed to be forgiven, then the Lord would bring them back again to their own land.

STORY 126

JERUSALEM IS BURNED

2 KINGS 25; 2 CHRONICLES 36; JEREMIAH

NEBUCHADNEZZAR appointed Zedekiah, the brother of Jehoiakim, as the king of the people he left in the land of Israel. Zedekiah had to promise to obey Nebu-

When the
Babylonian army
conquered Judah,
Nebuchadnezzar
ordered his soldiers
to burn the city
of Jerusalem
and the
beautiful temple
of God.

chadnezzar, but after Nebuchadnezzar had gone back to Babylon, Zedekiah rebelled against him. So Nebuchadnezzar came back again with all of his army and made forts around Jerusalem, from which darts and arrows were shot at the men defending the walls, and everyone was kept from going in or out of the city.

Jeremiah was inside Jerusalem with the rest of the people. King Zedekiah begged him to pray that Jerusalem would be saved. But the Lord told Jeremiah to tell the king that Nebuchadnezzar would capture the city and burn it. If the people would accept the punishment the Lord was sending upon them and would surrender to Nebuchadnezzar without fighting and be his slaves, they would not be killed. But if they refused to surrender they would die.

The Lord told Jeremiah to act out this message by wearing a wooden yoke on his shoulders. A yoke stands for service or slavery, so when the people saw Jeremiah wearing it, they understood that God was going to make them serve Nebuchadnezzar.

"Jerusalem will certainly be captured and burned," the Lord said. "This will punish the people for their sins."

Some of the leaders of Judah went to King Zedekiah and demanded that Jeremiah be killed for saying such things, because it discouraged and frightened the people.

"He says the Lord will send famine and plagues upon us, and will give the city to the king of Babylon," they told Zedekiah.

He told them to do as they liked with Jeremiah, so they put him into prison, and let him down by ropes into a deep well that was filled with mud at the bottom.

But one of the king's assistants went to the king and said, "My lord the king, these men are wicked to put Jeremiah into the dungeon, for he may die of hunger there."

So they took him out of the well but they didn't set him

free; he was still kept in another part of the prison.

Then King Zedekiah sent for Jeremiah again. He was brought to the temple where he and the king could talk secretly. The king said, "I want to ask you a question; don't hide the truth from me."

Jeremiah answered, "If I tell you the truth will you promise not to have me killed?"

"Yes," the king replied, "I promise."

Then Jeremiah told him, "The Lord says, 'If you will surrender to the king of Babylon and be his slave, you and your family will be saved alive, and Jerusalem won't be burned.'"

But King Zedekiah wouldn't obey the command of the Lord to surrender. So King Nebuchadnezzar's army attacked Jerusalem for eighteen months. By that time the food was all gone; there was nothing left to eat.

One night Zedekiah fled from the city with his army, but he was caught and brought to the king of Babylon for trial. That cruel king killed Zedekiah's two sons before his eyes, then put out Zedekiah's eyes and bound him with chains and took him to Babylon, where he was kept in prison until he died.

Nebuchadnezzar's army burned the temple and the palace and all the homes, and broke down the walls all around the city. He took the people away as slaves, except some of the poorest who were left to work in the fields and vineyards. Gedaliah was chosen as their governor.

So the kingdom of Judah ended as the kingdom of Israel ended, because of the sins of the people. It had lasted 388 years—ever since Rehoboam was made king over the tribes of Judah and Benjamin. Nineteen kings and one queen had ruled over the people during that time. Of these, fifteen were wicked, and five obeyed the Lord. But even when there were good kings, the people often worshiped idols.

And though the Lord waited and gave them time to repent, and sent his prophets to warn and persuade them, they wouldn't obey him. So at last he sent them into exile far away to Babylon, as he had already done to the other ten tribes.

NOBODY LEFT IN JUDAH

2 KINGS 25; JEREMIAH

THE LORD had promised that Jeremiah would be treated well when Nebuchadnezzar conquered Jerusalem. Now the Lord made this promise come true, for after the city was captured, the king of Babylon told the commander-in-chief of his army to be good to Jeremiah. "Don't harm him," he said, "and give him anything he wants."

The commander gave Jeremiah money and food. He decided to live with Gedaliah, the new governor of Judah, because he wanted to stay in the land.

Some of the Jews had escaped to other countries when Nebuchadnezzar captured Jerusalem. When they heard that Nebuchadnezzar had left some of the people in the land and had appointed Gedaliah as governor, they came back to the land of Judah to the city of Mizpeh, where Gedaliah lived. He couldn't live in Jerusalem, of course, because it had been destroyed.

Gedaliah encouraged them and said, "Don't be afraid to come back and live in your own land. If you will stay here

The prophet Jeremiah walked around wearing a heavy wooden yoke. This was God's way of showing his people that they must become slaves.

and sow your fields and harvest your grain and serve the king of Babylon, you will be happy and all will go well with you." So the people came back and lived in the land.

Then some men came to Gedaliah and said, "The king of the Ammonites has sent Ishmael, one of the princes of Judah, to kill you."

One of these men spoke secretly to Gedaliah and said, "Let me go and kill Ishmael, and no one will know who did it! Why let him kill you and cause all the people left in the land to be scattered and destroyed?"

But Gedaliah wouldn't believe what the man said. "No," he said, "leave him alone. I'm sure what you are telling me isn't true."

But it *was* true. A man named Ishmael came to Gedaliah's house, with ten other men pretending to be his friends. But after dinner they jumped up and killed him. Then Ishmael fled away into the land of the Ammonites.

All the people were afraid that the king of Babylon would come and punish them because Gedaliah had been killed. So they came to Jeremiah and begged him to ask the Lord to show them where to go and what to do.

"Yes," Jeremiah said, "I will pray for you, and whatever the Lord tells me, I will tell you; I will hide nothing from you."

Then they said to Jeremiah, "All that the Lord commands us, we will do, no matter whether we like what he says or not; we will obey the Lord."

So Jeremiah prayed and asked the Lord, and after ten days the Lord answered him, and told him what to say to the people. Then Jeremiah called the people together and

The angry leaders of Judah put Jeremiah into this well because he told the truth about their sins. Later the king decided to rescue him.

told them, "The Lord says, 'If you stay here I will bless you. Don't be afraid of the king of Babylon, for I am with you and I will save you from harm; and I will make him kind to you. He will let you live here in your own land and won't take you far away to Babylon. But if you disobey me and refuse to stay here, but go to Egypt to find food and peace, then the war and the famine you fear will follow you and kill you in Egypt. You will never again see your own land.'"

Then all the proud and wicked men among them answered Jeremiah, "You lie! The Lord didn't tell us to stay here and not to go to Egypt! You just want us to stay here so Nebuchadnezzar can come and kill us or take us away as captives to Babylon."

So they wouldn't obey the commandment of the Lord, but went to Egypt and forced Jeremiah to go with them.

Then the words came true that the prophet Isaiah had spoken more than a hundred years before: "The land of Judah shall be left lonely and desolate, overgrown with briars and thorns, and filled with abandoned houses."

Even after the Jews had been taken away to Babylon as captives, they refused to obey the Lord. Jeremiah the prophet wrote them a letter telling them to be loyal citizens of Babylon, and to be content, because they would stay there for seventy years. But instead of doing as Jeremiah told them, they complained and wanted to come back home to Jerusalem.

EZEKIEL'S STRANGE VISIONS

EZEKIEL

AMONG THE JEWS taken away to Babylon, before Jerusalem was finally destroyed, was a priest named Ezekiel. One day Ezekiel had a strange vision or dream. He saw a whirlwind and a cloud, and in the cloud were four angels beneath God's throne in heaven. On the throne was what looked like a man made of fire, surrounded by bright colors like a rainbow. It was the glory of the Lord that Ezekiel saw, and he fell face downward to the ground in worship.

Then the Lord told him to warn the other Jews who were with him in captivity, to obey God. "Give them my messages whether or not they will listen," the Lord told him. "Don't be afraid of them even though they seem as dangerous as poisonous snakes! I will make you strong and brave when you stand before them, so that you can tell them everything I want you to."

Then the Lord told Ezekiel to prepare an object lesson for the people still living in Jerusalem, to show them what was going to happen to their city. "Get a flat tile and draw a map of Jerusalem on it," God told him, "and put this tile on the ground with an iron pan in front of it to protect it like a wall. In front of the pan build a little fort. Now lie down on the ground on your side, facing the map, and stay there many, many days without moving. Eat only a little coarse bread each day, and drink only a little water.

Ezekiel was showing what would happen to Jerusalem:

369

Nebuchadnezzar would attack it with his army and build forts around it, and besiege it for many days. When the people saw Ezekiel eating only a little coarse bread every day, and drinking only a little water, they would know that the Jews in Jerusalem were going to suffer from famine. They would have hardly enough food and water to keep them from starving because the army of Nebuchadnezzar would be fighting against them.

After this the Lord commanded Ezekiel to take a razor and shave off all of his hair and his beard. Then he was to weigh the hair into three equal parts. One part was to be burned, one part cut into small pieces with a knife, and one part to be held in his hand until the wind blew it away.

The Lord told Ezekiel that this was an illustration of how the nation of Israel would be destroyed. The Lord had chosen Israel as his people, yet they had sinned against him more than any other nation in the world. Now he was going to punish them as he had never punished any other nation before. A third of them, like the hair Ezekiel burned, would die from sickness and famine; a third, like the hair he cut to pieces with a knife, would be killed by their enemies outside the city; and a third, like the hair Ezekiel held out in his hand for the wind to blow away, would be carried away from their own land and scattered over all the earth.

Then the Lord showed Ezekiel something worse yet. He brought him out to the court of the temple, and when he looked, he saw a hole in the wall. The Lord said to him, "Dig into the wall." When Ezekiel had done this, he saw a door leading into a darkened room. The Lord said, "Go into the room and see the things that are done there."

So Ezekiel went in, and there on the walls around him he saw pictures of all the idols the people of Israel worshiped. Before these pictures stood the seventy elders of

Israel burning incense to the idols. The Lord said to Ezekiel, "Do you see what the elders of Israel are doing? They are worshiping idols here in this darkened room. For they say, 'The Lord doesn't see us, he has gone away.'"

Then the Lord said to Ezekiel, "Now I will show you more of their sins." So he brought him to the inner court of the temple, and there Ezekiel saw about twenty-five men bowing down to the sun and worshiping it.

And the Lord said to Ezekiel, "Do you see them? Is it a little thing for the men of Judah to do all the evil they are doing here? For they have filled the whole land with wickedness, and now they have come back to the temple to sin against me and make me angry. Now I will punish them in my anger, and will not pity them. Though they cry out to me in their suffering, I won't listen."

Then Ezekiel was again, in his vision, lifted into the sky and taken back to Babylon, the land of his captivity. He told the captives all he had seen in the vision, but they didn't believe what he told them; they still chose to believe the false prophets who said that the people in Jerusalem would not be punished, and that their city would not be destroyed by King Nebuchadnezzar.

STORY 129

EZEKIEL DELIVERS GOD'S MESSAGES
EZEKIEL

NOW THE LORD told Ezekiel to act out what was going to happen to the people of Jerusalem. He was to pretend that he was moving out of his home in the darkness of the night. He was to dig a hole through the back wall of his house, and to go out through the opening, carrying his things on his shoulder. He was to cover his face as if he didn't want anyone to recognize him.

So Ezekiel did. As the people watched, he packed his things and carried part of them out of his house and left them in another place. In the evening he dug through the wall and brought out more of his things, with his face covered.

The next morning the Lord said to him, "If anyone asks you what this means, tell them that terrible things will happen to King Zedekiah and his people in the land of Israel. When you moved things out of your house to another place, it was a picture of their being taken away as captives to other lands. King Zedekiah's officer will break through the wall of the city so that he can flee away in the night, carrying what he can on his shoulder, and he will cover his face to keep the enemy from recognizing him. But he will not escape; I will see to it that he is brought here to Babylon as a prisoner, to die here, but he won't see Babylon!"

The Lord meant that King Zedekiah wouldn't see the land of Babylon because King Nebuchadnezzar would blind him by gouging out his eyes before taking him there.

Then the Lord told Ezekiel to eat some bread and drink some water, trembling as he did it, like a person who was afraid of his enemies. For the people in Jerusalem and the land of Israel would tremble when their enemies came. Some of the Jewish captives came to Ezekiel and asked him, "Is there any way to be forgiven for our sins? Is there any way to keep from being punished?"

Ezekiel answered them, "Yes, be sorry about the wrong things you have done and stop being bad. For the Lord says, 'I certainly have no pleasure in punishing the wicked. I only want them to turn from their badness and live. Turn, turn from your evil ways; for why will you die, O people of Israel?'"

Then one day the Lord told Ezekiel to mark that day on his calendar. "Today," he said, "the king of Babylon has begun his attack on Jerusalem." Ezekiel was hundreds of miles away from Jerusalem and there were no newspapers or TV in those days, but Ezekiel knew what was happening that day far away in Jerusalem, because God told him.

Three years later Jerusalem surrendered. A man who escaped brought word of its fall to the Jews in Babylon. Then everyone knew that Ezekiel had told them the truth when he said the Lord had abandoned Jerusalem; and everyone now realized that the false prophets had lied when they kept saying that Israel would not be punished for its sins, and that Jerusalem would not be conquered by the king of Babylon. The king of Babylon not only conquered Jerusalem, but broke down its walls, burned the houses, the palace, and the temple, and took away King Zedekiah and put out his eyes, and brought him and his people to Babylon. The whole land was left lonely and desolate.

And yet, although the Lord had sent all these troubles upon the people of Israel, his purpose wasn't to destroy them, but only to punish them so that they would be sorry for their sins and begin to worship him again. Then he could bless them. He told Ezekiel to tell his people that the day was coming when he would search for them in every land where they were captives, just as a shepherd searches for his lost sheep, and that he would bring them back again to their own land.

The Lord told Ezekiel
to say to the winds,
"Come, O winds, and blow
upon these dead bodies
so that they will have breath
and be alive."

DEAD BONES BECOME A LIVING ARMY

STORY 130

EZEKIEL 37

AND NOW ONCE MORE the Lord showed Ezekiel a vision. Ezekiel seemed to be out in a valley where the ground was covered with dead men's bones, old and dried. The Lord asked him, "Can these bones live again?"

Then the Lord told Ezekiel to say to the bones: "O dry bones, listen to the command of the Lord: flesh shall come upon you, and breath shall come into you, and you shall live!"

As soon as Ezekiel said this, a strange, rattling noise began as the bones came together to form their skeletons. Then flesh grew upon them, and skin, until the bones were bodies again. But there was no breath in them; they were still dead.

Then the Lord told Ezekiel to say to the winds, "Come, O winds, and blow upon these dead bodies so that they will have breath and be alive." And when Ezekiel did this, the wind blew over the dead bodies and breath came into them; they breathed and were alive, and stood up, and were a great army!

Then the Lord explained to Ezekiel why he had shown him this vision, and what it meant. He told him that all the people of Israel complained because of their punishment and their trouble. They said they were like bones that were dry and dead, and that they had lost all hope of ever being happy, or of seeing their own land again. But the Lord said he would raise them up out of their troubles, as he had raised those dry bones to life, and that he would bring them back to their land. When he had saved them from their misery and put his spirit into their hearts and had brought them back to their own land again, then the people of Israel would know that it was the Lord who had given him this vision and made his words come true.

After this the Lord told Ezekiel to get two sticks and give each of them a name; one was to be named for the kingdom of Israel, and the other for the kingdom of Judah. He told Ezekiel to hold the two sticks close together, and they would grow into one stick in his hand.

When the people saw this strange miracle and asked him what it meant, Ezekiel answered them, "The Lord says, 'I will bring back the people of Israel to their own land, and they will not be divided into the two nations of Israel and Judah any more, but I will make them one nation. Neither shall they worship idols any more or be wicked; for I will put my spirit into their hearts and make them holy, and they will be my people and I will be their God. They will live in the land where their fathers lived, and their children and their children's children will live there always. And I will be kind to them and give them a good king who will rule over them forever.'"

Jeremiah had told the people that they must stay as slaves in Babylon for seventy years, and then at last they could go back to Jerusalem. And this came true. After seventy years the Jews returned to their own country. But there they sinned more than ever, and made God more angry with them than ever before. So he sent them out of Canaan again, and scattered them among all the nations as they are today. But some of them have now returned to the land of Israel, for God has let them come back home again once more.

Ezekiel told them that the time will come when they will want to worship God and will believe him and obey him and accept him as their Savior.

DANIEL AND THE KING'S DREAM

DANIEL 2

KING NEBUCHADNEZZAR of Babylon decided that he needed some new advisors, so he started a school to train some of the Israeli boys who had been captured at Jerusalem. He said that all the students at the school must be handsome, quick to learn, and in perfect health. He wanted them to learn everything there was to know. They would attend his school for three years, and then would work for the king as his advisors and government officials.

Among those chosen to go to school were four Jewish boys whose names were Daniel, Shadrach, Meshach, and Abednego. These young men had a problem: they loved God and wanted to obey him, but the king didn't want them to. The king said that they should pray to idols before every meal and thank them for the food. But God said no. So what should they do?

Daniel and his three friends decided to ask the king for permission to eat other food, instead of food for which the idols had been thanked.

Daniel talked to one of his teachers about it. This man

liked Daniel a lot, but he didn't dare give permission. "I'm afraid it will make the king angry," he said. "If he notices that you look paler and thinner than the young men who eat the food blessed by the idols, he will be angry with me and kill me."

"Please let us try it for just ten days," Daniel begged. "Give us only vegetables and water, and after ten days see if we don't look as well as the fellows who eat the other food. If we don't, then we will go ahead and eat the same as the others do."

The teacher finally agreed, and they were fed vegetables and water for ten days. At the end of that time they looked better and healthier than any of the others! So from then on they could eat whatever they wanted to. God helped them become wise, and he made Daniel able to understand the meaning of dreams.

One night King Nebuchadnezzar wakened from a dream and couldn't get back to sleep. So he summoned all his wise men, and they came and stood before him. "I had a dream that worries me," he said.

"Well," the wise men replied, "tell us the dream and we will tell you what it means."

But the king said, "I can't remember it! And if you won't tell me what I was dreaming about, and what it means, you will be killed and your houses torn down and made into piles of ruins. But if you tell me my dream and what it means, you'll be the richest, most honored men in the kingdom."

"But you have to tell us the dream before we can tell you what it means!" they protested. "Why, there isn't a man on earth who can tell a person what he dreamed about, and no king or ruler would even think of asking such a thing. Only the gods could tell you, and they don't live on earth."

Then the king was very angry and ordered all of them killed because they hadn't told him his dream!

Daniel and his three friends hadn't been summoned before the king, but they were among the wise men, so the king's death order for all the wise men meant that they would be killed too. But when a soldier came to kill them, Daniel asked what it was all about, and when he found out, he told him to stop killing people and he would tell the king what he had dreamed!

Then Daniel went home and told his three friends to pray and ask God to show him what the king's dream was, so that they wouldn't be killed. And that night, in a vision, God showed the dream to Daniel.

Then Daniel praised God, and said, "I thank you and praise you, O God of my fathers, because you have heard our prayer, and have told me what the king wants to know."

Then Daniel went to the captain of the king's bodyguard and said to him, "Don't kill the wise men of Babylon, but take me to the king and I will tell him the meaning of his dream."

So the captain rushed Daniel before the king, and the king said to him, "Can you tell me my dream and its meaning?"

Daniel replied, "The wisest man on earth can't tell it to the king; but there is a God in heaven who tells secrets. God has told me what your dream was, not because I am wiser than anyone else, but so that you will know that he is the true God. He has told you in your dream what will happen in the future."

Then Daniel told the king the dream and its meaning. The king threw himself to the ground in front of Daniel to show him deep respect, and said to him, "Your God is a God of gods and a King of kings and can tell secrets for he has told you this dream."

Then the king made Daniel a great man and gave him gifts and appointed him ruler over the province of Babylon, and he became the head of the wise men. And at Daniel's request, his three friends became rulers too.

STORY 132 **THREE MEN WHO WALKED IN THE FIRE**
DANIEL 3

KING NEBUCHADNEZZAR of Babylon now made a huge statue of gold and set it on a plain in the province of Babylon. Then he sent for all of his princes, governors, captains, judges, and all the other rulers of his kingdom to come and worship it. One of the king's assistants told them, "It is commanded that as soon as the band begins to play, you must fall down and worship Nebuchadnezzar's gold statue. If anyone refuses, he shall be thrown into a flaming furnace."

Then the king commanded the band to begin to play and instantly everyone fell down and worshiped the gold statue.

Daniel's three friends refused to do it, because they knew it was wrong to worship a statue. Then some of the Babylonians went to the king and complained to him about them.

380

"Didn't you make a law that everyone must fall down and worship the statue when the band begins to play, and that if anyone refuses, he will be tossed into a white-hot furnace?" they asked him. "Well, there are some Jews holding high political positions in your empire, and these men haven't obeyed you; they don't worship your gods, and they refuse to bow to your gold statue. They are Shadrach, Meshach, and Abednego."

King Nebuchadnezzar was furious. He commanded that the three young men be arrested at once and brought to him. "Is it true, O Shadrach, Meshach, and Abednego," he shouted, "that you do not worship my gods, and refuse to bow to my gold statue? I'll give you one more chance. When you hear the band begin to play, *fall down and worship the statue,* or you will be thrown at once into a flaming furnace; and who is the god who will be able to save you from my anger?"

Then Shadrach, Meshach, and Abednego said to the king, "We won't do it! If you throw us into the furnace, our God is able to save us, and he will. But even if he doesn't, we will not worship your gods, sir, nor bow to your gold statue."

Nebuchadnezzar's fury became more fierce. "Heat the furnace seven times hotter than ever before!" he commanded his men. Then he called for the biggest soldiers in his army to tie up Shadrach, Meshach, and Abednego and throw them in. The furnace was so hot that the flames killed the soldiers, but after Shadrach, Meshach, and Abednego had fallen down into the fire inside the furnace, they got up again and walked around in the flames! For God wouldn't let them be burned. The only things that burned were the ropes they were tied with; these burned from their wrists!

King Nebuchadnezzar was surprised beyond belief when

he saw the three boys walking around in the fire! "Didn't we throw three men into the fire, tied tightly with ropes?" he exclaimed. "And now there are four of them, loose and walking around in the fire! And the fourth looks like the Son of God!"

Nebuchadnezzar got as near as he could to the mouth of the furnace and shouted to them, "Shadrach, Meshach, and Abednego, you servants of the Most High God, come out!"

So out they came. The princes, governors, and captains crowded around them and could see that the fire hadn't hurt them a bit; not a hair of their heads was even singed, and they didn't even smell of smoke!

Then Nebuchadnezzar said, "Blessed be the God of Shadrach, Meshach, and Abednego, who has sent his angel and saved these young men who trusted in him. Therefore I now make a law that anyone who says anything bad about the God of Shadrach, Meshach, and Abednego shall be destroyed, and his house shall be torn down and made into a heap, for there is no other God that can rescue people as their God can!" Then the king made Shadrach, Meshach, and Abednego even greater than they had been before.

Shadrach, Meshach, and Abednego were thrown into a furnace of fire because they refused to worship the king's statue. They were protected by the Son of God.

THE KING WHO ATE GRASS

DANIEL 4

KING NEBUCHADNEZZAR'S palace was very large, and was ornamented with many statues of men and animals. It was filled with objects made from gold and silver, and with all sorts of beautiful things stolen from the nations he had conquered.

Nebuchadnezzar was a mighty king, and his men flattered him by praising everything he did; so he soon forgot about God and thought only of his own riches and power. God was displeased with him because of this and sent a strange punishment upon him.

After it was all over, he told his people about it. This is what he said to them:

"I had conquered all my enemies and was enjoying life in my palace, with no worries at all. Then I had a dream that made me afraid. So I called together all the wise men of Babylon and told them the dream, but they couldn't tell me what it meant. At last I called for Daniel, who has the spirit of the holy gods with him, and I told him my dream. I said to him, 'I saw a very high tree standing in the center of a wide plain. The tree grew taller and taller until it reached to heaven, and its branches spread out to the ends of the earth. Its leaves were green, and it was filled with fruit. The animals rested beneath its shade, and birds nested in its branches, and everything that lived came to it for food.

"'Then, in my dream, I saw an angel come down from

heaven. "Chop down the tree," he shouted, "and cut off its branches; shake off its leaves and scatter its fruit. Let the animals get away from beneath it, and the birds from its branches. Yet leave the stump of the tree in the ground where the dew shall fall upon it for seven years." O Daniel, what does my dream mean?'

"At first Daniel was afraid to tell me, but I insisted, so finally Daniel told me:

"'The giant tree you saw, with the animals resting in its shade and the birds nesting in its branches—that tree means you, O king. You have grown great and powerful, and your kingdom reaches to the ends of the earth. And you saw a holy angel coming down from heaven, saying, "Cut down the tree and destroy it, yet leave its stump in the ground, and let it be wet with dew. Let him wander with the wild animals of the field for seven years." This is what your vision means, O king: You will no longer be in your palace to be waited on by your servants, for they shall chase you out to live among the wild animals. You will eat grass like a cow, and sleep on the ground and be wet with the dew, until you have learned that God rules over all the nations of the earth, and makes anyone he wishes be the king.'

"Everything came true just as Daniel said it would. Twelve months after this dream I was walking on the roof of my palace, and as I looked out upon the great city of Babylon with its high walls, temples, palaces, and gardens, my heart was filled with pride. I forgot that it was God who let me be king, and I said, 'Is not this great Babylon that I have built by my own power and for my own honor and majesty?' While the words were still in my mouth, there came a voice from heaven, saying, 'O King Nebuchadnezzar, to you it is spoken—the kingdom is taken from you. You will be chased away from human society and will live with the wild animals and eat grass like a cow for seven years, until you know that God rules over all the nations of the earth and makes anyone he wants to be king.'

"That very hour I became insane, so that I was no longer fit to rule my kingdom. I was chased out into the fields to live, and ate grass like a cow and slept on the bare ground, and my body was wet with the dew until my hair grew long as eagles' feathers, and my nails were like birds' claws. . . .

"But at the end of the seven years I looked up to heaven, and my reason came back to me. And now I praise God and honor him who lives forever, and whose kingdom shall have no end. He does whatever he wills, in heaven and on earth, and no man can hold back his hand, or ask why he does anything. And when my reason came back to me, so did my honor and my kingdom. For the rulers and governors sought for me and I was made the king again, and all my greatness was given back to me. Now I, Nebuchadnezzar, praise and honor God, the King of heaven, who does only what is just and true; and he is able to bring down the proud to the dust."

STORY 134

THE HAND THAT WROTE ON THE WALL

DANIEL 5

AFTER KING NEBUCHADNEZZAR died, King Belshazzar became the new ruler of Babylon.

One day Belshazzar invited a thousand of his political

officers to a great party, where they all drank a great deal of wine. Then he commanded his servants to bring him the gold and silver bowls and dishes which his father Nebuchadnezzar had taken from the temple in Jerusalem. When they were brought in, the king and his princes and his wives drank from them, and praised his idols.

Suddenly a hand appeared, writing words on the wall. But no one could read the writing, for it was in a different language. The king's face grew white with fear, and his knees trembled.

He screamed to his assistants to bring in the wise men, and said to them, "If you can read that writing on the wall and tell me what it means, I'll pay you a fortune." But none of the wise men could read or understand it.

The king was *really* worried by now, and his assistants didn't know what to do. But when the queen heard what was happening she came in before him and said, "O king, don't let this mystery trouble you. For there is a man in your kingdom who has within him the spirit of the holy gods. Your father Nebuchadnezzar discovered him and made him master of all the wise men of Babylon; for he has great knowledge and knows how to interpret dreams and predict the future. Call for this man, Daniel, and he will tell you what the writing says."

So Daniel was brought in before the king, "Are you the Daniel who was brought as a captive from the land of Judah?" the king asked him. "I have heard that the spirit of the gods is in you, and that you are very wise. My wise men can't read the writing over there on the wall, and I must know what it means. If you can tell me what it says, I'll make you very rich."

"Keep your gifts," Daniel replied, "but I will read it for you and tell you what it means. O king, the most high God gave your father Nebuchadnezzar a kingdom and glory and

387

honor. And because God made him so great, all nations trembled and feared before him. He killed or kept alive anyone he wanted to.

"But when he became proud and forgot God, God made him come down from his throne and his greatness was taken from him. He was driven from his palace and became like an animal, and lived with the wild donkeys. He ate grass like the cows and his body was wet with dew, until he learned that God rules over the nations of the earth, and that God alone decides who shall rule in Babylon.

"But you, his son, have not humbled your heart, though you knew all this. You have been proud and have sinned against God. And you have sent for the bowls from the temple of God, and you and your lords and your wives have drunk wine from them, while praising your idols that can't see, hear, or know anything at all. And you haven't praised the true God who lets you live, and gives you all you have. So, God has written these words: MENE, MENE, TEKEL, UPHARSIN. This is what the words mean: Your kingdom is ended; God has taken it from you. He tried you out as king, but you didn't obey him. He has given your kingdom to the Medes and the Persians."

Then Belshazzar commanded his assistants to clothe Daniel with royal scarlet, and put a gold chain around his neck; and he appointed Daniel as the third ruler in the kingdom. But that same night the army of the Medes and Persians entered the city and killed King Belshazzar and took over the empire. Darius, the Mede, became the new emperor.

DANIEL IN THE LIONS' DEN

DANIEL 6

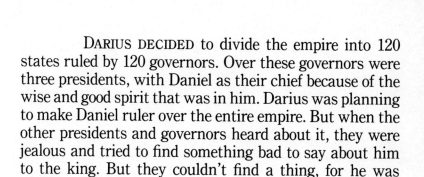

DARIUS DECIDED to divide the empire into 120 states ruled by 120 governors. Over these governors were three presidents, with Daniel as their chief because of the wise and good spirit that was in him. Darius was planning to make Daniel ruler over the entire empire. But when the other presidents and governors heard about it, they were jealous and tried to find something bad to say about him to the king. But they couldn't find a thing, for he was faithful to his duties and they couldn't point out a single fault. Finally they decided, "We'll never be able to complain about Daniel to the king except possibly about his religion."

So they came to the king and said, "King Darius, live forever! All the presidents and governors of your kingdom want a law made that any person who prays to anyone but you for the next thirty days shall be thrown into a den of lions. O king, make this law and sign it, so that even you can't change it." And King Darius signed the law.

When Daniel knew that the law was signed, he went home, opened the windows of his room towards Jerusalem, knelt, and prayed and gave thanks to God three times a day, just as he always had done before. Then the other presidents and governors got together and went over to Daniel's house and found him praying, and rushed back to the king and said, "Didn't you make a law that any person praying to anyone but you for thirty days must be thrown into the den of lions?"

"Yes," the king said, "I certainly did. It is now a law of the Medes and Persians which can never change."

Then they said, "That fellow Daniel isn't obeying you, O king, for he prays to his God three times a day!"

The king was crushed! Oh, why had he signed that law? He didn't want to punish Daniel. He tried every way he could to save him. But the presidents and the governors said to him, "You know perfectly well, O king, that no law the king has signed can be changed!"

So at last King Darius gave up, and Daniel was thrown into the den of lions. But first the king said to him, "O Daniel, your God whom you serve so faithfully will save you."

Then, after Daniel was thrown in, a great stone was rolled across the mouth of the lions' den so that no one could get Daniel out.

The king went home to his palace and refused to eat, and sent away the orchestra that played for him each evening. He was up very early the next morning and hurried out to the lions' den, and called sadly to Daniel: "O Daniel, servant of the living God, was this God of yours able to deliver you from the lions?"

Then Daniel called to the king, "O king, my God has sent his angel to shut the lions' mouths so that they haven't even scratched me!"

The king was overcome with joy and excitement and commanded that Daniel be taken out at once. So Daniel was unhurt because he trusted in his God.

And now the king ordered the men who accused Daniel to be thrown into the den of lions along with their children

Daniel's enemies said that if he prayed to God, they would throw him to the lions. Daniel prayed anyway. And God closed the lions' fierce jaws.

and their wives—and the lions leaped on them and killed them as soon as they fell to the bottom of the den.

Then King Darius wrote this letter to his people in all the nations of his empire: "I make a decree that in every part of my kingdom men tremble and fear before the God of Daniel. For he is the living God; his kingdom is the one that shall never be destroyed, and his power shall never end. He is the God who can save from danger—he saved Daniel from the lions."

So Daniel prospered in the reign of Darius, and also in the reign of Cyrus, who became king after Darius was dead.

While Daniel was in Babylon he read the book written by Jeremiah the prophet, and learned from it that the Jews would go back to their own land after seventy years of exile and captivity in Babylon where Daniel was living. Well, those seventy years were nearly ended! So Daniel fasted and prayed to the Lord asking that his people, the Jews, might return to the city of Jerusalem and build it again.

Three weeks later, as Daniel was continuing to pray this prayer, the angel Gabriel arrived from God's presence in heaven. It was in the evening, about the time when the priests had offered a lamb for a burnt offering at the temple in Jerusalem.

The angel told Daniel that the Jews would soon go back to their own land and rebuild Jerusalem, and that after 484 years the Savior would be born! But, the angel said, the Savior will be killed and his enemies will come again and destroy Jerusalem and the temple.

MANY JEWS RETURN TO ISRAEL

EZRA

AT LONG LAST the seventy years of captivity in Babylon ended, and the time came for the Jews to go back to their own land. Cyrus was king of the Babylonian empire at that time, and God made him willing to let the Jews go home again to Jerusalem. Then the words came true that were written long before by the prophet Isaiah, that God would raise up a great king named Cyrus who would send the Jews back to rebuild Jerusalem and the temple again. It had been nearly 200 years since the prophet Isaiah had said this! Cyrus had not even been born when the prophet told what he would do! And the Jews were still in their own land and didn't think anyone would ever capture them. But God knew all that was going to happen, and he told his prophet to tell about these things long before they happened.

So King Cyrus made a law and sent this message through all his empire: "The Lord commanded me to rebuild his temple in Jerusalem. Who among the captives from Judah wish to go back to their own land? Let them go now and rebuild the temple of the Lord; and let those who don't go help those who do by giving them silver and gold and cattle and clothing to take with them."

Then the Jewish leaders, the priests, the Levites, and all those the Lord made willing, prepared to start off on their journey to Jerusalem, rich with all the gifts given them by those who didn't want to go. King Cyrus gave them golden bowls taken from the temple by Nebuchadnezzar long before. In all, there were 5,400 of these gold and silver bowls and goblets. King Cyrus entrusted them to Zerubbabel to take them safely to Jerusalem.

Of the people of Israel, 42,360 returned to Jerusalem at that time, along with their 7,337 servants. They had with them 736 horses, 245 mules, 435 camels, and 6,720 donkeys.

Upon their arrival at Jerusalem they found it in ruins, for the army of Nebuchadnezzar had demolished it seventy years before, and no one had touched it since. Jerusalem's walls and houses, and the temple, had been broken down or burned.

The first thing the people did was to rebuild the altar of the Lord in the court of the temple, so that they could use it to worship God and to ask for his help; for they were afraid of the nations around them. They used the altar to offer burnt offerings to God every day—a lamb in the morning, and a lamb in the evening, just as the people of Israel used to do before they were taken away to Babylon as slaves.

Then they got ready to rebuild the temple. They hired workmen from Tyre, as King Solomon had done hundreds of years before, to cut down cedar trees on Mount Lebanon, making rafts of them and floating them down the Mediterranean Sea to the shore near Jerusalem.

When the very first stones of the foundation of the new temple were laid, the priests and Levites were so happy that they played on trumpets and cymbals and sang songs of praise to the Lord. Everyone was glad, and shouted with a great shout, because the rebuilding of the temple had begun. But many of the old men, who remembered the beauty of the temple that stood there before, couldn't keep back the tears of disappointment, because the new temple wouldn't be nearly as nice. So the shouting and the crying mingled together, and were heard far away.

THE PEOPLE REBUILD GOD'S TEMPLE

STORY 137

EZRA, HAGGAI

DO YOU REMEMBER that after the king of Assyria carried away the ten tribes of Israel as captives, he sent people from his own land to live in Israeli cities? These people, the Samaritans, worshiped idols, though they pretended to serve God.

The Samaritans were angry and did all they could to stop the Jews, and paid some men to tell the king of Persia that the Jews were disobeying him. Artaxerxes was now king of Persia, for King Cyrus had died.

They wrote this letter to him: "We want you to know, O king, that the Jews who came from Babylon are rebuilding the wicked city of Jerusalem. You should know that once they get the walls rebuilt, they will stop paying taxes to you, and will rebel against you. We don't want this to happen, so we suggest that you read up on the history of the city of Jerusalem, and see for yourself that it has always been a rebellious city, and has given much trouble to the kings who were before you; in fact, that is why Jerusalem was destroyed."

The king did as the Samaritans asked him to, and sent them this reply: "Thank you for your letter. I have checked into the matter and find that Jerusalem is, as you say, a very rebellious city that has always given us trouble. So tell the men of Judah to stop building the temple until I give them permission."

Then the Samaritans hurried to Jerusalem and made the people stop building. So the work ended during the entire time Artaxerxes was king.

After Artaxerxes' death, Darius II became king. But although the Jews knew there was another king in Babylon, they didn't ask him for permission to start building the temple again. For ever since the Samaritans had stopped them from building God's house, they had been building houses for themselves, and had become more interested in this than in finishing the temple.

The Lord was displeased with them, and sent Haggai the prophet to tell them, "You say, 'It isn't yet time to rebuild the temple!' Well, is it time for you to be living in beautiful houses while my temple lies in ruins? It is because you have left it unbuilt, and have all hurried to build your own houses, that I have not blessed you; that is why you have not prospered and been happy. Go up to the mountains and cut timber and build the temple, and I will be pleased with it."

Then the people obeyed the command of the Lord, and began to build it. But when the Samaritans heard about this, they came again to Zerubbabel and Joshua the High

As in the days when Solomon built the first temple, cedarwood was brought from Lebanon for the rebuilding of the temple.

Priest, and said to them, "Who has commanded you to begin building the temple again?"

Zerubbabel and Joshua answered them, "King Cyrus did. He sent us here with specific instructions to do this. And he gave us the gold and silver bowls which Nebuchadnezzar had taken out of the temple. 'Carry them to Jerusalem,' King Cyrus told us, 'and build the temple.'"

Then the Samaritans wrote a letter to King Darius II at Babylon, and told him what the people of Judah had said. And they asked the king to find out whether it was true that Cyrus had commanded them to build the temple. When Darius read the letter, he told his servants to search in the books where all the decrees of the kings of Babylon were written down. And sure enough, one of the books had this note in it. "In the first year of the reign of King Cyrus, he made this decree: 'Let the people of the Lord rebuild the temple at Jerusalem. Lay strong foundations. Get money from the king's treasury to buy whatever materials you need. And take to Jerusalem the gold and silver bowls which Nebuchadnezzar took from the temple; place them in the new temple when it is built.'"

As soon as King Darius II found this decree which Cyrus had made many years before, he sent word to the Samaritans to let the men of Judah build the temple of the Lord, and not to disturb them.

THE KING HELPS EZRA

EZRA

WHILE ARTAXERXES was the king of Persia, there was a Jew named Ezra who lived in Babylon with the other exiles from Jerusalem. Ezra was a good man who loved his people, and was very anxious for them to obey God so that he would give them his blessings. He asked King Artaxerxes to let him go to Jerusalem to teach God's laws to the Jews who were there, and to see that they obeyed them.

Artaxerxes gave Ezra permission to go, and gave him presents of gold and silver to take with him as gifts to God. And the king gave Ezra a letter which said, "I make a law that all the people of Israel who are still in Persia, and who want to go to Jerusalem, may go with Ezra. He is going to Jerusalem to find out whether the laws of God are being obeyed there, and to take the silver and gold which the king and his princes and the people of Babylon are donating to the God of Israel."

"And if you need more money," the king told Ezra, "get it out of my treasury. And I, Artaxerxes the king, command all the treasurers who have the care of my money in the provinces where Ezra is going, to give him, whenever he asks for it, as much as $200,000 plus 1,100 bushels of wheat, 900 gallons of wine, and as much salt as he wants. Help in every way possible to get God's temple built so that God won't be angry with me and send some disaster upon my kingdom."

Then he said to Ezra, "When you get to Jerusalem, select mayors and other public officials to rule the people. Be sure that the men you choose know the laws of God, so that they can teach the people who don't. Anyone refusing to obey God's laws and my commandments is to be punished with whatever punishment he deserves—death, exile, heavy fines, or prison."

Ezra thanked God for the king's kind attitude towards him. Then he called together some of the leaders of the Jews in Babylon, and some of the priests and Levites, for a meeting on the shore of the river Ahava. They brought their tents and camped there three days. They ate nothing during the entire time, for they spent their time praying to the Lord and asked him to direct their trip to Jerusalem and to protect them and their children and their money.

Then Ezra called twelve of the priests and counted out to them the money and the gold and silver bowls and dishes the king had given to the temple. "This silver and gold is an offering to the Lord," he told the priests, "so guard it carefully. Count it again when you arrive to be sure you have it all, and then give it to the priests and Levites at the temple."

So Ezra and all those returning with him to Jerusalem gathered at the river Ahava campground towards the end of April, and left from there on the long trip of many weeks' travel to Jerusalem. They had to go through wild desert country, full of bandits waiting to rob them. But the Lord watched over them and wouldn't allow their enemies to harm them, and in about four months they reached Jerusalem safely. There they rested for three days and then went up to the temple and counted the money and the golden bowls again, to see that none had been lost. Then they gave them to the priests and Levites at the temple. And how they thanked God for giving them a safe trip through the land of their enemies!

Ezra gave the letters from the king to the governors who ruled over the provinces in that part of the kingdom. And of course the governors obeyed the king and gave Ezra and the people with him everything the king had told them to.

BEAUTIFUL ESTHER BECOMES A QUEEN
ESTHER

NOT ALL THE JEWS went back to Jerusalem with Zerubbabel and Ezra; many of them still lived in the land of Persia. King Ahasuerus was now the Persian emperor. In the third year of his reign he prepared a great party for his officers in the garden court of his palace, in the city of Shushan where the kings of Persia lived during the winter.

Queen Vashti held a party at the same time for the women who lived and worked in the palace of King Ahasuerus. On the seventh day of the king's party, when he was drunk, he sent for Queen Vashti, to show everyone her beauty. In Persia the women lived in a separate part of the house, by themselves, and never came out before men unless they wore veils. So when King Ahasuerus sent for Queen Vashti to come before all the princes and people with her face unveiled, she refused, knowing that this would be quite wrong.

But the king was so angry at her refusal that he called

401

in his advisors and asked them, "What shall I do to Queen Vashti? How shall she be punished for not obeying me?"

One of the men replied, "Vashti has done wrong not only to you but to all the people of your kingdom. All the women of Persia will stop obeying their husbands when they hear that you commanded Queen Vashti to come and she refused. Let the king make a decree, and let it be written among the laws of the Medes and Persians which cannot be changed, that Queen Vashti shall never see the king again; and let the king choose someone else for his queen. Then, when this becomes known, wives everywhere will be afraid not to obey their husbands."

The king and his servants thought this was a good idea. So he sent letters through all the different provinces of his kingdom, commanding every husband to make his wives obey him.

Then the king's advisors said to him, "Let's have a national beauty contest to discover the most beautiful girls in Persia. Bring them all here to the palace to become your wives, and the one you decide you like best will be the new queen instead of Vashti." So that is what they did.

Among the government officials at the palace there was a Jew named Mordecai who had a young cousin named Esther. She was a Jewess. Her father and mother had died, so Mordecai adopted Esther as his daughter and brought her up in his house. She was very beautiful, so she was selected to be one of the king's new wives. But would she be the one selected as his queen? Everyone liked Esther very much and hoped she would be the one he would choose. She was given seven young girls to wait on her and was given a nice apartment in the harem, the place where the king kept his wives.

But Esther didn't tell anyone she was a Jewess, for Mordecai had advised her not to.

Sure enough, King Ahasuerus loved Esther more than any of the other girls who were brought to him, so he placed the royal crown upon her head and made her queen instead of Vashti. Then the king celebrated with a big party and gave gifts to all his servants.

HAMAN MAKES A BAD LAW

ESTHER

IT SO HAPPENED that two of the king's officers were angry with the king and wanted to kill him. Mordecai heard them talking and discussing their plans. He sent a message to Esther, telling her about the danger the king was in, and Esther told the king. The men were arrested and executed by being hanged on a gallows. Mordecai's deed in saving the king's life was written down in a book that told about all the main things that happened while he was king.

There was a man at the palace named Haman who was very great, for he was in charge of all the king's assistants. They all bowed to him, for the king had told them to. But Mordecai wouldn't do it. They asked Mordecai, "Why don't you obey the king and bow to Haman?" They kept asking him about this for several days, but he wouldn't listen to them, so they finally told Haman about it.

When Haman realized that Mordecai wasn't bowing to him, he was very angry and determined to punish him.

But he wasn't satisfied to punish Mordecai alone; he decided that since Mordecai was a Jew, he would punish all the Jews of Persia.

So Haman said to King Ahasuerus, "There are people called Jews scattered all through your kingdom, and they have laws of their own which are different from our laws; and they don't obey the king's laws. It is not good to let such people live. If the king will make a law to have them all killed, I will pay a hundred thousand dollars into the king's treasury."

King Ahasuerus agreed to this. He told Haman to make any law he wanted to against the Jews, and he would sign it.

Then Haman wrote a law declaring that on the thirteenth day of February the people of Persia were to kill all the Jews in the kingdom, both young and old—women and children as well as men and boys. Whoever killed a Jew could have the Jew's house and money for himself.

When Mordecai heard about the law Haman had made, he was filled with horror; he tore his clothes, and put on sackcloth and went out into the streets of the city and cried with a loud and bitter cry. And in every province where the messengers brought the decree, there was a great mourning among the Jews, and going without food, and weeping.

Queen Esther hadn't heard about this new law, but her maids came and told her that Mordecai was clothed in sackcloth, and crying out in the street. This made Esther sad, and she sent new clothes to him, but he wouldn't take them. So Esther called one of the king's assistants and sent him to ask Mordecai what the trouble was. Mordecai told him all that had happened, and about the money Haman had promised to pay into the king's treasury if the king would let him kill the Jews. Mordecai gave him a copy of Haman's law to show to Esther; and he asked him to tell the queen to go to the king and beg him to spare the lives of the Jews.

When he told Esther what Mordecai said, Esther sent back this message: "Everyone knows that anyone going to the king without being sent for will be killed instantly unless the king holds out his golden scepter. And he hasn't sent for me to come to him during the last four weeks. How can I go and speak with him?

But Mordecai returned this message to Esther: "Don't think that our enemies will spare you just because you are the queen, when they kill all the other Jews. If you don't try to save your people now, someone else will do it, but you and I and all your relatives will die. And who knows, perhaps God made you queen for just this purpose, to help the Jews at this particular time?"

Then Esther sent word to Mordecai, "Gather together all the Jews in this city, and tell them to go without food and pray for me. Do not eat or drink for three days, night or day; I and my maidens will do the same. Then I will try to go in and speak with the king. And if I die, I die."

So Mordecai called all the Jews together, and they did as Esther commanded.

THE KING HONORS MORDECAI

ESTHER

THREE DAYS LATER Queen Esther dressed herself in her royal robes and went into the inner part of the king's palace and stood before the king as he sat upon his throne.

And God was with her, for the king held out his golden scepter to her. So she came to him, and touched the top of the scepter.

Then the king asked her, "What is it you wish, Queen Esther? Whatever it is I will give it to you, even if it is half of my kingdom."

Esther answered, "Please come today with Haman to a banquet I have prepared for you!"

Then the king said to his servants, "Tell Haman to hurry and get ready."

So the king and Haman came to the banquet. The king knew Esther wanted to ask some favor from him, and so as they sat at the banquet he asked her again, "What is it you wish? I will give it to you, even if it is half of my kingdom."

Esther answered, "Please come with Haman to another banquet I will prepare for you tomorrow, and then I will tell you what it is I want to ask of you."

Haman was thrilled and proud to be invited—he and no one else except the king himself—but as he was leaving the palace he noticed Mordecai sitting at the gate refusing to bow to him. He was very angry, but said nothing.

When he arrived home, he called for his friends and for his wife, and boasted to them of his riches and greatness, and told them how the king had honored him above all the princes, and above all the king's other servants.

"Yes," he said, "and Queen Esther invited no one else but me and the king to come to her banquet. And tomorrow I am invited again, with the king! Yet I can't be happy while I see Mordecai the Jew sitting there refusing to bow to me."

Then his wife and all his friends said, "Make a gallows seventy-five feet high, and tomorrow ask the king for permission to hang Mordecai on it; then you can be happy at the queen's banquet."

Queen Esther was afraid to go in to see the king because it was against the law unless he asked her to. But she went anyway in order to save her people.

Haman was pleased with this advice, and he had the gallows made that very afternoon.

That night the king couldn't sleep. He told his servants to bring him the history book recounting the principal events of his reign. So the book was brought to him and as he was reading from it he noticed the item about how Mordecai had saved his life. For Mordecai had told him about the plot against his life.

King Ahasuerus asked his servants, "What reward or honor was given to Mordecai for this?"

"Nothing, sir," they replied.

While the king was talking about this, Haman arrived at the palace to ask the king for permission to hang Mordecai on the gallows. When the king was told that Haman was outside and wanted to see him, he said, "Yes, tell him to come in."

So Haman came in, and before he had a chance to tell the king his errand, the king said to him, "Haman, what is the highest honor I can give to a man who has helped me?"

Haman said to himself, "The king must mean me: I am the one he wants to honor."

So he said, "Let the man wear the king's robes and his crown, and let him ride upon the king's horse; and let one of the king's most noble princes lead the horse through the streets of the city and shout to all the people, 'See how the king is honoring this man!'"

"Good!" the king said to Haman. "Take these robes of mine and get my personal horse, and take the crown, and do as you have said, to Mordecai the Jew."

Well, Haman had no choice but to obey the king, so he took the king's robes, his horse, and his crown, and brought them to Mordecai, and led him on horseback through the streets of the city, shouting out to all the people, "This man is being honored by the king!"

Afterwards Mordecai returned quietly to his duties at the king's gate, while Haman hurried home, full of shame, hiding his face so that no one would recognize him.

BRAVE ESTHER SAVES HER PEOPLE

ESTHER

AT QUEEN ESTHER'S second banquet the king asked Esther again, "What is your wish, Queen Esther? What is your request? For it shall be given you, even to the half of my kingdom."

Esther answered, "If the king is pleased with me, this is my request, that the king will save my life and the lives of all the Jews. For we face death. I and all my people are to be killed; every one of us must die."

"Who would dare to touch you and your relatives?" King Ahasuerus roared.

Esther answered, "This wicked Haman is our enemy."

Haman turned pale with fright as the king rose from the table in great fury and stalked out into the palace garden. When he came in again, Haman had fallen down beside the queen to beg for his life. But the king had decided to kill him.

"Why not hang him on the gallows made for Mordecai?" someone suggested.

And the king said, "Yes, hang him there." So that is the way Haman died.

King Ahasuerus gave Haman's palace to Queen Esther, and Mordecai was called in before the king (for Esther now told the king that Mordecai was her cousin, and how kind he had been to her) and the king appointed him as his prime minister, the job Haman had had before.

Then Esther went to the king again, though he had not called for her, and fell down crying at his feet. The king held out the golden scepter to her and she stood before him and begged that Haman's law dooming all the Jews be changed. "For how can I bear to see my people die?" she wept.

But even the king couldn't change it, for no law of the Medes and Persians could ever be changed, not even by the king himself. Then King Ahasuerus had an idea! He told Esther and Mordecai to make another law giving the Jews permission to fight back against anyone who tried to harm them!

Mordecai sent copies of this new law to all the provinces of the kingdom. The message went by swift messengers on horseback, mules, camels, and young dromedaries.

So on the thirteenth day of February the Jews gathered together in every city, armed to fight for their lives; and they destroyed all their enemies. So God saved Esther and her people from those who had tried to destroy them. Then Esther and Mordecai sent letters to all the Jews telling them to hold an annual celebration of their victory, with parties and presents for each other and for the poor.

FAITHFUL WORKERS REBUILD THE WALL

NEHEMIAH

IT HAD NOW been ninety years since the exiles
had returned to Jerusalem from Babylon. Artaxerxes was
now the Persian king, and Nehemiah, a Jew, was one of his
trusted government officials. One day Nehemiah met some
men from Judah and asked them how things were going in
Jerusalem.

"Not very well," the men told him.

They said the walls of Jerusalem were still in ruins, and
the gates of the city had never been rebuilt at all.

Nehemiah cried when he heard this. Then he began
going without food as he prayed for the Jews, asking God
to make King Artaxerxes willing to help them. For Nehemiah had decided to ask the king to send him to Jerusalem to rebuild the city walls.

As King Artaxerxes was sitting one day in his palace,
and Nehemiah was there with him, the king noticed that
Nehemiah seemed very depressed.

"Why are you so sad today?" the king asked him. "Are
you sick?"

"No," Nehemiah replied, "but how can I help being sad
while my city of Jerusalem stands without walls?"

"Well, what do you want me to do about it?" the king
asked. At first Nehemiah didn't answer, but silently, in his

411

heart, he prayed again that God would make the king willing to help.

Finally he said, "Would you send me to Jerusalem to rebuild its walls?"

"How long will it take?" the king asked. "How soon could you return?"

And after they had talked about it for a while, the king told him to go!

Nehemiah then asked the king for letters to carry with him, addressed to the governors of the provinces he would pass through, telling them to help him; also a letter to the keeper of the king's forest near Jerusalem, asking for timber to make beams for the city walls and gates. So the king gave him the letters, and also sent soldiers to go with him and guard him.

But there were two wicked men named Sanballat and Tobiah living near Jerusalem, who were enemies of the Jews. When they heard that the king had sent someone to help the Jews in Jerusalem, they didn't like it at all.

Nehemiah arrived safely in Jerusalem, and after he had been there three days, he went out secretly at night, so that his enemies wouldn't see him, and examined the ruined walls of the city.

The next morning he called a meeting of all the people and told them, "You see the danger we are in, with no walls to guard us. Come, let us rebuild the walls as a protection against our enemies." Then he told them about the king's instructions to him.

"Yes, let's get started; let's build the walls," they said to one another.

Everyone helped—the priests, the Levites, and the people, and even some of the women.

But Sanballat was angry when he heard about it. "What are these weak Jews trying to do?" he mocked. "Do they

The temple of God
was rebuilt by the Jews
who returned from Babylon.
King Herod made the temple even nicer,
because he wanted to please
the Jews.

think they can build a wall right around Jerusalem? Where will they find enough stones among the heaps of rubbish left by their enemies?"

And Tobiah, who was with him, said, "If a fox walked on their wall it would fall down!"

But the Jews went on with their work until they had built the wall to half its height all around the city.

Then Sanballat and Tobiah and all the enemies of the Jews decided to attack suddenly and kill them before they had a chance to escape. But the Jews were told of the plot, so Nehemiah instructed the men of Israel to carry their weapons at all times.

"Don't be afraid," he said. "Remember, the Lord will help us. Fight for your wives, your children, and your homes."

But when their enemies heard that the Jews were prepared to fight them, they changed their plans and didn't come.

After that scare, half the men of Israel worked on the walls while the other half guarded. And even those at work carried their swords with them. Nehemiah kept a trumpeter near him in case of enemy attack, for it was a long way around the city, and the workmen were widely separated.

"If you hear the trumpet," he told them, "hurry to help."

So all the people worked hard from morning till evening. They didn't even take off their clothes, day or night, except for washing.

ENEMIES MAKE TROUBLE
NEHEMIAH

WHEN SANBALLAT AND TOBIAH heard that Nehemiah and the men of Israel were still at work on the wall, and that it was half built already, they were afraid to go into Jerusalem. So they sent word to Nehemiah to come down to one of the villages on the plain and meet them there. But Nehemiah knew they wanted to harm him, so he sent messengers to tell them, "I am doing a great work, and I cannot come down. Should I stop the work just so I can talk with you?"

They sent him the same message four times, but each time he gave them the same answer.

Then Sanballat sent a messenger to Nehemiah with this letter: "I am told that you Jews in Jerusalem are going to rebel against the king of Persia. I am told you are plotting to be their king; that is why you are building the wall around the city. Come and talk with me, or I will tell the king what you are planning."

But Nehemiah sent back this reply: "It isn't true, and you know it."

Then Nehemiah prayed to the Lord to help him, and prayed that the work on the wall would not be stopped by these enemies.

So Nehemiah and the people kept on working on the wall and finished it in fifty-two days. Then they held a great celebration. The priests, Levites, and the people walked along the top of the wall in two groups, going in opposite directions, with trumpets blaring and harps playing, singing praises to God as they walked around the city until the two groups met. Then they came down from the wall and marched together to the temple, and offered sacrifices to God with joy and gladness. So the wall was dedicated to the Lord to guard his temple and his people from their enemies.

Nehemiah now appointed leaders throughout the city and told them, "Shut the gates at night, and don't open them in the morning until the sun has risen high in the heavens. And each of you must take his turn at guard duty on the walls, to watch for our enemies."

A TIME TO CELEBRATE
NEHEMIAH

NOW IT WAS THE TIME for the annual Festival of Trumpets, which was a sort of Thanksgiving Day. The people met together that day to worship. They asked Ezra the priest to bring from the temple the book of laws proclaimed by Moses. Ezra brought out the book and stood outside the temple on a pulpit where all the people could see him. Then he opened the book and read out of it from morning until noon as everyone listened—men, women and even the children. And the priests and Levites explained what he read.

When the people heard God's laws and remembered how often they had disobeyed them, they began crying. But the Levites said to them, "Don't weep, for this is a day of happiness. Go home and eat and drink of the good things God has given you, and send presents to the poor." So all the people went home to have a big dinner and to send gifts to the poor. They were glad because the Lord had been so good to them, and because they had understood the words that were read to them out of God's law.

The next day they came to Ezra again so that he could read more of God's laws to them. This time he read to them from the part of the book commanding them to celebrate the Festival of Tabernacles each year. "Go up to the mountains," the book said, "and cut down olive, pine, and myrtle branches, and make huts and live in them all week." So the people went up and cut branches from the trees, and built huts on the flat roofs of their houses or in their yards, and in the courts of the temple, and even in the streets. Then they moved out of their houses and lived in the huts for the seven days of the celebration. And there was a great joy among them. There hadn't been such a celebration in Jerusalem for hundreds of years.

They remembered how often they had disobeyed God. So on the twenty-fourth day of the month they met in sorrow to go without food and to confess their sins to God; and they wore sackcloth to show their grief.

Their leaders then wrote out their promise to obey God; then Nehemiah the governor and some of the priests and many of the chief men of Israel signed the agreement. The people promised to obey all of God's commandments.

Nehemiah went back to Babylon after this, for he had promised the king he would. We are not told how long he stayed there, but when he returned to Jerusalem again he found that the people had already forgotten their promise to obey God's law. They had again made friends with the heathen nations around them, and had intermarried with them. And the people of Israel had stopped giving the priests and Levites a tenth of their fruit and grain; so the Levites had left the temple to work in the fields to raise food for themselves. Nehemiah was grieved, and called the priests and Levites back to the temple. "Why is the temple of God forsaken?" he asked.

Nehemiah saw the people loading their donkeys and bringing their grain in from the fields on the Sabbath. He rebuked their leaders. "Why are you so wicked?" he demanded. "Didn't God punish our fathers by destroying this city for doing these very same things?"

On the evening before the Sabbath, when it began to grow dark, Nehemiah commanded that the gates of the city must be shut and not opened again until the Sabbath ended. And he stationed guards to prevent any traders from coming into the city to buy and sell on the Sabbath day.

Then he spoke to the men who had married heathen women and said, "Wasn't Solomon a great and wise king? Yet when he married foreign wives he fell into the sin of worshiping their idols. Should we listen to you, then, when you want us to disobey God by doing this same wicked thing?"

This chapter completes the story of the Old Testament. The Bible tells us nothing more about the Jews until Jesus came more than 400 years later. We can find out from our history books at school what happened during those 400 years.

Now, as we read the New Testament, we will see how God kept his promises about sending the Savior.

GOD'S SPECIAL MESSENGER

LUKE 1

NOW THE TIME CAME for the Savior to arrive on earth. And how the world needed him, for everyone was selfish and unhappy! No one was pleasing to God. All the people in the world were sinners, just as Adam and Eve had been. When Adam and Eve sinned in the Garden of Eden, God promised them that a Savior would come someday to take away their sins. The prophets too had often told the people of Israel that this wonderful Savior was going to come.

The prophets said that someone else would come before the Savior did, to tell the people to get ready for his arrival by turning away from their sins. This was John the Baptist. Here is the story of his birth:

While Herod was king of Judea, an old priest named Zacharias worked at the temple, helping the people to worship God. His wife's name was Elizabeth. They were both careful to obey all of God's commandments, but God had never given them a child.

One day, when it was Zacharias' turn to burn the incense on the gold altar, he stood in the holy place at the hour of prayer. Suddenly he saw an angel standing beside the altar! He was terribly frightened.

But the angel said, "Don't be afraid, Zacharias. God will give you and Elizabeth a son, and you are to name him

An angel explained to Mary that she would have a baby even though she was a virgin, for God would place the baby in her womb. The baby would be Jesus, God's Son.

John. He must never drink wine or any other alcoholic beverage, and he will be filled with God's Holy Spirit from the time he is born. He will tell the people of Israel about the Savior who is coming, and he will persuade many of them to turn from their sins and obey him."

Zacharias was amazed! "How can I be sure you are telling the truth?" he asked the angel.

"I am the angel Gabriel," he replied. "I live in heaven and stand before God, doing whatever he commands me. He has sent me to tell you this good news. And now because you haven't believed me, you will be punished by being unable to speak until all that I have told you comes true."

Zacharias' wife Elizabeth had a young cousin named Mary. She was in the royal line of Israel, for she was a relative of King David who had lived hundreds of years before.

Six months after the angel appeared to Zacharias in the temple, God sent his angel to Mary. She was frightened, for she had never seen an angel before. But Gabriel said, "Don't be afraid, Mary! God has greatly blessed you. You are going to have a baby and his name will be JESUS. He will have no human father, for he will be the Son of God. And God is giving a baby to Zacharias and your cousin Elizabeth."

Mary didn't understand how she would have a baby, for she was a virgin, that is, she wasn't married and so she had never slept with a man. But the angel explained that this wasn't necessary, for God would do a special miracle to make her pregnant while she was a virgin. No other baby has ever been born without a human father. Jesus was different. How excited and happy Mary was at this wonderful news that she would be the mother of the Savior of the world!

She was engaged to be married to a kind man named

Joseph, who was a carpenter. But when he heard that Mary was going to have a baby, he was sad. He thought that she had sinned and that some other man was the baby's father. He said that now he wouldn't marry her. But God talked to him about it and explained that God was the baby's father, so it was all right for him to marry her after all; so he did. But he didn't sleep with her until after the baby was born.

Meanwhile, God gave Zacharias and Elizabeth the son he had promised them. When the baby was eight days old, their neighbors and relatives came to dedicate him to the Lord and to decide on his name. They wanted to call him Zacharias, because that was his father's name. But his mother said, "No, we will name him John."

"Oh, no," they said to her, "none of your relatives has that name." Then they motioned to Zacharias, asking him what he wanted to name the baby. He couldn't speak yet, and couldn't hear, so he took a sheet of paper and wrote, "His name is John." They were all very surprised, for Zacharias hadn't told them about the angel giving him this name in the temple.

Little John grew, and the Lord blessed him. When he was older he lived out in the lonely wilderness away from the rest of the people until the time came for him to preach to the Jews and tell them about Jesus. For this child God had given to Zacharias and Elizabeth was John the Baptist, the one who came to prepare the way for Christ.

THE BIRTH OF GOD'S SON
MATTHEW 2; LUKE 2

IN THOSE DAYS the Jews were under the rule of the Romans; they had to do whatever the emperor of Rome and his assistants told them to. Now he made a law that the name and address of every Jew must be written down. He instructed everyone to go to the city where his ancestors had lived, so that the Roman officers could record their names. Ancestors means relatives who lived hundreds of years before. So Joseph and Mary went to Bethlehem where King David used to live, because they were relatives of his, though he had lived hundreds of years before they were born.

But when they arrived at Bethlehem there was no room for them at the little hotel; it was already full. So they went out to the stable where the donkeys and camels were kept, to sleep in the straw on the floor. And while they were resting in the stable, Mary's baby was born. He was the little son that the angel Gabriel had told her about. Yes, Jesus was born out there in the stable; Mary laid him in a manger.

That same night some shepherds in the fields outside the town were watching their sheep to protect them from wild animals. Suddenly an angel surrounded by a bright light appeared to them. They were very frightened. But the angel said, "Don't be afraid; for I have good news for

you, and for all the world! Tonight, in Bethlehem, your Savior was born! His name is Christ the Lord.

"And this is how you will know him: you will find him wrapped in baby clothes and lying in a manger!"

Then suddenly many, many other angels appeared, praising God and saying, "Glory to God! Peace on earth between God and men!"

After the angels returned to heaven the shepherds said to each other, "Let's hurry to Bethlehem and find the baby!" So they ran into the village and soon found Mary and Joseph, and the baby lying in a manger! Afterwards the shepherds returned to their flocks again, praising God for what the angel had told them. They had seen the Savior.

When the baby was eight days old, his parents named him Jesus, just as the angel Gabriel had told them to. And they dedicated him to the Lord, for he was the Son of God.

Not long afterwards some men who study the stars came to Jerusalem from a distant eastern land. "Where is the baby who will become king of the Jews?" they asked. "For we have seen his star and have come to worship him." They knew in some way from seeing the star that Jesus had been born. So they came to Jerusalem looking for him, but they didn't know just where to search.

When King Herod heard them asking about a new king, he was worried, for he was the king and he didn't want anyone else to have his job! He told the men to find Jesus, and then to come and tell him where he was so that he could worship Jesus too. But what he really intended was to kill Jesus.

Shepherds were taking care of their sheep one night near Bethlehem, when suddenly the skies were filled with angels telling them of Jesus' birth.

King Herod now summoned some priests who had spent their lives studying the Scriptures, and asked them whether the Bible said where the new king would be born.

"Yes," they replied, "in the city of Bethlehem; that is what one of the prophets said."

So Herod sent the astrologers to Bethlehem. "Go to Bethlehem and search for the child," he said, "and when you have found him, come and tell me so that I can worship him too!"

So the men went to Bethlehem. And as they went, the star they had seen appeared to them again, and seemed to stand right over one certain house. They went in and saw the baby with his mother Mary, and they bowed low before him, worshiping him. Then they gave presents to the new king—precious gifts of gold and spices. Afterwards they returned to their own country, but they didn't go through Jerusalem, for in a dream God warned them not to tell Herod where Jesus was.

When Herod discovered that the astrologers had disobeyed him, he was very angry and sent his soldiers to Bethlehem to kill all the little children two years old or less. Since he didn't know which baby was the little king, he killed them all. But before the soliders arrived, the angel of the Lord told Joseph to hurry to Egypt with the baby and his mother. So Joseph wakened them in the night and they fled to Egypt and stayed there until King Herod was dead. Then the angel spoke to Joseph again and told him, "Go back to the land of Israel, for King Herod is dead."

Joseph did as the angel commanded, and he and Mary and Jesus came and lived in the city of Nazareth.

The hotel was full—"NO ROOMS," the sign said. So Joseph took Mary to the stable and made a bed of hay. That is where Jesus, God's Son, was born.

STORY 148

JESUS GROWS UP
MATTHEW 3; MARK 1; LUKE 2, 3; JOHN 1

JOSEPH AND MARY went to Jerusalem every year to celebrate the Passover. When Jesus was twelve years old, he went with them. After the celebration ended, they started walking back to their home in Nazareth, along with many other people. For friends and neighbors traveled together to the celebrations at Jerusalem. Some rode on mules and horses, but many of them walked. Joseph and Mary noticed that Jesus wasn't with them, but thought he was with some of their friends, so they didn't worry. But when they didn't see him all day, and evening came and still he wasn't back, they began looking for him and worrying, and asking everyone if they had seen him. But no one had. By this time they were *very* worried and started back to Jerusalem to search for him there. It took them a day to return and it was another day before they finally found him. He was at the temple talking with the great teachers there, listening to them and asking them questions!

These men were greatly surprised at how much Jesus knew, for he was only twelve years old, while they were college professors.

"Son!" his mother exclaimed, "why have you treated us like this? Your father and I have been searching for you everywhere."

428

Men far away
in a distant land
learned from the stars
that a new king of the Jews
had been born.
They traveled many weeks
to bring their gifts
to Jesus.

Jesus was surprised. "Didn't you know I would be here at the temple?" he asked.

Joseph and Mary didn't understand what he meant, but his mother always remembered what he had said and often thought about it. Afterwards she understood—he was the Son of God and naturally would want to be at his Father's house, which was the temple.

Then Jesus returned home to Nazareth with his parents and did all that they told him to do. And as he grew, God blessed him; and everyone loved him.

The next we are told about Jesus, he was a man thirty years old. But very few knew that he was the Son of God, for John the Baptist hadn't yet begun to tell them about him.

Meanwhile John was living out in the wilderness. His clothes were woven of coarse camel hair, fastened around his waist by a leather belt. He ate locusts for his food—they were plentiful out there in the wilderness—and honey from the wild bees.

But now the time had come for John to preach to the people, telling them to get ready for the Savior by turning from their sins. He began his preaching beside the river Jordan, and great crowds came there to hear him. He told them that the Savior would soon be coming to save them and to destroy the wicked. John said that they mustn't think their sins would be forgiven just because they were descended from a good man like Abraham! No, they themselves must obey God. Many who heard John preach turned from their sins and were baptized by him in the river.

Then Jesus came to John and asked to be baptized. John

At twelve years old Jesus was able to talk intelligently with these wise old men. He was God's Son, so he already knew more about God than they did.

didn't want to do it. "*I* need to be baptized by *you*," John told him; "why do you come to me?" Jesus had no sins to be washed away; why then should he be baptized? It was because he had come to earth to obey all of God's commandments for us.

Jesus told John to baptize him anyway, even though he didn't understand why, for it was necessary. So John agreed. Then, as Jesus was coming up out of the water after being baptized, the sky above him opened and what looked like a dove came down from heaven and lighted upon him. It was the Holy Spirit. At the same time God's voice spoke from heaven saying, "This is my beloved Son. I am very pleased with him."

SATAN TEMPTS JESUS TO SIN
MATTHEW 4; MARK 1; LUKE 4

AFTER HIS BAPTISM Jesus went out into the wilderness alone for forty days and forty nights. All that time he ate nothing, but fasted and prayed to God; and afterwards he was hungry.

Do you remember how Satan tempted Eve to disobey God? And when she did, it caused all the rest of us to have wicked hearts? Well, when Satan saw that Jesus had come to give us new, pure hearts, and to make us good, he thought he would try to stop him. So he went out into the wilderness to tempt Jesus, as he had tempted Eve in the Garden of Eden.

He came to him and said, "If you are the Son of God, change these stones into bread, so that you will have food, for you are very hungry."

But Jesus knew why Satan had come, and he refused to turn the stones into bread. He told Satan, "It is written in the Bible that obedience to what God has said is more important than food to eat."

Then Satan took Jesus into Jerusalem to a very high part of the temple. "If you are the Son of God," he said to him, "throw yourself down, for it is written in the Bible that the angels will keep you from hurting yourself."

But Jesus said it was also written in the Bible that we must not put ourselves in danger just to find out whether God will help us.

Then Satan tried again. He took Jesus up on a high mountain and showed him all the kingdoms of the world at the same time, with their beautiful cities, their mighty armies, and their great riches. He said to him, "I will give you all of these if you will only kneel down and worship me." For that is what Satan wanted most of all—to get Jesus to worship and obey him.

But Jesus said, "Get out of here, Satan, for it is written in the Bible, 'You shall worship only the Lord your God, and serve him alone.'"

Then, when Satan saw that he couldn't make Jesus obey him, he went away; and angels came and cared for Jesus.

Then Jesus returned to the river Jordan where John was baptizing. When John saw him coming, he said, "Look! There is the Lamb of God!" He called Jesus the Lamb of God because Jesus would die as a sacrifice just as lambs were sacrificed at the temple. Two of John's disciples heard him say this, and immediately followed Jesus wherever he

went. He talked with them, and invited them to his home. Then one of them, Andrew, went to get his brother Peter. The next day two others, Philip and Nathaniel, decided to go with him. So now Jesus had five disciples.

JESUS TURNS WATER INTO WINE

MARK 6; JOHN 2, 3

ONE DAY JESUS went to the city of Cana to attend a wedding. His mother and his disciples were there too. During the wedding supper something unfortunate happened: the host ran out of wine and the guests were disappointed. Jesus' mother told him about it, expecting him somehow to get some more. Then she told the servants to be sure to do whatever he told them to.

There were six large stone water jars there in the house, used to store water, for there were no taps in those days as we have in our homes now.

Jesus told the servants to fill the water jars with water, and they filled them to the brim. Then he said, "Take some to the master of ceremonies." And when they did, the water had become wine!

The master of ceremonies didn't know that Jesus had

The first miracle Jesus did was to turn water into wine at a wedding in the city of Cana.

435

changed it (but the servants did) so when he had tasted it, it was so good that he called the bridegroom over. "I've never heard of anyone's saving the best wine to the last!" he exclaimed. "Everyone else serves the best first, and after everyone has had enough, then they serve the wine that isn't so good!"

This was Jesus' first miracle. When his disciples saw what had happened, they believed that he was the Son of God.

Now it was time for Jesus to go to Jerusalem for the annual Passover celebration. This was a holiday week to remind everyone about the time when God used Moses to rescue the people of Israel from Egypt.

Nicodemus was one of the political leaders of the Jews. After dark one night he came to Jesus and remarked, "Sir, we know God has sent you, for no one could do the miracles you do unless God were with him."

Jesus replied, "Unless you are born again, you cannot be one of God's children!"

"What?" Nicodemus asked in surprise. "How can a person be born a second time? Can he enter into his mother's body again as a tiny baby and be born again?"

Then Jesus explained to him that by being born again he meant becoming eager to do God's will, and asking Jesus to take away one's sins so that God gives him new, eternal life.

And then Jesus said something else that seems very strange at first. He said, "As Moses lifted up the serpent in the wilderness, so must I be lifted up." What did he mean?

One dark night Nicodemus came to Jesus to talk to him about the kingdom of God. Jesus told him that he must be born again to enter God's kingdom.

Well, do you remember the time when the people of Israel were in the wilderness and God punished them by sending fiery serpents into the camp to bite and kill them? But then God told Moses to make a bronze statue of a serpent and put it on a pole and lift up the pole so that everyone who had been bitten could look at it; and when they did, they got well.

So now Jesus said to Nicodemus, "As Moses lifted up the serpent in the wilderness, so must I be lifted up." Jesus meant that he was to be lifted up on the cross so that we might look to him and be forgiven of all our sins. That is, we can thank him for dying for us.

Jesus also told Nicodemus, "God loves the people of the world so much that he sent his only Son into the world to die for them, so that whoever looks up to him in faith will not be punished for his sins, but is forgiven and goes to heaven when he dies."

By this time King Herod was dead. His son—his name was Herod too—was now the governor of Galilee. Like his father, he was a wicked man. He had married his brother's wife, Herodias, even though she was married to his brother. When John the Baptist told Herod this was wrong, Herodias became very angry and tried to get Herod to kill John for saying such a thing. But Herod wouldn't do it. Herod was afraid to kill him because he had heard him preach and knew he was a holy man. Yet, to please Herodias, he arrested John and put him in chains, and shut him up in prison.

While John was in prison, Herod's birthday came around and there was a big birthday party with all his government officials invited. During the party, Salome, the daughter of Herodias, came in and danced. Herod enjoyed her number very much and said to her, "Ask me for anything and I'll give it to you, even if it is half of my kingdom!"

So Salome ran to her mother and asked, "What shall I ask him for?"

"Ask him for John the Baptist's head!" she replied.

So Salome ran back to the king and said, "Please give me the head of John the Baptist on a tray."

Then Herod was very sorry for his promise, but everyone had heard him say it, so he didn't dare refuse. He sent one of his soldiers to cut off John's head in the prison. He brought it to Salome, and she gave it to her mother.

When John's disciples heard about it, they came and took away his body and laid it in a tomb, and went and told Jesus.

STORY 151

JESUS MAKES A SICK BOY WELL
LUKE 4; JOHN 4

ONE DAY JESUS and his disciples came to the village of Sychar. Just outside the city was a well, called Jacob's Well, where the people came to get water. It was hot, and Jesus was tired from the journey. He sat down by the well while his disciples went into the city to buy food.

A woman came from the city, carrying her empty pitcher to get some water from the well. This woman didn't love God in her heart, and had done many things to displease

This woman is talking to Jesus beside a well where she has come to get some water. Jesus tells her that he can give her eternal life.

him. Jesus knew this, for he sees all our hearts and knows everything we do. He talked with the woman and told her some of the things she had done that displeased God. She was surprised and said, "Sir, I see you are a prophet." She meant that he must be a person to whom God told things that other people didn't know. "I know that the Savior is coming into the world," she said to Jesus, "and when he comes he will tell us everything."

Then Jesus told her, "I am the Savior!"

The woman left her pitcher and hurried back to the village and said to the people, "Come and see a man who told me everything I have ever done! Could this be the Savior?"

The people rushed out to see Jesus and begged him to visit their city. So he stayed with them three days, and they listened carefully to what he taught them. Then they said to the woman, "We, too, believe he is the Savior, but not just because of what you told us about him; we have heard him for ourselves, and we know now that he is the Savior from heaven."

From that time on, Jesus began to tell the people that the judgment day was coming, and that they must turn away from their sins and trust him to save them.

He now returned to the village of Cana where he had changed the water into wine. While he was there a rich man from another city came to him and begged him to heal his son who was very, very sick. "Come quickly before my child dies," he pleaded.

But Jesus replied, "Go home, your son is already well again!"

The man believed Jesus, so he started back home. But before he arrived, his servants met him and said, "Your son is well!" He asked them what time the child had begun to get better and they replied, "Yesterday at about one o'clock in the afternoon, the fever left him!"

Then the man realized it was the same time that Jesus had said to him, "Your son is well!" So he and all his family believed in Jesus as the Son of God.

The Jews offered their sacrifices only at the temple of Jerusalem, but they had churches called synagogues in every city. When Jesus returned to Nazareth, where he had been brought up, he went into the local synagogue on the Sabbath day. He was asked to read aloud to the people from the book of the prophet Isaiah. So he read from the part where Isaiah told the people of Israel about the Savior who was coming into the world. After he had finished reading and had sat down, everyone in the synagogue was staring at him. So then he stood up again and preached to them. He told them that what he had just read had come true that very day, right before their eyes. He said that he himself was the Savior, the Son of God, whom Isaiah was writing about in the part of the Bible he had just been reading to them.

But when he said this, all the men in the synagogue, or Jewish church, became very angry, for they didn't believe he was telling the truth when he said he was the Savior. They jumped up and grabbed him and led him out to the top of a steep hill on which their city was built, to throw him off a cliff and kill him. For they thought it was very wrong for him to say he was the Son of God. But Jesus walked away from them, and they couldn't seem to stop him! This was, of course, another miracle.

TWO BOATS FILLED WITH FISH

MATTHEW 8; MARK 1; LUKE 4, 5

JESUS NOW CAME to Capernaum, a city beside the Sea of Galilee, and great crowds came down to the beach to hear him preach. There were so many people that Jesus was almost crowded into the water. So when he noticed two fishing boats pulled up along the shore, with the fishermen mending their nets, Jesus stepped into one of the boats—it belonged to Peter—and asked him to push it out a little way into the water. Then he sat down and taught the people from the boat.

When he had finished, he said to Peter and his brother Andrew, "Now go out into the lake and let down your nets."

Peter answered, "Sir, we fished all night and didn't catch a thing; but if you say so, I'll try again." And to their surprise, in just a little while they caught so many fish that their net broke! Then they shouted to their partners, James and John, who were in the other boat on the beach, to come and help them, and they filled both boats with fish until they almost sank!

When Peter saw the miracle Jesus had done, he knelt before him and worshiped. Then Jesus said to Peter and Andrew, "Come with me." And they left their boats, nets, and everything else, and went with him everywhere, for now they were his disciples.

Later Jesus went to the home of Andrew and Peter. James

and John were there, too, and Peter's mother-in-law, but she was sick, and had a fever. They all begged Jesus to heal her. So he went in and stood beside her bed and commanded the fever to leave. Instantly she was well, and got up and cooked dinner for them!

In the evening, at sunset, a great crowd gathered in front of the house, bringing him many sick people to be healed, and those with evil spirits. And he healed them all, and made the evil spirits come out and go away.

In the morning, getting up long before it was light, Jesus went out to a lonely place in the wilderness to pray. Although he was God's Son, yet he was on the earth as a man who felt pain and hunger, joy and sorrow, and needed to pray for God's help just as the rest of us do. That is why he went out into the desert that morning to pray.

While he was away, many people came to Peter's house looking for Jesus. So Peter and the other disciples went out to find him, and told him to come back because everyone was asking where he was. But Jesus replied, "I must go and preach the gospel in other cities, too."

Then he traveled all through Galilee, teaching the Good News in the synagogues and on the beaches. What Good News was it that Jesus preached? It was this: That he had come into the world to be punished for our sins, so that if we turn away from those sins and believe his promise to save us, we won't be punished at the Judgment Day, but God forgives us and takes us to heaven when we die, and we will be happy there forever.

A man with leprosy now came to Jesus and knelt before

Some of Jesus' disciples had been fishing all night, but didn't catch a thing. Then Jesus called to them from the shore and told them where to place the nets.

him. "Lord, you can heal me if you want to," he pleaded.

Jesus pitied him and put out his hand and touched him. "I want to!" Jesus told him. "Be healed!"

The leprosy left him instantly and he was well again! Jesus told him not to tell anyone who it was who had healed him, but to go to the priest at the temple and offer a sacrifice, as Moses had commanded those who were cured of leprosy. But as soon as Jesus was gone, the man told everyone what he had done for him!

One special group of Jews was called scribes, and another special group was called the Pharisees. They pretended to be very good, and told the people to obey all the laws in the Scriptures, but they themselves didn't bother with them. They obeyed some of God's commandments, like not working on the Sabbath, but they didn't obey such commandments as being kind and fair. They were hypocrites; that is, they pretended to be good but in their hearts they really weren't at all. So when Jesus told them to turn away from their sins and to obey God, they hated him and did all they could to keep the people from believing him.

STORY 153

JESUS CHOOSES TWELVE DISCIPLES
MATTHEW 9, 12; MARK 2, 3; LUKE 5, 6; JOHN 5

NOW JESUS CAME again to the city of Capernaum, and great crowds came to the house where he was staying, and he preached to them. The house was a one-story build-

Jesus talked to John and Peter on the beach.
Both of them decided
to become Jesus' disciples.
"Come with me and fish for men!"
Jesus invited them.

ing with a flat roof. Among those who came to him were four men carrying a sick friend on a stretcher. But there was such a crowd that they couldn't get inside. So they went up on the roof and took off some tiles, and used ropes to let the stretcher down carefully, with their friend on it, right into the room where Jesus was! In fact, the sick man landed right in front of Jesus!

When Jesus saw how much faith they had, he said to the sick man, "Your sins are forgiven!"

But some of the scribes and Pharisees who were sitting there said to themselves, "Who does this man think he is, forgiving sins as though he were God?"

Jesus knew their thoughts and asked them, "Why do you think such sinful thoughts? Is it any harder for me to forgive this man's sins than to cure him of his sickness? Now I will make him well." Then he said to the sick man, "Stand up and go on home!"

Instantly the man jumped up, stood there for a moment, then picked up the stretcher he had been lying on and disappeared through the crowd! The people who saw it happen just couldn't get over it. "We've never seen anything like this before," they exclaimed.

In those days the Jews had to pay taxes to the Romans. The taxes were collected by other Jews called publicans and everyone hated them, because most of these tax collectors were unfair—they cheated by collecting extra money for themselves. As Jesus walked along he saw a publican named Matthew sitting at his tax collection booth. Jesus told him, "Follow me." And Matthew did. He left everything and followed Jesus, and from that time on he was one of Jesus' disciples.

Soon afterwards, Jesus went to Jerusalem to attend the celebration of one of the Jewish holidays, and passed the pool of Bethesda on the way. This pool had five porches

THE LORD'S PRAYER
MATTHEW 6:9-13

Our Father in heaven,
we honor your holy name.

We ask that your kingdom
will come now.
May your will be done
here on earth,
just as it is in heaven.

Give us our food again today,
as usual,
and forgive us our sins,
just as we have forgiven those
who have sinned against us.

Don't bring us into temptation,
but deliver us from the Evil One.

Amen.

around it, all filled with sick, blind, and lame people. Jesus saw a man there who had been sick for thirty-eight years. How Jesus pitied him! This man and all the other sick people had been waiting there because every once in a while the water moved as if someone had stirred it, and the first person in the water after it stirred was healed of whatever disease he had!

"Do you want to be healed?" Jesus asked him.

"Of course!" the man replied, "but I have no one to help me into the pool after the water stirs; while I am trying to get down into it, someone else steps in ahead of me and I'm too late."

Jesus told him, "Pick up your sleeping mat and start walking!" And immediately the man was well!

But Jesus did this on the Sabbath, the day each week when no work was permitted, so the Jewish leaders scolded the man for "working" by carrying his sleeping mat that day!

"But the man who cured me told me to!" he answered.

"Who said that?" they demanded. He told them it was Jesus. Then the Jews tried to kill Jesus for not obeying their law.

On another Sabbath day he went into the Jewish church, or synagogue, and saw a man there with a shrunken hand. The Pharisees watched to see whether Jesus would work on the Sabbath by healing the man! But Jesus knew their thoughts and said to them, "If one of your sheep fell into a well on the Sabbath, wouldn't you pull it out? And if it is right to help a sheep on the Sabbath, how much more a man?"

Then he said to the man, "Reach out your hand!" And when he did, it was healed!

This made the Jewish leaders very angry, and they began to talk about killing Jesus. So he and his disciples left that

*This is a picture of Jesus
preaching the sermon on the mount.
He taught the people
about God's kingdom
and how to receive God's blessings.*

place and went away to the Sea of Galilee. Many people from Jerusalem and Judea and from countries far away came to see him when they heard of the wonderful things he did. The sick people crowded around him to touch him, for when they did, they got well!

After this he went alone into the desert and stayed there all night, praying to God. When it was morning, he called his disciples and chose twelve of them to be with him, and to preach, and do miracles, and to heal the sick and cast out devils. These twelve were called "apostles," or "messengers." These were their names:

PETER
ANDREW (Peter's brother)
JAMES
JOHN (James' brother)
PHILIP
BARTHOLOMEW
THOMAS
MATTHEW (the publican)
JAMES
THADDEUS
SIMON
JUDAS ISCARIOT.

THE HOUSE BUILT ON THE ROCK

MATTHEW 5, 6, 7; LUKE 6

WHEN JESUS SAW the crowds coming to him he climbed a hill and sat there with his disciples, teaching them. These are some of the things he told them:

"Blessed are the humble, for the kingdom of heaven belongs to humble people. They are the truly happy ones.

"Blessed are those who mourn, for they shall be comforted.

"Blessed are the meek, for they shall inherit the earth.

"Blessed are those who are anxious to do right and to please God, for they shall be satisfied.

"Blessed are those who are merciful to others, for they shall have mercy shown to them.

"Blessed are the pure in heart, for they shall see God.

"Blessed are the peacemakers (that is, those who will not quarrel and who try to keep others from anger and fighting), for they shall be called the children of God."

Jesus told his disciples that when they were treated cruelly because they were his followers, they should be glad, for they would get a big reward in heaven!

He also told them that they must not be afraid to let others know that they loved and obeyed God. Their example would help others to love and obey him too.

If we do the things God commands, and teach others to do them, we will be great in the kingdom of heaven.

Jesus also told his disciples that they must always be pure and good in thought and action; they (and we) must not even think bad thoughts.

And when others are unkind to us, and do us harm, we must not try to pay them back. Instead we must do good to them and pray for them and love them; for then we will truly be the children of our Father in Heaven. We will be like him, for he is kind even to those who don't obey him or love him.

Jesus told his disciples not to just pretend to be nice so that others would praise them for it, but to please God by being *really* nice to others. And when we give help to the poor we must not go around bragging about it.

Jesus said we must not want to be rich, but must send our money on ahead to heaven. How do we do this? By giving our money to the church and Sunday school, and to the missionaries, and to the poor. And then in heaven we will have more things to make us happy than all the money in the world can buy.

This is something else that Jesus said to the people at this time: "You can't obey both God and Satan. For if you obey God you will do what is right, but if you obey Satan you will do what is wrong. So you can't do both—you must choose one or the other."

He said that we should treat others as we want them to treat us. If we want them to be kind to us, we must be kind to them.

"Work hard to enter the narrow gate of heaven," Jesus told his disciples, "for the road to hell is wide and smooth." He meant that we must choose the road we will travel along through life. The road to heaven is narrow and rough, where few bother to walk. The road to hell is broad, well-paved, and popular, and stands wide open before us, welcoming us.

THE BEATITUDES
MATTHEW 5:3–12

Humble men are very fortunate!
for the Kingdom of Heaven is given to them.

Those who mourn are fortunate!
for they shall be comforted.

The meek and lowly are fortunate!
for the whole wide world belongs to them.

Happy are those who long to be just and good,
for they shall be completely satisfied.

Happy are the kind and merciful,
for they shall be shown mercy.

Happy are those whose hearts are pure,
for they shall see God.

Happy are those who strive for peace—
they shall be called the sons of God.

Happy are those who are persecuted
because they are good,
for the Kingdom of Heaven is theirs.
When you are reviled and
persecuted and lied about
because you are my followers—wonderful!
Be happy about it! Be very glad!
for a tremendous reward awaits you
up in heaven.

THE GOLDEN RULE
LUKE 6:31

Treat others as you want them to treat you.

Jesus said that not everyone who calls him Lord and Master will get to heaven, but only those who obey his Father in heaven. Many will come to him at the Judgment Day and call him "Lord" and will say they have worked for him and taught others about him. But he will tell them they have never truly been his disciples. And he will send them away with all the other wicked people because they only pretended to be his disciples but didn't really do what he told them to.

One day Jesus told his disciples an important story about two men who built two houses. One of them chose solid rock to build his house on. When he had finished it, a great storm came up, but the rain and wind could do no harm because the house had such a solid foundation.

The other man built his house on sand, and when the storm came, the rain washed the sand away from beneath his house, and the wind blew against it, and it fell down in a great heap and washed away.

Jesus said that we are either like the wise or foolish man. If we listen to his teaching and do what he tells us to do, then we are like the wise man who built his house on the rock. But those who listen to him but don't do what he tells them to are like the foolish man who built his house on the sand. Those who do what he tells them to will be saved, but those who disobey him will be lost, for the storm means the Judgment Day.

JESUS BRINGS A DEAD BOY TO LIFE
MATTHEW 8; LUKE 7

IN THE CITY of Capernaum there lived a Roman army officer who had a servant he dearly loved, but the servant was very sick and ready to die. When the officer heard that Jesus had come to his city, he asked some of the Jewish leaders to go and find Jesus and beg him to come to the officer's house and heal his servant. So they went and found Jesus and pleaded with him for help. "This officer is a Roman, not a Jew," they explained, "but he has a deep love for the Jews and has been very kind to us and has even built us a church with his own money."

Jesus started off with them to the officer's house. But before they got there, the officer sent him this message: "Please don't come! For I'm not good enough to have you in my house. Instead, stop where you are and just say that my servant must get well, and he will! I'm sure the sickness will obey your orders and go away, just as my soldiers obey me and do whatever I tell them to!"

Jesus was very greatly surprised. "I've never before met even a Jew with this much faith!" he exclaimed. "And I tell you, at the Judgment Day many people of other nations who have faith in me will be in heaven, while many of the Jews won't, because they don't believe."

So Jesus didn't go to the man's house, but healed the servant while he was far away. And when the officer returned home, he found that the servant was well again!

The next day Jesus went to the city of Nain. Just as he was entering the city gate, he met some people carrying out a dead boy to bury him. He was the only son of his mother, and she was a widow, that is—his father was dead. Many of her friends were with her.

When Jesus saw her, he pitied her. "Don't cry!" he said. Then he stopped the funeral procession and went over to the dead boy and said, "Young man, get up!" And the boy sat up, alive! And Jesus gave him back to his mother!

Everyone was frightened by this amazing miracle, and how they praised God! "Jesus must be a very great prophet indeed to be able to bring someone back to life again," they exclaimed.

One day a man named Simon asked Jesus to come to his home for dinner. But as they were eating, a prostitute came with an expensive bottle of perfume and knelt at Jesus' feet, crying because she was sorry for her sins and wanted to be forgiven. Her tears fell on Jesus' feet and she wiped them with her long hair and kissed them and poured the perfume over them.

Simon knew this woman was a sinner, and he said to himself, "If Jesus were really God's Son, he would know who this woman is, and how bad she is, and he would send her away."

Jesus knew what the man was thinking and said to him, "Simon, I have something to say to you: Two people owed a man some money. One owed him a lot, and the other owed him only a little. But neither of them had any money to pay him back, so he told them they could forget about it and they didn't have to give him back the money. Tell me now, which of these two men do you suppose will like him best for being so kind to them?"

Simon replied, "I suppose the one who owed him most."

"Yes," Jesus said, "that is correct." Then he turned to

the woman and said to Simon, "Do you see this woman? When I came into your house, you didn't give me any water to wash my feet, but she has washed my feet with her tears, and wiped them with her hair. You didn't give me the customary kiss of greeting on my cheek, but this woman has kissed my feet again and again. And so her many sins are forgiven, for she loves me so much. But those who have little to be forgiven for will love me only a little."

Then Jesus turned to the woman and said, "Your sins are forgiven; go home in peace!"

After this Jesus went through the entire country, preaching the Good News in every city and village; and the twelve apostles were with him.

STORIES WITH HEAVENLY MEANINGS STORY 156

MATTHEW 13; MARK 4; LUKE 8, 12

JESUS OFTEN TOLD the people stories that contained lessons. These stories are called parables. One of his stories made them see how foolish and wicked it was for them to put their trust in money. Here is the story:

"There was a rich man with many farms and orchards. When harvest time came, his crops were so large that his barns wouldn't hold them all. Then he said to himself, 'What shall I do? I haven't enough space to store my harvest. I know! I'll tear down my barns and build larger ones. Then I can eat, drink, and be merry, for I'll be rich enough to live for many years without ever working again.'

"But God said to him, 'Fool! Tonight you die! Then who will get all your wealth?'

"All those who live to get rich are like that foolish man. For death often comes when they are least expecting it, and they must leave their money for others, and go away to a world where nothing but sorrow has been stored up for them."

Jesus told his disciples not to be afraid of being poor. "Be like the birds," he said. "They don't plant seeds in the fields, or reap grain, yet they have enough to eat because God feeds them. And God cares more about you than he does about the birds! And look at the flowers! They don't need to work hard to get clothes for themselves, and yet they are more beautifully clothed and have brighter colors than Solomon the king of Israel! So if God gives such beautiful clothing to the flowers, which are of so little value that one day they are growing in the field and the next are cut down and burned, he will surely give you all the clothes you need. So don't be afraid to trust him. Your heavenly Father knows what you need. The most important thing for you to do is to obey him and to be his child. Then he will give you everything you need."

Great crowds surrounded Jesus as he walked along the shore of the lake, so he got into a boat and taught the people from there. He told them this story:

"A farmer went out into the field to sow grain. Some of the seed fell on the hard ground of a path that ran along beside the edge of the field, and the birds flew down and ate it. Some of the seed fell on stony places where there

Jesus told a story about
a farmer who planted his field
by throwing seed
across the ground.
He used the story
to explain
how different people
receive God's Word.

wasn't enough earth on top of the rocks to make strong roots, so in a few days the little plants withered away. And some of the seed fell where briars and weeds were growing; the seeds began to grow but the weeds were tall and thick and shut out the sunshine and used up the rain, so the little plants soon died. But the rest of the seed fell on good ground—plowed and harrowed and ready to receive it. The rain watered it, and the sun shone down upon it, and it soon grew; and after a few months there was a harvest of grain—a hundred times as much as the farmer had planted."

When Jesus was alone with his disciples, they asked him to explain this parable to them. He told them that the seed meant his words. Some of his words are heard by people with hard hearts who refuse to believe him. Satan comes and takes God's words away from them by making them think of other things, just as the birds ate the seed that fell on the hard pathway. Other people to whom Jesus speaks try for a while to obey him, but it is only for a little while. As soon as they have trouble, or are laughed at by others, they turn away from him.

Other people hear Jesus preach and are glad, but afterwards they begin to care more for their homes, their money, and their pleasures than they do for the things of God.

But there are some people who listen carefully to everything Jesus says, and remember it, and try every day to obey whatever he tells them to. They are like the good soil where the seeds grew well and there was a crop of a hundred times as much seed as the farmer had planted.

Jesus also told the people about a jeweler looking for pearls to buy at a bargain. He went to everyone who had any to sell, and at last he found a pearl that was larger and more beautiful than any he had ever seen before. But although it was priced at far less than its real value, he still didn't have nearly enough money to buy it. So he sold everything he owned and came back and bought that one precious pearl. This is the way people feel who want their sins forgiven. They cannot be happy until it is done, and they are willing to give up every sinful pleasure, and everything that offends God, so that they may come to him and ask him to forgive their sins.

One of the Jewish leaders came to Jesus and said, "Master, I want to be with you wherever you go."

Jesus replied, "The foxes have dens to live in, and the birds have nests, but I have nowhere to lay my head." Jesus meant that he was poorer than the foxes and the birds, for they had homes of their own, but he had nowhere to go when he was weary.

STORY 157

THE WINDS AND THE SEA OBEY JESUS
MATTHEW 8; MARK 4; LUKE 8

THAT EVENING JESUS and his disciples got into a boat to sail over to the other side of the Sea of Galilee. But suddenly it began to be windy, and soon there was a great storm, and the waves dashed into the boat and began to fill it with water so that it was beginning to sink. But Jesus was asleep.

"Master!" they shouted to him, "save us! We'll all be drowned!"

Then Jesus stood up and spoke to the winds and the sea, and said to them, "Peace! Be still!"

The wind stopped blowing, and the sea became very still and calm. Then he said to his disciples, "Why were you afraid? How is it that you have so little faith?"

So they went on to the other side of the lake, and when Jesus got out of the boat, there was a man there with an evil spirit in him. The man had torn off his clothes and was naked and very fierce, so that no one could go by him without getting hurt. His friends had often tied him with chains to keep him at home, but he broke the chains and went out and lived in a graveyard, crying out and cutting himself with stones.

While Jesus was still far out on the lake, the man saw him and ran to him as he stepped ashore and fell down at his feet and worshiped him. The evil spirits in the man were frightened when they saw Jesus, for they knew he could make them go away. They begged him to let them enter a herd of pigs feeding nearby, and Jesus told them they could. So the evil spirits came out of the man and went into the herd of pigs. Then the whole herd (there were about two hundred of them) ran over to a cliff and tumbled off into the sea, and were drowned.

The men who had been taking care of the pigs ran into the nearby city and told everyone what had happened. So all the people came rushing out to see Jesus. When they saw the wild man sitting there quietly—clothed, and in his right mind—they were afraid, and asked Jesus to go away from their country.

A terrible storm threatened to sink the disciples' little boat. Jesus was asleep, but they screamed to him to wake up and save them all from drowning.

So he got back into the boat to leave. The man begged to go with him, but Jesus said, "No, go home to your friends and tell them what great things the Lord has done for you." So the man began telling everyone how Jesus had made him well.

STORY 158

HEALED BY A TOUCH
MATTHEW 9, 13; MARK 5, 6; LUKE 8

AS SOON AS JESUS returned to Capernaum, one of the leaders of the local Jewish church came and knelt at his feet and told him, "My little daughter is very sick and I'm afraid she is going to die. Oh, please come and put your hands on her head, so that she will get well again."

Jesus went with him, and so did his disciples, followed by a great crowd. In the crowd was a woman who had suffered for twelve years from a disease no doctor could cure; she had given them all the money she had, but was no better—in fact, she was worse. But when she heard that Jesus was in town she said to herself, "If I can only touch him, I'll get well." So she pushed her way through the crowd and touched him, and as soon as she did, her sickness was cured.

Immediately Jesus turned around to the crowd and asked, "Who touched me?"

The disciples were disgusted with him. "Why ask such a foolish question?" they said. "The whole crowd is pushing and touching you!" But he still kept looking around to see who had done it. When the woman saw that he knew what she had done, she came trembling and fell at his feet, and told all the people why she had touched him, and how in a moment she was well.

"Daughter, don't be afraid," Jesus said to her. "Because of your faith in me you are healed."

While he was still talking to the woman, a messenger arrived to tell the little girl's father, "Your child is dead. It's no use for the Master to come now."

But Jesus told the father, "Only have faith and she will come back to life!"

When they arrived at the house, Jesus saw the people weeping and wailing and said to them, "Why weep? The child isn't dead, she is only asleep!" He meant that she would soon be alive again, like one wakened from sleep. But they didn't believe him, and laughed at him. Then Jesus told all of them to leave, and took three of his disciples—Peter, James, and John—and the father and the mother of the dead child, and went into the room where she lay. Then he took her by the hand and said, "Get up, little girl!" And the little girl—she was twelve years old—jumped up and started walking! Then Jesus told them to give her something to eat!

As Jesus left her home, two blind men followed him, calling, "Oh, son of David, have mercy on us." They called Jesus this because he was a relative of King David's, and this was a title of honor and respect among the Jews.

"Do you believe that I am able to make you well?" Jesus asked them.

"Oh, yes, Lord!" they replied. Then he touched their eyes, and immediately they could see.

"Don't tell anyone what I have done for you," Jesus told them, but they told everyone!

Now a man was brought to him who couldn't talk because of an evil spirit in him. So Jesus told the evil spirit to go away, and it did. Then the man could talk again! "What wonderful things are happening today," all the people exclaimed.

But the Jewish leaders were jealous of Jesus and hated him. They told the people that he was able to cast out devils only because Satan, the prince of the devils, was inside him. What a wicked thing to say!

Jesus now returned to Nazareth where he had been brought up, and went into the Jewish church on the Sabbath day and taught the people. They were amazed at his wonderful sermon. "Where did this man get such great wisdom and power to do such wonderful miracles?" they asked. "Isn't he the son of Joseph the carpenter, and of Mary? And aren't his brothers and sisters here with us?"

So they refused to believe he was anything special, because he seemed so common to them. And because they didn't believe, he did few miracles among them except to put his hands on a few sick people to heal them.

The daughter of the Jewish leader had died. But Jesus brought her back to life. How happy everyone was!

POWER FOR JESUS' DISCIPLES

MATTHEW 9—11, 14; MARK 6; LUKE 9; JOHN 6

JESUS NOW SENT his twelve disciples all through the land to preach the Good News. But he told them to go only to the Jews, for they were God's chosen people, and God wanted the Good News preached to them first.

Jesus gave the disciples power to do miracles so that everyone would believe what they preached. "Wherever you go," he told them, "heal the sick, make the lepers well, raise the dead, and tell everyone that Christ has come to save all who believe in him. But don't expect them to be kind to you! They will treat you as they have treated me. They will take you before their judges and whip you because you preach to them about me. But don't fear them, for they can only kill your bodies. Fear God who is able to destroy both soul and body in hell."

Jesus told them not to take any money or food with them on their trip, for God would give them all they needed. "God even cares about the sparrows and feeds them," Jesus said, "and not one of them dies without God's knowing about it. So don't be afraid that he won't take care of you! For you are much more valuable to him than the sparrows are! He remembers the smallest things about you, and knows even the number of hairs on your head. And he will notice everyone who treats you well. When anyone is kind to you, he is being kind to me, and whoever gives you even

470

a drink of cold water because you are my disciples will be rewarded for doing it."

When Jesus had finished talking to them, they went out to the cities and towns preaching to the people and healing those who were sick.

Afterwards, when they returned, they told him all they had done. "Let's get away to some quiet place where you can rest a while," he said. There were so many people coming and going that they scarcely had time to eat. So they all got into a boat and sailed across to the other side of the Sea of Galilee where they could be alone. But when the people saw where they were headed, they followed on foot, walking around the lake to the other side where Jesus was.

As soon as they arrived across the lake the people recognized him and ran to get those who were sick, so that he could heal them. And wherever he went, in villages or cities, sick people were laid in the streets and all who touched him became perfectly well!

In the evening his apostles came to him and said, "Send the people away to the villages to buy food, for it will soon be dark."

"They don't need to go away," Jesus said; "you feed them!"

"What?" the disciples exclaimed, "feed all this crowd?"

"How many loaves of bread do you have?" Jesus asked them. "Go and see."

When they knew, they said, "Five, and two small fish."

He told them to tell all the people to sit down in groups on the green grass. Then he took the five loaves and two fish, looked up to heaven and thanked God for them. Then he broke the loaves in pieces, and gave them to the apostles, also the two fish. Then they passed them out to the people. And the strangest thing happened! As the disciples broke off pieces of bread, the loaves were still the same size as before, so there was enough for everyone! And it was the same with the fish.

A MIRACLE AT A PICNIC

MATTHEW 15, 16; MARK 7, 8; JOHN 6

JESUS NOW RETURNED to Capernaum again, and went into the Jewish church to teach the people about God.

"What should we do to please God?" the people asked him.

"Believe that I am the Savior!" he replied.

But the Jews were expecting a Savior who would be a great soldier and set them free from the Romans, so that they could have their own king. But Jesus was a poor man, not some great hero. He didn't promise to make them rich, but told them they were sinners. Many people didn't like him for this, and refused to believe that he was the Savior, and went away and left him.

Then he said to the twelve disciples, "Are you too going to leave me?"

Peter replied, "Lord, where else can we go? For no one else but you can save us."

Then Jesus told them, "I have chosen you twelve to be my apostles, and one of you is my enemy." He meant Judas Iscariot, who was going to help the chief priests and elders of the Jews put him to death. They hated Jesus and did all they could to keep the people from believing him.

Jesus then left the country of Israel and went to Tyre and Sidon. The people who lived in those cities were not Jews, but Gentiles. While he was there a woman begged him to get rid of an evil spirit that was in her daughter. At first he turned away as if unwilling to hear her because she wasn't a Jew, but he did this only to find out whether she truly believed in him. Then she begged him more earnestly, and fell at his feet and worshiped him. "Lord, help me," she begged.

Then Jesus told her, "Because of your faith in me, your daughter is healed." And when she got home, the evil spirit had gone out of her daughter and she was perfectly well.

Jesus now returned to Israel. A deaf man who could hardly speak was brought to him to be healed. Jesus led him away from the crowd and put his fingers into the man's ears, and touched his tongue with spit, and looking up to heaven, said, "Be opened!" And immediately the man was well and could both hear and speak!

Soon many sick people who were lame and blind, or couldn't speak, were brought to him and laid before him so that he could heal them. And he healed them all. The people marveled as they saw the lame walking and the blind seeing. And how they thanked God!

The crowd soon became very large, and once again Jesus fed them with only a few loaves of bread and a few fish. The people had been with him for three days and had nothing left to eat, for they had eaten all the food they had brought with them.

Then Jesus said to them, "If I send these people away to their homes without food, they will faint along the road, for many of them have come from far away. How many loaves of bread do you have with you?"

"Seven!" they replied, "and a few small fish!"

Then he told the 4,000 people to sit on the ground, and he took the seven loaves and the fish and thanked God for them, and gave them to his disciples to give to the people. And they all ate their fill. Afterwards, seven basketfuls of scraps were picked up off the ground!

He went next to the city of Bethsaida, where a blind man was brought to him, and the people begged Jesus to touch and heal him. Jesus took him by the hand and led him out of the town; then Jesus touched the man's eyes with spit and placed his hands on him.

Jesus asked him if he could see. "Yes," the blind man said, "I see some men, but they look like trees walking around."

Then Jesus put his hands on the man's eyes again, and told him to look up, and now the man could see everything clearly.

Jesus fed 5,000 hungry people. He used a little boy's lunch of five buns and two fish to feed them all. And there was food left over!

WHO IS JESUS?

MATTHEW 16, 17; MARK 8, 9; LUKE 9

AS JESUS WAS GOING to the city of Caesarea with his twelve disciples, he asked them, "Who do the people think I am?"

"Some say you are John the Baptist, risen from the dead," they answered. "Others say you are the prophet Elijah, come back to earth again."

Then Jesus asked, "Who do you think I am?"

Peter replied, "You are the Christ, the Son of God." In other words, Peter was telling Jesus that he believed he was the Savior. But Peter and the other disciples were looking for a Savior who would save them from being ruled by Rome. They knew he was poor, but they expected him to become rich and great, and believed that he would make them great, too. Like the rest of the Jews, they had not yet learned that he had come to rule in their hearts. Instead of fighting battles for them as a king, he was going to die on the cross for their sins.

Now Jesus began to tell his disciples what was going to happen to him when he arrived in Jerusalem: He would be cruelly treated by the chief priests and other leaders of the Jews. In fact, they would kill him, but he would come back to life again three days afterwards.

When Peter heard this he exclaimed, "No, these things will never happen to you." But it was for this very reason—

to suffer these things—that Jesus came into the world. So when Peter said they would not happen to him, Jesus was displeased and called Peter his enemy. For Peter didn't want him to do what would please God, but what would please Peter.

One day Jesus took Peter, James, and John up on a high mountain to pray. As he prayed his face began to shine like the sun and his clothing glistened and became as white as snow. Suddenly two men were standing beside him, talking with him. They were Moses and Elijah, who had died many hundreds of years before. Now they had returned to this world to talk with Jesus about his being crucified at Jerusalem.

The disciples recognized these two men—we don't know how—and were too excited and frightened to know what to think. Finally Peter exclaimed, "Master, this is great! Would you like us to get three tents—one for you, one for Moses, and one for Elijah?"

But just then a bright cloud came across the sky and God's voice spoke from the cloud. "This is my beloved Son," God called to them. "Listen carefully to everything he tells you."

The disciples fell face downward to the ground in awful fear, but Jesus came and touched them and said, "Get up, don't be afraid." When they stood up and looked around, Moses and Elijah were gone, and no one was there except Jesus. Then Jesus told them, "Don't tell anyone what you have seen until after I have died and become alive again." But they didn't understand what he meant when he spoke of becoming alive again.

When they came down from the mountain the next day, many people were waiting to see Jesus. A man came and knelt before him and pleaded, "Master, please help my son, my only child. An evil spirit has got into him, and it tried

477

to kill him by making him fall into the fire and into the water. I took him to your disciples, but they couldn't heal him. Oh, please, help me."

"Bring him here," Jesus told him. But as the father was bringing his boy, the evil spirit threw the boy to the ground, foaming at the mouth. Jesus asked his father, "How long has he been this way?"

"From the time he was just a little child," the father replied.

Then Jesus said to the evil spirit, "I command you to come out of this boy and never enter him again!"

Instantly the spirit began shrieking and then came out as the boy lay on the ground, apparently dead. "The evil spirit killed him," everyone said. But Jesus took the boy by the hand and pulled him to his feet, and he was well!

When Jesus and the disciples went back to Capernaum, the tax collectors asked Peter whether or not Jesus was going to pay the temple tax. Jesus knew the men were talking to Peter about this, so when Peter came back into the room Jesus said to him, "Go to the Sea of Galilee and throw in a hook and a fishing line. Open the mouth of the first fish you catch, and you will find a piece of money in it! Give it to these men as the tax for both of us." So Peter did as Jesus said, and found the piece of money and gave it to the men!

ONE LEPER SAYS THANK YOU

MATTHEW 18; MARK 9; LUKE 9, 17

NOW ALTHOUGH JESUS had plainly told the disciples what was going to happen to him—that he would be treated cruelly and put to death at Jerusalem—still they never seemed to understand. They thought that even if he had to suffer, soon afterwards he would be crowned the king of Israel and become very great, and then they would be great too!

One day as they were walking along, the disciples began to argue with each other about which of them would be the greatest in Jesus' kingdom. When they arrived at the house where they were going, he asked them, "What were you arguing about out there on the road?" But they didn't answer, for they were ashamed to tell him. Then he called a little child over to him and gathered his disciples around. He told them that unless they put away their pride and became like the little child—humble and willing to obey—they could not even get into the kingdom, let alone be the greatest in it.

Jesus also told his disciples that whenever they met to worship him, even though only two or three were there, his Spirit would be right there with them. And if one of them did something wrong and afterwards confessed it and was sorry about it, the person he had wronged must forgive him.

Peter asked, "How many times must we forgive him—as many as seven times?"

"No!" Jesus answered, "not only seven times, but seventy times seven!" He meant that we must *always* be ready to forgive each other.

Then he told them another story: "There was a king," he said, "and a man who owed the king $1,000,000. But the man couldn't pay it back. So the king ordered him and his wife and his children to be sold as slaves, so that the money they were sold for could be paid to the king for the debt. That was the custom in those days. Then the man fell down on his knees before the king and begged him to be patient until he could repay the money and the king was sorry for him, and was kind—he forgave him the entire debt!

"But that same man went out and found another man who owed him only a few dollars. He caught him by the throat and said, 'Pay me what you owe me!' The man fell down at his feet and begged, 'Have patience with me and I will pay back everything I owe you.' But the first man wouldn't wait; he had him arrested and thrown into jail, to be kept there until he paid.

"When the king heard about this, he summoned the first man. 'How low can a man get?' he demanded. 'I forgave you all that huge debt just because you asked me to, and shouldn't you have pitied that other fellow just as I pitied you?' And the angry king sent him away to be punished until he paid back all he owed."

In this story, the king means God, and the man who owed so much means us, because we have sinned so often against God. And God will punish us if we don't forgive others, just as the king in the story punished the man who wouldn't forgive.

As Jesus and his disciples traveled to Jerusalem, he sent

two of them on ahead to find somewhere to stay for the night. They came to a village and asked where they could stay, but the men of the village told them to go away, for they hated all Jews.

When James and John heard what had happened they were very angry, and asked Jesus to let them ask God to send down fire from heaven to destroy the entire city. Jesus wasn't at all happy with James and John for talking like that. "I didn't come to destroy lives, but to save them," he said. So he and his disciples went on to another village.

As they were walking along, ten lepers came to meet Jesus. They stood at a distance and shouted, "Jesus, Master, have mercy on us."

When Jesus heard them shouting to him, he called back to them. "Go and show yourselves to the priest." For if lepers got well, they went to the priest to examine them, to say they were healed.

And as these ten men were going to the priest's house, they were healed. But only one of them came back to thank Jesus for making him well.

STORY 163

THE GOOD SAMARITAN
LUKE 10, 11; JOHN 8

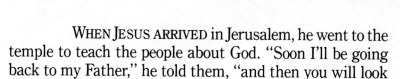

WHEN JESUS ARRIVED in Jerusalem, he went to the temple to teach the people about God. "Soon I'll be going back to my Father," he told them, "and then you will look

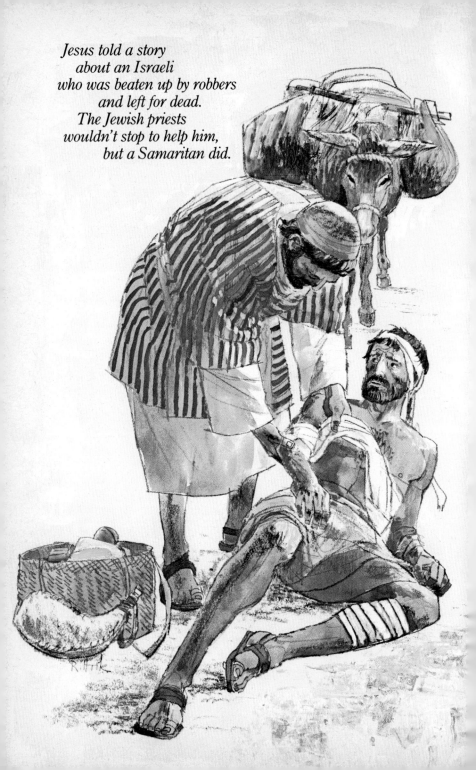

Jesus told a story
about an Israeli
who was beaten up by robbers
and left for dead.
The Jewish priests
wouldn't stop to help him,
but a Samaritan did.

for me but won't be able to find me. And you can't go where I am going because you refuse to believe that I am the Son of God. So you will die without having your sins forgiven. But if anyone believes me, he will never really die."

Jesus meant that those who trust him will have eternal life after death. But the Jews thought he was saying that they would never die at all. "Abraham died," they said, "and the prophets died, and yet you say that if a man believes you, he will never die! Are you greater than Abraham and the prophets?"

Jesus replied that Abraham knew about him and his coming to earth, and believed and trusted him.

"Of course!" the Jewish leaders sneered. "Why, you aren't even fifty years old—how could you have known Abraham?"

Jesus told them that he had been alive in heaven before Abraham was born. This made them so angry that they picked up stones to throw at him and kill him, but he just walked away.

Another day while he was teaching the people, a lawyer asked him this question: "Master, what must I do to be saved?"

"What does God's law say?" Jesus asked him.

The lawyer replied that the Bible told him to love God and his neighbors.

"Right!" Jesus replied. "Do that and you will be saved!"

"But who is my neighbor?" the lawyer asked.

Jesus answered by telling him this story: "A man was traveling from Jerusalem to Jericho, but some robbers stopped him and stole his clothing and beat him up. He was seriously wounded, and the robbers left him half dead beside the road. While he lay there on the ground, too weak to get up, a Jewish priest went by. He was a minister and a teacher of God's law, but instead of being kind to the wounded man, he crossed over to the other side of the road and went on, pretending he didn't see the man lying there. Next, a Levite came along (Levites were the men who helped people worship at the temple) but when he saw the man, he too went right on without trying to help him.

"But then, a Samaritan came by. The Jews hated the Samaritans so it wouldn't be surprising if this Samaritan had refused to help the wounded Jew. But when he saw him he pitied him, and pulling out his first aid kit, bandaged up his wounds, and put medicine on them. Then he helped him onto the back of his donkey, and took him to an inn and paid the man's bill.

"Which of these three men was a neighbor to the wounded man?" Jesus asked the lawyer.

"The one who helped him," the lawyer replied.

Then Jesus told him, "Go and do the same to everyone who needs your help." Jesus meant that people who say they love God must prove it by being kind to others.

Jesus now went out to the village of Bethany, a little way from Jerusalem, to visit two sisters named Martha and Mary and their brother Lazarus. When Jesus arrived, Mary sat at his feet to listen to him talking about the way to heaven. But Martha kept on working in the kitchen and was angry with her sister for not helping. She said to Jesus, "Sir, don't you even care that Mary has left all the work for me to do? Tell her to come and help me."

But Jesus said, "Martha, Martha, you get upset so easily. Only one thing is important and Mary has chosen it. And I don't think I should tell her not to." Mary had chosen to listen to Jesus, the very most important thing that any of us can ever do.

Jesus now taught his disciples how to pray, giving them this sample prayer: "Our Father in heaven, may your name be reverenced by everyone. May your kingdom come soon.

Martha is upset!
She wants Mary to come and help her make dinner
instead of just sitting there listening to Jesus.
But Mary was doing
the best thing.

May your will be done on earth as it is in heaven. Give us this day our daily bread, and forgive us our sins just as we forgive those who sin against us. And lead us not into temptation but deliver us from evil. For yours is the kingdom, and the power, and the glory forever, Amen."

JESUS MAKES BLIND EYES SEE
JOHN 9

Now JESUS CHOSE seventy more disciples besides the first twelve, and sent them out two by two into every city and town where he himself expected to follow later. He told them to heal the sick and to preach the Good News to people everywhere.

Afterwards they returned to him full of joy because they had been able to do wonderful miracles in his name. But he told them not to be glad just because they had power to do miracles, but because their names are written down among those whose sins are forgiven, and who will go to heaven when they die.

As he left the temple, he saw a man who had been blind ever since he was born. Jesus spat on the ground and made clay of the spittle, and put it on the eyes of the blind man and said to him, "Go and wash in the pool of Siloam."

He did, and when he came back, he could see! Then his neighbors and many others who knew him when he was blind, asked, "Isn't this the blind beggar?"

Some said, "Yes," and others, "No, he just looks like him."

But the man said, "Yes, I'm the blind beggar, but now I can see!"

"Wonderful!" they exclaimed. "Whatever happened?"

"A man called Jesus made clay and put it on my eyes, and told me to go and wash it off in the pool of Siloam, and I did, and suddenly I could see," he explained.

"Where is Jesus?" the neighbors asked.

"I don't know," the man replied.

Then they brought the man to the Jewish leaders. They, too, wanted to know how he had been healed.

"Jesus put clay on my eyes, and I washed it off and now I can see," he explained.

Then some of the leaders said, "The man who cured you can't be a good man, because he did it on the Sabbath day!" They meant that God had told his people not to work on the Sabbath, and they were calling healing work! Then they asked the man what he thought of Jesus.

"I think he must be a prophet," he told them.

But these Jewish leaders wouldn't believe he had been blind. Finally they called in his parents and asked them, "Is this your son? Was he born blind? Then how can he see now?"

"Yes," they said, "he's our son, and was born blind, but we don't know what happened. He's old enough to speak for himself, so ask him." The parents were afraid to say that it was Jesus who had cured their son, because the Jewish leaders had threatened to hurt anyone who said Jesus was the Savior.

Then the leaders talked to the man again and told him,

"God healed you, not that fellow who put clay on your eyes, for we know he is a sinner."

"I don't know whether he is a sinner or not," the man replied, *"but one thing I do know: I used to be blind, and now I see!"*

"What did he do to you?" they asked him again.

Then the man got mad. "I told you once," he snapped. "Why don't you listen? Why do you want to hear it again? Do you want to be his disciples too?"

They were furious. "You are his disciple, but we are Moses' disciples. We know that God sent Moses, but as for this fellow, we don't know who sent him," they sneered.

"How very strange!" the man replied. "Here's a man who can cure blind people, and yet you don't know who he is! Since the beginning of the world such a thing has never been heard of before, that a man born blind can see. If God didn't send this man, he couldn't have cured me."

"You dirty bum," they snarled. "Are you trying to teach *us*?" And they threw him out of their church, the Jewish synagogue, and told him never to come back again.

When Jesus heard what had happened, he found the man and asked him, "Do you believe in the Son of God?"

"I want to," the man answered. "Who is he?"

"He is the person talking with you!" Jesus replied.

"Lord, I believe," the man said, and worshiped him.

ANOTHER VICTORY OVER DEATH

JOHN 10, 11

ANOTHER TIME JESUS said to his disciples, "I am the good shepherd and I know my sheep." He meant that he was like a shepherd to his disciples, and they were like his flock of sheep. In that country the shepherd walked ahead of his sheep, and they followed him. Each sheep had its own name and knew its own shepherd's voice, and came when he called it. The shepherd stayed with his sheep night and day to keep them from being lost, and to guard them from wild animals. Yes, Jesus is our shepherd and is always with us to guard us from Satan and to show us the way to heaven.

Jesus now went again to the temple, and the Jewish leaders crowded around him and demanded, "If you are the Son of God, why don't you say so?"

Jesus replied, "I have, but you wouldn't believe me because you are not my sheep. My sheep listen to my voice and follow me, and I give them eternal life. They will never be lost—no one can ever take them away from me. My Father gave them to me, and no one can kidnap them. My Father and I are one." Jesus meant that he is God—not God the Father, but God the Son. He is as good and as great as God the Father, and he is to be loved and worshiped as such.

About that time Lazarus, Mary and Martha's brother,

became ill. His sisters sent a message to Jesus to tell him about it. Jesus loved Lazarus, Martha, and Mary very much, but when he heard of Lazarus' serious sickness, he didn't go at once to help them, but stayed where he was for two more days.

Then he said to his disciples, "Now, let's go to Bethany, for Lazarus is asleep and I will go and waken him." Jesus meant that Lazarus was dead, and that he was going to bring him back to life again. But his disciples thought he meant Lazarus was resting.

Then Jesus told them plainly, "Lazarus is dead."

Bethany is about two miles away from Jerusalem, and many of the Jewish leaders had gone there to be with Martha and Mary, to try to comfort them in their sorrow. When Martha heard that Jesus had arrived, she went out to meet him, but Mary stayed in the house.

Martha said to him, "Sir, if you had been here, my brother wouldn't have died. But I know that even now whatever you ask of God will be given to you."

Jesus said to her, "Your brother will live again."

"Yes, of course," Martha replied, "—at the Judgment Day."

Then Martha went back to the house and told Mary that Jesus had arrived and wanted to see her. So Mary ran out to where he was, and knelt down at his feet and said, "Lord, if you had been here, my brother wouldn't have died."

When Jesus saw her crying, and the Jewish leaders crying too, he was angry because they didn't think he could

Jesus said, "My sheep listen to my voice and follow me, and I give them eternal life. They will never be lost—no one can ever take them away from me."

help them. "Where have you buried Lazarus?" Jesus asked them.

"Sir, come and see," they replied.

Then Jesus wept.

"See how he loved him," the Jews said. And some of them asked, "Couldn't this man who opens the eyes of blind men have saved Lazarus from dying?"

Lazarus' body had been placed in a cave with a stone rolled across in front of it, to seal it.

"Take away the stone," Jesus said.

But Martha objected. "By this time his body has begun to decay," she protested, "for he has been dead four days. The smell will be terrible."

"Didn't I tell you that if you would only believe in me, you would see how great God's power is?" Jesus asked.

Then they took away the stone and Jesus shouted, "Lazarus, come out!" And he came out, wrapped up in the sheet he had been buried in. "Unwrap him," Jesus told them, and they did.

When the Jewish leaders who had come to visit Martha and Mary saw this great miracle, many of them finally believed in Jesus. But some went to the Pharisees and told them what they had seen.

The Pharisees and chief priests were terribly disturbed and called a meeting to discuss it. "What shall we do?" they said. "There is no arguing with the fact that this man Jesus does wonderful miracles. But if we let him alone, everyone will believe he is God's Son and make him their king; and then the Romans will be angry, and come and destroy our government."

So from then on the Jewish leaders began plotting how to get rid of him by killing him.

*Lazarus was dead
and buried in a cave
for four days.
But Jesus stood outside the cave
and told him to come back to life, and he did!*

R. Hook

THE RUNAWAY BOY
LUKE 15

ONE SABBATH DAY when Jesus was teaching in one of the Jewish churches, a woman was there who had been bent over for eighteen years and couldn't straighten herself up. When Jesus saw her he called her over to him and said to her, "Ma'am, you are healed!" Then he laid his hands on her, and immediately she straightened up. How she praised God, for she was well!

But the leader of the church was angry because Jesus had healed her on the Sabbath day. He said that this was wrong because people shouldn't work on the Sabbath, and healing someone was work. He said to the people, "There are six days for working; if any of you want to be healed, come some other day than on the Sabbath."

Jesus was angry. "You hypocrite," he told the man, "don't you feed and water your donkeys and cows on the Sabbath? If it is right to care for animals on the Sabbath, isn't it right to heal a woman on the Sabbath who has been suffering for eighteen years?"

Then the Jewish leader was ashamed, and the people were glad because of the miracles Jesus did.

When some tax collectors, who cheated people whenever they could, came to hear him, the Jewish leaders were disgusted. "Why does Jesus act kindly towards these bad men, and even eat with them?" they asked.

This was Jesus' reply: "If you have a hundred sheep and lose one of them, don't you leave all the others and hunt for the one that is lost? And when you find it, you take it on your shoulders and carry it home rejoicing. And when you get home, you tell all your neighbors and friends, and they rejoice with you, for you have found your lost sheep. Well, that's the way it is with these cheaters. I have come to save them too—I haven't come just to save good people."

Then he told them this story: "A man had two sons. The younger one said to him, 'Father, give me my share of the money you are planning to divide up among your sons.' So his father did, and soon afterwards this younger son took the money and went away to a distant country, and spent it all doing all sorts of bad things.

"When the money was gone, there was a great famine in that land, and he began to be very hungry. Then he hired himself out to a man who sent him into his fields to feed pigs. He was so hungry he wanted to eat the husks the pigs ate, but of course he couldn't digest them, so he went hungry instead.

"Finally he said to himself, 'At home even the servants have plenty to eat, while I am here starving. I'll go to my father and tell him, "Father, I have sinned against God and you, and don't deserve to be called your son any more; just let me be one of your hired servants."'

"So he returned to his father. And while he was still far away, his father saw him and ran out to meet him and threw his arms around him and kissed him. Then his son began his speech: 'Father,' he said, 'I have sinned against God and you, and don't deserve to be called your son any more . . .'

"But his father said to the servants, 'Bring out my best suit for him, and get him some shoes, and get the finest calf and kill it and let's have a party; for this son of mine was lost and is found.' So they had a big dinner to celebrate his son's return.

"When the older son returned home that evening from working out in the fields, he heard the music and dancing and called one of the servants, and asked him what was going on.

"'Your brother's back!' the servant told him, 'and your father has killed the best calf for a big party because he is back safe and sound.'

"But the older son was angry and wouldn't go in. His father came out and begged him.

"'Look,' he told his father, 'I've worked hard for you all my life, and in all that time I've never disobeyed your instructions, yet you never once gave a party for me and my friends. But as soon as this son returns after throwing away your money and doing all sorts of bad things, you kill the best calf on the farm for him.'

"The father replied, 'My son, I've always loved you dearly, and everything I have is yours. But it is right that we should be happy, for this brother of yours left us and has come home again; he was lost and is found.'"

By using this story Jesus was telling the proud Jewish leaders—who hated him for preaching to sinners—that God loved those sinners and was willing to forgive them, and was willing to have them as his children if they would only stop being bad and start obeying him.

Another story Jesus told was about a boy
who ran away from home
and was very bad,
but when he
finally came home,
his father
loved him
anyway.

JESUS LOVES CHILDREN

MATTHEW 19; MARK 10; LUKE 16, 18

ANOTHER time he told a story to those who love money and spend their time enjoying themselves instead of obeying God.

"There was a rich man," he said, "who dressed in beautiful clothes, and ate only the best foods. And there was a beggar named Lazarus, who was sick and covered with sores. Because he was so poor he had very little to eat, and his friends carried him to the rich man's gate and left him there to beg for the scraps from the rich man's table. Even the dogs seemed to pity him, for they came and licked his sores.

"The beggar died, and was carried to heaven by the angels. He wasn't poor there, for he ate with Abraham! Then the rich man died too, but he went where the bad people go. There, being punished for his sins, he looked up and saw Abraham and Lazarus far away. 'Father Abraham!' he shouted, 'have pity on me and send Lazarus to dip the tip of his finger in water to cool my tongue; for I am tormented in these flames.'

"But Abraham said to him, 'Remember that in your

"Love" is the best title for this picture. Jesus loves little children. No one can get into God's kingdom without being like a child.

498

lifetime you had everything and Lazarus had nothing, but now he is happy and you are sad. And besides there is a great gulf between us, so no one can come and help you, and you can't come to us.'

"Then the rich man said, 'Then please send Lazarus to my five brothers at home, to tell them to repent and obey God, so that when they die they won't come to this dreadful place.'

"Abraham replied, 'The Bible already tells them that.'

"But the rich man said, 'No, Father Abraham, that isn't enough. But if someone returns from the dead and tells them, then they will surely repent.'

"Abraham replied, 'If they won't listen to what God says to them in the Bible, they won't obey him even if someone rises from the dead.'" (Afterwards Jesus rose from the dead, but even so, few people listened to him.)

Then Jesus told a story to those who thought themselves better than others. He said, "Two men went up to the temple to pray. One was a proud Jewish leader and the other was a cheating tax collector. The Jewish leader stood where everyone would see him and prayed, 'God, thank you that I am better than other men, and especially that I am better than that bad tax collector over there. For I fast twice each week, and give the church a tenth of all I earn.'

"But the tax collector, who knew how bad he was, and was sorry for it, stood where he hoped no one would notice him, and bowed his head and beat upon his breast in great sadness, saying, 'God, be merciful to me, a sinner.'"

Then Jesus said a surprising thing about the two men.

A blind man, Bartimaeus, cried out, "Jesus, son of David, have mercy on me!" Jesus had mercy on him, and healed him. Bartimaeus could see!

He said that the cheating tax collector went home forgiven, while the Jewish leader didn't! "Everyone who is proud will be brought low," Jesus said, "but those who are humble and confess their sins will be honored."

Once when some mothers brought their little children to Jesus so he could put his hands on them and bless them, his disciples shooed them away. But Jesus didn't like this. "Let the little children come to me," he said. "Don't tell them not to, for little children are in the kingdom of heaven." He meant that only those who are humble and loving like little children, will ever get into his kingdom. Then he took the children in his arms and placed his hands on them and blessed them.

One day he took the twelve disciples aside and told them that the time had come to go to Jerusalem, and when they got there everything the prophets had said about him would happen: he would be laughed at, and whipped, and spat upon, and nailed to a cross, and killed; and the third day he would come back to life again.

But the disciples expected him to be crowned king of the Jews soon, so they couldn't understand what he was talking about.

JESUS RIDES A COLT

MATTHEW 20, 21; MARK 10, 11; LUKE 18, 19

WHEN JESUS ARRIVED in the city of Jericho, on the way to Jerusalem, the usual crowds pushed along behind him. A blind man, Bartimaeus, was sitting beside the road, begging, and when he heard the commotion he asked what was happening—what was all the noise and excitement about?

"Jesus of Nazareth is coming," someone told him.

As soon as he heard this he began to shout, "Jesus, son of David, have mercy on me!"

"Stop making such a racket," everyone told him.

But he just shouted louder, "Son of David, have mercy on me!"

Jesus stopped in the road and told Bartimaeus to come to him.

"He's calling for you!" the blind man was told. So he jumped up, tossed aside his old coat and went over towards where Jesus was waiting.

Jesus asked him, "What do you want me to do for you?"

"Sir, I want to see," the blind man answered.

"All right," Jesus told him, "because you have faith, you are well!" And immediately he could see! Then he followed Jesus down the road, praising God for the mighty miracle that had been done to him.

In Jericho there was a man named Zacchaeus who was

in charge of collecting taxes in that city, and because he cheated so much, he was very rich. As Jesus passed through the streets of the city, Zacchaeus tried to see him, but couldn't because of the crowd, for he was too short. So he ran on ahead, climbed up into a sycamore tree, and waited for Jesus to pass by.

When Jesus came along the road past the tree, he stopped and looked up into the branches and saw Zacchaeus sitting there. "Come on down, Zacchaeus," Jesus told him, "for I am going to your house for dinner!" So Zacchaeus happily took Jesus with him.

As I have already said, Zacchaeus and the other tax collectors were unfair, cruel men. They forced the people to give them more money than was right. But when Jesus came to Zacchaeus' home, Zacchaeus became very sorry for what he had done. He stood up before all the people and told Jesus that he would stop being unfair, and from then on he would be kind to the poor and would give them half of his money. And if he had taken more money than he should, he would give back four times as much as he had taken.

When Jesus saw that Zacchaeus was sorry and was ready to do whatever Jesus told him to, he said that all of Zacchaeus' sins were forgiven. But the Jewish leaders said Jesus shouldn't eat with a tax collector because he was a sinner. Jesus replied that he had come into the world on purpose to be among sinners, to teach them to repent and to save them from being punished for their sins.

Passover was now near (it was a happy time, a little bit like Christmas is to us) and many people went to Jerusalem

Zacchaeus, a tax collector with a bad reputation, climbed a tree to see Jesus. Jesus went home with him to have supper.

to celebrate it. Everyone wanted to see Jesus, and as they stood around in the courts of the temple they asked each other, "Do you think he will come?" For the Jewish leaders were saying that if anyone knew where Jesus was, he must tell them so they could have him arrested and killed.

Six days before the Passover, Jesus came to Bethany where Lazarus lived. Lazarus, you remember, was the man Jesus had brought back to life again after he was dead.

Then Jesus left Bethany to go to Jerusalem. When he had come as far as the Mount of Olives he sent two of his disciples to a nearby village.

"You'll see a colt tied there that has never been ridden," he said. (A colt is a baby horse.) "Untie him, and bring him to me. If anyone asks why you are taking the colt, just say, 'Because the Lord needs him,' and they will let you have him."

The two disciples found the colt just as Jesus had said. And as they were untying him, the owners asked, "What are you doing there, untying that colt?"

"The Lord needs him," the disciples replied. Then the owners let them have the colt for Jesus to ride on. They brought him to Jesus, and the disciples threw their coats across his back and Jesus sat on him.

As he rode the colt towards Jerusalem, a great crowd spread their coats on the road in front of him, while others cut down branches from the trees and made a green carpet for him to ride over. They did this to honor him, for that is what people used to do when a king rode through their streets. Then the crowd surrounding him began shouting, "Praise God for sending us a king!"

Jesus rode into Jerusalem on a donkey colt, and everyone celebrated. They waved palm branches and shouted, "Praise God for sending us a king!"

R. & F. Hook

But Jesus knew they didn't really love him, and that in a few days they would be shouting, "Crucify him!"

Upon his arrival in Jerusalem, Jesus went up to the temple and began healing the blind and the lame who were brought to him there. But the Jewish leaders were angry and jealous because some school children who were visiting the temple began praising Jesus for his wonderful miracles.

STORY 169

THE TWO MOST IMPORTANT COMMANDMENTS

MATTHEW 21, 22; MARK 11, 12; LUKE 20, 21

JESUS TOLD the people this story:

"There was a farmer who planted a vineyard and built a wall around it and built a guard tower to protect it from robbers. He leased it to a man who promised to give him part of the grapes when they were ripe. Then the owner went away to a distant country.

"When the grapes were ripe he sent someone to collect his share of the crop. But the man who was leasing the farm beat him up and scared him away. Then the owner sent someone else to collect his share, but the man on the farm threw stones at him and wounded him in the head, seriously injuring him. Afterwards the owner sent still other men to collect the rent for him, but some were beaten

508

up and others killed. The owner sent his only son, for he thought, 'They won't dare harm my son.'

"But when the tenant saw the owner's son coming, he said to his friends, 'That boy is going to own the vineyard someday; come on, let's kill him and then it will all be ours!' So they caught him and dragged him out of the vineyard and killed him."

Jesus asked, "When the owner of the vineyard returns, what will he do to those men?"

The people answered, "He will kill them and lease his vineyard to someone who will give him his proper share of the grapes."

In this story the owner of the vineyard means God, and the wicked man leasing the farm means the Jewish leaders. God chose them to be his people, and he gave them the land of Canaan. He taught them his laws, and they promised to obey him. But afterwards they turned against God and persecuted and killed his prophets whom he sent to warn and persuade them. Then at last God sent his only son, Jesus. And now in a few days they were going to kill him just as the wicked farmers had killed the son of the owner of the vineyard.

When the Jewish leaders heard this story, they knew that Jesus was talking about them. They were very angry and wanted all the more to kill him.

Then Jesus told the people another story. "A king's son was getting married," he said, "and there was a big party to celebrate the happy occasion. But the people he invited to the party wouldn't come. So he sent for them again. 'My dinner is ready,' he said. 'Come to the marriage.'

"But some turned away and wouldn't listen, and others tortured and killed his messengers. When the king heard about it he was very angry, and sent his soldiers to destroy those murderers and burn up their city.

"Then the king said to his friends, 'The wedding dinner is ready, but I won't let those I first invited come. Go out into the streets and lanes and invite everyone you see to come to the marriage.' So the messengers brought as many people as they could.

"The king gave a gift to each guest—a new outfit of clothes! And he required that the guests wear these clothes at the wedding dinner. But when the king went into the banquet room where the dinner was being served, he noticed a man who wasn't following instructions, for he had on his regular clothing.

"'Friend,' the king asked, 'why no wedding clothes?' And the man was silent, for he had refused to take them when they were offered to him.

"Then the king was angry and said to his servants, 'Bind him hand and foot and take him away, and throw him into the dark dungeon where people are kept who will not obey me.'"

In this story, the king means God, and the king's son means Jesus. Those who were first invited to the party and wouldn't come were the Jews, because they were the first to be asked to believe in Jesus, but many of them wouldn't do it. The people who were invited to the dinner afterwards are the people of other nations who believe Jesus. The man without the wedding clothes is anyone who pretends to believe and to accept God's invitation, but won't obey him. Such people may seem to obey God's Word, and might fool others, but God sees their hearts. We cannot hide our hearts from him, even for a moment.

One of the Jewish religion teachers now came to Jesus and asked him this question: "Master, which is the greatest of God's commandments?"

Jesus answered, "You must deeply love the Lord your God. This is the first and greatest commandment. And the

510

next most important commandment is, you must love your neighbor as yourself." Jesus said that all the other commandments in the Bible came from these two. If we obey these two great laws of God, we will be obeying all the other laws too; we will be doing everything the Bible tells us to.

STORIES ABOUT HEAVEN
MATTHEW 25

JESUS SAID always to be ready for the Judgment Day because no one knew when it would come. Then he told a story about ten girls at a wedding reception. In that country when a man was married, he brought his bride home after supper, and his friends would go out with their lamps to meet them and welcome them to their new home. That is what these ten girls planned to do. They lit their lamps and were ready, but because the bridegroom and the bride didn't come right away, the girls sat down to wait, and fell asleep. Five of them had been wise enough to bring extra oil so that if their lamps went out, they could fill them again. But five were foolish, and didn't have any extra oil.

Around midnight there was a shout, "Here comes the bridegroom! Go out and meet him." Then the girls woke up, but the lamps of five of them had gone out—the five who hadn't brought extra oil along. They said to the other girls, "Please give us some of your oil."

But the others replied, "We don't have enough. Some of the shops are still open—go and buy some."

While they were gone, the bridegroom came, and all those who were ready went in with him to the reception and the door was locked. When the other girls came back they knocked loudly at the door. "Sir, open to us," they called. But the bridegroom refused to let them in.

In this parable the bridegroom means Jesus coming back to earth. The ten girls mean all of us who call ourselves his disciples, and who want to meet him. Will we be ready? Do we really love him and obey him? Or have we forgotten to be ready when he comes?

Jesus then told his disciples another story, this time about a man who was preparing for a trip to a distant country. Before he went, he gave money to his servants and told them to use it to earn more for him while he was away. He gave $5,000 to one servant, $2,000 to another, and only $1,000 to the third.

The servant who had the $5,000 used it to buy things, and then he sold them for more than they cost him. He kept buying and selling like that until finally he had twice as much money as he started with! The servant with $2,000 did the same, until he had earned $2,000 more. But the servant with the $1,000 didn't use it. He hid it instead.

After a long time the master came back and called in his servants to find out how much they had earned with his money.

The servant with the $5,000 said, "See, I have earned $5,000 more." His master was pleased and paid him well for his fine service.

Then the servant with the $2,000 came and reported,

512

One of these girls
brought enough oil
for her lamp,
but the other one didn't.
The girl with enough oil
would be ready to meet
the bridegroom.

"See, I have earned $2,000 more." And the master was pleased and gave him a good reward.

Then the servant with the $1,000 came. "Master," he said, "I know how unfair you are and that you take what isn't yours. I knew you would take away all the money I earned, so I didn't earn any! Here is your money again, just what you gave me."

The master was angry. "You disobedient, lazy fellow," he said, "if I take all your profits, that is no excuse for your being idle while I was gone."

Then he said to his other servants, as he took back the $1,000, "He doesn't get even a tiny reward!"

In this story, the master means Christ. He has gone to heaven to stay for a while—we don't know how long—but he is coming back. The servants are all of us left here in this world to work for him. The money means whatever he has given us to work with. Some of us have many abilities and opportunities and some of us have few, but each of us has some ability God can use. When Jesus comes again, he will reward those who have used their talents well, but he will punish those who have not used them, or who have used them for themselves.

MARY SHOWS HER LOVE FOR JESUS
MATTHEW 25, 26; MARK 14; LUKE 22; JOHN 12

ONE DAY JESUS talked to his disciples about what would happen on the Judgment Day. He told them that he will come back to earth in all his glory at that time, and all the holy angels will be with him. Then he will sit on his throne, and the dead of all nations will rise from their graves and stand before him to be judged. And he will separate the righteous from the wicked, as a shepherd separates his sheep from the goats. He will place those who are good at his right hand, but those who are bad at his left.

Then he will say to those on his right hand, "Come, children of my Father, into the kingdom which has been waiting for you from the beginning of the world. For when I was hungry you gave me food; when I was thirsty you gave me a drink; when I was poor and naked you clothed me; when I was sick you visited me; when I was in prison you came to me and comforted me."

Then those who are good will say to him, "Lord, when did we ever see you hungry and feed you, or thirsty and give you a drink? When did we ever see you poor and naked, and clothe you? Or sick, or in prison, and comfort you?"

And Jesus will reply, "Whenever you did these things to any poor and suffering person who loved me, it was the same as if you did it to me."

515

Then he will turn to the wicked and say, "Go away; you are cursed, for I was hungry but you didn't feed me; I was thirsty but you gave me nothing to drink; I was naked but you didn't give me any clothes; I was sick and in prison but you didn't visit me."

They then will answer, "Lord, when did we ever see you hungry, or thirsty, or naked, or sick, or in prison, and not help you?"

And he will answer them, "When you didn't do it to the poor and the suffering people who love me, it was the same as if you didn't do it to me." They will be sent away into everlasting punishment, but the righteous to eternal life.

Then Jesus told his disciples that in two days, at the celebration, he would be betrayed and killed. For the chief priests were anxious to arrest him and kill him. "But we can't do it during the holiday when all the people are around," they said, "or there will be a riot."

Jesus ate supper that night at Bethany with Mary, Martha, and Lazarus.

While he was there, Mary took a bottle of very rare, expensive perfume and poured it over Jesus' feet and wiped them with her hair, and the house was filled with the fragrance.

But Judas Iscariot, the disciple who later betrayed him, complained about this. "Why wasn't this perfume sold, and the money given to the poor?" he growled. Judas didn't really care what happened to the poor, but he said this because he was the disciples' treasurer and carried their money, and often stole some of it.

But Jesus told him, "Let her alone. Why find fault with her? She has done a good thing. You will always have the poor with you, and whenever you want to you can do them good, but you will not always have me."

Jesus told his disciples that wherever the Good News

about him was preached throughout the whole world, this thing that Mary had done to him would be talked about.

Then Judas Iscariot went to the chief priests and asked them, "How much will you give me if I take you to Jesus when he is alone, so that you can arrest him quietly?"

They gladly promised him thirty pieces of silver. From that time on Judas was on the lookout for a time when Jesus would be away from the crowds, so that the chief priests could come and arrest him without starting a riot.

STORY 172

JESUS WASHES THE DISCIPLES' FEET
JOHN 13

THE PASSOVER DAY finally came. This was a national Jewish holiday to celebrate the night so long before when the Israelis had escaped from Egypt. The angel of death had killed all the oldest boys in each Egyptian family that night, but he had passed over the houses where there was lamb's blood on the door. It was because the angel passed over them that the celebration was called the Passover.

Each year during the Passover celebration, every Israeli family took a lamb to the temple and killed it as a sacrifice

517

Only slaves washed people's feet in Bible times. Yet Jesus gladly washed his disciples' feet. The greatest one of all became the servant of all.

before the altar. Then the priests burned its fat on the altar, but the rest of the lamb was taken home, where it was roasted, and the family ate it that night, just as the Israelites had done so many hundreds of years before when they left Egypt.

The disciples asked Jesus where they should go to roast and eat the lamb, since Jesus had no home in Jerusalem—or anywhere else.

"Go into Jerusalem," he told them, "and as you enter the city you will see a man carrying a pitcher of water. Follow him into the house where he is going, and say to the man who lives there, 'The Master wants you to show us the room you have prepared for us.' He will take you upstairs to a large room all set up for you. Prepare the lamb there, for that is where we will eat it."

The disciples did as Jesus said, and sure enough, they met a man with a pitcher, and he took them to the room Jesus had told them about. There they prepared the lamb.

In the evening Jesus arrived with his other apostles and they all sat down for the supper. "I have wanted very much to eat this Passover supper with you before I die," he told them, "for I will not again eat a lamb that has been sacrificed until I myself am sacrificed for the sins of the people."

But the apostles didn't understand him. They didn't know what he was talking about. They still thought he was going to become king of the Jews, and that the time for this was very near.

They began arguing among themselves, as they had before, as to which of them would be greatest in the kingdom. Then Jesus told them, "Here in this world the rulers and the wealthy are the greatest, but with you it is different. For whichever of you is the humblest will be the greatest. The one who wants to be the leader must be the servant of all!"

Then Jesus asked them which was greater, the master who ate at the table, or the servant who waited on him as he ate? They said it was the master. Then Jesus pointed out to them that he was their servant, even though he was their master; and they should serve each other as he served them. Then he demonstrated what he meant:

He got up from the table, wrapped a towel around his waist, poured water into a basin, and began to wash their feet and wipe them with the towel. When he came to Peter, Peter didn't want him to do it, for he didn't want Jesus to act like his servant. Jesus told him, "You don't understand now why I am doing it, but you will later."

"No," Peter told him, "you shall never wash my feet."

Jesus replied, "If I don't, you can't be my disciple!"

"Then, Lord, don't wash just my feet, but my hands and my head too!" Peter exclaimed.

But Jesus told him, "When you have had a bath, it is only necessary to rewash the feet!"

After he had washed their feet and returned to the table again, he said to them, "Do you know what I have done to you? You call me Master and Lord, and that is correct, for I am. If I, then, your Lord and Master, have washed your feet, you ought to wash each other's feet, for you should follow my example; you should do as I have done to you." He meant that we should help each other at all times.

THE LAST SUPPER

MATTHEW 26; MARK 14; LUKE 22; JOHN 13, 14

AS THEY ATE the Passover supper Jesus said to them, "One of you sitting here eating with me will betray me." He meant that one of his disciples would tell the Jewish leaders where he was, so that they could come and arrest him when the people weren't around to protect him from them.

The disciples were very much surprised and sad when they heard this. They looked at each other, wondering which one he was talking about. Peter motioned to the disciple sitting next to Jesus to find out who it was that Jesus meant. So he asked Jesus, "Lord, who is it who will do such a terrible thing?"

"It is the one I give this piece of bread to when I have dipped it in the dish," Jesus replied. Then he gave it to Judas Iscariot. After that Satan entered into Judas, and Jesus said to him, "What you are going to do, do quickly."

No one at the table knew what Jesus meant by these words. Some of them thought he was telling Judas to go and buy things they needed, or else to go and give something to the poor. Then Judas went out into the night. After he was gone, Jesus said to them, "I will be with you only a little while longer. Before I leave you, I want to give you this new commandment: *Love one another as I have loved you. Everyone will know that you are my disciples by your love for each other.*"

As they were eating, Jesus took a small loaf of bread and blessed it, and broke it apart and gave it to his disciples to eat. "This is my body, broken for you," he told them. He meant that his body was soon to be broken and crucified on the cross as a sacrifice to God for them.

Then he thanked God for the wine and gave it to them, and they all drank some of it. "This wine," he said, "is my blood given to God so that he will forgive your sins." For soon his own blood would flow like the blood from the sacrifices at the altar. Then he told his disciples to meet together often, after he was gone, and when they came together they should eat some bread and drink some wine as they had just done, to remember him until he returns.

This was the first Lord's Supper, or Communion, or the Breaking of Bread, as we sometimes call it. One of the reasons for doing this is to make us think of how our Savior was punished on the cross for our sins; and we repent of those sins and determine not to do them again, and we ask the Lord to help us.

As Jesus and his disciples were sitting there at the supper table, Jesus told them not to be sad about his being taken away from them. He was going to heaven, he said, to prepare homes for them. Afterwards he would come back again and take all of us who love Jesus to our new home up there with him.

Then he looked up to heaven and prayed for his disciples, and for all those who would believe in him afterwards. He prayed that they would be kept from sin, and would love one another.

Jesus is eating with his disciples for the last time. The next day he will die on the cross. He is breaking the bread for them to eat with him.

JESUS IS ARRESTED
MATTHEW 26; MARK 14; LUKE 22; JOHN 18

JESUS AND HIS APOSTLES now sang a hymn together and went out to the Mount of Olives, a short distance from Jerusalem. There they went into a garden called the Garden of Gethsemane.

"Sit here while I go and pray," Jesus told them. Then he went a little distance away and kneeled down and prayed. And now he began to be in terrible anguish as he thought about being punished for our sins and separated from God, for he knew that in a few hours he would be crucified. Great drops of blood fell like sweat from his forehead to the ground. Then an angel came to help him.

When he got up from prayer and went back to his disciples, he found them sleeping. "Asleep?" he asked. "Get up and pray so that you will not be tempted to do wrong." Then he went away and prayed again. When he came back he found them sleeping again. He went away a third time, and when he returned and they were asleep again, he told them, "Get up now, for my betrayer is near."

Judas had been watching when Jesus went to the garden. Because it was night, and because only a few of his followers were with him, Judas decided that this was the best

Jesus was in agony the night before he was crucified. He knew that he would die for the sins of the whole world. He spent the night in prayer.

time to betray his Master. So he went to the Jewish government officials and told them that Jesus was alone with his disciples in the Garden of Gethsemane. They sent a gang of men with Judas to capture Jesus.

Judas was bringing the men to the garden now, and Jesus knew it, but he didn't run. He waited for them to come because it was the time for him to die. While he was still talking with his disciples, Judas and the others arrived, carrying swords and clubs and lanterns.

"The one I kiss on the cheek is the man you want," Judas told them. "Grab him and don't let him get away."

So Judas came up to Jesus, pretending to be his friend, and greeted him with a kiss on the cheek, as is still the custom in eastern lands when men meet. Then the men grabbed Jesus and held him.

"Lord, shall we use the sword?" the disciples cried out. And Peter drew his sword, and struck a servant of the High Priest, cutting off his ear.

"Put your sword away," Jesus told him. "Don't you realize that I could pray to my Father to send thousands of angels to fight for me, and save me from death? But then how could the words of the prophets come true, which say that I am to die for the people?" Then Jesus touched the man's ear and healed it.

Turning to the men holding him, he asked, "Why the swords and clubs? If I am a thief why didn't you arrest me in the temple? I was there every day."

Then all the disciples left him and ran away into the night.

Jesus was first taken to Caiaphas, who was the High

Judas was a traitor. He brought the soldiers to arrest Jesus. Judas gave him a "friendly kiss" to show the soldiers which one was Jesus.

Priest that year. All the Jewish government officials soon gathered at the High Priest's palace and Jesus was brought before them.

Peter had followed Jesus a long way off, hoping no one would recognize him; so now he too came along to the palace, and sat down among the palace servants beside a fire they had built in the courtyard because it was cold.

A servant girl came over to him and said, "You were with Jesus of Galilee!" Peter strongly denied it, and said it wasn't so. Then he went out onto the porch. Just then he heard a rooster crow.

Another servant girl saw him there and said to the others who were standing around, "This fellow was with Jesus of Nazareth!"

Again Peter denied it. "I don't even know the man!" he said.

After a while one of the servants of the High Priest, who was a relative of the man whose ear Peter had cut off, said, "Didn't I see you with him in the Garden of Gethsemane?"

Peter denied it again. And just then he heard the rooster crow the second time, and Jesus turned around and looked at Peter.

Suddenly Peter remembered Jesus' words, "Before the cock crows twice, you will say three times that you don't even know me." And he went out and cried bitterly.

The High Priest asked Jesus about his disciples, and about what he was teaching the people.

"Why do you ask?" Jesus replied. "You already know what I teach, for you have listened to me in the temple. Nothing I teach is a secret."

One of the police officers hit him in the face for saying this. "Is that the way to talk to the High Priest?" he shouted.

"Should you strike a man for telling the truth?" Jesus asked him.

JESUS WEARS A CROWN OF THORNS

MATTHEW 26; MARK 14; LUKE 22; JOHN 18

EARLY THE NEXT morning the men who had arrested Jesus brought him before the Jewish Supreme Court. There the Jewish officials tried to get people to tell lies about Jesus, but no two of them could keep their stories straight. At last two false witnesses came who declared, "This fellow said, 'I am able to destroy the temple and build it again in three days.'"

Then the High Priest said, "I demand that you tell us whether you are the Christ, the Son of God."

Jesus answered, "I am. And I tell you this, that you will see me sitting at the right hand of God and coming back to earth again in the clouds of heaven."

Then the High Priest tore his clothes and said, "We don't need any more witnesses. You yourselves have heard the wicked thing he said—that he is the Son of God. What should his punishment be?" And everyone shouted, "Kill him."

Then they spat in his face and mocked him, and when they had blindfolded him, they struck him. "Tell us, you Christ, who hit you?" they laughed.

Now they tied him up, and the entire Supreme Court led him to Pontius Pilate, the Roman governor. "This man tells the Jews to rebel against the Romans," they lied. "He tells them not to pay taxes to the emperor, and says he is the king of the Jews."

"Are you a king?" Pilate asked him.

"Yes," Jesus replied, "but my kingdom is not of this world, for if it were, my servants would fight to save me."

Then Pilate went out and told the Court, "I find nothing wrong with this man."

But they were even more fierce, and yelled out, "Everywhere he goes he starts riots against the government, all the way from Galilee to Jerusalem."

When Pilate heard them speak of Galilee, he decided that since Jesus came from there, he would send him to Herod, the governor of Galilee, for Herod was in Jerusalem at the time.

Herod was glad of the opportunity of seeing Jesus. He had long wanted to, having heard so much about him, and he hoped to see Jesus do a miracle for him. Herod asked Jesus many questions, but Jesus remained silent as the High Priests and other Jewish leaders bitterly accused him of many sins. Herod and his soldiers now made fun of Jesus and mocked him, putting a royal purple robe on him, because he had said he was a king.

Afterwards Herod sent him back to Pilate again.

Then Pilate called together the Jewish leaders and said to them, "You have accused this man of starting riots, but I find him not guilty. Herod has also found him innocent. There is no reason at all to talk about giving him the death penalty."

Now every year, during the Passover, if any of the Jews were in prison for disobeying the Romans, the Roman governor used to set one of them free, and he let the Jews say which prisoner it should be. He did this to please them, and to make them more willing to let him rule over them.

At this time a Jew named Barabbas was in prison for murder. The people now began shouting to the governor to do as he had always done and set one of the prisoners free.

"Which one?" Pilate asked, "Barabbas or Jesus?"

While Pilate was speaking with them, his wife sent this message to him: "Don't harm that innocent man. I had a terrible nightmare about him last night."

The High Priest now persuaded the mob to demand the release of Barabbas.

"Then what shall I do with Jesus?" Pilate asked.

And everyone shouted, "Crucify him."

"But why, what has he done wrong?" Pilate asked.

"Crucify him! Crucify him!" they yelled.

When Pilate saw that he couldn't persuade them to ask him to free Jesus, he took some water and washed his hands while all the people watched, and said, "Don't ever blame me for this innocent man's death."

Then all the Jews answered, "Let the blame be on us and on our children."

But Pilate, by washing his hands, didn't rid himself of the blame. For he knew Jesus was innocent, but wouldn't let him go free. He was afraid that if he offended the Jews they might want someone else than him to be their governor, and he would lose his job. That is why he gave Jesus to them, to crucify him.

Before the Romans would crucify anyone they would whip him. He was stripped to the waist, his hands were bound to a low post or pillar in front of him so as to make him stoop forward, and while he stood in this way, he was cruelly beaten with rods or whips until his back was red with blood and open wounds. So now Pilate told his soldiers to whip Jesus in this way.

Afterwards, Pilate's soldiers made fun of him just as Herod's soldiers had. They put a purple robe on him and placed a crown of thorns upon his head. Then they bowed before him, pretending he was their king, and shouted, "Hail, King of the Jews!" And they spat on him and struck him on the head with a stick.

JESUS IS KILLED ON A CROSS

MATTHEW 27; MARK 15; LUKE 23; JOHN 18, 19

PILATE STILL HOPED the Jewish Supreme Court would finally let Jesus go, so he spoke to them again. "Once more, I tell you that I find no fault in him," he said.

Then he brought Jesus out to them, wearing the crown of thorns and the purple robe. But when the Jewish leaders saw him, they shouted again, "Crucify him! Crucify him!"

"Take him yourselves, then, and crucify him, for I find no fault in him," Pilate told them.

The Jewish leaders answered, "By our law he ought to die because he says he is the Son of God."

Now Pilate was even more afraid to put Jesus to death.

"Where were you born?" he asked Jesus. But Jesus gave him no reply.

"Do you refuse to speak to me?" Pilate demanded. "Don't you know that I have power to crucify you, and power to let you go?"

"You can only do what God will let you do," Jesus answered.

From that time Pilate tried to set him free. But Caesar, the emperor of Rome, was a jealous and cruel man and Pilate feared him. When the Jews saw that Pilate wanted to set Jesus free, they screamed out, "You are no friend of Caesar's if you free a man who claims he is a king. How will Caesar like that? What do you think he'll do to you?"

Then Pilate was afraid to let Jesus go, for fear the Jewish leaders would tell Caesar. So he gave Jesus to them to be crucified.

Then Judas Iscariot, the disciple who had betrayed Jesus, was afraid because of what he had done, and brought back to the Jewish leaders the thirty pieces of silver they had paid to him for telling them where Jesus was. "I have sinned," he said, "for I have betrayed an innocent man."

Then Judas threw down the thirty pieces of silver on the temple floor, and went away and hanged himself and died.

Then the soldiers took the purple robe from Jesus and gave him his own clothes again, and led him away to die. Jesus had to carry the heavy wooden cross up a hill outside the city, and when he stumbled, they made a man carry it whose name was Simon, who was coming in from the country. A crowd followed him out to Skull Hill or Mount Calvary, just outside the city gates, where he was to die.

There they nailed his hands and feet to the cross and crucified him. Yet in his agony he prayed for them. "Father, forgive them, for they don't know what they are doing," he pleaded. He meant that they didn't know how great their sin was in killing the Son of God, or how fearful their punishment would be. Then they gave him a mixture of gall and vinegar to drink. This was given to people who were crucified so that they wouldn't feel their awful pain quite so much. But when Jesus had tasted it, he wouldn't drink it, for he was deliberately suffering those pains for all of us. They crucified two thieves with him, one on his right side and the other on his left.

People who were crucified did not die suddenly; they lived in terrible pain for many hours, sometimes hanging on the cross for days before they died. Jesus was crucified in the morning, but hung in agony until the afternoon, while the soldiers who had crucified him sat down and watched him there. They took his clothes and divided them up among themselves, and threw dice for his coat.

Pilate told the soldiers to place this sign on the cross above Jesus' head: JESUS OF NAZARETH, THE KING OF THE JEWS. These words were read by many, for the place where he was crucified was near the city.

The people passing by felt no pity for him, but mocked him, saying, "If you are the Son of God, come down from the cross."

And one of the thieves who was crucified with him said, "If you are the Christ, save yourself and us."

But the other thief said, "Lord, remember me when you come into your kingdom."

Jesus told him, "Today you will be with me in Paradise." Jesus meant that the sins of the thief were forgiven, and as soon as he died, even that very day, his real self would go to the happy place where Jesus was going.

Jesus' mother and his disciple John were standing near the cross while Jesus died. Jesus saw them standing there and asked John to take care of his mother, since he was going to die and leave her. From that hour, John took her to his own home and cared for her just as though she were his own mother.

From twelve o'clock noon until three in the afternoon there was darkness over all the land. God sent the darkness because his Son was being killed by wicked men.

About three o'clock, Jesus called out with a loud voice, "My God, why have you forsaken me?" He said this because God seemed to have turned away from him, and it

Jesus is dying for our sins. He had been crowned with thorns and then nailed to the cross. It is noontime, but everything is growing dark because God's Son is dying.

was true. God had turned away from our sins for which Jesus was dying.

When one of the men standing there heard his cry, he ran and got a sponge and filled it with sour wine and held it up on a stick to Jesus' mouth so that he could drink it. Jesus tasted it and then cried out, "It is finished," and bowed his head and died.

When the Roman soldiers who were watching Jesus saw how he died, they were terrified, and one of them said, "Surely this man was the Son of God."

STORY 177

JESUS COMES TO LIFE AGAIN
MATTHEW 27, 28; MARK 15, 16; LUKE 23, 24; JOHN 19, 20

THE JEWISH leaders didn't want Jesus and the two robbers to be hanging on the cross the next day, for it was the Sabbath. So they asked Pilate to tell the soldiers to kill them there on their crosses, so that their bodies could be taken down and buried that day.

Pilate agreed, and told the soldiers to break their legs because this would make them die more quickly. So the soldiers broke the legs of the two thieves, but when they saw that Jesus was already dead, they didn't break his legs but instead they pierced his side with a spear, making blood and water flow out.

536

There was a garden near the place where Jesus was crucified, and in the garden there was a new burial place—a cave carved out of the rock. It belonged to a rich man named Joseph. Joseph was a disciple of Jesus, though he had never told anyone for fear of what people would say. But now after Jesus was dead he went boldly to Pilate and begged for Jesus' body, and Pilate said he could take it down and bury it. So Joseph took Jesus' body down from the cross and wrapped it in a new cloth he had bought, and laid it in the cave and rolled a huge stone across the door.

Meanwhile the Jewish leaders went to Pilate and said, "Sir, while that liar was still alive, he said, 'After three days I will rise again.' Please place a guard for the next three days at the cave where he is buried, so that his disciples can't come in the night and steal his body, and then tell everyone he has come back to life." So Pilate agreed, and soldiers were sent over to guard the cave so no one could get in and steal Jesus' body.

But two nights later the angel of the Lord came down from heaven and rolled back the stone from the cave and sat upon it. His face was as bright as lightning, and his clothes were white as snow. The soldiers trembled for fear and became as weak and helpless as dead men. Then they ran into the city, terrified.

Early the next morning, as it was getting light, Mary Magdalene and the other Mary, and Salome, came to the tomb bringing spices to embalm him, that is, to help keep his body from changing to dust. "But how can we ever roll away the stone from the door of the cave?" they were wondering; for it was *very* heavy. But when they got there, the stone was pushed aside! They went into the cave and there was an angel in a long white robe!

They were badly frightened, but the angel said to them, "Don't be afraid. Are you looking for Jesus? He isn't here;

he has come back to life again! See, that is where his body lay. Now go and tell his disciples that he is alive again and that he will meet them in Galilee."

The women ran from the cave in great fear, and yet with great gladness, and went to tell his disciples what had happened. But as they were running, Jesus met them. "Hello there!" he greeted them. They came and held him by the feet and worshiped him. "Don't be afraid," he said, "but tell my brothers—my disciples, including Peter—to go to Galilee, for I will meet them there."

When the women told the disciples what the angel had said, Peter and John ran to the cave to see for themselves. John got there first and stooped down and looked in and saw the linen sheet lying there—the one Joseph had wrapped around Jesus' body—but he didn't go inside. Then Peter arrived and went right in. So then John went in too, and finally realized that Jesus had come back to life again. Before that they hadn't understood what he meant when he had told them that he would be alive again three days after he died.

Meanwhile some of the guards reported to the Jewish leaders what had happened during the night. The Jewish leaders gave them money to get them to lie about what happened, and to say that his disciples had come during the night while they were asleep and had stolen Jesus' body! (How would the guards know what happened when they were asleep?)

"If the governor hears about it and wants to kill you for

Jesus was buried here in this cave. These women came to embalm his body—but he was gone. He had come back to life again!

538

*After Jesus arose,
   he joined two of his disciples
      as they walked along the road to Emmaus.
         But they didn't recognize him.*

sleeping," (for the soldiers were killed if they slept on duty), "we will persuade him to pardon you," they promised.

So the soldiers took the money and said what the Jewish leaders told them to. But of course, it was a lie, for they hadn't been asleep at all.

JESUS RETURNS TO HEAVEN
MARK 16; LUKE 24; ACTS 1

LATE THAT AFTERNOON as two of Jesus' friends were walking along to the village of Emmaus, which was about seven miles from Jerusalem, they were talking to each other about all the strange things that had happened that day. Then Jesus came and walked along with them.

But he looked different, so they didn't recognize him.

"What are you talking about that makes you so sad?" he asked them.

One of them, whose name was Cleopas, answered, "Are you a stranger here, that you haven't heard all the things that have been happening the last few days?"

"What things?" Jesus asked.

"About Jesus of Nazareth," they replied. "He was a prophet and did great miracles. We thought he was the one who would free Israel from the Romans. But the chief priests and other Jewish leaders crucified him. And now, early this morning, three days after he was killed, some

541

women who are friends of ours went to the cave where he was buried and came back reporting that his body wasn't there, and that some angels told them he is alive! Some of our men went to the tomb afterwards and found it was as the women had said: Jesus' body wasn't there!"

Then Jesus reminded them about what the prophets had written concerning Christ—that he would be killed, and afterwards come back to life again. Then Jesus began at the beginning of the Bible and explained all that had been written about him. But still his two friends didn't recognize him.

As they neared the village where they lived, he prepared to leave them and go on further. Thinking he was a traveler, they invited him to spend the night with them, as it was getting late in the day. So he went home with them. As they were eating supper together, Jesus took a small loaf of bread, and after he had thanked God for it, he broke it and gave it to them. But as he did this, suddenly they recognized him, and just then he disappeared!

Then they said to each other, "Didn't you feel warm inside while he was talking with us out there on the road, explaining what the prophets had said?"

They started back to Jerusalem and right away found Jesus' disciples and others with them, and told them how they had seen Jesus and talked with him, and how they had recognized him as he was breaking the bread at the supper table. And just then, while they were telling about it, Jesus himself suddenly appeared among them and spoke to them! They were badly frightened, for they thought he was a ghost.

Jesus ascended to heaven to see his Father! Once his work on earth was finished, he went back to his Father to live with him forever.

Then he said to them, "Look at the nail marks in my hands and my feet. Touch me and see that it is I, myself, for a ghost doesn't have flesh and bones as you see I have!" They could hardly believe it for joy!

A few days later Jesus appeared to his disciples on the shore of the Sea of Galilee. This is the way it happened: Peter, Thomas, Nathaniel, James, John, and two other disciples were there, and when Peter said he was going out to fish, they said they would go along. They did, but caught nothing all night. In the early morning Jesus was standing on the shore, but the disciples didn't recognize him.

"Did you catch any fish?" he asked them.

"No," they replied.

"Throw your net out on the right-hand side of the boat and you'll catch plenty of them!" Jesus told them.

They did, and now they couldn't drag the net into the boat, it was so full of fish! As soon as they came to land, they saw a fire burning, and fish laid on it, and bread.

"Come and have some breakfast," Jesus called. They were almost sure it was the Lord, but didn't want to ask him!

Another time he met them on a mountain in Galilee where he had told them to go, and when they saw him they worshiped him. He said to them, "God has given me all power in heaven and on earth. Go and preach the Good News to the people of every nation, baptizing them in the name of the Father, the Son, and the Holy Spirit, and teaching them to do everything I have commanded you."

Jesus showed himself not only to his disciples but to more than five hundred others at one time.

Forty days after he came back to life, Jesus appeared to the disciples at Jerusalem again.

Then he walked with them to a place near the village of Bethany (where Mary, Martha, and Lazarus lived) and blessed them. And while he was blessing them, he began to rise into the air until he disappeared into a cloud!

While the disciples stood there straining their eyes for another glimpse, two angels appeared, dressed in brilliant white, and said to them, "Why stand here looking at the sky? Jesus will return someday, just as you have seen him go!"

ARRESTED FOR PREACHING!

ACTS 1–4

AFTER JESUS had gone back to heaven, the disciples returned to Jerusalem to wait until the Holy Spirit came upon them, for Jesus had told them to do this.

When the annual Jewish holiday called Pentecost arrived, and the disciples were meeting together, suddenly they heard what sounded like the roar of a great wind. The noise came closer and closer until it was in every room of the house where they were meeting. Then what seemed to be flames of fire in the shape of tongues rested on the head of each of them and the Holy Spirit came into them as Jesus had promised, and they all began to speak in other languages that they had never known before!

At that time there were many Jews in Jerusalem who

had come from other countries to attend the Passover celebration. These men and women were amazed to hear the disciples talking in their own languages. But others, who didn't understand what the disciples were saying, mocked them and said, "They're drunk."

Peter replied, "No, they aren't drunk, but God has sent his Holy Spirit into them. You killed Jesus of Nazareth who did such great miracles, but now God has brought him back to life just as the Bible promised. And we, his apostles, have seen him alive again. His coming back to life proves that he is the Savior of the world whom the prophets told about."

Then everyone was sorry because they had helped kill Jesus. "What can we do now?" they asked Peter and the others.

Peter replied, "Be sorry for your sins and be baptized, and the Holy Spirit will be given to you just as he was to us, for God promised to send him to you and to your children, and to all who will obey him." Great crowds believed in the Lord Jesus that day, and about three thousand were baptized.

One afternoon Peter and John went together to the temple at the hour of prayer. A man who was lame from birth was being carried along the street by his friends, and placed at the gate called the Beautiful Gate of the temple. There he begged from all who came to worship. When he saw Peter and John about to go into the temple, he asked them for some money.

Peter looked down at him and said, "Look here!" The man looked up expectantly, for he thought Peter was going to give him some money. But Peter said, "I have no money! But I'll give you what I have: in the name of Jesus Christ of Nazareth, stand up and walk!"

Then Peter took him by the right hand and helped him

up, and immediately the lame man's feet and ankle bones were strengthened, and he leaped up, stood for a moment, and then started walking, leaping, and praising God as he went into the temple with them! He didn't even have to learn to walk.

When all the people saw him, and realized he was the man who had sat begging at the Beautiful Gate of the temple, they were filled with wonder at what had happened, and crowded around to see him. Then Peter preached them this sermon:

"You men of Israel, why be surprised by this? And why look at us as though we had made this man walk? It is Jesus who has given us the power to make him well. Brothers, turn to God and believe Jesus so that your sins will be forgiven."

There was one group of Jews who didn't believe there would ever be a Judgment Day, or that the dead would ever come back to life again. Some of these men belonged to the Jewish Supreme Court and were part of the government. They rushed over to stop the disciples from preaching about Jesus. They arrested Peter and John and put them in jail. But it was too late, for about five thousand people who heard Peter's sermon that day believed in Jesus!

The Supreme Court met the next day, and Peter and John were brought in. "By what power did you heal that lame man?" the Court demanded of them.

Peter answered, "He was made well by the power of Jesus of Nazareth, the man you crucified. You counted Jesus as worthless, but God has made him the ruler over all of us. No one else in all the world except Jesus can save us from being punished for our sins."

When the members of the Court realized that Peter and John were uneducated fishermen, and yet were so bold, they were amazed. And of course they couldn't deny that the man had been healed. Finally they told Peter and John to go out for a little while, so they could discuss the case among themselves and decide what to do.

They finally decided to tell them that if they ever again preached about Jesus, they would be punished severely. So they called them in and told them.

But Peter and John replied, "Should we obey you instead of God? We can't stop telling people about Jesus and what we have heard him say, and have seen him do."

Then the rulers threatened them again and finally let them go because they were afraid of riots among the people if they kept them in jail.

AN ANGEL OPENS PRISON DOORS

ACTS 4, 5

PETER AND JOHN now went to the other friends of Jesus and told them what the rulers had said. "Lord," they all prayed, "help us not to be afraid to preach the Good News; and give us power to do more miracles in Jesus' name."

Then they went out and preached again, unafraid of what the rulers might do to them. Many who heard them believed, and all of these new believers joined the others in their Bible study and prayer meetings, and in helping each other. Those who owned houses or lands sold them and brought the money to the twelve disciples to give to those who were poor.

But when a man named Ananias with his wife Sapphira sold some land, they decided to bring only part of the money they received in payment, but to say it was all of it.

They thought the apostles wouldn't know they were lying, but God told Peter about it. So when Ananias came with the money and told Peter the lie, Peter said to him, "Ananias, the land was yours. You didn't have to sell it. And the money you received was yours. You could have kept it all if you wanted it. Why have you let Satan tempt you to lie to the Holy Spirit?"

Instantly Ananias fell down dead! So the Lord punished him for his sin. Then the young men who were there carried him out and buried him.

About three hours later his wife, Sapphira, arrived, looking for her husband and not knowing what had happened. Peter asked her, "Was the money your husband brought to us the entire amount you received for the land?"

"Yes," she answered.

Then Peter said to her, "Why have you and your husband agreed together to try to fool the Spirit of the Lord? Look, the men who have just buried your husband are at the door, and they will carry you out."

Instantly she fell down dead at Peter's feet, and the young men came in and carried her out and buried her beside her husband.

Soon the apostles were in jail again! The Jewish leaders were deeply concerned about the wild enthusiasm of the crowds, so they arrested them. However, that night the angel of the Lord came down and opened the prison doors, and brought them out!

"Go back to the temple," the angel told them, "and

preach the Good News to the people." So, early the next morning, they went up to the temple again and began to preach.

Meanwhile, the Jewish leaders called together another session of the Supreme Court and sent for the apostles to be brought from the prison for trial. But of course they weren't there! The soldiers came back to say that the prison was shut and the guards were standing before the doors, but the prisoners were gone!

Instantly the Court was in great confusion, but while everyone was guessing how they had escaped, a messenger arrived to say, "They are preaching at the temple!" Guards were sent at once to the temple, with instructions to get the apostles, but to bring them quietly so as not to excite the people and start a riot. So the apostles were soon standing again before the Court.

"Didn't we tell you never again to speak about Jesus?" the High Priest yelled at them.

Then Peter and the other apostles replied, "We must obey God rather than men. You persecuted Jesus and cruelly killed him on the cross, but God has brought him back to life again, to be the Savior and to give the Jews new hearts, and to forgive them their sins. And we, his apostles, are his messengers of this Good News."

This made the High Priest and the others raging mad, and there was talk of killing them. But Gamaliel, one of the rulers and a man deeply respected, stood up to ask that the apostles be sent out of the council room for a little while so that he could speak freely.

Ananias was struck dead because he lied about the offering he made. He and his wife said they gave all *the money, but they kept some for themselves.*

Then he addressed the Court as follows:

"Rulers of Israel, be careful what you do to these men. Some time ago there was a man named Theudas who created a great stir by pretending that he was someone great, and about four hundred men followed him and became his disciples. But before long he was killed and all of his followers were scattered. Afterwards another man named Judas from Galilee persuaded many to follow him, but he also died, and his disciples were scattered. I say, let these men alone and don't harm them. For if what they teach isn't true, it will soon come to nothing; but if God has indeed sent them, you can't stop them. If you try, you will be fighting against God."

The entire Court agreed to what Gamaliel said, but they whipped the apostles anyway, and again told them that they must stop preaching.

STORY 181

STEPHEN IS STONED TO DEATH

ACTS 6, 7, 8

DO YOU REMEMBER about the Christians selling their land and bringing the money to the apostles to give to the poor? Some of this money was given to widows, that is, to women whose husbands were dead. But there was a complaint that some needy widows weren't getting as much help as others.

So the apostles called together all of Jesus' friends and

said to them, "It isn't right that we apostles should stop preaching the Good News in order to distribute this money; so you choose seven men who are honest and wise and full of the Holy Spirit, and let them take care of this business. Then we can spend all our days preaching and praying."

Everyone thought this was a good idea, and they chose seven men to decide who should get how much. Then the apostles prayed for them, asking God to help them and to give them wisdom in doing their work.

Stephen, who was one of these seven men, not only gave money to the poor, but also preached and did great miracles. But some Jews were angry with him for doing these good things, so they took him to court. They brought in witnesses to lie about him and to say, "This man is constantly saying things he shouldn't about the temple and against God's law."

The High Priest asked Stephen if it was true that he was saying these bad things.

Stephen talked to them a long time about how wicked the Jews had been for hundreds of years. They had killed God's prophets and had worshiped idols.

Then Stephen told the men of the council, "You are wicked men just like your fathers were. Which prophet didn't they kill, and now you have killed the Savior."

At this, the judges were furious, and gnashed their teeth at Stephen like wild animals. But he looked up into heaven and saw a glorious light, and then he saw Jesus standing there beside God. "I see the heavens opened, and Jesus standing at God's right hand!" he exclaimed.

Then the judges yelled and shouted and put their hands over their ears so that they couldn't hear his words. And they dragged him out of the city and killed him by throwing rocks at him.

But as they were stoning him, he knelt down and prayed, "Lord Jesus, forgive them for this sin."

553

The men who had lied about Stephen threw the first stones at him. They took off their outer robes so they could throw harder, and laid them at the feet of a young man named Saul, to keep for them until they had finished killing Stephen.

After Stephen's death everyone turned against Jesus' friends and tried to hurt them. But some good men dared to come and get Stephen's body, and to mourn over it and bury it. As for Saul, the young man who had watched over the clothes of the witnesses, he began a great campaign against the Christians, for he went into every home to find those who believed that Jesus was their Savior, and when he found them, he arrested them—men and women alike—and put them in jail. Many of Jesus' friends fled from Jerusalem to different parts of the country, and to other countries too; but wherever they went, they told everyone the Good News.

Philip, who was another of the seven men who gave the money to the widows, went at this time to the city of Samaria and preached to the people there; and they listened to him carefully when they saw the miracles he did. For evil spirits came screaming out of people when he told them to leave, and people who were sick or lame got well. So there was great joy in Samaria, and many people believed and were baptized.

When the apostles in Jerusalem heard how interested the people of Samaria were, they sent Peter and John to join Philip there, and to pray for the new Christians to

Stephen told the Jewish leaders that they were wicked because they rejected Jesus. This made them very angry, so they killed Stephen by throwing stones at him.

receive the Holy Spirit. And when Peter and John laid their hands on the heads of these new believers, God sent his Holy Spirit into them.

STORY 182 **SAUL SEES THE LIGHT AND FINDS LIFE**
ACTS 8, 9

IN THE CITY of Samaria there was a man named Simon who did wonderful things by magic. Everyone had always listened to whatever he said, for they thought God had given him special powers. But when Philip preached the Good News in that city, and many believed and were baptized, Simon did too! So Philip baptized him, and after that he stayed with Philip, marveling at the miracles he did.

When Simon saw that people received the Holy Spirit when Peter and John placed their hands on them and prayed for them, he offered money if they would give him the power to do this too. But Peter told him it was wrong to think that God's powers could be bought. "Repent of your sin and ask to be forgiven," he told Simon, "for I can see that you are not right with God at all."

Then Simon answered, "Pray that God won't punish me."

The angel of the Lord now told Philip to leave Samaria

and to go to the city of Gaza. He of course obeyed, but didn't know what he was supposed to do when he got there. But as he was walking along the dusty road towards the city, a black government official from the land of Ethiopia rode by in his chariot. He was a very important man in his country, for he took care of all the treasures of the queen of Ethiopia. He had been in Jerusalem to worship at the temple, and now as he sat there in his chariot returning to his own land, he was reading from the Bible at the part where the prophet Isaiah told the people of Israel that a Savior was going to come into the world to die for their sins.

The Holy Spirit told Philip to go over to the chariot and talk with the man. So Philip ran to the chariot and heard him reading aloud.

"Do you understand what you are reading?" Philip called out to him.

"How can I unless someone comes and explains it to me?" the man exclaimed. Then he invited Philip to come and sit with him in the chariot and to talk to him about it.

As they were riding along, the treasurer asked him, "What did the prophet mean when he wrote these words? Was he speaking about himself or someone else?"

Then Philip explained what it all meant, and told him that Isaiah was talking about Jesus.

Farther down the road they came to a pool of water beside the road, and the officer said, "Look! Water! What is there to keep me from being baptized?"

Philip replied, "If you believe with all your heart, you may."

"I believe that Jesus Christ is the Son of God," was the Ethiopian's answer. Then he told his driver to stop, and he stepped into the water with Philip, and Philip baptized him. When they came out again, the Holy Spirit took Philip away! He just suddenly disappeared! But the Ethiopian went home happy because now he had heard about Jesus and he was one of Jesus' disciples.

Meanwhile, how Saul hated Jesus' disciples! He finally went to the High Priest at Jerusalem and asked him to write letters to the Jewish leaders in the city of Damascus, demanding that they help him arrest any disciples of Jesus he found there so that he could bring them in chains to Jerusalem to be punished for believing that Jesus was the Savior.

The High Priest gave Saul the letters he asked for, and he started to go to Damascus.

But as he neared the city, suddenly a brilliant light from heaven shone around him, and Jesus appeared to him. Saul was terribly frightened and fell flat on the ground. Then he heard a voice saying, "Saul, Saul, why are you trying to hurt me?"

"Who are you, sir?" Saul asked.

The voice answered, "I am Jesus, the one you are persecuting."

Then Saul, trembling and astonished, said, "Lord, what do you want me to do?"

The Lord replied, "Get up and go on into Damascus. You will be told there what to do next." (The men who were with Saul heard the voice but couldn't understand the words.)

Then Saul got up, and found himself blind. He couldn't see a thing. Those who were with him had to lead him by the hand and bring him to Damascus. He was there for three days without sight, and did not eat or drink anything.

The Holy Spirit told Philip to go to a distant road where he would see an Ethiopian government official.
He was reading about Christ in the book of Isaiah.

F. R. Hook

SAUL ESCAPES IN A BASKET

ACTS 9

THERE WAS a disciple in Damascus named Ananias, and the Lord said to him, "Ananias, go down to Straight Street, and ask at the house of Judas for a man named Saul. He is praying to me right now, and he has seen a vision of your coming to him and putting your hands on him, and giving him his sight!"

Ananias answered, "Lord, I have heard about this man and of all the harm he has done to your people in Jerusalem. And now he has come here to Damascus with the letters from the chief priests, giving him power to arrest everyone who believes in you."

But the Lord said, "Go and visit him, for I have chosen him to preach my Good News to the Gentiles, and to kings, and to the people of Israel. And I will show him how much he must suffer."

So Ananias went to the house of Judas, found Saul, and laid his hands on him, saying, "Brother Saul, the Lord Jesus who appeared to you as you were coming to Damascus has sent me to put my hands on you so that you can see again, and so that you will be filled with the Holy Spirit."

Immediately Saul's sight returned, and he was baptized, and after he had eaten some food he was strong again. Then he stayed with the disciples in Damascus, and went into the Jewish churches and preached to the Jews about Jesus, telling them that he is the Son of God.

The people in the city could hardly believe what they heard!

"Isn't this the man who persecuted the Christians in Jerusalem," they asked, "and came here to arrest all those who believe in Jesus, to take them back in chains to the chief priests for punishment?" But Saul just preached all the more and proved from the Scriptures that Jesus is the Savior.

After several days the angry Jews began to talk about killing Saul. They watched day and night at the city gates to capture him if he went out. But the Christians heard about it and let him down at night in a basket from a window in the wall, so that he escaped and went into the desert for a while to talk to God. Three years later he went to Jerusalem.

When he arrived at Jerusalem he went to find the disciples of Jesus, for now instead of hating them, he loved them and wanted to be with them. But they were all afraid of him and wouldn't believe he was really one of them. Then Barnabas, one of the men who had sold his land and given the money to the poor, brought Saul to them and told them how Saul had met Jesus on the road to Damascus, and how he had boldly preached the Good News.

Then the apostles welcomed Saul, and he stayed with them and preached in Jerusalem.

But some of the Jews at Jerusalem, like those at Damascus, determined to kill him. When the apostles heard about it they sent him away to the far-off city of Tarsus, his birthplace. After this the Christians had no more trouble for a while, but were left in peace.

As Peter went through different parts of the land visiting the new churches, he came to the city of Lydda. He found

Jesus appeared to Saul
when he was on his way to Damascus.
He was going there
to persecute Christians.
Saul then became a Christian
himself.

there a man named Aeneas, who had the palsy and had been in bed for eight years.

Peter said to him, "Aeneas, Jesus Christ makes you well! Get up!" And immediately he stood up and was healed! Then many of the people who lived at Lydda and throughout that entire area believed in Jesus as their Savior.

At Joppa, a city not far from Lydda, there was a disciple named Dorcas. This woman was very kind and good, always helping the poor. But she became sick and then died. Her friends sadly gathered in an upstairs room to prepare for her burial.

When the disciples in Joppa heard that Peter was not far away, over in Lydda, they sent two men to ask him to hurry and come to them, and he did.

They brought him to the house where the body of Dorcas lay. All the poor widows she had helped were there, crying and showing the coats and other clothes she had made for them.

But Peter asked them all to leave. After they had left the room he kneeled down and prayed, and then, turning to the dead body, he said, "Dorcas, get up!"

And she woke up as though she had been asleep, and sat up, and he gave her back to her friends!

THE GOOD NEWS IS FOR EVERYONE

ACTS 10, 11

OVER IN THE CITY of Caesarea was a man named Cornelius, an officer in the Roman army. He was a good man who feared God, and even though he wasn't a Jew, he taught his family about God. He gave many gifts to the poor, and spent much time in prayer. One day Cornelius saw an angel coming to him and calling him. He was terribly frightened. "What do you want, sir?" he asked.

The angel replied, "God has heard your prayers and seen the gifts you have given to the poor. Now send men to Joppa to find a man named Peter who is staying in the house of Simon, a tanner, by the seaside. Bring him here and he will tell you what to do."

So Cornelius called two of his servants and a godly soldier and told them what had happened and what the angel had said, and sent them to Joppa to find Peter.

The next day as they were arriving at Joppa, Peter went up to the housetop to pray, for the house had a flat roof and the people in that country used these roofs for porches. As he was praying, he grew very hungry, and while lunch was being prepared, God gave him a vision. He seemed to see the sky above him open, and something like a great sheet of canvas came down to the ground in front of him. On this sheet were all kinds of wild animals and snakes and birds. Then a voice said, "Kill them and eat them for dinner, Peter."

Do you remember that Moses told the people of Israel not to eat certain kinds of animals? Well, some of these animals were there on that canvas sheet, and in the vision, God told Peter to eat them! So Peter answered, "No, Lord, for I have never eaten anything you have told me not to."

But the voice came again, and said, "When God says it is all right, don't say it isn't!"

This happened three times, and then the sheet was pulled back to heaven again.

While Peter was trying to understand what the vision meant, the servants of Cornelius arrived at the house where Peter was staying. They were outside at the gate, asking if someone named Peter lived there. Then the Holy

Cornelius and his household
were the first Gentiles
to become Christians.
Peter preached the Good News to them.
Here we see Peter
baptizing Cornelius.

Spirit said to Peter, "Three men are looking for you. Go with them without fear, for I have sent them."

So Peter went downstairs to the men and said, "I'm the man you are looking for. What can I do for you?"

They answered, "Captain Cornelius, a good man who fears God and is well thought of by all the Jews, was told by a holy angel to send for you to come to his home, so that you could tell him what to do."

Then Peter asked the men to come in and stay there that night, and the next day he went with them, and some of the Christians who lived at Joppa went along with them.

They arrived at Caesarea the following day. Cornelius was expecting them and had invited his relatives and friends to be with him when Peter came. As Peter walked into his house, Cornelius fell down and worshiped him. But Peter said, "Stand up! I am only a man like yourself!"

Then after talking together a while, Peter went inside and met many Gentiles—people who, like Cornelius, weren't Jews.

Peter told them, "You know that the Jews say it is wrong for us to associate with men of other nations, because we Jews think we are better, and we call everyone else heathen. But God has taught me in a vision that God loves all mankind, and not just the Jews. So I came as soon as I was sent for. And now, what is it you want? Why did you ask me to come?"

"Four days ago," Cornelius answered, "I was fasting and praying here in my house when suddenly an angel stood before me in bright clothing and said, 'Cornelius, God has heard your prayers and has seen your kind acts to the poor. Send messengers to Joppa to find a man named Peter. He is staying in the house of Simon, a tanner, living by the sea. When he comes he will tell you how you and all your family can be saved.'

"Immediately I sent for you and I appreciate your coming. We want to hear what God has told you to tell us."

Then Peter said, "I realize now that God doesn't choose one nation more than another, but in every nation there are those who worship him, and do what is right, and are those he receives as his children.

"God sent Jesus into the world, and he went about doing good. Yet the Jewish leaders put him to death. But God brought him back to life again on the third day and allowed us to see him. God has appointed Jesus to be the ruler of all nations; for all who believe in him have their sins forgiven."

While Peter was still speaking, the Holy Spirit came upon Cornelius and the other Gentiles who were with him. Then Peter asked, "Shouldn't these men be baptized, since the Holy Spirit has come upon them just as he did upon us?" So he baptized them in the name of Jesus. Then they begged him to stay with them for several days.

AN ANGEL RESCUES PETER
ACTS 11, 12, 13

SOME OF THE DISCIPLES who fled from Jerusalem at the time Stephen was put to death now went to the city of Antioch in the land of Syria and preached there to men who weren't Jews, and God helped many of them to believe.

When news of this reached Jerusalem, the apostles sent Barnabas to Antioch to investigate the matter. He was glad when he saw how many of the people there believed, and he encouraged them to continue to earnestly worship and obey the Lord. For Barnabas was a good man whose heart was full of faith and of the Holy Spirit, and through his preaching many more believed in Jesus.

Then Barnabas went to the city of Tarsus to look for Saul, and when he found him he brought him back to Antioch. They stayed there a whole year, preaching the Good News. (It was in Antioch that the disciples were first called "Christians.")

About that time King Herod began to persecute the Christians. He killed James, the apostle who was the brother of John, and because he saw how much this pleased the Jews, he arrested Peter too, and put him in jail, intending to execute him. Herod placed soldiers and guards all around the jail, night and day, so that Peter couldn't escape. But the church in Jerusalem kept praying for him.

The night before he was to be killed, Peter was sleeping between two soldiers, bound with two chains fastened to the soldiers' wrists, so that if he even moved they would know it.

Suddenly the prison was full of light and an angel was standing there! He touched Peter's side and wakened him. "Quick, get up!" he whispered. But the soldiers slept on as the chains fell off Peter's hands! "Dress yourself and put on your shoes and follow me," the angel said to him. Peter followed along behind him, but thought it was only a dream! When they had passed the guards, they came to

Peter was put in jail for preaching that Jesus arose from the dead. God sent an angel to save Peter from getting executed the next day.

the iron gate that led out of the jail into the city, and it opened for them by itself! They walked on together down the street, and suddenly the angel was gone!

When Peter collected his thoughts, he said to himself, "Think of it! The Lord has sent his angel to save me!" He went over to the home of Mary, the mother of the disciple Mark, where many Christians were praying for him. Peter knocked at the gate, and a girl named Rhoda came to see who was there. But when she heard Peter's voice she was so excited and glad that she forgot to let him in, and ran back and told everyone that Peter was out there!

"Don't be foolish!" they said. "Peter is in prison!" But she insisted he was at the gate.

"Then it must be his spirit," they said. They thought he had already been killed, and his spirit was out there in the street trying to get in! Meanwhile, Peter kept on knocking! They finally opened the door and there he was. Then what excitement there was! But Peter quieted them and told them what had happened and asked them to tell the other apostles. Then he left and went to find a place to hide.

In the morning when the soldiers woke up at the jail, Peter was gone. King Herod questioned them closely, but they couldn't tell him what had happened, so he commanded them all to be killed for letting Peter escape.

One day while the Christians at Antioch were worshiping the Lord, the Holy Spirit spoke to them and told them to send Barnabas and Saul to other countries to preach the Good News to people everywhere. They all fasted and prayed together, and then put their hands on the heads of Barnabas and Saul to bless them, and sent them away as missionaries.

So Barnabas and Saul left Antioch and sailed away to the island of Cyprus, taking with them a young disciple named Mark.

There they met a Jew named Elymas, who was a false prophet and was the advisor to the governor of the country. The governor was a wise man and he sent for Barnabas and Saul to come and explain the Good News to him. But Elymas spoke against them, and tried to keep the governor from believing what they taught.

Then Saul, who was now called Paul, looked at Elymas, and said, "You child of the devil, full of all wickedness, will you never stop speaking against those things the Lord has commanded us to teach? And now the Lord has sent a punishment upon you, and you will be blind for a time, not able to see even the sun."

Immediately his sight was taken from him. He groped around like a person in the dark, and had to be led by the hand. Then the governor, when he saw the miracle that Paul had done, believed in Jesus.

STORY 186

TRAVELING MISSIONARIES

ACTS 13, 14

PAUL AND BARNABAS and Mark now sailed away from Cyprus and came to the city of Perga in Turkey. There Mark left and went back to Jerusalem, for he decided the trip would be too hard. So Barnabas and Paul went on by themselves. They arrived at the city of Antioch and went into the Jewish church to teach. After the Scriptures had been read, the leader asked them to speak to the people.

So Paul stood up and said, "Men of Israel and all of you who fear God, listen to me. The God of the people of Israel chose our fathers to be his people, and by his mighty power he set them free when they were living as slaves in the land of Egypt. Afterwards he took care of them for forty years as they wandered around in the wilderness. Then he destroyed the wicked nations of Canaan, and divided the land among his people.

"And now, just as God promised, he sent Jesus. But the people of Jerusalem and their rulers didn't realize who he really was, and they killed him. But God brought him back to life, and we talked to him several times afterwards. And now we have come to tell you the Good News that this Jesus is the Savior who was promised, and that all of your sins are forgiven if you believe in him."

The Jews weren't very interested, and began to go away, but the Gentiles who were there begged Paul and Barnabas to preach to them again. And so on the next Sabbath almost the entire city came to hear them. But when the Jews saw the crowds, they were jealous and displeased and spoke against the things Paul said.

Then Paul and Barnabas spoke boldly to the Jews and said, "It was right for us to preach the Good News to you first, but since you won't hear it and don't care to be saved, we will preach it to the Gentiles instead. For that is what God has told us to do." They said that Jesus is the Savior of all the nations, not just the Jews. When the Gentiles heard this they were glad, but the Jews started rioting until Paul and Barnabas had to flee for their lives to the city of Iconium. But in this city, too, the Jews who wouldn't believe stirred up the people until they were about to stone Paul and Barnabas to death.

Then Paul and Barnabas fled to another city, called Lystra, and preached there. A man was there who had been lame ever since he was born, and had never walked. Paul saw that the man had faith to believe, so he shouted, "Stand up!" And the man leaped up and walked!

When the people of Lystra saw this miracle, they cried out, "These are gods who have come down to us from heaven!"

When Barnabas and Paul saw what was happening, they tore their clothes to show their dismay, and ran among the people shouting, "Sirs, why do you do such things? For we are men like yourselves, and have come to preach to you and persuade you to turn from worshiping idols. We want you to worship only the true God who made heaven and earth and the sea, and everything in them."

Just then some Jews from Antioch and Iconium arrived at Lystra and shouted out that Barnabas and Paul were wicked men who were trying to fool everyone. Almost at once the same people who had just been wanting to worship them, tried to kill them. They stoned Paul and dragged him out of the city and left him for dead. But while the Christians were standing around him he got up and went back into the city again!

The next day he went with Barnabas to Derbe. After preaching there they went back to all the cities where the people had persecuted them, and preached to the Christians who lived there. Paul encouraged them to keep on believing in the Lord Jesus, and reminded them that they must expect trouble and sorrow when serving God.

Then they appointed elders to rule over the churches in each city, and finally they went back to Antioch to report to the church that had sent them on this journey. They called together the entire church and told everyone how they had told the Good News wherever they went, preaching it to the Gentiles as well as to the Jews. They stayed in Antioch with the disciples for a long while.

PAUL MEETS YOUNG TIMOTHY

ACTS 15, 16

BUT NOW some believers from Jerusalem arrived at Antioch to preach, and they claimed that a person couldn't be saved without offering up animals as sacrifices.

For hundreds of years before Jesus came to earth, the Jews offered such sacrifices to show that their great Messiah was coming to save them. But when he came, there was no need for these sacrifices; we don't need anything to remind us that a person is coming when he is already here and we have seen him! Jesus is the Messiah, and he is the Lamb of God that takes away the sins of the world.

Paul and Barnabas talked with these men and tried to make them understand that sacrifices were no longer needed, but they wouldn't believe. So it was agreed that these men and Paul and Barnabas should go to Jerusalem to ask the elders of the church there to settle the question.

The apostles and elders met together in Jerusalem to discuss this problem, and the Holy Spirit told them that it is no longer necessary to offer up animal sacrifices.

Then the apostles and elders sent Judas and Silas to Antioch to tell the Christians there what had been decided. They also wrote a letter to be read to the Christians not only at Antioch, but in other cities too, telling them that they need no longer sacrifice lambs, oxen, or goats to the Lord. The time was past when the Lord wanted the people to worship him in this way. What he wanted them to do now was to turn from their sins and to believe in his Son Jesus—loving him in their hearts, and obeying his commandments.

So Paul, Barnabas, Judas, and Silas came to Antioch and called together all the believers, and gave them the letter from the apostles and elders, and explained it to them. Everyone was glad when they read it, for now they could worship God anywhere and not just in Jerusalem where the temple was.

After this, Paul said to Barnabas, "Let's go out again and visit our brothers in all the cities where we preached before, and see how they are getting along."

Barnabas was willing, and he wanted to take Mark with them, but Paul thought they shouldn't take Mark because he had deserted them and gone home when they took him with them before.

Paul and Barnabas disagreed so much about this that they decided not to stay together. Barnabas took Mark and sailed to the island of Cyprus, while Paul chose Silas and went to Syria to visit the churches there.

Arriving at Lystra, the city where he had healed the lame man, Paul met a young man named Timothy, whose mother was a Jewess, and a disciple of Jesus, but whose father was a Greek. Timothy was well thought of by the Christians there at Lystra, for he had lived a fine Christian life from the time he was a small child. When Paul saw how wise and good this young man was, he invited him to go along with him and Silas, and learn to be a minister and preach the Good News.

One night at Troas, a coastal city, Paul had a vision. In the vision he saw a man standing before him, pleading, "Come over to Macedonia and help us." Macedonia was over in Greece, across the Adriatic Sea. So Paul and those who were with him sailed from Troas and soon arrived in Philippi, a city of Macedonia.

On the Sabbath day they went out of the city a little way to a riverbank where people met to pray. They sat and talked with some women there, telling them about Jesus. A woman named Lydia, a saleswoman, was very interested and listened carefully to what Paul said, and believed in Jesus. When she and her family had been baptized, she begged Paul and his friends to come and stay at her home.

STORY 188

AN EARTHQUAKE SHAKES A PRISON

ACTS 16, 17

AT PHILIPPI they met a young woman who had an evil spirit in her. She earned a lot of money for the men who owned her by telling fortunes. She would tell people what would happen to them in the future.

She followed Paul and his companions and shouted, "These men are the servants of God; they will tell you how to be saved." This went on for several days.

But Paul didn't like it and finally turned around and said to the evil spirit inside her, "In the name of Jesus Christ, come out of her." And immediately the spirit came out and left her.

When her owners realized that she was healed and the evil spirit was gone, and that she could no longer earn money for them by telling people's fortunes, they were angry. They grabbed Paul and Silas and brought them before the city judge. "These Jews are disturbing the peace of our city," they shouted. "They are teaching the people to do wicked things."

This was enough to start a riot and the judges commanded that Paul and Silas and Timothy be whipped. After they had been beaten until they had many painful wounds, they were put in prison. Their jailer was told to keep them safe; if they escaped, he would be killed. So he took them into the inner prison and fastened their feet in the stocks so they couldn't escape.

In the middle of the night as Paul and Silas were praying and singing praises to God, with the other prisoners listening, suddenly a great earthquake shook the whole prison, and immediately all the doors opened of their own accord, and the chains that held the prisoners fell off! The jailer woke up, saw the prison doors open, and fearing he would be tortured and killed for letting the prisoners escape, he drew his sword to kill himself, for he supposed all the prisoners had run away. But Paul, down in the dark dungeon, knew what he was about to do, and shouted up to him, "Do yourself no harm, for we are all here."

Then the jailer called for a light and came trembling into the dungeon where Paul and Silas were, and kneeled down before them, crying out, "Sirs, what must I do to be saved?"

They answered him, "Believe in the Lord Jesus Christ, and you will be saved, and your family." Then they told him and all his family about the Savior, preaching the Good News to them. And they all believed and were baptized.

The jailer now washed the blood from their backs where they had been whipped, and brought them food. How happy he was because he and his family were Christians now, and all their sins forgiven.

In the morning the judges sent some officers to the prison to tell the jailer, "Let those men go."

When the jailer told Paul he could leave, Paul replied, "They had no right to beat us, for we are Roman citizens and had no trial. If they want us to go, let the judges themselves come and bring us out, so that the people will know we were unjustly whipped and thrown into prison."

When the judges heard that Paul was a Roman citizen, they were afraid they would be punished for what they had done to him; and they came and begged him to leave their city. Then he and Silas left the prison and went to Lydia's house. After meeting with the disciples there and encouraging them, they left Philippi.

From there they went to Thessalonica, where Paul preached in the local Jewish church, called the synagogue, for three Sabbaths in a row. He explained the Scriptures and showed from them that Jesus was the Savior. Some of the Jews believed, and many of the Gentiles too. But the Jews who wouldn't believe were angry at those who did, for they were deserting the Jewish religion.

Paul and Silas went next to the city of Beroea. There, too, they went into the synagogue to preach to the Jews. The Jews in Beroea were more willing to learn than those in Thessalonica. They listened to the Good News and then searched the Scriptures to see whether the things Paul and Silas told them were true. As a result, many believed, both men and women, Jews and Gentiles.

Paul and Silas sang and praised God in jail. God sent an earthquake to open the jail. The men didn't run away, and they told the jailer how to be saved.

579

PAUL, THE TEACHER AND TENT-MAKER

ACTS 17, 18

WHEN THE JEWS of Thessalonica learned that Paul was preaching in Beroea, they went there to stir up the people against him. As a result, the Christians decided it would be best if he left the city, though Silas and Timothy stayed.

Paul and those with him went on to the capital of Greece. The people of Athens were considered the best thinkers of that time, and were known all over the world for their learning; yet they worshiped false gods. They made beautiful idols and built splendid temples and altars in different parts of their city. Among the altars was one with these words on it: "TO THE UNKNOWN GOD." For though they had many gods they thought there might be a God they had never heard of. That is why they built this altar to him.

As Paul passed through the streets of Athens he noticed how full of idols the city was. He preached to the Jews in their synagogue, and went every day to the marketplace where the people of the city met to talk, and explained the Good News to them.

When the men of Athens heard him, some of them asked, "What is this fellow talking about?"

Others answered, "He seems to be telling about some new and strange god." They said this because he preached about Jesus and the resurrection.

So they invited him to Mars Hill, in the center of the city, to lecture to them about his religion.

"You are saying some strange things," they remarked, "and we would like to know what you mean." For the people of Athens liked nothing better than to tell or hear something new.

So Paul stood up and addressed them as follows:

"Men of Athens, I see that you think a great deal about the gods you worship, for as I walked through your city looking at your temples, altars, and images, I saw an altar with these words written on it: 'TO THE UNKNOWN GOD.' So now I want to tell you about this God you worship without knowing him."

Then Paul told them about God—that he had made the world and everything else, but he doesn't live in temples built by men. He is not like the idols of gold, silver, and stone made by men. "People don't know any better than to worship such idols," Paul said, "so God hasn't destroyed them for doing it, but gives them food and clothing and everything they need. But now," Paul declared, "God tells everyone to stop worshiping idols and to repent of their sins and to believe in Jesus, for God has set the time when he will send Jesus to judge everyone, and the proof that he will do this is that he raised Jesus from the dead."

Several of those who were there that morning believed, among them Dionysius, a member of the Supreme Court of Athens, and a woman named Damaris, and some others.

Paul now left Athens and came to the city of Corinth. There he found a Jew named Aquila, with his wife Priscilla, who were in the business of making tents. Paul was also a tent-maker, and whenever he needed money he made tents and sold them. So since he and Aquila were in the same kind of work, Paul went to stay and work with him.

But every Sabbath day he went into the Jewish church

and taught the people, persuading both Jews and Gentiles to believe in the Savior. When the Jews contradicted him and spoke against Jesus, he told them, "I have done my duty in telling you about him. If you won't be saved, the fault is your own; from now on I am going to preach to the Gentiles."

Corinth, like Athens, was a great city, but the people who lived there were very wicked. One night the Lord spoke to Paul in a vision and told him that many Corinthians would become Christians. He told Paul to preach boldly, without fear, for the Lord would be with him and would take care of him and no one would hurt him.

Paul stayed in Corinth a year and six months preaching to the people. But the Jews who wouldn't believe finally got together and brought him before the governor. "This fellow," they told him, "teaches people to worship God in a way that is very wrong."

Paul started to defend himself, but the governor turned to those who had arrested him and said, "If this man had done something wrong, I would need to listen to you, but since it is only a question about your worship, handle it yourselves, for I refuse to judge such matters." And he drove them out of the courtroom.

THE GOOD NEWS CAUSES A RIOT

ACTS 19

PAUL STAYED in Corinth a long time. Then, after saying good-bye to the Christian brothers there, he sailed to Ephesus in Asia. He was in Ephesus for three years, preaching the Good News until all the people in that part of the world had heard it, both Jews and Gentiles. God gave him power to do wonderful miracles so that handkerchiefs or aprons he touched could be taken to sick people, and they got well!

The people of Ephesus worshiped the image of a Greek goddess named Diana—they thought this idol had fallen down from heaven. It was enshrined in a beautiful temple built of cedar, cypress wood, marble, and gold. It had taken 220 years to build this famous temple, known all over the world as a tourist attraction. People came from every land to visit it, for it was thought to be one of the most beautiful and wonderful things ever made.

Little models of this temple, called shrines, with an image of Diana inside, were manufactured at Ephesus. In fact, this was one of the main businesses of the city. The men who made the shrines sold them to the tourists, and in this way they earned a lot of money. One day, Demetrius, one of these tradesmen, heard Paul telling some people that they shouldn't worship idols. Demetrius suddenly realized why his business was becoming so poor. The people

583

weren't buying his idols any more because of what Paul was telling them about its being wrong! So Demetrius called together all the workmen who made silver shrines for Diana, and addressed them as follows:

"Gentlemen, you know that our living depends on selling these shrines. But this Paul has persuaded many people here, and in almost every other city in this country, that the idols we make are false gods. So there is a danger that we cannot sell enough shrines to stay in business. But there is also danger that the great goddess Diana will no longer be worshiped, and that the people will not come to her beautiful temple any more."

When the workmen heard what Demetrius said, they were very angry and shouted, "Great is Diana of the Ephesians!" The whole city was soon in confusion. Then the workmen caught Gaius and Aristarchus, two men who had come with Paul to Ephesus, and rushed them into the theatre where a great mob had gathered. Paul wanted to go in and try to reason with the mob, but the Christians wouldn't let him, fearing what might happen to him. And also some of the city's leaders who were his friends sent word to him not to do it.

Inside there was a great uproar, some people shouting one thing and some another, and many didn't even know why they were there!

A man named Alexander stood up and kept trying to get the people's attention so he could accuse Paul, but the crowd just kept on shouting for about two hours, "Great is Diana of the Ephesians; great is Diana of the Ephesians!"

Then the mayor of the city came in to address the crowd and the people finally quieted down. "Men of Ephesus," he said, "everyone knows that the people of our city are worshipers of the great goddess Diana, and of her image that fell down from heaven. And since no one denies this, you

584

ought to be careful and do nothing in anger. For you have brought these men here called Christians, who have not robbed your temple nor spoken evil of your goddess. If Demetrius and the workmen who are with him have any complaint to make against them, let them go before the court and prove what evil they have done. We are in danger that the Roman government will send soldiers to harm us because of today's riot, for we can give no reason why we are here." Then he sent the people away and they left the building.

Paul then called together the disciples and said good-bye, and went to Macedonia, then on to Troas.

PAUL SAYS GOOD-BYE
ACTS 20, 21

ONE SUNDAY EVENING as he was preaching a farewell sermon at Troas (for he was planning to leave the next day), Paul kept talking until midnight. There were many lanterns in the upstairs room where the meeting was held, and a young man named Eutychus, who was sitting on a window sill listening to Paul, fell asleep and fell to the ground three stories below. Everyone thought he was dead, but Paul went down and put his arms around him and said, "It's all right; he is alive." And he was!

Then they all went back upstairs to eat together, and Paul preached another long sermon, until finally it was morning. Then he left to sail with the others to the city of Miletus, not far from Ephesus. He didn't want to go to Ephesus at that time, so he sent for the leaders of the Ephesian church to meet him at Miletus.

When they arrived he addressed them as follows:

"You know me well, for I stayed with you three years. I taught in the synagogue and in your own homes, telling both Jews and Gentiles that they must repent of their sins and believe in the Lord Jesus Christ.

"And now I am going to Jerusalem, not knowing what will happen to me there, except that wherever I go, the Holy Spirit keeps telling me that jail and persecution await me. But I am not afraid. I don't care if they kill me. I will die with joy, except for the fact that I will never see you again."

Then Paul kneeled down and prayed with them, and they all wept together, and as was the custom in those days, they embraced him and kissed his cheeks, sorrowing most of all because he said that they would never see him again. Then they went with him to the ship and watched him sail away.

Paul next came to the city of Tyre, where the ship was to unload. Finding some disciples there, he stayed with them seven days. When he left, they came with their wives and children and all kneeled together on the beach and prayed; then Paul and those traveling with him went aboard the ship and sailed on to the city of Caesarea. There

The leaders of the Ephesian church came to see Paul. He told them that he was going to Jerusalem and that he might be killed there. They sadly said goodbye.

587

they went to the home of Philip, one of the seven men appointed by the apostles to care for the widows of the church. This was the same Philip who preached the Good News to the Ethiopian as he rode in his chariot.

While Paul was in Philip's home, a prophet named Agabus came and took Paul's belt and bound his own hands and feet with it. Then he said, "The Holy Spirit has told me that the Jews at Jerusalem will bind the man who owns this belt, and give him to the Gentiles to torture him."

The Christians cried when they heard this, and begged Paul not to go to Jerusalem. But he said to them, "Why do you weep and break my heart? For I am not only ready to go to jail, but also to die at Jerusalem."

When they saw that they couldn't keep him from going, they stopped pleading and said, "May God's will be done."

Then Paul and his friends left Caesarea and went to Jerusalem, where they received a warm welcome from the church. Then Paul went to the temple. While he was there, some Jews from Turkey recognized him and grabbed him, crying out to all the people, "Men of Israel, help us! This man teaches the people to disobey the laws of Moses. He has brought Gentiles into the temple!"

Soon the entire city was in an uproar. A mob formed and pulled Paul out of the temple to kill him. But as they were doing it, someone told the captain of the Roman guard at the nearby barracks.

The captain took some of his soldiers with him and ran down among the people. When the men who were beating Paul saw the soldiers, they stopped, and the captain took him away from them and commanded him to be bound with chains, and asked who he was and what he had done. Some of the crowd yelled one thing and some another, so that no one could tell what the trouble was.

Then the captain ordered Paul to be taken into the barracks. As he was being carried up the stairs (for the soldiers were carrying Paul to protect him from the people), the crowd surged after him shouting, "Away with him! Kill him!"

PAUL SPEAKS BRAVELY FOR JESUS
ACTS 21, 22

PAUL NOW SPOKE to the captain. "May I have a word with you?" he asked. "I would like to speak to the people."

The captain said he could, so Paul stood on the stairs where the people could see him, and motioned for silence. Then he spoke to them in Hebrew (which made the people even quieter). This is what he said:

"I am a Jew born in Tarsus, and brought up here in Jerusalem. I was taught all the wisdom of Moses by the great Gamaliel, and I used to be as anxious for everyone to obey Moses' laws as you are now. In fact, I persecuted and tried to kill every Christian I could lay my hands on, binding them and sending them away to prison and death, both men and women. The High Priest and all the Council will tell you that what I say is true, for they gave me letters to the Jews at Damascus permitting me to arrest all the

Christians I found there, and to bring them in chains to Jerusalem to be punished.

"But as I was on the way to Damascus, one day about noon, suddenly a great light from heaven shone around me. I fell to the ground and heard a voice saying, 'Saul, Saul, why are you hurting me?'

"'Who are you?' I asked.

"He said, 'I am Jesus of Nazareth, the one you are hurting.' The men who were with me saw the light and were afraid, but couldn't understand the words that were spoken.

"'What shall I do now, Lord?' I asked.

"And he replied, 'Get up, and go to Damascus, and there you will be told what you must do.'

"I couldn't see, being blinded by the terrible light, so I was led by the hand into Damascus. After three days a disciple there named Ananias, who feared God and was well thought of by all the Jews, came and stood by me, and said, 'Brother Saul, receive your sight.'

"Immediately I could see him. And he said to me, 'God has allowed you to see Jesus and to hear him speak so that you can go and tell all the nations about him.'

"Later when I was in Jerusalem and was praying in the temple, I saw Jesus again in a vision, and heard him say, 'Hurry and get out of Jerusalem, for the Jews will not believe what you tell them about me, and I will send you far away to preach among the Gentiles.'"

The crowd listened quietly until he said these words about preaching to the Gentiles. Instantly they began shouting, "Kill him! Kill him! Such a fellow isn't fit to live."

The captain then commanded that Paul be brought into the barracks and whipped, to make him confess what evil he had done.

But as they bound him and got ready to whip him, Paul

said to the soldier in charge, "Is it legal for you to whip a Roman citizen before he has been tried and proved guilty?"

One of the soldiers ran over to the captain and warned him, "Be careful what you are doing, for this man is a Roman."

Then the captain came over and asked Paul, "Tell me, are you a Roman citizen?"

"Yes, I am," he replied.

"I am too," the captain said, "and I paid plenty for the privilege."

"But I was born free," Paul replied. Then the men who were about to whip him slipped away and disappeared, as did the captain, too! For he was afraid he might be punished for having even tied a Roman citizen.

The next day when the captain wanted to know for sure what the Jews were accusing Paul of, he commanded all the local Jewish religious leaders to appear, and brought Paul down and set him before them.

Paul looked at them very earnestly and said, "Men and brothers, my conscience is clear. I have done no wrong." Then Ananias, the High Priest, ordered those who stood near Paul to slap him on the mouth.

"You hypocrite!" Paul exclaimed. "God will punish you for pretending to give me a fair trial and yet commanding me to be hit before I am proved guilty!"

"Is that the way to talk to the High Priest?" they asked him.

"I didn't know he was the High Priest," Paul said, "for it is written in the Scriptures that we mustn't speak evil of those in authority over us."

Then Paul tried again to speak, but there was such an uproar that the captain, fearing Paul would be torn to pieces, told the soldiers to get him out of there and take him back to the barracks.

PAUL'S NEPHEW SAVES HIS LIFE

ACTS 23, 24

THE NEXT NIGHT the Lord Jesus came and stood beside Paul and said, "Don't be afraid, Paul, for as you have spoken about me to the people here in Jerusalem, so also you must speak about me in the city of Rome."

In the morning, forty of the Jews promised one another that they wouldn't eat or drink until they had killed Paul. Then they went to the Chief Priest and elders and said to them, "We have agreed with one another that we will not eat or drink until we have killed Paul. So tell the captain to bring Paul down before the council tomorrow as though you wanted to ask him some more questions, and on the way we will ambush him and kill him."

But Paul's nephew heard about their plot and went into the barracks and told Paul. Paul called one of the soldiers and said, "Take this young man to the captain, for he has something to tell him."

So the soldier took him to the captain. "Paul, the prisoner, asked me to bring this young man to you," he said.

Then the captain led him to a place where they could be alone and asked him what he wanted to tell him. The young man answered, "The Jews have agreed to ask you to bring Paul before the council tomorrow, pretending they want to ask him some questions. But don't do it, for more than forty of them will be hiding along the road. They have promised each other that they won't eat or drink until they have killed him."

"Don't tell anyone you told me this," the captain warned.

The Roman governor of Judea was named Felix. He didn't live at Jerusalem, but in the city of Caesarea on the sea coast, about sixty miles from Jerusalem.

When the captain heard that the Jews wanted to kill Paul, he decided to send him to the governor. So he called two of his officers and said, "Get ready 200 soldiers, and 70 horsemen and 200 spearmen, to go to Caesarea tonight. Have horses ready for Paul and the men who are with him to ride, and get him safely to the governor."

Then the captain wrote this letter to the governor: "The man I am sending to you was grabbed by the Jews and they were about to kill him. Then I went with soldiers and rescued him, for I heard he was a Roman. I wanted to know what they accused him of, so I brought him before their council, and found that he had done nothing worthy of death. When I learned they were still determined to kill him, I decided to send him to you, and have told the Jews who accused him to appear before you and tell you what they have against him. Farewell."

Then the soldiers brought Paul by night to the town of Antipatris, which was on the way to Caesarea. There the infantrymen left him and returned to the barracks at Jerusalem, but the horsemen brought him to the governor the next day, and gave him the letter. After reading it, the governor told Paul he would hear his side of the story when the Jews came from Jerusalem to accuse him. Then he commanded that Paul be kept in prison until they arrived.

Five days later, Ananias the High Priest and some of the council came down from Jerusalem to Caesarea, bringing with them a lawyer named Tertullus to accuse Paul before the governor.

"We have found this fellow to be a wicked man," Tertullus said, "stirring up trouble and disorder among the Jews all over the world. He is a leader among those who believe in Jesus of Nazareth, and he took Gentiles into the temple! We would have handled his case under our Jewish law, but the captain came with soldiers and took him from us by force, telling us to come to you to accuse him. Now we are here, ready to prove everything we charge him with."

Then Paul answered, "It was only twelve days ago that I went up to Jerusalem to worship, and they attacked me in the temple, but I wasn't arguing with anyone, or trying to stir up the people; neither can they prove the things they have accused me of. But I confess this: that I worship God in a way different from theirs, although I believe everything that is written in their Scriptures. And I expect the dead, both the bad and the good, to rise up at the last day, just as the Jews believe. Believing this, I am trying constantly to do nothing that my conscience tells me is wrong."

Then Governor Felix sent for the captain to explain what he knew about the affair. Felix told the soldiers to keep Paul in prison but to let him see any of his friends who might come to visit him.

Paul's enemies planned to ambush and kill him. His nephew found out about the plot in time to warn him and save his life.

594

PAUL PREACHES TO A KING

ACTS 26

SEVERAL DAYS LATER Felix sent for Paul to come and talk to him and his wife Drusilla, who was a Jewess, and to explain the Good News to them. As Paul spoke to them, persuading them to obey God and not to listen to temptation, and told them that they would be judged at the last day, Felix thought of his sins and was so afraid that he trembled. Yet he didn't repent of his sins, but sent Paul back to prison.

"Some other time when it is more convenient," he said, "I will send for you again to tell me more about these things."

Felix hoped too that Paul would offer him money to let him go free, and so he sent for him frequently to talk with him. But after two years, when another governor named Festus came to take Felix's place, instead of letting Paul go free, Felix left him in prison.

When Festus, the new governor, arrived at Caesarea, the Jews asked him to send Paul to Jerusalem to be tried, for they intended to have men hidden along the road to kill him.

But Festus said, "Paul shall stay here in Caesarea, and those who wish to accuse him may come here and say what they have against him."

So when they arrived, the governor commanded Paul to

be brought before them, and the Jews stood and accused him of many things, but Paul denied everything.

Festus wanted to please the Jews so he asked Paul, "Are you willing to go to Jerusalem to be tried there for the things you are accused of?"

Now it was a law that any Roman who was sentenced to death might ask to be taken before Caesar, the emperor, for a final decision as to whether he should live or die. When Festus asked Paul if he was willing to go to Jerusalem to be tried, Paul knew what would happen, so he replied, "Jerusalem is not the place where I ought to be tried, for I have done no wrong to the Jews, as you know very well. I ask to be taken before Caesar."

Then Festus said, "You want to be tried by Caesar, do you? All right, to Caesar you shall go." He meant that Paul would be taken to the city of Rome, where the emperor lived.

Several days later, Agrippa, who was the king of another part of the land of Israel, came with his sister Bernice to visit Festus at Caesarea. Festus told him about Paul. "There is a man here in prison," he said, "whom the High Priests and other leaders of the Jews have asked me to condemn to death."

Agrippa was a Jew and when the governor told him the Jews wanted to put Paul to death, he was interested. "I would like to hear what the man has to say," Agrippa said.

Paul told King Agrippa that he was very glad to plead his case before him because the king knew all about the laws of the Jews, and would understand what he was talking about.

Then Paul told him, "The Jews themselves know very well what I have been like since childhood. For I am a Jew, and if they would tell the truth, they would say that I used to be one of the strictest among them. I, too, once thought that I ought to do many things against Jesus of Nazareth. But one day at noon, as I was nearing Damascus, I saw a bright light from heaven, brighter than the sun, that shone around me and the men who were with me. And we were all afraid and fell to the ground."

Then Paul told Agrippa and Festus and all who were listening to him how Jesus had spoken to him from heaven, and had said he would make Paul a missionary and send him to preach the Good News to the Gentiles, so that they too might repent and have their sins forgiven.

While Paul was speaking, Governor Festus said in a loud voice, "Paul, you are crazy; you have studied so much that you have lost your mind."

But Paul answered, "I am not crazy, most noble Festus. I am only speaking the truth, and King Agrippa understands what I say, for I am sure he has heard all of these things."

Then Agrippa said to Paul, "With so little evidence do you expect me to become a Christian?"

Paul replied, "I wish that not only you but all these who are listening to me were Christians such as I am, except that they wouldn't have to wear these chains."

When Paul had said this, Agrippa stood up, and so everyone else did too, and Agrippa and Festus went off to talk with each other. "This man has done nothing worthy of prison or death," they agreed.

And King Agrippa added, "He could be set at liberty if he hadn't demanded to be taken to Rome, to appear before Caesar."

SHIPWRECKED BUT SAFE

ACTS 27

WHEN THE TIME came for Paul to be sent to Rome, Festus turned him over to one of the captains of his guard, along with several other prisoners who were being sent to Rome at the same time. They went by ship from Caesarea and came the next day to the city of Sidon. Here they stopped for a while and the captain, whose name was Julius, treated Paul kindly, letting him go ashore to visit some of his friends.

Leaving Sidon they came to the city of Myra. There the captain placed his prisoners aboard another ship headed for Rome. After sailing slowly for several days they reached a place called Fair Havens, in the island of Crete. It was winter and the time for storms, and Paul said to the sailors, "Gentlemen, I prophesy that if we go on, there will be great danger not only to the ship but also to our lives." But the captain of the ship didn't believe Paul, and since Fair Havens wasn't a good harbor to stay in for the winter, he decided to leave it and to try to reach a place called Phoenix. The wind blew softly from the south that day, so everyone except Paul felt good about it. So, leaving Fair Havens, they sailed out to sea again.

But soon there was a storm, and the wind beat against the ship until the sailors could no longer steer, and they had to let the ship run before the wind. As they neared an island called Clauda, they wound cables around the ship to keep it from breaking to pieces. The storm grew worse, and the next day they threw out some of the cargo to make the ship lighter, to try to save it from sinking.

The storm kept on day after day. No one could see the sun, moon, or stars at any time, because of the dark clouds that covered the sky. Finally everyone gave up all hope, thinking they would surely be drowned.

But after they had eaten nothing for a long, long time, Paul stood up among them and said, "Sirs, you should have listened to me and stayed at the island of Crete; then you wouldn't have come into this great danger. Nevertheless, don't be afraid, for there shall be no loss of any man's life among you, though the ship will go down. Last night the Lord sent his angel to tell me, 'Don't be afraid, Paul, for you will come safely to Rome and be brought before Caesar; and for your sake God will save the lives of all the men who are with you in the ship.' So, gentlemen, cheer up, for I believe what the angel told me. But we will be wrecked on an island."

On the fourteenth night of the storm, as the ship was driven along by the wind, the sailors thought they were near some land. They measured the depth of the water and found that they were right, for the water was getting more shallow. They were afraid of rocks near the beach, so they dropped four anchors out of the ship to keep it from being driven any further, and then waited for morning.

When it was morning Paul begged them all to eat something. "This is the fourteenth day since the storm began," he said, "and in all that time you have hardly eaten any-

God promised Paul that all the people on this sinking ship would reach land safely. He kept his promise, and not one person drowned!

thing. Please take some food, for not one of you will be hurt." Then he took some bread and thanked God for it before them all, and began to eat. Suddenly everyone was more cheerful, and ate some too. Altogether there were 276 persons aboard. After they had eaten, they threw some of the cargo of wheat into the sea to lighten the ship even more.

When it was day, they saw the shore, but of course they didn't know what country they had come to. There was an inlet in front of them, and they decided to try to head the ship into it so as to avoid the rocks along the coast. After they had pulled up the anchors and hoisted the sail they steered toward the land, but before they reached it the ship ran aground, and the front part was held fast on the bottom of the sea and couldn't be moved, while the back part was broken by the great waves that dashed against it.

The soldiers shouted to the captain to have the prisoners killed for fear some of them might escape. But the captain wanted to save Paul and told them not to do it. He told those who could swim to jump in and get to shore. The others followed, clinging to boards and broken pieces of the ship. So everyone reached land safely.

PAUL ARRIVES IN ROME

ACTS 28

THEY FOUND they were on an island called Malta. The people of the island were very kind to them and helped them light a fire on the beach, because of the rain that was falling and because of the cold. Paul gathered a bundle of sticks and laid them on the fire, but suddenly a poisonous snake slithered out from the sticks and bit him, coiling onto his hand.

When the people of the island saw it hanging there they said, "No doubt this man is a murderer, and though he has escaped drowning in the sea, he is being punished by the bite of the snake for the evil he has done."

But Paul shook off the snake into the fire and felt no harm. They watched him a long time, expecting his arm would swell or that he would fall down dead, but when no harm came to him, they changed their minds and said he was a god.

The governor of the island, Publius, invited Paul and those who were with him to his house, and they stayed there three days. Publius' father was sick with a fever, so Paul laid his hands on him and made him well. Then others who were sick came and were healed. They showed their gratitude by giving Paul and his friends many presents.

After three months the captain took Paul and the other prisoners aboard a ship that had been waiting at the island until the winter was over, and they sailed away to the city of Puteoli, where Paul was the guest of the local church for seven days. Then the prisoners were marched by land towards Rome. When the Christians at Rome heard that Paul was coming, they went out to welcome him at a place called the Three Taverns.

Upon arrival at Rome, the captain gave the prisoners into the care of the Roman guard. Paul was allowed to live in a house by himself, with the soldier who guarded him. Three days after his arrival in Rome he sent for the Jewish leaders who lived there and said to them, "Men and brothers, though I have done no wrong to the Jews, nor disobeyed the laws which Moses gave to our fathers, yet the Jews at Jerusalem gave me to the Romans as their prisoner. When the Romans tried me, they wanted to let me go because I had done nothing for which I deserved to die. But when the Jews still wanted to kill me, I asked to be taken before Caesar. Now I have sent for you so that I can tell you what I believe, for it is because I believe in the Savior whom the prophets wrote about that I am bound with this chain."

The Jews replied, "We have had no letters about you, and the Jews who came from Jerusalem have not spoken against you. But we would like to hear what it is you preach—for we know these Christians are spoken against everywhere."

So they set a date and on that day many of the Jews came to Paul's house and he explained to them in an all-day Bible class what the prophets had written about Jesus. Some believed, but some didn't. As they argued, Paul told them that the prophet Isaiah had spoken the truth when he said that although a message from God would be brought to the people of Israel, many of them wouldn't listen to it because their hearts were wicked, and they didn't want to be God's children. Then he said that the

Good News refused by the Jews would be preached to the Gentiles, and the Gentiles would accept it.

Paul stayed two years in Rome, living in a house he rented for himself. There he welcomed all who came to hear him, and he taught them fearlessly about Jesus, and no one tried to stop him.

The Bible does not tell us where Paul went after this, or how he died at last. But from accounts given in other books it is thought that he was set free at Rome and went back to Jerusalem, then traveled through other countries preaching the Good News and finally returned to Rome again.

Not many years after that, there was a great fire in Rome which continued burning for six or seven days. The people believed that their wicked emperor, Nero, had ordered the city to be set on fire. To save himself from the blame, Nero accused the Christians of doing it. Then the people rose up in a great fury against the Christians, and killed many of them. Among those who were killed, we are told, were the apostles Peter and Paul. Paul, it is said, was beheaded, and Peter crucified.

LETTERS FROM THE APOSTLES
ROMANS

WE HAVE SEEN that as Paul traveled to many places, telling people the Good News that Jesus wanted to be their Savior, a lot of them believed in Jesus and became Christians. They started churches, usually small groups in their homes, where they could talk about the Lord and help one another grow strong in their faith.

Even though Paul couldn't stay with each group and keep on preaching to them, he continued to teach and encourage them through letters. Other apostles—Peter, James, John, and Jude—did this too, and the letters they wrote form about half of the New Testament. We often call the letters "epistles." God told the apostles just what he wanted his followers to do, and when we read their letters, we learn a lot about how Christians should live.

Paul wrote a long letter to some people he didn't know personally—the believers in the city of Rome. He wanted them to know what he taught and to become acquainted with him by reading the letter, because he was hoping to visit them soon. He told them he was not ashamed of the Good News about Christ, because it was God's powerful method of bringing all who believe it to heaven.

He reminded them that all people are sinners. He said, "No one is good—no one in all the world is innocent. No one has ever really followed God's paths, or even truly wanted to. Every one has turned away; all have gone wrong. No one anywhere has kept on doing what is right; not one."

They could have been terribly discouraged to hear that, because they knew their sins kept them from pleasing God. But Paul didn't leave them with the bad news. He told them the Good News that if they trusted in Jesus Christ, God would declare them "not guilty" and take away their sins. God sent Jesus to take the punishment for their sins and to end all God's anger against them. Both in Paul's day and in ours, people are not saved because of good things they do, but because they believe that Jesus died for them.

Paul used Abraham as an example of how this works. The Scriptures say that Abraham believed God, so God cancelled his sins and declared him "not guilty."

The letter told the Christians in Rome that they could have peace of mind and be absolutely sure they were God's children, because the Holy Spirit would speak to their hearts and keep reminding them how God had forgiven and accepted them.

Then Paul told them practical ways in which they could show their love to God and to other people. He begged them to use their energy to serve God and not to act like the unbelievers who lived all around them. He even said they should be kind to their enemies—and we all know that is not as easy as being nice to our friends!

One of the hardest things he told them to do was to obey the government and its laws. Since the government in Rome was not at all helpful to Christians, but actually wanted to get rid of them, this must have sounded like a difficult rule to keep. Paul always reminded his friends that the power to do hard things comes from the Holy Spirit who lives in all God's children.

When your family gets a letter from someone who loves

you—like your grandmother, for instance—the letter often ends like this: "Grandpa and I send our love to everyone, and special hugs and kisses to the children." Paul wrote like that to his friends: "I send my love to all the Christians there in Rome. Give my greetings to all those who meet to worship in Priscilla and Aquila's home; give my best regards to Rufus." And he greeted many others by name. He cared very deeply for all his fellow believers.

GOOD PEOPLE IN A BAD CITY

1 AND 2 CORINTHIANS

IN EACH of his letters Paul talked about the special problems or needs of the church he was writing to. Corinth was one of the largest and most important cities of Paul's time, but it was very evil. Most people who lived there did wicked things, and the local laws and customs permitted and even encouraged every kind of wickedness.

When citizens of Corinth became believers in Jesus Christ, they wanted to change their habits and live the way they should. They no longer fit into the sinful life of Corinth, but their neighbors made it hard for them to change.

Paul understood their problem and he wrote two letters to encourage them and to warn them. He said they couldn't expect their unbelieving neighbors to understand how they felt, because it is the Holy Spirit who searches out and shows us all of God's deepest secrets. The person who isn't a Christian can't understand and can't accept these thoughts from God, which the Holy Spirit teaches us. They sound foolish to him, because only those who have the Holy Spirit within them can understand what the Holy Spirit means. Others just can't take it in.

Some of the Corinthian Christians were quarreling and splitting up into unfriendly little groups. Paul said they were acting like babies who just want their own way. He asked, "Don't you realize that all of you together are the house of God, and that the Spirit of God lives among you in his house? If anyone defiles and spoils God's home, God will destroy him. For God's home is holy and clean, and you are that home."

Another problem in the Corinthian church was that a certain man was commiting a serious sin, and the group of believers was not doing anything about it. Paul sternly ordered them to punish the man by refusing to let him be in their church until he corrected his sinful behavior. The good news is that later on, the man was sorry about his sin and stopped doing it. Then the Christians gladly took him back into the church.

Some of the sinful behavior in Corinth was in the relationship between men and women. For that reason, Paul wrote a lot about what makes a good marriage—one that is really pleasing to God. He said that no matter whether they were married or single, they must be pure and loving and obedient. They should put the feelings of other people ahead of their own comfort and pleasure.

Both to the Corinthians and later to the believers in

Ephesus, Paul said God had given each one of them some special ability. No matter who they were or what they could do best, there was an important job for them in the church and in the world. He compared the church to a person's body. We all know that each part of our bodies does some special thing that is necessary. We need our eyes for seeing and our ears for hearing. Our hands do one kind of job and our feet do something entirely different. In the same way, each believer is like one special part of the "body" of Jesus Christ. God gives some the ability to be church leaders; others can preach or teach well. Some are good at financial matters and can handle the church money wisely; some can do miracles or heal the sick. And some can speak in a special language God gives them.

In our physical bodies, our eyes should not try to do the hearing. That would be silly, wouldn't it? In the same way, we should be glad for our own gifts in the church body, and should not be jealous of someone else's special assignment.

Then Paul said that even though all these special gifts had value, the greatest gift of all is the gift of love—and we can *all* have that gift!

Did you know that Paul had a serious physical problem? He didn't say exactly what it was, although some people think he had an eye disease. But we know *why* he had it. He said God gave him this physical condition to keep him from becoming proud of himself and also to provide God with a special chance to show his strength even though Paul's body was weak. God said to him, "My power shows up best in weak people!"

THE LOVE CHAPTER
1 CORINTHIANS 13:4-7, 13

Love is very patient and kind,
never jealous or envious,
never boastful or proud,
never haughty or selfish or rude.
Love does not demand its own way.

It is not irritable or touchy.
It does not hold grudges
and will hardly even notice
when others do it wrong.
It is never glad about injustice,
but rejoices
whenever truth wins out.

If you love someone
you will be loyal to him
no matter what the cost.
You will always believe in him,
always expect the best of him,
and always stand your ground
in defending him.

There are three things that remain—
faith, hope, and love—
and the greatest of these is love.

FOOLED BY FALSE TEACHERS
GALATIANS

ALTHOUGH PAUL was a loving friend and teacher, he could also speak out very firmly when he was disappointed in something the new believers did. A good example of this is in his letter to the Christians in an area called Galatia. It was what we now call Turkey.

He had visited there on one of his missionary trips and many people had become Christians. He taught them for awhile, then he had to move on to another place. After he had gone, some other teachers began to tell those new believers that in order to be saved from their sins, they had to keep the law—not only the Ten Commandments, but dozens of other laws that God had given through Moses.

Well, when Paul heard about it, he wrote a letter to the Galatians, and he told them he was amazed that they had turned away from the Good News he had told them and were following a different "way to heaven." He said, "It's as if a magician had cast an evil spell on you!" He told them that the different way didn't really lead to heaven at all, but that they had been fooled by the false teachers. He reminded them that the Good News he preached was not based on some human imagination, but had come from Jesus Christ himself.

He thought some of them might ask, "Well, then, why were the laws given, if we aren't saved by keeping them?"

His answer was that the law was given to show people how guilty they are, because it really isn't possible to keep the law in every detail. He compared the Jewish law to a school teacher who gave them rules. The law was a guide until Christ came to give them right standing with God through their faith. Paul added, "But now that Christ has come, we don't need those laws any longer to guard us and lead us to him. For now we are all children of God through faith in Jesus Christ." Like the believers in Paul's day, we too can enjoy our freedom—not freedom to do wrong, but freedom to love and serve each other. After all, the real point of all the commandments was that we should love others as we love ourselves.

Then he urged the Galatians to follow the Holy Spirit's instructions in their hearts. If they insisted on having their own way, it would probably lead them to do wrong things: to worship idols instead of the true God, to hate and fight with each other, to be drunkards and murderers. But if they let the Holy Spirit control their lives, he would give them the ability to live as they should.

Paul compared our lives to a fruit tree. Do you have an apple tree in your yard, or a pear tree or cherry tree? You know it will bear good fruit each year if it is properly taken care of. Can you imagine what the tree would look like if it bore nine different kinds of beautiful fruit? That's not likely with fruit trees, but Paul says that when the Holy Spirit controls us, he will produce these nine qualities in us: love, joy, peace, patience, kindness, goodness, faithfulness, gentleness, and self-control.

When the believers in Galatia read those words, they must have been glad that the Holy Spirit would help them be more loving to each other, or to be patient with their wives and children. Some needed to be faithful in their work and not become discouraged when things did not go well. Others had hot tempers or other bad habits and wanted the Holy Spirit to help them control themselves and be gentle with everyone. And because Paul wrote these encouraging words to them, they learned to let God's Spirit do these things for them.

WELL-ARMED SOLDIERS FOR GOD

EPHESIANS; PHILIPPIANS; COLOSSIANS

IN AN EARLIER CHAPTER you read that Paul preached in Ephesus, where the main business of the city was selling idols—statues of their goddess named Diana. When many people believed Paul, the business men were angry, because they thought the Christian faith would spoil their business. If people believed in Jesus and worshiped God, they wouldn't buy statues of Diana!

In spite of this trouble, a church was formed in Ephesus. While Paul was in prison in another city, he wrote to tell the Ephesian Christians some helpful things.

He advised them to be holy, good people who wouldn't

lie to each other. He said that if they were angry, they shouldn't let the sun go down with the anger still in their hearts, but they should get over it quickly. He warned them not to steal, but to work and earn money for their needs and the needs of the poor. He said, "Be kind to each other, tender-hearted, forgiving one another, just as God has forgiven you because you belong to Christ."

Paul told them how a happy family can please God. The wife should follow the leadership of her husband and should obey, praise, and honor him. The husband should love his wife the same way Christ loved the church—enough to die for it! And what should the children do? They should obey their parents, because God has placed parents in authority over their children. He also had instructions for the parents. They should not nag and scold their children and make them angry, but should use loving discipline, giving good suggestions and advice. And then he said that slaves and masters (today we would say employees and employers) should work together, respecting each other.

From the very beginning of the Bible, we have seen that Satan is the worst enemy of God and of human beings. When we try to live for God, Satan does everything he can (and he is powerful!) to keep us from doing right; it's like a long, hard war all through our lives. Paul told the Ephesians something we should learn too. He said they would be able to fight Satan successfully if they would use some of the equipment soldiers had in those days. And he described that equipment this way:

First there was a wide belt that protected the middle part of the body; Paul said that truth is like that belt. And God's approval is like a breastplate—that is, metal armor that protects the heart. Faith is the shield that stops the arrows Satan shoots at us, and salvation is the helmet that protects our heads from injury (just the way a motorbiker or football player is protected by a helmet). He said we can move swiftly if we wear the shoes of the Good News of peace with God. All those things are like protective or defensive equipment. What can we use as a weapon against Satan? Paul said our best weapon is the sword of the Spirit—the Word of God, the Bible. And then he told them one more good way to win the battle with Satan: *Pray all the time!*

Paul talked about prayer in another of his letters—one to the believers in Philippi, the city where he was once in prison with Silas. Remember how the jailer believed in Jesus when God sent an earthquake to shake up the prison and open the doors and remove the chains from the prisoners' arms and legs? No doubt that jailer was now a member of the church to whom Paul wrote the epistle to the Philippians, and he and his friends must have been happy to read these words: "Always be full of joy in the Lord; I say it again: rejoice! Don't worry about anything; instead, pray about everything. Tell God your needs and don't forget to thank him for his answers." Paul promised that if they did that, they would experience God's peace, which is far more wonderful than the human mind can understand.

He also told the Philippians to fix their thoughts on what is true and good and right. Paul told them to think about things that are pure and lovely, and to dwell on the fine, good things in others. We must not forget that the things the apostles wrote to the churches then are things God wants us to know and to obey nowadays too. If we pay attention to what Paul told the Philippians, we will know that we must stay away from magazines that picture sinful behavior. And we must not listen to dirty stories or bad language. We will also be very careful about what kinds of

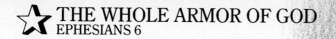

THE WHOLE ARMOR OF GOD
EPHESIANS 6

The strong belt of truth

The breastplate of God's approval

Shoes that speed you on
as you preach the Good News
of peace with God

The shield of faith to stop
the fiery arrows of Satan

The helmet of salvation

The sword of the Spirit,
the Word of God

TV programs we watch, and even the thoughts we think, so we can keep our minds on things that are pure, true, good, and lovely.

Another church in that part of the world was the group of believers in Colosse, a city in Greece. In a letter to the Colossians, Paul poured out his heart, reminding them to be faithful to Christ. He also urged them to keep their minds on the glory that would someday be theirs when they would go to live in heaven, where Christ sits in a place of honor, beside God the Father.

STORY 201

JESUS WILL COME AGAIN!

1 AND 2 THESSALONIANS; 1 AND 2 TIMOTHY; TITUS

PAUL WROTE twice to the believers in Thessalonica, and one of the most exciting things he said was that Jesus is going to return someday! Of course, the disciples had first heard about this on the Mount of Olives soon after Jesus had risen from the grave. They were with Jesus when he suddenly began to go up into the sky. He disappeared into the clouds, leaving the disciples staring after him. Then two angels appeared to them and said, "Jesus has gone away into heaven, but someday he will come back in the same way you just saw him go."

In his first letter to the Thessalonians, Paul told them more details. He said that when Jesus is ready to return, he will appear in the sky and will give a great shout of victory. An archangel will cry out loudly and there will be the sound of a trumpet call. What an exciting thing to see and hear! But something even more exciting will happen next.

The believers who have already died will rise and be taken up into the sky to meet Jesus. Then all the people living on earth who love him will rise into the sky too. All the believers will then be given new bodies that will be perfect and pure in every way—they will never sin or get sick or die. And from that time on, they will be with Jesus forever.

Paul said that these amazing things will happen very, very quickly—as fast as you can blink your eyes.

Paul wanted everyone to know what is going to happen on that day so they would not be worried about what happens to Christians who die. Although their bodies are dead, and they are separated from their loved ones for awhile, they are safe in God's care. Everyone can look forward to that day when Jesus will return and will bring all his people together, to be alive with him forever.

The letter said believers must never forget that Jesus is going to come back. They should keep watching for him and obeying God as they wait for that wonderful day. Almost two thousand years have gone by since those words were written, but they are just as true today as they were then.

Most of Paul's letters were to churches, but he also wrote

Paul told the Ephesians
that Christians need
to be armed like warriors
in order to fight
against Satan.
With all the armor on,
Christians can
defeat Satan.

four letters to individual friends: two to a young man named Timothy, one to Titus, and one to Philemon.

Timothy was a very special friend to Paul. We think Paul was never married, so he was especially glad to have Timothy to take the place of the son he never had. In fact he said to him, "You are like a son to me." As we would expect, he gave Timothy a lot of fatherly advice about his life, urging him to fight well in the Lord's battles and to cling tightly to his faith in Christ, always keeping his conscience clear and doing what he knew was right.

Paul could see that Timothy was the kind of young man who would become a leader of other people, so he told him many important things about how a church leader should live. He should be a steady, honorable man with a well-behaved family and obedient children. He should not have any bad habits, and he should have a good, happy marriage. Paul also told Timothy always to be respectful to older people.

Timothy's father was not a Jew and probably didn't worship the true God, but his Jewish mother, Eunice, and his grandmother, Lois, were Christian believers and they had brought Timothy up to know and love God. They had taught him carefully, and had told him all the Old Testament stories about how God had been with his people ever since he had first told Abraham he would have as many descendants as there are stars in the sky!

Then they taught him that Jesus had come to be the Savior of all who believed in him and wanted their sins forgiven. And Timothy listened, just as you are listening to these same stories in your home, or are reading them for yourself.

Paul was in prison when he wrote to Timothy. He said he was suffering there, but he was not ashamed to be in prison. He was there because of his faithfulness to Christ.

He told Timothy to take his share of suffering, too, like a good soldier of Jesus Christ. He urged him to work hard so God could say to him, "Well done!" He said, "Be a good workman, one who does not need to be ashamed when God examines your work. Know what his Word says and means."

Above all, Paul told Timothy to preach the Word of God at all times—even at those times when he didn't feel like it or it wasn't convenient—so he could bring many people to Christ.

Paul also wrote to Titus, a very short letter but one that contained some good advice for that Christian leader. Paul had appointed Titus to strengthen the churches on an island called Crete (you can find it on a map of the Mediterranean Sea) and to find good pastors for them. He said Titus should be a good example to them of how a Christian should behave, showing love and good deeds to everyone—good advice for all of us!

STORY 202

PAUL HELPS A RUNAWAY SLAVE

PHILEMON

PAUL WROTE some of his letters while he was in jail for faithfully preaching about Jesus.

Among the visitors who came to see Paul in prison was

a slave named Onesimus. Paul told him how Jesus could become his Savior, and Onesimus believed. He did helpful things for Paul, probably buying food for him to eat and telling him what was going on outside the prison.

But Onesimus had a serious problem; he had run away from his master. When Paul heard about it, he was surprised to learn that the master was one of his good friends, a man named Philemon. A long time before, Paul had told Philemon about Jesus, and Philemon had become a believer.

When Onesimus became a Christian, he decided he should return to his master and be his slave again. But he was fearful about what would happen to him, because runaway slaves were usually punished severely by being whipped or even killed. So Paul wrote a letter to Philemon for Onesimus to take with him.

In the letter Paul thanked Philemon for being such a helper to the church—in fact, the church met in his home. Then Paul asked a favor. He asked Philemon to treat Onesimus with kindness, and to forgive him for running away.

The name Onesimus means "useful." Paul said that although Onesimus hadn't been very useful in the past, from now on he would live up to his name. After all, Onesimus was now like Philemon's brother, since both belonged to God because of their faith in Jesus.

Paul said he had wanted to keep Onesimus there with him as his helper, but of course he couldn't do that because Philemon was really his owner. He said, "If Onesimus owes you any money, I will pay it for him." But then Paul reminded Philemon how much he owed Paul, because Paul had helped him find God—and nothing could ever repay that debt!

At the end of the letter, Paul said, "I hope to get out of jail soon and come for a visit, so please keep a guest room ready for me."

We don't know for sure whether Paul ever got out of jail or whether he ever saw his good friends Philemon and Onesimus again. But we can be quite sure that Philemon treated Onesimus well and that Onesimus didn't run away again!

AN UNSIGNED LETTER

HEBREWS

ONE OF THE LETTERS in the New Testament is different from all the rest because it is not signed. It doesn't say, either at the beginning or the end, who wrote it. Many people think it was Paul, but no one is able to prove it. It doesn't really matter; we can read it and learn a lot from it, whoever wrote it.

One of the writer's messages is that Jesus Christ is like the High Priests of the Old Testament. The High Priest was the one who was allowed to go into the most holy place in the temple, and he could offer to God the blood from sacrificed animals. Then God would forgive the sins of the people who had sacrificed those animals.

But when Jesus came and died to become our Savior, animal sacrifices were no longer needed. Instead of the

624

blood of animals, he gave his own blood and made sure of our eternal salvation. Because he made that sacrifice of himself, we can go right into God's presence and speak directly to him in prayer.

It is faith in Jesus Christ that assures our salvation. The person who wrote the letter explained what faith is. He said it is being sure something is going to happen, even though we are not able to see it happening right now. We sometimes hope and dream about something nice in the future, but that isn't really faith. Faith is being just as certain as if we could see it now!

Then the writer gave a lot of wonderful examples of people whose lives showed they had this great gift of faith. As you have been reading this book, you have read stories about these people and you know about the ways they served God. The letter mentions Abel, Enoch, Noah, Abraham and Sarah, Jacob, Joseph, Moses and his parents, the Israelites who followed Moses out of Egypt, and the soldiers who marched around Jericho. The writer talked about Rahab, Gideon, Barak, Samson, Jephthah, David, Samuel, and other prophets. What do you remember about each one in that list of names?

At the end of the letter, the writer says we live our lives as if we were running a race in a stadium, and all those Bible heroes of faith were sitting in the grandstand, watching us. We would like to run our race as well as they ran theirs. Just as an Olympic athlete runs to win a medal, we run the race of life to win God's approval. How helpful it is to know we have the encouragement of other Christians around us, including those who lived long ago!

JOHN'S LETTERS ABOUT LOVE

1, 2, AND 3 JOHN

THREE LETTERS in the New Testament were written by the apostle John. You remember that John and his brother James were fishermen until Jesus asked them to follow him and be his disciples. These two brothers and Simon Peter were especially close to Jesus, and John was even called "the disciple Jesus loved." Of course, we know Jesus loved all his disciples, but John was a special friend.

John was one of the four men who wrote biographies of Jesus, which we call Gospels. It is in the Gospel of John that we read these wonderful words, "For God loved the world so much that he gave his only Son so that anyone who believes in him shall not perish but have eternal life."

Knowing these things about John, we are not surprised that when John became an old man and wrote letters to Christian friends, he had a lot to say about love. In his longest letter he told them that the best way we can show that we love God is to love other people. God *is* love, and if we are God's children, our lives will be full of love.

John warned believers that if they hate other people, they are really murderers at heart, and no one who wants

Living the Christian life is like running a race. All the Bible heroes of faith are sitting in the grandstand watching us. Let us run a good race.

to murder has eternal life. We can tell what real love is from Christ's example in dying for us. In this same way we ought to be willing to lay down our lives for our Christian brothers and sisters. This *might* mean actually dying for them, but it can also mean being willing to give up our own way and our own comfort to serve and help them.

John said some people talk a lot about loving others, but their actions don't prove that their love is real. This is especially true if they see others in need or in trouble, and don't reach out and help them. John's letter says they should practice showing love to others; you know that when we practice something over and over (like shooting baskets or playing the piano), we keep getting better at it!

Another warning John gave was that many preachers and teachers might tell them things that are not true, even though the teachers pretended to be Christ's followers. He said there are ways to test those teachings, to find out if they are dependable and true. One way to be sure a message is really from the Holy Spirit is to ask: Does it agree that Jesus Christ, God's Son, actually became a man with a human body?

Loving God means doing what he tells us to do, and that isn't hard, for God's children can obey him by trusting Christ to help them. Whoever has God's Son has life, but whoever does not have his Son does not have life. John said he wrote his letter so those who believe in the Son of God may know for sure that they have eternal life.

In another letter, addressed to his friend Gaius, John praised Gaius for being kind to traveling teachers and missionaries and for inviting them to his home and taking care of their needs. He said when Christians are hospitable and helpful to their fellow believers, they are partners with them in the Lord's work. How encouraging that letter must have been to Gaius!

WHAT DAMAGE THE TONGUE CAN DO!

JAMES; 1 AND 2 PETER; JUDE

THE APOSTLE JAMES was one of Jesus' own brothers, and at first he didn't believe that Jesus was really going to be the Savior of the world. But when he finally did believe, he became a faithful follower and a leader among the Christians.

The letter James wrote was addressed to "Jewish Christians everywhere," so it was probably passed around from one church to another so many people could read it. He told them how important it is for believers to have patience and to ask God to tell them what he wants them to do. James said God is always glad to give us wisdom when we ask for it.

James had two very important messages for the readers of his letter. The first was: *You must control your tongue.* The second was: *If your faith is real, you will prove it by your actions.*

He pointed out that though the tongue is one of the smallest parts of the body, it can do a lot of damage if it gets out of control. Here is some of his advice about the tongue:

It is best to listen much and speak little.

If a person doesn't control his sharp tongue, his religion isn't worth much.

Don't be too eager to tell others their faults.

If a person can control his tongue, he can control himself in every other way.

Just like a tiny spark that can set a great forest on fire, the tongue is a flame that can turn our lives into a blazing fire that hurts or destroys others.

It is harder to tame the tongue than it is to tame wild animals.

The tongue is full of wickedness and can poison the whole body.

Don't criticize and speak evil about one another.

Don't grumble and complain.

Don't swear, but just say a simple yes or no.

Then James gave his friends instructions about making their faith practical. He said it wasn't much use to say they were Christians if they weren't proving it by helping others. It isn't enough just to have faith; believers must also do good things, to prove that they have faith. We all know a body is dead when the spirit leaves it; James said that's the way it is with faith. It is dead if it is not the kind that results in good deeds.

Unlike James, Peter was one of the very first men to become Jesus' disciple. He was one of the three who were especially close to Jesus and were with him at certain times when other disciples were not there, for instance, in the Garden of Gethsemane.

Peter wrote two interesting letters, also to Christians in many different churches. He told them that believers should be like one big, happy family. Like Paul, he said some good things about marriage. Wives should respect their husbands. A woman shouldn't think too much about how she looks, but should think about the kind of beauty that comes from having a gentle, kind heart. And husbands should be thoughtful and kind to their wives. In fact,

Peter said that if they didn't treat their wives well, God would not answer their prayers.

Peter warned the believers to watch out for Satan, their great enemy, who prowls around like a hungry, roaring lion, looking for a victim to tear apart. And in another letter he warned them about false teachers—the same kind Paul had warned the Galatians about.

Apparently Peter had heard some people saying it didn't look to them as if it was true that Jesus was going to come back. They said, "Well, where is he? Years have gone by and he still hasn't come. Probably he isn't really going to keep his promise!" Peter said not to worry about people like that and not to give up expecting Jesus to come. In God's plans, time isn't the same as it is to human beings. In fact, Peter said that to God, a thousand years are like one day. Jesus has a good reason for delaying his coming, but when the right time comes, he *will* come just as he promised.

The last epistle in the Bible is a very short one—only a page or two—written by Jude, another of Jesus' brothers. He, too, wrote to warn believers about teachers who gave false messages and led the Christians into making serious mistakes about what they believed. Jude promised that Jesus was able to keep them from slipping and falling into those mistakes.

JOHN'S AMAZING VISION OF HEAVEN
THE REVELATION

WHEN THE APOSTLE John was very old, he was a prisoner on an island called Patmos, in the Mediterranean Sea. He wasn't kept in a jail cell, but he wasn't allowed to leave Patmos. One morning a strange and wonderful thing happened to him. He saw a vision—a vivid picture in his mind of things that weren't really there on the island. A vision is like a dream you have when you are awake.

And what did John see in this vision? He saw Jesus in his glory. "His eyes were bright like flames of fire," John wrote. "His feet gleamed like polished bronze, and his voice thundered like storm waves against the seashore. He held seven stars in his right hand and a sharp, double-edged sword in his mouth, and his face shone like the brilliant sun on a cloudless day."

John fainted at the sight and fell down in front of Jesus, but Jesus put his hand on John's head and said to him, "Don't be afraid. I am the First and Last, the Living One who died but is now alive forevermore. I have the keys of death and hell, but you need not be afraid of me."

John saw a door standing open in heaven. And a voice from heaven said to him, "Come up here and I will show you what must happen in the future."

Then John saw a door standing open in heaven. The same voice that had spoken to him before, in tones like a mighty trumpet blast from heaven, spoke again: "Come up here and I will show you what must happen in the future."

Instantly John's spirit was there in heaven, although his body did not leave the island. "Oh, the glory of it!" John exclaimed as he wrote about it afterwards. "There was a throne and someone sitting on it. Great bursts of light flashed forth from him as from a glittering diamond or from a shimmering ruby, and a rainbow glowing like an emerald encircled his throne. Lightning and thunder came from the throne, and there were voices in the thunder. Spread out in front of the throne was a shining crystal sea."

Then, in his vision, John heard the singing of millions of angels gathered around the throne, giving praise to Jesus. After that, an angel flew across the heavens, carrying the Good News about Jesus to every nation, tribe, language, and people. "Fear God," the angel shouted, "and praise his greatness. For the time has come when he will sit as judge. Worship him who made the heaven and the earth, the sea and all its creatures."

Then, after seeing many terrible things happening on earth, John saw the Holy City, the new Jerusalem, coming down from God out of heaven. It was a glorious sight. He heard a loud shout from the throne in heaven: "Look, the home of God is now among men, and he will live with them, and they will be his people. He will wipe away all tears from their eyes, and there will be no more death, sorrow, crying, or pain. All of that has gone forever."

The city was so filled with the glory of God that it flashed and glowed like a precious gem. John says it was made of pure, transparent gold, like glass!

John was told this important message about that city:

Nothing impure will ever be allowed there, nor can anyone come in who does what is wrong. Only those whose sins have been washed away by the death of our Lord Jesus Christ can come in. Their names are written in God's Book of Life.

Let us all be sure we believe in the Savior, so we can say eagerly, "Come, Lord Jesus!"

INDEX OF IMPORTANT PERSONS IN THE BIBLE

CLEOPAS Believer on the Emmaus road *Story 178*
CORNELIUS A Roman soldier who sent for Peter *Story 184*
CYRUS King of Persia *Story 136*

DANIEL A prophet and writer *Story 131*
DARIUS (THE MEDE) King of Persia *Story 134*
DARIUS II King of Babylon *Story 137*
DATHAN A rebel against Moses *Story 50*
DAVID Second king of united Israel *Story 78*
DEBORAH A judge in Israel *Story 64*
DELILAH A Philistine woman who betrayed Samson *Story 70*
DOEG A servant of King Saul *Story 83*
DORCAS Christian woman in Joppa *Story 183*

EHUD A judge of Israel *Story 63*
ELKANAH Father of Samuel *Story 74*
ELI High priest of Israel *Story 74*
ELIJAH A prophet *Story 101*
ELISHA A prophet *Story 106*
ELIZABETH Mother of John the Baptist *Story 146*
ENOCH Man who did not die *Story 3*
EPHRAIM Son of Joseph *Story 26*
ESAU Brother of Jacob *Story 13*
ESTHER Jewish wife of Ahasuerus *Story 139*
EVE The first woman *Story 1*
EZEKIEL Prophet and author *Story 128*

FELIX Roman governor of Caesarea *Story 193*
FESTUS Roman governor in Caesarea *Story 194*

GEHAZI Servant of Elisha *Story 108*
GIDEON A judge of Israel and military leader *Story 64*
GOLIATH A giant Philistine warrior *Story 80*

HAGAR Maid of Sarah; mother of Ishmael *Story 9*
HAMAN Enemy of Esther and her people *Story 140*
HANNAH Mother of Samuel *Story 74*
HEROD King of Judea when Jesus was born *Story 146*
HEZEKIAH Twelfth king of Judah *Story 120*
HIRAM King of Tyre *Story 89*
HOPHNI Son of Eli *Story 74*

ISAAC Son of Abraham and Sarah *Story 9*
ISAIAH Prophet and author *Story 123*
ISHMAEL Son of Abraham and Hagar *Story 9*

JACOB Son of Isaac *Story 13*
JAMES An apostle; son of Zebedee *Story 152*
JAMES Another apostle *Story 152*
JEHOIADA A high priest in Israel *Story 117*
JEHORAM Fifth king of Judah *Story 116*

DATE DUE

DE 9			